REBOUND

LIBRARY SYSTEM RESET
BOOK THREE

K.T. HANNA

For everyone who ever dreamed of a magical Library
Don't ever give up on your dreams
Even if they talk back

PREVIOUSLY IN THE LIBRARY

After being isekaid into the Library of Everywhere, Quinn and Lynx (the Library manifestation) begin the arduous task of restoring the Library.

Milaro the grandfatherly king of the elves, and his grandchild Malakai become an integral part of the hunt for overdue books. This includes retrieving some very dangerous and important books, one of which is held by Kajaro who ends up not dying the way they think he does.

Quinn busies herself stocking the library with the specific golems it needs to run. Between Misha, Cook, Farrow, and the shelving golems Tim and Tom the Library begins to run smoothly and even gets some assistants - Eric and Geneva, Jim and Bob, and Dottie the talking bench, as well as Narilin the book doctor. Don't forget Aradie the Nightowl.

After retrieving some restricted books on the Dabilian home world, torn apart by rampant chaos magic, Quinn and Co. heal up and start working toward activating more filtration pillars and fulfilling the different Library branch opening requirements. After replacing some of the filters and fighting miasma drones, the filtration system is back online and ready to increase output and help the mana levels of the world rise, because they were dangerously low.

Now that's fixed Quinn synchronizes with the Library, resulting in a huge revelation about her heritage that she wasn't expecting, but that explains so much. After which they begin to retrieve the last of the books needed to open the culinary branch, and encounter missing restricted books along the way that the Library has no recollection of.

The Library and Lynx realize they have gaping holes in their memories and are missing literal chunks of time.

In retrieving some of the necessary books, they encounter a dimension manipulation series of books that poses very specific danger to the Library.

Even though the prerequisites for the Culinary branch opening are reached, there seem to be more problems just around the corner.

1

STILL MARKED

BOOKS LAY STREWN ALL OVER QUINN'S BEDROOM. THOUGH SHE'D absorbed many of them, they lay open for her to reference specifics. Things like ice could be manifested anywhere there was a hint of water, for example.

Which included inside living, breathing things.

For medicinal purposes, it required a very steady mind and will to maneuver something she couldn't see. Diagrams were easier for her to understand when they were drawn on paper, rather than simply rotating in her mind.

Right now, she felt like an over-absorbed sponge, practically bloated to the point of spilling.

Two weeks wasn't even remotely enough time for Quinn to power up and become invincible, but it was all the time she'd got. So she'd made the best of it.

Quinn pulled her hair into a messy high ponytail as she stood at the top of the staircase looking out over the Library, ready for another new day. She glanced down to see Lynx standing at the bottom of the stairs. Instead of taking them two at a time and risking breaking her neck, she simply leaped over the railing and floated gently down to stand right in front of him. She grinned at him.

"Well, now you're just showing off," he said, but there was definitely a twinkle in his eyes.

"I've got magic. Why shouldn't I show off?" Over the last couple of weeks, she'd found a new appreciation for all things magic-related.

Lynx disappeared for a moment and then tapped on her shoulder from behind her.

Quinn laughed. "Fine. You can show off too. Anyway, what's up? Why'd you call me?"

"I need you to go over a few of the new timetables so we can allocate all the newly trained assistants to the roster." He moved to stand in front of her again.

"Can't you do that?" she said.

"Yes, I can do that and have done that, but I need you to look at it and tell me if you're okay with it." He paused and continued when she raised an eyebrow. "To finalize it."

"Wow, Lynx," she half joked, "copping some attitude there."

He raised an eyebrow. "You've been very busy, which is fine, but you can't always fob all of your responsibilities onto me. I *do* have a few of my own."

"I'm aware of that," Quinn said, and she really meant it. But she'd been trying to play catch up on her magical affinities as well as on digesting all the information she'd absorbed since arriving. "Thank you for all your help while I've been training."

"How are your powers, then?" he asked. "Are you still feeling some of the affinities more than others? Do you feel better equipped to defend yourself and the Library now?"

"Some of the affinities are definitely more viable than others. Not sure why. Library and I will have to figure that out. But I definitely feel ready to defend everything." She said the latter smugly and flexed her hand once. A sheet of very hard, very cold ice appeared around it that she managed to render flexible. Underneath it was a tiny air pocket between her skin and the ice that protected her skin from ice burn. She displayed it with pride, but then sighed and muttered under her breath. "Capable, however? Well, I'm working on that."

She'd learned so much in the last two weeks from compartmentalization theory to finding strength in dodging, parrying with mind magic, forceful mind segregation, telekinesis, and even advanced telepathic techniques.

Her favorite so far was the speed enhancement and control she'd learned. Especially the speed as applied to elements that could allow her to instantaneously cause the blizzard she'd previously been using with the ice balls. The blizzard balls had been her own manifestation of that type of ability. And now she'd devoured three books with a specific focus on blizzards.

And then there were the ice, water, and air intermediate teachings. Not to mention the fact that Milaro had drilled her every single day for the last two weeks on her mental protections, her mental retaliation, and her ability to mentally access the compartmentalization without turning into a cold sociopathic killer.

Hopefully, anyway.

Sadly, she'd only just gotten into some aspects of chaotic magic theory in the last couple of days. Chaos affinities were largely found innate in creatures like imps that stemmed directly from chaos. She still had a lot to learn in that regard. Overall though, her progress had been fantastic. Now she just needed to keep practicing the useful applications.

"Yeah," Quinn said again. "I think the training has been going really well."

"Great. There's a lot to do. Let's go down the list. We have a very slight problem. The culinary branch is in full operation now and we've been able to alert all of the people who have overdue books from that specific branch."

"But that sounds like a great thing," Quinn interrupted, not understanding.

"And if you'll let me finish . . ." he continued, ignoring her interjection. "Word of mouth is finally starting to work. Before, it seems, many thought the books were malfunctioning and the Library wasn't actually back. Now, however, we're starting to get people coming in and bringing books back that are very obviously ours and that the Library recognizes, but those tomes are from the other, still closed branches. Thus we are starting to build up a stockpile of books that require the outstanding branches be opened to be returned in the first place."

"Oh," Quinn said. Given how many books were still missing from just the main branch and now the culinary branch . . . "Do we have a lot of them yet?"

"Well, not so many, yet. It's only started over the last few days. We have"—he paused and checked something—"ninety-eight books so far, in four days. I can only assume it'll start compounding as time goes on. While it's a good thing that people no longer think the return of the Library is just a rumor, right now those books must be placed in holding until we can reopen those branches."

"But when those branches open, we'll already have a head start, right?" Quinn asked, clinging to that silver lining.

"True." Lynx frowned in thought. "Anyway, people who know they have a book or that their family has a book have started returning them whether they've been pinged or not."

"We should provide a specific storage room for those. Maybe off of Narilin's book infirmary?" Quinn asked, directing the question to the Library.

Done. You also have yet to make time for me.

Sorry. Been busy. Quinn cringed.

I'm aware.

Quinn sighed and spoke to Lynx again. "Doesn't that mean we're getting some of the original books back much quicker now?"

"Yes, you'd think so, wouldn't you? You'd be right, too. It's just that I never foresaw the branches being closed at all, so this problem is yet another thing I overlooked." Lynx sounded positively dejected.

"Hey." Quinn reached over and patted his currently solidified shoulder. "Your overlooking things had nothing to do with you. We're going to get to the bottom of this and you'll be back to normal in no time."

Lynx laughed softly. "Thanks. I know it'll work out, it has to. It's just that I'm frustrated.

"And I get that. I'm upset for you. I know Harish and Siliqua will find a way to rectify this. In the meantime," Quinn raised an eyebrow. "Well, I guess I should take care of the Library today and not necessarily jump head first into . . ."

"Jump head first into what?" Milaro said, appearing suddenly the way he seemed to sometimes. "You know, I've talked to you about all this head nonsense."

Quinn rolled her eyes. "You know that's not what I'm talking about."

"I know, but I couldn't resist."

Quinn smiled despite herself. Milaro and her were back exactly where they used to be. She was used to things now. Used to this ridiculous propensity she had for absolutely every single affinity out there. And used to the fact that she was the Librarian and that it was a good feeling. Quinn decided she very much liked being part mystical creature.

"Before you get started on Library stuff, though," Milaro said, "Cadre, Siliqua, Harish, and I need to speak to you."

Quinn raised an eyebrow. "And just what do you need to speak to me about?" She wasn't trying to be facetious; there were many things they could talk to her about. From Library protections, to re-sequencing, Librarian mind protections to filtration chamber problems . . .

"The Serpensiril we have in stasis." He grinned at her. "It's still being maintained by six of your security golems."

"Oh," Quinn said. "Yes. Progress on that front?"

Milaro sighed. "I, unfortunately, am not able to, shall we say, dive into his mind anymore. There is an alert set up specifically aimed at my magical signature. Any time I get close to his mental space, shall we say, it's like he begins to react whether or not he's in stasis. We cannot afford for him to break out of that stasis given what happened last time."

"Can't you just kill the bastard?" Eric butted in, his wings making more of a hissing noise than their usual humming. It made Quinn wonder if the sound reflected his moods.

Quinn laughed. "We're not prone to killing people."

"He ripped his friend apart," Eric said flatly. "I would think he's classified less as people and more like a monster."

"First you love fining people. Now you don't mind killing them? Where does that end?" she asked.

But the imp didn't answer the question. He just barreled on ahead. "Quinn, he's taking up too many of the Library's resources. Keeping him in stasis, if we can't get anything good out of him, is only going to make things worse in the long run."

Quinn blanched. Some of that was due to the fact that they'd had this conversation about half a dozen times over the last two weeks and Quinn refused to kill him outright. Maybe it was because part of her remembered how close she'd come to doing it herself. There was a part of her that was terrified of killing other beings. If she started condoning it, how much would the line blur? How much would she change if life became inconsequential as a means to an end.

Self-defense was one thing, and she could twist Tenejo's previous action to mean his death would protect the Library and more . . . and yet that was a type of trauma she wasn't ready to deal with.

Yet.

"I know, I know," Eric said when her pause went on too long. "Stop being such a bloodthirsty Eric."

Quinn sighed and tried very hard not to laugh. She almost failed. "Anyway, we do need to go over what we're doing with Tenejo."

Lynx piped up. "That's going to have to wait, Milaro. She has to check on the assistants and code them into the system."

"Fine. I'll see you this afternoon. We'll meet in your office to start with, and then we'll venture to the dungeon as it has been prepared by the Library."

Quinn shuddered ever so slightly. "You know I hate that word."

"Well, you can hate it all you want, but that's the reality of it, Quinn. The Library has enemies and we need to figure out who they are." Milaro's tone was grave, heavy even.

"I know . . ." Quinn sighed.

"Sometimes I forget how young you are," he said kindly.

"Thank you, oh millennia-old grandfather figure of mine," Quinn said, and turned her attention back to Lynx, her back pointedly in Milaro's face.

Eric chuckled. "I still think we should be fining people more. I can't believe you gave the culinary branch a thirty-day grace period, too!"

"There's only like twenty days of it left. Start thinking up awesome, scrumptious fines, will you? And I'll even let you hand out the first one." Quinn waved him away, trying to focus on the rest of her conversations.

That appeared to mollify the imp somewhat. "Thank you," he said. "Also, my uncle will be delivering an information packet, I guess you could say, in person in the next few days."

"What?" Quinn said, already hating the day. It had gone from planned-more-training-like-the-past-two-weeks, to a nope-you're-done-with-rest-here's-everything day. "Information packet? Can't he just send it?"

"No, my uncle . . . anyway, you're going to get to meet him, and you'll understand why I think he's just the best person ever." The sarcasm practically dripped off Eric's words as he darted away before Quinn could say anything else.

Quinn pinched the bridge of her nose and let out a long-suffering sigh.

"Hey," Lynx said, nudging her again. It was like he'd picked up Malakai's bad habit. "It's okay, let's just go and give all of these assistants the access they need and bump the other three supervisors you were going to bump up."

"How many new assistants did we end up with?" she asked, grateful to have Lynx request something specific.

"Oh, there's like a dozen of them."

"A dozen? I guess we have expanded a bit, right?"

"A lot," he said.

"Oh." She smiled. "You had to get people for the culinary branch and some to help Cook in the kitchen, right?"

"Yes. We are very close to filling those two hundred seats in the dining hall on a semi-frequent basis now." By this time, they'd slowly walked to the reception area where the grand welcoming check-in desk stood. There were three lines leading away from the right-hand side of it.

Quinn blinked. "Okay, is it just me or is the check-in desk bigger now?"

"Oh, it's not just you. Of course it's bigger now. The Library accommodates what it needs to function." Lynx grinned, and pride in the Library practically oozed from his . . . manifested form. The runes in his hair were practically churning with joy.

"Oh," Quinn said. "That's kind of awesome."

"Yeah, it leaves us room to do all of the admin and be on hand if we're needed by the assistants and supervisors on the left-hand side, and it allows all the books to be checked in." But he stopped short when Quinn gasped ever so softly.

"Wait," she said, "Is that . . . is that a line going back into the Library?"

"Oh yeah, those are inquiries. So the other side is now . . . look, just come up."

They walked into the check-in desk and Quinn realized it was more spacious inside too.It now had two distinct areas. One where people could make inquiries and the other where people would check in their books.

"Oh," Quinn said, "I think I could get used to this." As they went over all the information of each assistant and transferred the information fully into the system, Quinn noticed several species listed that she'd not seen before.

"Wow," she said, "we reached a lot farther with the applications this time, right?" The names meant practically nothing to her without visuals. She'd have to inspect all the new assistants in short order so she could understand them better.

"Yes and no. Three of these only have five of the prerequisite affinities that we require. They will basically just be taking returns if we end up accepting them once they've interviewed. They're not going to be capable of doing anything serious."

Quinn hesitated and then asked the question on her tongue. "I don't suppose you've found anyone who has the Library affinities?"

"Nope, not another one yet. Not even one," he said. There was a strange flicker over him, and all the joy from the runes was gone.

"How are your memories going?" she asked on impulse.

"Well, I have sat down with Cadre several times now. I've been back to the Core a few times and I think, you know, I think eventually it's gonna be all okay." He sounded like he was trying to stay upbeat.

She watched him for a second and wondered if he realized how transparent he was being. She shook her head. "You don't need to make me feel better, Lynx, but I'm sure it will be okay. In the end."

"Of course, I've got the amazing Quinn looking out for me, right?" His dark violet eyes sparkled again.

"Yeah, we'll get your memories back. Yours and the Library's." Quinn meant every word. "So, has there been any news on ways to get those missing books back sooner?"

"Look, you're probably going to have to talk to Siliqua and Harish. The Core is trying its best to figure out ways to trace the books that were once the Library's."

"They're still marked as the Library's, so there's got to be ways to trace it using the name." Quinn frowned. "I mean, we have tracking systems back home. There had to be a tracking system here too. Just magical."

"You would think so," Lynx said. "No, there . . . there is, and that's what we'll talk to Eric's uncle about when he gets here."

"Oh," Quinn said, "well, that makes sense. So we're doing pretty good here."

"Yeah, if you can just okay the allocation of Deflin, Malice, and Argo to a supervisory assistant role. That's all I need from you right now. You have a lot of tasks to get done."

"Lynx, are you okay?"

"I'm as well as can be expected right now, Quinn. Thanks for asking." He went back to work and Quinn felt, for just a moment, ever so slightly out of her depth.

It had been two weeks since they opened the new branch. And

while they'd made some progress, they still had so much to do. They'd even had to resort to Eric's uncle in order to figure out the intricacies of the missing restricted vault books and how to locate them. They also still had to figure out the Ashiron pillar. There were also a couple of things she needed to talk to Misha about in that regard.

Finding the Serpensiril's allies was coming up a dead end. Everybody knew there was no way the Serpensiril had orchestrated this whole thing all by themselves.

She was going to have to take Jasper up on her offer of seeing if she could divine for them. After giving Jasper back access to the Library, the woman had promised Quinn to come to their aid at any time should they need her.

The Librarian sighed and looked around her home. Books had always been such an integral part of her life. Now they had the perk of being magical. She made a small ice sculpture of Kajaro in the palm of her hand and crushed it with her fist.

Despite all Quinn's best efforts, it was looking more and more like the Library needed all the allies it could get.

2

SHIFT IN THESE MEMORIES

QUINN SCANNED THROUGH A LIST OF BOOKS THAT SHE HAD BEEN USING over the last couple of weeks to enhance and expand her knowledge base as she leaned over her desk, grateful for her comfortable chair. The only thing she'd really gained new knowledge on was Chaos, yet she didn't understand everything she'd learned. There weren't many opportunities to practice mastering control over chaotic elements.

And understandably so.

All the other books she'd absorbed were of skills already in her repertoire as beginner texts or, she supposed, beginner abilities, which she'd now managed to expand on. After cross-referencing the best books to enhance the current skills that she had, she'd realized there were woefully few that met her precise specifications.

Maybe she'd end up writing her own books and combinations just like Milaro had.

Her connection with the Library was constantly deepening. She could feel all the people streaming in through different doors. If she concentrated just right, she could even tell where her assistants and the golems were, not to mention her favorite people in the Library like Milaro, Malakai, Dottie, Misha, and, of course, Lynx.

Aradie was, as usual, sitting on the perch in her office. This time she actually looked like she might be asleep. Quinn realized the bird was probably very bored lately with all of Quinn's lack of adventure and time spent inside the Library.

Quinn didn't mind being in the Library at all. This was something she could get used to. Checking in the books, making sure they were healthy, going and dinging anybody who deserved a fine, chatting to some patrons, working on her skills, training montage for a few days now and again, eating endless amounts of Cook's food. It all seemed surreal yet also like a distant future dream. She sighed.

What's the matter? the Library asked.

"Oh, you're paying attention."

I've been busy.

"You're always busy," Quinn said, feeling petulant for a second.

Are you going to tell me what's troubling you, or do I have to try and guess?

"As long as guessing doesn't mean you try to pry into my head, then maybe we could make it fun."

The Library chuckled ever so slightly, and the sound echoed through Quinn's head.

She relented. "Okay, fine. I'm just wondering about my future and where I came from and entirely if there's anything I should know about what we are that I might have to watch out for."

That's very clever, Quinn, the Library said. *If I wasn't paying attention, I might even have answered that question.*

"You're still not going to tell me outright? I have to just make my guess?

I'm sure I recall you telling Lynx that you already had a guess.

Quinn shrugged. "I do. I'm just double-checking something. In the meantime, is there anything I should be aware of?"

The Library seemed to pause for a moment and mull that over. *Just make sure that you don't let anger get the better of you.*

"Anger?" Quinn asked.

Yes, tempers are an especially volatile thing.

"Well, I know that, but last time I tried to seal off my emotions, I almost turned into a sociopath, so I've got to watch that too," Quinn deadpanned.

The Library chuckled. *I meant that tempers are an especially volatile thing for us in particular. Also, we would have stopped you before anything bad happened.*

"Well, you almost didn't," Quinn said absently, her thoughts darting to the very minor clue.

But you did stop, the Library said. *Look, Quinn, just do what you're doing. We're all working on trying to figure out everything so the Library can return to the days of happy, magic-sharing, occasional fine-handing out. There'll be much less stress and far more rejoicing.*

"It's like you read my mind," Quinn said, narrowing her eyes at nothing in particular.

It's almost like I'm a part of you, the Library said. *Just don't stress too much, and when you've got a chance, we should probably have another chat.*

"Another synchronization?" Quinn asked, slightly apprehensively, considering everything she'd learned and the mild amounts of pain she'd experienced in the last one.

No, just a recalibration of sorts. We haven't spoken in a few weeks, in close quarters.

"You're right," Quinn acknowledged. Then she turned her head toward the door, cocking it to one side. "Oh, I think, yep, they're coming."

I'll leave you to it. Thank you, Quinn.

This left Quinn wondering exactly what the Library was thanking her for, and what it was that Quinn had somehow agreed to, and not entirely realized that she was doing so. She looked up as Cadre, Milaro, Harish, Siliqua, and Lynx entered her office. She silently thanked the Library again for having made her office much larger after they implemented the old jail that they'd had.

"Nice to see you all," Quinn said, pretty sure this wasn't going to be nice in the slightest. Every single one of them had a grim expression on their face, even Cadre, all four feet of him, constantly, usually, looked like he was smiling non-stop with a gecko-like grin.

"It's not all bad, Quinn," Milaro said, grinning at her, allowing some of the tension to leak out of the room. "Really, it's not."

"Fine," she said, not believing him at all. Milaro had a way of giving the truth without actually giving all of it, so he never actually lied, but more omitted the whole truth and didn't feel guilty in the slightest.

Must be an elf thing.

Cadre cleared his throat. "We are still looking into the sequencing. It's coming along. There are several other tests that I will need to run that will take some time. I can say, however, that right now I am approximately 97% sure the suggestion you made will work."

Quinn sat up straighter at that announcement. "Are you serious? It'll work?"

"Well, not a hundred percent yet, but all signs indicate that any damaged memory segments can be replaced. However, that is only to do with the functioning of the system - to get it back to operating at an optimum level." He glanced sideways to the others. "I'll let Siliqua explain further."

"Okay, give it to me," Quinn said, leaning back in her chair as if to brace herself for the crash landing she knew was about to come. This sounded a little too good to be true. After all, she'd been totally reaching when she suggested genetic sequencing. Considering she had no science background at all, her comment was made off of some vague media sensationalizing she recalled.

Siliqua gave her a sad smile. "See, we can replace any malfunctioning part of the overall system with the same undamaged sequence. However, in doing so we'll remove any corrupted information or memories or files that we currently cannot see. That sequence will then replace those permanently. Since we don't want to delete those memories forever yet, we are endeavoring to pull the remnants of them, the files behind them, I guess you could say, the memories that were deleted. We are aiming to retrieve them before we attempt to repair the functioning portions of the sequence."

Quinn blinked. "So it's gonna take a while."

"Yes," Cadre said, "it's going to take a long while."

Quinn blinked at Cadre, then thought over his words and realized that figuring out what memories had been wiped might be easier now if they could potentially repair them too. Unless she'd misunderstood. "Does that mean we'll probably be able to repair the missing pieces as well? I mean, to restore them so we can ascertain what information they didn't want us to know?"

Cadre's eyes lit up. "Precisely. At least theoretically. Again, the success chances are very high right now, but I cannot deal in absolutes when I have yet to test the process out."

Quinn nodded slowly as she took it all in. "And when you say it's going to take a long time, what do you mean? Years?"

"I wouldn't estimate that it will take years. However, I would caution that it may take several months for us to retrieve the memories we seek. I'm cautious to overpromise and underdeliver." It was obvious that Cadre was trying desperately not to offend Quinn.

"You know, Cadre, I think you're pretty cool. I come from somewhere that had no access to magic. Somewhere, well, you're all fantastical creatures to me, so it's kind of less about me getting upset with you and more about me going, 'Oh wow, magic can pretty much do anything.'" She smiled as non-threateningly as she could.

Cadre laughed and seemed to lose some of the tension that was spread across his shoulders. "Oh, well, that does make a lot of sense, Librarian. I will endeavor to retrieve those memories. Harish and I have been working on this as well as the sequencing."

"Fantastic," Quinn said.

"Speaking of which," Harish said, "there has been an interesting turn of events."

"How interesting?" Quinn asked.

"We've been breaking down Lynx's missing memories and have been sorting the gaps into a timeline of sorts. It's not perfect yet and we still have a lot of work to do, but it does appear these gaps started approximately six hundred years before Kor retired. At least, that appears where Lynx is frequently missing chunks. Once we've figured out exactly how to catalogue and determine that we've found all of them, we should be able to apply the same principle to the Library."

Quinn looked at Lynx. "Are you okay?"

He shrugged, seeming completely and utterly defeated. "I'm still here," he said. "I think I'm still me, but right now it's my priority to try and recall some of those instances. I'll push through."

"What sort of information are we talking about?" Quinn asked as a thousand questions popped into her head at once right alongside the worry for Lynx. "Does this correspond to times when there are gaps in the Library's recollection as well? Or you won't know until you've applied the same methods to the Library too?"

Harish nodded and handed her several pieces of diagrammed paper. Quinn looked up at him and said, "Couldn't you just send that to me?"

"No, no, this is something I mapped out by hand. With all of the corruption and missing information we've been encountering, I don't want to risk anyone else accidentally or deliberately gaining access to our current process. Right now I'm trying to account for all possibilities." He gestured to the pages. "This is the surest way I know to keep it only in our hands."

"So you mean there's someone potentially monitoring the entire Library system through outside means. Like a backdoor into a system?" Quinn asked.

The alarm on Siliqua and Cadre's face told Quinn that they hadn't even contemplated that possibility and that they were horrified by it. But Harish simply nodded.

"Great." Quinn took a deep breath. "I guess we really can't trust that inputting information into the system right now will mean it A: remains for our eyes only, and B: remains at all."

"Exactly," Harish said. "There is a pattern, time-wise. I'm sure once we can allocate these memories to their specific subjects or to the specific things that were viewed, recorded, or occurred, we will be able to piece together a timeline of incidents that led up to the shutdown of the Library . . ."

"And," Siliqua interjected, "this will also enable us to hopefully pinpoint perhaps some of the Serpensiril's allies or collaborators, conspirators, however we want to call them."

Quinn could feel a massive headache coming on. This was so much information for her to take in, even welcome as it was.

"Anyway," Lynx said, clearing his throat, and Quinn thought perhaps doing his best not to sound forlorn. "About six hundred years before Kor sought to retire, there was a shift in these memories and the blanks. They began to appear semi-frequently."

"Not before then?" Quinn asked.

Lynx shrugged. "I can't guarantee that, but we have a minor starting point."

"Were there any signs that something had changed?" Quinn asked. "For her, I mean."

"None that we noticed at the time," Milaro finally spoke up. "I've always been a frequent visitor of the Library, at least once a week, sometimes more."

"And now you hang around like a bad smell," Quinn quipped with a grin.

"Well, it's not my fault you don't give me time for a shower, is it now?" the king said and smoothly continued the discussion. "Anyway, looking back now at the mapped missing sections, it seems obvious that something happened. Lynx, do you remember her behavior changing or anything like that?"

Lynx shook his head. "Not suddenly or anything. It's just . . . there were . . ." His face scrunched up as if he was trying his hardest to remember details.

Aradie hooted long and low, coming in to land on Quinn's shoulder again. She nudged Quinn.

"Oh, what? You remember something?" Quinn scritched under her neck.

Aradie nodded and then did something she very rarely did. She spoke to the whole group, not just in imaged into Quinn's mind. *Korradine had a visitor around that time, perhaps a few years before it.*

"What, didn't she usually get visitors?" Quinn asked.

Not in general, Aradie said.

"Your owl is correct," Lynx piped in. "Kor loved the books, and was obsessed with magic and all forms of its knowledge. She may as well have been married to the Library. She loved her job so much. But I . . . I don't remember this visitor," he said, looking at Aradie.

The bird fluffed her wings and gave Lynx an almost human stare down.

"Oh," he said, "maybe it did start a few years before we think, then."

It is odd that Lynx does not remember, Aradie said, *because he was there. He was there when her visitor came in. I didn't think anything of it at the time. It wasn't a species we generally have problems with. In fact, it was a Daríghâhnish.*

"Wait, what?" Quinn said. "A Daríghâhnish?"

Exactly.

Milaro's expression darkened. "Pray tell, Aradie, can you show us an image of this specific Daríghâhnish?"

Yes, but you can't react right now until we have all of the information. There was hesitation in Aradie's words.

"But maybe that's where it started, Aradie," Quinn said. "Do you think they did something to her?"

Not this person in particular, but it was an odd encounter. And Aradie showed everybody the image of a gorgeous, purplish-bluish skinned Daríghâhnish with black hair, so dark it looked like an ink bottle had spilled on it. Their eyes were bright red and shone like a thousand rubies.

Milaro gasped, and his face suddenly resembled a thundercloud.

"I take it you recognize her?" Quinn asked dryly.

"Yes," he said, his eyes still fixated on the image. "That's Malakai's maternal great-aunt."

3

MUCH MORE TO RECALL

QUINN SHOOK HER HEAD AS IF TRYING TO DETERMINE WHETHER SHE'D mishcard Milaro. "Wait a second. Malakai's maternal great-aunt?" Not having had family for the longest time, familial relations weren't exactly her forte.

"Yes," Milaro confirmed, avoiding her gaze, which was unusual behavior for him.

"You're saying she's part of your extended family?" Quinn asked, just to clarify.

Milaro nodded, cringing slightly. Quinn couldn't help feeling surprised and immediately suspicious, not of Milaro, but of the circumstances surrounding this person's visit to the Library. Especially given that Malakai didn't like talking about his mother's side of the family.

Harish interjected, "You mean Ardenil?" He pointed at the frozen image. "That's Ardenil?"

Milaro sighed. "Yes, that is one hundred percent Ardenil."

"Well, that's just . . ." Harish stuttered, glancing at Siliqua, who was fidgeting with her hands and avoiding eye contact.

Quinn cleared her throat, completely lost. "Can someone explain to me the significance of this person being Ardenil?"

Milaro sighed again, a habit that was beginning to irritate Quinn. "Ardenil was banished several hundred years ago, I'd say about seven hundred?"

Harish shook his head. "More like seven hundred and fifty."

Quinn held up her hands to stop their conversation. "Rewind. Why?"

"It's a bit of a long story," Milaro cautioned.

"Then make time to tell the long story," Quinn insisted. She was determined that people would fill her in earlier rather than later. *We really need to get a history section,* she said, addressing the Library.

We have historical magical texts.

No, just a history section, so I can absorb knowledge about everything, and you guys will stop leaving me out of the loop.

You can't just absorb random knowledge. It has to be magical.

Then it should be! Quinn realized she was trying to take the easy way out, but it would make things much easier if she could.

The Library remained silent.

I know, that was silly of me. I just need to know this stuff.

We all do. The Library sounded a little sad.

Milaro heaved a heavy sigh. "Well, she had a great falling out with Malirsha, who was my son's grandmother, about their, shall we say, species inclinations, way before my son married into the family, but they are technically kin."

"Oh, tell it properly," Siliqua interjected, crossing her arms. "She was of the Chaos Faction."

Quinn raised an eyebrow at the name that sounded very much like a video game. "What do you mean, Chaos Faction?"

"Well, you see, the Darigháhnish have a lot of factions. They're more segmented than most of our cousins. They have chaotic factions, fervent religious factions, and don't forget the militantly strict monitoring of the sector faction whose name I can't quite recall. And then there are the anti-magic factions. Those ones are fun." Siliqua's sarcasm spoke to the reality being the precise opposite.

"What do you mean, anti-magic factions? How can you be anti-magic when everyone on your planet knows magic exists?" That made absolutely no sense to Quinn.

"They believe the body should be used as intended without enhancements or assistance from magic." It appeared to be taking Siliqua considerable strength not to roll her eyes. "Let's just say they often end up having to trade crops with those who have had some magical assistance in producing them. You'd think that made them hypocrites but it's not something they'll even debate. Anyway, we're digressing. Now you know they have factions."

"Thank you," Quinn said to Siliqua. "I seem to recall when we went to the Dabilian home world that Malakai mentioned he had a chaotic affinity of some sort."

"Yes, exactly," Milaro confirmed. "He got that from his mother's side of the family. The Darigháhnish have always had a sympathetic chaotic origin, shall we say." Milaro's expression was thunderous, clearly annoyed. There was some serious history there, but it seemed they would be discussing that later as well.

Still, Quinn understood she'd have to take her wins where she could. She waved everything away and asked outright, "So what does this visit between this Ardenil person and our Librarian mean?"

"Well, I'm not a chaos theorist, but Ardenil was, and she was very devout about it. She attempted multiple times to get Malirsha to renounce the family's path and veer away from all other affinities, to only take on those with chaotic elements, which several bloodlines have done. But all of the combinations can be extremely dangerous without being tempered by others, especially when combined with a pure chaos affinity."

Quinn scowled and narrowed her eyes at him. "You made me believe that chaos affinities just weren't a thing."

"No I didn't. We just don't encourage them." Milaro didn't even seem fazed that he'd been caught in an omission. "They are a rare thing and extremely species based. It has a lot to do with your genetic makeup."

Quinn cringed. "Yes, my genetic makeup. Okay, that's great."

Quinn looked at the image again and replayed it. "Could this have been just a regular visit?"

"Look at the tension in their shoulders," Siliqua said, leaning in as the image was replayed yet again. It was only a few short seconds and didn't show much but an overview as Aradie had moved through the Library. Probably thinking nothing of it at that stage. "That doesn't look like a friendly chat."

"Maybe she had an overdue book," Cadre suggested, "which we cannot currently check because of the state of the Library's recollection of its collection."

Quinn sighed as the Migalexutal began to crack up. Cadre wasn't wrong, it was just frustrating and he horrid comedic timing. She ended up choosing to ignore it. "Okay then, did she frequent the Library?"

"Of course she frequented the Library," Lynx chimed in. "If I recall correctly, which we all know may not be the case right now, she semi-frequently checked in on the restricted section. Although I do recall barring her from that several times because she spent too much time in there."

The words came out slower and slower as realization dawned until Lynx finally just shrugged. "I don't know. I just know she was here as a pretty frequent visitor. What, maybe a thousand years ago? Five centuries before we had to shut down?"

"But you do recall her being here? Not just because of this projection, right?" Quinn tried to prod gently.

"I mean, yes, I recall her as an individual. And I don't recall this particular event. As you can see, I'm not in the image." His voice grew softer as he spoke until he sounded thoroughly confused. "Well, maybe. Really, Quinn, I'm just not a reliable source anymore."

"It's okay, Lynx. We'll get things sorted again, okay?" She gave his arm a brief squeeze and realized it wasn't as tangible as usual.

"I know," he said, but she couldn't help feeling like he was just saying that. They needed to help him.

"Well, the image isn't clear enough for us to read their lips," Quinn said, as she bent far too close to it, peering at it.

Aradie hooted indignantly.

"I'm sorry, I'm not being critical. I'm just making an observation."

Aradie flew back to her perch. Now Quinn had to deal with an irritated owl later on after they'd figured out what to do about this image. Why couldn't anything just be easy for once? This just made it one more thing that Quinn had to add to the list.

"Malakai won't know anything about this, will he?" she asked, even though she was aware of the base emotions he had for his mother's side of the family.

"No, she was banished about seven hundred years before my son and his wife even met, way before Malakai was born." Milaro chuckled. "I realize the scope of years must seem absurd to you."

"Perhaps a little," Quinn conceded. "You said Malakai is thirty, right?"

"Yes, he's still a baby." Milaro winked at her.

"Yeah, young," Quinn said. Couldn't this have just been straightforward? She had missing books to get back to the Library and its new branch. There were lost books from the restriction vault that she desperately had to get back because they were magically dimensionally evil. There were branches to open, fabricated memories, lost memories, warped memories to regain and retrieve. The system was damaged and those were all just starting points. It seemed like the lists just kept getting longer and longer and there was more and more to do.

And very little of it felt like it was getting resolved.

It felt infinitely impossible to complete all the tasks in front of her.

"Quinn," Milaro said, and she looked up, focusing on him. "It's okay. I realize it all feels very overwhelming right now, but you're not alone in this, at least, right?"

"Yeah," she said. "At least I'm not alone." She glanced down at the picture again and squinted. "Is Ardenil even speaking to Korradine in this?"

They all peered a lot closer and Aradie hooted.

"You don't think so? Well, I'm glad you decided to tell us this now," Quinn said irritably.

Another hoot.

"Of course, I would have listened to—" she said to the owl. "Whatever . . . we're talking later."

Aradie shrugged and turned around on her perch, giving Quinn the cold shoulder. She sighed and counted to three in her head before turning back to the image and speaking. "It doesn't look like they're talking."

"It looks like Ardenil is speaking to Korradine. Korradine doesn't appear to be reacting at all, except for the tension in her shoulders," Siliqua said. "This is actually quite fascinating."

"I'm glad you find the Librarian ignoring a patron to be so exciting," Quinn said. "And it's only a few seconds. For all we know there could have been a very heated response mere seconds after this interaction."

"No, no, Quinn, that's not it. Why would she be standing there talking to her without having an actual conversation? Ardenil was never a patient person. There should be books flying around, which she wouldn't have cared to damage. Probably some fists flying." Siliqua's eyes narrowed. "She was a little bit of a violent person. Probably where Malakai gets his fighting streak from."

Quinn angled the image differently. "Well, she's certainly speaking to Korradine."

Cadre perked up at that and leaned forward, peering closely. "Hmm, it almost seems like she's speaking *through* Korradine, perhaps. Maybe my eyes aren't what they used to be. There are other options. Just because it's the two of them doesn't mean it *is* the two of them."

"What?" Quinn asked, shaking her head to try and clear up what she just thought she heard.

Cadre grimaced. "Let me try to explain. Lynx, could you please become Ardenil for a moment?"

Lynx sighed and suddenly in the blink of an eye, Ardenil was not only in the image in front of them, but also well . . . in front of them.

Cadre cleared his throat. "See. Just because it's the two of them, doesn't mean it's them."

"So it could also be shapeshifters?" Quinn asked.

Cadre shrugged. "Or something convincing perceptions that events occurred."

"Just like when it showed Lynx taking the book from the restricted section in that owl's memories?" Quinn asked, suddenly remembering.

"Precisely." Cadre smiled this time.

"Oh . . . I remember reading something," Quinn said as another idea struck her, compounding with Cadre's revelation. The problem with filling her mind with so many new books in the last two weeks was that it was more difficult to locate some of the older information she'd read. It wasn't that it disappeared or that she replaced the space it had taken in her brain. It was more that there was just so much more to recall. It meant Milaro teaching her how to speed up her inner thoughts before almost anything else had been a brilliant idea.

"There was something. This is . . . this is really familiar," she continued, trying to pull up the relevant information in her mind.

"What do you mean it's familiar?" Siliqua asked. "Is this something that would happen on Earth where people just ignore each other? I . . . I don't feel like she's ignoring Ardenil. It's something else."

"You don't need to just make excuses for Korradine," Lynx said. "It's enough for us to know now that she betrayed us. The whole Library, me, all of us. I just wish I knew when she turned. When they managed to convince her that to help destroy the Library."

"I'm sure that's not what they did," Quinn said to Lynx even though she didn't even have a gut instinct. But she wanted to lessen that blow for him. "I'm positive that she still loved the Library for a very long time."

"Well, it's very obvious that she didn't when she started doing this to us." Lynx blinked out of the room abruptly.

Quinn sighed. "Well, that didn't go well."

"Did you think it would?" Milaro asked. "Right now, he's having to juggle the fact that somebody who he worked closely with for thousands of years literally betrayed everything Lynx stands for. Everything he is made of and somehow manipulated his memories and the

Library's memories of those events. Even worse, she took those memories. Altered, deleted . . . she stole from them."

"That's it," Quinn said. "Exactly. There was . . . there was a mention. Oh. Can we figure out if Ardenil came before this time? Maybe a few years? Aradie, please, please, when is one of the most recent times before this visit that Ardenil entered the Library?"

Still not turning her back around to the front, Aradie finally projected another image.

"This is about two years earlier?" Quinn asked her.

Aradie nodded.

"Oh great, you're not even speaking to me in images anymore," Quinn muttered.

Aradie turned her head around and winked before turning it back. They were gonna have a long talk later.

"Oh, but she's not interacting with Korradine?" Quinn asked.

Aradie shook her head and then hooted once, low and mournfully. "Oh, you don't know if she saw her. That's odd. Did she take out any books at that point in time?"

"No, there's no record in the system," Milaro said slowly. "Not that that necessarily tells us anything anyway."

Harish gasped, "But there is one of those gaps."

Quinn had this idea in her head and she wasn't sure if she should pursue it, but some of the actions she'd seen Korradine eliciting in these projected memories from Aradie spoke against everything Lynx had said about her. "Do you think it's possible that she cast a spell on her or, perhaps that none of this is Ardenil at all and just some shapeshifter insert who is giving us a red herring? Or . . . I don't know, inserted like a brain-eating parasite to control her with?" Quinn asked, just throwing some ideas out there.

Milaro blinked at her, a sad smile tugging at his lips. "Yes, those are all possibilities, Quinn. But I would also think them highly unlikely given later events."

"Oh," she said, not entirely sure what she should say next because she had no idea how to determine any of the ideas she'd come up with after so much time had passed. But she was suddenly extremely tired.

4

ALMOST SUFFOCATING

The air around Quinn thickened when she opened her eyes. Not even simply like a fog, but instead, like an actual cloying air density all around her. There was dampness to it, almost suffocating, and no matter where she looked, haze shrouded everything.

Not the obscured-by-mist type either, but more like she had very bad eyesight and had forgotten to wear her prescription glasses. Nothing was recognizable, and for several seconds Quinn almost forgot to breathe.

Muffled sounds reached her ears, as if something was climbing around in the walls, perhaps scuttling about on the floors. Yet she couldn't see any of these creatures. Hell, she couldn't even see the floor properly. It, too, was a hazy grey mass.

That's when she realized a few things. Aradie wasn't perched on her shoulder, nor was she wearing the leather perch for her to do so. Quinn had gone to sleep ages ago and remembered this distinctly because she'd had a long, relaxing bath beforehand. And this wasn't the same room she'd fallen asleep in.

In fact, as she glanced down and realized there was a couch beneath her and not a bed, things began to twist into focus from the haze of the unrecognizable.

The hall was long and wide, and the only furniture in it was the red couch she'd been asleep on. The grey stone walls, floor, and pillars emanated a coldness she felt through to her bones, and as she stood up somewhat shakily, she realized she had bare feet.

She was back in her dream world. Or, more precisely, the world Kajaro had coaxed her into when he initially triggered the mind bomb he'd planted. Only the last couple of times she's ventured into it, it was clear it no longer belonged to him.

Instead, she'd made it her own.

This was where the tomes she'd absorbed came in handy. Time moved differently in her dreams, and she'd devoured a lot more information and practiced since the last time she'd set foot in one of these.

Usually, they were triggered by something. At first, it came from the implanted device that Kajaro had planted. Then it came because he was alive, and she was drawn to reveal his machinations. But back then, she'd only had rudimentary mental and dream skills.

Now, she felt much more prepared.

Except for the fact that this was a medieval-type reception hall and not the hallway she'd been in the last time she visited. She closed her eyes briefly to send out her senses into this dream world. It was her mind, therefore what she wanted to accomplish should work.

She didn't sense anything out of the ordinary, but she did still hear the scuttling and that wasn't something she'd dreamed up on her own. So it was either someone trying to reach her again, which meant likely Tenejo or Kajaro, or else there was something she'd noticed subconsciously and needed to try and figure out.

Quinn cast part of her mind to sorting through all the observations she'd had recently, pushing through the haze to envision things she'd witnessed in the Library. The whole incident with Tenejo flashed into her mind. He hadn't touched her, not even come close to her.

And yet, shadows lingered around that memory that didn't make sense to her. Something she could pry into. Perhaps something that her previous actions allowed to gain a foothold in her subconsciousness.

But those shadows weren't making the noises that grew more insistent every second she spent considering something else.

There didn't appear to be any trace left of Kajaro anymore, and her link to him had faded over the last two months so that she would have to focus very hard to see if she could locate his mind. To be honest, trying to do so seemed reckless.

Then there were yesterday's or last night's events or however time references worked in relation to her dream world. This whole Ardenil visit felt almost like a red herring to her, and still needed to be investigated just in case it turned out to be something.

But that wasn't pressing enough to trigger this world. Was it? To trigger this state of mind of hers?

Instead of panicking like she could feel trying to bubble up in her throat, Quinn plopped herself on the ground and sat cross-legged, closing her eyes in order to try and center herself. Time warped weirdly in dreams, and in a way, she knew she had all the time in the world right now.

Or as little of it as she allowed herself.

She let herself relax and reached tentatively for those sounds that appeared to skitter out of her hearing just when she thought she'd finally gotten close to them. The more she listened and focused, the clearer the sounds became until she finally realized they were dry branches blowing in the wind, insects scuttling through rotting vegetation.

Rotting vegetation, bloodied tree limbs, remnants of wings and appendages dangling from the bark . . .

"We've been waiting for you, Librarian. Won't you stay a while?"

How had this specific memory managed to dangle in the back of her mind so much that it had finally pulled her into this? What was it about that memory, apart from the sheer grossness of it? Were there clues she should have picked up on?

Obviously. Of course.

Otherwise she wouldn't be here.

Once she'd latched onto the reason for her dream world, her senses began to pick up on other things. Slight shifts in the air, an adjustment in the hall she was currently in, and a definitive sensation of decay coming from outside of the hall.

She pushed herself up from the ground, aware now that instead of the initial haze, she'd arrived in here with, there was now a sense of miasma seeping in through all the stones that made up her fortress.

Seeping through cracks she couldn't see.

"I want you to disappear."

Those words echoed through her head, through the halls, bouncing off the stone walls to create a cacophony of sound that threatened to split her head.

And then it stopped, and complete silence descended upon her. Quinn shuddered.

She had no idea how this one had got through to plant a seed into her mind, but then it wasn't like the mind bomb. This was like a memory trying to get her attention, perhaps to study it in more detail, to see it in more detail.

Because the devil was in the details.

As she walked out of the hall, it opened up into a misty version of the copse of trees they'd found the demonic tree in originally.

And there, right in front of her, was the tree.

The tree groaned in that horrific humanoid way. The one that made her wonder if it was in fact a person that had been warped into this bloodletting thing.

This time when its branches moved, it was more like shaking itself awake from a long slumber instead of shaking pests loose from itself. There was more blood too, dripping constantly in congealed strands as it slowly dribbled down.

Its two wide and gaping eyes held more malevolence and were entirely red and black now. Some of the serrated, jagged teeth had been broken. Several of its branches appeared to be covered in ice. Just like when she'd frozen it.

Only then she'd exploded it, and this shouldn't be possible. Thus, this was a remnant, a memory, either of hers or its. Somehow it had cemented itself into a position in her mind. She just wished she didn't have to figure out the why while having to deal with the visage of that tree all over again.

It was one of her least favorite Librarian moments so far.

Then the voice spoke out again—a roar in that guttural tone, like fingernails on a chalkboard down her spine.

Villain! We are no villains. It is you who seek to contain the true power of the universe, who seek to limit chaos. You are the misguided ones.

Misguided for not wanting things to be overrun with chaos. That really was a unique take. While Quinn now remembered this portion of the conversation, she wasn't entirely sure what it meant. There seemed to be more meaning behind the words than she'd initially attributed to it.

Quinn wracked her brain as the words echoed through the halls over and over again as if it was trying to fill her mind with only that.

For just a split second she truly wished Milaro was there with her. He had a way of making these things make sense, of helping her out of her own head.

And then she remembered something Milaro said while she was synchronizing with the Library last time. He'd been speaking to the Library directly and thus it was an in-passing comment between the two of them. But it rang through her head now, as loudly as a bell.

You were simply part of original creation.

But wasn't chaos the origin of creation? And wasn't the whole point of filtering the chaotic elements so that chaos didn't overwhelm in volume and start devouring all that it had created again?

She scanned through all her knowledge gained from the books of the Dabilian homeworld. *Laws of Chaos, Upside Down, Chaos Theory, Myth and Legend, Reality Combined, Chaos Fever Dream* and *Mastering Your Reality Through Chaos.*

Chaos was the originator. It was the very first spark that created everything else. She'd had this pounded into her head by the Library, Lynx, and every book she'd picked up on the subject. With the Serpensiril confirmed as enemies, they'd been seeking their allies for a long time.

Logically, with the phrasing, the voice in the tree had to be one of the original species then. One of the originals. Which meant she had to figure out which species those were.

Quinn walked right up to the tree, taking in everything about it. Trying to push past the gag reflex that immediately triggered. Her recollection was eerily accurate. Right down to the membranes of the wings sticking out from the portions of the tree that had devoured the Esposian Furionas.

The fae species who had fallen victim to the tree and the book of sacrifice. Who Geneva had been taking care of ever since.

There was a niggling in the back of Quinn's mind. Something unsettling, something that wasn't quite sitting right. Geneva's shock over the appearance of her cousins had been genuine. But Quinn had never thought to ask why. It seemed that Furionas were relatively fragile, so of course if a bigger and more powerful opponent appeared they'd be obliterated if their magic was also stronger.

But the only creature in that clearing had been the tree. And its shadows, of course, but for all intents and purposes as she glanced around her recreation, Quinn could tell the shadows were simply an extension of the tree's will.

So who had forced the Esposians into their plight?

The Furionas were a conglomeration of ancient species who all shared similarities. But as Geneva said, and as Lynx and all the information Quinn had seen led her to believe, those factions or differing tribes lived separately from one another.

Quinn's stomach heaved as realization hit her. She didn't want to be right, but it was the only solution she could think of. What was worse, was that she didn't know how she'd been blind to it in the first place. Why hadn't she seen it to begin with?

She could feel Tenejo's memories that she'd extracted in the back of her mind, like they too wanted to get out as if they had so much to tell her. But right now, she needed to wake up and let the others know what she'd gleaned from going over that horrific memory several times.

Tenejo was going to have to wait a bit longer.

Her list of things to do just got even longer.

She had to figure out precisely how to prove, outside of her head, that the Esposians rulers had brought their citizen's demise on themselves.

5

COMPLEX SITUATIONS

QUINN CLUTCHED HER HEAD IN HER HANDS, TRYING TO MAKE SENSE OF all the information she had at hand. Not to mention the fact that she had lists and lists of books. Thousands of them still had to be retrieved in order to open up the other branches, which would then have thousands of books of their own to retrieve. She glanced over the list and sighed.

Main Branch Tome Report

6,997 are still outstanding from the initial overdue amount. 11,045 books returned. 5 books being reproduced. 16 missing restricted books.

Horticulture: 503/720

Bardic Musical: 580/897

Crafting: 472/730

Alchemical/Medicinal: 289/384

Combat: 604/837

Academy: 542/785

Culinary Arts: 282/282 - Culinary Branch Open – 3,654 Books of 3,795 remaining. Would you like a categorical breakdown?

Yes or No?

"No," Quinn muttered out loud, suppressing a groan.

Would you like a current listing of borrowed books?

Yes or No?

"No." Quinn let her head fall onto her arms. She could sense she was about to get visitors and at least that saved her from having to go over too many numbers.

Milaro knocked on the door and poked his head into her office. "How are you doing today, Librarian?" He asked, flashing her a grin.

"I've been better," she said, barely looking up at him. She had summoned him after all. "Thank you for coming. I had one of my weird dreams last night."

"Really? Do tell." He sounded full of curiosity, which was basically how he sounded on a daily basis.

"That's why I asked you to come." Quinn recounted the dream in detail, shuddering as she recalled the tree yet again and the way the voice grated against her spine like it was trying to rip out her spleen. When she was finished, Milaro looked incredibly thoughtful.

"Well?" she said, not feeling her most patient, which wasn't really patient at all anyway.

Milaro shrugged. "I don't know what to make of it. It feels more like your subconscious examining a memory than any real insidious trespassing into your mind. I do think we need to look into the Esposians. Have you seen Geneva recently?"

"No." Quinn sighed and leaned back in her chair. "She's been helping with their recovery and took a short leave of absence to do so. Hopefully she'll be getting back soon."

"You should summon her back, you can do that with your assistants."

Quinn shook her head. "I'm not so sure. I think she might need some time. She seemed pretty shaken up." Quinn wasn't unaffected by what they'd experienced, but these were a species variant of Geneva's – somewhat closely related. It was probably all too easy for her to imagine the same happening back on her own world.

Milaro nodded, a shadow passing over his gaze. "I think we need to look deeper into the Esposian islands. This didn't just happen over a short period of time, Quinn. That sacrifice is not something you slap together on a Friday night and have done by Sunday with a group of friends while drinking a few ales."

Quinn chuckled despite the gravity of the subject matter. "I didn't think it was. Okay, so we're now adding the Esposians to our list. Is that correct?"

"It wasn't like they tripped and fell on the book and accidentally sacrificed most of their population. I mean, that's a hefty book for them to have, right?" Milaro frowned.

"Definitely," Eric said, sweeping into the room, bowing with a flourish in the air toward Quinn, winking cheekily at her when he hovered upright again.

"You have like a sixth sense when it comes to stuff that is relegated to those five books, don't you, Eric?" Quinn asked.

"Well, to be fair, I actually have thirty-five senses." He quipped.

Quinn gaped at him. "Wait, thirty-five?"

He waved the question away with his hand. "Yes, but it's an imp thing, you probably wouldn't understand most of them anyway. So let's not get into that right now."

Quinn blinked at him, suddenly not sure she wanted to know what the other senses were. "I'm going to quiz you about at some point."

He shrugged. "You could just find a book on it."

"Speaking of books," Quinn said, glancing at the list that was still in front of her. "The returns appear to have slowed down. Although some of the culinary branch books have already been returned. Not many yet, but they've only got like two weeks left to give them back without a fine."

Eric's eyes glowed, and he rubbed his hands together. "I'll take care of all those fines for you, don't you worry, Librarian."

She didn't say anything but tried to hide the amused smile fighting to appear on her face.

"All right," Milaro said, pulling them back on track. "Malakai will be here shortly. I think we need to make a list by order of importance."

"Have we found the location of the other restricted tomes yet?" Quinn asked, suddenly feeling weary.

"No, but Siliqua seems to think we're fairly close to establishing where a couple of them are. We have general quadrant areas but nothing definitive enough where it would be marginally probable to locate the book in an acceptable time frame."

"I'd like to contact Jasper, she said she'd refine a couple of rituals that can help pinpoint a location, and see what we can figure out. Is that acceptable?"

"Jasper, Jasper . . . yes," Milaro said as if he only just remembered who that was. "I approve of Jasper, even though she is somewhat eccentric."

Quinn raised an eyebrow. "She's eccentric?"

"Hush now." Milaro grinned.

Lynx suddenly popped into view. "I also know we could technically restart another filtration pillar, but I looked at our energy levels and I think we need to get them up a little higher before we do so."

Quinn blinked at him. "Have you been practicing the sudden entrances?"

"Yes," he said smugly. "I actually have." Then he grimaced. "Come on, I've got to find some form of entertainment considering some of my memories seem to have taken time off."

"Focus," Milaro said.

Quinn rubbed her temples. "Okay, so we're on the same page, we need to approach the Esposians. Well, first of all, we need to talk to Geneva and see how their recovery is even going. Shouldn't we have sent people out to check the Esposians on the other islands?"

Milaro blinked at her. "Of course, we sent scouts out to the other islands. As surreptitiously as I could, just to pop their heads in and check. There didn't seem to be any evil, blood-sucking speaking trees that were using ritual sacrifice books, but we could always look again."

Quinn groaned. "I guess that's a good thing."

"Of course it's a good thing. Okay, so number one, can we get in contact with the Esposian king?"

"He's more like a lord. Probably wouldn't like it if you called him a king. It's very, what do you call us? Elfish?" Milaro grinned smugly.

"Yes, that's right," Quinn said, trying not to let Milaro's current playfulness get on her nerves. She was just stressing a little bit and she knew he made light of things to try and ease that tension, but right now it wasn't achieving that. "Okay, so we need to see the Esposians. We have to get those three books back as soon as we have locations. We need to check in on the Darigháhnish, right?"

"Ah, that is a familial matter and Malakai will be—"

"What am I going to be doing, Grandfather?" Malakai said, leaning against the door frame, arms crossed.

"Ah, yes, speak and he appears. It's like I summoned you."

"Well, you technically did like half an hour ago, but I was busy. I only just got here. What did I miss?"

"I'm going to send you to your mother's."

Malakai's face took on a hue that made it look as if a dark thundercloud had taken up residence in his face. Quinn shuddered at the look and vowed to avoid her friend's bad side. She spoke up cautiously. "He doesn't have to."

"Yes, he does. He has a standing invitation. It would make the questioning go much, much easier." For once Milaro's expression was hard and unwavering. Nothing like the kind dad joker she was used to. This was the king speaking. "And he hasn't seen his mother since his father died ten years ago."

"Oh," Quinn said. "Well, that's not awkward."

"Yes, it is," Malakai said. "It's extremely awkward. How could you think it's not?"

Quinn shrugged and looked away, unsure how to respond, considering she'd been using sarcasm. Probably not the best time to point that out.

Malakai, still scowling, turned to his father and grandfather. "Do you really think it's a good idea for me to take her with me to see Mom?"

Milaro looked like he was about to speak and then stopped short, casting a glance between Quinn and his grandson. He sighed. "Yeah, I didn't really think that through. But she could have some insight into your great-aunt. And right now, that's something we sincerely need. Probably more than we need to keep a lid on Quinn's origin."

"I guess I could ask her to keep it between us for now. You know she's going to sense everything, right?" Malakai sounded sullen.

Milaro hesitated and then sighed. "She usually does." He turned to Quinn with an apologetic smile. "There are multiple reasons why Malakai's mother is not currently in the picture."

"Why don't you just tell her? I mean, it's not like she was ever much of a mother anyway," Malakai spat out.

"She does love you in her own way." Milaro said, trying to smooth the waters over. Quinn cringed at that because in somebody's own way, didn't necessarily mean anything good.

"Yeah, well, maybe when I was like five, if I'd have understood what loving me in her own way meant, then maybe it would have been okay."

Quinn impulsively reached out and gave his arm a quick squeeze. "It's okay, we'll get this sorted."

Malakai at least gave her a half smile for her effort.

Lynx, as if he was tone deaf and completely oblivious to every-thing, which he probably was, butted into the conversation. "I don't know, from what you've told me, Arnekai is a pretty good mother. After all, she's made sure to give him his best chances by leaving him with Milaro. Makes sense to me." He shrugged.

Malakai scowled. Milaro rolled his eyes and Quinn decided that she and Lynx were going to have a very detailed conversation conven-tion about societal norms. Not that she was a universal expert on it, but he was so close to humanoid sometimes that Quinn often forgot he was a magical entity. She took a breath and spoke. "Okay, then, now that we've got that awkwardness out of the way . . ."

"Trust me," Malakai said, "it's not out of the way yet. However, what gives, Quinn?"

"Well, first of all, I'd like to go visit your mom. I think that would be pretty cool."

"Speaking of which, why don't we go visit *your* mom?" Malakai asked.

Quinn raised an eyebrow, trying not to let her memories tab her with pain. "Because the people who served as my parents on earth were killed when I was twelve and I grew up in foster care. Not completely unloved but, you know, not with parents who were really served as parents. They were just adults who made sure that we had what we needed and stayed safe."

"Oh," Malakai said, "well, I guess now it's really awkward, isn't it?"

Quinn laughed. "No, it's all good. I came to terms with that part of my life a long time ago. It's actually a lot better than a lot of people out there ever got. And I don't have many complaints."

"Don't you want to go back to Earth?" he asked.

Quinn thought that over for a few seconds. Did she want to go back to Earth? She'd already missed her deadline by two months for picking her major. She'd had a handful of sort of friends because she spent most of her time studying and the rest of it reading. And she didn't have extra spending money because everything went to room and board while her scholarship paid for the rest. She occasionally called her foster parents to let her foster mom know, at least, that she was doing pretty well. But that was like maybe once every month or two. She didn't think her foster mom would care much if she didn't call at all. And a foster dad definitely wouldn't. There were a couple of foster siblings who checked in with her every few weeks.

"Maybe," she said, wondering why she honestly hadn't thought of this before. "Maybe I should go back soon just to let people know that I won't be around anymore so they don't worry."

"You've been gone for like two months. Don't you think they'll already have worried?" Malakai asked.

Quinn blinked at him and said, "I don't know. What usually happens when the Library sucks somebody into this dimension? Does like a truck hit me or a building collapse on me?"

Lynx piped up. "No, we pretty much just kind of reached through and grabbed you. Except it was really hard to because there's no ambient magic on your world. It took a lot more malachite crystals to get you through to here than it would from anywhere else. Because it has to feed on the actual magic contained within them. And Earth has no ambient magic to help fuel the process, whereas most worlds do."

"Oh, is that why Earth has no magic users?"

"Pretty much, that's why you were kind of safe there." Milaro spoke softly.

"Yeah, I don't think, I don't think my guardians would have agreed with you," Quinn said, a flash of sadness at their passing constricted her chest. She took a moment to recover before speaking again. "Yeah, maybe I should go back and just let people know that I'm okay. I mean, I've still got my phone. I could easily just find somewhere to charge it and text people and say, 'Don't look for me. I've started a new life. I'm absolutely fine.'" With any luck, the auto debit had continued to take money out of her account. She didn't have a lot, but she did have some emergency savings.

"I'd love to see some of these devices you've talked about," Malakai said, suddenly perking up. "I mean, I think that would be fun."

Quinn raised an eyebrow. "You mean nobody else has technology like that in the universe?" She found that very difficult to believe.

"Of course they do. Not quite as you seem to have described it, though because most places use magic as a means to fuel things. So, I want to see a world that functions fully without magic. That's just bizarre to me." His eyes lit up and it was like he'd forgotten they were going to see his mother. That subject change had been all sorts of obviously deliberate.

"Well, how about we go see your mother? And then we go question the Esposians. And if we haven't found any of the books' locations by then, I'll make a quick trip home and you can come with me. As long as we disguise your skin tone and ears. Maybe put your hair in a ponytail." Quinn looked at him critically. If all else failed he could probably pass as a cosplayer with a few tweaks.

"In a ponytail?" Malakai asked incredulously.

"Yeah, in a ponytail."

"Seriously, I guess you're going to ask me to wear jeans next."

"Well." She looked at his baggy fighting pants and grimaced. "You can't turn up in those pants."

"Really?" he said. "There's nothing wrong with these. These are like the height of fashion."

Quinn cut in. "For a sword-wielding, bow-wielding Darigháhnish, maybe?"

"Ah," he said, "I see your point. You promise we'll go visit your world and make sure people realize that you're okay and not dead?"

"Yeah," Quinn said. "I promise."

Lynx grumbled under his breath. "I miss out on all the fun."

"But that's okay, Lynx. We'll get you sorted and maybe make another trip. We just won't have to send anybody messages."

"Well," Milaro said, "this all sounds like a plan. Let's get you ready to go and visit Arnekai."

"Okay, so let's redo it. Visit Malakai's mom." Malakai scowled at Quinn's words. "Talk to the Esposians. Make sure the people on my end don't think I'm dead. Find the books. Figure out who's trying to kill us all. Live happily ever after."

"Quinn, my dear, you always know how to simplify such complex situations," Milaro said.

Quinn rolled her eyes.

6

LOOSE ENDS

Several things bugged Quinn about the Library's current status. Even though she was glad word had spread that the Library was open again for business, she wasn't pleased with the fact that so many of the visitors were just there to sit and enjoy the books.

This was totally within their rights, but the return of books had slowed significantly. This meant she'd probably have to send people, including herself, out into the universe to retrieve the books people weren't bringing back, or to find the books that were having a difficult time making their way to the Library.

She found herself obsessed with the idea of hundreds of little books on the same planet, all taking part in a trek across a desert to get to a door that would see them reach the Library. Their little covers inching across like they were crawling.

She needed to get out more.

Quinn stood surveying the Library, her senses reaching out, noticing more and more doors opening. More people now frequented the culinary branch and the dining hall in front of it, which provided wonderful food. People sat in the seating areas all around, many involved in book discussions. It was a wonderful sight to behold.

There were hundreds of thousands of books in this part of the Library, and some of these people didn't ever want to borrow one. They enjoyed coming to the Library and soaking up the atmosphere.

Suddenly, Lynx tapped on the desk next to her. She turned toward him and blinked. He stood on her left-hand side, his eyes filled with curiosity.

"What?" Quinn asked.

"Sorry. You were really deep in thought there. Is everything okay?" he asked.

"I'm just slightly worried about the whole Library thing," she replied.

"How so?"

"Well, didn't we only have like eighteen thousand books that we had to retrieve in total?" She asked. She knew the Library had so many books she couldn't personally count them without the system. Was there a reason only eighteen thousand had been missing?

"Yes, for the main branch of the Library anyway." Lynx smiled, obviously trying to make her feel better.

"But there are heaps more books in the Library. We have hundreds of thousands of books. Is that even enough for a universe?" she asked.

"Ah, yes and no. Remember, we can duplicate books. A lot of the books on the shelves have duplicates. Rudimentary beginner books especially. We have a plethora of them. The thing is, the books we have to retrieve, while beginner, intermediate, and advanced, have many that are more complex, advanced versions. While some of them are copies, they've soaked up excess magic in the world. We could make another copy if we couldn't retrieve them, but that would cost us energy. Instead of bringing in the ambient energy they have been soaking up for five hundred years, which is why we want the books that haven't been returned," Lynx explained.

"Now you've completely and utterly spelled it out for me like I was five. Now I understand," Quinn said. She knew he'd given her a similar explanation before, but this held more detail and helped her head.

"I'm sure I'd already explained it to you," Lynx replied.

"You kind of sort of did, but to be fair, I think my brain glossed over it. I've been taking in a lot of information lately." She smiled at him.

"Plus, there's going to be another twenty, thirty thousand books in total from all the other branches that we have to get to get them fully operational. Don't worry, we're not going to run out of work anytime soon," Lynx said, grinning at her.

Quinn sighed. She could already feel the throbbing starting in her temples. "Yeah, I wasn't worried about us running out of work."

"Oh," Lynx said, "then what was the problem?"

Before Quinn could answer, however, another source of headache approached.

"Are you kidding me?" Malakai said as he strode across the foyer toward the check-in desk, oblivious to the patrons gathering to return their books. "She hasn't bothered to reach out to me for a decade. Her son. And she said she doesn't have time right now."

Milaro looked like he probably wished he was anywhere else but talking to Malakai right then. "I know you're disappointed."

"Oh, I'm not disappointed. There is nothing she could do to disappoint me more than she already has," Malakai retorted.

"Malakai, your mother is—"

"Don't deny it. You hate her too." Malakai practically spat the words out, finally resting against the counter inside the check-in area.

"Well, it's no secret that I severely dislike her," Milaro said as he climbed into the check-in desk and nodded at Quinn and Lynx. "But she is your mother. And Miyago was very, very much in love with her. So sometimes I feel myself being more lenient with her than I would be with almost anybody else in the universe."

"Except for Quinn," Malakai interrupted, crossing his arms and glaring at his grandfather.

"Yes, except for Quinn. But we all know those are extenuating circumstances."

"Want to fill me in?" Quinn asked, hating to be talked about when she was standing right there with them.

"Well," Milaro said, shaking his head as if to clear it.

"My darling mother," Malakai said, "told me that she won't have time for me for a few days. She'll contact us when she's free."

"Oh," Quinn said, "is she royalty? Has lots of, like, business?"

Malakai laughed and Milaro shot him a glare that didn't shut his grandson up even slightly. Then the king sighed and answered. "Not quite. She's part of the ruling clan, but she's a researcher. A chaotic magic affinity researcher. She and her family have contributed a very large portion of the knowledge on the chaos affinity."

"Because the Darigháhnish have a chaos immunity or something like that, is that correct?" she said, remembering information without accessing it for once.

Malakai grunted, Milaro glared at his grandson again and nodded. "That would be correct. Obviously, it's a lot easier to research and observe something dangerous when you're at least partially immune, to a lot of its effects."

"Okay, so she doesn't have time. That's fine. Why are you so upset?" Quinn asked, keeping her tone even. She didn't want to sound too interested in his family drama. He could be fairly volatile about it.

"Because she—"

"Not now, Malakai," Milaro snapped.

"Well, if not now, when?" Malakai snapped right back. "Look, Quinn, my mother decided ten years ago, when my father died, that there were a lot more important things than her son. And she's just staying true to that, even today."

"I'm sorry, Mal," Quinn said, her voice soft, hoping it soothed a little bit. "We'll just go see her next week, okay?"

"Yeah," he said. "I guess we will."

She could tell he wished they didn't have to go and see her at all.

"It's just not the way I wanted it to go," he said.

"Hey, it's not the way any of us wanted it to go. But we have other leads and we have a lot of other things to do. How's the locator for the books going?" Quinn turned to the Library manifestation.

Lynx shook his head. "Nope, not ready yet. Probably be another few days before we're ready for it."

"Okay. Jasper is busy with a special harvest for one of the magical plants right now, so I know she can't come. I could just do some train-ing. Because Geneva is . . . when was it, Lynx?"

"She'll be back at the end of the week and apologizes profusely. But the Esposians that she rescued were in a little bit more dire straits than we anticipated. Those were her words."

Quinn pondered that. "Hmm. Well, I guess that'll be useful for us before we go and talk to the Esposians, right?"

"True." Malakai actually smiled and then he grinned at Quinn.

She knew there was nothing good going to come from that grin. "Fine, spill it. What?" She crossed her arms.

"Why don't we go take this opportunity of a couple of days of free time and visit *your* home, Quinn?" His eyes sparkled.

Quinn could feel the color draining from her face, even if it was only a bit. She'd talked pretty big the day before about going home and letting people know that she was fine, but in all honesty, being missing for a little over two months was not ideal in human society.

When had she started thinking of Earth as the home to a human species? That felt . . . odd. Quinn had to stop herself from going down that rabbit hole.

Still.

They probably missed her. Why hadn't she gone earlier? She hadn't even really thought about it. She'd been so caught up in this adventure where she was an important figure. But he was right. She needed to at least put people at ease if she ever wanted to go back. Sure, she could go whenever, but in order to do so, she needed to not be a missing person.

"Okay," she said. "I guess that's a good idea."

"There's one problem with returning to your homeworld." Lynx spoke up. He hesitated before elaborating. "You won't have direct access to Library and system functions, or at least you won't have much access."

Quinn blinked at him. It made sense. Earth didn't have magic. "So how did you pull me here? Did you pull on my magic?"

"No," Lynx said. "We used the Library's last vestiges of magic to boost the signal to grab you."

"But you didn't pull me through a door."

"Yes, I did. I made a trapdoor appear underneath you and I pulled you through the floor."

"Oh. That's why I fell down." The memory flashing through her mind.

"Yes, that's why you fell down," Lynx conceded. "I seriously thought you'd already figured all this out." He sounded somewhat put out.

Quinn ignored his pout. "So, you literally just yanked me through the floor. Wouldn't everybody have seen it?"

"There would have been a momentary sort of earthquake sensation for most people and maybe disorientation." Lynx shrugged. "And because the world doesn't have magic and they wouldn't have believed a trapdoor suddenly opening in the middle of a floor where there had never been a trapdoor before, and a person disappearing into it and not reappearing again."

Quinn blinked. Milano chuckled. "It's a perception thing, Quinn. If people don't believe in magic, they often simply won't see it. Or else they'll perceive it as something else."

"But I believed it when I got here."

Malakai laughed. "That's probably because you literally just got sucked through an emergent trapdoor and into a massive star-like chamber, right?"

Quinn nodded. He made sense. It was very true. The core chamber had seemed supremely magical when she arrived. "So you mean I won't have access to the interface or anything like that?"

"Probably a rudimentary version, considering your actual heritage," Lynx said. "Ooh, I may have to run a couple of analyses on that. I wonder if Siliqua would help me." He started muttering under his breath.

"Hello," Quinn said, clicking her fingers. "Can we focus on me for a second?"

"Quinn," Milaro said, "now the real you comes out. I always knew you were a bit of an attention hog."

She glared at him.

He laughed. "If looks could kill."

"Stop it." But she felt better. Her trepidation was mostly gone and she knew she had Milaro to thank for that.

"Okay, so if I don't have access to the Library interface as a general rule, how am I going to come back?" she asked, because that was when the real panic started bubbling. How was she going to get back to the Library if she didn't have power?

"You need to take this," Eric said, hovering over to her and dropping a disc about the size of her palm and about an inch thick into her hand.

"What's this?" she asked, looking slightly up at him. "Magical gate device?"

"Yeah, pretty much," Eric said. "We use them all the time in Halschius. Sometimes the amount of impenetrable rock we have down there just interferes with the signal. It's a chaos thing."

"Oh." Quinn hefted it in her hand. It was pretty heavy.

"Precisely," Eric grinned at her again. "Pity I can't come with. I don't think I can come up with a good disguise."

Lynx was eyeing the disc gleefully. "This is fantastic!"

"Gee, thanks," Eric said flatly.

"No, you know what I mean. Now I don't have to try and find one or create one of those. Thanks, Eric," Lynx said. He turned to Quinn with a big smile. "That's a door key. Literally, a Library door key. It's infused with power, sort of like a battery would be in your world, and you'll have to affix it to the door you want to use. It'll expand slightly and you'll need to place your hand on it and it will feed on *your* energy levels. Which is fine because you have a ridiculous amount of energy and that, plus pulling on the Library's malachite stores, will allow you to come back through to our little pocket dimension."

"Okay, I guess I can go back then. So maybe we should just go and do this," Quinn said, not liking the butterflies that were in her stomach slowly turning into intestine-eating worry. "I'll be ready in an hour."

"I don't think you should take Aradie," Milaro said. Aradie glanced from Quinn's shoulder at him with what could be referred to as a bit of a death glare.

"Yeah, Aradie, I'm sorry," she agreed reluctantly. "People don't walk around with massive owls on their shoulders where I come from."

There was a shimmer on her shoulder as Aradie became about half her usual size, which was still pretty big to be sitting on her shoulder, but much smaller than usual.

"Seriously, now you let me know you can morph," Quinn asked incredulously.

Aradie shrugged.

"I still don't think that's gonna work," Quinn said softly. "Will you be okay leaving me?"

If you're okay leaving me, Aradie said.

Quinn smiled. "I'll be right back, I promise. Well, guys, I have to go and grab some stuff and get ready, and then we'll head out." But she stopped before she left frowning as she looked at Malakai. "Oh, we need to get you jeans and like a T-shirt and some sneakers and some form of . . . do you have anything that can run on batteries and adjust his facial features? He's very much an elf. And I don't think any comic cons are going on in my city right now. So having him pretend to cosplay isn't going to work."

Malakai opened his mouth, but his grandfather beat him to it. Milaro grinned. "I believe I can take care of that for you."

"I'll be right back, then," Quinn said. She dashed upstairs, her stomach still roiling. She grabbed her phone that had been sitting on her side table ever since she'd come to the Library.

In a little mag wallet on the back of it she had key cards, a little bit of cash, and her driver's license. Things she'd honestly never thought she'd need again. An easy acceptance of her life here in the Library that spoke volumes.

She'd need to talk to the core and examine precisely why she'd simply dismissed her homeworld so easily. Now that she thought about it, she'd practically forgotten about her home. That couldn't be normal, could it?

Maybe a side effect of synchronization . . . or something else.

Still. That could wait. The Library felt like more of a home than anywhere she'd ever known. It was time to go and say goodbye to people and tie up loose ends.

She was nervous to see what her friends thought happened to her. But maybe she was most nervous to find out that they hadn't thought of her at all.

7

MAGICLESS WORLD

QUINN BLINKED AS SHE STOOD NEXT TO THE CHECK-IN DESK, LOOKING at Malakai.

"Well, what do you think? I did a pretty good job, didn't I?" Milaro preened proudly next to his grandson.

Quinn blinked again. Nope, Malakai was still standing in front of her, still about six and a half feet tall. Milaro disguised the salt and pepper elements of his hair so he wouldn't stand out. His black eyes didn't extend through the sclera, even though they were so black you couldn't see the pupil, which was fine.

Hopefully, no one would get close enough to notice the oddities.

He wore jeans and a T-shirt that looked out of place on him. He was so tall and lanky that it didn't exactly sit right on him, although the combat boots looked pretty good. His ears appeared human too. She looked him up and down and frowned. Even his hair pulled back into a ponytail was too long. It would stand out too much.

"Can you tweak the illusion a little bit?" she asked.

"Why?" Milaro asked, blinking in surprise. "He looks great!"

"Can you make his hair a little shorter? Hair that goes that long down to his butt is going to stand out a lot. We're trying to be incon-spicuous." Quinn was worried that along with the hair and his looks, people would gawk at them everywhere they went. Elves were ethe-real, and Malakai was pretty striking in appearance. It was odd how she'd become so used to it.

Malakai scowled. "You already asked me to do a ponytail instead of a braid. Why can't I just braid it?"

"Well, I guess you can do whatever you want..." Quinn frowned and waved the question away. "Just adjust the illusion so it's not quite as long. It'll stand out and I don't want us to draw more attention than we already will when we're there."

"Fine," Milaro said grumbling as he adjusted it.

"And it's probably pretty cold back home so you might want a jacket to go over that T-shirt."

"Oh, thank you," Malakai said, relief in his tone.

"I'll probably call you Mal while we're there," Quinn added, trying to ignore the rising nerves.

"You've started calling me that here anyway," he said. "Just keep it up."

"Malakai is a name people would give a nickname too on Earth," Quinn said. "Makes more sense to call you Mal."

"Are you really planning on seeing some of your old friends?" Lynx asked, his interest piqued.

"I'll probably run into them. Plus, I'm gonna text them once I've charged my phone when I find a charger, I hope."

"Well, is he acceptable?" Milaro asked, still sounding a little put out.

"He'll do. It's fine now. I think I'm maybe overly sensitive." She squinted up at him. "He's very tall."

"No, I'm not, you're just very short. There's not much I can do about that," Malakai said.

"I can't really adjust stature with this illusion," Milaro grumbled.

Quinn walked around Malakai satisfied that he'd pass for human. "How will you maintain the illusion?" she asked.

"Well," Milaro explained, "what happens is the brooch he's wearing—"

"Oh, that button's a brooch?" Quinn asked curiously.

"Yes, the brooch that he's wearing has its own mana source with enough power to allow the illusion to stay without any excess ambient mana for several days." Milaro sounded smug as he explained how it worked.

"Oh," Quinn said, "we're gonna be there like maybe a day. I'm not planning on going for a long time. Just enough to get there and text people that I'm not dead. I'm pretty sure my dorm room and all my stuff will be either in storage or have been sent back to my foster parents now. I don't plan to go get anything, I guess. I might see if I can access my email, pull some pictures, print them out, that sort of thing."

"Print out pictures? Can't you just make them happen?" Malakai asked incredulously.

"No, Malakai. I can't just make them happen in a world without magic." Quinn paused thoughtfully for a moment. "I guess printing them would be making them happen."

"Sorry," he said. "I'm just curious."

"It's fine." She turned her attention to the manifestation. "Lynx, how do we go about this?"

"Oh," he said, his eyes opening wide in surprise, "that's right. You've never opened a door for yourself."

"Got it in one. You keep sending me to places. I don't choose to go there myself," she muttered.

"Hmm." Lynx frowned like he was trying to figure out how to explain things.

"It's a lot easier than he's making out," Malakai said. "You just have to precisely picture the door you want to open."

"I need to picture the exact door I want to open?" Quinn repeated.

"Well, yes, otherwise you'll get sent somewhere vague. Who knows? You could even get stuck somewhere."

"Oh, so this is all like a visualization thing?"

"Well, of course. How did you think it operated?" Malakai asked.

"To be honest, I thought you kind of just gave it a location and it found a door and it opened it." Quinn shrugged.

"Well, that's how the Library works. When we seek to find books,"

Lynx butted in. "You see, it locates the book or the holder or where it was last pinged. Then the Library sends out its frequency to that area and finds an appropriate location within a minimal amount of distance from said book. That is how I've been sending you to the places you've needed to go to retrieve the books."

"So when we have to walk a ways, does that mean there's nowhere else you could make a trapdoor or anything?" Quinn asked, curious about the theory behind it.

"Well, trapdoors are pretty easy to make, but sometimes you have to be careful." Lynx paused for a moment as if searching for how to express himself. "Like, for example, when you went to the Esposians, I might have been able to get you closer, but I could have also accidentally hit an underground spring and drowned you by sending you. So generally, we try to find upright areas to put doors in. And sometimes the last ping can be a distance away."

"So when you pulled me from my Library to here, opening the door in the floor had been your best option?" Quinn asked.

"Pretty much. You can't put a door in a table." Lynx scoffed. "That doesn't work. It doesn't have the right framework for it."

"Okay, Fine. Let me think," Quinn said. "I think the best place would be the door at the back of the library that opens into the trash alleyway."

"Trash alleyway," Malakai said. "You're going to take me to a trash alleyway?"

"Well, I don't want us to be seen stepping out of a door from a magical Library. That might be a little hard to explain." Quinn raised an eyebrow at him as she spoke.

"Will the Library need to pull power from me to open our door there?" Quinn asked suddenly.

"No," Lynx said. "We have enough power in the Library that this isn't a problem at all. It's just going to take several hundred, maybe a thousand or so malachite crystals."

"Really?" Quinn said. "That's a lot."

"Well, it was when we didn't have many. Now it's just barely a drop in a bucket." Lynx shrugged. "It's fine. We're good."

Quinn looked around and tested the weight of the bag at her side again. "Well, I guess. I guess we should get going."

"We really have everything?" Malakai asked. "I can't take weapons through with me . . . will we be safe?"

"Safe enough. We should be good." She patted the small bag on her side that she'd gotten from Dottie. "I have my phone, my wallet, and the door opener thing, and hopefully I'll be able to go and get some memories."

"Picture the door you've chosen in your mind with as much detail as possible and reference the location. Activate it by placing your hand on the door." Quinn walked up to her favorite door to exit through, even if it was a little ostentatious, placed her palm on the door, and visualized the alleyway and the door that opened out onto it.

The sun was high in the sky when they stepped through the door onto the asphalt, a sensation she hadn't experienced for quite a while. Quinn wondered about the fascination most of the cultures she'd encountered had for cobbled streets. Wasn't asphalt a much better option? Was it a magic thing? Regardless, she hadn't even considered time. There had to be different time zones all over the universe too, right? There were different time zones on Earth, let alone in the galaxy, the universe, or whatever.

Still, the alley was just as she remembered. It wasn't your standard trash alley. It was nestled between two academic buildings, one filled with lecture halls, the other a library. Most of the trash consisted of paper, books, and things that didn't necessarily smell bad.

Malakai cleared his throat, and she turned around to see their Library disappearing behind them as the door closed. She clutched her bag for a split second, relieved to feel the weight of the door opener inside. It needed a better name, something like "Disc of Library Access." "Door opener" just sounded mundane and non-magical, not exciting in the least.

She felt the nerves in her stomach. This was Earth. She reached out with her senses and got absolutely nothing, which was quite disconcerting. She'd grown so used to having access to her senses and interface, no matter where she was, and being able to feel things about an area or sense incoming people or items or tremors. This sudden silence inside her brain was disquieting.

"Well, I guess my idea of a trash alley, as you call this, wasn't exactly the same as yours. So Quinn, why are you just standing around?" Malakai asked softly, standing next to her.

"I'm trying to get my bearings," she said, because it was truer than she'd intended it to be. There were all sorts of things she'd grown used to in a magical world that she no longer had access to, and it was a very odd sensation.

She pulled up her HUD, trying to get a grip on just how much was missing. It flickered, obviously soaking up her own energy, and she quickly shut it down. But not before a few scattered images flickered across her sight. She couldn't afford to run out of the energy they needed to get home though. Although her body produced its own energy, it was literally the only magical thing here. She knew it was going to take forever for it to fill back up.

Those brief images sparked an odd memory in her mind, her parents and the car accident. How had she survived? She'd been in the same car, after all. That was odd, and something to look into a little later when she didn't have to go and find a phone charger. "Let's go check my bank account and make sure it's still open, although I do have some cash on me."

"Bank account? Like, you give money to a bank, and you can access it anywhere?" Malakai asked.

"Well, yes, can't you?"

"Well, of course we can, but you don't have magic here. I want to see how you do everything without energy and mana." Malakai's eyes were shining with genuine curiosity.

"I just . . . we have electricity and the internet; they're pretty much the same thing, Mal," Quinn said.

They walked out of the alley, and suddenly the bustle of the university was there. So many people walking between buildings and between classes, but hardly anybody needed to go to the industrial trash bins. It had been the perfect place to pick, even if it meant they had to travel a ways to get to the places she needed to go.

"Okay, we need to go to one of the shops on campus and get a charging cord, then we'll sit down and have a coffee," Quinn muttered half to herself. "Oh, I have missed coffee. And while we charge my phone, yeah, that's a good idea."

They headed off and entered a store that sold textbooks and other paraphernalia. It had everything you could need, from books to paper, to pens, to laptops, to just everything. She walked to the back, where all the charging cables were kept, and sighed with relief.

Malakai looked around. "This just looks like any bookshop I've ever encountered with a few other things."

Quinn glanced at him, and realized, somewhat belatedly, that he was getting glances from a lot of people. She put that down mainly to his height, but also partially to the pony tail that fell halfway down his back. Plus, she looked at him in this human light. He was definitely attractive.

"Well, it's a bookshop. It has computers too," she said, making sure he didn't wander too far.

"Computers?" he said.

"Over there." She pointed at the laptop display.

He looked at them and said, "Oh, wow. You've talked about these." He inspected them and navigated with the mouse after several seconds of studying. "This is like a rudimentary system!"

Quinn paused and thought that over. "I guess it is. It's how we access the internet. Look, we'll talk about this over coffee. I've cables to get."

She grabbed a charger for her phone, and on a whim she also got a power brick, paid for them at the counter, and left with Malakai sulkily following behind her.

"So, computers. Could you just buy one of those?" he asked after they'd walked a minute or two.

"Yes. But that would leave me mostly broke."

"Oh," he said, "Are they expensive?"

"Well, some might not think so, but not everyone is made of

money." On their way to the coffee shop, Quinn stopped at an ATM, looked at the balance in her account, and was extremely relieved to see that her savings were still intact, minus a couple of cell phone bills that had been auto-debited. Since she hadn't used her meal card and it was the only other thing that came out of the account, it was still pretty healthy.

"Oh," she said, "that's good. Let's go get a coffee,"

And they walked into the coffee shop. Quinn took a long, deep breath of all the caffeinated smells and walked up to the counter to order. "I'd like a chocolate chip cookie," she said, "And a small soy latte, please."

She looked at Malakai, and asked, "What do you want, Mal?"

"Whatever you're having," he said.

"Make that two," she said to the girl as she handed over her card to pay.

Quinn smiled as they waited for her order, but she was nervous. There was something wrong with this lack of being able to perceive things around her, this lack of being able to tap into magic. How had she become so dependent on it in such a short window of time? By anybody's standards, two months wasn't long. She frowned.

"Quinn, coffee's ready."

She picked them up and walked with Malakai over to one of the tables next to a charge point.

"Eat up," she said. "We're going to be here for a little bit."

She plugged her phone in, and after several seconds, it registered the charging. She sighed in relief, "This'll make stuff much easier."

"So," Malakai said biting into the cookie and cooing appreciatively. "Talk to me about this computer thing."

"They're generally several hundred dollars for a decent one, or a few thousand for an amazing one, and they hook up to the internet." She shrugged.

"Will you show me the internet?" he asked eagerly.

"Of course, I can show you the internet on my phone as soon as it's charged enough." Quinn thought this was sort of endearing. He was so interested in how a magicless world worked.

Then she heard someone call out her name and she looked around, trying to locate the source.

"Quinn? Is that you?"

This time it was closer and easier to locate.

She sighed, took a deep breath, and turned with a smile on her face. "Hey, Hallie, how you doing?"

Her one persistent friend stood in front of them, her wide blue eyes open in shock. "I thought you were dead."

8

PARTS OF HERSELF

"Hallie, don't be silly. What do you mean you thought I was dead?" Quinn said, trying her best to be friendly and brush off the very real fact that she'd been missing for two months. She'd never been overly friendly to anybody, preferring to keep to herself. Which meant Hallie probably thought this was highly unusual behavior from her.

Hallie's eyes darted from Quinn to Malakai and back again. She frowned. "Who's this?"

"This is Mal," Quinn said.

Malakai inclined his head and said, "Nice to meet you, Hallie."

"Huh, is it?" she said, narrowing her gaze at Malakai. Then she turned her attention back to Quinn. "And you're not being held by him against your will?"

Quinn blinked. "What? No. Not at all like that." She waved her hands for emphasis.

"Then why did you disappear? You were speaking to me one moment and then you were just gone the next. How could you just not contact me? The police even said you'd withdrawn cash the week before, and there were no signs of foul play so you probably just cut ties." Hallie sounded slightly panicked.

Quinn racked her brains. She was sure they hadn't been the best of friends. She was absolutely positive she'd kept her at arm's length like she did with most people. But maybe Hallie hadn't had many great friends either and thus, well, that kind of counted as her friendship. Plus she couldn't remember what she'd withdrawn cash for. "I'm really sorry. I just sort of got caught up in stuff."

"In stuff? I've never met anybody more studious than you, more boring than you. You wouldn't even come out to parties with me," Hallie lamented.

"Well, I don't really like parties. I prefer to sit and read," Quinn mumbled out an excuse that wasn't a lie at all. Oh, now she remembered. She'd splurged and bought a brand new high-end tablet for school and reading. She really hoped that was with her other stuff in storage. She couldn't remember if she'd had it at the library with her or not.

"Look, even your mom contacted me asking me if I knew where you were. The fact that I told her that the last time I'd seen you, we had been discussing majors seemed to settle her down a bit. But Quinn, even your work called around for your friends. I mean, you couldn't have just told us or your dorm mate where you went? Even Jordan contacted me!" Hallie seemed a lot more bothered by it than Quinn had expected.

Quinn actually felt guilty for not having given home more thought, especially since even her foster brother had reached out. "I . . . that's why I came back. I realized that I should have said goodbye to everybody."

"Goodbye to everybody?" Hallie crossed her arms. "Are you leaving? Are you going somewhere?"

Quinn took in a deep breath. She was not good with this improvisation.

"Well, I'm extremely glad that I found Quinn," Mal said, smoothly interjecting.

"I . . . I'm sorry this has caused you so much trouble," Quinn added.

Hallie turned to Mal and gave him a very quizzical look. She slowly looked him up and down and then it was like a light bulb went off in her mind and her eyes widened. She looked back at Quinn, pulled the chair up from a vacant table next to them, and sat down.

"Are you serious? He's why you left? I would never have thought a guy would get you away from the university." There was a conspiratorial grin on Hallie's face. It lit up her eyes too.

Quinn didn't like lying. She was about to disabuse her friend of that notion when Malakai spoke up. "I've been a bit of a bad influence on her."

Quinn had to suppress a laugh because he really had been. She'd fought a giant cephalopod; she'd gone to a chaotic magic lava rock world, barely survived a vortex assault from a snake man. There was so much she'd done since she'd met Malakai. He was a hundred percent telling the truth, just not the truth Hallie thought she was hearing.

"I'm sorry," she said again. "I just . . . I guess I got carried away." Again, that wasn't exactly a lie because Quinn had been carried away through to another dimension or dimensional portal or whatever it was classified as.

"Okay, but you need to sit down and catch me up. And don't . . . don't be such a stranger. What . . . I mean, you're back here?" Hallie's tone downplayed the question, but her body language portrayed more eagerness than her voice.

"Oh, I just wanted to catch up on some stuff and check some things," Quinn said evasively.

"Like what? The fact that you missed the deadline and thus got unenrolled?"

"Yeah, pretty much that." It was hard to believe Quinn had been planning her entire life and now it was gone. Everything was different and she couldn't even come back if she wanted to because she'd screwed it up. Well, she hadn't completely screwed it up, but her scholarship would be gone. She couldn't afford this university without it. She hadn't really thought of that. It made her feel melancholy.

Although she was fairly certain the Library technically paid her to be the Librarian.

"But are you happy, Quinn?" Hallie's words pulled her out of her thoughts.

"Yeah, I . . . I am actually," she said. It was one of the first truths she'd uttered since sitting down to coffee. "I'm actually really happy with the way my life is turning out. So don't worry about me."

"I'll only not worry about you if you tell me what you've been doing." Hallie's words were soft and serious.

How was Hallie so concerned about her? But it felt good that someone had worried about her. So, instead, she asked, "Did you pick your major?"

"Yes," Hallie said, her smile brightening. "I chose theater and I'm loving some of the choices I get to take next semester. It's going to be amazing, Quinn. I'm going to be the best actress ever."

"You know, Hallie, I bet you will be. You'll surprise everyone."

"I know, right?" Hallie's laugh sounded so carefree. Like she didn't have the weight of an entire universe on her shoulders.

Quinn wanted to put her even more at ease. "See, Mal is kind of family."

Hallie's eyebrows shot up. "So you're not an orphan anymore?"

"Well, I mean, yes, but in a way, I found family," Quinn said, which wasn't a lie because they'd become just like family. Considering Milaro treated her like his grandkid too, and they had the same ability essence. She just made it sound a little more related than not.

"Yes, I'm a part of her family," Mal said.

"Oh, really? He's a cousin?" Hallie raised an eyebrow.

Quinn could practically see the thirst in her eyes and moved to head that train of thought off. "Close enough. Mal's my friend and family," Quinn finished hurriedly.

Malakai chuckled. "That I am, but I'm also devilishly handsome, am I not?" He leaned into the role a bit too much.

"Don't say that, you're being an idiot."

"You wound me again," he mocked.

Hallie laughed. "It's good to see you smile, Quinn. You don't . . . you've never really done that. I think this is the most I've heard you talk in the eighteen months I've known you."

"Really?" Quinn said contemplating that in more seriousness than she wanted to admit. "I'm sorry. I guess I just like my own company."

"That's okay. Will you promise to text me just sometimes? Let me know how you're doing? Are you here to pick up your stuff from your dorm room? I think they put it in storage when you didn't come back after a month. They . . . they usually do that for a while anyway." Hallie trailed off, looking at Quinn expectantly.

"Yeah, I might go see if I can have a look through," Quinn said, suddenly eager to find some of the small mementos she might be able to keep. "Hey, Hallie, thanks for worrying about me."

Hallie laughed. "Of course I worried about you. You saved my ass so many times with lecture notes. I don't know what I would have done in that first year. I've had to grow up a little bit this year because you kind of disappeared. But I get it, not everything's as easy as it appears to be to others, is it?"

For a second there, Quinn just wished that she had spent more time with Hallie, maybe more time developing friendships, less time focusing on getting out and getting herself set up for the future. "Yeah," she said to Hallie, "sometimes I think it's like that."

"Look, Quinn, I gotta go. I've got a class in five minutes and I'm gonna have to run all the way across campus now." Hallie stood up and paused. "Text me, please."

"I will," Quinn said, and watched her one friend walk out of the coffee shop.

"From the way you spoke back in the Library, I didn't think you would be so attached," Malakai said. Quinn pulled herself out of the thoughts that were spiraling in her head right then and looked at him.

"You know, neither did I. That was weird. She was always so annoying. She always asked for my notes, and insisted on talking to me when I was trying to study. I just, I guess she grew on me more than I realized," Quinn said thoughtfully.

"People have a way of doing that, you know," Mal said. He paused for a few seconds before speaking again. "Okay, so what next?"

"Drink your coffee and eat your cookie," Quinn said, suddenly feeling quite vulnerable. She pulled her phone over, which was now sitting at about forty-eight percent. They had talked to Hallie long enough that the supercharger had decided to actually do its work. And that's when she realized that she had like eighty thousand emails. Okay, she didn't have eighty thousand emails, she just had a lot.

"Hey, Quinn, what's the other thing you've got charging there?"

"Oh, it's a power bank. It should let me still access information on my phone for at least a little while once we're back," she said absently.

"Hmm, I wonder if we could adapt that," he said, studying it curiously.

Quinn perked up. "What do you mean adapt it?"

"You're bringing it back with you, right?"

"Yeah, I am."

"Okay, let's—yeah, just bring it back. Magic is magic, right?" He winked at her mischievously. "I could do with a little side project."

"Okay," she said, not exactly understanding what he was talking about. But she finally went to her messages and realized that her mother had actually sent her about fifteen over the last two months, which was about five times more than she usually sent her. She sucked in a deep breath and sent a text.

Hey Mom, so sorry for not contacting you earlier. My phone was fritzing with messages. I finally got it fixed. I want you to know I'm doing really well. Don't worry about me if I don't contact you for long periods. Just know that I'm doing absolutely fine.

She sent the message and then said, "Mal, come here." She turned the camera around and took a selfie of them and sent it to her mom straight after the message. She was relieved to see that Mal's illusion held up in a photograph too.

"There, that should at least let her know that I'm actually alive. It is me talking to her and not somebody who's stolen my phone and is trying to impersonate me."

"Your mom would think that?" he asked.

"Let's just not get into her crazy conspiracy theories that she sometimes comes up with." Quinn chuckled. "Okay, anyway, now I've just got a couple more to send."

"That's a pretty cool instant picture thing," Malakai said, obviously curious.

"Camera," Quinn said as she sent her next texts. She sent one to her foster brother Jordan. He'd been the closest thing to an actual sibling she'd had. Letting him know that she was okay. Sent the same photo. And then to her youngest foster sibling who was about fifteen right now in tenth grade and had contacted her five times throughout the last two months. The others were spam or just the library checking to see where she was for her shift a few times before they obviously fired her. The dorm contacting her . . .

She took a long swig of her coffee and watched the battery on her phone slowly tick up. She scrolled through the photos, not really wanting to talk and extremely grateful that Malakai wasn't necessarily the most talkative person either. Right now he appeared to be people watching. It was going to take a little while for the phone and the power bank to charge. At least it was half charged when she bought it.

"What are you thinking, Quinn?"

"Just . . ." She was about to speak when her phone dinged. "My mom texted me back."

She took a deep breath and opened the message. It was long.

How could you not contact me sooner? I'm grateful that you sent me photographic proof. And it's good to see that you didn't turn off the location information on the photo. And I can tell you're actually at the university. You realize that they halted your enrollment when you didn't turn in your finalized choices, right? And they've said they've put the scholarship on hold for now. You should go and see the administration and please text me a little more frequently. I've been worried about you.

Quinn cringed. Her foster-mother for the last three years before she graduated had been a decent sort—genuinely caring. The foster father, however . . . not a nice guy. "I don't suppose I can come back like once a month and just send a message to people, right?"

"I don't see why not." Malakai shrugged. "I mean, the Library is getting copious amounts of energy now. And you can refill your own energy well whenever you're in the Library. So that's easy ports back."

"Yeah, that might be a good option. Anyway," she said, hitting the table, standing up, and then she texted her mom quickly.

I will try to text you more frequently, but don't worry if it's been a couple of months. I'm going to be absolutely fine. I've found exactly what I want to do with my life.

The phone was almost fully charged. She'd probably plug it in while she was going through her stuff in storage to get it the rest of the way. The power brick had dinged up to three notches.

"Okay," she said, "let's get going."

"Where are we going now?" Malakai asked, raising an eyebrow.

"I need to go to dormitory storage and get my stuff or look through my stuff and see what I can take with me."

"I thought you weren't getting anything," he asked, almost as impishly as Eric would.

Quinn glowered at him. "I changed my mind."

It was about a ten-minute walk to get to the dormitories. Quinn pointed out a couple of other locations on campus. "That place has the best sushi even though it's just a little store and I used to take English in that building over there. It's a pretty awesome building."

"I would have assumed a language building would be closer to the library," Malakai mused.

"Well, we assume a lot of things and we don't always get them right."

He chuckled. "Did you text Hallie?"

"Thank you," she said. She texted Hallie a simple, *I'm texting you* and got a smiley face back immediately. She sighed. "Friends I didn't realize I had."

At least part of her felt warm at the sensation that somebody had actually missed her. It was better than she'd hoped. She reached the dormitory and went to find the TA, rapping on his door when she got there.

Bushy brown hair peering at the pages of a book moved at the sound, and he looked up, his dark eyes framed by thick glasses. His mouth opened in an O of surprise. "Is that you, Quinn?"

"Yeah, Gary. Sorry I disappeared." Quinn had never apologized so much in her life as she was doing today.

"You had us worried. It's good to see you in one piece. Is it his fault?" Gary asked, gesturing toward Malakai.

"No, it's not his fault," she said sheepishly. "I should've contacted you sooner."

"Yeah, you should have, but I kept your stuff." He smiled and fished out a key from his draw before standing up. "It's in about three boxes and a tub of bedding. I'll take you to the storage."

Quinn followed with Malakai trailing behind and got to the storage room.

"There you go, those ones in the corner in the back, right." He smiled. "Take your time, just bring me the key back and don't disappear with it."

"Thanks." Quinn watched him go and then walked in and knelt in front of the boxes, absent-mindedly plugging the phone and the charger into the wall as she did. She leafed through some of the stuff, picking out a couple of picture frames that she always held on her desk, pictures of her parents and the grandmother who had obviously come with her to this world, people who had raised her.

Memories flickered through her mind at the sight of them. Fragments she'd forgotten, distorted and fuzzy images she couldn't quite recall. Her head started to ache. She shoved the items in her bag.

"I don't think I can take the rest of this," she said, looking mournfully at the rest of the boxes. It really was just sentimental stuff. "I can't fit it. I don't know how to carry it."

"Why don't I just open my storage and put it in there," Malakai said.

"Because we don't have magic?" Quinn answered.

"No, it can pull on my mana and my energy and I can open it at least."

"But you won't regenerate it quickly, Mal."

"No, I won't. But we'll be home soon and we're using your energy for that. Plus I brought a few energy balls and that way even if it sucks everything to open, insert, and close, I'll be okay." He smiled at her.

"Oh," she said.

"Just let me do this for you, okay?" he asked.

"Yeah, thanks." Quinn couldn't help the smile. This was super sweet of him. Maybe she didn't have to leave parts of herself behind after all.

With her boxes all secure in Malakai's inventory and his energy replenishment at least partially started by an energy ball, Quinn stood and brushed her jeans off, grabbed her phone and the charging bank.

A wave of dizziness stole over her as she did so, and she had to reach out and grasp onto the cold stone wall as images flashed through her mind.

Sitting happily in the back seat with her grandmother while her parents drove to their favorite park. There was a picnic basket next to her, and her grandmother was teasing her about her love for apple and cinnamon muffins.

A sudden blaring of light and an impact that smashed her head against the window of the car so hard it shattered.

A flash of blue and gold light suffusing her entire body.

A glimpse of scales.

And everything went black.

9

NOT A VISION

THE DARKNESS OVERCAME QUINN SO SUDDENLY THAT IT JOLTED HER. A mist hung around her, although perhaps it was more shadowy than mist-like. Starry portions of sky blinked in and out from complete darkness as if someone created a star shooter that could plummet her into an abyss. Her thoughts were jumbled.

Slowly, in front of her, in those shadows, no, those images flickered through her mind. They were static, with interference, as if she wasn't supposed to remember, or as if there hadn't been enough capacity in her mind at the time to recall the events in detail.

She remembered the day and the house. The house was adorable, a small brick Tudor-style house in the older part of town. It had fake shutters on the outside and a merry little flower garden that her mother tended to all the time. Quinn watched as if outside herself, observing as her mother planted the garden. She wondered, for the first time, why she looked nothing like her parents.

Although she was completely aware of it now, they weren't technically her parents. Her father, with his blonde hair and blue eyes, and her mother, with light brown hair and a smattering of freckles, and brown golden eyes, laughed with her. Her grandmother had grey hair, grey eyes. That's all she remembered, except for the kind smile when she baked cookies. But the flowers, that was something her mother took pride in.

"Quinn, come here, show me your report card," her mother called. Quinn walked over and giggled at her mother. She had to be, what, twelve?

"Mom, it's online, like it always is. What are you talking about?"

"Fine, fine, give me the hard copy anyway." Her mother attempted to smile sternly, but it was, as always, just filled with contentment.

Quinn handed over the hard copy to her mother with a big grin on her face.

"You did it again! All As, I'm so proud of you." The smile her mother gave her showed both love and pride.

"Thanks, Mom."

"Now, do you know what you want for a reward?"

Quinn laughed. It felt beautiful with the sun shining down on her, a memory she hadn't recalled at all, playing out in front of her as if she was watching a television show. "Ice cream, like always." Quinn couldn't remember ever having smiled so big.

How had she forgotten all of this? They always went to the same ice cream shop, the one that mixed the different ingredients into whatever flavor you chose. The place that let her have that tangy, sour taste in something so cold and sweet.

"Okay, Dad will be home soon and we'll head out." Her mother stood up, brushing grass from her skirt, dusting off her hands. She gave Quinn a hug around her shoulders, nice and firm, even if it was quick. And then she walked into the house, and the memory faded.

Quinn felt suddenly cold at the loss of warmth. Shadows swirled in front of her, fragments of memories flickering past again like the static on an 80s television at 3 a.m.

"Well done! You're such a clever kid, Quinn," her father said, as he ushered them all out of the house toward the car. The garage was detached from the house, barely room enough for the larger modern vehicles. Small, but beautiful. Quinn loved the house.

She wondered why hadn't thought about it for so many years. They piled into the car, her and her grandmother in the back, her parents in the front. It was a small SUV, red in color. But it was that bright red, almost like freshly dripping blood. Not the weird orange red that always set her teeth on edge. They pulled out and turned on music and began to sing with it, until her father decided that chatting was more fun. The ice cream shop was only about fifteen minutes away.

"So, Quinn, tell me, did you cheat?" It was almost like a ritual question, a joke shared among all of them.

"No, Dad, I didn't get caught. Oh, I mean, I didn't cheat." Quinn grinned, completing her part of the tradition.

Dad laughed, her mom laughed, her grandmother laughed. The sounds were like music to her ears.

They headed through the intersection closest to the ice cream shop—they were so close she could practically taste it. The lights were green. They had the right of way.

And then time seemed to slow down for her . . .

It was as if Quinn could see the truck barreling toward them. It came from the passenger side, beyond her mother. Quinn always sat behind her father. Her grandmother and her mother were the first ones to be impacted.

Everything occurred as if in stop motion.

She could see the truck hit them side on, fully plowing into the side, shattering the windows into her grandmother and mother, the glass ripping them to shreds as Quinn's head hit the window next to her. It shattered too. She couldn't see her father, just the back of his seat. The sound of the airbags deploying.

All she remembered was the shock that ran through her body and the sudden blinding blue-gold light that shrouded her in what felt like a second skin. When she looked down, her entire body was covered in thick blue-gold scales like armor to protect her.

It emanated out from her, not far, maybe a foot, pushing any debris and anything else away from her suddenly, shielding her inside a cocoon from projectiles.

However, it didn't save her from impact damage.

When she woke up in the hospital six weeks later, she was an orphan and the room was empty. No relatives . . . they'd all been in the car with her. No friends, not even a social worker or nurse. Not that that was to be expected. It was the middle of the day when she woke up, so nobody would have been visiting anyway.

She couldn't remember anything, not even from the days leading up. And there was this bone-weary exhaustion that funneled through her as if she could barely even lift her head. She didn't know how long she'd been out until later. In her mind maybe it had been a day, or five, or fifty. There was no memory of how she'd survived, nothing to indicate any type of magical defense like blue scales had saved her.

The accident left her with a sense of foreboding she couldn't shake.

Like maybe, she should have died too.

Like maybe she should have died instead.

Q uinn opened her eyes to see stone walls around her, oddly earth-like.

"You're awake?" Malakai's tone was tightly controlled, his eyes darted wildly, bleeding through some of the illusion that kept them hidden.

She wondered how long she had been unconscious. Those memories felt like they might have taken an age to experience. "How long was I out?"

"Maybe ten minutes. It was barely anything, but I was getting worried." He spoke softly, his breathing began to calm, and he was still patting her shoulder absent-mindedly. His eyes reverted to the human illusion again.

"I didn't mean to worry you," she said, trying to gain her bearings. "Where exactly am I?"

"You're in the storage room. I just put your boxes in my storage and you kind of pulsed blue and gold and blacked out. I caught you before you hit the floor," Malakai said, his gaze now intense as he studied her. "You look really pale right now."

That's when Quinn realized she was resting against his thigh. She sat up quickly. Her head spun as she did so and she had to lean forward and rest her hands on her knees until the vertigo slowed down. Maybe that's what all her vertigo episodes had been. Perhaps her subconscious attempted to retrieve her memories frequently and sent her balance spiraling. Admittedly, she was probably reaching with that.

"Sorry, I . . . " She tried to figure out how best to articulate what had happened.

"What was it? Did you see something?" Malakai asked, and his concern was still obvious. From the way his brow furrowed to the ever so slight tremor in his voice. Then he paused as if a switch had been flicked. "Wait. Did you get a vision in a non-magical world?"

"No, no, nothing like that. Not a vision or communication or anything like that." Quinn sighed and pushed her hand through her unruly ponytail. "I just had to dig up some very painful memories that my brain managed to block out until now. Memories about my parents and the accident we were in."

"Really?" Malakai asked, raising an eyebrow as he stood back up. "You remember now?"

"I mean, I knew they died," Quinn said, taking his offered hand as she climbed to her feet. "I knew they died in an accident, but I was there, Mal. I was in the car at the time. They were pulverized. I don't . . . I never understood how I survived if I was in that wreck with them. No one understood. It was a miracle. And yet now that I know, I wish I didn't."

"What?" he asked as he leaned against the wall and watched her.

She could tell he was bracing himself. She didn't blame him. Hell, she wasn't even sure how she could come out and say the thoughts that were floating around in her head. "In the split second that the impact happened, my power manifested somehow. It threw a shield of scales over me and protected me, but only me, no one else."

Malakai just blinked at her.

The silence grew deafening, so bad that Quinn wished she hadn't said anything at all, except all the images were still playing in her mind. The crash, every detail, the glass breaking, splintering, slicing through flesh. She shuddered.

"Sorry, Quinn," Malakai said, "I didn't mean to—"

"It's okay," she cut him off. It was suddenly far too cold in here, in this basement room made of concrete. It was almost suffocating. "I get it. There was kind of a lot."

"No, it's a lot to digest." He held up a hand. "Just hear me out. I had to think back to what I know about you and who you are."

"Oh?" she asked, not confident that he had anything she wanted to listen to, but it couldn't hurt.

"Let's just say, I don't believe any of this was your fault." There was a steely determination in his eyes now. It hadn't been there but five minutes earlier. Not before she told him of the memory.

"What do you know?" she asked, crossing her arms to fend off the chill she felt crawling all over her skin.

Malakai sighed. "Look. Right now I only have supposition, and that's not going to help either one of us. This isn't my area of study or expertise, but I've been around my grandfather enough to pick up a few things here and there."

"You're beating that bush you're dancing around to death," she deadpanned.

Malakai chuckled and flashed her a grin. "That may very well be. But right now I want you to try and accept that it wasn't your fault. We need to get back to the Library, and you need to speak to the Core. And you need to talk to my grandfather. Because if my hunch is right, then I think this is all way more than you realize."

It was the first time that she'd seen Malakai unsure of himself in a way that he felt the need to get others to reinforce his own knowledge. No matter what, he'd always been decisive and knew precisely what to do. This new side of him wasn't helping her confidence any. The fact that he wouldn't tell her until he'd had his information confirmed scared her more than she wanted to admit.

Quinn nodded, trying to push the images back down in her mind. But now they were recalled, it was like her mind was trying to bring back all of the detail and more. Perhaps that was a good thing? But it really didn't feel like it. "Okay, give me a few while I go and hand the key back to Gary. I'll be back and maybe we'll just use this door to get home, hey?"

"Sounds like a plan, Librarian," Malakai said, but he paused and reached out to her arm, gently touching her wrist. "Don't get too in your head. I just don't want to tell you my theory and have it be wrong. Okay?"

Quinn smiled, a portion of her tension releasing. "Yeah. I know. But it feels better to have you say it out loud."

He grinned and her phone dinged. A message from her brother.

Just promise you won't be a stranger. I know we didn't see eye to eye all the time, but you're still my little sister.

Quinn tried her best not to choke up. Jordan was the only big brother she'd ever really connected with. She hoped he'd be okay. All she sent back was a heart emoji. Words were too difficult right now with how much her mind was spinning.

Once she dropped the key back with Gary and returned to Mal, they closed the storeroom door and stood in the room. It was easier this way too. No one would see them walking into a strange pocket dimension Library.

Quinn pulled the door key out of her bag, placed it in the center of the door, where it clicked on like a magnet, and fit her hand in the slot.

"Library, I need you." she muttered under her breath, aware of how very true those words were.

All of her energy whooshed out of her so fast she felt like she was about to pass out.

The key thrummed and glowed and finally activated.

10

LAST GLIMPSE

QUINN HAD BEEN SO FOCUSED ON SIMPLY GETTING BACK TO THE Library she hadn't really noticed that she'd opened up the doorway into her office. Granted, it was the door she most frequently went through during the day. And to be honest, her mental state felt marginally fragile—all things considered—she hadn't wanted to spill into the main part of the Library. Those memories had left her feeling drained and conflicted.

"Quinn, did you mean to come here?" Malakai spoke softly.

She nodded but felt like she was gulping in air after the transport or teleport, or however it was classified. It was amazing how the energy rushed back into her, replenishing the well she'd just drained. She'd been starved of magical energy on Earth, as if it didn't exist. Opening the door had bottomed her out in a huge rush. Usually, energy didn't leave her body at such speed. Her head was spinning.

"Do you think—" She tried to speak, but it wasn't working. Quinn shook her head, still trying to gain her equilibrium again. She couldn't figure out why the energy was rushing back into her so hard. Or was it magic perhaps? Was this because she'd been so used to the magical environment that being allowed back into it set her balance off?

"Don't ask. You need to just readjust first." Again, there were layers of concern to Malakai's voice. "Let's get Lynx and my grandfather. Frankly, I think you need to talk to the Library herself."

I am listening, the Library said and the voice echoed through the room.

"Good," Malakai snapped. "Maybe you could finally clear up some crap for her instead of keeping her in the dark so much for 'her own good.'"

The Library, perhaps wisely, didn't respond to that.

Not long after, Quinn sat with Aradie on her shoulder, scritching the back of her neck while the owl cooed in her ear. Malakai stood at the far end, leaning against the wall, a scowl on his face. His form reverted to that of his Darigháhnish heritage.

Lynx had arrived and paced back and forth alongside the conference table. "Can't you just tell me what the problem is?" he practically growled at Malakai

"No, I'm not repeating myself. I'm waiting until Milaro is here." Malakai kept his tone cool and even, but Quinn could tell that was only because of tight control.

"Speak of the devil," Milaro said, stepping through the door. He didn't seem as joyous as usual, as if a portion of his smile was ever so slightly forced. His hair was slightly tattered, like he hadn't had time to take care of it properly.

Quinn was immediately suspicious. "What have you been up to?"

He sighed and pushed some stray strands of hair back behind his ear. "I've been working with Harish and Siliqua on helping Cadre refine the sequences we need to retrieve the memories Lynx has lost and the rest of that stuff. Not to mention taking care of the affairs of the entire civilization I'm entrusted with safeguarding." He sounded so tired.

Quinn felt that blanket of guilt creeping back over her. Milaro was a king. He had people and an entire society to protect, and yet she called him to help all the time. "It's okay," she said. "We don't have to do this right now."

"Yes, we do," Malakai said, that same ironclad tone brooking no argument. "It wrecked you back there. For like ten minutes, I thought you weren't going to wake back up. You were shaking and sweating. You barely breathed. Your entire body went rigid multiple times. It was pretty scary, Quinn. So, we're getting to the bottom of it and figuring this shit out regardless how any of you feel about taking the time to do so."

"I didn't realize," she said. Probably because she'd been unconscious. Still, though . . . Those images began to try to assault her again from behind the barriers she put up. "It might just be easier if I show you, Milaro, Library, Lynx."

"Oh," Milaro said. "I'm sorry. Show us what?"

She blinked and then laughed softly. It was more of a stress relief than holding any actual brevity. "Sorry. It was slightly traumatic for me, so I think I just assume you know what happened. I'll diminish my shielding toward the Library and you momentarily so you can see what we're talking about."

"Are you sure?" Milaro asked gently as he walked up to the desk.

Quinn shrugged. "Can't really deal with it alone, can I? Might be memories from the past, but I think they're important. You might be able to find more contained within them than I realize. Even now as I examine them, they hurt like they did when I was twelve. Even with knowing as much as I know, it's difficult to separate my consciousness and memory and approach this logically." She gave him a sad smile.

Milaro returned the expression. "Then show us, show me? Maybe we can help."

"That's the idea," Quinn said and gave him her hands, for easier access to her memories. For Lynx and the Library, she allowed them to hear the tumultuous recollections that swirled in her mind, stirring up more and more as they swept along like a tornado.

Milaro held her hands and dove in. They both closed their eyes and there was a swirling vortex of images and death playing on loop. But with Milaro by her side, they didn't seem nearly as scary as they had the first time they'd played on repeat.

Now?

Now it felt manageable.

After several minutes that felt like seconds to Quinn, he squeezed her hands and she opened her eyes to look at him.

"I'm so sorry, Quinn. I didn't know." He moved around the table and reached to give her a very gentle hug.

She leaned into it, surprised by the pain that caught in her chest. "Yeah, I know. Neither did I. They died because of me, didn't they?"

"You can't blame yourself for that, Quinn. I think a lot of people have died because of this. It's not you, it's bigger than you." Milaro started, but she cut in.

"But I couldn't save them. Whatever these stupid scales are save me and nobody else." She balled her hands into fists and looked up at Milaro beseechingly. "Doesn't that make me inherently selfish? Subconsciously, even?"

"There's nothing you could have done, Quinn. That's a species survival mechanism." Milaro crouched down so he was eye to eye with her as she practically burrowed her body into that chair. "Your body, your latent nature, protected itself in the only way it knew how. There was nothing you could have done to protect the others, but this . . . I'm pretty sure your dormant genes saved you."

Quinn tried to process what Milaro was saying. It wasn't that it was difficult to understand, but rather that she was grappling with the memory of her parents' death while she was in the car. Even though she'd known that was a fact, it had never really sunk in.

"Do you think that was a targeted incident or was it just an unlucky human, like, happenstance?" Quinn asked.

Milaro hesitated. "No, I don't think it was just unlucky. I don't know exactly how they found you and I'll need to talk to the Library."

I'm uncertain how they located her. We barely found her signature.

"Could she have had more magic present in her system at that earlier point in time?" Lynx asked suddenly.

Milaro shrugged. "I mean, of course she would have . . ." He looked thoughtful.

"We were locked away," Lynx said. "We weren't even aware of what you'd done. We didn't know until she'd been here for weeks."

Milaro stood up and patted Quinn on the shoulder, then joined

Lynx for some pacing alongside the conference table. "Okay, so we know that we sent you to a magicless world for a reason. We assumed that no one would try to locate you there. When we figured out how to get back in touch with the Library, we were going to fetch you. However, after some years passed we could no longer locate your magical signature. Frankly, we thought we'd failed. That's why I didn't mention anything for so long. Not even I was completely certain, to begin with."

Milaro sighed. "So whoever it was . . ."

"Well, we know the Serpensiril were involved," Malakai snapped. "Obviously. Probably the Esposians or whoever it is who's taken over them. But what we need to make sure Quinn understands," he said, glaring at her a bit, "is that it wasn't her fault. She had no way of knowing that would happen."

"It doesn't make me feel any less guilty, though I appreciate your effort," Quinn said. Malakai simply shrugged and went back to scowling at the entire room. "What does this mean?"

"Well, it means, Quinn, that you had a built-in genetic defense mechanism that's familiar to all cosmicisodracus and you managed to save yourself at the expense of every drop of magic your body had in it at that point in your life. Frankly, with the damage around you, you probably overspent."

"Would that explain my coma and why I was so weak for so long?" Quinn asked softly.

"Yeah, pretty much. Your body regenerates energy and mana naturally." Milaro answered. "That's just how it works. However, if you're on a world that isn't magically inclined or has no magic presence in it, then it's going to take your body a significant amount of time to regenerate even one or two energy. What your body did, protecting itself in that completely and utterly subconscious and, well, primordial way, drained your entire being of energy and magic. There wouldn't have been a drop of mana or energy left, until you managed to, I guess, regenerate some measure of it on your own."

"You think that's why I woke up?" she asked, a tight pain in her chest.

"Likely. Probably took you six weeks to get back one or two energy and the more you filled up, the longer it would have taken to regenerate more. There's no way we could have sensed you from that distance with, say, under a hundred energy. Too little and it's just a blip on the radar. A glitch even. It wouldn't have even pulled the Library in if they had scanned that quadrant earlier." Milaro was focused on her with a soft intensity and underlying sadness.

"Oh," Quinn said, trying to calculate that on her own. "So there's like every possibility that I could have gone my entire life without knowing about the Library or you."

"Pretty much," Lynx inserted. "I mean, if we hadn't sent out that last-ditch pulse and actually found your admittedly very weak signature, we wouldn't have pulled you to us. The Library would probably be gone in the next month or two and we wouldn't have had the energy to continue the search. Not with that little amount of power that you exhibited at the time. Like I said, it was a crapshoot. We were lucky."

"Okay, wait, wait." Quinn felt entirely too confused. "So you wouldn't have been able to find my affinities before then?"

Well, not much before then, the Library said. *Maybe a year? If we'd have scanned a year earlier, we might have found you. But as it stands, you were still extremely low on energy levels when we pulled you in.*

"That's true. You pulled on our power reserves as soon as we made contact with your immediate vicinity. Like you were thirsty for the energy," Lynx said, watching her thoughtfully now, having paused his pacing.

"Wait, but don't you scan for affinities?" Quinn asked.

"Yes, but affinities don't mean anything if you don't have magic to fuel them," Lynx said, as if it was the most natural thing to be aware of in the world.

"Oh," Quinn said. "So basically, because I'm mostly Library, my defensive mechanisms triggered when I was in danger and saved my life, depleting all of my magical stores, which left me alone for seven years until my magic levels finally rose enough to be detectable again."

"Nice summary. Why did you summarize it?" Milaro asked, his eyes smiling.

"Because I need to make sure I understand this. Couldn't my guardians have triggered their own defense mechanisms?"

"Not every species has a defense mechanism that's going to coat your entire body in an armor that will repel an impact like that collision, Quinn. They were going at full speed from your memories. They didn't even try to brake." Lynx sounded somber.

Quinn frowned. "That, that seems highly dangerous and sort of suspect."

"Yeah, it really does," Milaro mused. "I wouldn't be surprised if they found you guys by scanning when you were younger and surrounded by three other people with a magical signature. Maybe we shouldn't have sent you there. Maybe it made you all sitting ducks."

"Or maybe," Lynx piped up, "maybe it gave her the one chance she had to survive. They obviously thought she was dead. There was no magic left in her signature after that accident. There couldn't have been. That shield had to use so much power. It's frankly amazing she woke up from it at all."

"You're saying they thought I was dead?" Quinn asked, so many of the puzzle pieces clicking into place in her mind.

Milaro spoke up, obviously none too pleased about Quinn's accident or what it could mean. "I'm saying they thought they'd eradicated the last glimpse of a signature that could synchronize with the Library."

11

—————

SO MUCH MORE NOW

Eradicated had now become Quinn's least favorite word, at least for the moment. They'd found her, killed the people she'd grown up with as family, and assumed she was dead too.

It was a lot of information to take in at once, changing the very way she remembered a huge chunk of her life. Something she needed time to process, yet her gut was roiling as if trying to tell her that time was something she didn't have. There were no moments for wallowing or time to just take it easy. She'd spent two weeks doing that anyway. What she needed now was action. Except everything she wanted to do relied on somebody else having to take part in that thing.

She sighed.

Milaro leaned closer to her, peering at her face. "You seem very down, Quinn." His words were gentle, well-meaning, but somehow irritating at the same time.

"I mean, I don't know about you, but if you'd just been told that your parents' death was all your fault"—Quinn tugged on her ponytail —"I guess you're old enough for it not to affect you."

Milaro stepped back, a frown on his face and opened his mouth to say something but Quinn forestalled him.

"No, don't even try to tell me that it wasn't my fault, because we all know that it had to do with me. Without my being there . . ." She paused, taking in a deep breath. "I didn't make their choices for them; they did, in fact, choose to be dickbags, but that doesn't change the fact that without me this wouldn't have happened. Those people who were like family to me would have still been alive."

"Well, without you they wouldn't have even been there to begin with," Malakai said.

"Thanks so much for reinforcing that for me, that's just what I needed," Quinn snapped.

"Look, Quinn, they spent great years with you, right? You have happy memories with them, correct?" Milaro attempted to soothe past his grandson's faux pax.

"True," she said. "Okay, fine, fine, I'm gonna stop dwelling on it for now. Instead, we're going to get revenge, because I feel like revenge is one of the best motivators out there. So now we need to figure out what to do next."

Milaro chuckled. "You know, this proactive Quinn, that's the Quinn we like."

"What, you hate the other Quinn?" she asked sullenly.

"No, she's got her place too, but this one, this one can be a lot of fun." He winked at her.

"Thanks," she said, not really knowing if she should be grateful for that or not. A thought occurred to her. "How did they reach Earth with the Library closed?"

Milaro gave her a sad smile. "The Library isn't the only way to travel or locate someone. You've seen me teleport directly into the space without using a door. Many magic users have access to teleportation."

"Oh," Quinn said, trying to digest that information. She sighed before changing the subject. "Okay, do you know if we have any progress on Tenejo's memories?"

"Not as of yet," Milaro said. "We've been prioritizing the Library regaining its full functionality over getting Tenejo's memory sorted."

"No," Quinn said, "I feel like that's entirely the wrong way to go about this. We need to know whatever that encryption stuff in his brain is."

"Ever think it could be a trap," Malakai asked?

Lynx snorted. "I think we've now come to realize that everything could be a trap."

"I wasn't asking you, furball," Malakai said.

Quinn cringed. "Hey, can we not call each other names?"

"But he is a furball when he's not in humanoid form. Not even lying," Malakai said.

"Yes, but now you're being childish," Quinn reprimanded him. "What is it you wanted to say?"

"I just, I personally, with my wealth of mind magic experience," Malakai said sarcastically, "am worried that these memories you were permitted to extract from Tenejo are actually nothing more than a trap. I don't think hooking those memories up to the system is a good idea given the current state of things. I think we need to figure out ways to ward anybody and anything around it from any type of leakage, just in case. They're sneaky and conniving."

Quinn stared at Malakai for a second. She had to admit he was being entirely logical. More logical than she'd been, frankly. When she got that memory, she just thought she'd struck gold. She had been like, "Oh look, we extracted amazing, codified information from him. What a stroke of luck."

But what if that had been Kajaro's plan all along? Just like her mind bomb implantation had been. What if Tenejo was just completely and utterly a plant? They could have been playing the long game this whole time. She didn't even understand how she'd discounted such a possibility.

"Maybe it's already working," she said.

"What do you mean, already working?" asked Malakai.

"I didn't even once stop to think that that might actually be a trap. Maybe that's all a part of it." She couldn't even think straight right now. So many possibilities presented themselves.

"Well," Malakai said, "to be fair, I am much farther removed from the incident than you were."

She turned to Lynx. "Is there any sort of containment device we could use that the Library has on hand in order to keep it safe while we examine the item?"

Lynx raised an eyebrow. "You know you have access to the inventory too, right?"

"Yes, but I don't know what such an item would be called. Stop being pedantic."

"The answer is maybe." He frowned. "I'll have to look into it. We might want to reinforce or craft a new one."

"Well, if we can get a containment device so we can fiddle with the code without fear of imploding the Library, that would be ideal. Then we can see if it is a trap, or if it's actual information." One problem down, eighteen thousand more to go. And she didn't mean books.

Milaro frowned. "That's a good idea. I don't know if the Library will have one, but I do have one back in my vault. I could fetch that and bring it here. That way we have at least one option."

Quinn suddenly had a thought. "Speaking of which, Milaro, aren't you supposed to be doing like, kingly stuff?"

He waved a hand. "No, no, I've sorted out all the main tasks and delegated several of my usual duties to the current crown prince and his siblings."

"Wait . . . you have more children?" Quinn asked, blinking rapidly.

Milaro paused. "Of course I do. My wife and I have been alive a very long time." He shrugged as if it was self-explanatory. He continued on smoothly as if she hadn't interrupted. "You have to understand, Quinn, that as part of the council that helps regulate Library affairs, I also have duties other than being a king."

Quinn raised an eyebrow. "That's its name. Helper of regulating Library affairs?"

"No, it's long and it's arduous and it's annoying, so I truncated it. I'm just saying, I have more than duties as a king. I just have certain obligations that I had to organize first."

She still didn't quite believe him, but she was ready to move on. "Okay, so Jasper is still harvesting. Malakai, do you think we could visit your mom tomorrow or something?"

"No." Malakai shot her down. "It's only been like a day and a half and she said she wouldn't even be home for three days at least, so I think we don't want to head there before the end of the week, maybe."

Quinn sighed. And still there was that impetus just ringing inside her that they had to do something. It wasn't enough to just sit around and wait because if they waited it would turn out the way it had last time and nobody could afford for it to turn out that way. "Okay, then any development on the other books that we need from the Restricted Vault?"

"Nope, we're still missing about a dozen," Lynx said. "I think . . . maybe . . . could be entirely wrong. I have been wrong a lot lately."

Quinn wanted to tear her hair out and scream. This was not the productive afternoon she'd wanted after coming home. From home? Well, from Earth. And she really needed something to do to distract her from what she'd learned there. Remembering the accident in such vivid detail hadn't been on her bucket list.

"Fine," she said, "We don't know anything more about the Restricted Vault, we don't know . . . and how does that number keep going up? Wasn't it like six books last time?"

But she didn't wait for an answer. She stood up and paced to the door herself. Her entire body suddenly felt itchy. Like she'd been sitting in one place for too long. "I need to stretch my legs. I'm feeling cooped up and I—I'm gonna go and man the check-in desk for a while. I just—I need a break, guys."

She left the room without another word. Thankfully, they let her.

The bad news, as Quinn discovered when she stepped into the main portion of the Library, was that the Library wasn't overly busy. Not returns or enquiry-wise anyway. There were a few people at the check-in counter. She walked over, not recognizing the two assistants who stood there checking people in.

She glanced over to see Jim, separated from his twin for once, and frowned.

"Are you watching over these guys?" she asked.

"Yes," Jim replied, his many eyes darting back and forth. It was like he wasn't so good at replying when his twin wasn't there to finish his sentences.

Her frown deepened when he didn't say anything more, and then she walked to the other end of the counter and pulled up the console. She wasn't even sure what she was looking for. Perhaps it was time to check on her own progress as the Librarian. She'd absorbed a lot of books during her two-week downtime and now she needed to see the fruits of her labor, which were substantial. Her energy levels were high. No wonder they'd let her energy fuel the door key from Earth.

Name: Quinn
Age: Irrelevant
Heritage: Earth, Sector 12942
*Species: Librarian**
Energy Capacity: 2,289/2,289
Mana Levels: 1,898/1,898
Alignment: 101%
*Affinities: 1722***
Tome Knowledge: 118
Affinity Level: 12
Determination: Rising
**Awaiting determination*
***As far as the Library can determine*

She combed through her stats, eyeing each one, trying not to be disappointed that they weren't as advanced as she would have liked. Quinn sighed.

"Well, at least I've made some progress," she muttered.

"Quinn?" Dottie nudged against her leg. "You're sort of mumbling to yourself. Are you feeling okay?"

"Yeah, I'm feeling better now, Dottie."

"Now?" Dottie asked.

"Well, now that you're here." She winked at the bench.

"Oh, Quinn, don't be so silly," Dottie said. But Quinn was fairly certain that if the bench had a face, it would indeed be smiling at her.

"You know, Dottie, is there a golem that can encrypt or decrypt stuff?"

"I don't know, Quinn. I don't have access to that sort of information. You'd want to ask Misha that."

"Yeah, I would want to, wouldn't I?" Quinn couldn't explain the sudden melancholy that came over her. She was tired. She felt run down. And almost like everything was impossible. There was so much on her list that they needed to do. There was so much she didn't understand about this world still, about herself. It was almost as if Gloom was settling back over the Library.

"Quinn," Dottie interrupted her spiraling thoughts. "I think maybe you should go and take a nap."

"But Dottie, I've been sleeping. I can't keep using being tired as an excuse."

"I think you're a bit overwhelmed, dear. I think most people would be in your shoes." Dottie always reminded Quinn of her grandmother. Well, yeah. She still deserved to be called Grandma. "Have you gone to the new culinary section? Because Cook has been, well, whipping up a storm in there. You should go."

Quinn glanced at the counter where Jim of the Aracnio Brothers stood with the two assistants she couldn't even be bothered inspecting right now, chatting because there were no people returning books. For a fleeting moment she wondered why Jim wouldn't talk to her like that.

She glanced down into the Library and realized that there were a lot of people gathered around chatting amongst themselves, discussing books, discussing theories. And she sighed, a little bit of happiness sneaking back into her sadness.

"Yeah, Dottie, let's go." Quinn really wanted a donut.

She wandered down past some of the couches and tables and gave a little wave to people as she went past. She entered the dining hall, which had, yet again, taken on a slightly different form. It appeared more formal and less cafeteria-like now, almost like the big beer halls in the inns in Germany. She'd seen pictures of them when they studied the Oktoberfest.

Quinn walked through, marveling again at how amazing the culinary branch was. It sent a tingle up her spine, making her immediately want to open more of the branches because ultimately the Library was only kind of half done. It wasn't in its full grandeur.

She moved in and saw Cook manning two stoves at once. She watched them for a couple of minutes. They were stirring pots, flipping ingredients, measuring ingredients, and chopping things up. It seemed like they were in seventh heaven.

"Ah, Librarian," they said without even turning her way. "What brings you to my humble kitchen?"

"Hunger." She grinned at them. "Is the kitchen from the dining hall gone?"

"It is unnecessary now, Librarian." Cook gestured all around them. "We have so much more now."

"Oh," she said, not entirely sure how she felt about that. She sniffed the air and immediately forgot about the donuts. "Is that Hungarian goulash?"

Cook smiled at her. "Why, yes, yes it is." They ladled out a bowl and set it next to the stove. "I would advise you to eat it while it is hot and then, perhaps, take a stroll around the Library. Take it in. I think you would benefit.

Quinn eyed Cook for a second before nodding slowly. "Will do." she said as she picked up her food. Bread and bowl of goulash in hand, Quinn took a seat. Not out in the dining hall, but next to the bench where Cook was still doing their thing.

Dottie had trotted and was sitting beneath her. "Now don't you feel better, Librarian?"

Quinn nodded and sat taking in the atmosphere. Cook wasn't the only person at a stove. There were so many of them in the area. And people were browsing the books, sniffing the herbs. It was like a magical, botanical cooking garden. Quinn chuckled to herself at the thought.

"Are you a bit better now, Librarian?" Dottie asked.

"You know, I think . . . I think I feel a lot better now. Thanks, Dottie. I needed this. Thank you, Cook."

"I could tell," Cook said. "You miss home."

"No." Quinn pondered that for a moment. "I miss Earth. This, this has definitely become home."

"Very well, Librarian," Cook said. "Very well."

12

PRETTY SIGNAGE

Cook was right.

Wandering around the Library and just soaking in the atmosphere to decompress was the perfect solution. So far, other than frantically learning as much as she could about everything, Quinn hadn't really taken the time to just wander around and enjoy the fact that she was in a magical Library.

This time, as she walked through the Library, Quinn felt a sense of peace. It wasn't necessarily that the Library was in the back of her mind. It wasn't even the amazing connection they'd had since the synchronization. It was the atmosphere, the sensations, the very soft muttering from people that leaked through the entire interior like a wave of murmuring, calming and soothing. People sharing knowledge, people discussing books. Tomes being taken off shelves and returned to shelves. The smell of books and the sense of just so much coming together.

She walked into the main hall of the Library, which was as long as several football fields. Beautiful pillars rose up, reminding her that she really needed to check out the second level too. She'd never been up there. She'd been to a training room, and she'd been down that little hallway where she'd learned how to use a sword only to prove that she was really bad at it. The training room, the Restricted Vault, and all the doors that constantly opened. The Library was massive.

No wonder it needed its own little pocket dimension.

Quinn walked past the gathering of chairs and tables where they usually sat while interviewing new assistants. Several species were sitting at that table. They'd dragged some more chairs over, or maybe the golems had done it for them. She glanced at her HUD to see their species. One of them looked entirely human until she looked dead on at Quinn. Her nose just had two little slits. Her mouth was as wide as a Cheshire cat with fangs for all of her teeth. And her eyes, well, she had three of them. And yet when she smiled and waved, it felt more natural than anything.

Indelit - Subterranean species

Located in the: Illukai Region

Library Allies for: 329,000 years

They were from the same region as the Aracnios. The sheer scope of the people who visited here took Quinn's breath away, not to mention the time spans.

She walked down past about a couple dozen gathering areas, slowly taking in her surroundings as she went. Aradie was a comforting presence on her shoulder. She waved at Tim, who stopped and bowed briefly as he brought a couple of books to one of the tables. Quinn glanced over and frowned ever so slightly. These patrons weren't Salosiers, but their species had to be a very close cousin. But they also weren't the Tecopsis she'd encountered previously, either.

She wanted to know more, more about all of the species in this universe and about all the books they held in the Library. On sight, without having to reference the system.

Just randomly allowing her HUD to assess the people she came across wasn't any way to retain the information properly. She needed to absorb this.

She walked a little farther and summoned Misha. Aradie cooed in her ear.

"You summoned me, Librarian," Misha said. There was a smile on

Misha's face, and Quinn realized that she had barely been speaking to her supervisory golem lately.

"So this section," Quinn asked, "What is it?"

"This is the beginner's hall. Down here in this section, we have all of the books. All of the beginner magic books. But you knew that, correct?"

Quinn nodded because she had known the main branch housed beginner books, so this was nothing new. The bookcases were mostly full. She still knew there were thousands of books missing, but there were also like two hundred feet of hall.

Probably more. She wasn't very good at guesstimating distances.

"So, every single book on these shelves is a different beginner magic book? Different affinities?"

"Yes and no," Misha said. "On this level, they are all beginner magic books in all of the magical affinities."

"So, the cookbooks and alchemy books aren't on this level?"

"The magical combat beginner books are down the hall you traversed, I believe, when you were culling the bookworms. But other than that . . . the upper level houses all of the alchemical, musical, horticultural and other beginner books," Misha clarified.

"Oh," Quinn said, "the magic section is huge."

Misha looked over at her and blinked. "What did you expect? It is a magical Library, and so all of the affinities that are related directly to magic are in the main branch, and that is why you do not need to open a magical branch, because the main branch *is* the generic magical branch."

"Yeah, I got that." Quinn had understood that, yet seeing it all in place was entirely different. She'd known some of this stuff, but to be honest, she now regretted not taking more time to truly understand it.

Just browsing through the books instead of searching and directly locating them felt rejuvenating. Although she couldn't deny the convenience that was simply summoning a golem or cart to get her the books she'd looked up. But it took away some of that charm.

"If you go on further, when you get up those steps that lead to where the initial bookworm onslaught was, you will find the intermediate magical section, and it varies from there."

Quinn glanced around, frowning when she didn't see any clear indicators of subject matter anywhere. "Do we have signs showing people what's where? Signs to say, 'here are these affinities'?"

Misha blinked at Quinn, "Generally people ask the golems for the books."

"Isn't that highly inefficient,?" Quinn asked, genuinely curious. The golems couldn't split themselves up, after all. And the Library was starting to get a lot busier.

"Interacting with the patrons brings the golems who serve here great joy. It is why they are here, and they enjoy it." Misha sounded a bit impatient.

"Oh." Quinn thought that over and suddenly felt guilty. Did these golems have other dreams? Or did they want to simply be bookshelving golems forever? "Do we have enough golems? The Library's pretty busy now." Quinn paused again and looked back toward the main lobby. It was practically bustling now.

"Hmm. Would you like me to produce more shelving and assistance golems, Librarian?" Misha asked, sounding much more comfortable with the direction of this topic.

"I think Tim and Tom might need a little bit of help."

Misha smiled and bowed. "Very well. I will see to that immediately." And then they vanished.

Quinn still wasn't quite used to that happening, especially in cases like right now where she'd thought they were still mid conversation. She paused on the threshold of stepping into the intermediate section. "Aradie, these books. I'm confused. On Earth, libraries get multiple copies of popular books. I know we have some multiple copies, but otherwise, do we just have one copy of everything?"

No, Aradie said into her mind. Perhaps the owl had decided that simply spamming her brain with images wasn't always the way to go. At least for this conversation.

"Then the more popular books will have multiple copies?"

Yes.

"What about the ones that we had to retrieve? Were those books that have copies?"

Some of them had copies, but for the most part, those books needed to be retrieved because they were either our only copies or just because the copies out in the universe would thus have gathered a large portion of energy during the time the Library was in stasis. Even the copies that were out in the world soaking up energy and mana are important. Retrieval was determined on their potential energy contribution to the Library, not their content.

"Oh," Quinn said. "I learn something new every day."

Quinn took her time walking through the Library. She wasn't entirely sure she could afford downtime, but, at least for a little while, she was taking some. Sure, she'd walked past a heap of these bookcases, touched some books, saved some books, and read a lot of books. But usually, those books came to her via Tim and Tom, or Misha, or Carty, or even Dottie sometimes. She hadn't really taken time out to get used to her new home. Which, considering how much she'd loved her library back on Earth, was a true shame.

"Why does Cook always have the best ideas?" she muttered out loud. Aradie cooed in her ear. "Yeah, I know, shouldn't judge a cooking golem by their cover." She swore Aradie chortled.

The intermediate magic section was sort of underwhelming, in that the pillars were built into each wall as supports. But it was full of books. The shelving rose all the way to the ceiling and there was no second level as such. But there was a sort of level about halfway up with a slim platform that housed the next section's rolling ladder. She'd always loved those ladders. The small platform did indeed have a railing, but it wasn't like the majestic sweeping second-story level back in the beginner section. Perhaps it required less grandeur this way.

After all, it was purely about the books back here.

Because anyone who came back to the intermediate section was likely not just dabbling in magic.

She looked around, wishing that they had signs. "Why don't we have signs in the Library?" she asked, pointedly directing the thought at the Library itself. The whole lack of even row indicators really got on her nerves.

That's neither here nor there. We have a service where golems will retrieve the books for those who need them.

"But I've seen people walking into the beginner section and just retrieving books themselves." Quinn would have glared at the Library if it was effective.

Those people know where the books are that they want and they can find them. It's just—

"It's just the way it's always been done," Quinn finished for the Library.

Well, yes.

Quinn wasn't about to give up. "I would really like to add some pretty signage. You can make it look as magical as you want, but I feel it would make the Library a little bit more approachable and feel less like it's trying to exclude people, perhaps."

You think we exclude people here, Quinn? The Library sounded genuinely curious.

"No, not as such." Quinn sighed. "It's just I could understand how others might get that impression."

Oh, the Library said. *Well, it's not a difficult thing to do.*

Before her very eyes, Quinn watched as a couple of signs began to appear. They were small but big enough to see from the ground and they had things like ice tomes, earth tomes, and mental magic manipulation tomes. They became more obvious if she focused on them for a split second.

Quinn took a deep breath. "Yep, that's pretty much what I meant. That way people can come into the Library and find books for themselves. It's not like we're not constantly watching them anyway. They can't escape with the books."

That's true.

"It might allow people to think of the Library more as a cozy home and place to be. Maybe they'll stay longer. Maybe more people will feel comfortable here," Quinn said.

Well, we'll see, Quinn, the Library said. But Quinn could tell that it wasn't so skeptical anymore. The Library just needed some proof of process.

The intermediate section led Quinn up to the training room. She poked her head in to notice that it had reverted to the way it was before they attempted to view the memories of the owls.

"Are they done with the memories of the owls?" she asked Aradie.

But it was Eric who answered and almost gave Quinn a heart attack. "Mostly, just a few more to go through, but you know, there are other spaces we can use."

Quinn, shaking slightly, turned and glared at the imp. "Seriously, dude, why did you scare the crap out of me?"

"Because I am me," Eric said, flashing her a wink. "Come on, you should be used to me by now."

"Sadly, I almost am. Anyway, what do you mean there are spaces?" Quinn asked, mostly recovered now.

"You know, the Library can make any room we need, right?" he asked, raising an eyebrow.

"Well, yes, but . . . oh"—she grimaced as she finally had the light-bulb moment—"you needed a room to view the memories without impacting any other area of the Library, so now you have, like, an office."

"Exactly! Look at you, kid, you catch on real quick." Eric winked again. He really seemed to like winking.

"Oh, shut up, Eric."

"Come on, you love me and my impish ways." His wings hummed as he spoke.

"You really like playing that up, don't you?" Quinn asked, genuinely curious. He seemed to bring it up a lot.

"Why, yes, I do. I'm an imp, and you know something? I'm damn proud of it." His eyes flamed momentarily as he made his dramatic statement.

"Mm-hmm, proud of it, along with that fiery little tail you've got." This time it was Quinn's turn to wink.

"That's enough, Quinn. You don't insult an imp's tail." He crossed his arms as they walked slowly, and glared at her.

Quinn pressed her lips together, trying her best not to let her laugh to get out. She pushed it just that little bit too far. He really was sensitive about his tail being a torch.

"Anyway." He cleared his throat and continued as if she hadn't insulted him. "I thought I'd come and keep you company. You have yet to reach the Advanced or Legendary sections. You know where the Restricted Vault is. You haven't even found the area where specific species sections are relegated."

"What do you mean, specific species sections?" she asked, immediately interested. Aradie hooted softly. It sounded like a laugh.

"Well, you see, I'm an imp."

"You don't say," Quinn said.

"Oh, stop it. I'm actually being serious for once."

Quinn laughed. "You know, you should probably like hold up a sign in front of your face that says 'serious mode' so that people know that you're being serious and you're not just pulling our leg as usual."

"What would the fun in that be?" Eric said. "Anyway, listen. We prefer warmth and brimstone and, well, just an environment that is more attuned to us. The Library seeks to fill those demands and give us a place more suited to our species to browse the books, allowing us to relax in an environment that is more what we're used to."

"Oh," Quinn said. "Like, people from more watery worlds would prefer to breathe in water?"

"Yes, and the books are magically protected from climate, so it doesn't matter." Eric got that fire in his eyes he always did when he was excited.

"Wow," Quinn said. "Talk about private Library rooms. That's freaking fantastic."

"You would think so, wouldn't you," said Eric.

"Well, why wouldn't I think so?" Quinn asked.

"Oh, no, you would. I'm just saying. It's what you'd think. That it's amazing." Eric grinned and then sobered up to solemn before speaking again. "The point is, sometimes people don't leave the Library."

"You mean we get like Library reading room squatters?"

"Yes, and we currently have a couple of patrons who are treating us like a hotel."

Quinn shrugged. "Let's go see, then, shall we?" After all, patrons treating the Library like a hotel sounded a lot better than the mind-bombing and Library-destroying conspirators she was trying to chase down otherwise. Right?

13

PEOPLE UNDER THE STAIRS

QUINN WASN'T EXACTLY SURE HOW TO REACT TO WHAT ERIC HAD TOLD her, considering she probably had a very different view of squatters than Eric did. Were these people homeless? Did they need somewhere to stay? In which case, shouldn't the Library shelter them since it could? However, they couldn't just have everybody come and stay.

That wasn't even a viable option.

Was it?

Maybe. How big was a pocket dimension?

"Quinn," Eric said. She looked up at him, where he hovered directly in front of her.

"I'm sorry, my mind went places." She couldn't help it. Images flashed through her mind from horror movies she'd seen growing up where the call was coming from inside the house, or there were people under the stairs.

One she vividly remembered with a single-white-female-type stalker who entered the house, became the same person as the main character, and attempted to kill them constantly. Not that this was probably the case in the Library, but Quinn needed Eric to narrow down what this meant for her. "You're saying that people have come into the Library, ordered and used specific species allocated Library rooms, and are reading books and just staying here?"

"Yes," Eric said. "Sort of like we're a hotel. And they come up and they go, they use the dining hall multiple times a day." He sounded so indignant.

"Is that it?"

"Mostly."

Quinn paused a second before speaking as gently as she could. "But it sounds like the Library doesn't have much of a problem with it. Perhaps they need a place to stay?"

"Well, maybe," Eric said begrudgingly.

"Have you asked them if they need a place to stay?" Quinn pushed the matter further.

"Well, it's not as easy as all that," he stuttered.

The Library sighed, and the sound rippled underneath Quinn's feet all the way up her spine.

In times gone by, the Library began, and Eric could obviously hear it as well because he looked quite surprised to be in on the conversation. *We frequently had scholars who spent time, very large amounts of time, in their own rooms. It's perfectly normal, Eric,*

"Oh, so I don't have to kick people out after ten days of being in the Library and being a drain on our resources?" he said, the hum on his wings went up half an octave with his level of annoyance.

And how would you think they are being a drain on our resources, Eric? the Library said, its temperament just as even as always.

She realized she hadn't spent much time talking to the Library lately. In fact, the Library had been downright silent about a lot of things, which in and of itself wasn't necessarily bad, but given their current dire situation and the five thousand things she had on her list, it definitely wasn't the optimum thing for the Library to remain mostly silent.

We are a center for knowledge, a learning facility, a place that allows people to come and sit in silence or come and have scintillating academic discussions over books. They can take in the knowledge, learn the spells, learn the magic. They can ask somebody. They can ask one of the assistants if they're having issues understanding some of the material they're reading. We can direct them to the next book that might better help them understand whatever area of expertise they're pursuing. That's what the Library is, Eric. And if, as I suspect—the Library paused for a second—you are talking about the Slothilis, then they have been allies of the Library almost as long as your kind. And I do believe it's Carafax who is currently occupying the room you're speaking of.

Eric blinked. He didn't really have anywhere to look because the Library was simply speaking into both his and Quinn's minds at the same time. Although Quinn was fully aware the Library could speak to the entire Library at once if it so chose, doing so right now when it was a private conversation would be a major breach of etiquette.

Quinn chuckled. "So you're saying it's absolutely fine for researchers to be here researching knowledge like you do in a Library," Quinn said, her gaze punctuating with each word as she looked at Eric.

Precisely, the Library said, *you should just ask me these things, Eric. Quinn, while having access to much of the same information, still needs to adjust to how to process it quicker than she currently does.*

"Sure, how do I do that? Do I just ask for the Library to listen to me?" Eric's wing hum had risen another half-octave.

Quinn watched in amusement. It was probably the first time that she'd seen Eric practically lost for words. The little imp never seemed to lack the ability to talk under six feet of wet cement. However, in this case, he seemed slightly flustered.

Just speak to me, the Library answered as if it was the simplest thing in the world.

Quinn interrupted the conversation. "So, the Slothilis, is it possible for us to perhaps meet this Carafax person?"

Oh yes, the Library said. *I am sure, give me just a second. There you go.*
Lynx popped into view.

Here you go. Lynx will lead the way much easier than me trying to give you directions while I am currently processing multiple operations to figure out the entire list you've given me, Quinn.

"You sound a bit annoyed with me," Quinn said.

Just irritated that I have obviously let someone pull one over on me. Perhaps I was too trusting. Maybe I grew too complacent. Of which neither are a good thing nor are they an excuse for what has happened. I have to hold myself responsible and I may be having some difficulties doing that right now.

Quinn realized that the Library was now only talking to her and not to Eric, as he stood there in the air hovering with his arms crossed and quite a scowl on his face. He didn't appear to enjoy being corrected, and the Library had most definitely come out on top.

So, Quinn asked the Library telepathically, *are you okay?*

To be honest, Quinn, no. I've lost memories, I've lost data, which is knowledge, which as you can imagine for me, a hoarder of knowledge, is the equivalent to losing a limb. Right now I am focused on tracking down which books are missing, where they are located, how we can fix the memory holes as Cadre, Harish, Milaro, and Siliqua constantly give me new information to process to see if we can access things in different ways. I don't feel like there's enough time or enough information available to me to figure all this out.

You know we can do it together, right? We're working on it from our end. We will figure this out.

Thank you, Quinn. I feel I should just be older and wiser, and the former is barely even possible, the Library said. *You are appreciated. Now, go visit Carafax.*

Your wish is my command.

She could practically feel the Library grinning at her.

Right then and there, Quinn decided that she needed to go and speak to the Core sooner rather than later, perhaps tomorrow, or at least within the next few days. There were many things she needed to clear up before she tackled some of the larger items on their list, not least of which was figuring out exactly what she was capable of, now that her new heritage had been revealed. Then again, she had so much coming up in the next few days.

For now, she wanted to meet this so-called squatter, as Eric had called them, or academic, as the Library insisted they were.

"Quinn, are you done daydreaming? Can I take you now?" Lynx asked, his tone sharp.

"Wow, temper, temper, Lynx." She grinned at him.

"Look, I got interrupted in the middle of inventory, okay? I've saved my progress, but I still need to get back into the swing of things, and that takes me a little while," he said grumpily.

"Can't you just, like, automatically count stuff?" Quinn asked.

"Well, yes, but it still takes a while to get warmed up." He sighed. "You wanted to go and visit Carafax, right?"

"Yes, I did." Quinn couldn't help but feel a little excited to meet another new species, another new knowledge seeker.

Eric seemed disgruntled. He flew with his arms still crossed, muttering under his breath.

"What was that, Eric?" Quinn asked as Aradie leaned into the side of her head. Sometimes that threw her equilibrium off completely, but she was getting used to it.

"Nothing. Just bloody all-knowing libraries. It's very frustrating."

Quinn chuckled. "You know, it's probably a good thing that you don't know everything. Otherwise, what use would it be for you to be here, in a Library, of everything?"

"It's not *of everything*. We don't have romance novels in this branch," Eric muttered.

"No, I'd imagine we don't, because they're not technically magical. Do we have any love potion sections?" Quinn asked suddenly.

"Only the alchemy section, but I don't believe infatuation potions are what you're looking for. Now, just follow me," Lynx said. "This way."

They'd already long gone past the training room. Quinn hadn't realized quite how big the Library was. She'd never been past this point before. How negligent she'd been.

"Here on the left-hand side, we have advanced magical texts. If you haven't been cleared for this level of magic, you can't even touch these tomes," Lynx explained as if he'd suddenly become a tour guide.

Quinn suppressed a smile. "Well, that's enlightening," she said. "So, where is . . ."

But she didn't have to ask any more. Further in, there was a series of doorways that just screamed private chambers. As she looked at it, a sign appeared over them, and she chuckled. "Private reading rooms. That's excellent," she said.

You're very welcome. The Library echoed in her ears.

"Did you have something to do with these signs?" Lynx asked, as he opened the leftmost door.

"Yes," Quinn said. "Yes, I did. It was a pretty good idea. Thank you very much."

They opened the door, and yet it didn't open into another room. It opened into another corridor, which went however many feet long, and then they turned into the first door on the left. Lynx rapped on it sharply.

"Come in," a voice said. It was a very gruff voice, it sounded kind of like a *Sesame Street* character who lived in a bin.

Lynx opened the door, and heat swept out. It wasn't like a fire and brimstone heat like she assumed would be in an imp home world. This was more like the moistness of the earth, and the way it retained the heat and the water, keeping it ripe for crops, and apparently for this Slothilis.

It was true, at first, she thought the being in front of her looked quite like a sloth, a very large sloth, almost the size of a horse. He was hunched over, and that's when Quinn realized that he was more of a hedgehog sloth where some of the fur was indeed spine-like. He had long limbs that moved languidly as he turned the pages.

He looked up from a very large desk, and a slow smile spread across his hedgehog-sloth-like face. He grinned. "Ah, to what do I owe such esteemed company?" he said slowly. His irises were kind, dark, dark brown, and they took up most of his eye, like a cat's eye, or maybe like a sloth's eye, she wasn't exactly sure. She'd have to bring up an image of one in order to be sure, but she found herself smiling back easily.

He didn't speak slowly or exaggeratingly like they demonstrated sloths to be in movies and cartoons, but he spoke with deliberation and caution as if making sure that each word he chose was the exact word he meant to choose. She liked him instantly.

"Hi, I'm the Librarian. It is nice to meet you." She flashed him a genuine smile.

"Ah, Lynx, I like this one, she is sweet, unlike her predecessor," Carafax said, nodding slowly.

Quinn immediately had about eighty thousand questions. Lynx, on the other hand, scowled very briefly, as if it was almost a reflex reaction, and then he sighed. "Well, if you have any insight from your interactions with Korradine," he said, "we'd welcome any information you have for us."

Slowly, Carafax raised an eyebrow and then shifted his position languidly. Quinn could hear the needles on his back shift against one another. It was a pleasing sound, almost like a soft xylophone, slightly musical in effect.

"Excuse me," she asked, "I couldn't help but notice. Are you researching musical texts?"

"Why, yes," he said. "I am, my dear. Do you appreciate good music?"

Quinn nodded. "I really do. I'm hoping we can get the bardic musical branch open as soon as possible."

"I would appreciate that. I do believe I have sent my assistants to return several books that I borrowed from the Library to teach former students. I will return them and pay the fine appropriately." His grin widened, revealing blunt, white teeth.

"Oh, you've been here for ten days and you haven't returned them yet?" Quinn asked before really thinking it through.

"I must admit, I was so excited when I realized that the Library was truly back, that in my joy I forgot to bring them with me. I have sent for them. Rest assured they will be in excellent condition." His smile never seemed to fade.

Is there anything else we can get for you?" she asked.

"No, no, I am quite happy to head into the kitchen myself." He turned toward Lynx, his expression suddenly changing to one of seriousness. "Now, dear Lynx, you mentioned wanting to know things about Korradine. How much time do you have?"

Quinn's spine tingled in an almost premonition-like way. This didn't sound good, but at the same time, she thought this might be their best chance for more information.

She just had to hope Lynx was ready to hear it.

14

SLOTTING INTO PLACE

LYNX BLINKED AT CARAFAX BEFORE LETTING OUT A LONG-SUFFERING sigh. "To be honest? At this moment we really don't have much time for anything in-depth." He sounded somewhat dejected by his own answer.

Carafax simply nodded in that sagely way that spoke of age and wisdom. Frankly, her gut feeling told her there wasn't a secret Quinn wouldn't feel comfortable sharing with the Slothilis. She found him fascinating.

"Then, shall we take a truncated approach to things?" he asked, the smile never leaving his face.

"What do you know about Korradine?" Quinn asked, preferring to be direct and stop the somewhat overly eloquent Library guest from becoming sidetracked.

"As you wish," he said, his merry eyes twinkling as he focused on Quinn. He paused and glanced very slowly down at a bag next to the large desk he occupied, before picking up without any urgency whatsoever.

Or perhaps this was him moving with urgency. Quinn was so fascinated by his movements that she really didn't care. His spines rippled as he moved, leaving behind a soothing lullaby with those faint xylophone sounds.

He pulled out a thick journal and splayed it open on the desk. Its thick pages held scrawling handwriting flowing from edge to edge. A small chuckle escaped him, sort of like a loud rumbling purr.

The thing was, she knew it wasn't mind magic effects like both Narilin and Malakai could utilize because her mental defenses didn't sound off any alarms. But she did realize there was something magically fascinating about Carafax.

"Ah yes," he said, jabbing a finger on a page and beckoning Lynx and Quinn to come over. "You see, right here. This is when I first noticed that something was strange."

Quinn peered at the page but didn't really understand anything about the dating system in the universe yet. Which, in hindsight, was likely something she had to correct. But as she glanced at Lynx, she realized he'd grown pale.

Then his eyes shot back into focus and he practically growled out the next words. "Are you sure this is accurate?"

Carafax didn't appear to be perturbed in the least. He simply smiled and nodded. "Yes. This is undoubtedly correct. I am very astute with my journal entries. Observations are what fuel a part of my magical work. It's essential that I notate those down that I observe while I'm studying as well.

As Lynx digested the information Quinn could feel the Library processing it as well. "And you're entirely certain this is when you began noticing changes?" Lynx asked again, this time more insistent. Quinn could practically hear the Library talking through him.

She wanted to know what the big deal was, but she could still feel the effect the information was having on the Library as a whole. An uneasiness and uncertainty that she'd yet to experience as it rolled through her entire nervous system. Being connected to a universal magical Library might sound like a lot of fun, and it was. At least until you began to feel in sync with it and the entire being started having mega feelings.

What is it? she asked, pushing her voice out to the Library.

A few seconds of awkward silence in the real world passed before the Library begrudgingly answered. *If what Carafax says is true, Korradine's behavior changed a long time before we remember it.*

Is there any reason to disbelieve this? Quinn pushed for an answer.

None. Carafax is a longtime Library patron. With thousands of years of contributions to a few of our branches. He's very methodical and observant. I would say this is about as accurate data as we can get. The Library didn't sound happy about any of that.

Remember though, this could just be one of the memories you're missing.

The Library didn't respond, but Quinn hoped it considered her words.

Carafax had turned his attention back to the books he was leafing through, that same content smile still on his face. Eric's scowl was so deep Quinn was worried it might swallow his face, but she'd seen him bounce back from it before so it should be good.

She wasn't entirely sure how she should phrase what she wanted to ask, so a part of her just thought she should go ahead and ask it. "Can I ask . . . is it possible to get a replica of any of the days you happened to notice anything about Korradine at all?"

Carafax blinked up at Quinn slowly, his smile turning into a thoughtful half frown. Frankly, with his face, she wasn't entirely sure he was even capable of a full-on scowl. He just seemed so happy. Although, she could imagine him being terrifying in some capacity to his enemies. If he uncurled from how he'd positioned himself at the desk, she was quite certain he'd be massive.

"Yes," he said finally, sounding pleased. "I believe I can do that right now."

Before Quinn could ask, Lynx answered the question on the tip of her tongue for her. "He's got a magical chronicling affinity. Long story short, he can magically recreate events and happenings he's witnessed, and his magical journal technically qualifies as an official observation."

"Come now, Lynx. You take all the fun out of me pretending it's an amazing feat." Carafax's eyes sparkled as he picked on the Library manifestation. "Anyway, young Librarian. You are indeed correct!

Give me a few minutes and I should be able to locate them and produce them for you. I am feeling somewhat peckish. I think this would be a good time to go and visit Cook."

Carafax muttered under his breath, and his eyes took on a golden bright hue as a flash of power ringed around him. Several moments of pulsating light later, and he'd produced said documents. He handed them to her with a flourish of his long-clawed hands and Quinn took them gingerly in her own, quite astounded at the way his magic worked.

It was better than a Xerox.

She was also quite impressed at the sheer mass of papers.

She blinked up at Carafax as he leveraged himself out from behind his desk. He was a couple of feet taller than her and took up so much more space that she felt positively tiny.

Quinn rifled through the documents and paled. Now she understood why the Library reacted in the way it had.

Carafax leaned forward, a small frown tugging his smile down. "Is something the matter?"

She shook her head. It wasn't even that. "These are from . . ."

He smiled. "Oh, I took them from the last two visits where everything seemed normal, and then included the changed observations. I mean I've got bits on everyone, even on you, Aradie." He winked at the bird.

She pointedly looked away from the Slothilis, as if he wasn't worth her time.

Quinn would have found it amusing if she didn't feel like Carafax's powers of observation bordered on the creepy.

"Are you wary of me now, young Librarian?" he asked, and a little bit of melancholy tinged those words, immediately causing Quinn to suffer from mega guilt.

"Not as such," she started to say and then sighed. "It's not what I mean. It's just this is all very . . ."

"Clinical?" he asked.

"Sort of." She shrugged. "Like we're all just being watched and will never know."

Carafax nodded very slowly. "I am a chronicler. It's very lonely work. We observe, we compile, we discover. I'm fascinated by everything I do not yet know, and every bit of knowledge that could potentially be discovered."

"Is there a reason you didn't come forward with this information at the time?" Eric snapped like his scowl had finally won out and taken control over his willpower.

Carafax cringed. "To be honest? At the time, I had several projects on my plate. I meant to pull dear Korradine aside and see what it was that troubled her, but it never appeared to be something dire . . ." He paused and bowed to Lynx apologetically. "At least, that is, until it was. Now I know better. Should something occur again, I will endeavor to not make the same mistake."

Quinn tried to flash him a smile, but she couldn't help the sadness she felt. Maybe if he'd noticed, maybe they could have done something about it.

But then, she wouldn't be here, would she? Quinn wasn't entirely certain how she felt about that side of it. Before she could think farther up that track, the Library spoke into her head.

Hindsight is always best. We can't change anything now. But we can move forward.

Even the tone inside her head sounded melancholy.

"There could be some hints in these notes that directly relate to why." Carafax pointed out not unkindly. "I cannot pretend to know what she was thinking. Had I? I would have spoken up much before this. It wasn't until I returned last week and heard whispers of Kor's betrayal that I truly put two and two together and got a surprising result of four." He chuckled at his own joke before sobering back up.

"Honestly, though . . . I wish I'd been more inquisitive in nature and less observant. Please let me know if I may be of more assistance in this matter. I am truly grateful that the Library has been returned to us." His smile reached so wide it crinkled his eyes into practical non-existence.

"Thank you," Quinn said, meaning it, but wishing she knew what to ask to get to the bottom of it.

"Ah, new Librarian. Quinn. You are an interesting mix yourself, aren't you?" His eyes suddenly lost their friendliness and sent shivers down Quinn's spine.

There was nothing hostile in the look, but more of a hunger. One of knowledge and less about devouring something whole. Still, Quinn wondered if this species had carnivorous tendencies, but she was too scared to ask the system and find out.

"I do believe I'm a bit of an interesting mix myself." She said it with a laugh, trying to make light of it. But she could tell from Carafax's shrewd gaze that he didn't believe her for a second.

He paused as if seriously considering speaking to her about something. He glanced to either side of them and the smile settled back over his face. "I will be staying in the Library for a while to catch up on the work I have missed out on in the last few centuries. Should you ever feel bored, Librarian, please let me know and I would love to regale you with my adventurous findings."

Quinn smiled and suddenly wanted to know what he meant by that. But they'd delayed him from his food for long enough already. "It was wonderful to meet you," she said instead as they all proceeded out into the hall.

He walked on two legs as they exited, which she found odd since his arms were so long and she realized she'd judged a part of him on preconceived notions that he'd walk like a sloth or gorilla. She really needed to get better about that.

He moved slowly out of the doors first and then began to slowly waddle toward the kitchen.

Quinn watched him go, a frown on her face.

"I feel exactly the same way," Eric muttered, hovering next to her.

Quinn nodded. "I only wish I knew how I felt."

Eric moved to hover directly in front of her and crossed his arms. "Sometimes, you just have to go with your gut, Quinn."

"If I went with my gut, Eric, I'd have run screaming from the Library at the sight of you and never returned." She shrugged. "You're not exactly commonplace or welcome mythology in my world."

He hovered there for several seconds before he finally burst out laughing. "Touché. Well. That lightened the mood. Shall we continue the tour?"

Quinn still clutched the papers in her hands and shook her head. There was too much to get done, too much to do. Especially with some new pieces of the puzzle slotting into place.

"No. I think I need to get a full night's rest. I've got a feeling the next week is going to be very hectic." She sighed as she headed back toward her office to leave the pages there.

Eric shrugged as he followed her. "Suit yourself."

"I wish that's all it was," she muttered under her breath. Lynx trailed along, uncharacteristically silent.

She understood it. If she'd just found out one of the people she'd trusted most in the universe had been planning to betray her for millennia longer than previously thought, she'd be shaken too.

15

GATES OF HALSCHIUS

Lynx was nowhere to be seen while Quinn poured over the information she'd received from Carafax in her office. She could understand it though. He'd yet to come to grips with the betrayal.

Totally understandable, to be fair.

Even if he'd suspected on some level, he'd likely never contemplated such a long duration, nor its irrefutable confirmation.

Quinn thought she'd react in a much stronger manner. Then again, she wasn't as old as most of the universe.

Aradie, however, perched on her shoulder, peering at the pages with her as if she too was trying to understand the sheer magnitude of what Carafax's observations meant.

"Does this really mean that she was planning this for thousands of years before she retired?" Quinn asked.

Aradie cooed for a moment before answering in Quinn's mind, *Not exactly. More like one thousand two hundred years, if my understanding is correct that is.*

"Fantastic," Quinn said, her frustration bubbling over. Aradie, perhaps wisely, chose not to dignify that comment with a response.

Scouring the pages, trying to read through sections and find clues she hadn't seen before, Quinn felt completely out of her depth.

There were subtle shifts in her behavior from about twelve hundred years before she announced her retirement. Very subtle shifts, and differences in the way people reacted to her. Short-temperedness, irritability, classic signs that something had changed, often in a chemistry type of way, Aradie explained what Quinn could see, leaving no room for other possibilities.

Leaving her no room for even the wish of a different outcome.

Quinn didn't know enough about Korradine's species, the unusceros, to know if that was common, but she was willing to bet that mood and personality changes weren't species inherent and thus it had been out of the ordinary, or else Carafax probably wouldn't have noticed it. He recorded multiple interactions where her greeting towards him changed, her demeanor from friendly through to almost openly hostile when he requested restricted section information, or else advanced section information from any of the branches.

As much as the universe appeared to be magical now, it was a fact that high-level magic was still only the purview of a relatively small number. Not necessarily because others didn't have an affinity that would allow them to pursue such magical heights, but that perhaps not as many people *wanted* to pursue those heights.

The sheer magnitude of the books in the Library began to take its toll on Quinn. She thought she'd understood before they opened the culinary branch, but now she realized she did, in fact, not.

She hadn't even absorbed a fraction of the Library's contents. For all intents and purposes, Quinn was still a rank amateur when it came to magic and magical defenses. Her ability to safeguard the Library currently relied on the generosity of those people around her, and the more she realized that the more uncomfortable she became.

The more she sort of yearned to just curl up with a good fantasy adventure that didn't involve a magical Library. That was something for future Quinn to worry about, though.

She had more urgent matters to figure out first. Like just when did Korradine turn bad? And more so, at least in Quinn's opinion, why did she turn against the Library? Because the why very obviously involved all of the bigger picture elements they were scrambling to figure out.

Any shortcut to finding out the identities of all of their detractors should help them solve the entire problem.

In theory at any rate.

She dove back into the notes. 1,232 years before Korradine announced retirement. Carafax made note of her being ill.

"She was sick," Quinn muttered. "How many times was Korradine sick over the years she was Librarian?" She directed the question at the Library.

There was a moment of silence before an answer came. *Twice. The first time was right after her arrival here due to the dimensional shift and the rolling effect it had on her at first. Completely expected.*

"And the second time?" Quinn asked.

That would be close to 1,750 years ago, the Library said. *Give or take a few.*

"That makes these dates coincide, right?" Quinn glanced at the information flashed up on her hood and frowned, answering the question herself. "Yeah, that would coincide with the date. What's Ariticavia fever?"

It plays with the mind. It gives you an extremely high fever that basically causes hallucinations and sweats and a healthy bout of paranoia. While you're sick, you tend to believe that ninety percent of the people coming anywhere near you are out to kill you, or worse.

"Oh, well that sounds like a very pleasant illness." she said, not commenting on the worse aspect.

The worst thing is its duration. It can last up to three months. Pretty long time just for what would amount to a common flu?

"There's nothing common about influenza. Do you mean a cold? Just a head cold?" Quinn corrected before asking.

The Library paused for a moment and then backtracked. *No, I meant influenza.*

"Well, influenza sucks, so this would just be like a prolonged version of that?" Quinn wanted more clarification to understand the illness. Even if she felt like she was grasping at straws.

The hallucinations can take many forms.

An idea came to Quinn, one that she wasn't precisely sure where she'd heard it. She'd read some pretty sketchy mind magic books, however. She was pretty sure it came from one of those.

"Could it be that those hefty hallucinations might have hidden specific attacks?" She spoke the words slowly, sounding out the thoughts in her mind.

I'm not sure I follow your train of thought. Clarify?

"Could this illness have hidden mental attacks that were disguised as hallucinations so that not even Korradine would realize that the ideas that began to start in her mind and blossomed as time passed, weren't necessarily her own?" It sounded convoluted and fantastical even to Quinn's own ears.

The Library was silent and Quinn realized that she had inherently been reaching for multiple straws then, but it was an idea that wouldn't let her go. From the way Lynx described his relationship with Korradine, down to most people's initial impressions of her. She had been a fantastic Librarian, an all-around nice person, generous, excellent at her job for thousands of years.

There had to be some origin point that changed her behavior and that needed to be either an immediate realization that she'd been living her life completely wrong, which should have resulted in a complete one-eighty that was immediately noticeable by everyone. Or else something so subtle it wasn't necessarily her own doing, or even her own thoughts, but a type of influence.

It could even have been a combination of any of the types. Or none of them at all.

But, as the recipient of a mind-bomb implantation in her head in her first encounter with somebody who knew anything about mind magic, Quinn wanted to cover all their bases. She didn't feel the need to defend Korradine. She just felt the need to find a logical explanation for the things that had happened.

You know, the Library suddenly spoke up, *that could be a possibility. Let me see if we can figure out if anybody other than general Librarian staff came to see her.*

"What about an assistant?" Quinn asked, trying to push the idea further. For the sake of Lynx and his current level of dejection, she was willing to entertain a lot of avenues. "Was she particularly close to any of the assistants?"

Suddenly, Lynx appeared in front of Quinn, blinking at her. "Yeah, yeah, she had maybe three or four really good assistant friends, one of whom started maybe fifty years before she got sick."

Another idea occurred to Quinn. Maybe she'd just watched too many CSI dramas, but she had to ask. "This fever, is it common enough that it could be deliberately triggered?"

He frowned. "I mean, most viruses being contagious means you can trigger them, right? So technically, I guess. But it could also have been an illness that just opened an opportunity." Then he paused and frowned. "Though I guess that sounds naive."

Quinn offered him a commiserating smile. "Tell me about the assistant."

"Daphne," he began. "Daphne was an Esposian who came to us about fifty years before this date . . . forty-eight, to be precise, if I go off the system information. She was with us for, oh, maybe a thousand years, until shortly before we had to shut the Library down. She quit just after Korradine triggered her retirement."

"Doesn't that sound a little bit too coincidental?" Quinn asked.

She realized, of course, that she hadn't been close to the whole situation. That meant she was able to look at all of the information they got without being emotionally attached to whatever outcome they had. The thing was, Lynx was still extremely emotionally attached to his memories, what remained of them, of Korradine.

Lynx sighed and looked up at Quinn, a sad smile on his face. "You know, I really do appreciate that you are trying so hard to find a reason that she betrayed everything, but that doesn't negate the fact that she did what she did."

"But sometimes it might not be her actions that did it. If these thoughts were planted in her head, like that bomb was planted in mine, then it wasn't of her own volition. She didn't consciously make this choice herself if it was inserted for her. At least initially. Insidious whispers in your head can be dangerous." Quinn didn't know if this was true yet, but she did have a strong inkling that it might in fact be.

Because accounts of who Korradine had been didn't line up. And things that didn't work factually sincerely bothered her.

Lynx perked up a little bit at that and then he flagged again. "Korradine had amazing mental facilities. She was one of the best mind magic users I've ever witnessed."

"Including Milaro?"

"Including Milaro."

Quinn couldn't get around it. "Wait, could that fever lower any of your basic defenses?"

The Library paused. *Yes and no. It just makes everything more difficult than it was in the beginning. It makes it difficult to maintain any long-term magical defenses of offenses of your own. So it's possible that her mental defenses were weakened at the time. I mean, it's very plausible.*

Lynx grinned. "Well it might be plausible, but I feel like this is a total reach on our behalf. You're trying to justify her actions. While perhaps she was influenced, I don't think she could have been blindingly swayed to something she wouldn't believe in herself."

"I'm just throwing out ideas from these descriptions that Carafax has given us. It's great that it pinpoints a timeline for us. It also pinpoints a timeline we can research. We can find perhaps more memories from the owls in these specific windows about the whole thing." Quinn sighed. She'd wanted Korradine to be more innocent than she appeared, just for Lynx's sake. "If your memories and recollections were tampered with, I figured perhaps others were. Maybe, though she did betray you in the end, she didn't mean to. Or if she'd been herself, she never really would have."

Lynx watched her for several seconds, so much so that Quinn thought maybe he'd figured out a way to multitask without getting that odd blank stare in his eyes. And then he smiled. "You know, Quinn, even if it turns out that we have no evidence, that anything was planted or that her mind was screwed with in any way, the fact that you're willing to entertain that she wasn't just some secret, manipulative, conniving Librarian, that means a lot to me. Thank you."

"Of course," Quinn said. "What are friends for?"

"Yeah," he said. "Thank you." And he was gone.

"Wow," Quinn muttered out loud, leaning back in her chair. "Sometimes he can be almost human."

Don't insult him that way, the Library chuckled. *Anyway, there's a lot of work to be done, Quinn. You need to—*

And that was when the alarm began to blare overhead. Quinn paused. "What *is* that?" She couldn't sense any movement coming from anywhere in the Library, which meant that sound was for her alone.

The Library sighed audibly in Quinn's head just before the announcement.

The gates of Halschius have opened. Arrival imminent.

Quinn blinked. Eric shot into the room faster than she'd seen him move in quite some time. "What's this?" Quinn asked.

"That would be my uncle," he said. "He likes fanfare, and I wasn't expecting him now."

"Oh, well, we were expecting him soon, right?" Quinn smiled at him, trying to put him at ease. "So this isn't all that unusual. But what about the gates of Halschius? I know we've had other imps in here. It has never given me an alarm like that before."

"That's his direct door from his throne room." Eric's eyes were fully fired up, and his tail end sparked as he flitted around the office. "He's literally the king of Halschius. And he's definitely not an imp."

"What should I call your uncle?" Quinn asked, feeling some nerves start to fray in her stomach right then.

"You should probably—" He paused for a moment as if pondering whether she'd be able to pronounce the name in the first place. Since Quinn knew that she couldn't actually pronounce Eric's real name, she didn't have much hope for his uncle. Eric grinned at her like he knew exactly what she was thinking. "You should probably just call him Uncle Hal."

She crossed her arms and glared at him. "Seriously, Uncle Hal?"

"Yes," a voice intoned from the doorway. The sound filled the room with majesty and danger, shaking the floor under her feet. Quinn shivered.

She looked up. She wasn't sure what she'd been expecting. Maybe a slightly larger imp floating in the air. Not what appeared to be a black-furred, red-horned, and red-eyed satyr standing in the doorway that had miraculously enlarged itself to accommodate the King of Halschius. His lava hair dripped down his back only to evaporate just before it hit the ground.

He smiled wickedly before he spoke. "You may call me Uncle Hal, and I want to know how the hell the Library lost the books I entrusted to it."

16

TWO OR THREE OR SEVEN

THERE WERE A LOT OF ANSWERS SITTING ON THE TIP OF QUINN'S tongue as she stared at Uncle Hal. She could have answered him honestly. She could have told him they quite literally had no clue how these books had not only gone missing from the Library but somehow had also been wiped completely from the memory of the Library and anybody who had come into contact with them who worked in the Library. But she didn't, because she was too busy pouring every ounce of energy into not gaping at the eight-foot-tall satyr who now stood in front of her desk.

Upon closer inspection, she realized he had flames licking the horns on his head.

Fire.

In a Library.

Was that not dangerous? Couldn't the Library and everything in it be burned to ash in a heartbeat? She was pretty sure his fire was formidable.

I'm not going to burn down, the Library's voice inserted into her mind. *I'm not that type of flammable.*

Quinn suppressed a laugh, finally freed from the tension she felt when Uncle Hal appeared.

"Let's start from the beginning," Eric said, breaking the silence as he darted in to hover above her desk. "Uncle Hal, this is Quinn, the new Librarian, and Quinn, this is my Uncle Hal, for want of easier pronunciation for you."

Quinn smiled as much as she could around the nerves she still felt building in her gut. She stood up and reached a hand forward to shake.

Hal raised an eyebrow. "Hmm, that's a very Earth-human custom. Aren't you somewhat far from home, young lady?" His eyes narrowed as he said the latter, and it made her feel like she was being X-rayed.

Quinn balked at the look in his eyes. He wasn't monstrous; that wasn't the right term, but he was regal and powerful and dangerous. She could feel it emanating off him in waves. And yet, the Library's reaction to his presence was almost nonchalant, as if he was inconsequential in the grand scheme of things as far as the Library itself was concerned.

As far as Quinn was concerned, she was having a lot of trouble controlling her bladder.

His eyes raked her up and down, but not in a creepy way. It felt more like he was assessing her capabilities and ended up finding her wanting. He scowled for a second. "How long has the new Librarian been present?"

Eric tsked under his breath. "How long do you think the Library's been operational again? What, two months? Do you think they've changed Librarians again in the meantime?"

"Do not take that tone with me, Eric," Hal said. But she thought there was more levity in his words although it was difficult to tell.

Quinn could sense the lightening of his mood as his nephew spoke to him with the same lack of deference as always. It wasn't just the way Eric behaved around her. He appeared to behave like that around everybody, regardless of status.

The King of Halschius, which came way too close to the King of Hell for Quinn's comfort, might rate a little bit more respect than Eric was currently showing. Hal shifted his stance and crossed his arms, looking at Lynx and at Eric, and then pinpointing Aradie with his glare before he spoke. "Why was I not informed that the experiment was taking place? What has the council been doing?"

For several seconds, there was absolute silence in the room. Not even their breathing intruded. Quinn could quite literally hear nothing. It was so overwhelming that it felt suffocating. Just as she was about to speak, a swirl of wind erupted in the middle of the room and left, leaving Milaro standing in its wake.

"About time you showed up," Hal said, his scowl deepening if that was even possible.

Milaro shrugged, his good-natured smile coming to the fore. But there was a tension that remained in his shoulders, and Quinn could see that the smile, for once, didn't reach Milaro's eyes. "I believe you were asking about the experiment," he said, a smile tweaking the corners of his lips. "I came as fast as I could."

It took every ounce of willpower for Quinn not to high-five that use of sarcasm.

"You know exactly what I'm asking," Hal said, his voice somehow deepening. It resonated through the floor, through the entire room, but Quinn realized that the Library didn't allow that force to penetrate the outer walls of her office. It was good to know that level of control was possible within the Library.

Again, you could always just ask me.

Quinn didn't dignify that with a response.

"Well, as you can see, it happened." Milaro shrugged. To anyone outside, it might appear that he was being dismissive, but Quinn could tell he was tense. "You were a little busy."

"What do you mean, I was busy?" Hal sounded incensed. Offended, even. "You could have summoned one of my aides. I could have helped. You've made her weak."

"She's not weak. We gave her all of the components we discussed initially."

"What? You mean you actually broke down the Seveshall family essence to give her your abilities?" Hal began the statement with an air of flippancy, but grew serious as Milaro's stone face confirmed the sarcasm to be true. "Wow, Milaro, you have grown up."

"Oh, shut up, Hal," Milaro said, and Quinn suppressed a gasp. This was the most heated argument she'd heard Milaro in yet. "You could have stayed around. You were the one who told us to go ahead and form the emergency council and do what we thought needed to be done. You had too much unrest at home."

Hal scowled at him, but as seconds passed and nothing else happened, Quinn realized that he couldn't seem to argue with Milaro, for whatever the elf king meant obviously hit home. She tried to open her mouth and speak again, but this time Hal cut in again.

"Regardless, you should have informed me." At least now he seemed only disgruntled and not angry.

"We did. Maybe check your messages every now and again," Milaro said, "and to be frank, we didn't know it had succeeded until the Library reopened. So just cool your temper. Everything will be fine."

The tension leaked back out of Hal's shoulders, and he sighed, turning his attention back to Quinn, assessing her yet again. "You did turn out quite well," he said, pursing his lips thoughtfully. "I would have designed you slightly differently."

"Just because y'all decided to give me ABC whatevers doesn't mean I'm not my own person." All this talk about her as if she wasn't there was truly getting old. "Give it a damn rest."

Hal very elegantly raised his right eyebrow. "You have a spine and some fire. You are welcome to visit Halschius whenever you would like. I would give you a tour. I think you'd get on well with some of my children. Not him, though." He pointed at Eric.

"Uncle Hal, give it a rest." the imp said, the hum of his wings edging ever so higher.

"What? You can be cantankerous, annoying, and belligerent." Hal grinned at him, and chills ran down Quinn's spine. Those serrated, shark-like teeth were going to give her nightmares.

"All traits I learned from you, dear uncle," Eric said, putting his nose up into the air and fluttering his wings even harder than usual.

Instead of scowling, Hal actually laughed, a booming, mirthful sound Quinn was not expecting to come out of an eight-foot-tall, burning-horned satyr.

Quinn sighed and cleared her throat. "As fascinating as this discussion of me is, I want to direct our attention away from me for just a moment. Let's talk about the books I'm sure you're here to berate us about." She was trying to smooth over the fact that she was quite certain Milaro and Hal had a lot to talk about and if she gave them ten minutes now, it would turn into hours, and they'd keep arguing. She already existed. The Library was open. Everybody should be happy.

Quinn, however, felt very tired.

"Yes, the books," he said, as if he'd forgotten, even for a split second, what he'd come here for. "I would love an explanation for how you let the five most important books in my arsenal disappear. You were supposed to be safe, Drevicia."

"Don't use my real name, Hal," the Library intoned, its voice ringing through the entire office.

"Ah, what should I call you then? Library?" He said the last word disdainfully as if it was a lesser thing.

"You know that's what I am now." There was steel in the sound as the Library spoke, and the walls practically shook with the power.

"No, you are s—whatever. Such a stupid charade," Hal muttered under his breath. "One of these days, it's going to come back and bite you, if it hasn't already, by the fact that I can tell just from walking in here that you are broken, almost beyond repair."

The Library gasped. It was a forceful sound, heartbreaking almost, like something shattered around them.

Quinn felt it in her soul.

"You don't know that," the Library spat. Quinn noticed the shadows coalescing into a form as the Library presented an equally tall form in front of the satyr. A tail jutted out from it, elegantly dangling down as the Library stood on two feet. Quinn could tell the fingernails were elongated into claws. The Library was elegant and beautiful, powerful and somehow completely melancholy.

"Do not name me again. You no longer have permission. You gave that up eons ago." The Library practically spat the words out in a low tone that hummed in time with the Library's usual flow of power.

Quinn could have cut the tension with a spoon, let alone a butter knife. She took a deep breath and tried to play peacemaker again. "Can we redirect the attention to the matter at hand first, and then you can all go to your own room, dig up your past that you still don't want to share with me, and have at it, okay?"

Three heads turned in Quinn's direction. The ones with eyes, Hal and Milaro, blinked. Quinn was fairly sure that if the Library's shadow self had been able to blink at her, it would have too.

"Quinn speaks the truth," the Library said. "You need to help us figure this out. What exactly are they going to use those books for?"

Hal leaned back, studying the shadow in front of him. "You honestly don't remember the discussion we had when I brought those books to you?"

"No. So much of it is gone." Suddenly the Library sounded almost defeated. "You don't understand."

"And you have the nerve to stand in front of me and tell me that you're not broken, and be upset that I pointed it out?" Hal's voice had lost most of its anger. In its place was genuine worry.

"No. But you don't need to remind me of something I'm already painfully aware of."

"And how are you going to rectify it without my help? Why has it taken you so long to fetch me? And you didn't even fetch me. You sent my nephew to inform me." Now Hal sounded wounded by the fact that his . . . maybe friend hadn't sought out his help.

"Actually," Eric piped up, a mischievous grin on his face, "the Library didn't send me either. I just kind of went, 'I'm going to go tell my uncle that the books are missing.' For shits and giggles."

"Eric, this is grown-up talk, and you've already interfered enough," his uncle said before turning back to the Library and Milaro, leaving the imp to gape at the back of his head.

Hal's tone was now full of concern, and much less oppressing than when he was angered. "You had to know I can help."

"But you've been so busy. Those wars have waged for millennia," Milaro began.

"I always have a war or two or three or seven raging on." Hal shrugged easily. "That's how Halschius works. You know it. I know it. The entire universe knows it."

"Even if this set's been particularly nasty?" the Library asked gently.

"What?" Hal laughed again, but softer this time, perhaps it rated as a chuckle for him. "Because one of my sons is trying to kill me? Again? Do you think that's anything other than commonplace for me?"

"Well," Milaro said, "maybe if one of them actually meant to kill you instead of just whiling away the hours of boredom of eternal life, perhaps."

"Oh, will you shut up? You're worse than your grandfather." But the King of Halschius smiled as he spoke.

"I'll take that as a compliment," Milaro said. "We'll discuss this later."

"Everything later. But right now, dear Librarian," Hal turned around, crossing his arms, "to answer your question . . . if you combine *Ririn's Dimensional Distortion Through Sacrificial Means*, *The Parsneauvian Theory of Spatial Dimension Manipulation*, *The Crown and Fall of Pocket Dimensions Due to Spatial Interference*, *Machmüller's Theory of Dimensional Dissolution and Disintegration through Ritual Sacrifice*, and *DeKarlyle's Thesis of Spatial Distortion*, you can essentially create or even unmake dimensions regardless of the type of magical input. You could technically even dissolve dimensions despite the copious protections that have been put in place. If you tweak it correctly. Technically."

Quinn gasped as the puzzle pieces that were the books all slammed into place in her mind. "Like the pocket dimension the Library sits in?"

"Precisely," Hal agreed. "And I hate to say it, but given the report of the state of the tree you found Machmüller's book in, and how long these books have been outside of the Library for . . . I think whoever means the Library harm might be close to fully capable of inflicting it."

17

WILD PLAN

Quinn wasn't entirely sure how to respond to Hal's statement and was acutely aware that what he said wasn't even catastrophizing the situation but was instead a purely factual statement.

How did she refute the fact that someone having access to all of those books together for more than five hundred years spelled big trouble for everyone? Or better yet, was there any way that she, in this position, could reassure people that everything would be fine?

No. No, there was nothing she could say.

Not yet, anyway.

The silence lingered, growing heavier and deeper. Much more uncomfortable with each passing second.

Eric piped up, his voice carrying through the quiet room. "Oh, come on people. It's not the end of the universe."

Quinn couldn't help the laugh that barked out of her in surprise. Because it could, in fact, wind up being the end of the universe. Wasn't that the whole point?

His statement and her laughter broke the tension, and she shot him a grateful smile before speaking, her head finally mired in less doom. "Does that mean that the combination of those books can essentially undo the Library?" she asked softly, racking the knowledge she'd absorbed for any sign of meaning in it.

Hal frowned. "Well, yes and no. It's not like it's an easy feat."

Quinn raised an eyebrow. "Then why catastrophize it?"

"Just because it's not easy doesn't mean it can't be done." Hal shrugged, almost contradicting himself. But he paused for a second before moving on to clarify. "Shock value lets you assess your situation on a heightened level. Right now, you don't seem to have initiated the production of more security golems, either."

He frowned after that statement and stood in all his eight-foot glory, accessing what Quinn could only assume was a HUD like hers. Which begged a gazillion questions about how and why Eric's uncle Hal had such detailed access to the Library.

Even more so, access that Quinn wasn't aware of and couldn't precisely pinpoint outside of a vague sensation of him having it and currently accessing aspects of the Library. Usually, it was easy enough for her to sense the people and their activities in the Library.

She'd even found during her downtime that if she wanted to, and she concentrated really hard, then she could actually figure out what it was the people were accessing. Within the Library anyway. It let her keep an eye on everyone and everything. Have a measure of control.

Keep the Library as safe as possible.

Frankly, sometimes it felt a little overpowered.

That is, until she remembered that some very dangerous magic books had gone missing, and she realized being a bit nosy about people's borrowing habits was probably a safe way to play it.

After all, she was the Librarian, right?

She shook her head. Realizing that she wasn't voicing her thoughts and that everyone was looking at her. "Why would I be able to summon more security golems? Misha said we had eight at our disposal."

In that instant, two things happened.

Misha appeared directly in front of Quinn at the mention of their name and bowed immediately upon seeing Hal. And the second, was a loud laugh from the satyr.

"Greetings, King—"

"Call me Uncle Hal." Hal grinned at Misha, his fiery eyes practically dancing.

Misha blinked once and inclined their head. "Very well. Uncle . . . Hal."

The satyr burst out laughing so hard he clutched his stomach. "Misha. You are priceless. Even in a renewed form. I approve of your name."

Quinn was pretty sure her supervisory golem scowled, even if it was difficult to tell.

They turned to Quinn and spoke, their tone colored by a hint of irritation. "You mentioned my name. Did you need something?"

"Are we able to establish more security golems now we have another branch?" Quinn figured she may as well get them started if that was the case. It was the only plausible explanation for why he'd think there could be more. And the tension emanating from Misha seemed in need of diffusion.

"Yes." Misha cocked their head to one side. "We do not currently have all of the necessary components. Thus, I have not yet begun their construction. I would have approached you when we were ready for it. These will be new constructs unlike the reawakened ones currently serving. The others were in stasis awaiting commands for a while first. We reestablished what we could from the old stock. Right now, they have all been utilized."

Quinn nodded and glanced over at Milaro who sighed. Good. It appeared he realized what she was getting at without her having to verbalize it.

"Fine. I'll send a message. Misha, check with my seneschal about our stock levels for those components you're missing. If you're lacking any of your previous suppliers, just let us know so we can assist with that." Milaro ran a hand through his hair and turned to Hal, his expression morphing into a scowl. "And you . . . don't need to be filling her head with ideas of woe. The situation isn't nearly as dire as you're making it out to be."

"Yet," Hal said, a smug smile on his face. "There's always time."

"Which you're saying we don't have, old man," Milaro said, smiling his own brand of smugness.

Hal laughed again, but this time it only seemed to scratch the surface instead of penetrating deep. In fact, Quinn thought he sounded somewhat offended. Even though it seemed he might be as old as the universe itself, it probably wasn't a good idea to call him old. She silently thanked Milaro for taking the satyr's ire on himself voluntarily.

She was pretty sure he'd done that intentionally.

"I get that you two might need to catch up. But again. Standing here, not quite knowing what's going on." She waved a hand out to make sure they paid attention to her and not to whatever silly feud the two of them had going on with one another.

Uncle Hal turned to her, giving her his full attention for the first time since glancing her over as he walked into her office initially. There was something unsettling in that gaze of his, apart from the fiery depths being mesmerizing, that is. She just couldn't quite put her finger on what it was.

It made her feel slightly uncomfortable, but more in a *this person is highly dangerous and could probably crush me in the palm of their hand* sort of way than anything creepy or slimy.

Ah, that was it.

Quinn felt entirely out of her depth.

Overpowered by the age, wisdom, and might in the room.

"So. Let's get a good look at you, little Librarian," Uncle Hal said. His tone had changed. Gone was the condescension, the glimpses of anger he'd released while speaking with Milaro, and the extreme standoffishness she'd experienced up until now.

In its wake was this strange warmth, with an undercurrent of caring that took her by surprise as much as it made her wary. Behind her, both Milaro, Eric, and the Shadow of the Library shifted ever so slightly. She could practically feel their surprise, their cautious anticipation.

"Do you need me to do something specific?" she asked, proud of the fact that her voice didn't waver despite an odd onset of nerves.

"No. I can see what I need to see." His eyes, while still swirling pools of fire, actually felt more welcoming than destructive. It calmed her.

Warmth enveloped her body from head to toe. She felt like she was wrapped up in a binding of pillowed hugs. It lasted for all of two seconds before she was free of it, and as it departed she couldn't help but wrap her arms around herself to fend off the sudden chill that rushed in.

Hal frowned. "How long have you been here? When did you arrive? Have you even synchronized yet?"

Quinn paused, wondering why and how he knew so much. Then again, he was probably as old as the Library. What had he called it? Drevicia? "I've been here just over two months, and I've connected, and synchronized once each, I think. So far." She felt an odd need to justify her progress.

Hal scowled. "Training?"

"I'm not the most coordinated when it comes to weapons, so we've been concentrating on elemental attacks with ice, wind, and water as my main focuses, as well as mental magic control." Suddenly it felt like there was some final test she should have studied for and forgot all about. This was worse than being dressed down by a lecturer because your phone rang in class.

Something flashed through Hal's eyes, but she could tell it wasn't directed at her. Slowly, he turned around to the rest of the room. "How is the Library even still here? You should know better than this." His tone was even, but Quinn could tell it was only so smooth because he was tightly controlling his anger at the situation.

At least he had control. That was a blessing in itself.

Milaro sighed, and the Library remained silent.

"Look," Milaro began. "You, like every single other being with a magical affinity in the universe, were notified that the Library was back in business. Which meant that, of course, we'd have a new Librarian. You could have checked in sooner, so how about you take a step back and don't criticize the hard work she's put in."

"It's not her I'm concerned with." Hal snapped, he flexed his hands open and then balled them back into fists. "You know that's not my concern."

"How about we tell me this concern so that I, too, will know it," Quinn snapped.

Both Hal and Milaro turned to look at her, blinking rapidly as if she'd shone a bright light on them. At least Milaro had the good grace to look sheepish. Hal on the other hand seemed slightly shellshocked.

"Sorry, Quinn. I forgot myself." Milaro bowed with a flourish in front of her, his usual smile back as he reached over and tried to ruffle her hair. Quinn, for her part, managed to dodge it expertly. "She's not prone to letting you think for her. Might want to get to know our new Librarian before you get all righteous."

Hal glanced at Quinn and sighed. "I apologize. But . . . the fact remains that you are woefully underprepared. It's like you never even used any of your magical affinities until you got here or something, which is just ridiculous to contemplate."

When Quinn didn't laugh but held his gaze seriously, Hal actually paled.

She wasn't sure how he managed that exactly considering his skin was an odd hue of red. But he did.

"She was based on Earth, after all. It's not like she *could* use her powers," Eric chattered gleefully. He seemed to delight in his uncle's discomfort. "Not without fully depleting her entire energy and mana store and plummeting her into a six-week coma, anyway."

Eric finished his last statement off with a flourishing somersault and fluttering of his wings. He bowed in mid-air and barely escaped the swipe of his uncle's claws. Then he flitted back behind Quinn, hovering there just behind Aradie so as to avoid his uncle's wrath.

Hal's expression changed from one of consternation, to annoyance, and straight into thoughtfulness. "Still, two months . . ." He turned to the shadow of the Library and asked very pointedly, "Why haven't you simply mirrored everything into her mind? She's fully capable of withstanding that much information transfer. All of the copies of the texts, everything—you have it all. Why haven't you imparted it?"

There wasn't any anger in his tone anymore, just this weird sort of quiet resignation that things were way behind schedule, or not precisely to plan, or something.

It took several seconds for the Library to respond. Agonizing seconds, in fact. Where Quinn stood next to Misha waiting for an answer she hoped would explain why Hal was so upset.

The Library let out a sigh that echoed through the entire structure. It rippled like the faint sound of a melancholic breeze. "Before the shutdown, the council came up with the wild plan for her creation. It was a chance in a trillion that we could get it to work in time if at all. It was the last-ditch effort."

"Took a few hundred years, I might add," Milaro interjected with a grin.

If the Library's expression had been visible, Quinn was fairly sure it would have been scowling.

"One of our fail-safes was to include other abilities. To take some of the most prominent specialties and combine them to make her even stronger in those areas," the Library said. "Ways for her to protect herself."

"Yes, yes." Hal waved a hand, "I'm aware." But he was cut off mid-sentence.

"One of those was the distillation of the Seveshall mind magic abilities. Condensing them down to their purest form," Milaro said smugly but before anyone else could interrupt him, he continued. "The others we took from the other lineages. She has a specific alchemical affinity enhancement, elemental combat enhancement, and several bardic traits that we determined would enable her to fight the strong chaotic elements we couldn't avoid in her creation."

"So, you meant to give her an amplified chaos affinity?" Hal asked incredulously.

The Library's shadow shrugged. "I am, after all, a product of chaos. Most of us are. It wasn't something that could be avoided if they were to use my own genetic code as the origin."

Hal pinched his brow in his fingers. "All of this makes simply transferring the vast Library catalog from the system nigh impossible.

I get it. I just think you made a huge mistake." He shot a glare at Milaro, who shrugged it off with a smile.

"Frankly, I think she's pretty cool," he said, flashing Quinn a wink.

Uncle Hal sighed, but it was a defeated sound. "Fine. I guess I'll have to help you with your fire affinity, then."

Quinn felt that dangerous unease come back. "I love using ice, water, and air. Is fire really necessary?" She giggled nervously, not the least because she wasn't sure if her coordination levels were a good match for wielding fire.

Hal grinned and his mouth opened wide enough to reveal all his teeth. "That's no good. Can't you hear the fire singing out to you? It's in your veins."

"What is?" Quinn asked before she could think better of it. She knew she didn't want the answer as soon as she'd finished asking it.

Hal let out another gutsy laugh. "Why, destruction of course. You are a creature of chaos, after all."

18

EXTRACTING MORE INFORMATION

Quinn frowned. Her head began to pound with levels of stress she could barely comprehend. "Creature of chaos" didn't exactly sound like a good thing to be.

Nor did she like the sibilant whispers she could hear just out of her reach and the fact that she couldn't tell where they came from. Heightened senses allowed her to identify where everything was going on in the Library, but if the whispers came from there, this was a new turn of events.

They stood in the training area. Yet again it had transformed itself to meet her needs.

Instead of the usual training room, which consisted of padded floors, padded walls, and training dummies, this time it hadn't been transformed into a media facility for viewing owl memories and sifting through them.

No, this new room was darker.

The walls were lined with a brimstone-type material, and the pools of liquid on the floor appeared to have been pulled up from the filtration area below to demonstrate to Quinn exactly how chaotic energy manifested when there was enough of it.

She'd seen the sludge before, and some of it sat on top of the pool of beautiful blue mana right in front of her.

"Is that how it always appears on purified mana?" she asked, resisting the urge to reach forward and touch the sludge.

Hal let out one of his boisterous laughs. "Oh Gods, no," he said. "No, this is just what we currently have access to here that I can pull to you without endangering the Library and everything in it."

The liquid seemed calm, simply floating there biding its time. "Is it really that dangerous?"

"Yes, in its purest form, chaotic magic will seek to regain power by unmaking creation. Do you understand what that is?" Hal asked softly.

"Well, yes," Then something she'd learned earlier floated to the surface in her marginally overtaxed memory. "Didn't they tell me that if I understood how something had been made, I would be able to unmake it?"

Hal raised an eyebrow. "Well, I guess they didn't completely keep you in the dark."

Quinn scowled. "I'll be the judge of that."

He chuckled. "Listen, kid, because you are a kid in my eyes, frankly, you're barely a blip on the radar right now. I'm sure that'll change in several millennia. Don't be too harsh on them. The need to keep the Library safe wars with their need to keep you safe. It won't always align perfectly."

Quinn could feel the color draining from her face at that statement. It wasn't something anybody on Earth would have told her. No, the only reason he could say this with a straight face was that for Hal, it was fact. Both her age and her presence were minuscule in the grand space of eternity. She cleared her throat and spoke. "Anyway, what's it usually like?"

Uncle Hal seemed to give that some serious thought. "Chaos is pushy and creeps and seeks and finds."

"Okay, I get that, but what does it look like?" She gestured at the sludge. "I mean the crusty black look is kind of gross, but not the most intimidating or creepy thing I've seen."

Hal reached a hand into the disgusting blackened sludge and picked it up. He rolled it in his palms until it became a ball and then it spread all over one of his hands, except it was smokey and mildly translucent as it did so. The solidity receded and it came alive in his hand, dancing like living slime.

Quinn shuddered because at first, it just looked like slime and then it appeared to have a life of its own. It was malleable and able to form at will. She could tell Hal wasn't directing it. The power of chaotic magic, seemed to have a wee bit of a will of its own.

Quinn gestured toward it. "And the people who are against us preventing this type of magic from devouring the universe are aware it's like this?"

Just as she finished saying that, the slime globule gathered itself so fast she barely saw it coming. And it was only with his super quick reflexes that Hal caught the ball of slime as it launched itself in midair toward Quinn.

"Ah," he said, "it likes you. I can see why."

Quinn crossed her arms. "I can't. Care to enlighten me?"

He sighed. "In order to make sure the transfer took place when they created you, they had to include a couple of excess chaotic elements. The Library's, shall we say, sample of genetic material, I think is how you would classify it, included every single affinity currently known or created. It also has the ability to adapt to more, to combine and create more, and to seek out new affinities. In doing so, it also gifted you an innate ability with chaotic magic."

"Oh," Quinn said. "Well, I sort of knew that, but that just reminds me of when everybody was like, 'Oh you have every affinity, that's odd.'"

He chuckled, "Yes, that is very odd."

"Is that when they knew, or at least when they suspected?"

"Suspected what?" he asked.

"That I was actually the experiment." She paused. "They didn't all appear to know at first . . . or at all."

"Perhaps. I can't tell you what's on their minds. You should probably just sit down and talk to them about it. That's going to be the easiest way for you to get your answers." For a moment, Hal actually sounded like a kindly old uncle, and then he grinned again, and the spiky shark teeth showed through.

Quinn wondered how she had ever thought that he was just a kindly old uncle.

"Be that as it may, Quinn, you need to concentrate. You need to understand how chaos feels, because sometimes it can slip in with things you eat, drink, wear, see, even the air you breathe. You need to understand where it is, how it feels, how it smells, and how it reacts. Because the one thing you don't want to do is inadvertently become addicted to it."

She eyed the strange smoky substance. "It's addictive?"

"Yep," Hal said, "sort of like a drug."

"Or exactly like a drug," Quinn said.

"Well, yes, precisely like a drug. The more you use it, the more you want to use it, and then the more you use it, the more it grabs a hold of everything you are, and subverts the ideals that may have driven you." He winked at her. "So, hold out your hand."

Quinn did so very hesitantly, still not entirely sure this was a good idea, but Eric and Aradie sat on what appeared to be bleachers, watching, and it made her feel just that little bit safer. She glanced over at them, and . . .

Hal noticed her division of attention. "Aradie would protect you, even if I suddenly went rogue."

Which didn't help Quinn's trust issues with the damn King of Hell any at all. "Thanks," she said dryly. "I trust you so much more now."

The slime spread itself across her hand, and Quinn instantaneously stored the sensation, the prickly feeling, as if it was trying to enter her system through the pores in her hand and still send chills down her spine, at the same time. That was how chaos felt.

It smelled oddly like cloves and cedar.

"That's a pungent smell," she said, pulling her hand away and allowing the ball of chaos slime to fall back into Hal's open palm.

"Excellent," he said. "Now you know how it smells and feels. We're not doing a taste. We're not going to invite that in. But you need to remember these sensations, Quinn. They could save yours, and the lives of others. That being said, you'll need more experience with all different levels of filtered chaos, right through to pure raw chaos. Do you understand?"

Quinn shrugged. "What, you want me to go down into the filtration chamber and try to get a feel for it? Perhaps mimic what the filtration system does and that would help me understand the properties. Maybe I could break them down?"

"No," Hal cut her off. "While those do sound like very worthwhile experiments on your own time when you have time. What I mean to tell you is that you're invited to come and visit me. I'll assist you in close combat and association with the chaotic lakes of my home."

"Halschius is situated on chaotic lakes?" Quinn asked.

Hal grinned. "That they are. What did you think it was, a happy playground?"

"No, I didn't." She shook her head for emphasis. "I'd love to take you up on that when I get some time."

"Well, you'll know when you're ready, just tell Eric and he'll bring you down. He'll stay with you, too. So you have somebody familiar, somebody you can trust to a certain extent." Hal grinned again.

Quinn laughed. "I know exactly what you mean."

He flashed her a grin and leaned his eight-foot height down to her level. "Between you and me, my nephew's pretty fond of you. He thinks you're like the little sister he was never going to get."

Quinn laughed a little nervously and stepped away. Hal radiated extraordinary heat. It was tightly controlled and held within an aura around his body from what she could tell, but he was likely hellfire and brimstone personified. She changed the subject. "Hey, can I ask a question? It's kind of personal."

Hal shrugged. "Worst I can do is not answer, correct?"

"Very correct." She took a deep breath. "Are you really this size or did you shrink yourself down?"

"That's for me to know right now and you to find out when you have the time to come and visit. I must be gone. I have a lot to do, wars to fight, people to maim, people to interrogate." He paused, looking back at her, the fire in his eyes flaring. "Are you sure you don't want to get rid of that Serpensiril you have in here? I have ways of extracting more information than you probably even considered he had."

Quinn blinked at him and for a moment, seriously considered handing Tenejo over. "You know what?" she said.

"What?" Hal asked.

"If I haven't figured out how to get that information on my own by the time we visit you, then I will gladly bring Tenejo with us wrapped in a bow for you to figure out instead." Quinn wasn't sure how she should feel about the fact that she meant every word she'd just said.

"That, my dear," Hal said, "sounds like the beginnings of a beautiful friendship."

And then he disappeared. Quinn stood there, watching as the chaos pool shifted back down through the bowels of the Library, obviously being returned to the filtration chamber. Slowly, the gym changed back to how it was before, and she could hear as Aradie flew in to land on her shoulders, while Eric hovered just behind her.

"Your uncle is very unique," Quinn said after several seconds of fascinated silence watching the pools recede.

"Yeah, I've heard that before," Eric replied. "I've heard him called worse things as well."

Quinn laughed. "I can imagine. We need to go see Geneva and the Esposians, right?"

"Is that really the most urgent thing?" Eric asked quietly.

"No," Quinn wanted to shout the words out. The lists were compounding worse than sketchy loan interest. "I have no idea what's the most urgent. I have so much on my plate. We have too much to do, it's . . ."

Settle, Aradie spoke into her mind. *All you can do is take one thing at a time. Even if you could split yourself in two, it would mean everything would be less efficient because it would also split your processing and brain-power. You cannot be in two places at once yet. So just breathe.*

Quinn had another thousand questions emanating from what Aradie said to supposedly calm her down. It was possible for her to split in two? Quinn shook the thought out of her head. For the most part, Aradie's tactic worked. She breathed a few times, steeled herself, and accessed that portion of her brain Milaro helped unlock, that let her methodically and logically speedily think through things, so it wouldn't take forever.

"Out of everything on my bingo card," she muttered under her breath, "I didn't expect to meet the King of Halschius today. Anybody else have that?"

Eric chuckled. "Nope, but I think I might make one with it on it."

"That, my friend," Quinn said, "sounds like an excellent idea. In the meantime, we still have two days before Malakai's mom is available to see us, which I don't like, by the way. She might have answers we need to solve this whole conundrum and she's too busy."

"Careful, careful. Boys love their mothers," Eric said, sarcasm dripping from every syllable.

Quinn shot him a partial death glare. "And we all know how much that is not true of Malakai."

Eric shrugged. "Not much I can do about that."

"I know, so we can't go and see Arnekai yet," Quinn paused as she thought things through. "I need to contact . . . I'll send Geneva a message about whether we can visit the Esposians with her yet. She'll have pertinent information we need."

Misha popped into view right next to Quinn making her practically jump out of her skin.

"You have a visitor, Librarian," Misha said, inclining their head slightly. For a split second it looked like her neck was bent unnaturally, but then it was gone, happening so fast Quinn thought she might have imagined it.

"Why would you come and tell me that?" Quinn said, slightly breathless.

Misha shrugged and looked around the training room. "I was there when your visitor arrived and thus I thought I would bring you the news since I could just appear right next to you."

Quinn half smiled, resigned to the fact that those who could instantaneously teleport, would. Which was another skill she was determined to obtain. "Thanks, Misha."

"Anytime, Librarian." Misha didn't even budge.

"Who is it?" Quinn asked before Misha could disappear again.

"Oh, that odd gardening mage. The hedge witch." Misha paused as if recollecting something unrelated to the Library was a chore. "Jasper, I believe her name is."

Quinn brightened. She liked Jasper. Maybe this day wasn't just going to be full of chaos and stress and overwhelm and complete and utter confusion. It'd be nice to talk to somebody who made sense and explained things without laughing themselves silly. She headed out into the main part of the Library and toward the check-in desk. She didn't make it the full way there as she spied Jasper leaning against the wall outside her office.

Quinn waved and called out Jasper's name. "Hey, Jasper!"

The tall and elegant anime-eyed woman turned to face her and raised a hand in greeting as well. Not quite like a wave, but Quinn would take whatever intergalactic greeting she could get.

"What brings you here?" Quinn asked, genuinely happy to see the witch.

Jasper's large eyes blinked slowly. As if she was trying to process a question she didn't fully understand. "The ritual, of course. I promised I would assist you. You wanted me to perform the location ritual, right?"

Quinn grinned. "Yes. Yes, I do."

19

RIPPLES THROUGH THE UNIVERSE

After the Esposian enslaving tree incident, Quinn developed a bit of a blind spot when it came to rituals.

Perhaps *aversion* was the better term for it.

When Jasper first mentioned it during her original visit, Quinn thought it was a brilliant idea. However, the more she pondered, the less appealing the idea of a ritual seemed. Especially if it was to find books that could potentially create rituals capable of tearing apart the very fabric of the Library itself.

Wasn't that ironic or something?

"So, the ritual?" she asked Jasper, trying to keep the tremor out of her voice.

"Yes, the ritual," Jasper echoed. "Oh, don't worry, Quinn." Maybe she could see that Quinn wasn't exactly enthusiastic about performing it and hurried to reassure her, "It's not like a *bloody* ritual or anything like what you're thinking. Although maybe it is like what you're thinking. We'll need a ritual space that's big enough for us to draw diagrams using runic language."

"Diagrams using runic language? You're not going to summon a blood tree that's going to devour everyone in the Library, are you?" Quinn asked, half joking, but the other half of her was deadly serious.

Jasper had the good grace to throw her head back and laugh heartily. When she was done, Quinn already felt a bit more relaxed. "No, we're not planning on enslaving your Library patrons. That'd defeat the purpose of finding the books you say you're missing."

"Okay, then," Quinn said, a little less harried now. "What do you need from me?"

"Well, first of all, like I said, I need a space. Somewhere we can go to draw on the ground, have access to the main vestiges of power of the Library, and hopefully, it needs to be on a surface that'll allow me to use magical charcoal to sketch out the runes." Jasper finished listing off her needs with a smile on her face.

Quinn could tell she was excited. She frowned. "Okay, we just need to ask the Library. It'll give us a room with those specific criteria."

I heard you, the Library said into Quinn's head. *You need a ritual room, preferably close to the mana filtration system would be your best bet. I mean, you could do it down there . . . I think I know the perfect space.*

We have four filters going now, right? Quinn asked. *Shouldn't that mean that we have a lot of available energy?*

The Library paused before answering. *We have a lot more energy than we had, but we still aren't operating at optimal levels or even medium levels yet. We are getting there, though. So as long as this doesn't pull inordinate amounts of power, it's unlikely that it'll impede the Library's recovery.*

Do you know what ritual Jasper's talking about? Quinn asked.

I have a few ideas about what it could be. I don't believe the power drain will be so great as to eliminate the gains we've already made. Frankly, we need to get those books back. This seems as good an idea as any. It has to be a priority for us. They can't be left out there, especially not in that combination, not from what we've seen so far. It could even already be too late.

Quinn paused and turned her attention back to Jasper, whose brow had creased showing some worry lines.

"Are you all right, Quinn?"

"Just got a lot on my mind," the Librarian said. "Sorry, I probably spaced out there for a little bit. Okay, so what else do you need apart from the ritual room? Library's taken care of that. We can go down to the filtration chamber level close to where the mana stores are and should make it easier for us to, well, locate the books, I guess. What else then?"

"Okay, we're going to need a list of the approximate duration the books were in the Library so I can figure out the level of Library saturation the books will have. I'll need their titles, their approximate content, because every affinity gives off different wavelengths, different locators, different ripples through the universe, if you will." Jasper's eyes shone as she spoke about something she was passionate about.

"Ripples through the universe . . ." That made Quinn pay just that little bit more attention. Frankly, the ritual sounded fascinating. Much less scary than she'd anticipated. "So it's kind of like a locator spell?"

"Yes. And if we have all of that information that I've asked you for when we go to locate each specific book, I should be able to narrow down the location with a decent amount of accuracy." Jasper spoke eagerly. "On top of that, if we know the approximate time period that the really important ones went missing in, then I can generalize a locator spell to find the other books that went missing around the same time. It might assist you in figuring out which books you're not yet aware of."

Quinn blinked. It sounded oddly like an app on her phone back home, but they didn't use that type of technology here. "That's amazing. How would you even do that?"

"Well, I'll gladly take you under my wing and show you if we can just get started as soon as possible." Jasper grinned.

"Are you on a time crunch?" Quinn asked, hoping that she wasn't. Mixing technology and magic might be right up her alley . . . when she got time for it.

"No, actually, I've taken care of the starweed replanting. People are under orders to keep Savinth away from them."

Quinn chuckled at the consternation in her voice. "Would she really do that again?"

Jasper sighed. "Probably not. And I understand why she did it. It was in retaliation to us not keeping our promise. But sincerely, our promise wasn't worth destroying our crop of starweed. That was measures above what we did. I'm sure we could have come to a peaceful solution."

"But didn't you ignore her? Wait a second. Let's not get into it," Quinn said. She decided that getting in the middle of that argument was a no-win situation, regardless of everything else.

Jasper shot her a shy smile. "Do you have any idea how many of your books are missing? The dangerous ones?"

"I think we've counted sixteen of them now. It could be more. We haven't yet been able to track down the when, why, who, what, which. But we do have sixteen names at least." Three of which are highly dangerous. Quinn thought to herself but didn't say.

"You have sixteen names?" Jasper asked, her eye shining even brighter.

"Yes," Quinn answered and then continued. "Names make them easier to locate?"

"Not necessarily. But it generally gives the, shall we say, the vibe that surrounds the book its own special signature. And that will help locate the precise tomes we're looking for."

"Oh," Quinn said.

"Well, at least that's something. Maybe we'll find books you didn't even know you were missing."

Quinn knew Jasper was trying her best to be reassuring, but for some obscure reason, maybe not so obscure at all, Quinn didn't feel comforted by the fact that, as a whole, the Library didn't know where a lot more books were. "What can I do to help you with this ritual?"

Jasper paused for a second, as if mentally ticking something off a list, then grinned. "Do you think you can get me resin dust? Charcoal? But I need charcoal from a seared winwood tree. I also require salt so that we can form a protective circle. Not that I'm expecting trouble. But just in case, considering we're close to so much power, we don't want to take any risks."

"How risky is this going to be for the Library itself?" Quinn asked, cautious now.

Again, Jasper paused for a second. "You know, the Library has a lot of protections. I doubt it's going to be actually dangerous for the Library, especially if it's putting us somewhere far away from people."

"And if potentially things could go wrong?" Quinn asked. "Does that mean to us and the people in the Library?"

"I mean, there's always a possibility."

"But is it probable?" Quinn asked.

"No, not probable at all, but everything's possible, even if it's only by a fraction of a fraction." Jasper winked at her.

Quinn smiled. She couldn't help it. Jasper was pretty easy to get on with. It made her wonder just what Savinth had done that Quinn wasn't aware of. Well, anyway, maybe she'd ask Jasper about the recipes at a later time.

"Misha," Quinn called, and Misha turned up right in front of her.

"What can I get for you, Librarian?" Misha asked, giving a little bow. She seemed more herself than she had been around Hal, which was a relief.

"Did you hear what she just said?" Quinn asked.

"No, I am not omnipotent, not even here, Librarian. I am simply able to go anywhere in the Library on a whim." There was no sarcasm in Misha's inflection, but Quinn could have sworn she almost heard it.

Quinn almost rolled her eyes, but instead she listed off the things they needed, and Misha frowned. "Um, might I make a suggestion? I do have a few level-three barriers in storage. I think it might be pertinent for you to use these just in case something goes awry."

"Well, the salt should do," Jasper said.

But Misha held up a hand and stopped her. "It should do, but there is every possibility that it won't do, and I will not put the Librarian in such danger. Since we need her there for you to access a portion of the power from the Library, we must also put her safety first."

"Very well," Jasper said. "Then shall we head to this miraculous place?"

Misha inclined their head toward Quinn and said, "I will meet you down there." And then she was gone.

Quinn watched where the supervisory golem had stood, pondering the exit. She hadn't been aware Misha was able to travel down to the filtration area. As it was, it required special permissions for others to enter.

Aradie came in for an almost crash landing on Quinn's shoulder, barreling so hard into the brace that Quinn actually stumbled to the side and lost her train of thought. "What's with you, girl?" The owl tweaked at her hair and butted her head against Quinn. "Now, now, I really wasn't going anywhere without you. You've just been off chatting with your mates?" Quinn asked.

Aradie leveled a very even glare at her.

Quinn chuckled. "Fine, I won't ask."

But Quinn had already begun walking toward the stairs to go down the mana pools. She paused and asked the Library, *Why can't we just have an elevator straight down to the pools from this level?*

Well, I mean, there's nothing stopping me from doing that. It's just that originally there'd been so much chaos emanating off the entire filtration area that it was a little dangerous to activate magic so close to it.

Quinn nodded. *I don't feel like walking down a heap of stairs. How about we extend the elevator?*

Very well, Librarian, the Library said. But Quinn thought she could detect some amusement in the tone. A corridor appeared behind the spiral staircase, and Quinn walked in it as if she'd done so every day of her life in the Library.

Jasper followed. "This wasn't here before, was it?" she asked, absolute wonderment in her tone.

"Nope, it wasn't," Quinn said. "The Library has a habit of doing that."

Especially when you ask. The words echoed with amusement through the Librarian's brain.

They headed down the corridor, which was fairly long, and now that Quinn thought about it, it had taken a while to get to the stairs in the core level when they were going to repair the filtration system. She was going to have to ask the Library one of these days just how it maintained structural integrity in light of all the different movements made with the interior. Although Quinn was fairly certain the answer was going to be "It's magic," which she was really starting to get tired of.

Finally, they came to an opening, and on the left-hand side were massive elevator doors. They opened with a slight whooshing sound, and they stepped in. "Okay, let's get us there."

It took maybe twenty seconds to get down all the way. Eight or nine stories meant a whole lot of space. The doors opened, and Quinn stepped out. She could see the stairs that they would usually take directly next to her and glanced out toward where the mana pools were.

She couldn't see Ashiron, but she could feel the dearth of a pulse from it much closer than usual. It didn't breathe like the others, not even the ones that were still offline. Ashiron was like a ghost. Quinn hesitated to move toward the area.

No, no, said the Library in her head, *just go straight ahead, slightly to the right, and you'll find exactly what you're looking for.*

Meanwhile, Jasper had already done so. There was a gasp, an intake of breath of surprise and eagerness from the sound of it. "This is perfect, Quinn," Jasper said. "We can easily sketch out the diagrams I need. There's plenty of room just in case it smokes up. You know, sometimes you just . . . rituals aren't the most reliable thing all of the time."

"Now you're telling me this," Quinn said.

"Oh, pish posh, it'll be absolutely fine. We have twenty-foot ceilings, and there is sufficient room for us all to move around." Jasper's eyes were glowing. "This is fantastic! I'll get started right away."

Quinn lingered in front of the cavernous room.

Now, it wasn't cavernous like the filtration chamber with its however many-foot-high ceilings and massive filtration pillars. It was just a tiny room by comparison that was for them to practice safe magic in. Before she could stop herself, Quinn peered around the corner and looked out over the filtration chamber.

The corner of it she could glimpse was beautiful with that iridescent glowing mana shade of blue now. There was barely any topical sludge, nor a chaotic feeling to the air whatsoever. It was lighter, even the air she breathed into her lungs felt weightless. She could sense all the pillars and that they'd have to activate a fifth one soon.

Her eyes drifted in the direction of Ashiron, but this wasn't the time right now. That empty and ominous feeling stayed in the back of her mind like a reminder alert.

She turned back to Jasper, who was frantically writing out runic symbols on the floor.

Quinn's gut rumbled and it had nothing to do with hunger.

Suddenly, this all seemed like a very bad idea.

2 0

RUNES AROUND HER

THIS TIME, QUINN COULDN'T EVEN BLAME THE WEIRD PREMONITION ON having said it out loud and jinxed herself. No, this time the bad feeling came from the thrumming she felt through the floor, as if it was trying to shake her loose, to get through to her bones, maybe shake her meat suit off.

It was an angry throb, like something had gone inherently wrong in the entire process.

Inside of the Library.

And then it faded.

Quinn paused and took a couple of steps toward the cavernous ritual room they'd been given. Jasper looked up at her from the middle of it, a frown on her face.

"That wasn't supposed to happen. I haven't even activated the circle yet," Jasper said looking around in bewilderment.

Quinn glanced at the runes that were sketched onto the ground. They weren't connected fully yet. "Well, I can see that you're not even finished yet."

"How do you know that?" Jasper asked. "I thought you didn't know about rituals."

"Because it looks incomplete and if there's one thing I've understood about magic since I got here, you can't leave any type of magic incomplete. That's just a recipe for disaster." Quinn shrugged. She'd begun to understand more of the intricacies of magic ever since the synchronization. Or at least the wheels and cogs.

Jasper chuckled. "It would be nice if people who grew up with magic were as logical as you in that case."

Quinn shrugged. "It was either learn fast or die. Kill the entire universe with me. Had to, you know, take my wins where I could."

Quinn reached out with her senses. An uneasiness permeated the entire Library. As if something had shifted and was out of place.

Is everything okay? she asked the Library.

There was no response.

That wasn't a good sign. Not when she spoke directly to it anyway. She double-checked that her shields were down and tried again. *What was that? What happened? Is everything okay?*

I need to concentrate. Just let me deal with it.

You know, we can stop if what we're doing is causing . . . Quinn offered.

It's not exactly what you're doing. Just . . . I will deal with it. The Library interrupted, as Jasper continued drawing runes on the ground.

The charcoal, which glowed in a very non-charcoal way, practically burned into the stone from what Quinn could see. Jasper was chanting under her breath words that Quinn couldn't decipher and yet they looked so achingly familiar that she thought she should understand them.

"Okay," Jasper said, her voice slightly strained with exertion, "getting there."

Quinn leaned against the doorway looking out toward the sliver of the mana lake she could see. It was serene being so far underground and yet being able to see an ocean of power in front of her. A vast body of churning energy that she'd helped reestablish. That felt good. Maybe Kajaro had been right about one thing. Subterranean worlds were pretty cool. She shook her head, clearing that thought out of it and turned to watch as Jasper drew more.

The Alyenarvor had just begun to sketch one very complex rune when the ground began to shake again. It rumbled this time like there was something trying to bubble up from underneath, explode out toward them and wipe everything out. Quinn moved in toward the arch at the other side, closer to the lake, watching it while shielding herself from potential danger.

The mana began to churn as if somebody had thrown a heater into the mix, increased the temperature and caused the liquid within to literally boil. It bubbled and spurted and crashed against the shore. Even the elements of chaotic sludge still visible here and there seemed to scatter off as if they feared the power the mana underneath it held.

"Uh-oh," Quinn said as she felt the very foundations of the Library begin to tremor. This didn't bode well. "Aradie?" she asked but the bird just shook her head, bewilderment coming across their connection. *Library?* Quinn asked, suddenly feeling ever so slightly frantic. Not completely, but this defied logic and the Library wasn't listening to her.

"Uh, Quinn, should I stop this?" Jasper asked, a tremor in her voice.

"Might be an idea. I don't know if it was that rune you just finished in particular, but better be safe than sorry."

The thing was, this time, the ground's heaving didn't subside. She wondered if it extended above to the Library as a whole. And as she reached her senses out, she realized that, to her relief, everybody upstairs was doing just fine. It was only them down here, stuck in the bowels of the pocket dimension, where the entire Library could crash down on top of them, who were having difficulty standing in the tremors underground.

Maybe that was just another portion of the Library magic, protecting the patrons and books for as long as it could. Cushioning impact, really.

She told herself to breathe, to be logical, to search for the reason. She reached out again and this time, she reached down with her senses. And that's when she realized they were almost directly above the dungeon the Library created to contain Tenejo.

That couldn't be good either.

Yes, you found it. Stupid damn Serpensiril's making it so I can't even put a ritual cavern where I want to put it without double-checking that there won't be detrimental magical reactions, the Library grumbled in Quinn's mind.

What do you mean, interrupting something? Quinn asked softly in her head.

I didn't foresee that the runic magic Jasper is invoking would interfere with the completely polar opposite runic magic that keeps Tenejo tethered in the dungeon. They are clashing and I am currently . . . The Library actually sounded sort of out of breath, which was extremely strange given the fact that it was an ancient Library being and Quinn hadn't realized it needed to breathe.

Are you moving it? she asked softly.

Yes, I'm relocating the dungeon currently. Far enough away so Jasper may finish the ritual. We need to find those books.

We need to figure out something to do with Tenejo, Quinn said.

Well, you're the one who didn't end him when you could have, the Library snapped. There was a pause. *I apologize. I didn't bring you here just to start killing people.*

Quinn shook her head. *No, no, you're making a pretty good point. All he's done since I spared him is cause us trouble. Maybe I need to switch those emotions off more often.*

No, Quinn. Maybe you just need to keep being yourself.

Quinn didn't answer that. She did reach up and scratch her bird behind the ears as the tremors beneath them began to lessen slightly. Aradie snuggled into her face and slowly the tremors in the ground subsided, leaving the people above completely unaware as to the disturbance that had been caused downstairs.

Jasper eyed Quinn warily. "Was that me? Did I cause that?"

"Not really." Quinn smiled, just glad nothing had disturbed Ashiron. "Inadvertently. And there was nothing you could do about it. It's okay. I think the Library has settled things now."

"Oh," Jasper said, "that's good, right?"

"Yeah," Quinn said. "Now let's see if we can find those books."

Jasper nodded. "Did you have that information I needed?"

Wordlessly, Quinn shared the names of the books and their approximate duration in the Library using the date *DeKarlyle's* book was checked out as a rough guide, just like she'd done with her abilities and Malakai so long ago. It sure came in handy to be able to share information with chosen people that easily.

Jasper grinned. "Thanks for that." and went quiet for a few moments as she took in all the information.

Is everything under control now? Quinn asked the Library mentally.

It's about as under control as it's going to get, the Library said. *We sincerely need to sit down and have a chat about removing Tenejo from this location. I cannot in good conscience keep him here, Quinn. He is volatile and dangerous and frankly wants to see yours and my head on a platter. I don't have time to mollycoddle somebody who wants to kill me and destroy everything I've worked for.*

Quinn could feel herself pale and she felt lucky that Jasper was engrossed in finishing the runic circle she needed to engrave around the entire cavern. *I'm sorry,* Quinn said. *I should have been more decisive. I think I'll take Uncle Hal up on his offer. I don't know if we can retrieve anything else safely from Tenejo anyway.*

Given that those memories are, at worst, a definite trap and, at best, going to infect us with something again when we're only just digging ourselves out of that hole, please visit Hal as soon as you can.

Quinn sighed mentally. Aradie snuggled up close to her head. Quinn wondered, just for a second, how she'd gotten so used to such a massive owl sitting on her shoulder all the time.

I lightened my weight, Aradie said to her in her mind. *It's simple magic. It's a displacement theory.*

Quinn side-eyed her bird. "Simple, huh?" She chuckled.

At least, the Library said as if the owl hadn't interrupted their conversation, *try and get to see Hal as soon as you can. I know you have a lot on your plate. As soon as we've got Lynx back to his usual form, he should be able to help you more, shoulder some more of the burden. Usually, my manifestation and my Librarian work in such close proximity and in such synchronicity that it's like a well-oiled machine, and then there are the assistants who should lighten your load further. I'm terribly sorry, but none of this has gone to plan, Quinn. The system's still fried, and we're finding more and more holes. Hopefully, that just means it will help us know what we need to do to fix them.*

Quinn could hear a very slight undercurrent of frustration from the Library. Regardless of everything else, the Library had rarely been actually frustrated, perhaps annoyed, perhaps a little bit irritated. But this was something the Library couldn't do anything about, and Quinn wasn't entirely sure how to help.

We'll get there. She tried to reassure the Library but was pretty sure it fell flat.

As if in answer, Lynx suddenly stood directly in front of her. He'd been solid for quite a while now, and she could appreciate the magical being that he was. He was very human in appearance, with slightly pointed ears. His purple sclera eyes were fascinating to watch, especially when he sometimes plugged into the system and had to multitask too many things at once, and the way the runes danced around in his hair, constantly rotating.

Magical.

She needed to figure out how to charge her phone with mana and how to text her friends. Surely texting would be cheaper than attempting to send through a whole person every time. There had to be some magical means she could use for telecommunication purposes. She didn't understand how that sort of magic worked.

"Quinn," Lynx said, looking directly at her.

"Sorry," she said. Not sure why she'd suddenly started thinking about adapting Earth technology. It was probably the runes in Lynx's hair.

"Are you okay?" he asked gently, peering at her with concern.

"Fine, I just had about seventeen stray thoughts," she said. On the bright side, it appeared that Jasper was about finished with her preparations. "Did you come down to help?"

"Yes," Lynx said. "I can easily locate or translate the locations to the actual map system, and that way we'll have definitive locations on the books that Jasper finds."

Quinn smiled. "Excellent. How are you feeling?"

"I feel isolated from portions of my functions. But otherwise, I'm glad to be mostly whole, and I'm glad to be here."

Quinn knew what he wanted to add was that he was glad that the Library hadn't sought to completely disregard him. That'd be almost worse than death itself. Being suspended in a stasis of nothingness had to be horrible.

"What do we do now?" But Quinn was cut off by Jasper's massive grin.

"Just you watch, Quinn." She sounded so excited. "This is how you do magic."

Jasper was tall and slender and ethereal looking like all Alyenarvor, especially in the glowing light of the runes that completely encircled her which had to be at least twenty feet in diameter. All around the edges were filigree shapes and beautiful runes practically etched into the rocky floor. In the center, stood Jasper, her hands under her chin to start with, and then she spread them to either side as she gazed up at the ceiling another fifteen odd feet above her.

Quinn couldn't understand a word the woman chanted. Nothing. But she could feel the magic coursing through the runes as they began to light up, as they began to swirl, as they continued to move and almost vibrate with a frequency that she could practically feel against the hairs on her skin.

A black glowing blue mist luminesced around each individual rune as Jasper rotated from side to side, chanting, never stopping.

Aradie made a low coo in her throat, and Quinn patted her absent-mindedly as she couldn't tear her eyes away from the spectacle in front of her. Jasper glowed with the same blacky blue as the runes around her. It gave her this otherworldly quality like she'd come from the other side.

She chanted, she called out, and then she stopped. But the runes continued to glow, and Jasper grinned widely.

"Now, all you need to do is speak the name of each book that you want to locate. If we can locate it, we will find it."

2 1

LIKE A PREMONITION

UNSURE IF SHE NEEDED TO SAY THE BOOK NAMES IN A SPECIFIC WAY, Quinn was confident Jasper would have given her more detailed information if necessary.

Quinn took a deep breath before speaking the first book name.

"Ririn's Dimensional Distortion Through Sacrificial Means," she said and watched as the entire circle lit up. The runes swirled, the power spiraled. She could feel it surging beneath her feet into the circle, through the runes, through Jasper who lit up with this black and blue glow of magic that resonated throughout the whole room.

That's when Quinn understood why the Library made them their own cavernous room. The energy in here felt rejuvenating. Quinn was about a hundred percent sure they didn't want this type of energy leaking through to the normal masses far above them. Most of them wouldn't be able to process it.

"Very well done," Jasper managed to breathe out. Her eyes glowed, her skin had an iridescent sheen under it, and above the runic circle, a massive, vast map of stars was all Quinn could see. For a second, a point very distant in the corner from her lit up like a shooting star and then it was gone.

"Next one," Jasper breathed out.

Quinn took another breath. This was exhilarating, the feeling of so much power coursing through her body, whipping around her head and simply inputting itself into this circle was amazing, and perhaps slightly terrifying. The next thing she wanted to learn was rituals.

She stepped forward, speaking the next name clearly. *"The Crown and Fall of Pocket Dimensions Due to Spatial Interference."*

Again, the runes lit up brighter than she'd ever seen them before. Her hair whipped around her with the vicious way the wind suddenly leapt into the space. Runes glowed vivid black and blue with an undertone of purple this time, ripping across the circle but they stayed put like Jasper who stood steadfast in the middle as if nothing could shake her resolve.

Quinn spied a light sheen of sweat on the witch's forehead now. Jasper's jaw clenched hard. Suddenly, the starry map appeared again, an additional blip in a completely different area this time shone brightly to join the other, and then the map was gone again.

Quinn couldn't wait for the all three locations to be filled in.

"These are hard to keep in place, Quinn. Are the rest of the books this same caliber?" Jasper ground out the words as if she was fighting to maintain this level of power.

Quinn shook her head, "Just one more like this and we can rest. Right now, these are the most important."

"I've got another one in me. Let me reset." Jasper paused for a second before answering, sounding stronger when she did. "You're good now. Do it."

Quinn watched Jasper carefully and finally got up the energy to name the last book they needed. *"The Parsneauvian Theory of Spatial Dimension Manipulation."*

This time, the wind whipped up and the power pulsated so strongly to the edge of the room that it rebounded back into the center where Jasper stood. It hit her as a focal point and rippled back out toward Quinn again. She watched as the grimace hit Jasper's face on impact, but the witch stood steadfast, strong and true. A manic grin crossed her face as she wielded the power back into itself.

The ripples continued converging back and forth until finally the entire energy sphere went still. The runes swirled restlessly, similarly to how Lynx's hair runes moved whenever he accessed his power. It was mesmerizing. Quinn found it difficult to tear her gaze away from the spectacle in front of her.

And then the runes glowed brighter. The blue, the black, the purple, and suddenly a white sheen around the edges of it. It flared and flared brighter until it reduced itself suddenly back to the black and blue.

This time, the map rotated in 3D the entire diameter of the runes and the third book's blip flared to life far away from the other two again. This time the dot that depicted where the book was seemed larger than the others.

And this time the map remained where it was, settling into a gently rotating half sphere that took up the majority of the air space in the room.

Jasper's underlying chant faded slowly until it stopped. The runes glowed softly with no power whipping them around anymore. Nothing but a gentle sense of accomplishment filled the cavernous room.

And the map.

It was like a 3D holographic diagram or something, like she'd expect to see on one of the space series she'd so eagerly watched as a child. This was amazing and really hit home how she was a hundred percent not in Kansas anymore.

The stars in the map shimmered gently and it rotated ever so slowly as if showing off its different aspects. If she reached out, she could probably direct it, position it, and figure out exactly where those books were located. Three blips on the radar of books.

Quinn couldn't help the shiver that ran down her spine. Jasper panted in deep breaths and stumbled to the edge of the runic circle. Quinn reached out a hand to steady her and Jasper gladly took it. She stumbled to the edge of the room and sat on the floor, resting her hands on her raised knees.

"I always forget how much locator spells take out of me," Jasper said.

"Are you okay?" Quinn asked, her eyes darting between Jasper and the massively revealing map that she wanted to play with.

Jasper chuckled as she noticed. "I will be. This didn't harm me. I'm simply bereft of energy. The more powerful an object, the more power it takes to locate it."

Quinn reached into her storage and pulled out an energy ball, handing it to Jasper.

"Oh, thank you," Jasper said, biting into it greedily. Color began to flush her face again and the sheen of sweat covering her entire body began to recede.

"Are you feeling better?" Quinn asked, slightly concerned even though Jasper didn't seem to be.

"Yes, but you and Lynx need to study the map and commit it to the Library's memory so I can let go of the spell."

"I'm so sorry," Quinn said. "I thought this was just a map room now."

Jasper chuckled. "No, it's not a map room now. However, if the Library is willing to leave the room where it is, I can come and easily re-engage the runes again. I won't have to recreate the circle now that I've established it."

"That would be fantastic, Jasper," Quinn said. She was grateful for her newly found friend. "We really appreciate this."

Just to be safe though, she sent out a thought to the Library. *We can leave this here, right?*

Well, I'm not making a new one anytime soon. The Library sounded a bit disgruntled but then a sigh rippled through Quinn's mind. *But sure. Yes. I will leave this here.*

Jasper shrugged, not noticing Quinn's preoccupation. "You know, I misjudged a lot of things about the Library and perhaps about Savinth, too. Maybe we'll have to have a chat."

Quinn laughed. "You know how that's gonna go."

"Yes, but I still think it's worth it." Jasper grinned and then smoothly changed the subject. "So, does the map help?"

"Well." Lynx interrupted their conversation appearing suddenly in their midst. "I mean, it looks like a map, it reads like a map, and I can input it right into the system here. The books are a lot farther away from each other than I would have suspected." He frowned, his eyes doing that strangely distant thing where he was looking into multiple avenues at once.

Quinn, as usual, itched to put something on his head to see if he would notice it was there before he knocked it off when he moved. But she wasn't in the office and now wasn't the time.

Even if she could really do with a tension breaker.

He blinked back into the present and glanced across at Jasper. "The spell fed off all the information we had available, correct? As well as the exact name of the book, is that right?"

"That's the only way I can locate them," Jasper confirmed. "I have to have knowledge of the most prevalent signature from before the item was removed from its rightful place. Hence the history of the books that I asked for, their duration in the Library, and all that."

"Hmm," he said. "We've got two pretty good locations, as far as I can see, even though they appear to be . . . I'll have to . . . I'll have to look into the areas these are in. It's not . . . it's not making as much sense as I want it to."

"Okay," Quinn said, looking between Jasper and Lynx, completely confused as to what he meant. "What about the third one? Didn't you say that two of them are quite clear?"

"Their location is probably, I'd say, continent-based. It would take us a while to find the book. We'd probably have to get there, cast another ritual, find a tracking spell." He paused for a second as if a thought just occurred to him. "Use you. You're like a tracking signal towards these books, remember? That's how you found it back with the Esposians."

He paused again and frowned, his eyes flickering, his runes spinning around his head. Quinn looked down at Jasper, who was still sitting, regaining her breath and equilibrium.

"Do you know what that's about?" She asked.

Jasper shrugged. "You should know what that's about. Aren't you connected to the Library?"

Quinn gave her another energy ball. "Yeah, I'm connected to the

Library, all right. Doesn't mean I understand it half the time or anything." She watched Lynx, running a thousand different scenarios through her head at once.

"Surely, couldn't . . . and the third one is what?" she asked as she noticed that his eyes flickered back into their usual focus.

"The third one is planet-wide. Maybe a little more? Sector specific only, if I'm correct?" He walked up to it and actually maneuvered it as if it was a 3D hologram. He pulled it out so that the stars moved and became closer to the exact location he was trying to find. "Yeah, this is more of an entire sector location basis than planet. We might have to figure out a way to pinpoint this before we go after this book because this is even less specific, especially for an extremely specific ritual."

Jasper shrugged. "It was the last one. We probably pushed it a little bit. It does pull on my energy. Maybe I should have had some energy balls between the last two of them. I just . . . I thought it would be enough."

"Well, you created a vast image here. A vast accurate image. I mean, I can see how it pulled a lot of energy from you." Lynx gave her a nod of approval, even though he frowned. "I'm inclined to believe this is as accurate as its particular signature wants to allow you to be."

Jasper shrugged. "It is what it is."

"It also pulled from Library power which just has a much larger pool." Lynx's voice trailed off like he was thinking about something that just didn't mesh with his current train of conversation.

Quinn studied the map too. Even if she had no idea how to ascertain locations, she was a bit curious. Geography had never been her strong suit on Earth and now that they were on a different—well, *universal*—stage, it wasn't like she could learn it instantly without a tome at her fingertips.

Food for thought for later.

"But if I had to say"—she frowned as an idea came to her—"You know, I mean, I'm new at all of this, so this is probably completely out of left field and wrong, but couldn't it be that the people who have each of these books are part of the conspiracy, right? Like, the first one was with the Serpensiril, or with Kajaro at any rate, and the second one was with the Esposians. Even if we're still trying to figure out their relationship to the Serpensiril and the whole chaos-magic-must-reign-supreme thing. Doesn't it stand to reason that these other worlds, these locations where the books we're missing from this group are, could be potential collaborators with the Serpensiril?"

Lynx turned and blinked at her, his eyes doing that weird lizard thing that they sometimes did. He didn't stop staring at her, almost like he was looking through her, and she knew he knew he wasn't, but she was also fairly certain the Library was meticulously analyzing what she just said.

"That is the logical conclusion," Lynx muttered. "Mostly what we were leaning toward."

"It makes perfect sense," Jasper said, springing to her feet with what appeared to be renewed vigor.

Quinn turned and glanced at her. "Right? I thought so. Logic and I are old friends. I just—I don't know who these worlds belong to, or what quadrants or areas they're in."

"Let me get that information sorted for you." Lynx went quiet for several seconds that seemed a lot longer to Quinn in her mind as she ran through a thousand different scenarios, and the fact that they were going to get answers whether these collaborators wanted them to or not. Quinn felt particularly stubborn today. She wasn't about to let anyone get the best of her and the Library.

Not in the long run, anyway.

Lynx gasped. "This is worse than I thought."

He paused, and it went on so long that Quinn was tempted to shake him by the shoulders so he'd continue. But she didn't have to.

"So far we have the Serpensiril and Esposians. Even if Kajaro wasn't located in Serpensiril territory when we confronted him. While this planet isn't species specific, it is located literally next to a circle of planets inhabited by the Ilgonomur, which is very odd. We've had a brilliant relationship with them for hundreds of thousands of years. I just . . ." Lynx shook his head as if trying to clear it. "Still, it's not *on* their home world, just close to it. This requires some research."

"Ilgonomur?" Quinn muttered. "So, like, Finn?"

Lynx nodded and continued speaking. "The second book is located in an area that, well, I'm not largely familiar with. It isn't inhabited by any of our allied species, but it is somewhat close to a few. I'll have to look into the second book's location more. It's the last one that's more concerning."

"Why?" Quinn said. "Who lives there?"

Lynx raised an eyebrow. "I mean, you could just inspect it yourself."

Quinn rolled her eyes. "It's a huge 3D holographic map. I have no idea how to use it. Just tell me."

Lynx cracked a small smile at that, but then the frown was back. "Well, it's just, that's the same solar system that the Aracnio planets exist in."

"The Aracnios? Like Jim and Bob?" Quinn asked incredulously.

Lynx nodded. "Yeah, just like Jim and Bob."

"Oh." A cold sensation crept down Quinn's spine. Not like a shiver, but more like a premonition. One she didn't want to have. "That's not good."

22

WARM AND FUZZY

A THOUSAND DIFFERENT THOUGHTS FLEW THROUGH QUINN'S HEAD AS she contemplated the gravity of the situation. The Aracnios species home world was located close to a book. Or basically in that star system, but not necessarily right where the book was perhaps because of the lack of definition in its location. It shouldn't mean anything. But it might be an idea to examine alliances and relationships of species in those sectors, just in case. "It doesn't necessarily mean we can't trust them, right?"

Aradie hooted and shrugged her shoulders in an oddly human sort of way. Her words and images conveyed through Quinn's mind. *I didn't find anything out of place when I scanned them. They weren't lying, and they definitely didn't have bad intentions toward the Library. Could it be that they're . . .* But that's where the owl left it.

Quinn, however, voiced those words. "It could even be an individual that hid the book. Or that the twins are unwittingly being used to monitor the interior goings-on of the Library?"

Lynx watched her closely. "You're putting a lot of thought into this."

"What, and shouldn't I?" Quinn asked. "They've been working with us for months now. We would be naive not to look into things. But I also think Jim and Bob might deserve the benefit of the doubt?"

"Perhaps," Lynx said. "This is something we have to look into. These are factions that we've been allied with for tens of thousands, no, hundreds of thousands of years. If it was accidentally misplaced, it's important we find out. However, if it was deliberately hidden then it's unexpected and, frankly, unwelcome. Being gone for five hundred years shouldn't make any difference to our alliances, but perhaps we need to be open to the possibility that it did."

He paused, and Quinn could see the recognition pass over his face in such a way that he paled back into an almost translucent figure that she could partially see through.

She felt a pang of sorrow for him as she saw the penny drop for him. "Yeah. Just because they've been allies on paper for that long doesn't mean they were happy with everything. Heck, I mean, the universe is ancient, right? Like, I mean, eons old. *Billions* of years. Older than ancient history. Older than the Cretaceous period. Older than everything. Surely, inside of so much time, two hundred fifty thousand years is nothing, right?"

Lynx nodded his head and some of his pep disappeared. "It's just a drop in the oceans. I guess . . . I guess we've been extremely naive."

Don't I know it, the Library echoed, the voice sounding through the room.

Jasper stood up straight, looking all around them, trying to find where the voice came from. Quinn shook her head and held up a hand for Jasper. "That's just the Library voicing individual concern."

It's not just my concern I'm voicing, the Library muttered softly, like a rumble through the room. *I don't really do that.*

"Yes, but you rarely do so out loud, where everybody and their dog can listen to you."

Fine, the Library said. *I'll just keep my thoughts to myself.*

"This is the first time I've ever heard you sound petulant, and it doesn't suit you." Quinn would have crossed her arms and glared at the Library, but . . . it was hard to do that when it was everywhere.

The Library sighed and the sound echoed through Quinn's mind, bouncing off each side until it stilled. *You have a point. I'm in a very bad mood.*

"We should probably sit down and chat about why you're in a bad mood," Quinn said.

We should probably sit down and chat anyway, the Library responded. *It's getting late. You should return to the main level and I will . . . I'll see you tomorrow. I have things to take care of.*

Jasper was still staring at Quinn, and she grinned at the witch. "You should probably close your mouth, I'm not sure any insects down here that might fly into it would be healthy."

Jasper laughed. "So that was the Library actually speaking."

Lynx laughed. "You'd be surprised at how much my boss speaks."

The Library's presence dulled in the back of Quinn's mind, and she knew she'd have to sincerely yell at the Library to get its attention in its current state of focus. She also knew the Library wasn't just sitting there idly pouting, but instead was trying to figure out exactly how to deal with all the new factors that kept springing up.

"Is . . . let me check." Quinn reached out with her senses, trying desperately to figure out if she could sense where the Aracnio twins were. Because of the roster, she knew they were supposed to both be on the front desk today, but the last time they'd been supposed to be there, they hadn't been.

She'd only seen one of them, without the other recently. It made her cautious and oddly suspicious. They'd been so kind and nice to her at first. She wondered now how much of everything was purely an act. "Aren't they supposed to be rostered on today?"

"Yes, yes, they are," Lynx replied, shaking his head.

"I'm guessing them being absent isn't a good sign."

"It could be a lot of things, Quinn. Let's not jump to conclusions yet." But with every syllable, Lynx sounded more defeated.

"Well, the big map with the blips on it makes me think we should be jumping to a lot of conclusions." Then she sighed, realizing how fanatical that sounded. Assumptions were the mother of all screwups, and they needed to be better than that. After all, they couldn't risk being wrong.

She took a deep breath. "Okay, what we need to do is figure out exactly where these are located. Can you do that, Lynx? Like home in on the actual location, especially of the Parsneauvian book?"

"I can narrow it down, but it'll take some time." He frowned, zooming in again. "I can research the other potential allies and precise species who live in the region of the Parsneauvian book. I'm unsure how else to approach this."

"We need more information. Don't we always just need more knowledge and more magic and more power? Isn't that how this works?" Quinn asked. Up until now, just having more abilities, having more power at her disposal, and knowing more had helped her through every hoop she'd had to jump.

"Pretty much. You just also need more time."

"That's fine. I'll figure that out," Quinn said. She was determined to make it so. "So, if you can concentrate on narrowing down the potential suspects, I think that would help us greatly."

"I'll do that."

"Just remember," Quinn added, "just because the book is near a specific home planet, doesn't necessarily mean anything. For now it's a starting point for us. After all, it could also have been planted there to make them look guilty."

Lynx nodded and then frowned. "You said you noticed the Aracnio brothers had been acting differently."

Quinn shrugged. "Just not always together and not as responsive to me as they were in the beginning. Not necessarily suspicious, but more standoffish than before, which at first I didn't think anything of. I thought maybe I'd done something to piss them off because I'm fairly adept at doing that. But since the realization that these books went missing and everyone knowing about it . . . perhaps that led to some of their reaction to me? Although Finn hasn't acted any differently. I'm not sure how to interpret it as a whole."

"We knew there were probably spies in the Library, so this just narrows it down." Lynx sighed.

"Do you have all the information you need from the map?" Jasper asked, and Quinn could see the sweat beading her brow again.

"Does it feed off your energy to maintain that map?" she asked her eyes widening with recognition.

"Well, it doesn't have to, but the Library's had enough problems with power, so I was letting it." Jasper shrugged.

Quinn shook her head. "You should have told me. It could have leeched off me. Mine regenerates oddly fast, and I have a ridiculous amount of it."

Jasper raised an eyebrow. "Your abilities and statistics are something I would love to discuss at a later date."

"Sure," Quinn said. "Want to help me flush all the traitors out of my midst first?"

"I thought you'd never ask," Jasper said, a grin positively lighting up her face.

Quinn turned to Lynx. No matter how she looked at it, she couldn't figure out if the Aracnio twins were, in fact, traitors or if Finn was. She hadn't really seen enough of Finn, but every time their aid was needed they'd performed an admirable job, especially when it came to Tenejo and imprisoning him.

"I think we should monitor them closely," she said to Lynx.

"Obviously," Lynx said, raising an eyebrow.

"Aradie, will the owls help monitor them? Make sure they're not sneaking in places and planting tapping devices?" Quinn asked her owl.

Aradie twisted her neck around, looked at Quinn, and Quinn could have sworn that she raised an eyebrow.

"Look, it doesn't matter if you think it's plausible or not, or probable or not, the fact is that everything is possible, if people find a way. And given enough desperation and wildly fanatical theories, most people are capable of anything." She could hear herself sounding more and more cynical with each word.

"You're sounding extremely jaded there, Librarian," Jasper said with a wink.

"Well, maybe, maybe I've got a reason to be jaded right now. A magical Library that lets everybody come and access all the magical knowledge they could want at any time, all the time no matter where in the universe they come from and has been sabotaged by people that it trusted. Like what? You can't give people free food and knowledge and a safe space to be? Because it's wrong or something?" Quinn was a little upset. The Library seemed like a safe haven to her.

"That people take issue with this makes me so angry on so many levels I can't even articulate it! Anyway, it doesn't matter. That's a me thing." Quinn paused, counted to five under her breath and then continued. "What we need to do is preserve the Library, keep it where it needs to be, and make sure that we fight off any of these naysayers. Anyway, I've got to get upstairs."

"I'm coming with you." Now Jasper's voice sounded raspy.

Quinn glanced at Jasper again. Despite the energy balls the witch had eaten, Jasper looked particularly haggard. The often-translucent sheen that her skin held had dulled, so that she just didn't look as revitalized as she usually did.

"Lynx," Quinn asked, "are you done with the map?"

"Of course," he said looking up irritably until he spotted the state the Alyenarvor was in. "I'm so sorry, Jasper. I'm done. You should release it."

"Thanks," she said. And it winked out of existence, the runes suddenly silent and dull once more.

"I guess if we need to locate some more books that we're technically not supposed to have anymore, or whatever, we'll just come back here. Is that okay?" Quinn asked.

Jasper grinned widely as she spoke. "That'd be fantastic, and it won't take nearly as much energy if the books aren't as powerful as the ones that you just had me locate. Those were some pretty hefty chunkers. I'm excited to see what they're about."

"Well," Quinn said cautiously, "they're books that contain a great deal of powerful information that's lethal in the wrong hands. A reason that apparently didn't help keep them in there. Anyway, you look like crap. Let's get you into the elevator, get you fed by Cook. They'll be no doubt delighted to feed you anything you want, and then

I think it would behoove you to stay here the night, eat in the morning, and go if you have to then. I don't really trust you to traverse through a dimensional gateway in the state you're currently in. That's not gonna mesh well with your magic system."

Jasper turned to Quinn as they got into the elevator and looked at her. Very long and hard. "That's very insightful of you. How did you know what sort of magic I was managing?"

Quinn shrugged. "I can sense every single affinity. It doesn't always mean I know what I'm sensing, but I'm pretty sure you access some type of chaos magic in order to make that whole ritual work."

"In a very controlled manner," Jasper said, "and you did have some lying around down here. I kind of helped filter it."

"I like that," Quinn said. "You should be an assistant too. I think a chaos affinity should be a must for a Librarian. It's far too involved in the universe for it not to be."

Jasper eyed her as if she was weighing the proposition. "Well, I might take you up on that. After getting the starweed back to my commune, I feel like something is missing. We should talk about this later."

Quinn grinned. "I'd like that, Jasper."

Lynx rolled his eyes and disappeared out of the elevator. Quinn chuckled as they stepped out themselves not a few seconds later. The Library bustle drifted to her. Discourse and discussions on tomes, on magical theory, on the use of different types of affinities and how some were so much superior to others.

The arguments were light and filled with various branches of knowledge. Quinn loved the atmosphere created in the Library and was glad the Aracnio brothers hadn't infected it if they were in fact spies. She glanced around, unable to see them, and motioned to Eric.

He flew over, a scowl on his face and his arms crossed. "Oh great, it's you? What do you want?"

Quinn raised an eyebrow at his greeting and decided to ignore it. "You don't happen to have noticed where the Aracnio twins are?"

Eric watched her for a moment. "What do you mean? Where are the Aracnio twins? They're sick. They took the day off."

"Oh," Quinn said, not liking the way her gut roiled. "What about Finn? Is Finn here?"

"Yeah, Finn's filling in. Look." And he motioned over to the check-in desk and Quinn sighed with relief.

"Okay then, that might not be as bad as I thought." She tried to process the information. If all of them had been obviously guilty, it would have been nightmarish. If maybe one of them was actually honest and a genuine part of the Library, she could deal with that.

Aradie nudged her with a wing. "What?" she asked the owl. "Oh, Finn is fine? As far as you can tell."

Aradie hooted and nodded her head slightly.

Quinn felt marginally mollified. She wandered with Jasper into the kitchen, into the culinary wing, through the dining hall, Jasper's eyes darting everywhere.

"Hey, Cook," Quinn said.

Cook glanced up and turned around, a grin crossing their face. "Ah, it is my favorite Librarian."

Quinn chuckled. Cook always made her feel lighthearted, even if only for a moment. "Aren't I the only Librarian?"

"That is a moot point. I have memories of previous Librarians embedded in my matrix and thus, I would like you to know that you are officially my favorite Librarian."

"Oh," Quinn said, getting a little warm and fuzzy. "Thanks."

"You are very welcome. Even if you still need to get stronger." Cook kept making food without skipping a beat.

Quinn colored slightly and changed the subject since she was very well aware she needed to get stronger. "Could you see that Jasper and I have some food?"

"What have you been doing, Librarian?" The cook asked, even as they switched tasks smoothly to prepare something else.

"We had some books to locate," she mumbled, eyeing the food hungrily.

"Ah, excellent. From your visage, I assume that you have had success."

"Yes," Quinn said. "I'd like to think so, anyway."

Quinn took her food and sat down with Jasper. They didn't talk much, probably because Jasper was exhausted. But from Quinn's point of view, she was already focused on what she and the Library Core would be speaking about the next day.

They'd delayed this conversation for far too long.

23

SOMETHING IS LURKING

QUINN COULDN'T GET A RESTFUL NIGHT'S SLEEP. SHE GOT UP MUCH earlier than usual, had a nice hot shower, pulled on her comfy clothes, and headed down to grab a cup of something very similar to coffee. She nodded at Cook, beckoned to Aradie, who alighted very easily on her shoulder and headed downstairs to speak to the Library.

If she wasn't going to sleep, then at least she could be productive.

The core room of the Library, where Quinn originally landed when she was pulled here from her university, was breathtaking as usual, especially now they had power to spare. The glimmering lights lit up overhead like leaves and raindrops on a tree.

She walked from the stairs onto the soft ground, looking up, and realized that the gentle winking of overhead lights weren't lit up as beautifully as she'd expected. There were gaps in them, and some of them flickered into red and orange, a few of them yellow. Quinn had no idea what that meant, except perhaps that it had to do with the Library's memory.

She'd wondered if there'd be obvious signs, but this was a lot more than she'd assumed.

Before, when there wasn't enough power to turn everything on, those little discrepancies had been difficult to notice. Frankly, the

Library hadn't had access to everything. But now, they stood out, and it only made Quinn more concerned, as the patches were obvious.

She moved toward the core, which glistened with luminescence in front of her. The ground shifted, and from behind, or perhaps within the trunk of the tree, as it were, a shadowy figure stepped.

"You're taking on corporeal form?" Quinn asked, a smile in her voice.

The Library shook its head. "Not necessarily. Sometimes I feel maybe it's easier to speak to a visage than to the trunk of a tree."

Quinn let herself laugh, and Aradie cooed softly. "Well, I'd ask you what brings you here, but I would say that that's painfully obvious. So, Quinn, ask me your questions, and I will do my very best to answer them."

Quinn observed the Library shadow for several seconds, because she wasn't exactly sure how to phrase all of the questions in her head. But she guessed she may as well start at the beginning. "How are you a Library, if you're really a dragon?"

The Library smiled, but it wasn't something Quinn could see. It was just a sensation she felt from all around her. "I see you jumped straight into it. You would be mostly correct."

"Mostly correct?" Quinn asked, quite curious.

"Well, mostly correct, because yes . . . I am a type of dragon, one of the first creations in the universe, along with four of my brethren, and we are what is known as a cosmicisodracus. We have differing main abilities, magic, and affinity inclinations, technically, but we also have all of them. Our strengths are distinctive, and frankly, we are all personally ourselves."

"There are five of you? Have I met any of the others?" Quinn's interest suddenly piqued.

"Not to my knowledge." The Library paused, and Quinn could feel the grin emanating from it. "And not yet."

"Oh." Quinn couldn't help but be oddly disappointed that they hadn't been hiding somewhere close by.

"I do believe"—the Library paused for a few seconds—"Yes, I do believe that two of them are actually hibernating right now." Another pause. "Wow, they've been hibernating for a very long time."

"So dragons hibernate?" Quinn blurted out her obvious question.

"We can. We don't have to, but we've been alive for a very long time, and sometimes we get a little bored," the Library said in a gentle tone.

The nerdy part of Quinn's brain that made it relatively easy to accept the magical Library when she first got there was in overdrive. She had to stop herself from going down a tangent that she didn't need to right now. "Okay, wait, so what are you?"

"I am a lunar cosmicisodracus, which basically means I am a primordial lunar dragon."

"Moon-based?"

"Mm-hmm. There's moon-based tides, waters, that's me. That's why the filtration system works for me. It's part of why I became the Library," the Library answered and immediately instigated a thousand new questions.

"Okay, so we've established that you're a dragon, which means I'm part, or mostly, dragon, but I can be completely and utterly over-whelmed by that in a bit." Quinn pushed the curiosity down for now, keeping it for later. "First of all, why are you a Library? Why aren't you a dragon flying around the universe?"

The Library, actually, chuckled. "Well, you see, I was always a bit obsessed with knowledge. For as long as I can remember, I wanted to know everything and how it worked, and why magic did A, B, and C, and how I could therefore make magic do D, E, and F. I wanted to know where everything came from, where everything was going, where there were potential hiccups along the way. Absolutely all knowledge appealed to me. Maybe being the youngest of my brethren boosted my curiosity into trying to keep up with everyone else. But when the universe began, and we sprung into being the equivalent of a split second later, we were a family who sought out the meaning of the universe and of who we were. We initially followed along as everything was created. We fell in love with some of the species and their development."

For a moment, stars passed through the shadow in front of Quinn, like the rush of a universe passing them by. "Oh, Quinn, you don't even understand."

And suddenly, it was like a movie playing into Quinn's mind. She could see it, one of the most beautiful sunrises she'd ever seen, from a mountainous region, with purples and blues and yellows just stretching across the horizon as two suns rose one after the other. There was water and waves and mountains. And down below in the valley of the vision were, well, people. Not humanoid. They looked very similar to centaurs, except they had six legs.

And then the vision was gone.

But the sense of majesty and wonder and the beauty of creation, that lingered in Quinn's mind. The forming of a world, the life bestowed . . . magical.

It blew her away. She wanted to see more.

"I'm not here," the Library said gently, "to give you a visual tour of the entire universe. You have doors you can open to reach those places. You know that, right?"

"Yeah," Quinn said, the wonder still lingering so close to her skin she got goosebumps. "'So, tell me, how did you become the Library?"

There were several seconds of silence, and then the Library sighed. "Yep, that's a good question. So let me start . . ."

"At the very beginning?" Quinn asked.

"Eh, give or take several thousand millennia." The Library laughed softly before continuing. "Well, you see, it took a long time for us to realize that the chaotic elements of creation magic were actually more dangerous than they were helpful. That they needed more power, and that with every creation, the spark of chaos began to burn out. Naturally, originally there was so much power, so much magic, that we didn't notice."

"Didn't notice what?" Quinn asked.

"We didn't notice that the spark slowly began to regurgitate, I guess, or starting to draw power back into itself because of how much it had output. It didn't regenerate fast enough naturally. Not at the rate it was expending energy to create worlds and solar systems and the rest. We were all too giddy being mostly new in life and figuring out our own idiosyncrasies and how our own abilities manifested to notice that the spark was starting to, well, feed on itself. It began to devour anything in its path that could boost extra power allowing it to create bigger and better things. But in order to do so . . ." The Library paused.

"You mean it basically steamrolled over already established creations—those being species and worlds?" Quinn asked, wondering just how that was possible. "Sort of recycling in the worst way possible?"

"Exactly like that. And in doing so, it devoured everything on those planets, all life, including any species it had created. Now it didn't do this constantly. It took us maybe a millennia to notice and by then we'd lost around a dozen civilizations completely. So we had to convene an emergency council."

"Is that the council that Milaro's on?" Quinn butted in.

"Precisely," the Library said, smiling into Quinn's senses again. "Or at least its original incarnation. We convened and we decided that in order to temper the magic that was loose in the universe, we needed to remove the dangerous element from it because it devoured everything, Quinn, everything in its wake. It didn't care, it didn't discriminate, it didn't pick a special planet or a specific species. If we'd gotten in the way, we'd be gone too. In fact, it got several of our cousins, much younger, much more reckless, and it just gobbled them and all their power up, lending more to its own gathering momentum. We had to do something and this is what we decided on." The Library gestured to itself and all around them.

"We realized we needed a filtration system, something through which to filter the magic so it didn't try to devour itself and its creations. So that it didn't contaminate everything it touched. After some research and realizing what that would entail, I volunteered because water is my main element, it's what I'm best at, and the mana, while not water, is still a type of liquid. Its viscosity is something I innately understand. I set up myself as a filtration depot, so to speak. I mean, you've seen the size of it. It can expand anytime I want. As long as I have power incoming."

"And that was just the start?" Quinn asked, "What about the Library? You're just telling me how you became a filtration station."

"Just let me get there. It's taken millennia for this to happen." The Library sounded ever so slightly irritated. "I can't convey the scope in five minutes."

Aradie cooed. And even though Quinn couldn't see facial features, she was pretty sure the Library just squinted at Aradie.

"You know, your owl can sometimes be very intrusive," the Library said.

Quinn laughed. "You don't say. She's always in my head."

Aradie hunched her shoulders up and looked away from Quinn. "Now there's no need to be offended. Just let me listen to the Library."

"Having the filtration system in place helped immediately. At least it did when we took on the chaotic elements causing the power to feed on itself, and manage to calm down the initial spark. The universe was mostly complete by then. I mean, this is eons before Earth and many other planets were created. But we did it. It stopped seeking out the excess energy and allowed the filtered energy to be gathered in one spot and to flow out into ley lines and ley pools from there to the entire universe. With this offset, the spark could create without feeding off the negative void energy until eventually it just became the magic within the universe, as long as the chaotic element was tempered by the filtration." The Library paused thoughtfully before continuing. "Then we realized people needed ways to harness all of the different affinities. Back then there were only several hundred. Maybe, I think we started with 812."

"812? That still sounds like a lot," Quinn said.

"It is, but not compared to 1,722."

Quinn laughed. "You make a very valid point.

"In order to help people harness magic, we created magical tomes —a way for them to access information and knowledge safely because we couldn't to have people lose control or accidentally trigger chaotic elements due to a lack of affinity. To create magical tomes, we set up a system that allowed for careful creation of magical tomes that anyone could have access to, but that wouldn't sit around becoming potential stagnant pools for chaotic magic to fester in. Because that, that would be food for disaster and over expenditure all over again. We couldn't afford to have it unregulated at all. But we could make it so that everybody had access to that knowledge. So that's what I did. I volunteered to shift into a magical Library. And I did. And now I am a massive Library. Voila."

Quinn narrowed her eyes. "Yeah, but that's not everything. You don't just Library and voila. You would have needed different powers to help, right? Because you don't specialize in spatial manipulation yourself, or you didn't back then right?"

"Well, every dragon has at least a bit of spatial manipulation. We can shift our corporeal forms around quite a lot. But yes, you're correct. My siblings assisted me and poured copious amounts of their own energy into me in order to create the Library, to make it into what we, what the universe required to survive . . . to thrive. We started with like fifty tomes. And it just grew. We had several people help us along the way. And the whole venture continued to expand. Then we divided the sections into new branches. We arranged new deadlines, new facilities. And my very, very own pocket dimension. It was the only way we could make the Library accessible to everyone from everywhere. When they so desired. We weren't trying to gatekeep the magic. We were just trying to make sure that the chaotic elements didn't get out and start devouring and thereby unmaking the damn universe again." The Library paused and sounded a little melancholy when it continued. "We'd already lost so much to chaotic magic running rampant."

"Well, I mean, sounds really noble and all," Quinn said. "But obviously, not everybody agreed."

The Library sighed. "You're correct. One of my brethren, my siblings. He didn't. He wasn't overly fond of the from the very beginning and only aided us begrudgingly. While believed that those who were strong enough would come out the other side unscathed, he also realized that chaos needed some form of control. His opinion of how to achieve the chaotic control over the long term different, but since up to that time, not even one planet survived the reappropriation of power, not even one individual—he relented."

Quinn waited a few seconds before trying to approach the question delicately. "Do you think he could have anything to do with . . ."

"To do with . . ." The shoulders on the Library's shadow slumped and they shrugged. "I would like to answer that with a no, or at least an *I don't think so*. I've tried to convince myself that that's not the case. But something lurks behind this whole conspiracy. And even I have to admit, my brother is probably the prime suspect."

24

VULNERABLE

QUINN WANTED TO GRAB THAT TRAIN OF THOUGHT AND RUN WITH IT AS
far as they could. Find him. Stop him, and live happily ever after in the
Library gathering overdue books, opening branches, and drinking tea.

Except that seemed like it'd be something the Library would have
already done if it could. And, right then, Quinn needed more information. Acting rashly wasn't an option. Knowledge about what
exactly made up her heritage was too important to push to the side.

It couldn't wait.

"I'm going to put a pin in this brother thing that could be our arch-
nemesis because we have other stuff to address," she said. "But we are
going to come back to this, because . . . that's a bit of information I feel
should have been revealed to me sooner."

The Library chuckled. The sound resonated through the space and
made the lights above them shimmer ever so slightly. "You make a
good point, on all fronts, but right now it's just supposition. I do think
we should have more than just us present to go into detail about my
brother as well as more than just an inkling on my behalf."

Quinn frowned and then nodded. "Fine. Quick segue, are you able
to appear to me like this now because of the excess power that the
Library has?"

"In a manner of speaking," the Library said, "I could always generate this shadow, but in emergency and critical mode, it drains too many resources that are necessary for other functions. Our power levels are stabilized this is now a negligible level of power usage. It allows me some vanity."

"Couldn't you appear as a dragon instead of a person?"

"I could probably form my shadow into a dragon, but no," the Library said, smugly, "I don't want to. I quite like being enigmatic. Don't go around spreading rumors, okay?"

"Well, it's not a rumor if it's true," Quinn said. She could almost feel the glare from the Library this time. "Fine, I won't say anything."

"You said you had other questions? Do they have to do with your family?"

Quinn shook her head. "No, they have to do with everything."

"That's quite an encompassing list."

Aradie punctuated the Library's statement, very unhelpfully, transmitting brief images of the accident Quinn had been in as a child, followed by the magic as it suffused her body when Kajaro chose to try and attack her. Quinn waved the images away. "There's no need to shove them in my face. I remember them very well now."

Aradie cooed slightly apologetically, and Quinn sighed.

"As my owl has attempted to demonstrate, I want to understand what I am and how the hell I survived that accident?" For several seconds, the Library was silent, but Quinn knew it wasn't avoidance. It was simply trying to organize the copious amounts of information and thoughts the Library contained.

"You were created, in theory, because I didn't put it into practice personally, by using part of my initial unmodified-by-anything genetic source material. We all, before the establishment of the Library, took our own samples to be stored, just in case, in the event of a disaster, a fatal injury or something, that we could regenerate aspects of ourselves if necessary.

"There were a lot of reasons to do this, and they were all very good. So, when we were theorizing a possible solution, the idea was that because it's my genetics, whatever we created, whoever we created from it, would also become completely aligned with all affinities, no matter what they were. That due to the proclivity of our heritage for all the affinities including new ones, that the genetic sample would also evolve just as we have and continue to. And thus, the need to specifically locate a Librarian would no longer be necessary." The Library paused for a moment, as if it knew Quinn needed time to digest everything before she could take in more.

It *was* a lot of information, and to be honest, the time given to Quinn to digest it wasn't quite enough before the Library continued.

"However, since you weren't born into dragon form, there were certain other aspects we had to include. We needed to temper the pure affinity compression with mental strengthening, specifically chaotic manipulation abilities are necessary for the cosmicisodracus species, and a magnification of the ability to bind, create, and absorb tomes of magic. That was the theory behind creating a Librarian. We'd exhausted everything else. There were no other options. This was our last hope. And that was before the shutdown."

It was a lot of information to take in. Quinn took her time trying to process that and didn't speak for a bit. "Okay, so I'm not actually blood related to Milaro, right?"

"That's correct. You received what I would call a distillation of the essence of the familial bloodlines' abilities from a few species. Not actually their genetics, but the abilities themselves were refined down to a concentrated form for you, so that we could highlight the specific areas that required strengthening. Given that the disappearance of every single being with Library compatible signatures couldn't have been a coincidence, we realized anyone with those signatures would be placed in imminent danger."

Well . . . the Library wasn't wrong there.

"So I have the Seveshall mind magic line because?" Quinn was trying to grasp the meaning behind each ability.

"To give you greater ability to reinforce your own mind, so that nobody could influence you or target you."

"Did you already suspect that Korradine had been compromised?" Quinn asked.

The Library shrugged its shoulders. "I'm not entirely sure. I think maybe on some level we all did. But we also wanted to find ways to mitigate any possible circumstance changes."

"Okay, I've got that. Who else?"

"Well, you also have the species affinity for chaotic magic, which is ever so slightly different from the cosmicisodracus innate ability. We took that, I believe, and distilled it down from the Darigháhnish line, so you'd have a higher affinity with chaotic energies, and be protected from them. That could even be why you've been having sort of like a radar reaction when you come in the vicinity of those specific tomes that belong in the Restricted Vault."

"Okay," Quinn said, digesting that, trying her best not to drown in the sea of information. Frankly, she was a bit more excited than overwhelmed. Figuring out who and what she was meant she could figure out what she could do and how far she could push. Just how strong could she get? "And I'm guessing, lastly, if you gave me a magical essence ability for the books, you distilled Salosier affinities?"

"Well, like I said not necessarily affinities. You see, people like Narilin, they have this innate ability to manipulate the magic word to . . . well, basically, anyone creating magical tomes, wants a scribe who's a Salosier. We got super lucky that she applied when she did. That probably feeds into your ability from the Darigháhnish as well, allowing you to home in on the books that we didn't even know we'd lost. Does that answer your questions?" the Library asked.

"It answers some of my questions." Quinn mulled everything over. She could understand what they'd attempted to achieve. Magic made so much possible. Even if she was magical, she'd been raised in a world without it. Sometimes it was still difficult to grasp the concept properly. "So far these haven't emerged harmoniously."

"You're the only one of you; I can't tell you how things will mesh completely," the Library said softly, "but you are also sort of a part of me."

"Maybe a bit." Quinn smiled. Perhaps they were family. "But I'm not fully a dragon like you."

"Well, not exactly, because you were created in a different way, but you still have all of the pertinent genetics involved."

Quinn thought that over and finally asked, "How did I survive that car wreck? I mean, I know from the memories that something kicked in and saved me, but it doesn't make sense to me. I know I should probably have died and instead managed to protect myself even though my family didn't make it." That was harder to ask than Quinn realized. She hadn't initially thought about how voicing that question would make her feel. Her stomach tied itself in knots.

"It's pretty simple," the Library said. "You are a dragon. Essentially, at your core. That's what your entire physiology is based on. You've just lived in this form your entire life. There's so much you'll have to learn to understand your powers, like shapeshifting for example. Maybe after the next synchronization. Your body needs to learn to process more power before we can do too much. Some of it may happen instinctively, especially if you're in mortal danger."

"So that means when I was fighting Kajaro, I wasn't actually in danger of dying?" Quinn asked.

"Probably not. If the failsafe didn't kick in, it was unlikely you were in any real danger. Staying in the subconscious like that with no true way to be activated means it's basically on a spring coil—it'll activate when the trigger is flipped. You'd already increased your energy levels after all. But then you would have also given away to him what you are, and that wouldn't have been a good thing."

Quinn nodded, taking all of that in. "Basically, when the car got hit and death was close to certain, *then* the self-preservation kicked in?"

"Exactly. Do you remember when you first got here, and Lynx noticed that your energy levels were higher than expected?"

Quinn nodded. "Yeah."

The Library's shadow leaned forward eagerly. "If you'd never utilized magic before your pool should have been tiny. But not only was it unexpectedly large, but you also already had mana. So, I theorize, that when the shielding triggered it drained every single drop of magic it could from you to fuel that barrier, and thus protect you from imminent death. Because dragons, well, I mean, we probably could die, but you've got to get through a lot of magical protection to kill us. Makes us *mostly* invulnerable."

Quinn pondered that for several seconds. "Do we have weaknesses?"

The Library shook its head from side to side, very slowly, like it was thinking. "We probably do. I'd say we definitely do by now. Everybody's always trying to find ways to kill things that are unkill-able, because then you understand why it's not unkillable in the first place. However, even with my wealth of knowledge, I'm not aware anything other than sheer annihilation.

"Did they come close to it with what they did to the Library?" Quinn asked.

"Not precisely . . . yet I could feel the power fading. It felt wrong." The Library's tone had shifted, and the light dimmed briefly around them.

But Quinn still had so many question. "And you? Are you that intrinsically bound to the Library? Would destroying the Librarian connection seriously ultimately kill you?"

There was another pause before the Library responded. "Well, what would have killed me is if all the filters stopped and the backlash of chaotic energy within the mana pools was magnified by the amount of mana that we have down there. I don't even think I would have survived that sort of eruption. But then again it would be enough to annihilate the pocket dimension and thus I'd have been anni-hilated."

Quinn raised an eyebrow. "And why did you all make it so that a Librarian had to be linked to you?"

"That should be a conversation for another day, Quinn."

"Yes, but I'm here now, and therefore it should be a conversation for now."

Aradie hooted. It sounded more like a laugh. She obviously agreed with Quinn.

A soft sigh escaped the Library before it responded. "The Librarian was introduced so that the Library wasn't above others. By that I mean that I have to work in concert with the Librarian. We must synchronize. We must be on the same page, and we can veto each other. That's important. Important that I don't suddenly go senile and start trying to amalgamate everybody into books. Or that you don't go power crazy and start trying to burn all the books so nobody else gets the information."

"Or get on a power trip about how chaos is so much better and we should destroy the Library and everything it stands for?" Quinn managed to deliver the line in a completely dead pan manner.

The Library chuckled. "Valid point."

Quinn grinned and asked her next question. "How long on average were other people Librarians?"

"Oh," the Library responded, "a few thousand years, some ten thousand or so."

"So was Korradine a Librarian much longer than most?"

"Well, yes, she loved . . . she was a Librarian a lot longer than most people ever made it," the Library said, a sadness underlying the tone. "That's . . . I mean, I knew that, but I didn't really connect the dots properly."

"Sometimes," Quinn said, "it's all about perspective. Right now, I feel like my perspective on our dear Korradine is perhaps a little less biased than yours and Lynx's and everybody else's."

The Library chuckled. "You know, I think it's good that you're here, Quinn."

"Well, that's great because I seem to be stuck here."

"Well then, is that it?"

"Yes, I think so." Quinn paused. "For now."

"I'll summarize for you," the Library said.

"Oh, gee, regale me with your summary."

"No need to be so sarcastic. You are technically a newly improved version of me. You have all of the affinities, and you have complete and utter access throughout the Library to everything, no matter what. You are codified in a way that my own signature recognizes yours on a personal level. There are things you can access that nobody else has been able to access. Maybe even some things I might have forgotten about."

Quinn caught her breath, trying to tamp down on the wave of excitement that began to engulf her. "And where would I find these things?"

"I thought you'd never ask. Once we're in a slightly more stable place, you'll need to visit my vault."

Quinn frowned, confused that the Library appeared to have forgotten something. "I've been to the Restricted Vault."

"No, I mean my vault. It contains the histories of everything, of everyone, and of everywhere, but most importantly, of myself."

"Every when, too?" Quinn asked.

"In a sense," the Library said, "but nothing about the future, sadly."

Quinn felt a lump form in her throat. "Can I bring Lynx with me?"

"Of course you can take Lynx with you. It's not like he's feeding information to anywhere. He's just lacking many of his memories, as am I. Perhaps there's a way you can help piece them together by accessing the vaults."

"Is there a reason you haven't let anybody else consult this vault?"

"Yes," the Library answered vaguely.

"Well, what is it?"

"The vault is an actual part of me. In a sense, a part of the cosmicisodracus heritage. Because you were made from my own genes, you can pass into the vault. I can only allow people I can trust into this space. There is information there that I wouldn't want others, with perhaps less stellar motives, to access." There was an air of vulnerability around the Library for a moment. "Maybe something I have to entrust you with.

"I get it." Quinn nodded. None of them needed anyone else to know how to make the Library feel vulnerable.

2 5

SEVERAL INSTANCES

Milaro looked down the massive conference table in front of him. It was perfectly smooth, ancient wood, the grain bold and beautiful. Twenty chairs ran down each side, his own at the head for a total of forty-one.

He ran a hand through his hair, styled as he usually wore it when conducting official state affairs. A silver circlet sat on the top of his head, just as uncomfortable as always. He'd been wearing it infrequently of late, having spent an inordinate amount of time in the Library.

While he was ecstatic that the Library had returned, he wasn't impressed with the fact that he'd been oblivious to Quinn's existence, even if that meant their enemies also had no idea she existed at all. It didn't matter. He felt like he'd failed as a creator. He wasn't a god; he wasn't under any delusions like that, but he'd put a lot of effort, time, magical research, and probably in Quinn's eyes, scientific research, into creating a being that would circumvent the constant disappearance of potential Librarians.

If she managed to survive until adulthood.

Because the whole point was, there had been plenty of people with the affinity, and suddenly there were none. It didn't take a genius to figure out someone orchestrated the disappearances.

Perhaps her creation wasn't the reason the Library's genetics were sampled, but it ended up being their only option.

Finally, the door at the end of the hall opened and people filed into the room interrupting his train of thought.

Milaro observed them, watching closely as they moved in, speaking to each other in hushed tones, holding folders full of papers as they stuck together in small groups. Quite a few of the council members still preferred to use handwritten documents just to keep things in their head that little bit better.

Milaro looked past them at the gilded walls of the conference hall. It could seat hundreds of people, but right now, the massive thirty-foot ceilings, the arched windows, the beautiful silk drapes, it all felt like such an extravagance in the face of everything else.

In this huge room, there was a long table with enough seats for forty-one people. The council, however, currently only had twenty members, and none of them were the original members. For those longer-lived people, they'd simply retired and passed the responsibility off.

In the case there was no heir? The spot simply faded.

The Seveshall family could almost be traced back as far in the council as its inception. But only almost . . . nothing was as ancient as the cosmicisodracus and the sprites.

Which made him wonder about the Library's siblings. Two of them were hibernating, but none of them knew where. He wasn't even sure if they could be woken should the Library require aid.

"Milaro, are we starting?" Harish asked, speaking softly, oddly impatient for his usual self.

Milaro inclined his head and said, "Just give me a moment, I'm gathering my thoughts. We'll start shortly."

Nobody else paid attention to what Milaro said. They were all busy gossiping, catching up. He wanted to watch them a while longer, see if he could pick up on anything out of the ordinary.

It was always amazing to see the amount of people that came together for this council. However, now, in watching them, Milaro couldn't help but feel like maybe some of them shouldn't be a part of the council. It gave him pause and caution. He watched the Fae Furionas' representative Nishpa, the aunt of Geneva who worked in the Library. He didn't think there was anything going on there, but could he be completely sure?

He'd known her for more years than he could count. But he'd also known Korradine as well, and look at how that turned out.

Knowing the Seveshall had such powerful mind abilities often caused people in his vicinity to obtain items or magic spells or other ways to protect their thoughts from his potential intrusion. Not that he couldn't slip under defenses. But he'd promised himself he wasn't about to intrude on anybody's privacy without permission unless there was a dire emergency or a matter of life and death.

Though technically he guessed he could claim the latter right now on behalf of the entire universe.

None of that felt like any sort of justification for prodding so deep without consent, no matter how much he might want to, just to safeguard everything else.

At least, not yet.

His eyes passed over Ikeshal. He was a satyr. Hal's right hand down in Halschius. It was odd for him to be here and away from his domain. Even when the council was called, he didn't usually strayed far away. Perhaps Uncle Hal, as he was going by now, had more than a passing interest in the current state of the Library. He had seemed to take a liking to Quinn, which was perhaps fortunate. He was the one person Milaro could be certain would never betray the Library.

The Overseer of Halschius knew the stakes better than almost anyone else.

Milaro spied Escadril, a Salosier who only attended intermittent council meetings. Not that the council met very often. It was one of those hereditary things that was passed down to the oldest heir when the previous council member passed away or retired. Part of their function was to monitor the Library's direct spheres of influence and to verify that the mana it filtered met the necessary standards.

If the mana became tainted, repercussions extended to all wielders of magic . . . which was most of the universe.

Right now, there was a lull. The Library had returned and many people were still waiting to see the aftermath caused by its absence.

So, while he set out forty seats, Milaro didn't expect all forty members to attend.

Finally, Dasken, the sedimentite stone species, shuffled in closing the door behind him. That made it everyone Milaro expected. Dasken moved slowly, cumbersomely due to the way his pieces of rock formed together. His beady onyx eyes darted here and there like he was worried he'd be chastised for being tardy.

The old rock man had always been a bit stodgy.

Every single person who filed in was a different species. They represented so many different planets and solar systems. Not every species or region sent a delegate. Milaro thanked whatever fortune had graced him that there were no Serpensiril on the council to start with.

Though, at the same time, that might have been a brilliant way to keep an eye on them. Short of throttling one of them and wringing out of them exactly what their faction was after . . . Milaro knew they couldn't even attempt to read their minds. They'd been far too clever if Kajaro and Tenejo were anything to go by.

Surely it couldn't be as simple as a fanatical need to cull the weak and allow the strong to survive. There had to be so much more to it than that.

Right?

Especially since there was no guarantee it wouldn't wipe out their very own home worlds.

Still, it was time. Milaro cleared his throat. "Let's bring this to order. We have several things to go over right now, including the summary of the Library's return."

Dasken made a rumble in his throat. It was the way he cleared it, which always sounded like rocks grating against one another. The sedimentite lifted an igneous rock-like hand and waved it briefly pulling attention to himself.

"Yes," Milaro said.

"I recall my son returning books." Dasken drawled slowly, his voice gravelly, almost brittle. "Why was the Library offline in the first place? Why could we not access it? What happened? Is it damaged? Should we be looking into alternate filtration methods?"

He spoke each word very deliberately, slowly, almost achingly so.

Milaro filed the question away. Until these literal words, he would have trusted Dasken as far as he could throw him. But something flickered in his aura, an ability Milaro couldn't quite turn off.

It didn't always give him answers, but it was a fairly good judge of something being off or not right. In this case, Dasken's questions weren't borne out of his need to know, but instead a need to ask. Which made no sense, and yet might indicate a level of mind manipulation Milaro hadn't been expecting.

It was something he needed more time to look into, and so he shifted his own perception to begin cataloguing precisely how Dasken, and every other person in the room's auras reacted. It'd take a lot of energy, but be worth it.

"What would make you ask that? We've been monitoring the filtration levels for centuries." Milaro asked, keeping his voice as level as possible so as not to give away his suspicions.

"It was gone for so long, I thought it was destroyed. That perhaps all it left behind were the filters," he grumbled, like a storm in the distance. "The mana quality has been going down for the last several decades, after all."

"You know better than most of us," Milaro said, wondering just how skewed Dasken's perception of time was, "that the Library is nigh indestructible."

Dasken shrugged. "It's not a matter of understanding or believing," he began, his voice echoing in the grand hall. "It's a matter of the fact that the library was gone. Everything can be destroyed. Even my species can be destroyed. Therefore, it's not foreign to assume that something is or was very wrong with the library especially when the mana quality diminished."

Siliqua clucked her tongue, her eyes twinkling with amusement.

"That's a mighty fine observation you've got there, Dasken," she said. "However, I've been working with the Library for the past few months and I can tell you it's fully functional, up and running for both returns and borrowing, believe it or not. It is doing fine. Its functions are still complete. And its filtration systems have been repaired."

Dasken turned his deep black eyes on Siliqua. She smiled, beaming back at him. He shrugged again. "Then that will satisfy my curiosity."

But Milaro still couldn't shake the odd feeling he got from the sedimentite. His aura was practically crackling, but the king couldn't tell why. Yet another thing he was going to have to look into. "Anyway," Milaro said wanting to move the meeting along, "the agenda today is the library and the books that were taken just before it had to close its doors."

"What do you mean, the books that were taken just before it had to close its doors?" That was Nishpa. Geneva's aunt had a very clipped way of speaking and she didn't brook any nonsense whatsoever. However, Milaro knew how to deal with that. They had, after all, been friends for millennia.

"What I mean there are hints of sabotage to the Library's contents shortly before it was forced to temporarily close." He probably should have thought that through before speaking.

Why was it forced to shut down?

I don't understand why it shut down in the first place!

Isn't it supposed to be a universal Library?

I thought the pocket universe kept it separated from everything else?

How are we supposed to guard things if the Library itself can't?"

Everyone spoke at once, and Milaro could feel another headache coming on. He'd been getting them a lot lately. He held up a hand, wondering again if this meeting had even been a good idea. "Please pay extra attention to the outskirts of your territories and neighboring territories. Keep an eye on known problem areas. Any upheaval, any ill-conceived magical ventures, even if it seems mundane at first glance. Let us know so we can look into it." He tried his best to forewarn them while also encouraging them to bring information to him personally—without ever actually giving them sensitive information.

Since he wasn't certain who he could trust, he had to make sure all the information filtered through himself and a select few others.

Spreading himself too thin?

Never.

The rest of the room quieted down, all their attention on Milaro. He didn't particularly want it, but he had it, and for the time being, that would be enough. "The Library, as you've no doubt realized, has repaired its problems. It's returning to full power and you should have noticed the improvement in mana filtration already."

Harish stood up and cleared his throat, allowing Milaro to take a seat. At least having his own right-hand man in the meeting always helped. "The focus right now will be on replenishing the library stocks. We need the council members to return to our usual Library supply contracts. During this last half millennia, and the Library being so quiet, I realize that many of you stopped or minimized production on the items required for the Library trades and the agreed-upon supply lines from the inception of this council. I want to touch base and make sure you have everything you need in order to begin replenishment of the clay blocks, the metal blocks, the malachite crystals, and everything else the Library requires to function at an optimal level."

Nishpa sighed loudly. "You understand mana came dangerously close to being corrupted, right? As fae, we are bound by magic. We can't escape it. Our entire existence relies on it. I have sick children from the contamination that began to seep into the mana when they were born."

"Will they be okay?" Milaro asked, a pang of unease flooding through him.

"Yes. But," Nishpa continued, "it's not the Library's fault. As far as I am to understand it, as my niece briefed me, there is a faction who wants to destroy the Library. Is that correct, Milaro?"

As another wave of rampant questions broke out throughout the room, Milaro wished, for just a second, that he'd pulled Nishpa aside earlier and spoken to her. She was always a little hot headed, strong willed. It was probably part of her charm. Right now, it had been an inopportune statement.

Why haven't you told us this?

I thought that was why we had the council, to protect the Library?

Who on earth would wish for that?

Milaro paused and took in everyone in the room again, noting down those who didn't protest at all, and those who protested too much.

Nishpa met his gaze and gave him an imperceptible nod before he addressed the topic. Ah, that was good to know. She was being deliberately disruptive. He'd have to talk to her after the meeting. "As always, some factions are not in line with the general consensus. This is always to be expected. I apologize for not mentioning it sooner."

"We'll help where we can help. If the Library stops filtering that mana, and we're all in the dark. The gravity of the situation is not lost on us," she said gravely.

Escadril nodded. The boughs on top of his head were massive, like a beautiful oak tree. His nine fingers on each hand tapped gently as he moved them against the wooden table. "My grandniece has been extremely happy working at the library, and yet extremely sad and angry that so many of the books were damaged during its downtime. What can we do, Milaro? Tell us, what do you need from us?"

At that moment, Milaro had to make a very difficult decision. Either he kept everything secret and tried to do everything himself, which was obviously not working out, considering he also had a kingdom to run.

Many of these people had been with him for a long time, a few of them even knew about Quinn. If some of them, one of them, any of them, had been pulling strings behind his back to make the Library collapse, then he didn't know who it was. Wasn't it better to keep enemies closer? And maybe if they knew more, if they thought they were getting away with it, if there was a traitor on the council, then perhaps, just perhaps, they might even slip up.

He made the decision in a split second and turned, "What we need to do is monitor the Serpensiril and the Esposian fae, please, Nishpa."

"My niece has already briefed me on this. We are still in the process of trying to heal the survivors." She sounded sad, but with an underlying tone of anger and determination. That pretty much summed up Nishpa.

Milaro nodded. "We need all of you to keep an eye out. Everybody needs to be alert and vigilant. We are missing several pertinent tomes and have locations for them." He didn't want to let out all of the information, least of all that which painted the Library in a bad light. Even if he knew it would come to the fore eventually, he needed to buy time and at least give them a chance to rectify the situation.

"You have locations?" Ikeshal, the satyr who'd been sent by Uncle Hal, said.

"We have approximate locations."

"Ah," he said, "better than nothing."

Milaro could tell he meant, better than he'd hoped for. "Precisely. Any information on practices that are attempting to halt mana filtration, or disrupt the magical balance we've only precariously maintained is appreciated."

Escadril cleared his throat. "I'll have my aide prepare a report for you. Our scouts have several instances on file that might interest you." He glanced around the room, the leaves in his hair rustling ominously. "After all, we wouldn't want to encourage anyone to destroy the universe."

His flat statement fell across the silent room, but the Salosier's gaze rested on Dasken the Sedimentite, who shifted almost imperceptibly in his seat for a moment, eyes downcast. He didn't say a word.

He didn't really have to.

His aura crackled with static.

Milaro took note and continued on as if there had been no pause at all.

26

IT'S A MYTH

M ILARO LET HIMSELF FALL BACK ONTO THE COUCH, HEAVING OUT A massive sigh. Full council meetings always took it out of him. He much preferred the smaller crisis council they'd convened when the Library couldn't find any compatible affinity signatures.

The members of the latter were people he trusted infinitely.

Or at least, they had been. Recently though, he'd begun to sense changes in several auras like Dasken displayed in the previous meeting.

It was enough suspicion he second guessed everyone now.

"You realize," Harish said, butting into the king's thoughts, "you probably could have handled that a little better."

Milaro shrugged. "You know, I really don't care. It was eye-opening, realizing that Dasken may not be the ally we always thought he was. He's always been a bit of a loner, never overly friendly to any of us. But this, this is just some food for thought. I don't think I have doubts about any of the others, to be honest. You know, we're going to have to analyze everyone, suspect everyone, and hope we're wrong in ninety percent of the cases."

Harish chuckled.

Milaro raised an eyebrow. "Where'd your better half go?"

"She's gone back to the Library. She was running some tests with Cadre." Harish shook his head. "Frankly, she didn't even want to leave there to come for the council meeting, but I convinced her to do so."

"Thanks."

"Don't thank me yet . . . you know she'll get something out of you."

Milaro did, in fact, know that. But the fact still brought a smile to his face. He wasn't sure what he'd do without his childhood friends by his side.

There was a light knock on the door. Milaro sat up so that it didn't look like he had just fallen into the couch, even though he'd gladly do so.

Nishpa opened the door and poked her head around. She was very similar in coloring to her niece. The golden hue of her hair was lighter, more like a smattering of early morning sunlight than the deep golden hair that Geneva had. Her skin also had a polished hue to it, more golden pearl-like than faintly gold like the precious metal. She didn't choose to wear red like Geneva either. Instead, she wore a bright indigo, a striking blue purple that offset everything.

She had more of a mezzo-soprano voice too when she spoke too. Melodic in a lulling way. "Milaro, how long are you going to pretend that you're absolutely okay?"

Milaro raised an eyebrow and chuckled. "I can never pull one over on you, can I?" he said, conscious of the relief he could hear in his own voice. He'd been relying on his mind magic far too much to navigate this current dilemma, and it'd begun to take its toll.

"No, and I don't know why you'd want to." Nishpa hovered into the room and positioned herself on the coffee table to look him directly in the eye as he sat. "You do understand that you hold a lot of the council's responsibilities in the palm of your hand. Not to mention you have your own lands to worry about. You must take care of your health. And right now, well, you're a bit of a wreck, aren't you?"

Her last words were soft, and her half-smile took the sting out of them.

Milaro grumbled slightly, even though he was secretly grateful for the fact that somebody called him on his own bullshit. Lissenia had done so for thousands of years. He felt a pang of loss at her memory. He missed his wife.

"Seriously," Nishpa said, settling down and brushing off her outfit as if there were specks of dust on it. "You know I'm supposed to take care of you. I promised her I would."

"Well, you've been doing a pretty crappy job of it lately, haven't you?" Milaro muttered, only half serious.

Nishpa chuckled. It was like a silvery bell went off in the room. "Oh, I'm so glad to see you still have that same sense of humor I warned her away from. You're no fun."

"No, *you're* no fun." Milaro sighed.

But the fae Furionas grew serious. "Okay, so what's all this about? Why are you . . ." She narrowed her eyes. They did the same thing that Lynx did when he connected to other parts of the system while multitasking.

The color flowed into the sclera, pulsating and half rotating while she inspected him.

Only Milaro knew that Nishpa wasn't looking up information. Instead, she was basically giving him a brain scan. She paused and blinked her vision back to normal. "You've really messed some stuff up in there."

Milaro sighed. He was completely and utterly aware that he'd been somewhat complacent when assisting Quinn at first. While he'd originally suspected her to be their experiment, he hadn't been completely sure. Given the distance, and the lack of communication in the past decades. He just hasn't expected her to appear before him.

"So how did you do that? Tell me before I get angry and just read your mind." Nishpa was becoming irritated.

Milaro raised an eyebrow at her. "You know, you can't get beyond my defenses."

"Are you kidding me?" Nishpa said. "Have you seen the tatters of your defenses lately?"

"What do you mean?" Milaro paused and looked inward. It took but a split second for him to realize what she was saying. His own walls *were* in tatters. "Damn it," he said. "I didn't . . . is this? Oh, no."

"What is it this time, Milaro?" Harish said, as if this times were a regular occurrence.

"It's just . . . Kajaro's mind bomb for Quinn, for want of a better word, was well placed. We had to contain it to an extent where when it exploded in on itself, it didn't take her entire mind with it. I didn't realize it nicked my defenses as well. Did it let him in?" Milaro muttered to himself, suddenly a hint of panic in his voice.

He took a second to center himself, only just realizing how tired he'd become. His energy reserves, magic reserves, and hell—his mental reserves were all running low. If he didn't take the time to recuperate, he was going to put a lot more than just himself in danger.

"I have to check," Milaro said. He raised his legs up, crossed them, and sat, eyes closed, taking in deep breaths while he focused his attention inward to himself and all of his defenses. The thing was, Milaro's mental defenses didn't only encompass his own mind. They were directly linked to the entire Areiltháhnish defenses. It was simply the way the Areiltháhnish king approached everything. A familial bond with basic mind magic superpowers that made sure the entire society remained protected.

And, where possible, extended out to protect anyone and everyone he could.

He was shocked to find the crack.

A crack that Nishpa saw while he himself remained oblivious. While it raised concern that he hadn't noticed it himself, he did realize that Nishpa was one of the foremost experts in mind medicine. Still, he opened his barriers with a sigh and began to repair the crack. It didn't try to resist him. There was no residue around it. There was no hint that anything had escaped into his mind. Simply that there was a blemish there to begin with was worrisome enough.

One that got past his usually meticulous maintenance too.

He paused and opened one eye, looking directly at Nishpa. "I don't suppose you'd fancy a look in just to double check with me that I haven't accidentally allowed detrimental leeway?"

"I thought you'd never ask. I was going to do it anyway." She smiled gently at him, not voicing the danger implied in Milaro's request.

He took both of her tiny hands in one of his, the connection solidifying when she peered into his mind.

Her presence felt less like a runaway freight train, which was a very accurate description of Quinn's, and more like a gentle summer breeze with pale golden lights trickling through. It soothed everywhere it touched, and he was grateful he hadn't realized quite how stressed he'd become since the Library reopened. Since he'd discovered the potential conspiracy behind why the Library had closed in the first place. And since he'd realized that if they couldn't protect Quinn until she came into her own powers properly, everything in the universe was still doomed, and the experiment meant nothing.

After all, they didn't have the time to do it again.

Careful, Nishpa's voice spoke into his mind. *You're walking the edge pretty finely here, my friend. You can't take everything on your shoulders. Haven't we discussed this before?*

There's just suddenly so much to do. I wasn't expecting it to blow up to this extent. Milaro felt whiny, but it also released an unbelievable pressure in his mind to simply tell someone else the extent of things.

On the bright side, we have the Library back and you should be patting yourself on the back for that accomplishment, because without your tenacity and insistence, it wouldn't be here. So just take it easy. Your grandson's depending on you.

Milaro let out a soft, low sigh. *Well, he's not the only one, but my other son and grandchildren are neither here nor there right now. I just . . .*

Hasn't he come back? I mean, it's been a decade. He's technically in line for the throne.

Technically, I'd prefer to give it to Malakai right now.

Nishpa tsked under her breath. *Ah, never mind. I am going to ignore that for now, and you need to be quiet. I've almost got this.*

Milaro went silent again, letting his thoughts simply flow. But they kept returning to the Library and who the hell partnered with the Serpensiril? He had suspicions, especially based on the new map information he'd received from Lynx. He didn't like any of it. People who'd been their allies for hundreds of thousands of years. Had they ever really been allies? He couldn't be sure anymore. Finally, he felt Nishpa's presence wane and disappear.

He finished patching up the crack in his mind, refreshed his entire network of mental protections, extending out to refresh the connection to the kingdom's defenses, and finally opened his eyes again.

"Oh, that's much better," Nishpa said, scanning him once again. "Now you look almost like the Milaro I know, except for the obvious preoccupation. Stop letting it get to you, we'll figure it out."

"But we didn't, Nishpa. We let it get to a stage, without even realizing it, that the Library had to shut down. We had no solution, no other way to perform the filtration the universe literally needs. To top it off, now it seems as though, well, look at it." He gestured around vaguely. "People we'd never have suspected in a million years may have been pretending for a million years to be our allies. This is not a good thing."

"You need to stop jumping to conclusions," Nishpa said. Harish grunted his approval.

"I'm calm, I'm just frustrated. This isn't how it was supposed to go."

"Well, how was it supposed to go, Milaro?" she asked, crossing her arms. "You tell me. How was this world supposed to go?"

"Well, everybody was supposed to just want to learn magic and do good with it, and like sunshine and lollipops." He bit off his sarcasm and continued softly. "But this is so much bigger than that."

"It is. But you know, I've already dispatched some, shall we say, observers. It's okay. Dasken won't get away with anything if he's one of them."

"But won't he notice?"

"No, he won't notice what I've done. He rarely notices anything not integrally tied to rock formations." Nishpa winked at Milaro.

"Then I look forward to your report. Or not. I'm hoping it eliminates him as a threat."

"Either way, there'll be some elimination." This time she grinned, and it held a positively sinister air.

"You know, Nishpa, I try to take you seriously all the time, but that line coming from you is just adorable."

"How many times have I told you not to call me adorable?" She stomped her foot on the table for emphasis.

"A lot," he said and smiled. "Thank you, my friend, for checking up on me and making me feel better."

"Do you think, Milaro, that this Librarian would be eager to see me? We did so much work to bring her here." She smiled a little sadly.

"What do you think Dasken would do if he knew what we'd done to bring a Librarian to the Library?" Milaro asked suddenly.

Nishpa paused, giving her answer some real thought. "I'm not sure. After all, it was only a few of us who did it."

"True. Nobody ever likes to go and speak with the Core. It has a way of looking into your soul and that medicine is hard on your body. I guess we'd have found out sooner if he was an ally or a traitor. I'm not wrong, right?" Milaro said. "I mean, it was pretty weird the way he acted in today's meeting."

"Oh, no, you definitely weren't wrong," Harish said. "Even Siliqua noticed it. Sometimes she can be oblivious, especially when she's thinking about new ways to apply specific technologies. But this . . . it's like there's something foreign in his aura."

Milaro stood and began pacing around his antechamber. "Okay, well, I'm going to need some help. I can't expect the Librarian to do everything. She's new. She's got what, thirteen or fourteen thousand books that have been overdue for five hundred years and need to be returned. She has, I think, five more branches to open. She has to figure out what to do with a Serpensiril hostage they've got. Not to mention, she needs to learn more books, get more magic, gain more power." He paused in frustration at the list. "I can't give her more to do. The list is huge. You don't even understand. Plus, she's got to go see my daughter-in-law."

"Oh, wow. She's got to go and see Arnekai?" Nishpa asked, her voice trembling ever so slightly. "That is—oh, are you sure that's a good idea?"

"Well, it has to be a good idea. Malakai's going with her, luckily."

"Are you sure that's *luckily*?" Nishpa asked incredulously. "He gets on with his mother about as well as dry grass and a spark."

"Well, I mean, you're not wrong," Milaro said, feeling somewhat defeated. "Look, there's nothing I can do. She has her heart set on solving five thousand problems. The thing is, I don't want her to know that there's five thousand and ten, so how about we just take the remaining ones off her?"

"Okay, what's your plan?" Nishpa said. "I promise I won't let Geneva know. She's currently not in a good state. The discovery of the Esposians and the subsequent inability to make their ailments magically disappear has thrown her for a loop. She's been tending to them in their homeland for weeks now. They've been infected for what I believe is centuries. That particular settlement was practically wiped out, or controlled. We've sent more people to investigate some of the islands, but so far it's looking bleak. We can't allow this to happen again. So what do you propose, Milaro? You have our full backing." Her words had lost their playfulness. She was serious now.

"Quinn needs to speak to the Esposians at some stage, likely soon. I'd like to have that organized for her so that she has to do as little of the work as possible."

"And what should we do? Not everybody is aware of the council. Most people think it's a myth." Nishpa said.

Milaro shrugged. "Your guess is as good as mine, but you're also pretty high up in the Furionas fae, and so I would think you should be able to pull some rank there. Plus, I mean, it's not like you can't drop my name too."

"Very well. I'll start looking into it and applying a bit more pressure than I have been. I'm extremely concerned because even with my healing abilities, it's taking these Esposians a lot longer to recover than I would have thought." Nishpa sounded worried. "Their torment spirals run deeper, and we will make someone pay for it as soon as I know who to target."

Milaro nodded solemnly. "But for now, let's not let her know that either."

"Very well." Nishpa inclined her head and launched into the air. "I'll be in touch."

Milaro watched one of his oldest friends leave, his mind overrun with the sheer magnitude of work they had to do. He was grateful to have her in his life, and yet concerned that he somehow hadn't detected the crack in his mental defenses before she did.

27

PERPETUAL TWILIGHT

QUINN EMERGED MOSTLY REFRESHED FROM HER CHAT WITH THE LIBRARY Core. Armed with more information and understanding of what she was, of what it meant to be the Librarian, she felt much better about herself.

Even if completely out of her depth.

She stretched her arms out in front of her and cracked her knuckles. Her neck ached a little and she felt stiff, and hungry.

Very hungry.

It was already past midday, and she was starving. She headed over to the kitchen, wondering exactly how she was going to access the vault and just when she'd have the time to.

All you have to do is ask, the Library said, *and to be honest, right now, it's not a big rush. I just wanted you to be aware.*

I know, Quinn replied, *but I just, you know, I like to think about things.*

You like to think about way too many things sometimes. Maybe let me do the thinking for you sometimes.

Quinn laughed and waved at Cook who simply, wordlessly, handed her a plate full of what looked like potatoes and sausage gravy. Quinn could practically taste it already.

"Thank you," she said. Cook simply flashed her a grin.

"Now where was I?" Quinn muttered to herself. She put a plate down, sat down, and took two beautiful, delicious mouthfuls of food. The potatoes were perfectly crispy on the outside and soft and fluffy on the inside. And the gravy complemented them wonderfully.

Suddenly, Malakai sprinted up to her table and slammed his hands down on it.

"Why are you in such a rush?" she asked, looking up at him, only very slightly irritated by the interruption of her meal.

"My mother is waiting for us." he gasped out, still trying to regain his breath. There was a strange quality to his eyes. As if he was a caged animal looking to escape.

She cocked her head to one side and gave him a really long look. He seemed to be sweating slightly. In all their training together, in the few fights they'd been in together, even when they fought that bloody tree, she'd never once noticed Malakai sweat. Granted, she wasn't always looking to see if he was sweating, but she tended to notice a lot about him.

"Are you okay?" she asked.

He practically flopped onto the bench on the other side of the table and shrugged. "I don't know," he said, and he seemed super worried. That little line between his eyebrows was totally pinched.

Quinn took another bite and thought over his words. "I think you're worried about seeing your mother."

He glared at her sullenly. "Really, Quinn? That took you all of ten seconds to deduce, right?"

"There is no need to get snarky with me." She grinned at him, knowing she'd figured him out eventually.

He sighed. "You're right, I'm just, I'm not . . . I don't think I'm ready to see her."

"What do you mean you don't think you're ready to see her? You probably have a lot to say to her, right?" Quinn asked gently.

He groaned in frustration. "Oh, you wouldn't believe it. I have a lot I need to get off my chest."

"Well, isn't this the perfect time, then?" she asked between bites of food.

"No, Quinn, it's not the perfect time. We have other things we have to ask my mother. More important things."

"What, and your childhood trauma isn't important?" Quinn said, "I think you've got that a little bit back to front, Malakai."

He sighed and leaned back. "I actually think I prefer you calling me Mal."

"Mal? Mal it is, then. It's pretty easy for me to do. It's also truncated and not three syllables long. I like that." She smiled, trying to make him feel more at ease even if she was fairly certain it would take her ages to remember to just call him Mal consistently.

He chuckled. "See, I knew you'd make me feel better."

"Always." She paused, chewing another bite. "You should go get some of this. Potatoes and I think it's biscuit gravy, but I'm not sure. Whatever it is, Cook, as per usual, has completely captured my taste buds."

Malakai chuckled and Quinn began to finish off her food as he went to get his own. He plopped back down as she'd almost finished.

"So," she said, "you feeling a bit better now?"

"Marginally, still stressed. We have a lot to do before we go and see my mom, I guess."

"Define, 'we have a lot to do.'" She raised an eyebrow.

"Well, you see, my home world, or my mother's home world, or however you want to put it, has very thick oxygen. There's a couple of books you need to absorb so it's easier for you to breathe and it won't exhaust you. If you're trying to process the weight of that oxygen on your own, it will likely make you extremely… hmmm euphoric I think is the term."

"Okay," Quinn said, raising an eyebrow. "Did you happen to know the names?"

"Yes. We returned all of our books so it should be in the collection."

That took Quinn by surprise. "Did you have a lot of them? I didn't realize. I thought you guys only had the combat one."

"Well, that one was a restricted book and my grandfather was stressed about not having returned it to the Library in the last five hundred years." Malakai shrugged. "We had like three or four others out. We returned them the first day."

"Oh, fantastic." Quinn smiled as she cleaned her plate. "What's it called?"

"It's a really boring title, Quinn. It's just *Air Density Manipulation: Facts and Findings*."

"Oh," Quinn said. "You're right, that is a pretty boring title. I thought you guys were all about interesting and captivating titles."

"Yeah, mostly. Sometimes I think the authors just wanted to get the books out there with as relevant a title as they can."

Half an hour later, after they'd both eaten, Quinn sat in her office with the book open in front of her. Splaying her hands on either side of the open book, she breathed out and back in to absorb all the knowledge contained within. There was a lot about micro-density, about how the air moved in and out of her lungs, how to adjust it before it entered.

It was a lot of work to process the information, but there were spells she could activate that would simply take care of it for her. "Modify" seemed like a good trigger word. "Thinning" seemed like something out of a horror novel. So she concentrated on "Modify" and the spell cast. It didn't do anything, but she could tell that there was this faint filter over her mouth and nose where she'd take in the air.

"Well," she said, "that was anticlimactic." And she closed the book and pushed it away.

Aradie swooped down, sat on her shoulder and chatted in her ear. "You know I can't understand you when you coo and hoot as well as I can when you actually speak into my mind, right?"

Aradie shook her feathers.

"Well, are you up for going to this world?"

Aradie raised an eyebrow. It was very disconcerting seeing an owl raise an eyebrow, but it was also very effective. Quinn leaned back and sighed. It was still early afternoon. She didn't really have a reason to put off going to see Malakai's mother today. Speaking of the devil, she knew he was approaching. She thought he had a backpack or two in hand as well.

Her senses, as far as the Library interior was concerned, extended easily now, but they still weren't as detailed in information as she'd have liked.

Yet.

"Oh, is there going to be hiking involved?" she asked the empty room. But even Aradie only gave her a side-eye.

He knocked on the door but walked straight in since it was open. "I've got our supplies."

"Supplies? What do we need supplies for?" Quinn asked, slightly suspicious.

"Well, you know, food just in case and because Cook also loves to cook for you. I'm not sure Darigháhnish cuisine will be your forte." He offered an apologetic smile. "It's barely something I can stomach myself. Anyway, there's also a change of clothes each. I just had the Library give me one of your outfits and that's about it."

"Do you think we'll be there for a long time?" Quinn asked.

Malakai shook his head emphatically. "Not if I have anything to do with it. We'll be there for the bare minimum. I don't enjoy visiting the Espinar Peninsula region. It is not my favorite place. There's something about it that always sets my teeth on edge."

A shudder ran down Quinn's spine. He hadn't even said that about the destroyed Debilian Homeworld.

"Okay, so maybe two days?" Quinn asked.

"We should probably leave now," he said, evading the question.

"Are you okay, Mal?" Quinn asked, actually concerned now.

"Look, this is probably as hard for me as going home was for you. Except I haven't seen my mother in a decade, and we've never been on the best of terms as it is." He paused and took a breath. "I'm glad you're going with me. I think it'll make it a little easier. But I should forewarn you that I'll probably be extra . . ."

"Moody?" Quinn offered."

"Yeah, 'extra moody' is a good way to put it." He chuckled softly.

"Okay, I can put up with that," she said.

Malakai offered her a soft smile. "Thanks, Quinn."

"Anytime. I mean, you even packed for me." A thought struck Quinn even though it was still early afternoon. "Should we wait until the morning to go?"

Malakai blinked at her. "Well, it *is* the morning there, right now."

"Oh," Quinn said, having completely and utterly forgotten that the same time zone wouldn't be applicable everywhere in the universe. "That's a good point. Okay, so oxygen modulation in place. I guess you know where to open the door to, right?"

"Let's just let Lynx know we're going." Mal seemed torn between wanting to go and wanting to procrastinate.

Quinn cocked her head to one side. She was pretty sure Lynx knew they were going, but common courtesy dictated they should probably let him know in detail. Also, it seemed like Malakai wasn't quite ready to go anywhere yet.

He was stalling.

She could let him do that for a bit.

"Well, he's at the front counter, and you know I like to exit through the main doors."

Malakai chuckled. "Don't forget to hover when we go over the threshold, eh?"

"I won't. No more falling on my face!" She glanced down at her jeans and shirt. "Am I dressed appropriately? Jeans? Boots?"

"Yeah." He glanced at her and shrugged. "I mean, you'll do."

"I'll do?" she asked skeptically.

"You're not prone to wearing the same type of clothes I do."

"That's true," she said as they walked through the Library to the front desk. Lynx stood deep in conversation with Eric and Dottie. "Lynx, we're heading out then."

He turned and raised an eyebrow. "I know."

"I know you knew, but we thought we'd tell you anyway," Quinn said.

"Just be careful, Quinn. Don't . . . just be careful," he said, his expression softening somewhat.

"I will," she said. And with that, Malakai opened the double doors, and they stepped through without any problems at all. It was dark beyond the doors. Dimmer than she'd expected for somewhere where it was supposed to be morning.

"Why is it so dark?" she said, as the doors closed behind them, cutting off any light source from the Library.

"It's not dark. Oh," Malakai said as he turned to her. Then he blinked. "Sorry, that was remiss of me. I guess it is for most people. I kind of forget that a lot. Still, it's not as dark as you think. This is just our daytime."

"But it looks like twilight." Quinn gestured around them to the dim lighting and shadowed surroundings.

"Our daytime is sort of like a perpetual twilight, the way our suns and moons work. They're more lunar based than solar. The system is very unique."

"You said it was the Espinar Peninsula?" Quinn asked, determined to look up books on it when she got back. If there was any magic involved in the region, they always had information on it. Perhaps it was a good idea to get some informational sources into the Library that weren't involved with magic.

Maybe it'd be a good idea to get several new, mundane areas in the Library. Probably some therapy books with the mounting violence. Some entertainment, some plain fiction. Good old escapism. She shook the irrelevant thoughts out of her head. But then if this place was a peninsula . . . "Your tides must be kind of crazy here."

He nodded. "You have no idea. Luckily, it's the wrong season for you to witness just how crazy it can be."

She grinned and now her eyes had adjusted, she realized they stood in a small clearing in a large forest. But not like one she'd ever been in before. In between the massive black tree trunks, she could see and the deep green, and she was fairly certain some of the leaves were blue, Quinn could see twinkling lights not far off.

"This is an interesting town," she said cautiously.

"Well, it's not the town yet. That's, um . . . that's a little bit farther ahead. I didn't want to appear directly in the middle of town," he said sheepishly. "This way, it gives us a few moments to acclimate to the different air texture and that way we're not going to get blindsided by my mother immediately."

Quinn could tell this was taking its toll on her friend. "It's okay, Mal, we've got this."

He grinned at her. She squeezed his hand and let go. "See, I'm right here, so are you. We're fine."

He raised an eyebrow.

"A little bit too far?" she asked.

"Yeah, a little bit too much." He chuckled. "But appreciated."

"Well you know, you win some . . ."

Malakai actually laughed. "Thanks, Quinn. Thank you for grounding me and letting me realize that not everything needs to be serious a hundred percent of the time."

"Stick with me, kid," she said and the levity helped them both get rid of some tension.

As they began to walk toward the smattering of lights ahead of them, the trees moved in ways Quinn wasn't used to trees doing. The way the branches and leaves stirred, they almost seemed alive. It was a little bit scary, this perpetual twilight, this area of trees that almost seemed tormented.

"It's the chaos magic," Malakai said softly, answering her unasked question. "It's not everywhere, but it is there. Just little bits seep in through to us here. The Espinar Peninsula is known for that. Anybody who lives here, which is basically all of the Darigháhnish, has come to terms with how to function and become adept at living with it. Frankly, we thrive. I've spent relatively little of my life here, maybe five years when I was very young. I can innately manipulate the chaotic energy in my surroundings; it's a species-specific skill. I don't mean to do it. I don't even think about doing it, but I do perform these little intricate spells, I guess, or little intricate diversions so that chaos can't consume me. It's an innate trick we learn to unlock. It's why you received some of the Darigháhnish innate ability filtered down as well. My grandfather explained that to me too. You know, right?"

"Yeah, I know. Distilled essences of the Seveshall bloodline and distilled essences of the Darigháhnish species traits, and I think

Salosier is in there somewhere too. Don't worry, I'm a bit of a mixing pot." Quinn stopped walking for a moment and winked at him to make sure he understood she was fine with things.

He laughed and smiled, and then the expression on his face went blank. Quinn turned to see where his gaze landed. Directly ahead of them, their path opened out into a beautiful, wondrous tree city.

It was breathtaking. Nothing like the Esposians'. The city had dwellings down at the bottom, and in the trees, everywhere. Light shone through myriad windows at all differing heights, flicking like joyous fairy lights were dancing around. There was a bustle of people as well.

Well, except for the one who stood directly in front of Malakai and herself.

She was taller than him, almost as tall as Milaro, perhaps just shy of seven feet. Her stark, white, long hair fell all the way down her back in thick waves, and she wore hunter's garb that clung to her body, leaving little to the imagination. Her darker, almost navy skin stood out in stark contrast to the white eyes that matched her hair.

And when she spoke, even the trees shivered. "You are late, Malakai."

Then she turned that imposing gaze on Quinn. "I am Arnekai, and you are?"

Quinn had never felt so intimidated in her life.

28

CHILDHOOD ADVENTURES

Funnily enough, Quinn had pictured this moment in a variety of ways, but for the life of her, she couldn't think how to approach it now that it was happening. She'd wanted to say something like, *Well, I'm the bloody Librarian,* but that felt a little too cocky for this situation. Instead, she gave a sort of half-smile and said, "I'm Quinn. I'm the new Librarian."

It was like night and day on Malakai's mother's face. Arnekai's imposing gaze disappeared and when she smiled, and it was as if the entire woods lit up. It was such a beautiful expression.

It took away all of the sinister air, all of the trepidation Quinn had felt, and put her at ease. That's when she remembered that the Darigháhnish had an innate mind-soothing ability, and she made sure to strengthen the wards protecting her own.

"I've been dying to meet you. I've heard so much about you," Arnekai said, her smile reaching her eyes.

Quinn was mildly confused. "You've heard about me from . . . ?"

"Well, you know, grapevines being what they are, and people do talk. They talk a lot about you. You're apparently very nice." Arnekai gave a little wink.

Quinn couldn't take a step back because Malakai was directly behind her, but she wanted to. She smiled, not knowing quite how to take the compliment. "Um, thanks," she said.

Arnekai laughed, and it was a beautiful sound, just as amazing as she looked when she smiled. The transformation that came over Malakai's mother was decidedly odd. Like she was two different people.

"Anyway, has Malakai been giving you any trouble?" she asked, winking at Quinn.

Quinn took a step to the side and looked between the son and the mother, and patted Malakai on the shoulder. "See, I told you it wouldn't be that bad."

He sent a ferocious scowl in her direction, and didn't say a word.

Instead, Quinn answered the question. "He's never been any trouble."

"Well, that's wonderful, isn't it," Arnekai said. "Come on, come, come, I've prepared a lovely morning feast. I thought you'd really enjoy sampling some of our food."

Quinn glanced at Malakai, who simply shook his head almost imperceptibly, and followed after his mother. Quinn didn't have to run to catch up, but the underbrush did give her some pause. Roots broke the surface here and there just enough to lend caution to her steps.

Pale blue and purple light streamed off Arnekai, sometimes mixed with the occasional white brightness. It lit the way better than the twilight that permeated the rest of the woods. Quinn sensed the people all around them. They looked at them, the curiosity in their eyes practically breaking through her skin. She locked her gaze directly on Arnekai's back and followed, lest she either lose her temper or embarrass herself.

They made their way to one of the houses built into the trunk of a massive tree. It wasn't anything like the redwoods in California, but it reminded Quinn of them, size-wise. However, the coloring was all wrong. Blacks and blues, deep greens and purples.

She followed Arnekai onto what appeared to be a sort of patio. It had a table, multiple chairs, with an awning overhead bedecked with tiny lights. Food Quinn couldn't identify by sight was arranged in different dishes spread out on the table and it smelled fantastic. All these different scents mingled together to make what Quinn thought of as absolutely appetizing.

Malakai's scowl, however, had deepened further.

Arnekai gestured to a seat on her left and Quinn took it. "So, Miss Librarian, tell me all about yourself."

"I'm Quinn. The Library found me and now I'm a Librarian." She wasn't exactly sure what to say except the bleeding obvious. She didn't want to give anything away about her heritage or where she'd lived. And nothing in her past life was particularly relevant here anymore.

Arnekai's eyes widened slightly with surprise. "Well, that's a little bit dull. What did you do before this?"

"I was studying to be a librarian . . ." Quinn said, realizing that maybe this was a huge step up from her life on Earth. Not that she hadn't already realized that. Libraries on Earth had nothing on this one. She had to admit to being pretty lucky that the Library found her even if a part of her wondered about what would have happened if it hadn't. Would her mythical side ever have been unlocked? Would she be traveling through dimensional doors? Nope, probably not. "Yeah, I've always loved books."

"That seems very interesting." Arnekai didn't sound like she meant it at all. "And tell me, what planet was it again?"

"A non-magical planet. It was lucky that they found me," Quinn said. For some obscure reason, she still didn't feel like giving out all of the information, even if this was Malakai's mom.

"It's okay, Quinn. She knows," Malakai said, his voice strained.

"Oh, you know," Quinn said. If Arnekai already knew, that was a different story. Even if she kind of wished it wasn't so.

"Who do you think gave them the Darigháhnish essence to distill? I had to extract it myself. And I had to make sure it came from the most reliable sources. It's a very difficult thing to do. Milaro should have told you this." Arnekai sighed, but there were no theatrics to it this time. "He's never been overly fond of me, or my kind."

"Stop it, Mom." Malakai snapped. "You know the reasons Grandfather isn't fond of you."

"Well, of course I do, but he's also extremely mistaken and has always been so very judgy." A smile played across her lips before she continued. "You've always been my little snuggums. You know I adore you. But there are just so many reasons why you couldn't come and be with me. And we all know that I'm right."

"Really, Mom? Really?" Malakai crossed his arms. "You're right all the time?"

"Well, yes, actually. As it turns out, if your father had listened to me, he'd still be here." All of Arnekai's levity was suddenly gone, and her tone could have cut through stone.

Malakai pushed his chair back so fast it fell over and stood, glaring at his mother. "That's not fair. You know it wasn't his fault."

"No, dear, it wasn't his fault. But he shouldn't have died and left us alone. He shouldn't have been there in the first place. I warned him about the dangers, and he went anyway. Now he's gone." All emotion disappeared from Arnekai's expression.

Quinn was overcome with fascination as she watched them discuss the subject as if she wasn't there. Arnekai's whole demeanor had changed. She was serious, not intimidating this time, but there was a melancholy that swept over her, through her. It was infectious. It hurt Quinn in her chest like it was attacking her heart. There was no doubt Mal's mother was deeply affected by whatever had happened to his father.

The woman sounded distant as she spoke. "You don't know the half of it, son. You have no idea what we went through to get to that stage and how much I pleaded with him not to go."

"But he had to, Mom. It was important." Even Malakai sounded defeated.

"Yes, but we were important too. At least. We should have been." Arnekai ran a hand through her magnificent hair. The only sign of frustration she showed. "And now, now I have other responsibilities that pull me away and I can't be with you the way you need me to. Don't mention your father again. I do not wish to speak of him."

And then, as if night was changing into day, the melancholy sensations suffusing the area dropped and were replaced by that brightness once again. She turned to Quinn. "I'm terribly sorry to bore you with our family drama, but you are, while not related by blood, sort of family, considering Milaro's little experiment. Now, tell me, how well has Snuggum's been doing? Or would you like to hear about some of his childhood adventures first?"

Quinn thought that given enough time, she might get along very well with Arnekai, as long as she didn't mention Malakai's father.

Ever.

Malakai, on the other hand, didn't seem to be vibing with his mother in any way whatsoever. He glowered in the corner, irritated and angry at her if Quinn was any judge. Still, they had come for her help, and Quinn wasn't about to blow that deal.

She smiled gently, determined not to waste this trip. "We did have some questions about Ardenil, your great-aunt, I believe it was."

That's when Arnekai's countenance changed slightly again. She glanced at Quinn, her expression closed off. "I do not wish to talk about that yet. We will have a nice breakfast, some good discourse, and then we will see."

Quinn felt pressure against her, as if Arnekai was trying to coax her into doing what she wanted. However, Quinn wasn't easily coaxed anymore, but she did understand the reticence to talk about something one wasn't comfortable with yet. After all, they'd only just met, so Quinn couldn't exactly blame her.

A small smile softened Arnekai's face. "Now, I thought you might like to hear some stories about when Malakai was a little snuggums."

Quinn grinned, despite the thoughts echoing around in her head. Surely they could offer Arnekai a few hours of company, considering she seemed to miss her son more than Malakai let on. Even if there was something about her that set Quinn's teeth on edge.

Maybe he missed her more than he'd let on, too, although she wasn't entirely sure. Her reasoning for leaving him behind didn't seem to wash well with Quinn. It made her wonder what the real reason was, because this seemed quite selfish and fabricated.

She wanted to know more, but was quite certain after this first encounter that Arnekai wasn't about to elaborate. So she just widened her smile. "Sure, tell me stories. I can always use more ammo to tease him with."

Arnekai chuckled. "Yes, that's a very healthy friendship to be able to make fun of one another and know that you're safe." She sighed, another pensive sound from her. Perhaps Malakai reminded her too much of her dead husband. Arnekai's dazzling grin was back. "You see, when he was four, Malakai picked up his first bow . . ."

"Oh no," Malakai groaned. "You're not going to tell her this one, are you?"

"Eventually, I will tell her all of the stories, my little snuggums." Arnekai grinned impishly. "I've got a feeling Quinn will be around for a very long time."

"You know she will," he said irritably, even though a small smile ticked up the corners of his mouth. "You know she's going to be here for ages. It's not like she's got a specific lifespan anymore."

"Well, provided you can power her up in time." Arnekai pulled herself back and squinted at Quinn. "Right now you're still pretty weak."

"Thanks," Quinn said dryly. Stating the bleeding obvious seemed to be a skill a lot of people had.

"I don't mean that in a bad way. It's just that you have access to so much power." Arnekai gestured all around them, vaguely, in an encompassing way. "You have the ability to absorb more power than I've ever seen before."

She squinted at Quinn this time, really as if she was looking over her, into her, through her. "Yes. Oh dear. You are a bit of a conundrum, aren't you? The Library has its hands full."

Quinn scowled. "I thought we were talking about Malakai, not about me."

"You're new and interesting. New and interesting is always my thing." Arnekai winked at her once again.

There was a loud rumble off in the distance. Arnekai's eyes

narrowed, and for a moment her eyes flickered. And then the smile was back, almost like it never left.

"Anyway, when he was four, Malakai picked up a bow for the very first time. You know, he had little"—she sort of measured out a short length with her hands—"arms and they didn't reach everything very well. But he insisted he wanted to learn how to shoot that bow. His father taught him. And well, he was so proud when he came to show me that he got really excited and accidentally shot his dad in the butt. It was the funniest thing, Quinn. Miyago was hopping around, yelling and cursing, saying 'Ouch.' Malakai stood there, put the bow down and screamed loudly and started sobbing. Have you ever heard my son scream?"

Quinn shook her head, fighting the urge to smile, but she couldn't help herself. The story was ludicrous, and Malakai's expression was the icing on the cake. His skin had a beet-red undertone, so embarrassed. Quinn needed to keep this in her pocket for a future time.

"I have *not* heard him scream," Quinn said, fighting the urge to giggle.

"Well," Arnekai said, glancing over at her son, "I don't think he'll offer to do so right now."

Malakai sighed as if he couldn't win and then chuckled. "You're very right."

"I doubt my son will offer to show us how he screamed back then." She needled him, a smile on her face. "Still, his voice is a little deeper now. It wouldn't have quite the same effect. It was wonderful, though. It drew half of the village to us. And my poor husband had to yank the arrow out of his butt cheek. It didn't take long to heal. He had innate healing powers. It's a pity Malakai didn't inherit it."

"Hey, I got some of his healing ability, okay?" Malakai said defensively. "I can heal small injuries."

"Yep," Quinn said, "he's actually helped me a couple of times."

"That's refreshing." Arnekai didn't sound like she meant that at all. "He's actually helped somebody, not just stayed in a study or in a training hall."

"I've actually been quite active since Quinn arrived." Now he sounded indignant.

"Really? Has Milaro let you out of your cage?" Arnekai's scorn was barely concealed. Quinn suppressed a cringe.

There was a lot more in that statement to unpack than Quinn was willing to dive into. But right now, probably wasn't the time to bring that up.

Malakai crossed his arms and stood proud. "Grandfather has apprenticed me to the Library. I am Quinn's trainer."

"You're training the Librarian." Arnekai's words were full of derision.

The little bit of the tolerance she'd won from Quinn vanished. She shouldn't be deriding her child like that. Malakai had been integral in her acclimation to the Library and everything it needed from her.

"Yes, Mother, I'm training Quinn. You haven't seen me for ten years. You have no idea what I'm capable of anymore." There was an edge to his voice that hadn't been there before.

Arnekai leaned back in her chair. Her eyes focused on her son, her expression actually serious. She wasn't taking the mickey out of him this time. "Very well, you've made your point. Perhaps later, you will show me some of the improvements. I would like to see that."

"You would like that, would you?" Malakai said, his tone heated. "It's supposed to be all to your convenience, is it, again? Look, we came here for a reason. You don't have to pretend to be the perfect mother."

"I've never pretended to be the perfect mother. All I've ever done is try to show you that I love you," Arnekai snapped, her beautiful face twisted ever so briefly in what looked like pain.

"Well, sometimes you kind of suck at it, *Mom*," Malakai muttered.

"I'm not perfect," she reiterated, like she had to understand that herself.

"Wow, can I get that engraved on a key ring so I can carry it around and shove it in your face when I need to?" Malakai said.

Quinn, very wisely, kept quiet.

"Well," said Arnekai, pushing herself up, "I guess that's the end of the lovely reminiscent breakfast. I have rounds to do, Malakai. I'll be back in time for lunch."

She turned to Quinn. "I am sorry for the reception. I will, however, be available to discuss the pertinent information that you came here for once I have seen to my duties."

And with that, she took off, leaving Malakai stewing in his own frustration and Quinn wasn't sure what to say. Despite the tension, she couldn't help that tiny seed of sadness that she wished her parents were still alive to argue with.

2 9

THE OLD WAYS

Quinn decided that, despite the eeriness of the perpetual twilight that settled over the Espinar Peninsula, she found it quite to her liking.

It was calm, and there were no bright flashes of light. Although occasionally, white flashes illuminated more here and there, the lighting level was ultimately soothing. A serene energy underlay everything around them.

Quinn and Malakai walked through the village, and all around it. The place wasn't as large as Quinn had expected, but more like a small town where everyone knew one another. There were a few small shops with banners waving from the tops of their doors proclaiming the wares within. While outside there were several stalls, like a farmer's market. They sold fruits and vegetables that Quinn couldn't recognize. One of which had a definitive pungency that reminded her ever so slightly of durian fruit, but tamped down.

She grinned at Malakai, who wouldn't stop frowning, trying to lift his spirits up somewhat. "It's okay," she said to him. "I think maybe we were expecting a bit much."

He shrugged and his shoulders fell dejectedly. "That's just it, Quinn, I never really expect much from her. I know better by now."

Quinn wasn't entirely sure how to react to that. While in foster care, she'd simply kept her head down and done what needed to be done. And she'd had one of the better families. Before that, she distinctly remembered parents who loved her and always showed it. She nudged him in the arm, just gently, trying to let him know she was there.

Whatever instinct guided her to do that was right. Malakai sighed and spoke. "I was fifteen the last time we were all here." He gestured around at the way nobody quite met his eyes, at the way nobody quite talked to him. He was definitely not one of the bunch. "I mean my parents and me. All together."

"I guess that explains why nobody's running up to you and hugging you. You were in your angsty teens," she said with a smile so the edge didn't hit.

He chuckled. "To be fair, we both know nobody would be running up and hugging me anyway. I'm not really the hugging type."

Quinn laughed this time. "I'm glad to see you haven't lost your sense of humor just because you had a fight with your mom."

"Quinn, don't go there." He looked away, like the subject was just annoying for him. "I always have a fight with my mother. Being a mom never seemed to be her priority."

Quinn shrugged. "Everyone has different priorities. But that doesn't mean you can't learn things from her. Even if she doesn't realize she's teaching them."

He watched Quinn for a moment. Perhaps he realized that she'd never really had a mother either, at least not in a time scope of things. Then he reached down and squeezed her hand gently, smiled, and spoke. "This is getting heavy. How about we change the subject?"

"Excellent idea. How about we go back to talking about the fact that there's a faction out there trying to destroy the universe as we know it and put the Library out of commission?" She winked at him.

Malakai laughed. They were far enough away from the rest of the settlement that nobody noticed quite how forced that laughter was.

She nudged him again. "Maybe we just need to give her a chance."

"A chance to do what, Quinn?" he asked with a long suffering sigh,

"Help us," Quinn said.

He paused and watched her for a moment before continuing their walk. "You're rather upbeat for someone that got pulled into a situation that is do or die."

"Is there at least a little bit of sarcasm in that?" she asked.

"Maybe a tiny bit." He sighed. "I'm not sure how you've managed to stay on top of everything and not just scream and run away."

"It's been marginally better than ceasing to exist because the universe imploded and I didn't know why." Quinn shrugged. "It's true that I might have had several panic moments, especially when I found out that I'm not what I always thought I was. But you know . . . it doesn't change the person I am. My values, my motivations . . . they're all the same. And frankly, life would be rather boring by comparison if I were back on Earth."

"You wouldn't have any comparison for it," Malakai said. "I mean, honestly, you wouldn't. You'd probably be happy with your life or at least content."

"Not now and knowing I wouldn't be, though. I know how big the universe is and I know that we're just a speck of dust out there in it." Quinn grimaced. "Although I could really do with a little bit of downtime to cement myself, get myself in the right frame of mind for the rest of it."

"Hey, you had a couple of weeks." Malakai flashed her a grin.

"I had a couple of weeks where I devoured books every day." They'd begun meandering back toward Arnekai's house. "I'm getting a little hungry."

Malakai fished into his backpack and pulled out what looked like a protein bar. Quinn raised an eyebrow. "Something Cook made for us to take with us on journeys, so we don't get hungry and we get all the nutrients we need or something like that."

"Oh, great." Quinn chomped down into it. It tasted like it had hints of white chocolate and macadamia nuts in it. She'd have to ask Cook how they kept reading her mind. "Anyway," Quinn said around a mouthful of food. "What should we do next?"

"I guess we wait for my mother to return so we can talk or whatever." He let himself fall into the chair on the porch and watched as the village bustled around doing their daily tasks, coming and going from hunting and patrols, people gathering around the farmers market section, chatting, exchanging wares and foods, maybe even recipes.

Quinn was pretty sure she saw a couple of casseroles change hands.

"Have you been waiting long?" Arnekai's voice sounded so suddenly Quinn was surprised she hadn't noticed the elf's approach. She sounded less imposing and a bit more trepidatious as if she wasn't entirely certain of how she'd be received.

"We really haven't been waiting long at all," Quinn said. "We've just been watching. It's quite nice here. It has this serene and comfortable feeling to it. Relaxed."

Arnekai laughed. "I guess it does." She sat down next to Quinn and took a deep breath with closed eyes. When she opened them again, Arnekai was smiling. "Yes. You're right. It's quite comfortable here. I guess that's what we get for maintaining constant vigilance."

"Then you've done a very good job," Quinn said.

Arnekai sighed and leaned forward, her elbows on the table. "I owe you an apology," she said, directing her attention to her son. "I'm not the best when it comes to communicating with people in general, let alone people I care about, namely you, Malakai. I owe you an apology for not being there, for not explaining the why to you in a way you'd understand, and for my never clarifying it. I'm sorry. Maybe one day you can forgive me, but I don't expect you to. I just hope you'll understand that sometimes we do things for reasons others won't always understand."

Malakai, for his part, paled slightly. His mouth hung open in shock, and his eyes looked like they were being held open by somebody. For a couple of seconds he sat like that and then he shook himself and nodded, looking away from his mother's gaze. "Sure, I bet I'll understand more when I'm older."

"Maybe . . . hopefully," Arnekai said and turned her attention back to Quinn. "Anyway, I promised I would help you with information about my great-aunt. Milaro and the Library requested nicely, and thus I need to stop putting off the inevitable and talk about a very uncomfortable familial situation. You need to understand, however, that I'm just a few hundred years old and thus a lot of this will be hearsay and things I've read in our history books and retellings and in my other aunts' and grandparents' journals. I guess now is as good a time as any for you to ask me your questions about Ardenil."

Quinn didn't need magic to sense that Arnekai was extremely uncomfortable talking about this subject matter. It might be better to get the whole thing out of the way sooner than later. "Would there be any reason you can think of that Arnekai might have removed a Restricted Vault book from the Library without permission from, you know, the Librarian, the Library itself, Lynx, or anyone?" Quinn asked, not bringing up how she might have gotten it out of the Library in the first place.

"Ardenil was never your commonplace person." Arnekai sighed. "She was contrary, rebellious, deliberately combative, and refused to do anything she was told. I've only ever met her three times in my life because by the time I came along, she was already in disgrace. I do, however, have access to our official chronicles."

"Ooo!" Quinn butted in. "Is that like an official chronicler? Like the slothilis?"

Arnekai blinked at Quinn. "Being a chronicler isn't restricted to a species . . . even if the slothilis are extraordinarily capable."

"Oh." Quinn felt entirely clueless. She'd just thought maybe Carafax had been around more of the histories than just the Library. "Of course. Sorry, carry on."

"Reasons, Mother," Malakai said trying to regain her attention. "We need reasons why she was banished and why she would have been lurking around trying to figure out where to get these books from. We need to know why she took it."

"Ardenil, she . . . well, it might be better if you wait and talk to *my* mother."

Malakai sighed. It was a deep, almost irritated sound. "And where, pray tell, is Grandmother?"

"Well, you know her. She's busy." Arnekai avoided eye contact.

"Okay, fine. She's very busy. Doing what, Mother?"

"She's on an expedition."

Quinn's eyes narrowed. She was pretty good at telling when people were evading questions even if they weren't being this blatantly obvious about it. Arnekai didn't want to give out any more information than she had to. Given the situation, though, this wasn't a good sign.

Quinn stepped in before Malakai boiled over. "Maybe we can talk about the expedition later. Can we focus on the chronicles you gleaned your information from?"

Arnekai nodded, shook herself ever so slightly, focusing on Quinn. It was as if Arnekai was too embarrassed to talk about it. She sighed before finally starting. "Ardenil was known for . . . she'd always been a little bit of a troublemaker. My grandfather never really managed to keep her under wraps. She was a willful spirit, which is fine, usually, except a few millennia ago, maybe three-ish, she ran into a group of people that weren't exactly people my family approved of. She was simply not in good company, I guess."

"Most kids don't like being told who they can be friends with," Quinn mumbled.

"She was several hundred years old at that stage," Arnekai said softly by way of excuse.

"Elaborate," Malakai asked.

"She met this group of people when she was going through her apparently never-ending rebellious stage. They dimension jumped, they caused havoc wherever they went, they basically acted like children, despite the fact that they were all several centuries old. It was a big melting pot of people, too. There were Serpensiril, Ilgonomur, Esposians, some Furionas fae, some centaurs, Sedimentites, even some Tecopsis which I always found odd, and probably several I'm not thinking of. If they'd been productive and industrious, it would have been magnificent, but instead, they were a big interspecies group that caused mischief. It culminated in my great-aunt attempting to steal one of our lineage's sacred texts."

"Sacred texts? Like magical texts?" Quinn asked, this being the first she'd heard of them.

Arnekai shook her head. "Not quite. They're the histories of our people, and specific exercise techniques for our lineage and the chaos manipulations that allow us to dwell in this sector. Exercises that won't work for other species or even clans . . . or they shouldn't."

Quinn felt oddly disappointed, despite the fact that it held some chaotic manipulation techniques.

"There will be a copy in the Library. In one of the vaults. Or there *should* be," Arnekai clarified before continuing. "This book holds techniques that help us maintain the boundaries around our domain, which is what I was scouting earlier. If you don't have these skillsets nailed down, if you aren't attuned to and can't control those chaotic waves, then you can't patrol the grounds. Then our entire space becomes vulnerable. It'll bleed farther and farther into the universe, infecting everything. Because of that, the sacred texts are very specifically important to our species."

"And she attempted to steal these?" Quinn asked, making a note to herself to ask about other vaults. Just how many were there?

"They're similar to the magical texts that the Library has, but they are species-specific, and are guarded heavily here in our stronghold. After she attempted to steal them, she was banished, and they asked her not to come back."

"Did they ask her not to come back," Malakai said, "or did they very strongly suggest that there might not be a welcome reception for her, should she choose to return?"

"Got it in one," his mother said. She gave Quinn a wan smile. "Our history is not what I would call unblemished."

Quinn nodded and paused to gather her thoughts. "Why did she try to steal it?"

Arnekai winced. "I was hoping we wouldn't get into this. I can't stand politics."

"No one can." Quinn chuckled. "But we have to understand what we're up against."

"The universe is vast, and there was never any way everyone was always going to agree on everything," Arnekai began. "Even before things went awry with the Library, there were factions. The Serpensiril, Esposian fae, and Ilgonomur have always had a close relationship. Just like the Furionas, Darigháhnish, and Areiltháhnish. Even if the degree to which they think it varies, those are three regions of space, three species that have always held that chaos just makes magic more powerful. Most of the factions anyway."

"So those are good starting points to investigate, right?" Malakai asked, and for the first time Quinn could hear some actual enthusiasm in his voice.

"Very good starting points. But by now, there will be more people in cahoots with them, perhaps more obvious about it than before. And just because I didn't list a species as having direct contact with our aunt, doesn't mean they didn't." Arnekai paused. "But I guess it's a good place to start."

"Better than what we had," Malakai muttered. "Anything else you can think of."

Arnekai hesitated momentarily. "If you get to a point where you need assistance, know that the Darigháhnish will always offer aid to the Library." Light flashed around her and a rune appeared briefly in front of Quinn's face, before pushing into her forehead and vanishing along with a short, sharp pang of pain.

"Ow!" Quinn glared at Arnekai.

"Wow," Malakai said. "I was not expecting an oath, Mom, thanks." His smile in her direction was genuine.

"Thank me when the time comes. For now it's just an empty promise that I hope doesn't come to fruition." She held up a hand to forestall any irritation. "But we will fulfill it if it becomes necessary. For the good of us all."

"Thanks," Quinn said, genuinely happy at the gesture. "Any other hints or tips?"

"Just be aware that those I listed are simply those who stood out and it was by no means the entire species. There are factions even in our own that don't agree with everything I do. So all of those mentioned could be involved or none." Arnekai gave Quinn a small smile. "Always be cautious and careful. They are a conglomeration that believes magic shouldn't be filtered, because it's supposed to weed out the weak, and thus leave the survivors stronger for it. It's a fanatical viewpoint on life, but for whatever reason, Ardenil believed in it. The last time I saw her, she left an impression. It was at my grandfather's funeral about two centuries ago."

Arnekai paused, as if she didn't want to keep going, but steeled herself before speaking again. "Ardenil stood up in front of the whole gathering and tapped her staff on the ground. It sent out a pulse that effectively froze every single person there for several seconds. Her voice extended as if amplified and she cursed the entire gathering. She said, 'Rue the day you let your closed mindedness banish me—you will be punished by my hand or by chaos as it tears the flesh from your bones and leaves your weakness to rot in the waste that remains.'"

A few seconds of complete silence followed.

"Wow. She sounds like the life of the party," Quinn said softly.

Arnekai smiled sadly. "I only wish it were as simple as that. Curses aren't taken lightly anywhere in the universe."

30

A COINCIDENCE

Even though they left the Espinar Peninsula after lunch, it was dark by the time they walked into the Library. The daytime and atmosphere differences were a little jarring at first. It was simply disconcerting to step from a bright twilight afternoon into the slightly quieter depths of the night in the Library.

Granted, given the different time zones around the universe, the Library was never actually closed. And even when it might seem late in the Library, there were always patrons lingering, looking up books, chattering in groups now that the Library had been open for a while.

It was amazing how busy the culinary branch had become too. The number of chefs who wanted to try new magical recipes at all hours as well as discuss potential palate cleansers and recipe changes with each other was astounding.

Bustling.

That was the right word. The Library had become a bustling hive of activity on a constant basis.

Quinn felt a surge of affection for the Library. Although she was extremely tired from having been dragged on patrols with Arnekai that morning, this morning, whatever. She didn't know how the time zones worked when crossing dimensions. What she did know was that she had been taken around the whole perimeter of the Espinar Peninsula and was shown exactly how the Darighähnish spent their time protecting their sector.

Quinn could feel the chaos when she was there, palpitating just outside the boundaries, waiting for them to slip up so it could pour inside. It made her skin crawl.

So when Malakai indicated they should return to the Library, Quinn wholeheartedly agreed.

Quinn was effectively exhausted after spending so much time with Malakai and his mother, and the tension that anything blunt could have cut through. She was even too tired to think of a good analogy. Quinn barely made it up the steps to her quarters and stumbled through the doors. Aradie cooed from across the room, full of concern, but not enough concern apparently to come and help her magic herself up the stairs.

Which Quinn realized belatedly she could have done herself. Had her brain been capable of functioning, she would have remembered that she could in fact use magic to not only hover but also bloody fly, and she wouldn't have had to walk up steps in the first place.

It might not sound difficult. But three flights of stairs, while wildly tired, were just not fun.

Quinn threw herself onto the bed, not giving two craps about whether she was dirty or sweaty or whatever. She was just tired. She closed her eyes and felt herself sinking into the beautiful soft bed, ready to dream of everything nice like sugar and spice with cherries on top.

She waited for the darkness of sleep to claim her.

Then she waited some more.

And then she opened her eyes.

Because while she was absolutely exhausted and completely bone-tired, she wasn't actually sleepy. Her brain was running nineteen to the dozen. She was fascinated and scared, and worried about the Library as a whole. There was so much, especially after speaking to Arnekai, that she had to go over and rectify and change and figure out.

"Take a breath," she said out loud to herself. Breathing was a very good practice in any being that required oxygen after all.

"Okay, Quinn, come on." She sat up and slapped her cheeks very lightly. Tomorrow. Tomorrow she would need to convene a meeting. But right now, while she was still thinking of it, well, all of the information they'd gathered from Arnekai was still fresh in her mind.

Quinn needed to figure out the traitors in their midst. She wrote down the potential names. Frankly, after speaking to Arnekai, there was more potential betrayal than she'd thought possible. There was Finn, and Jim, and Bob. And well, technically even centaurs had been hanging around with them back in the day.

Furionas fae too. Although she doubted Geneva. There was Danio, the very first centaur they'd hired. Then there was that other Aracnio she'd interviewed, called Steve of all things even though he hadn't been hired in the end. She'd found the name a little unusual for a fantastical universal Library applicant anyway. But then again, Jim and Bob were very commonplace back on Earth too. She noted that down for herself, something to look into later as well.

Maybe they thought only leaving a couple of spies behind might keep the Aracnios far from suspicion. And yet, the twins began behaving differently since the moment Tenejo and his kin walked into the Library, or thereabouts. Perhaps not the precise moment, but close . . .

Quinn frowned. The Tecopsis visitors they'd had wouldn't have been spies or they'd have stayed longer, or at least attempted to. Quinn knew that despite the minuscule likelihood of patrons beings spies, she'd end up having to replay so many of the Library readings, and Aradie's readings, to determine whether or not they could have posed a threat.

Speaking of which . . . she wondered if any of the memories tampered with had been more recent ones. That was food for thought. Any memories since the Library had reopened? Quinn jotted that down too.

And then there was Larry, the sedimentite. She'd liked him. He was a really good assistant. From his demeanor and the actions she could recall, he was probably also innocent. Just because they were from that species didn't necessarily mean that they were in cahoots with the Library saboteurs. It would have been much easier to just blame the entire species. But you couldn't do that. That wouldn't be fair, right?

Because everything in life was *so* fair . . .

Quinn fell back onto the bed again. This time her brain felt a little bit calmer. She had her list of all the things she needed to look into. First thing in the morning, she'd call a meeting and get her supervisors in, and figure out what the hell they were going to do with all of this information.

Aradie swooped down to sit and coo next to her head.

Quinn waved the concern away. "I'm fine. I'm just very tired and there's a lot to do."

Of course, there's a lot to do, Aradie said into her mind, not making Quinn interpret more coos, for which Quinn was extremely grateful, given the fact that her brain felt like mush.

You did well. Sometimes I believe the reason I chose you was definitely right. The owl sounded smug.

"You chose me, huh?" Quinn muttered as her eyes grew heavy.

Well, you didn't exactly choose me. I had to give you a push in the right direction, didn't I?

"I didn't realize Librarians got their own familiars," she mumbled.

I'm not your familiar. I'm your friend, guide, and guardian. I believe that is a far more accurate assessment, Aradie said, sounding slightly indignant.

"How come you're so much better at talking to me now?" Quinn asked, suddenly.

Our synchronicity is higher. It's not quite the same wavelength as the Library, but on our own. It'll allow us to communicate over greater distances.

"Oh" was all Quinn managed.

You need to rest. Aradie patted her gently with a soft wing.

"Yeah, I think I'll sleep," Quinn murmured with a smile before passing out.

The light that shone through the upper windows in Quinn's bedchamber the following day was very bright. So bright, in fact, that Quinn, knowing it was technically artificial light in this little pocket dimension, thought she should probably talk to the Library directly about it. Maybe, just maybe, it wouldn't wake her up by glaring in her face.

However, once she pushed herself to her elbows, she realized that she'd woken up much later than she usually would. She glanced around. Aradie wasn't in the room. She frowned, looked down at her side table and realized her phone was also not there, which was quite odd. She guessed the power bank had probably run out, or Malakai was fiddling with it to get it to work on magic. He'd mentioned something about that previously. She really wanted to know if mana and magic could restore the electrical capacity.

Quinn sighed, pushed herself up, and stretched. She felt a little stiff, which meant the activity she'd done yesterday, or today, or whenever it was with Malakai's mom on the border patrol, had definitely taken its toll. It probably meant Quinn should be a little bit more active around the Library too. It wouldn't kill her to get a little fitter, and maybe she could also have some coffee.

A juxtaposition for most, but purely logical for Quinn.

She showered, dressed, and decided a tracksuit was definitely on point for the day. One of the perks of being the magical Librarian was simply that she could pick whatever she wanted to wear to work that day, because nobody could tell her not to.

Down in her office with a sandwich in hand, she realized it was already lunchtime. Not that she minded the sleep-in. Sleep-ins were, to be fair, one of the best things out there. One of the advantages of adult life that had nothing to do with bill paying, which, no matter what anybody said, was definitely not a perk.

She began her workday by pulling up all the information she'd gathered the previous night. She made sure to get all of Finn, Jim and Bob, Danio, Steve, and Larry's information that they had available to them through the Library system. She checked their checkout histories, their ages, their habits, observations by the Library, anything that had set off the Library's radar. Anything at all, to be honest. Nothing out of the ordinary. Nothing to flag them.

She tapped her pen against the table, lost in thought.

"Pray tell, what are you doing trying to drill a hole through the desk at this hour of the day?" Quinn glanced up and saw Malakai. A rush of relief went through her. Somehow, when he was around, it always seemed a little easier to take everything on. It was nice having somebody who didn't judge her, who joked with her, who didn't seem to pity her—at least not outwardly, anyway.

"Thanks," she said. "What brings you here?"

"Well, I assumed you'd want to talk about what we spoke to my mother about."

Quinn chuckled. "Yes, you'd be correct."

She sent a silent message to the Library to summon Dottie, Eric, Narilin, Aradie, and Lynx. She still didn't know where Aradie had gone this morning. She'd been there during the night; Quinn was sure of it. She knew they'd talked, or she thought they'd talked. Maybe that was all in her head and part of a vivid dream. Quinn really didn't need to start hallucinating right now.

She watched and waited.

"What are you waiting for?" Malakai asked.

"I just expected people to come sooner." It was at this point Quinn realized she might be overtired.

"The only one you need to talk to right now who can literally pop in is Lynx, right?"

"Yes, I know." Quinn sighed; her head felt a little fuzzy. "I'm just a bit scattered this morning."

"I bet you were up all night. That's why you're up late this morning, isn't it?" Malakai moved to lean against her desk.

"Well, I was up fairly late. I couldn't sleep when we got back," she admitted.

"I don't blame you. I always find the time shift a little weird. But I slept like a baby." He winked and grinned.

"Of course you did," Quinn said. "Anyway, what do we do while we wait?"

"I don't know. I mean . . ."

Lynx's appearance cut him off, and Malakai seemed quite relieved.

Dottie trotted into the room a second later. Quinn thought she was smiling. She was exuding an aura of happiness around her. Made Quinn wish she could give the bench a bit of a hug.

"Dottie," she said by way of greeting.

"It is wonderful to have you back, Librarian." Dottie trotted over. "How was it? Were the seats comfortable?"

Quinn couldn't help but laugh. Dottie was pretty entertaining even if she didn't realize it.

Narilin walked in next, a serene smile on her face. Quinn raised an eyebrow. "Wow, my Salosier friend, you seem rather happy. Like the cat that got the cream."

Narilin looked around for just a moment, slightly panicked. "Cat," she said.

"No, it's an expression from Earth. I'm sorry. No cat." Quinn tried to calm her but couldn't help asking, "What's wrong with cats?"

"They just, they sometimes try to sharpen their claws on me," Narilin said. "I'm not very fond of that."

Quinn had to suppress a laugh because that didn't sound like a pleasant experience at all—even if it was pure cat in nature.

Next, Aradie swooped in and sat on Quinn's shoulder. And finally, Eric also came in. He was grouchy, scowling as per usual, his arms crossed as he hovered over Quinn's desk.

"Wow, you're in a fine mood," she said. "What's bugging you?"

"It's nothing. We have some disagreements over appropriate fines. I'm just getting a little sick of it." If possible, he crossed his arms even tighter.

Quinn smiled. "I'm sure everything will iron itself out in the end. Anyway, I wanted to pick your brains about Finn, Jim and Bob, Danio, and Larry."

"Finn, Jim, Bob, Danio, and Larry," the imp said, sounding decidedly even angrier.

"Eric, what's wrong?"

Eric was practically dripping lava. "Jim and Bob are gone, aren't they?"

"Really? Like, what do you mean gone? Like one hundred percent they've left? I thought maybe they'd just taken a couple of their days off." Quinn felt like something cold was crawling up her spine.

"Wouldn't you think it was rather coincidental for them to do that?" Eric asked irritably.

"Well, yes, it was a bit of a coincidence," Quinn admitted. "I guess I was just hoping for the best."

"Well, don't hope for the best because it's not going to come. They've disappeared. They've run off and just . . ."

"That's enough, Eric," Lynx said. "We know."

"I guess that proves that they're traitors, then, not much to dig up about all that then," Quinn said. She couldn't help feeling disappointed. She'd really wanted to give them the benefit of the doubt. They'd been nice for the most part. "Is it odd that a part of me sort of hoped they weren't?"

Lynx hesitated slightly before answering. "Well, we can't be completely certain, but I also don't think they were the only ones."

"What do you mean?"

"I think we let our guard down a little bit too much with the newest batch. There's been . . . there were a few incidents while you were gone the past couple of days," Lynx said, refusing to make eye contact with her.

Quinn groaned. She didn't like the sound of that.

3 1

ANOTHER LIST

"JUST WHAT INCIDENTS ARE YOU TALKING ABOUT?" QUINN ASKED, despite wishing she could curl up with a good book and ignore all the crisis currently occurring.

"Well, it started maybe a day before you left to go and visit Malakai's mother, but you were very busy and we did not want to bother you," Narilin said, looking everywhere but directly at Quinn. The Salosier was even wringing her hands, a sure sign that there was something they were keeping from Quinn.

"Okay, what problems?" Quinn was really trying to keep her tone even.

"There have been some problems with the bookworms. They are having trouble producing several affinities, despite Farrow's best efforts." Narilin still wouldn't meet her gaze.

Quinn frowned. "What do you mean?"

"Because some of the books have been in the library for so long and much of their leftover essence was also devoured by bookworms. The engorged ones you fought off, very bravely might I add. The bookworms that were salvaged are not reproducing." Narilin paused as if trying to think of what she needed to add. "Right now, we do not have all the affinities represented, and some of those that we do have aren't producing the correct wavelength yet. We have reached an impasse."

Quinn paused for a moment digesting the information. She really wished they'd tell her this stuff as soon as it happened. "There has to be something we can do to rectify that, correct?"

Narilin hesitated before answering and Lynx stepped in. "There are, of course, many things we can do. However. There has not been much time to take a trial and error approach to figure out what's gone wrong with the breeding."

Quinn glanced between the two of them. Both Lynx and Narilin looked positively mortified. While Quinn wanted to pretend it was just about worms, she knew that, in fact, it wasn't. It was about yet another thing in the Library that was supposed to function but wasn't.

The more they thought they fixed the Library, the more broken elements they seemed to find.

"Okay, then. Let's see what we can do." With her mind, she called Misha, who popped immediately into the middle of the ever growing gathering. A part of Quinn thought it might be a case of too many cooks in the kitchen. But what other option did they really have?

"What can I do for you, Librarian?" Misha asked, giving a brief incline of their head by way of greeting.

"How are we on the bookworm front?" Getting straight to the point was the only way Quinn was getting through this.

"Ah, that is not my area of expertise. I shall fetch Farrow for you," Misha said, and an instant later, Farrow stood in front of them.

Quinn massaged her temples, still not used to the instant teleportation thing. "Look, Farrow, I'm sure you're very busy."

Farrow looked around herself, inclined her head to Narilin and the others, and then glanced at Quinn before irritably looking at Misha. "You know I don't like it when you do that. Sometimes I have specimens in my hands."

"I checked this time," Misha said, a bit of smug impertinence in their tone. They looked strangely bored, their eyes briefly flickered in much the same way Lynx's often did.

"Well, check better next time, thank you," Farrow said. She turned her attention to Quinn, finally. "What was that you asked, Librarian?"

"I've heard there's been some incidents, that the bookworms aren't reproducing, for one." Quinn paused and her eyes narrowed.

"The bookworms are my main concern right now, but did Narilin not tell you about the owls?" Farrow sounded less whimsical than usual. As if she was all about business and solving the problems she was having.

"No," Quinn said. "Neither did Aradie, who is an owl." She glared at the owl who was perched on the back of her chair. Aradie wisely looked away, and Quinn turned her attention back toward Narilin. "And Narilin told me essentially nothing. So, please, what do I need to know?" Quinn asked.

"Very well," Narilin said, cutting in on anything Farrow might have said. "We are having difficulties with the quills as well. With such a long downtime, hibernation time if you will, their sturdiness has decreased."

"And in plain language?" Quinn asked as calmly as she could.

Aradie hooted in her ear and spoke in her mind. *A lot of the feathers are being prematurely offered and thus do not have the strength required to maintain the magical script in its entirety.*

Quinn blinked. "How do we alleviate this?"

Narilin shrugged and, funnily enough, so did Aradie. Quinn sighed and counted to three because she didn't really have time to count to ten.

"Maybe just make sure the owls don't get overeager. Not yet. It hasn't been long enough. And we all know they understand us," Quinn offered. "I mean I realize we need the quills especially since we need to replicate damaged tomes. But we can't get ahead of ourselves. It's only going to make more work in the long run."

"We have tried reasoning with them; they are just overexcited," Narilin said. "I'm sure they will stop immediately if I simply tell them the Librarian has told them to."

"There's no need to snark at me, Narilin," Quinn snapped, then calmed herself and took a breath before looking around and gesturing at everyone else. "None of you offered anything else. I haven't even known about magic for three months yet. How am I supposed to solve these problems?"

Every single one of them at least had the decency to look contrite.

Narilin finally met Quinn's gaze and inclined her head. "Sorry, Librarian, I am frustrated as it is difficult to increase the output to what I need right now."

"Do you think this could be part of the sabotage?" Quinn asked.

"I would like to say no, but Jim and Bob were the ones feeding the night owls for me, as I had been extremely busy. Even with my cousin's help, I was swamped and determined to get all the books back on their feet as soon as possible. I just . . ." The beautiful Salosier shrugged helplessly.

"Narilin, it's okay," Quinn said. "We didn't know we couldn't trust them. We all know it's not on you. I would have thought the owls might have noticed something amiss with their food."

"It might not have been the food. It is just the only thing I can think of." Narilin shrugged, looking a little lost.

"You're doing a great job," Quinn said softly. The book doctor had a lot on her plate. After helping restore a handful of books, Quinn couldn't imagine the amount of work with the volume of damaged books Narilin had to fix.

Narilin looked up and blinked. "Thank you. I think I needed to hear that."

Quinn still had a shred of hope deep down that maybe the twins were just on a holiday. But it was all so coincidental she realized she was being foolish. She shrugged. "Sometimes, you know, we all need to hear that. Thank you for your hard work. Anyway, now that Jim and Bob are gone, is the situation salvageable?"

"I would say so. Their feed and bookworm supply is something Farrow and I can manage." Narilin seemed partially mollified and turned to Farrow with a small smile. "Sorry. I got a little carried away with the quills."

Quinn hid a smile at the interaction.

"It's quite all right," said Farrow. "Anyway. The bookworm

problem is something I'm working on right now. It will take several generations to get us back to where we were before the Library shut down. Unless . . ." They added the last as if they'd just had a lightbulb moment, which, perhaps, they had.

"What is it, Farrow?" Quinn prodded, really hoping they'd perhaps figured out a solution.

"Well . . ." Farrow seemed to be searching for the right words to express what was on her mind. "I'm unsure if we can get them from their birthplace. The Sepulcher of Cariad has long since lost its guardians. I'm not even sure if the histories mention it. But there is a slim chance we could retrieve some from their place of origin. I mean, it's a long shot, but a possibility."

Quinn perked up at that, but Eric beat her to speaking. "Wait. The Sepulcher of Cariad has long since been devoured by the Moonlit Wald. I mean, it's possible to go in there . . . but I'm not liking your chances of even locating the worms."

Farrow shrugged. "If I could be spared for a few days, I could take a team and attempt it myself. After all, I do have assistants now."

Quinn's eyes widened with surprise. "I'm all for it, but let's nail down some particulars before we start planning the rescue-the-bookworms expedition."

Farrow smiled. "Thank you, Librarian."

"Now, that's a solution for the bookworms, or at least a potential one. And perhaps something we can at least talk to the owls about—" Quinn started saying only to be interrupted by Narilin.

"Yes, but that is not the only—"

Quinn sighed. "Can we get a list? I'm really good with lists. Give me a list. I will tick, strike, delete things off it, and check it twice just to be sure. Just get me one made up and we'll address the rest of this at a later date once everything is out in the open, please."

She took a deep breath and smiled. "I know we have other stuff that's just as important, but right we have to deal with flushing out the people we can't trust. Determining if more of the assistants in the Library are spies takes precedence. I have to know who is trustworthy or not."

"Isn't it just better to get rid of all of them?" Eric spat out. "I mean, you can't a hundred percent guarantee that they're not going to be in cahoots with their governments or leaders or their underground or whoever is deciding all of this."

"You can't just assume they're a part of a minority faction. Sometimes people surprise you and I think that's a beautiful thing." Quinn could feel herself choking up. Damn those emotions. "If we don't believe that people as a whole can be good . . . then we really have nothing to hope for."

"That's a bit naïve," Malakai muttered. "But I see your point."

Eric opened his mouth as if to say something, thought better of it, crossed his arms and harumphed, but she could tell there was a little bit of a smile in his eyes. Maybe Eric wasn't quite as gruff as he always let on.

"Anyway," Quinn said, "let's get to the end of this so I can cross stuff off different lists. I need to know—"

There was a rapid knock at the door before she could finish what she was saying.

"Come in," Quinn said, and Finn dashed in, harried, sweaty even.

Finn stood there, their massive anime-like eyes wider than Quinn had ever seen them, frantic. Their hair stood out a little bit more than Quinn was used to, almost like they'd put their finger in an electric socket.

Still small and petite at barely four feet tall, they looked so worried and so scared that Quinn's heart went out to them. Like a rabbit fleeing a predator.

"Finn, what's wrong?"

"Please, I don't want to go back home. Don't make me go back again." Finn's eyes darted to each of them, pleading. They threw themselves to their knees in front of Quinn. "Please just keep me here, keep me safe. Please."

3 2

KEEP PEOPLE SAFE

QUINN didn't need anyone to tell her FINN was telling the truth. She could feel the tiny vibration of fear resonating through the room, through the entire Library. Subtle, but strong, and very obviously there.

From that very first encounter when Finn approached the check-in desk back before the Library opened as one of the first assistant applicants, Quinn had had a gut feeling back then about them, and all the assistants she'd hired, like Geneva and Eric.

And her gut was telling her that Finn's fear right now was real.

Now, whether that fear was a truth Finn believed because they'd been brainwashed into it or a truth that was fact, Quinn didn't know. She also didn't care.

Finn had come to the Library and won a little bit of her heart. Perhaps it was that they were shorter than her and resembled one of those eager, shy anime characters. Finn had never been a larger-than-life presence, only a small one, quietly doing their job.

They'd helped out, as an assistant should, but even in difficult situations like the one with Tenejo and maintaining that shield until Quinn's emotionless state took care of things, Finn stepped up and filled in shifts when necessary, caring and loving in their handling of all the books. Quietly going about their job, eyes always filled with endless wonder.

Unobtrusive and quiet.

Always there.

The perfect spy.

Could they be very good at their job and weaseling in under their target's defenses? If Quinn were sending a spy to get inside the Library's security, Finn would be the perfect choice. Or at least, someone who presented just like Finn.

Despite that, there was something about Finn and their passion for Library books—any books. Something that stood out from the first moment she'd interviewed them. It made Quinn quite certain that Finn, while perhaps encouraged to apply by their elders in order to spy, hadn't actually been aware of their initial motivations.

It was a strong feeling. And right then, Quinn was counting on it.

"Finn, what's wrong?" she asked, lowering her voice and making it as soothing as possible.

Finn's gaze darted all around, their already large eyes impossibly bigger. They still trembled even as they looked around as if they were trying to find something. "I just had my day off . . . I usually just spend it in one of the species-specific rooms, but I was called home this time. Asked to visit."

"Did they give a reason?" Quinn asked, as gently as she could, trying to put reassurance in the tone.

Finally, something clicked for Finn, and a visible wave of relief shot through them. The tension in their shoulders dissipated. "They said there were important family matters to discuss and since I had not been home in a while, I had to come home as soon as possible. I was so worried. My grandfather has had a few health scares. But when I got there . . ."

The tension ramped up again, so high that it was palpable and made Quinn's skin crawl. It was panic, rolling off the Ilgonomur in waves. Finn was close to a complete and utter panic attack. Quinn walked over to the couch, beckoning Finn to follow. After a second's hesitation, the Library assistant followed. Even doing such a small thing, seemed to calm them ever so slightly.

Quinn sat on the couch first, patting the seat next to her gently. "You know no one with ill-intent can get into the Library, right?" She just had to hope that Finn counted as a part of the Library being an assistant, and that the security would thus also screen out anyone who intended Finn harm too.

Finn nodded slowly.

"Come, sit with me. My legs kind of hurt." Quinn gave her best soft smile.

Finn eyed her cautiously, and then shrugged and sat down, still focusing only on Quinn. Her anxiety levels had evened out ever so slightly.

"Can you carry on? What happened when you got there?" Quinn asked gently.

Finn paused, and took a deep breath, as if they were centering themself. "They asked a lot of questions. All at once. My parents, my uncles and aunts, cousins I've never even seen before in my life . . . no one has ever been all that interested in me. Books have always been my thing. That's why I was so excited when the Library reappeared!"

Quinn noticed that Finn wasn't the best at staying on track. Probably why they occasionally lost themselves in the Library and research. She had to suppress a smile, because this situation required that she be serious. Instead, she gave her best look of understanding before speaking. "That had to be confusing. Do you recall what sort of questions they asked?"

"Assistants. They asked how many we had. If I had access to the restricted sections, or if I could be a supervisor and gain more console access that way. At first, they made it sound like they wanted to see if I could have a good career here, but then they started asking about removing restricted texts, which I thought was sort of odd." Finn paused, as if they were still digesting all the information themself. "Isn't that all in the Library rules? I mean, I thought it was. Their questions confused me so much. It started feeling like it wasn't me they wanted to hear about but the ins and outs of the Library."

Quinn patted the top of their hand gently, trying to pull them back on topic. "They've never taken that much interest in your goings on before?"

Finn shook their head and laughed ruefully. "Never once."

"Did they ask anything else?"

Finn frowned, like they were trying to bring their own brain back on track. "They wanted to know if anything in the Library had been strange recently." Finn scrunched up their face. "Why would they ask that, and why would they think I'd talk about it? I told them that even if it did happen, I couldn't tell them. It was work information."

Quinn cringed ever so slightly, certain how badly that would have been received. "Did they say why they wanted to know all this information?"

"No!" Finn spoke vehemently. "That's what's so confusing. They gave me no reasons for their need to know. But they wouldn't stop asking. Over and over . . . it felt like an interrogation. When I wouldn't elaborate, they didn't care that I didn't know. Instead, they told me to bring them back that information. But it wasn't a question, it was a demand. They seem suspicious about the Library being back. Their tones, the way they loomed over me . . ." Finn muttered the last few words, their gaze darting all around again as if to check that their relatives weren't hiding in the shadows. They whispered the next words. "I didn't feel safe anymore."

Quinn watched the way Finn wrung their hands, the way their eyes darted back and forth. They were legitimately scared, and Quinn was quite certain that they weren't scared of *her*.

What do you think? she asked the Library.

Genuinely scared, you're right.

Do you think they put them up to this? Quinn asked

No. I mean, yes, The Library corrected itself, *but I don't think Finn reacted in a way that their superiors thought they would.*

I get that same feeling, Quinn said. "Finn, it's okay, we get it. You can relax. Everything will be okay."

Finn relaxed into the couch a bit more, their eyes darted to everybody in the room, with Misha and Farrow there, Malakai and Dottie,

Eric, who was like a thundercloud at that point in time, Aradie and Lynx. The room was full of the main people of the Library. It seemed to calm the Ilgonomur somewhat. Maybe it made them feel safe. Quinn could only hope so.

Finn cleared their throat and gave everybody a very nervous, wan smile before leaning right back into the couch down and taking a glass of water from Lynx who'd briefly disappeared and reappeared.

"Is it okay if I ask you a few questions?" Quinn asked as gently as possible. When Finn nodded, she continued. "Let's take this back a bit. Who told you to apply for the Library?"

Finn's eyes lit up at the question. "I've always wanted to work at the Library, but for years, for centuries that is, for so long, it was something I didn't have a chance of dreaming about. I just worked at the Ilgonomur main branch Library. So boring, barely a magical text anywhere to be found. It's difficult for normal libraries to contain them without contaminating other aspects of the Library, you know."

Finn's expressions just lit up their face whenever they spoke about books. It was a demonstration of joy for knowledge Quinn was ninety-nine percent sure she had on her face whenever she spoke about books. It was part of the reason Quinn was certain Finn hadn't meant the Library any harm.

"So," Quinn said, "it was your idea to apply?"

"Once I found out, yes. But they encouraged me. They knew I loved books. They said that the Library opening at this time was unexpected and that if I got an assistant position in the first batch, I'd secure a prestigious future!" Finn said, a small smile on their face.

"Who told you this?" Quinn asked, storing away that it had been unexpected. Perhaps that was the almost five hundred years speaking, but it could also have been more.

"Oh, Gershan. He's the lead librarian for the Ilgonomur main branch library," Finn said importantly, then they paused, frowning. "He'd never paid much attention to me before this."

Quinn filed that away as well, and smiled, hoping to keep her assistant at ease. "Wonderful. So, you filled out the application?"

"Oh no. It was filled out for me. Which was great because, you know, there were things in there that I didn't exactly know what I should say." Finn paused, as if unsure what to say next. "I might read a lot, but I'm not a good writer. It was nice to have someone phrase things for me."

"Interesting," Quinn said, mulling that over in her mind. The application had little bearing on why she'd accepted Finn, but now she wanted to go back and look at how it was filled out just in case there were any hints.

This time, Lynx spoke up. "Why are you asking us to keep you safe?" Lynx said.

Finn began hyperventilating again, as if, for just a few moments, they'd forgotten how panicked they'd been earlier.

Quinn could sense the fear rolling off them in waves. "What else happened? Can you tell us?"

"At first I was excited. Everyone asked me all about the Library and what I did, but then the questions were more specific about how the book retrieval was going, if anything was still wrong with the Library." Finn frowned for a second. "I think Uncle Nort even asked about a filtration chamber? I answered that I didn't know anything about something like that. His aura flared when he heard that." Finn shuddered.

Quinn raised an eyebrow.

Finn shrugged. "I mean it would make sense to be curious after so long, right? But they didn't like it when I said no."

They asked the question like they wanted it to make sense. Quinn smiled. "Some people are naturally curious."

Finn's expression hardened for a brief second. Like they suddenly realized natural curiosity wasn't something their family ever exhibited. "When they got to the more strange and obscure questions, I stopped answering. I didn't know why they insisted on a core and the filtration chamber. Nor what they meant by dangerous books. But when I wouldn't answer, they began crowding around me. All of them this time. I don't like crowds, I don't like too many people. It's why I love books so much. Books let you read, they let you learn, and they show you things you didn't think were possible."

"Finn," Quinn said gently. "Focus."

"Oh. Yes." Finn cleared their throat. "When they started to offer me rewards to find these things, I really started to get worried. I don't want to get fired. I like it here. It didn't sound like something I was supposed to be doing here." Finn looked down at the ground and sighed.

"It's okay. Maybe we can find something in what they said to help figure out why they were so insistent," Quinn said soothingly.

Finn nodded and took a deep breath. "When I refused the rewards they began pushing me. One of my uncles, I think it was Uncle Nort again grabbed me by the arm. Look . . . it bruised." Finn was biting back tears now.

Quinn didn't react fast enough to disguise her gasp. There were multiple red and purple bruising all over Finn's right upper arm. Some cuts too where it looked like nails had bit into them. She had to push down her temper so Finn knew they were safe. "I'm so sorry, Finn. Go on."

As if bolstered by Quinn's reaction, as if relieved to find out they weren't overreacting, Finn continued. "They were vying for my attention. All of them. Reaching out, tugging me . . . I couldn't think, there were so many of them crowded around me. I was scared. It didn't feel safe." Finn looked up at Quinn as if searching for something.

Quinn nodded in what she hoped was an encouraging way. Even if she wanted to find Finn's family and punch them all.

Finn nodded. "Some of them started tugging me toward the debriefing chamber, telling me they knew just what could help jog my memory. But I've seen the change people go through after being in there. I wasn't entering that wing under any circumstances."

Quinn waited patiently while Finn took a few deep breaths before they continued.

Finn almost looked trancelike when they continued speaking. "I said I had to use the bathroom. It was all I could think of and it wasn't really a lie. I felt so nauseous. They scattered enough to let me go. Barely. I had to wrench my arm out of a couple of grasps. When I got to the bathroom, I went through the first door, but I used my Library pass on the second entry door. I'm quite certain they'd activated the external location locks on all the doors. My badge flashed red before it allowed me access. I don't think they knew an assistant badge could do that . . . and neither did I, but I'm so grateful. The Library saved me. I think."

"An assistant or higher's pass will override anything attempting to keep you from the Library if you seek to get back to it," Lynx said, his voice gruff.

Finn paled ever so slightly. "I don't think they wanted me to return here before they'd made me help them. Please don't let them come and get me."

Finn was shaking so much the couch was moving. Quinn leaned forward and patted them on the shoulder very gently.

"It's okay. You're safe here." Oh, how she wished she could be a hundred and fifty percent sure they were going to be safe here. So much had happened to put the Library and its assistants in danger, that she was beginning to truly question hers and the Library's ability to keep people safe.

Quinn motioned for Narilin and Dottie to come and help. "It's okay. You've been staying here in the quarters most of the time, haven't you?"

"Most of the time. It leaves me closer to the books and I like that." Finn smiled, although it wasn't as blinding as usual. "I just wanted to go home and see my parents, but they weren't even there when I arrived which is why I went to the offices because that's where they work."

Quinn heard the tremor in Finn's voice. She understood. They were worried about their parents, their family, and what it meant that they'd run away. Even if some of that same family had been attempting to coerce them, they were still family. And, for a lot of people, that could get very complicated, very fast.

But at the same time, Finn had been scared and hadn't wanted to be hurt or hurt something they cared about.

"You did the best you could with what you had," Quinn said. "It's okay. We'll make sure you're safe here. Dottie and Narilin are gonna take you upstairs. Maybe we'll get you a soothing soup, something to calm your nerves. Does that sound good?"

Finn nodded and a few tears escaped from their big, beautiful eyes. "Thank you." They sighed and held the sobs in, before turning to follow Dottie and Narilin upstairs. Quinn watched as they left the room and then she turned to Lynx and Misha.

"We need to go over the security elements for the Library. If we have to scan every damn person who walks through a door, we will, etiquette be damned. We're not letting anyone else who works to keep the Library going go through something like that."

"You know they could be . . . embellishing, right?" Lynx asked carefully.

"Of course I know, but sometimes my gut instincts just work well. And right now my gut is telling me that Finn is genuinely scared. I'll do whatever I need to, so I can keep the promise to keep that they're safe," she said, her tone hard as stone.

"Very well. I just wanted to make sure you'd considered all avenues," Lynx said, softening his words with a soft smile.

"I know, and I appreciate it. I'm not about to give them access to the filtration chamber or anything. But I believe Finn. And we're not letting them go back home. That—that was terror. Whatever information they want from Finn, they're not getting, and I'll be damned if I let anybody else infiltrate this place."

33

UNETHICAL WAYS

IT WAS LATE AFTERNOON BY THE TIME QUINN FINISHED MAKING SURE Finn was safe and sound and comfortable upstairs. Even though Aradie said Finn was telling the truth, Quinn still wished the tale could be a lie.

Imagine trusting your family and finding out they were using you. Surely there had been signs before? She wasn't about to take every word as truth, but there was no way to fake such fear that fed through to her from Finn and the Library. So, at least for now, keeping Finn safe here was about the best she could do.

Especially since Quinn was fairly certain Finn's only mistake was being oblivious to anything not book related.

Everybody else had tasks to perform. Apart from Aradie, Quinn was mostly alone, and her owl was particularly silent right then.

It made her feel oddly adrift.

The easiest way, of course, to deal with that was to make a list for herself and figure out precisely how she could approach the rest of the problems in front of her. Being active meant making sure she didn't just sit there and dwell on things that she couldn't change, and take care of the things that she could.

That was proactive, right?

Wasn't it?

She sighed. Security golems. Yes.

That's what she needed to concentrate on. She settled herself into her big comfy office chair and wrestled herself into the right frame of mind to work.

She extended her senses to the Library with her thoughts, absent-mindedly reaching up to scratch Aradie behind her neck. The owl cooed softly, slightly disgruntled as she had been fast asleep. Quinn removed her hand and wondered why the Library hadn't answered her yet.

You do realize that I do more than just talk to you, right?

Oh, sorry. Quinn wasn't sure how else to respond.

No, I'm sorry, the Library said. *It's been a very long few days and I'm finally seeing some light at the end of the tunnel. I'm a little short-fused lately. On top of everything else, we've actually been trying to figure out the different reasons why the Ashiron filtration pillar is so silent. Anyway, what was your question?*

Security golems. Where do we stand on the production right now? Quinn asked and filed away the comment about Ashiron to check on later.

A couple of seconds passed, and the Library chuckled. *Well, it seems we've just gotten in the correct components, I guess you could call it, to create the new security golems that will extend to the culinary branch.*

How many can we make?

Six. Six per branch. Eight for the main branch.

So what, thirty-six? Or wait, forty-four security golems is all the Library can have? Quinn asked, not entirely sure she'd got the math right. Not to mention that didn't sound like enough for when the Library was fully powered and operational. Who came up with that arbitrary number?

Well, we need to hit the next power level before we can have more. That's as much as we can have on this power level if all of the branches are open.

"Which they're not," Quinn mused out loud.

Well, whose fault is that? The Library chuckled.

Actually, Quinn said, *it's not mine, it's yours.*

I beg to differ. The Library let out a sigh. *Although, I guess by way of being too trusting it was my fault.*

None of us know whose fault it is . . . that's what we're trying to figure out, Quinn grumbled. *Anyway, where is Milaro? I haven't seen him for what seems like days.*

You realize he runs an entire sector, right?

Quinn knew this. She knew it very well, in fact. She just didn't really want to admit it. *I know he has other things to do, I understand. I just . . .*

Well, this line of questioning would suggest you don't. What's troubling you, Quinn?

Quinn sighed. "Nothing, he just . . . he was here so often he became a staple and I got very used to having him here. I'm just . . . I miss him. I miss his company. It's like the grandfather I never had."

But you know you're not actually related to him, right?

Of course, I know that. I'm just . . . I'm feeling a little out of my depth. Quinn really hated admitting that.

The Library's tone was soothing when it spoke. *Quinn, anybody in your position would feel out of their depth.*

Thanks for the pep talk, Mom.

The Library chuckled, and it was a warm sensation. It echoed through Quinn's office softly. A joyous sound.

You're in a good mood now, Quinn said.

I am in an excellent mood now, actually.

Why? Tell me.

You just reminded me that I don't have to be completely serious and focused all the time. And that breaks, even small ones like this, can do a lot of good.

There's a lot to do, but you can't pour from an empty jug. Quinn had never understood the analogy. Pouring from a cup. Why would you pour from a cup anyway? Jug was much better. Or tea or coffee pot.

She could practically feel the Library smile.

The security settings need to be upgraded because Siliqua, Harish, and

Cadre, in applying their theory or your theory of the sequencing, have figured out that well, let's just put it this way, I haven't evolved enough with the times.

This time, Quinn chuckled. *Well, I mean, you've been around for like eons. It's not like it's easy for you to change.*

But it needs to be. And I mean, I can technically change into anything, so why can't I adapt to other things?

Quinn laughed. *Wow, I like you in this frame of mind.*

I confess, I'm fond of this mood myself. I believe Harish, Siliqua, and Cadre will want to speak to you a bit later, tomorrow probably. They've come across several things that'll help us immensely in the long run.

Thanks for being vague. Quinn rolled her eyes

I'll let them explain it. I don't want to spoil anything, plus there are several experiments they're still running that won't be done until oh, late into the night tonight. So just in case, I won't spoil anything simply because it could be that I'm completely and utterly wrong and nothing is working the way they said it probably would.

I appreciate that forethought, Quinn said. *Anyway, talk to me. What do you mean they found new ways to adapt your security?*

I'm pretty much stuck in the ways from when the universe was much smaller, less populated, less diverse. There are specific brainwave patterns I haven't scanned for. As in, I haven't adapted to the evolution of many species. Therefore we're going to modify the security system to be more aware and well, teach an old dragon new tricks.

I like that, Quinn said. *Why do you think you haven't changed up until now?*

Do I have to admit it out loud? the Library grumbled. *I've been somewhat oblivious. Being what I am, having had all of my siblings' assistance in becoming what I am, having the amount of power that I've had, I believed wholeheartedly that I knew best what to do, where to do it, how to do it, and who to do it with. The thing is that as time has changed, so too have civilizations. They've risen, they've fallen, some have been annihilated. Chaos crept out during those five hundred years we were gone, which is a speck of dust in the grand scheme of time, and destroyed or annihilated at least seven species*

I've been able to track so far, Quinn. It's all so much bigger than me and I never realized it. These last couple of months have been extremely eye-opening. As much as I may be oblivious to change, there are some things that are going to have to.

That's very astute of you, Quinn said. *I don't think you're as stubborn as you think you are.*

Thank you. Coming from somebody who is probably one of the least stubborn people I've met, I appreciate the compliment.

How about we just work toward fixing the problem? Quinn grinned to herself.

Now that, Quinn, is a little bit naive, but I do love the sentiment and so I shall agree.

Misha has the components for the security upgrades, then? Quinn asked.

Misha popped right into being directly in front of Quinn's desk. "Yes, Librarian?"

Quinn laughed. "You know, I don't think I'll ever get used to saying or sometimes just thinking your name and having you simply appear. I can't even talk about you behind your back."

Misha cocked her head to one side. "Why would you talk about me behind your back? Are you not satisfied with my work?"

"It's . . . never mind. It's just a silly thing from a silly time in my life," Quinn said, suddenly feeling decidedly melancholy. High school had often felt lonely.

Misha blinked at her, waiting.

"Anyway, you have the components for all of the security golems we need, right?" Quinn asked, glad to change the subject.

"Yes. Milaro has arranged for our supply levels to be boosted. This means as the next branches or power capacities are reached, we will have sufficient parts."

"How close are we to that?" Quinn asked herself more than anyone else and accessed the information through her HUD. "Hmm. We only need like ten percent more."

Yes, the Library said. *We could do with opening another filtration pillar, but that pulls a lot of power anyway. I'd prefer to surpass into the next level first. Right now I believe we're sitting at five pillars, and that should be enough for now. We'll want to be at eight by the time we finish the next level of power and we need to have fixed Ashiron by the time we are at optimal levels, which will then allow us to flush the universe's magic system continuously without pause.*

"Great," Quinn said, "so everything's on track in that. Any idea what's wrong with Ashiron yet?"

"No," Misha said flatly. "Still a mystery. It is not functioning and your ordering its seal to be increased was likely a good call. We will likely have to go down and inspect it properly, perhaps extract it, maybe quarantine it, perhaps even rebuild it. We must ascertain if its problem is contagious."

"That would be horrific," Quinn said.

"Everything is sealed and in place and has been for quite some time," Misha continued. "Whoever initially sealed it, knew to cut it off from everything else."

You have no idea how bad it could get, the Library responded. *Contagion means, not only would it spread to the other filters, but also through the filtered mana that goes out into the rest of the universe. That's just a whole debacle we need to avoid.*

"I guess our path forward is easy enough for now," Quinn said. "Thanks, Misha. I didn't mean to interrupt what you were doing. I was just curious about our security levels."

Misha nodded. "I understand, Librarian. I did not want to leave you waiting. I will get back to my duties."

Quinn watched as Misha disappeared again. Her instincts told her something was slightly off . . . not right but she couldn't pin point it. She frowned. "Did that take a lot of energy to do?" she asked the Library.

No, it doesn't. Misha is an integral part of the Library. She is an extension of the console in a way.

"But not like Lynx, right?" Quinn asked not bothering to speak in her head since she was in her office anyway.

Very right. Lynx is . . . he's special.

"I get it," Quinn said.

We'll leave it at that. The Library chuckled.

"Anyway," Quinn said, "I might take some time for myself. I should probably get some books to absorb."

Actually, the Library said, *you should probably be absorbing a few books a night. You're at the intermediate level for the most part now, except for any new areas you begin. It's probably best for you to continue on this path first. Intermediate skills take more time to process. It's best to process them while you sleep. Helps them stay in your mind better.*

"Will you recommend specific books for me every night?" Quinn asked, half-jokingly.

I can if you'd like me to.

"Well, you are the Library. You *don't* think it would be a good idea for you to be the one to recommend what will help me the most?" Quinn asked.

Malakai would be your best bet for combat-related items, and Milaro would definitely be the best to train your magical elements, especially the mind tomes.

Quinn rolled her eyes. "Do you see either of them here? It's getting late. I'm hungry and I'm inordinately tired right now. I think I should grab a few books, go up to my room and relax for once."

I'm sorry, Quinn.

"For what?" Quinn asked the Library. She was genuinely surprised by the comment.

I realize you have a lot on your shoulders.

"Yeah, but you know, I would have had to choose a major back on Earth and probably been bored for the rest of my life."

But you wouldn't have known that you were bored, said the Library matter-of-factly.

"Maybe not, but this is okay." She grinned gesturing vaguely all around her. "After all, give me a few more months and I'll be super powerful."

The Library chuckled. *Yes. Yes, you will.*

"So, recommendations?" she prodded.

Fine, the Library said. *I think you should try* Contemporary Ice Magic *since you seem to work well with that.* Ice Magic as a Missile: The Untraceable Killer *is also an excellent volume.*

"Wait, wait," Quinn said. "*Ice Magic as a Missile: The Untraceable Killer.* Is this like a how-to murder mystery book?"

No, it's simply a delicate subject in the advanced ice section. That should allow you to hone the blast that you've been perfecting, without making ice balls float everywhere first. But I also think you should read the following book along with it just in case. Focus on You: How Not to Get Distracted and Accidentally Impale People.

Quinn blinked. "Is that really a book or are you pulling my leg?"

Oh no, that's really a book. Sometimes you have to explicitly spell out what a volume contains, otherwise a lot of people don't understand what you're getting at.

Quinn laughed. "Okay, so that's three."

Yes, and the other two are from the Restricted Vault. I know I said maybe you don't need to get books out of the restricted section, but I think these two would be important for you. Especially at this juncture in time.

"Well, spill, tell me what they are," Quinn said.

Discussions on Temporal Mind Manipulation, *for one.*

"Temporal mind manipulation?" Quinn asked, a shiver down her spine at the implications of the title.

Yes, you know how you speed up your thoughts and you try to have an entire conversation in your head while somebody else is talking to you?

"Yes," Quinn said, not realizing that the Library had caught on to her innermost thoughts when she did that.

Oh no, Quinn, I wasn't reading your mind.

"You're doing it again," Quinn said.

No, it was your facial expression. Those are like an open book, but of course I knew what Milaro was teaching you. I know you can speed up your thoughts. After all, I know every single book you've absorbed up until now.

"Oh, valid point." Quinn said, "plus we've had a few conversations in that manner."

True.

"What's the other book?" Quinn asked.

It is Thesis on Distilled Essence Utilization.

"Wow, that's very specific to me."

We might have used some of that book as a wee guideline for the theory behind how you were created. It holds integral theories that could easily be misused or applied in unethical ways.

That information didn't sit easily with Quinn. She wasn't entirely sure how to process it. But she got an urgent feeling that she should read that book specifically.

As soon as possible.

3 4

PARALLELS TO DRAW

THE PILE OF BOOKS IN FRONT OF HER MADE QUINN SECOND GUESS asking the Library to make recommendations.

After absorbing *Discussions on Temporal Mind manipulation*, *Thesis on Distilled Essence Utilization*, *Contemporary Ice Magic*, *Ice Magic as a Missile: The Untraceable Killer*, and *Focus and You: How Not to Get Distracted and Accidentally Impale People*, Quinn's brain felt like it was full of dense fog.

Thesis on Distilled Essence Utilization plagued her thoughts somewhat. She didn't quite grasp how they'd done what they'd done. The sheer scope of stripping down and refining bare essence seemed an overwhelming process. Perhaps this one would take a while longer to sink in.

She meandered downstairs and into her office, glancing over at the check-in desk where Dottie ushered a few of the newer assistants around. Quinn frowned. She didn't really recognize any of them, which wasn't necessarily a problem in and of itself. It was just that she was pretty sure it was rude to inspect her own assistants.

They were the Library's employees, after all.

First things first, she said to herself as Aradie flew in with what looked like a breakfast sandwich packed in a nice little brown bag sent by Cook via Aradie post.

"Thank you," she said to the bird who settled on the perch on the back of Quinn's chair. Quinn looked around her office for a moment. She'd definitely been spending a lot of time in it lately. She wondered if it was possible to spend too much time in her office.

There was a knock on Quinn's door and she looked up, surprised to see Eric hovering there.

"What's up?" she said.

"I came to give you some news." The imp refused to meet her gaze, looking everywhere in the office except directly at her.

"Okay, you're being oddly somber for, you know, yourself." Quinn watched him intently. He was hiding something. "What's the problem?"

Eric shrugged his shoulders, kind of looked from side to side, and finally met her eyes. "Geneva is almost finished with her work. You can probably visit the Esposians relatively soon."

Quinn leaned forward, putting her chin on her hands, and watched Eric closely. The imp had a very specific way of speaking when he wasn't telling her the entire truth, and that was precisely what he was doing right now.

"So you're telling me that Geneva isn't ready for us to come yet, is that correct?" She reorganized what he'd said.

"Yes."

"Well, I knew that already. What aren't you telling me?" She leaned back in her chair, never breaking their eye contact.

Eric finally sighed and then shrugged. "I'm not telling you that Uncle Hal said you're still welcome at any time."

Quinn pondered that for a moment. Why would he not want to tell her that? "I'm glad. I plan on heading there as soon as I mark a few more things off my list. I have several things to organize here, and then I have to visit the Esposians, and we still have to check on what Harish and Siliqua's work has yielded with regards to Ashiron. But after that, tell him I will be there as soon as I can. I'm really looking forward to the visit."

Eric raised an eyebrow. "You're sincerely looking forward to visiting Halschius?"

Quinn raised an eyebrow at him. "Should I not be?"

"Well, no." Eric paused as if trying to get his head around what he wanted to say. "It's just we don't get many willing visitors, shall we say?"

Quinn laughed. "Well, I'm sure the fiery presence of your uncle and the constant, what is it, two, three, or seven wars he has to deal with probably helps contribute to that whole unwelcome sensation."

"True," Eric said, and then he winked. "But we'd love to have you, Librarian. We might not let you come back to your Library."

"I don't think you're gonna have a choice. Lynx will pull me back," Quinn said smugly.

"You spoil all my fun, all the bloody time." Eric actually threw his head back and laughed his maniacal little laugh.

Quinn just grinned at him.

"Librarian," Eric said, as if he meant to change the subject so easily. "What is it you're looking at?"

Quinn raised an eyebrow. "What do you mean, what am I looking at?"

"Well, I mean, you've got your HUD pulled up." He gestured in front of her.

"Oh, no, I was just looking at the books I've absorbed and the ones I've got to try tonight." The sheer number of textbooks she still needed to learn was overwhelming. What she wouldn't do for a nice escapism novel right then. Perhaps she needed to arrange that. "I was just . . ."

"Do you have any questions? I can try and answer questions. I might not even charge you for them." Eric's grin widened.

This time, Quinn raised an eyebrow and sincerely contemplated his offer. "Look, I just . . . I have a lot of skills and it's just a lot." She paused as she said that. "I think I say that more than anything else."

"Well, except for books," Eric said.

"Except for books," she repeated. She smiled. He somehow usually made her stress disappear. "You do have a way with words, Eric."

"I know," the imp said, grinning evilly. "How about you review stuff a little later? I believe Narilin wants to see you."

"And how long have you believed Narilin wants to see me?" Quinn asked.

"From the moment I came in here. It's just that then there were other things I wanted to talk to you about that I feel are slightly more important than what Narilin wants to talk to you about." The imp was still skirting around the edges.

"You think what you want to talk to me about is more important than the repair and replacement of a heap of necessary Library books?" Quinn asked, leaning back in her chair.

"Well, when you put it that way, it makes me sound selfish," Eric said.

"Maybe a little," Quinn replied and pushed herself to her feet. "Okay, I'll go see Narilin and find out what she wants. I might pop by and see how Farrow is doing with the bookworms and her assistants."

"You want some company?" Eric asked.

Quinn met his gaze properly, really giving him a good look over. "I'm sure Aradie and I would appreciate company."

Walking through the Library never got old. It was so active and alive. All the people, different species intermingling, both levels filled with patrons.

It was one of the first times she didn't stop by the kitchen before doing anything else, which was all thanks to the breakfast Aradie flew in for her. She reached up to scratch the owl on the back of her neck before stopping by to see Farrow on their way to the book infirmary.

Farrow's tree likeness was different in many ways from the Salosier's. She was, after all, a golem, but her form was still slender and elegant and reminded Quinn of the trunk of a birch tree, even if the coloring and texture weren't quite the same.

Farrow turned and greeted Quinn with a smile. She was perhaps the most expressive of all the golems, at least all of the *original* golems they'd summoned.

"What brings you here, Librarian?" She inclined her head.

"I just wanted to see how you were going and how Marilyn and

Arilin are doing helping you now they've been here a while." Quinn genuinely wished she had more time to spend in this section of the Library. It had such a rich and earthy feeling. A magical vibe that was more genuine than anywhere else.

"They're doing fine." Farrow gestured to the back corner where the twins, cousins of Narilin, were currently working on what looked like . . .

"Is that a bookworm habitat?" Quinn asked, intrigued.

"Yes, it is." Farrow sounded so enthusiastic, it was contagious. "The twins have devised an experimental method for us to acquire the correct bookworm affinities we are lacking."

"That sounds wonderful," Quinn said.

Farrow nodded. "It is, actually. If you want, I can go into the theory behind it. I think you'd find the fact that we don't actually need to mate them right now, that instead as long as we . . . oh." Farrow shook her head. "I am sorry, I can get carried away. I know you're busy, Librarian."

"Oh no, Farrow, you're fine," Quinn reassured. "To be perfectly clear, if I had a little more time on my hands, I'd sit and chat with you about this. Keep everything stored up, because as soon as I do have some time, I'd love to sit and have a coffee, or a tea, or some sort of beverage or food with you."

Farrow cocked her head to one side. "Well, I do not require sustenance in the way that you do, Librarian, but I would be very happy to sit and spend time with you."

"Thank you," Quinn said, quite taken with Farrow's sincerity. "Is there anything we can get for you, anything you need that can help you in your research on how to replenish the bookworms, the silverfish, all that sort of stuff?"

"As soon as I know, Librarian, I will pass it on to you."

"Thank you," Quinn said. "We're going to go and see Narilin now."

"Say hello for me." Farrow inclined her head like a sort of mini bow.

"Yes," echoed Marilyn and Arilin. "Say hi to Narilin for us."

Quinn smiled, trying not to laugh again, but the names were so similar, they tripped her tongue up more than she liked to admit. And they were all so nice. Narilin was definitely more at ease in the Library now she had her family around her, which Quinn thought could only be a bonus.

Today felt easy. Peaceful.

Sort of like the calm before the storm.

But Quinn refused to dwell on how portentous that could be as they made their way to the book infirmary.

Stepping through the ornately carved doors with their depictions of books and trees and reading and writing, Quinn paused. There was this feeling every time she entered that annex, this beautiful, over-whelming sense of love for knowledge and books.

It put Quinn at ease, almost like nothing could disrupt it in the universe. Sadly, she knew much better than that. However, the sensa-tion was encompassing, revitalizing. She'd have to remember that next time she was feeling oddly depleted by, well, the circumstances around them.

Maybe just sitting here for an hour would replenish her reserves. Calm her energies down.

"Librarian," Narilin said, her voice bright and lofty. She was in a good mood. Jane stood next to her and grinned over at Quinn before going back to binding the book she was working on.

"It's good to see you, Narilin," Quinn said, glancing around. Apart from slightly fewer books being present, it looked much the same as it had last time she'd visited. "Tell me, is there anything we can do for you? Do you need anything from me? I haven't seen you for a while and I was curious as to how things are progressing here and what I might do to assist you."

Narilin shook her head. "There is really nothing I can think of. As a general rule, I go to Misha with any requirements I have. Farrow has been working with me and my cousins and, well, we almost have things solved. Everything will be in tip-top shape extremely soon. Is there something troubling you, Librarian?"

Quinn blinked. "Well, no, just trying to make sure that I'm doing my job."

Narilin laughed and it really did sound like the breeze on a spring day. It smelled like it too, and the relaxation that came along with the birthing of a new season washed over Quinn, making her feel beautifully relaxed. She knew the Salosier species had certain abilities that allowed them to soothe the nerves of people, but this was very welcome. It wasn't as intrusive as the Darígháhnish mind-soothing powers.

Quinn had been more stressed than she liked to admit.

"Eric did mention you had something to talk to me about?" she asked, prodding gently.

"Actually, there is one book we are having difficulty repairing, Librarian," Narilin said, her tone suddenly concerned.

"Oh, really?" Quinn perked up, glad to see there was something she could help with. Perhaps. "What's it called?"

"Oh, it is called *Jeshua's Tome of Revival.*" Narilin glanced at her cousin as if asking her if she should talk about it. Jane nodded. "The problem is, I believe it might have been a Restricted Vault book."

Quinn blinked. "What makes you think that?"

"We have the cover, but the pages were completely devoured or disintegrated. I'm not entirely sure how either. There is no recollection of it in the main collection, but the spine has a Library stamp. So I thought I would ask if you know of it," Narilin finished with a small smile, as if she was glad she'd found something the Librarian could help with.

"Could those pages have been ripped out?" Quinn asked.

Narilin cocked her head to one side as she pulled the binding up to show Quinn. "Well, that is a possibility, by somebody very strong with an affinity for canceling magic, perhaps."

"But wouldn't that destroy the tome?" Quinn asked, reaching forward and running her fingers over the leather. She'd hoped it would give her a spark. But there was a dull and lifeless quality to it. No connection sparked at all.

"Technically, removing the content pages destroys the knowledge." Narilin paused before continuing. "But not its intrinsic magic, because the cover is still intact."

"So it technically wouldn't destroy the tome?" Quinn asked.

"Exactly. It is merely missing its interior," Narilin confirmed.

Quinn sighed. "And where was it?"

"It was in one of the massive piles from the intermediate section of the magic division."

Quinn suppressed a sigh. "Thank you for letting me know."

"You're welcome." Narilin's smile widened and Quinn felt a brief rush of affection for the Salosier.

Do you know that tome? Quinn asked the Library.

I have no recollection of the tome in question, the Library said. *But if it's in the Library, the odds are that I should know.*

The Library sounded so defeated, Quinn wished she could give it a hug. *Don't get sentimental on me now, Quinn.*

It's very hard not to, Quinn shot back.

Eric still hovered at her side. He paused. "I've been called to the front desk. There's a somebody doesn't want to pay their fines." His glee was practically palpable.

Quinn looked up at the imp who was grinning so widely he looked like a Cheshire cat. Quinn realized there were a lot of parallels to draw in this Library. "Well, you look happy."

"I'm ecstatic," he said.

"I guessed as much." She laughed.

"I'm off to impose a fine, Librarian. I'm excited—oh, and there's someone waiting for you at the front desk too!" he said the last as he'd already begun dashing back to the check in desk.

Quinn sighed and took one more look around the Infirmary. One of these days she was going to improve her restoration abilities. Today, however, was not that day. Aradie pecked at her hair.

"Yes, yes," she muttered. "I know I've got a visitor."

Retracing her steps to get back to the Library, Quinn meandered somewhat slower than usual. She could smell amazing fragrances coming from the dining hall attached to the culinary branch and barely resisted the urge to stop and get some food. She had a visitor, after all. It wasn't Milaro; that was certain. He would have just teleported to her precise location.

She moved reluctantly toward the front desk when she heard her name called.

"Quinn! Wait up! I'm taking you up on that offer!"

She turned toward the voice, unable to prevent the huge grin she felt spreading across her face. "Jasper," she said. "It's so good to see you."

And she meant every word.

3 5

THIS IS NORMAL

Jasper's arrival brought joy to Quinn's day. Even after all the ritual problems, she was glad to see her newfound friend. "What do you mean you're here to take me up on my offer?" she asked.

"Exactly that!" Jasper replied. "You said I could be a Library assistant, and so I've decided that's precisely what I'll do."

"What was that I hear?" Malakai asked, suddenly standing next to them.

Quinn glanced around. "How did you get here?" she asked.

"I've been standing here the whole time," Malakai said, avoiding her gaze.

Quinn narrowed her eyes, peering at him. "Are you pulling ninja tricks on me again?"

"Pretty much. You should probably pay more attention to your senses in regards to people's proximity through the Library, because that's going to come in handy one day," he said with a smirk.

"What?" Quinn said, "When we're playing hide-and-seek?"

Jasper laughed. "You two have the best interactions. I could record them and conjure them for people and they would pay money to see them."

Quinn scowled.

"Anyway," Malakai said, leveling a glare at Jasper, "what's this I hear about you becoming a Library assistant?"

"Exactly that!" Jasper said. "I might be a little bit overqualified, but I think I'd do a pretty good job."

"So do I," Quinn said. "In fact, I think you and Dottie would get on amazingly well."

As if summoned, Quinn could hear the tiny footfalls that told her Dottie was nearby.

"Did I hear you mention my name?" Dottie said, bright and cheery and perhaps slightly suspicious.

"Yes." Quinn grinned. "We were talking about you, not to you."

"Quinn," Dottie said, "that is just horrid of you, and I thought we'd become friends since you accidentally sat on me so many weeks ago."

Quinn chuckled, unable to stop herself at Dottie's dramatic statement. "You know I love you, Dottie."

The chair preened. "Yes, I suppose I do."

"Hey, rewind," Malakai said. He pointed very deliberately at Jasper. "Why does she get to be an assistant? She tried to attack you and kill you in a swamp."

"But she didn't *mean* it," Quinn said, dismissing his concern. "It was all a misunderstanding. And we got that whole fiasco sorted out. It wasn't even really Jasper's fault."

"What, it wasn't really Jasper's fault that they lied to Savinth and told her that they'd give her stuff that they never meant to?"

Jasper sighed. "I admit that was very wrong of me, of us. It's just, you know, we're very possessive about our recipes. Most of them are specifically species oriented. They've taken millennia to refine and condense into their most potent formats. In the wrong hands they could cause a lot of trouble for, well, for a whole slew of people."

"Wait . . ." Quinn interrupted her. "Are these recipes in the Library?"

Jasper shrugged. "Many of them probably are. But there'll be quite a few that aren't given how long it was closed and how many we've worked on in more recent years." She paused as if thinking for a moment, and then shook her head before continuing. "Probably shouldn't have offered them to Savinth in the first place. But we really wanted to get our hands on that book."

"Why?" Quinn said. "Why did you want that specific book?"

"You know," Jasper said, suddenly looking extremely confused, "I'm actually not sure. My grandmother told me we needed it, and I haven't seen her for a couple of centuries now. Anyway, all's well that ends well. And now I'm here because Quinn told me I should be an assistant."

"Do you really think it'll be that easy for you to become a Librarian's assistant?" Malakai practically growled out. He crossed his arms and glared at her.

"Why won't it be?" Quinn asked. "I mean, *you're* a Librarian's assistant and you didn't even want to be one. Milaro's the one who dobbed you in and made you an assistant regardless of what you wanted."

Malakai scowled. "It doesn't matter. I'm supposed to be training you in combat. Are you ready today or are you going to blow me off today like you did yesterday?"

Quinn paused. She'd only been having fun, but he seemed quite out of sorts with what she'd said. "I'm sorry, Mal. I was just playing."

He glared at her. "Anyway," he said, turning his attention to Jasper, "just what makes you think that you'd make a great Librarian assistant?"

"The fact that I love books, and that I can already use my own type of magic that doesn't even require books. At least not most of the time. And the fact that Quinn told me I'd be a good assistant." Jasper paused and looked thoughtful for a second. "Hey, I haven't seen the Aracnio twins since the first time I visited. They've never been the bookiest bunch, and I wanted to talk to them."

Quinn felt her mood sour. "Yeah, probably won't be seeing them ever again."

"What do you mean?" Jasper asked.

"Let's just say"—Quinn made the decision to trust Jasper with the news—"we discovered we have potential discord in our midst only to have them conveniently disappear."

"Pretty nasty coincidence that," Jasper said. "Never mind, we'll get to the bottom of it."

"I think *you* seem a bit suspicious," Malakai said. "After all, I mean, you didn't like the Library either. How do we know you're not secretly planning something?"

"That's when I thought that Korradine spoke for the Library. Now I've realized something was seriously haywire with that whole situation. I feel bad. Maybe if we'd realized sooner . . ." Jasper shrugged. "Well, whatever, the past is the past. I was thinking, Quinn, what about an assistant for you?"

Quinn looked at Jasper, quite puzzled. "What do you mean, what about an assistant for me?"

"Exactly that, a personal assistant, not a Librarian's assistant, like a personal Librarian assistant." Jasper scrunched her face a bit, like she was trying to wrap her mind around what she'd just said.

"Oh, like to help me with stuff that I specifically do around the Library?" Quinn gave that some thought. *Is that something I can do?* she asked the Library.

Technically, you can do almost anything you want in the Library, Quinn, except for destroy it. I'd be extremely put out if you destroy my Library after all the work I've put in.

Quinn chuckled. "I mean, that's a possibility, but I'm not exactly sure what you would do as my assistant."

"Oh, I could teach you ritual magic?" Jasper's huge eyes lit up with her smile.

"Well, you were going to do that anyway," Quinn said.

"I know, but now it would be in an official capacity."

Quinn laughed. "Okay, you can teach me ritual magic. I'll definitely need a bit of help with some stuff, too. I'm not the best remembering to talk to people, and you really have a way with them. You could maybe see what people feel about the current situation with the Aracnio twins, and all the upheaval."

"Sure, but they don't know me at all yet."

"I'll do it," Dottie said. "Everybody loves me."

"That they do," Quinn said. "Sounds like a good solution if you don't mind?"

Dottie practically preened. "Excellent. I'll be off, then."

Aradie plucked out one of Quinn's hairs. "Ouch!" Quinn said. "That hurt."

Aradie leveled a glare at her.

"Oh," Quinn said, "I'm so sorry, you're so much more than an assistant, Aradie."

The owl cooed ever so slightly, only barely mollified by the reassurance.

"Fine then, I guess." Quinn laughed. "You can be the Librarian's assistant assistant."

Jasper laughed. "That is perfect."

"No, actually wait until you hear what I need you to do for me," Quinn warned. "One of the things I most need help with is for someone to take over the roster and room allocations for the assistants."

"But that sounds boring, Quinn." Jasper pouted.

"Do you want to be my assistant, or did you just come here to try and have fun, discover new magic, and see what trouble you could get up to?" Quinn asked, crossing her arms.

Jasper's cheeks coloring slightly.

Malakai laughed. "See, I told you she's not going to be a good assistant."

"I'll be a fantastic assistant, Malakai, much better than you as a trainer or whatever you are," Jasper retorted.

"Thanks to me, she's not dead yet," Malakai shot back.

Jasper ignored him and looked at Quinn, slamming her fists down on the table in Quinn's office. "I guarantee you, I'll be the best assistant Librarian assistant ever. We really need to come up with a better name for that."

"How about Personal Librarian Assistant?" Quinn suggested. "No, wait, that sounds really sort of creepy."

Jasper actually laughed.

"Okay, fine. I'll need you to meet with Mal and Dottie, Eric, Geneva . . . and Danio has been promoted since the twins left. They only ever did their shifts together anyway. The one I really need you to help me keep an eye on is Finn."

"Finn, the Ilgonomur?" Jasper asked.

"Yes, our aim is to keep Finn safe. No allowing any strange visitors access to them on the grounds that they might know them." Quinn made sure her tone held the right level of serious in it. She wasn't sure they'd need an extra set of eyes, not with the amount they were beefing Library security, but it couldn't hurt.

"I can do that. Consider it done," Jasper said, her tone serious. Quinn wasn't entirely sure how to take that.

"Okay, we'll probably also have to meet with Carafax soon," Quinn said.

"Who's Carafax?" Jasper asked.

"Oh, Carafax is the most lovely slothilus I've ever met," Quinn replied.

Malakai cleared his throat.

"Fine," Quinn said. "The only slothilus I've ever met, but still the best. And they're helping us piece together some of the missing bits and pieces we need for the Library puzzle."

Jasper's eyes narrowed. "There's something you're not telling me, right?"

"Maybe a little bit," Quinn said. "You're brand new, and even though I'm glad to have a friend . . ."

"You don't trust me yet, do you?" Jasper said, a little bit of a pout in her voice.

"To be honest, not quite. I want to, and it'll come as long as you don't try to burn the Library down in the next little while." Quinn tried to cushion the reveal with a smile. "Aradie thinks you might be trying to muscle in on her territory, but you're not lying about things, and you're very honest."

Jasper preened a bit. "I am, you know, very honest, blunt even. Not everybody likes that," she added.

Quinn nodded. "I totally understand. Anyway, if you could take care of those things, I'd super appreciate that. Mal, could you show her where she'll be staying?"

He leveled such a blistering glare at Quinn that she almost reconsidered asking him to help out.

"Fine, but you owe me," he said.

Quinn suppressed a sigh. "Don't I know it." She waited until they'd left.

Dottie trotted back in and around behind her desk. "Are you okay, Quinn? You seem a little bit down today."

"You know, just so much to do, so little time," Quinn replied.

"It's not all that bad. You can do it. I know! How about I stay and keep you some company? I've got a few reports to read through on my HUD, and I would love to spend time with you," Dottie offered.

Quinn, not for the first time, wished that Dottie could take a different form, because she had this complete and utter certainty that Dottie would be one of the best huggers in the universe, and while Quinn wasn't often a hugger, right then, she could really have used one. "Thanks, Dottie."

"No problem," Dottie replied.

Quinn pulled up her HUD and looked at her own statistics.

Name: Quinn

Age: Irrelevant

Heritage: Earth, Sector 12942, Cosmicisodracus

*Species: Librarian**

Energy Capacity: 2,493/2,493

Mana Levels: 1,985/1,985

Alignment: 101%

*Affinities: 1,722***

Tome Knowledge: 135

Affinity Level: 13

Determination: Rising

**Awaiting determination*

***As far as the Library can determine*

She had exceeded her energy even more now. She frowned at it. How was her energy still climbing at the original rate?

"What seems to be troubling you?" Lynx asked, peering at her HUD from behind her.

"Can you really see that?" Quinn asked, barely phased by the fact that he had appeared so suddenly. She was really getting used to the way people popped up everywhere. What with Malakai, Lynx, and occasionally Milaro . . . it was practically common practice.

"Not everybody can see details unless you will them to," he said, "but I can, because I'm the Library."

"Nice. I thought you said most people slow down when they reach two thousand energy."

"Ah, but Quinn, haven't we established you're not most people?" Lynx replied.

"Yeah," she said. "We really have, haven't we?" She paused for a second, taking a deep breath to center herself. "Okay, so for me this is normal."

"You'll have ridiculous amounts of energy by the time you're done."

"Great. So here we are." She leaned back in her chair's cushioning; it was sort of like a hug. Almost what she needed.

"Here we are." Lynx studied her for a few moments. "What's wrong, Quinn?"

"I don't know. I feel like things are a little too quiet. Everything's a bit too smooth."

"And you just had to go and say that again, didn't you?" Lynx teased. "You warned me the first time and now you do it all the time.

Quinn couldn't shake the feeling she was maybe forgetting something important. "I think we need to check on Finn."

"Finn was fine the last time I checked on them," Lynx said. "I've been doing it periodically. They're just holed up with books and they've come down to do a few shifts. Whenever they get around books, they lose all their anxiety."

"I know how they feel," Quinn said. She stretched and leaned forward again, studying all the information. "Okay, great. Let me go through filtration status. We need to reboot another pillar."

"Probably a good idea," Lynx said.

"Let's put that on the list too," Quinn muttered as she searched for the lists. "Yeah, pillar filtration status." Her eyes lit up and she let out a little gasp. "Oh wait! Are we close to the next power level now?"

"We are." Lynx had that damn Cheshire grin on his face again. "Very close to the next level." A rush of relief that ran through Lynx's face and he smiled. "Maybe a week or two."

"Well, that is some of the most excellent news I've heard all day." Quinn smiled. "So we should probably wait on that pillar, I guess."

"I'd agree with that," Lynx said.

Quinn nodded. Suddenly, she felt like everything they'd been doing had a purpose. She glanced down at the long list of items that she still had to nail down, glad to see a few of them had made progress.

Priority listing - Librarian: Quinn.

Prioritize:

Strength - progress halted - immediate attention required

Fine Definition - in progress 65%

Pillar Activation - in progress 4/10

Task Delegation - in progress 43%

Library Returns - in progress

Energy Amplification - missing components

She frowned. *Strength – progress halted* was always a bit concerning. Despite trying to, she hadn't been able to figure out the why of that. She sighed and closed the list. There was still work to do, but everything was moving along. "You know maybe this isn't as overwhelming as I originally thought."

"Good," Lynx said. "Because I need you not overwhelmed."

Quinn didn't like the sound of that. "Oh, no. Now what?"

"It's not because of what you said before. I came in with this information. Geneva's ready for your visit the morning and she'll be waiting for you with her aunt Nishpa."

"Nishpa? I don't know a Nishpa."

Lynx paused for a moment before responding. "No, you don't, but Nishpa knows you."

36

ALMOST EMPTY

When Lynx mentioned that Geneva and her aunt wanted to see Quinn, she'd anticipated that Geneva would come to her. There were several Library pertinent matter they needed to go over since her absence.

She hadn't expected to be woken up early by Aradie, and then rushed to the doors by Malakai and Lynx, before she'd even woken up properly; before she'd even had time to get breakfast from Cook! Not to mention, she wasn't prepared to traverse through the Library doors before her brain had fully woken up.

As they prepared to walk through the portal Malakai nudged her. "My grandfather wanted you to know that Nishpa is a longtime friend of his."

Quinn blinked up at him. "That's it? Nothing more informative?"

"Nothing at all. But logically that's how she knows you." Malakai grinned like that was cause for amusement.

Quinn sighed and prepared herself for a fall through the doors.

However, this time, perhaps because Lynx came with them, the door opened perfectly, exactly where they needed to be, nice and even with the ground. It didn't open a foot off the ground and send her falling flat on her face.

Two things struck Quinn as odd when she stepped into the world of the Esposians on Ishiposa Isle. First up, she wasn't expecting it to look like it had been ripped straight out of a fantastical game world. Although, in hindsight, given how their last visit to the area had gone, she should have expected it. After all, when they found the books and the afflicted Esposians, it'd been on a world with floating islands and fantastical skies.

Quinn still didn't understand the physics. She assumed it was just hand-wavy magic, but there was something slightly unsettling about looking off into the sky and seeing multiple floating islands with massive building structures and bodies of water that simply fell over the side of them.

The second thing she hadn't been expecting was the sheer opulence of the city they ported into. Right at the front gates with the entire thing stretching up in front of them. Majestic, and oddly quiet.

Gold etchings and coatings gleamed from the top of the walls and gates.

Their entrance from the Library opened up right in front of Geneva and . . . another Furionas fae who resembled the Librarian Assistant in a remarkable way, as if she was a pale copy of Geneva. That had to be this Aunt Nishpa.

Nishpa offered her hand to Quinn in the form of a greeting from Earth. "Well met, Librarian," she said. Her voice was a lower timbre than Quinn would have thought given her size, but then she guessed that was speciesism. Just because the Furionas fae were indeed diminutive didn't mean they couldn't have alto voices.

She smiled. "Thank you for having us," Quinn said as politely as she could with a slight incline of her head.

Nishpa laughed, and it reminded Quinn of Geneva, who hadn't said a word yet, and hung back. Her wings, even while they were fluttering rapidly, were somehow also drooping.

"This isn't my abode," Nishpa said self-deprecatingly. However, she gestured to the mass of buildings, the town, how high the wall around them stretched up in a representation of sheer power, not to mention the castle beyond the town. It was straight out of a fairy tale. There were multiple stone houses, inns, double stories, single stories with gardens and children playing in the front yards, and right up behind everything else rose a massive castle.

It reminded Quinn of some of the dwellings she'd seen in documentaries on England and Germany. It was majestic, but not in ruins. Perfectly preserved. Something whispered in the back of her mind and Quinn frowned. No one was trying to break through her defenses. She couldn't quite pinpoint what it was.

Quinn forced her smile a little. "Then I'm grateful you're here to greet us, because we wouldn't know where to go." She realized she was nervous, and had spoken as such. She glanced at Geneva again. "Hey, there."

Geneva raised her eyes, and Quinn had to stop herself from gasping in shock. Her assistant looked so tired. Even her beautiful golden skin had a much paler hue to it, not quite as light as her auntie's, but the beautiful red of her outfit even seemed duller than usual. And her gorgeous iridescent wings as well. Everything just seemed to be toned down a notch. She'd obviously been through a lot in the last several weeks. Quinn wished she could do more to help.

"You doing okay there, Geneva?" she asked.

"I am doing as well as can be expected, Librarian," Geneva answered, not even a fraction of her usual self evident in the words.

Quinn frowned.

Aradie cooed in Quinn's ear, and she nodded. She spoke to the bird telepathically. *I'm aware. She's obviously given a lot of herself to help the healing of her cousins. I only wish there was something I could do.*

Aradie cooed several more times, and punctuated it with a hoot. Quinn raised an eyebrow. *If you want me to understand that, you're going to have to actually speak to me.*

Aradie huffed. Quinn decided it probably wasn't important enough if the bird wasn't going to actually put things in words for her.

Malakai stepped forward. "Well met, Aunt Nishpa."

"Malakai," Nishpa said, a beautiful smile spreading across the woman's face, even if it did reveal extremely sharp teeth. "It has been an age since I've seen you. I think you were, well, as tall as me last time I saw you." She laughed again. That self-deprecating manner that seemed to come so easily to her, Quinn thought, really came easily to a lot of people, including herself. She took note of their interaction, watching intently.

"Well, I mean, I've grown," Malakai said. "You mean you and your standing-on-the-ground height, right?"

Nishpa laughed yet again. "How are you doing? Have you seen your mother recently?"

Malakai scowled.

"Ah," Nishpa said, "then I guess the rumors are true. You got left with Milaro, didn't you?"

Malakai rolled his eyes. "You know, as well as I do that he's been training me for the past decade."

"Yes, yes, I do know that. Apparently, you've done very well." Then she paused, and her expression grew serious. "I was very sorry to hear about your father."

"Not as sorry as the rest of us. Not as sorry as me. Anyway," Malakai said, changing the subject. "What's the agenda? Are we going to stand here at the gates all day, or do we get to enter the city?"

"Don't be so rude," Lynx snapped.

"Don't be so moody," Malakai shot straight back at him.

Quinn laughed. "Guys, we're here to visit, and I'd really like it if you don't chase the people off with your antics."

"What do you mean, our antics?" Malakai said, but Lynx looked thoughtful. That was when Quinn realized they'd really taken Lynx with them. He was corporeal. He was separate from the Library. Was that truly okay? For him to be out here with them despite his current memory situation not being resolved yet. She could feel panic rising in her.

Don't panic, Lynx shot at her.

Wait, you can just talk through my shields?

No, I can't. I'm not in your shields. I'm in the surface of your mind.

Oh, she said, but extended her senses and realized what he'd said was true, even if she didn't fully understand it.

I couldn't make you do anything if I tried.

Oh, she said again. *So you're here in the Library's stead?*

I have a better connection to it, makes sure this information gets back as fast as possible. Don't worry, you'll catch up to this level of intricacy next time you synchronize and as you get stronger, but just . . . I used to be able to do this all the time.

You sure it's safe to be doing it now? Quinn asked.

It's about as safe as it's going to get, until they completely fix me.

Well, don't accidentally link up to any systems and infect them or something.

Again, Quinn, not a machine.

Yeah, yeah, got it in one. She smiled at Nishpa, who was still talking to Malakai. "I have to ask, is Malakai right? Are we moving into the city anytime soon?"

This time Geneva laughed. But even that sounded exhausted. She finally did flash a half smile at Quinn. "No, we were originally going to take you straight to the castle, but I thought it might be better if you came and saw the people you helped save first. I think this is something you all need to see, and I have to admit, I'm very glad Lynx can relay it directly to the Library."

Before Quinn could respond to Geneva's comment, she noticed a shadow passing over them and glanced up. It must have been a mile or two up in the sky, but an island was directly over them, floating ever so slowly past.

She paused. She'd always assumed the islands were stationary. "Did they always move?" she asked, slightly shocked.

"Of course they all move. They're not tethered to the ground," Nishpa laughed. "You didn't think they just hung in the sky, did you?"

"Well, I didn't feel the one move that we were on last time we were here. Neither of them." Quinn was floundering a bit here.

Nishpa chuckled. "They don't move fast. Doesn't your Earth rotate? You don't feel that rotating, right?"

"No, I don't feel that rotating. I guess I never really thought of it."

"Don't worry, this'll pass in several hours," Nishpa said in a gentle tone. "Every now and again, there's just a little bit of extra shade."

Quinn's mind was suddenly alive with questions. "What about storms? Do clouds form next to islands, underneath islands, over islands? Some islands block it out for other islands?"

Nishpa laughed again. "Sometime . . . I promise, Quinn, one day I will sit down and teach you all about the physiology of the floating worlds. It's quite fascinating and very magical. But right now, Geneva is correct. We need you all to come with us and observe the victims yourself. They have . . . I'm just going to let you see them before I take you to see my cousins, the Prime Minister and his wife. Is that acceptable?"

"Well, of course. I mean, we rescued them, right? Sort of? Kind of?" Quinn said, recalling the state they'd been in when Geneva found them. They'd appeared almost bereft of the will to live. She often wondered if they did them any favors by saving them.

"I don't know," Malakai said. "I kind of think it was a fate worse than death. I would have liked to be put out of my misery. They looked like they were in agony."

"Don't say that near them, thanks," Geneva said. "It's taken a lot of work to get them to even the stage they're at now. You wouldn't understand."

"No, I probably wouldn't," Malakai said. "I just don't like to see people suffering. The pain they were in makes me furious, and I want to make someone pay."

Nishpa patted him gently on the arm. "We'll find them, and I'll make sure you're with us when we confront the culprits."

"Is there any way we could help them?" Quinn asked, reaching for some hope.

"I'm not sure at this stage. There could be some obscure knowledge deep in the Library and that's why we're extra glad Lynx is here. Perhaps seeing their state will trigger a memory of a text or an observation in a text." Geneva looked at the manifestation with hope in her eyes.

Lynx simply nodded. "I'll do my best to help."

"How about you take us to them?" Quinn asked.

Nishpa waved their group on. "Come on, let's go."

Quinn smiled as they walked through the beautiful town. She could still see the amazing islands in the distance. All the wonderful towns above them, below them, out beyond them. And then there was the city they were walking through. The thing was, she could hear every single footstep she took. It resonated against the pavement, yet the timing of the sounds felt slightly off.

Even though she could see children, there was no shouting or merriment. No chatter. And they weren't playing boisterously, or at all, really. None of them looked at her. They didn't seem overly aware of her. But every single one of them appeared to be extremely cautious.

Like they were all acting on their best behavior.

Quinn slotted that away for later.

"Are we welcome here?" Quinn asked, her voice soft as they passed several stalls that were selling all sorts of fruits and vegetables. At least, she thought they were fruits and vegetables. They looked very fruit and vegetable-y.

"Well," Nishpa said, "our cousins are a distant branch of the fae, and perhaps slightly reticent, but open to possibilities."

"Beautifully diplomatic answer," Quinn said.

Malakai snorted a laugh. Lynx, on the other hand, looked like he wasn't paying any attention to them. He seemed to be engrossed in his surroundings, taking everything in around him. And that's when Quinn knew he was aware of what she'd observed. They'd probably compare notes later or else he was already feeding information back to the Library. Aradie shuffled slightly closer to her head as if she didn't like the atmosphere around them.

Just when Quinn was starting to feel extra uneasy, Geneva pulled one of the curtained doors aside and ushered them into a building. It was made of a type of sandstone, Quinn thought, although she was no expert on building materials. Still, she thought it looked like sandstone. And it was much cooler inside, which was very welcome because the humidity had started to rise in the main part of the city.

They walked through what appeared to be a communal living area, where several people mingled, but no one spoke.

Another curious occurrence.

But Quinn kept her attention on Nishpa, whose shoulders seemed to hold an odd tension as they went through that room to a larger one where there were six beds. Quinn pushed down her gasp of horror. These Esposians, she recognized them.

She got the distinct impression that they weren't being told everything, and she didn't like the sensation one bit.

The patient's wings were still translucent, even though they were supposed to be sort of ghost-like in a way, this was another step past that. As if all the color had been sucked from them. All of their energy drained.

They had a sickly pallor, and they stared blankly at the world around them.

"Hello, everyone," Geneva said, her voice almost impossibly gentle with a hint of sadness. "The Librarian is here. She came to see how you're doing."

They didn't register any of the words, apart from perhaps blinking once or twice more than usual. A couple of them gradually turned their heads to look at Quinn, and that's when she realized their eyes were all blank. There was no expression, no feeling, nothing in them, no recognition, no will, no want.

On the bright side, it seemed the pain had left them as well. They were almost empty husks, except for one.

She seemed younger. She had very long, pale white hair with a hint of gold spun through it.

A tear rolled down her cheek.

Quinn moved before she realized it, acting on instinct. Something hummed through her body, through her mind. Right behind her eyeballs, it rolled all the way down through her body. She could feel it.

And she knew exactly what to do and how to do it.

She visualized it in her mind, reached out her hand toward the crying Esposian and placed it on her shoulder.

"*San abitur,*" she said.

A rippling wave of energy left Quinn's body in a rush, winding her so much she fell to one knee. It swept over the Esposian, spreading out from the point of contact all the way over her body, right up to the wing tips.

Quinn opened her mouth to speak, but her throat was too dry.

She couldn't even hear what people were saying before everything around her blurred.

3 7

OFF KILTER

Instinctively, Quinn knew she hadn't passed out. There were parts of her—muscles, blood vessels—that felt like they were moving around, finding a new level of comfort. While she could sense her body, her extremities, everything within felt slightly displaced. It was as if her eyes had stopped processing information. It was strange inside her head, as if all time had slowed down.

Her body shifted.

Off kilter.

She couldn't quite pinpoint the sensation, but it was uncomfortable on one end and yet felt like she was coming home on the other.

System messages started flashing across her vision in her mind, as if she was seeing them inside her head.

Calibrating . . .

Calibrating . . .

Quinn didn't quite understand. She knew that when she tapped into the system originally and it was about to completely shut down, it required calibrating. She also knew the Library wasn't actually a machine and thus, because she was quite literally a part of it, she wasn't one either.

Which was good, because otherwise seeing the messages in her mind, and not just in front of her vision could really have upset that tenuous belief. And knowing that didn't stop her from being quite scared about the fact that her own system, her own body . . . was currently calibrating something she'd done.

Just like the Library.

Something she didn't even understand how she'd done.

She pushed down on the rising panic and took a moment to mentally clarify herself, forcing herself to breath and assess her situation logically while separating herself from overwhelming immediate reactions. The skill would really have come in handy during exams back on Earth.

Calibrating . . .

Assessing . . .

New mental fortitude healing affinity established

Calculating . . .

Calibrating . . .

Refining . . .

Investigating . . .

Affinity 1,723 has been established

Mental Chaotic Fortitude Abolition

Strength progress resumed

Please report to the Library as soon as possible to verify and establish a line of advancement for this affinity.

Quinn would have blinked if she hadn't had her eyes closed already. As it was, her inner eye, since that's what she was calling it, kept watching the words until they faded. A new affinity? That didn't make any sense. She just, well, as usual when she pulled something out of thin air, simply acted on instinct. And now she needed to deal with it.

Suddenly, a rush of cool air ran through her entire body and the whole shifting process stopped. It made the uneasiness halt and she felt more like herself again.

Finally, she blinked her eyes open.

Less time had passed than anticipated. She knew that because she wasn't passed out on the floor, but had merely stumbled against the bed with the Esposian she'd healed in it. Her bright blue eyes focused on Quinn, and Quinn knew, maybe instinctively, that her name was Eugea. In more clear hindsight, she probably knew her name because of the momentary connection during the healing.

Malakai and Lynx simply stared at her, agape.

The Esposian continued to study Quinn and Quinn took in her visage as well. She was no longer as transparent as she had been before. Her wings held a very faint green shimmer to them now that made her blue eyes all the brighter. There was a strange expression on her face, one of hope, one of confusion, and definitely some caution mixed in there. Like she didn't understand what Quinn had done.

Well, Quinn thought to herself, *that definitely makes two of us.* She wished she understood what she'd done far better than she did.

The Esposian didn't speak. Eugea seemed unaware of precisely what had happened or perhaps was still trying to feel out this new awareness. Tears still ran down her cheeks, but they had slowed now. Some of them were drying, leaving saltiness behind on her skin.

Quinn swallowed. Eugea was younger than Quinn expected. She could sense how shy and shaken she was. How simply shell-shocked she'd become after being healed. Frankly, everybody looked at her like that, including the two nurses who'd been in the room when they entered. Those two vaguely resembled flying goldfish.

Quinn cleared her throat trying to cut through the tension. She wasn't entirely sure what to say or how to act after the whole thing. She could hear the voices of the nurses around her.

No.

It wasn't voices.

It was their thoughts.

They were loud and intrusive despite Quinn's copious shielding.

How did she do that?

What happened?

How is Eugea aware?

A sudden wave of anger rippled through the room.

She shouldn't be aware.

The voices around her were clamoring inside her head. Quinn

could hear them no matter how much she didn't want to. And she could feel all the emotion involved too. She focused on Eugea's bewildered elation to avoid the surprising rage she could sense.

What did she do?

Who is she?

The litany continued until Quinn forcibly thickened the shielding over the surface of her mind to shut them out. But before she could, she'd gleaned enough to know that these nurses, these supposed caregivers were here to keep an eye on the patients, not to heal them. Not to help them regain what they'd lost. It made Quinn's hackles stand on end. She made sure to etch those Esposian caretakers into her mind so she wouldn't forget them.

Because she couldn't forgive this type of calculated apathy.

"Well," Nishpa said, breaking the silence. "That was very interesting."

Geneva focused on Quinn, her tone disbelieving when she spoke. "Librarian, what did you just do? How did you know how to do that?"

Quinn half shrugged. "It just came to me." She wasn't entirely sure how much she should be giving away. The atmosphere around them wasn't friendly, and she couldn't let on that she'd had no clue what happened initially. That wasn't information anyone outside her inner circle should have. If that.

Malakai said nothing, and Lynx, well, he was obviously in extremely deep conversation with the Library, because his eyes were doing that weird flickering thing. Not that she could blame him. This was important.

Nishpa stood back, contemplative. Malakai still hadn't said anything, and Quinn was desperately trying to figure everything out. She couldn't decide if this was a good or a bad thing, that she'd lost enough control of her everything that her body had moved on its own and acted on some weird cosmicisodracus freaking instinct that allowed her to exert power and attempt to heal somebody. Which turned out fine this time, but what if it hadn't?

Don't let them know you didn't purposefully heal her, Lynx's voice said over the top of her mind.

Am I being loud? For a second Quinn worried that she was broadcasting her thoughts. She thought she'd gotten a handle on that.

No, but your face is full of shock and confusion, and it's probably not the best that these people see you in that state of mind.

Oh, Quinn said, realizing he was right.

Anyway, I know you don't know how you did that, but please know that your affinities with the Library shouldn't allow you to ill harm someone if you're trying to heal them.

Quinn glanced at him, wondering how Korradine got around that. *Are you sure you can't hear my thoughts?*

I'm used to your moods and your facial expressions. The latter of which is usually very plain to see. At least for me.

Thanks, Lynx. Quinn sighed. How did she have a healing proclivity now? Healing others? She'd absorbed all of like, what, two or three healing books? All beginners? Then again, this did mention a chaotic element, so maybe that was part of it.

Still, Eugea wiped away the rest of the tears and looked up at Quinn as if she'd pulled herself back together. So maybe it was worth it all.

The newly healed Esposian motioned for Quinn to come closer and then whispered, "You need to be careful. The others aren't open to help right now. I was. I wasn't lost in despair, but the rest of them are. I was desperately trying to climb out. That's why you could help me.

"Well, maybe if I can repeat it . . ." Quinn trailed off at the look in the girl's eyes.

Eugea's jaw was set, and she quivered ever so slightly. Fear shone out of her gaze, but tempered by an odd note of determination. "No. I don't think it's wise to try and help them right now. It probably wasn't wise to help me in the first place."

"Can you explain that to me?" Quinn asked. She glanced around furtively, but the nurses appeared to be checking the other patients, even if it felt like they were aware of them. Almost like they were trying to observe them without appearing to be watching.

Healing shouldn't be a bad thing, but Quinn got the feeling none of the people here were supposed to be healed. She pressed a little harder than she perhaps would have usually. "I need you to make me understand what you mean when you say I shouldn't heal the others," Quinn said, keeping her voice as soft as possible.

"I don't think you can," Eugea whispered. "I think I was ready. They're all lost in there, but my state of mind was desperate to escape the nothingness."

"They're stuck in nothingness?" Quinn asked.

"In a manner of speaking. It's a lonely, sad place. It's broken. The world doesn't float. It's not synchronized, and you have to run or you get gobbled up. Always." Eugea shivered. "It's a nightmare. It's like a continuous, circular, never-ending nightmare. I could barely sense the outside world and that was with pushing so hard I cried with the pain. Trying to will my way out was pure torment. I wouldn't even wish it on somebody I hated."

Quinn watched tears trickle down Eugea's face again, the way her eyes blinked like a blue bottomless sea. "It's okay. I understand."

"You don't. They're going to come and fetch me. I'm . . . I'm sure of it." She glanced around furtively. "I'm still supposed to be in there."

On impulse, even though she was quite sure of the answer, Quinn asked. "Do you have mana?"

"Of course I have mana. I'm an Esposian. I have forty-seven affinities," the tiny fae said proudly.

"Great. Take this." Quinn gave her one of the door openers just in case, shoving it into her small hand and closing Eugea's fingers around it as if she was just consoling her. "If you need to. Even if they lock you out. You can get to us."

Eugea's already big blue eyes opened impossibly wider. She nodded her head and suddenly the door opener was gone from her hands. Quinn was relieved to know that she must have some sort of subspace storage in her possession.

"Will that help?"

"Maybe. I should be able to retrieve it in time if something happens." There was a sliver of hope in Eugea's voice.

"Could you pretend that this was all . . ."

But Eugea shook her head. "No. They test us, too. Intricately." She paused for a moment, a wave of pain coming over her face before it vanished. "We were aware of everything done to us from the outside, you know. It's . . ." Eugea shrugged and splayed her hands out to the side.

"Are you serious?" Quinn said, settling onto the bed right next to the other fae.

Eugea nodded solemnly. "You weren't bad. You were really trying to help. So were the women who came with you. I could sense that. There are others who have not been so kind."

"We have to save them." Geneva hovered close to them, her face drawn and pinched with worry.

"I can't just step in and take people away," Quinn said.

Nishpa harrumphed off to the side. " I'll see what we can do, but this was very bad timing."

Quinn sighed. "I realize this now. Let's just double-check that you're really gonna be okay," she added as soothingly as she could.

Eugea nodded.

"How do you feel?" Quinn asked, loud enough for the nurses to hear.

"I'm okay. I'm very tired," Eugea said, making a show of a yawn.

Quinn managed not to cringe at the fact that Eugea was a bad actress. Still, hopefully it'd be enough for the nurses to run with. "I'm glad we could wake you up. I don't seem to be able to wake anybody else. I think you probably were just about ready, right?"

Eugea nodded very emphatically, actually. "I'm just lucky you were here," she said.

Quinn suppressed a groan, and Malakai stepped in. "I've seen this before," he said, drawing the words out. "Happens sometimes when Darigháhnish are shocked into a catatonic state by a magic spell. Occasionally, just the very presence of someone can trigger the release." He said it in such a way that it sounded utterly like the truth, and if Quinn hadn't been aware that he was bullshitting, even she would have believed him.

She nodded as if deep in thought, like she was agreeing with every word he said. Even though she was a hundred percent certain it wouldn't do any good. It was worth a try to attempt to reinforce what he said.

She glanced at Nishpa, who shrugged, and she looked at Geneva. *Is there anyone we can trust to watch over her?* Quinn said, directing her mind speech to all of the people with her. Nishpa shrugged, but Geneva hesitated.

There is one nurse I would . . . trust, she said haltingly over the mind speech connection.

How far would you trust them?

Farther than I could throw them, Geneva said with a very slight laugh.

Quinn was happy to see she'd begun rubbing off on people. *Well, if you can trust them that much, they may be worth a shot.*

I'll get them. You stay here with Eugea until I'll be back shortly. And Geneva left the room.

The shortly ended up being fifteen excruciating minutes while Quinn sat with Eugea and Nishpa. Lynx was back in connection with the Library, his eyes flickering ominously. Malakai leaned up against the wall, his lips pursed, observing everything.

Quinn knew him well enough to know that he was on guard. As jovial as he might be around her most of the time, as much of a friend and close confidant as he'd become, he was still her guard and her trainer. He was ready to fight any threat at any possible moment, and Quinn had a horrible feeling he'd get to do just that before they left this world.

Geneva returned, followed by another fae, except her color was brighter, not so transparent. Quinn raised an eyebrow. She wasn't entirely sure if this person was Esposian or Furionas even if her brighter, more definitive coloring hinted toward the latter. "This is my cousin, Galetta. She will watch over Eugea."

"Your cousin?" Quinn glanced at Nishpa, who raised an eyebrow.

"She has more than one auntie," Nishpa said. "This is another one of my nieces. Galetta, you make sure you take care of this young lady."

Nishpa dropped her voice in volume when she spoke. "This is vital. If she needs to leave, you must help her."

Galetta nodded very solemnly.

"We can't wait any longer, Quinn." Nishpa poured exasperation into her tone as she made sure the whole room could hear. "We were expected about half an hour ago." And then her voice dipped into the surface of Quinn's mind. *I wanted you to see them, see what handiwork had been done so you could maintain your resolve when we went and met the Prime Minister. I didn't think you'd heal one of them like you were working a miracle.*

"Sorry for the delay." Quinn grimaced, and added, *Do you think they've heard?*

Oh, Quinn, I think they've more than heard, Nishpa said, and motioned for them to follow her.

Even as they all trailed after the regal Furionas fae, Quinn couldn't help the sinking sensation she felt in the pit of her stomach.

Eyes watched their every movement, ears probably reaching for every word.

They were not among friends here.

38

SECOND TREE ON THE LEFT

WITH ONE LAST GLANCE BEHIND HER, QUINN DECIDED THAT LEAVING Lugea where she was right now was probably the best solution. Nishpa and Geneva appeared to trust Galetta, and they all had somewhere else to be.

Quinn didn't like the sensations roiling through her gut as they exited the house where the sick Esposians were sheltered. It no longer felt like a haven for the patients, but almost like a prison.

The group made their way farther through the town inching closer to the majestic palace steps. They were the focal point, almost funneling any visitors to the main place of state.

"Are we safe to talk out here?" Quinn asked, her voice low in the bustle around them.

In a low voice probably, or else you could use mind-to-mind speech like you have been, Nishpa said, commenting mentally on the surface of Quinn's mind. The aunt didn't make direct eye contact as she constantly scanned the surroundings.

Quinn could barely hear it over her barriers, and adjusted her shielding to include her current companions, should they want to speak. Nishpa, Lynx, Malakai, and Aradie became their own pieces of light static in her mind.

You have some strong shielding there, Nishpa said. *Milaro taught you well.*

Thanks. Quinn liked being able to speak mind-to-mind as they meandered through a city she realized was full of eyes all focused on their party. The children weren't playing, weren't loud, and were definitely not behaving quite like children. She'd originally thought them to be kids but, well, the Esposians were of the same diminutive stature as Geneva and her ilk. Thus, to be honest, her companions weren't exactly much taller than the ones she had assumed were children. So she couldn't even be sure of their ages. *Is everybody watching us here?*

Pretty much. It's only due to our interspecies familial bonds that extend back eons that we were even allowed to accompany the Esposians Geneva rescued here. They initially didn't even want us to bring Galetta. Anger underpinned Nishpa's words.

Why couldn't you just take them home?

Nishpa hesitated, but Quinn realized it had nothing to do with her answer to Quinn and instead was more in line with watching the people around them, inclining her head by way of greeting so as not to openly offend anybody. She reacted to everyone, observant and alert. *Esposians require detailed and specific care in order to recover from all types of illnesses. They're immune-compromised when it comes to other atmospheres, including, sadly, our own. Galetta is only an exception because of her mixed fae heritage.*

Oh wow, seriously? Quinn hadn't expected that answer, but she could imagine it. She'd already had magical food help her adapt to multiple different atmospheres: oxygen densities and chaotic magic levels. It stood to reason a whole species might get sick because of such an adjustment too.

It's difficult to explain and probably part of the problem involved with the tree and the book and the infection that spread through all of them and took control. There are many species that would fall as well. But in this case, the Esposians were an extremely easy target. While they're wary of other magic as a whole, any chance to bring them back into a normal scope would be something they'd jump at. Easy to bait. Nishpa sounded saddened.

Quinn hated the implications. *Do you think that whoever left the book there or planted the book there knew?*

Oh, definitely, Malakai piped in. *I don't think you understand how deliberate it would have to be, to ascertain the results we witnessed. Whoever did this is cruel. Although, we've established this since they were likely behind the attempt to destroy the Library in the first place.*

Quinn thought it over for a few seconds. Images she'd gleaned from her patients' mind while the instant of healing flowed through her. *I saw inside Eugea's mind. Whoever did that, they were beyond cruel. The sort of suffering caused deserves pain, repayment, revenge on such a level . . . but I wouldn't hesitate to do it.*

Now we've settled on their attacker being cruel . . . even though we already knew whoever targeted them was, Malakai said, then he paused slightly before continuing. *I mean, it was obvious to anyone who saw that tree.*

Mal, get to the point, Quinn said, almost tripping over a piece of ground that jutted out just below her foot. She frowned and focused harder on the area. It swam before her eyes for a split second, warping before it reverted to appearing smooth. She took a sharp intake of breath. *Is there an illusion placed over this area or something?*

Nishpa sighed mentally. *Yes and no. It is minor cosmetic adjustments to make the city seem more majestic than it actually is. Less run down.*

Quinn raised an eyebrow, despite the fact they were talking mind-to-mind. They'd just hit the bottom steps leading up into the palace. There had to be at least 150 of them. But her vision played tricks on her. What had once appeared like perfect white marble, now seemed overlayed over rough concrete and was partially broken in places. With her mind aware of the illusion, it had to fight hard to trick her. *They're trying to keep up appearances for the Librarian?*

Not just you. Milaro's grandson is here. I mean, his grandfather is the King of the Areilthähnish. He governs an entire sector. A powerful sector. Most planet rulers want to impress him, not to mention Lynx has accompanied you. So not only do we have the Librarian, the manifestation of the Library, but also Malakai is here. They need to make it seem as if everything is perfect. Nishpa's disapproval of their actions was evident in every syllable she spoke.

Quinn knew as soon as she set foot on that massive staircase up to the entrance to the palace, that the appearance wasn't the only illusion.

A sensation of malevolence tried to force itself inside her skin. It left her feeling slimy but it backed off almost immediately, perhaps realizing that she'd noticed. If she hadn't been paying attention, she might have thought it a wave of nausea or something equally as nasty. But this? No. There was something more than just keeping up appearances and trying to stay on the good side of the Library at work here. There was nothing okay on Ishiposa Isle.

Quinn, were you going to say something? Malakai asked cautiously.

I just . . . there's more than just appearances here. There's something inherently wrong. It's nothing blatant, just underlying. I can feel it, and I think we need to get Eugea out. Frankly, we need to get out of here too. Apprehension made Quinn tense and worried. She knew she couldn't leave quite yet, not if she didn't want to offend these rulers and make whatever was hanging over the city even worse.

Didn't the Library tell you to report when you healed Eugea? Didn't the system tell you to report to the Library? Lynx interjected.

Well, yes, it did.

Excellent. As soon as we get back, you'll be able to unpack precisely what it was you did, and hopefully you'll be able to heal the other five. Lynx's tone held a soothing note.

You think? she asked, as she affixed a fake smile to her face for outward appearances. The slimy feeling continued to assault her wards. It was all she could do not to shudder visibly.

Well, I assume. I hope. I don't know, though. I can't go on what's always happened before anymore. Lynx shook his head ever so slightly.

None of us really know, do we? Quinn said, an odd note of melancholy washing over her.

As they marched up the steps, there was a landing about halfway, where a whole troop of guards waited for them. Well, there were at least half a dozen of them. Quinn glanced from side to side, and Nishpa shrugged almost imperceptibly.

Is this a normal escort? Quinn asked.

Within reason. There are several of us here.

Quinn nodded. *I suppose.*

Nishpa also plastered a smile on her face, even as she thought at them. *Still, be alert, be on the lookout, and don't let any of them know that we sort of know that they're watching us.*

Do you think they already know about the healing? Quinn asked, trying to keep the anxious laugh she could feel bubbling up at bay

Yeah, I think they definitely know.

Someone's already reached them and told them that we healed one of the afflicted? Quinn schooled her face to appear as passively as she could.

Oh, definitely, either physically or telepathically.

Not exactly what I wanted to hear, Quinn said.

You don't know me well, but I know Milaro very well, Nishpa said kindly. *He's prepared you for a lot of things, just not everything yet.*

Quinn sighed.

Prime Minister Adrito and his partner Latia are, well, they're not going to be what you expect. You need to be wary. I cannot read them. They are distantly related cousins. They go back so many thousands of years that we may as well not be related at all. But they are calculating, and worth keeping an eye on.

Aren't you different species? Quinn asked, even though she knew they were intrinsically similar.

Yes, but we are both fae and we are also capable of interspecies copulation, which is fairly standard when you are closely related as a subspecies.

I'm going to pretend I understand what you mean by that, Quinn said, trying to lighten her mood as she climbed probably the hundred and twentieth step. Her knees wouldn't thank her in the morning. It was a good thing she'd be able to help soothe the muscles with healing.

The guards had wordlessly fallen into step with them, two in front of them, two on either side of them and two in the rear, were really starting to make her feel anxious. She didn't feel safe in the least. *These guards, are they supposed to protect us?*

Well, they're supposed to, Malakai said. *I'd assume that's what they're there for, but in reality . . .*

Yeah, Quinn said.

I think they're trying to protect others from us, Lynx said. *I don't believe anyone we're heading to see will be grateful that you healed Eugea.*

Gee, what gave that away? Quinn asked, her exasperation shining through.

You could be nicer about it, Lynx grumbled.

I could be, but I'm stressed and I don't feel safe.

Well, I believe that makes all of us, Lynx said. *They'll be putting on a lot of pomp. They'll be presenting and trying to live up to all appearances, Quinn. They'll also be trying to maintain a sense of dignity and majesty. They are the equivalent to a king and queen. They're simply called the Prime Minister and his partner. You are here in an official capacity as the Librarian, so that does buy you some leeway. Act like the healing, if they bring it up, is nothing worth mentioning, as if it's just something you could do any time of any day and explaining it isn't worth your time.*

Quinn frowned. *I mean, sure, I can do that, I guess.*

You're going to have to. The Library wanted you back immediately, and if you don't play it how we need to, we might be in a little bit of trouble. Lynx paused. *Even me.*

Well, when you put it like that . . .

They made their way to the top of the massive staircase and approached the huge entrance doors. Quinn wasn't entirely sure what she expected when they opened but she really wished her instincts would stop taking over like they had when she healed Eugea, or when she fought the miasma drones, or marginally controlled the Serpensiril situation.

She needed to pause, slow down, and understand what she was doing and how she was doing it. Not to mention being able to repeat the episodes would be mightily beneficial for everyone. Even though she knew on some level she was subconsciously, fully, and utterly aware of what she did, it still didn't make it better.

It made it more complex and difficult to recreate.

The guards in front of them, in all their finery, pushed the doors open, walking with them as they opened inwardly. They stood at attention once the doors were fully open and watched as the entire group marched by, still flanked and followed by the remaining four guards.

The entrance aisle was probably about a hundred feet long, with a huge red carpet rolled out in front of them going back into the receiving hall.

Although, if Quinn really paid attention to it, to the way her feet fell on the carpet, it looked finer than it felt, not nearly as plush as the image would have her believe. But these illusions, they were magnificent, convincing, almost impossible for her to see through. If she hadn't tripped back then, she wouldn't have given the validity of her surroundings a second thought. She frowned, but wiped the expression off her face as fast as she could.

That's just right, Nishpa said. *Keep your poise. Be friendly, but not a friend. Don't be too aloof but be confident. You need to convince these people that you are as powerful as they fear.*

Quinn took in a very slow, subtle, deep breath. She could do this. She'd acted in the occasional school drama production as a convincing second tree on the left. This was just like that. Sort of.

Still, she looked at the two figures sitting on the thrones in front of her. They inclined their heads ever so slightly by way of greeting. Which Quinn was fairly sure was an insult considering the depth of the gesture and the fact that they remained seated.

She was three long steps down from them. Two could play at that game. She inclined her head just a fraction and introduced herself.

"Well met. I am the Librarian. Thank you for seeing us."

The first person who spoke was a very pale shade of green and not the pretty shade that Eugea had been. It was more a khaki green but with a sickly tint. Their hair had the same hue at the very ends, as if the white had been bleached and discolored in chlorine. He inclined his head in return, slightly deeper this time.

"Well met. I am Adrito, Prime Minister of the Esposian people." He spoke very formally, but his eyes, his eyes were dead. They held nothing. There was no passion, fire, or any type of emotion in them. Quinn didn't understand how to respond, but she offered a smile.

The person next to him, Latia, Quinn presumed, also inclined their head. They were a sickly yellow that looked almost like bile. The color did nothing for the already-ghostly complexion of the Esposians. "I am Counsellor Latia, First Spouse to Adrito."

"Now, we have a question," Adrito said, and he smiled, but not even that expression reached his eyes.

Quinn felt the malice try to seep into her bones again, and she instinctively knew to extend her shielding to her companions this time. None of them needed to be infected by whatever this was. She did it in the blink of an eye, covering them in another layer of protection, because she knew, without a shadow of a doubt, even though she didn't know how she knew, that they were about to be attacked. It didn't even matter if the answer she gave to the question was right, wrong, or fabricated.

Adrito continued as if something nasty hadn't just tried to take over his guests. "Thank you for saving our people, agreeing to see us, and for this visit. But we must know, how did you manage to cure Eugea?"

Quinn smiled, and chose to play it off in a self-deprecating manner. "It was a mere healing spell. Nothing more, nothing less."

Adrito tsked under his breath. "Ah, Librarian, I wish you hadn't said that. It would have made everything so much easier."

39

DELIBERATE STEPS

ADRITO'S TONE OF VOICE SET OFF ALARM BELLS FOR QUINN. FOR A SPLIT second, she wished she'd answered entirely differently. But then her curiosity and stubbornness got the better of her. She studied Adrito, trying her best not to insult the ruler of an entire species.

"It would have made what so much easier?" she asked. Okay, so maybe that wasn't trying her best. It was a small attempt. The thought counted, right?

Adrito looked shocked for just a second, enough that Quinn knew he hadn't expected her to respond in any collected way whatsoever. She felt like she'd won that point, even though she wasn't sure what she was winning. What she did know was that fluctuations of power emanated from both Adrito and Latia. The energy flowing from both of them held neither friendliness nor goodwill.

"Tell me, please, what would it make so much easier?" she asked, already starting to lose her patience. Not that that was a difficult thing to achieve. Her patience was in tatters lately.

Adrito gave a cocky smile and said, "It would have made what comes next much easier."

Quinn really didn't appreciate it when people refrained from answering very simple questions. Thus, she didn't even dignify his comment with an answer. Malakai began tapping his foot, and Quinn simply raised an eyebrow.

"Are you dense? Can you not read the room?" Adrito spat out, crossing his arms as he hovered in the air above his throne.

Quinn glanced around to see what she now realized were full-sized guards. The armor covered their entire bodies, including hands and head, and they stood almost as tall as Malakai. She couldn't quite tell what was underneath the armor. There were approximately two dozen guards in the large room now and they all stood directly behind the group. Quinn turned from side to side, taking it all in. Two rows of twelve guards behind them.

They definitely didn't seem like a welcoming committee.

"Are you going to explain or am I just supposed to guess?" Quinn asked.

Adrito scowled. "You need to tell us how you removed Eugea from her prison."

Quinn paused, latching onto his wording. Prison? Did that mean they'd deliberately placed their people into a damaging mental stasis? Or simply that they'd maintained them there?

Anger threatened to take control of her better judgment for a second. She had to calm herself with a deep breath. They'd get to the bottom of that after whatever it was Adrito was cooking up for them. She shook her head and shrugged again, trying to let all the implications roll off for now.

First things first. She had to deal with this prime minister. She chose to answer the question. "It was a healing spell. Eugea was sick." She tried to play it off, as if she'd simply done what any healer would be able to do. But she knew she wouldn't get away with that. Adrito had already proven himself shrewder than anticipated.

"Stop the games, Librarian. We're fully aware she's the only one you healed," he practically spat that last word out with disdain.

"Some patients are more open to being healed than others." Which wasn't exactly a lie on Quinn's behalf, just sort of a half-truth. Eugea had certainly been receptive to escaping the hell visage she got trapped in. Desperate, even.

"Enough," Latia said, an air of power echoing around them.

And Quinn realized suddenly that maybe Adrito wasn't the true ruler here. Or if he was, Latia also possessed great power.

Latia leaned into Adrito, whispering, and Quinn pushed her hearing as far as she could. She caught words like, *He will not be pleased,* followed by, *There's nothing we can do,* and followed by, *more than enough.*

Quinn cringed. That wasn't the best conversation to overhear. Regardless of the true content, she'd heard enough to be even warier. Plus that whole gut feeling thing was trying to churn her from the inside out like it was making butter. She could feel from the minds of her friends around her that they were all ready for combat, regardless of the outcome of this whispered conversation between the Esposian rulers.

They just had to wait. They couldn't be the instigators, but they could end the conflict. And she was positive they would.

Because she couldn't let these people win.

Quinn had sort of hoped for a peaceful outcome when Adrito turned his attention back to them. She had to stop herself from laughing. Because he really was tiny. About two and a half feet tall, if he was standing on the ground, his wings took up the same height behind him, and they fluttered with beautiful iridescent light shining off the sickly greens and yellows of his and Latia's coloring. She preferred the ghostly see-through white of most Esposians.

"Are you even listening to me, Librarian?" he demanded, in his high pitched voice. It wasn't very commanding.

Quinn rolled her eyes. "Get on with it. What is it that I'm supposed to have told you?"

"How you healed Eugea!"

If he'd been standing on the ground Quinn got the distinct impression he'd have stomped his foot. She sighed. "We've been over this. I healed her. I simply healed her. Nothing more, nothing less."

"Well, if you won't tell us, we're going to have to wrest it from you." He snarled. Sort of. Although the pointed teeth definitely helped.

Quinn almost bit out an *I'd like to see you try*, but Malakai beat her to it.

"I'd like to see you try and take anything from my charge." Malakai on the other hand, managed to sound both regal and commanding.

She'd never heard his voice so deep or so angry. It made her feel protected. Not that she needed protecting, but it was nice to know someone cared. Especially if that someone was Malakai.

At that point in time, Nishpa sighed. "I'd hoped it wouldn't come to this," she muttered.

"Come to what?" Latia frowned, her voice full of derision. "You presume so much simply because you're here on behalf of the fae emperor."

Nishpa shrugged. "It is what it is. I can't deny that. You know it. I know it. I was sent here to see what you were up to. And I have to say, I'm not the least bit impressed."

Somehow, her voice projected across in a more regal way. Quite majestic, actually. It made Quinn want to know exactly how Nishpa was related to the emperor and empress of the fae kingdom. Furthermore. Didn't that mean Geneva was related, too?

Just how many royals did she have in the Library?

"And they're just titles," Nishpa bit out as an afterthought. "You know they don't like to be referred to as such."

"They are weak. They should be stronger," Latia mocked, "then we'd call them whatever they wanted."

"What? As strong as you?" Geneva asked divisively. "Strong enough that you won't even help your own people heal. That you'd sooner conspire to keep them hurting and injured? Imprisoning them? Going so far that you'd consign them to torture instead of letting us aide them?"

Quinn glanced sideways. This was a new side to her supervisory Library assistant, and Quinn was here for it. Geneva's golden attributes positively glowed. Her deep golden hair shimmered with a pearlescent overtone and red undertones. Her eyes flashed, and she drew herself up to her full height, which, while flying, was actually quite tall.

"You will pay for the neglect you have shown your people. How dare you threaten your guests? You spied on those who came to your aid. And you have harmed your subjects for the last time." Geneva's voice resonated throughout the entire entrance chamber.

Quinn stopped herself from giving a round of applause to her Librarian assistant. Geneva was handling it quite well on her own. Even Nishpa looked proud.

"Very well then," Adrito said. Quinn was quite sure his voice was shaking. "Let's end this and we'll see who comes out on top."

Only something told Quinn, after Geneva's outburst, he wasn't quite as confident in his own abilities as he had been. But that was all the time she had to think of it. As the two rows of guards behind them launched into an attack on the six of them.

The guards moved with an oddly staccato rhythm, heir heavy armor unwieldy. Quinn found herself wondering if they were piloted armor systems, and if there were fae inside.

They attacked with clumsy swings, their coordination lacking. Not that Quinn was in a position to critique when it came to hand-to-hand combat. Still, she had to use all of her wits to dodge them, as their numbers were overwhelming. Each of them had to fend off four of the damn guards, and that was only if she included Aradie as an opponent.

Being air bound gave the owl a distinct advantage.

Adrito and Latia flung spells at the group. The guards, thankfully, only attacked them physically. Quinn could dodge their physical attacks in her sleep after all the training she'd done with Malakai. The movements were clumsy, exaggerated, and felt like they were following a set pattern.

Malakai was on an entirely different level – like an elf from one of the movies she'd seen as a child. He leapt in the air, firing his bow, neatly taking out two of the guards directly in the visors and sending them plummeting onto their backs. But then the rest of them were too close to him, so he swapped out his bow for his sword, with which he was just as lethal. He swung it wide, and she could see the way his muscles worked.

Magic or no magic, it seemed swords still had weight to them and required muscle mass to swing. Probably one of the reasons she was so bad at wielding a sword herself.

Quinn loosed her ice balls, still her favorite form of attack, sending them straight into the faces and helmets and joints of any of the guards that approached her. Some of her reading enabled her to infuse the balls. They shot out shards of ice, deadly, and mostly accurate.

Aradie used her laser eyes, which Quinn still really needed to talk to the bird about. Her aim was exacting and she went for the eye slits. One after another, the guards fell over. They were oddly weak. Quinn raised an eyebrow as they'd gotten rid of a dozen of the guards already in the space of a couple of minutes.

"Is this what you're throwing at us? Did you really think we'd be this weak?" Quinn was angrier than she thought she'd be. In fact, she was downright pissed off. How had they taken them so lightly? Why were they not giving her group the respect the strength of the Library was due? Did they not realize how far the Library had come in recovering since it found her?

Well, obviously the answer to all of that was no. Which led her to wonder if they could play that to their advantage? She desperately wanted to reach for that off switch in her brain that'd simply let her react, but she couldn't afford to do that right now.

She might end up killing these two rulers. She wasn't ready for an intergalactic kerfuffle quite yet.

"These are just the beginning," Adrito snapped out as he hurled yet another, what Quinn thought was supposed to be a miniature hurricane, toward her. She wasn't entirely sure. But it was relatively easy to bat it away with focused wind of her own. For somebody who was thousands of years old, he was less adept at wielding his powers than she would have thought.

Unless he was doing something else simultaneously . . .

Don't get distracted, Nishpa said. *Esposians are crafty and cunning and they will lull you into a false sense of security. Whatever he has next for us is going to be bad.*

Quinn nodded, chastising herself for getting ahead of herself, even as Geneva flitted around from armored guard to armored guard, speaking one word in a low and guttural voice that froze them. Not in an ice sort of way. It simply stopped them in their tracks, just like she'd done with the Esposians on the island.

Quinn glanced at Nishpa. She fought in a martial arts style, but with wind cutting through everything in front of her as an extension of her own body, of her own wings, almost like the air was a weapon of her own. She twirled in the air like a mini cyclone herself.

But Geneva made their attackers stop, and crumple to the ground, as if it was all they could do to obey her command. She'd gained confidence since the Isle . . . perhaps some of it fueled by anger.

So many intricacies to go over after they'd finished.

Lynx led everything that tried to engage him on a merry chase. She was surprised to see he could teleport both away from the Library and in the Library. Fine, the way he teleported during the fight was over much shorter distances, but he was successfully running all of the guards into each other and leading quite a merry chase.

Quinn almost let herself get distracted watching the others when a sword came down a hair's breadth from her head, and she only moved instinctively because her senses allowed her to do so.

"Quinn, watch out, I've got my own guards to fight," Malakai yelled from across the hall.

Quinn nodded, knowing full well that she needed to get her head in the game.

"Love to see what you've got up your sleeve," Quinn said, focused on the area around her now as she goaded their hosts. "I'm getting a little bored."

"Oh, don't taunt them, please don't taunt them," Nishpa muttered.

"Why not?" Quinn asked, "nothing else is fun." Although she was feeling a bit strained. She'd used her ice balls quite liberally and it felt as if she was overheating. She allowed her hands to ice over and for ice to form over her forehead, trying to keep the heat at bay. Were they doing something to her body temperature? Suddenly she felt quite out of breath and Aradie alighted to her shoulder with an inquiring coo.

"I'm fine girl, I'm fine," Quinn watched around them and noticed the floor was shaking. Quinn glanced over at Adrito who was being protected by Latia. She was fighting with Malakai, holding her own quite admirably, while Quinn and the rest waylaid the last of the guards that were sent to fight them. Yet the vibrations continued as if something ever so large was taking slow and deliberate steps toward them.

Again that slimy sensation wound its way up her spine, and she tightened everyone's mental shielding. The ominous pressure only eased slightly, lending her some anxiety she didn't need.

"It's okay Aradie, we've got this." But she wasn't sure they did. She kept her eye on the downed guards even as she popped one of her regenerative snacks into her mouth to chew so that her energy and mana replenished while they fought. The others did the same, keeping wary eyes on Adrito.

Quinn ran up the steps to assist Malakai, but stopped as she realized Latia and Adrito had a force field protecting them. At least that explained why Malakai hadn't already made short work of them. She could probably pierce the barrier with a lance of ice, or perhaps even stop the shield using a mind bolt. She'd never used that before, but she knew all the theory behind it.

But even as she had that thought, she turned toward the entrance because the whole floor under them practically buckled, including the stairs leading to the thrones.

It caused both Malakai and Latia to stumble, and Quinn fell to one knee.

She turned just in time to see a colossus emerge from outside.

No, that wasn't quite right.

It actually broke through part of the palace door and sent the arched ceiling crumbling to the floor where mostly injured guards scrambled to get out of the way, screaming as they did so. Many of the sounds cut off as they were struck by rubble falling from fifty odd feet high.

Definitely unexpected.

She watched as the twenty-foot tall monster moved laboriously. It seemed to be made up of a type of sandstone or perhaps a pale clay. And it was completely oblivious to the multiple guards it crushed under its feet as it walked toward them.

40

AT THE MEMORY

"W**ALKED**" MIGHT HAVE BEEN TOO GENEROUS A TERM. THE MASSIVE stone golem shambled toward them, destroying the entrance hall in the process, or at least the entry arch, the ceiling around it, and the beginnings of all structural integrity.

From what Quinn could see, anyway.

The illusions cast over the floor beneath the damage faded away, no longer able to keep up appearances. Each step the golem took dug into the floor, sending rocks, torn carpet, and dust flying up, along with pieces of armor.

Quinn could see that there were indeed Esposians operating the full body-sized armor inside. Or at least, she got to see the remnants of their bodies after they were squashed by the feet of the massive golem that seemed oblivious to all else in its approach.

The golem took one very languid, massive swipe at Nishpa, which the fae easily dodged. But the hand went right through the floor. The golem almost overbalanced but righted itself just in time. That's when Quinn realized it was Adrito who was controlling the movements, like he was piloting the golem from outside. Which was probably why Latia was protecting him.

Malakai still fought the sword-mage, trying to break through the barrier and reach Adrito. But Latia was much stronger than Quinn expected. Still, Malakai appeared to be holding his own quite well. Right now, with the size of that golem and the sheer destruction all around them, Quinn knew that the rest of them needed to focus on it.

So far, they'd mostly avoided injury, a few scrapes, a few bloody cuts, a lot of bruises. But this was far more dangerous than the guard navigated by Esposians who didn't quite get how to move with elongated limbs. The golem, while slow, moved erratically, and at that size . . .

Chunks of floor flew and scattered like its own weaponry every time it stepped closer.

Quinn studied it. Stone, what was the best thing to damage stone? She knew that she could hit it with a hammer and a pick and break into it that way, but this was protected by magic and she didn't have a large enough hammer on hand.

She could probably freeze it, but that wasn't going to penetrate the interior of the stone and thus wouldn't be able to break it apart when shattered. Even though it appeared sandstone like in appearance, that didn't make the stone immediately weak.

Quinn frowned. Her understanding of thermodynamics was rudimentary at best. Plus, this wasn't Earth, so if this was magical based rock, then anything she knew probably wasn't applicable.

They'd have to weaken it. She racked her brains even more, trying to come up with the best way to deal with the monstrosity in front of her.

That's when Geneva spoke up, flitting next to her ear for just a few seconds. "It's made out of malleable archonite. It's a magical type of clay sandstone. Steam is its worst enemy. I'll try to provide distraction."

Quinn blinked at the Furionas as she darted away again and decided to try soaking the golem first then. She had some access to fire—drench it and heat it to make steam. Didn't sound too hard, right? It did have openings here and there, not to mention if it was similar to sandstone then it was definitely more porous.

She frowned as she watched the massive creature swing again.

Nishpa's wind swords were cutting through it very gradually—sawing away was more accurate. Quinn tried to aim water into any of the holes she could see.

She scanned the creature, dodging here and there, even as she watched Aradie fire at it with her laser eyes and Geneva pelt it with her wind powers. Then Nishpa would allow her wind blades to saw away at the exact same spot. She was attempting to remove one of its arms and her precision was actually terrifying.

Quinn was quite glad the Furionas Aunt was on their side.

On the other hand, Quinn launched water at it in spears, tiny spears, so it would go in through any of the holes and suffuse the whole thing. The process was arduous. At first it barely felt like she was making headway, and time stilled in her mind as she worked the water with as much finesse as she could.

If she wanted to steam it out, the entire thing needed to be soaked.

It swiped, cumbersomely at anyone who dared come close to its body. But Aradie, Lynx, and Nishpa were far too agile to get hit.

As the water levels increased, it stumbled more, the soaked surfaces adding to its original weight. Quinn piled all the water she could into the thing, practically willing it to soak into the porous magical clay.

She wondered where Adrito had pulled the magical clay, that seemed oddly mismatched in pieces all over the golem's body, from.

Remembering how the city was built, she had the worst fears.

The creature rumbled and roared and swung a fist again at Nishpa again. This time its speed was fueled by the controller's desperation, and she didn't dodge quite well enough. It caught the fae's foot. The small Furionas yelped in surprise as she tumbled to the ground, momentarily stunned out of flight. Lynx dove in to pick her up and fetch her out.

Quinn wasn't sure if the fae had her own healing spell, but she didn't have time to pay attention because despite all the powers ripping into it, the golem seemed to have gained momentum. Perhaps it was a frantic speed that it now fought with, but it almost clipped Quinn and her hover ability barely yanked her out of the way in time.

She rolled to the side, barely avoiding another direct strike. Even as she did, some debris jumped up in rebound from the golem's fist hitting the ground, scraping and tearing at the skin in her cheek.

It hurt. But she could heal it with a thought. Disinfecting it and closing the wound in one go.

She glanced back to see that Malakai and Latia were still locked in a head-to-head battle and Adrito was now on his knees, hands on the ground, muttering as the force field wavered ever so slightly. Sweat poured down his face, and he was even paler than he had been.

Quinn, her senses extended, could feel the power was still rushing into him, but she knew it wasn't his own.

And she wasn't entirely certain where he was pulling it from.

Naturally, as a magician, he probably had reserves stored somewhere, but even as she watched as the golem gathered itself for another attack, she didn't understand how this was all going down. Even as they'd wandered the streets, as they'd approached the palace, she'd been acutely aware that this was a trap—even then she hadn't anticipated this.

Perhaps that's where experience came into play.

Aware that this city, this entire planet, was on the last vestiges of magic. The illusions were cast because it was easier than rebuilding, as well as less costly energy and mana-wise. It felt to her as if the energy around them was barely enough to keep the islands afloat in the sky.

Abject horror hit her when she realized the implications of her observations, of where Adrito was actually pulling his power from. But she didn't have time to dwell on those because it seemed the golem was ready to go another round.

What she wished for was a hammer she could bash it with, but none of them were adept in that weapon. Maybe Malakai could use it, but he was busy sparring with the silly cow who was protecting the idiot who was bleeding the magic in the atmosphere dry.

She glanced at the shields covering them and then back at the golem and at Nishpa limping with Lynx by her side. She darted over to where they were narrowly avoiding another fist. She placed her fingers gently on Nishpa's ankle and exerted the heal that she'd only known how to use on herself.

It stood to reason that she could use it on others if she understood how to use it on herself. Directing the flow of energy was a minor adjustment. All she did was enable the blood vessels and muscles in the foot that she touched to rejuvenate themselves faster than they usually would. It'd still be weaker and require more healing, but it should enable Nishpa to move for the duration they needed to.

Then the golem suddenly sprouted spikes.

They gleamed in the ever-expanding light that poured in through the broken opening of the building—through the slowly crumbling ceiling.

Obviously, Quinn's water barrage had been working, but that wasn't all. Not only did they gleam wet, but they appeared to be tiny javelins. And by tiny, she meant only in respect to how large the golem was. The spikes that began firing toward all of them were approximately a foot long and so very sharp at the tip, if spongy toward the end. Maybe the soaking was working.

The first one directed at her passed through Quinn's calf in its entirety before she even managed to scream.

The scream, when it came, tried to rip her throat raw.

It seemed as though things had a penchant for impaling her legs. She exerted a healing spell on herself and could literally feel the interior of her leg knitting back together. She was only glad that it hadn't nicked the bone because that would have hurt ten times more and been something she had no idea how to fix.

She was panting now, sweating ever so slightly with the exertion of healing. It wasn't nearly as magical as she'd first imagined from the cut on her cheek or helping Nishpa. It took energy and effort directly from her in bucket loads to close a wound like that. She popped an energy ball into her mouth.

Now she was angry.

Looking up, she realized Geneva hovered above her with a hand outstretched towards the golem, a thick shield protected their group from the onslaught of other spikes. But even as she watched, she noticed that Geneva began to perspire. Wordlessly, she handed the Furionas fae one of her many rejuvenation treats and flashed her a smile.

"Thank you, Librarian," she panted out.

"Always," Quinn said. "So what do we do now?" she asked, starting to feel a little bit uncomfortable. It wasn't going nearly as well as she'd hoped.

"We've got this," Nishpa said. "It's a lot easier than I think you imagine. You're already weakening it internally. We just need to figure out a way to combust it as well as the man back there who lacks complete and utter intelligence."

Quinn laughed. "Yeah, he does a bit, doesn't he?" She wondered if it was time to try and steam it out. Even though the spikes were pretty spiky, she got the feeling the rest of the interior was water logged. That's how it felt to her senses.

The group fought together. They coordinated their attacks. Both Quinn's water and Nishpa's wind. Lynx and Aradie worked on a series of lasers and what Quinn thought might be a type of explosive Lynx was throwing.

The lasers and explosions generated some levels of steam, but not nearly enough. Geneva concentrated on protecting them all, shielding from the inevitable spines that kept jettisoning from the massive creature.

Several of them broke through, but with their momentum slowed considerably, the wounds they left were mostly negligible. At least they were with healing at hand.

The golem swung and barely missed. The flooring jumped up more than several times, some of it cutting massive swaths into the person it hit. Quinn found herself healing more often than she'd anticipated, and kept an eye on her energy and mana levels.

Luckily, Lynx could dodge completely by making himself momentarily incorporeal.

"Can you do that all the time?" Quinn asked.

"No," he said. "It's draining the energy I have that keeps me here. I can't afford to run out of energy while we're here." He bit out the words, most of his concentration going to dodging incoming attacks.

"And you can't absorb it by eating either," Quinn mused for a second. But then had a thought as she yet again guided water spears inside the slowly growing holes of the golem. It seemed it couldn't replenish the material it was using to rain down spikes on them and was thus weakening itself even more, rapidly. "Why don't you just transform into a bird and do what Aradie's doing?"

For a second Lynx paused and looked at her, then morphed into an owl and followed Aradie into aerial attacks. Quinn sighed.

"Focus, Quinn. We need you. Can you heat it up?" Nishpa brought her back to the moment of the fight.

"Well, I can certainly." Quinn answered dubiously. She wasn't as confident with fire as she'd had little chance to use it . . . but she couldn't help the feeling of excitement that ran through her when she thought about its power.

"Then do what you do best and adapt it for the current set of circumstances." Nishpa flashed her a smile, but even as she did, a shard of flying floor caused her to dodge out of the way hastily. It barely missed her, and that's when the Librarian noticed her allies were all pale and likely getting to the end of their energy reserves despite the regenerative foods they'd consumed.

Or they were super worried.

Or both.

This golem was a formidable creation. They were only lucky that the person piloting it wasn't the sharpest tool in the shed. If it had been someone like Kajaro? They'd all be dead.

Quinn frowned. That was a very sobering thought. But using fire? When she knew the bare minimum? She'd already been overheating through most of this battle. She didn't understand why.

"Fine," she said. "I'll heat it up then."

The moment she said the words, it was like something clicked inside of her. Quinn envisaged a ball of flame igniting in the center of its core, fueling faster and faster until it became a ball, spreading through all of the passages with a white heat so hot it negated anything that could extinguish it. And then she released the thought and muttered "Burn."

She wasn't expecting it to do much, especially since she'd used her home tongue, but after several seconds the golem glowed red like coals did when they were hot. As if it was being engulfed by flames from the inside out. She'd soaked it purely so steam could help ruin its structural integrity and make it easier to kill. She'd never intended to burn it from the inside out.

Water wasn't fuel, definitely not for a fire.

Except, it seemed, in malleable archonite.

The flames moved, jumping from one leg to another, almost like it was alive, gleefully devouring its prey.

The golem tried to jettison spikes, but they melted down each time it made an attempt—dripping down its torso and arms.

A scream sounded behind them and Quinn turned to see Latia falling to a well-aimed sword strike from Malakai just as Adrito gripped his head and rolled on the ground in absolute agony. She could feel his pain from where she stood, emanating out in waves. But the shield was still there, wrapped tightly around the king or prime minister or whatever he was. Power rushed into it, replenishing it from an outside source.

The golem swayed from side to side, and Quinn could practically see even more power flying toward it, trying to undo the damage her flames had wrought.

Clarity hit her, and the blue gold scales flared to life, coating her body in a protective shield that she instinctively knew nothing could penetrate. She held out a hand and made one motion from above her head to the ground. "Incinerate."

The flames shot up from the ground, from the inside of the golem through the holes its spikes had created. The creature let out a mournful groan. Pity shot through Quinn's heart at the memory of some of her golems back at the Library, and it only made her angrier at Adrito.

The power he pulled on rushed in even faster as the golem began to fade, and Quinn felt a massive rumble underneath her feet through the hole the golem made when it crashed into the throne hall. In the corner of her view, she could see one of the islands in the sky hurtling downwards, narrowly missing the island they were on.

Anger surged through her at the confirmation that Adrito had pulled energy from the entire planet, the atmosphere, and everything that helped his people survive.

The flames engulfing the golem turned white.

41

USHER IN A NEW AGE

The golem in front of her burned.

Quinn blinked for a few seconds, fascinated at the white-hot flames engulfing its body. It writhed, the surface broke and cracked, and the malleable archonite turned brittle and white. The massive construct crashed around, destroying seating areas, statues, and anything in its way.

Its arms flailed around even as portions of them broke away and it roared with frustration as it smashed a fist through the floor. The sound of its scream echoed throughout the room, rumbling all the loose stone. She felt right through to her bones. Desperation and a tinge of sadness echoed in the sensations. The rebound of the action scattered the remnants of what had once been the Esposian-driven guardians.

Even though they'd attacked her, she knew they'd been compelled to do so, and she felt a wrench of anger toward their ruler.

Another piece of the ceiling crumbled away and fell. With a good forty to fifty feet to fall, Quinn knew it'd damage whatever it hit severely. With speed she didn't know she possessed, she dove and pushed Geneva out of the way, rolling them both to safety, while being as careful of her wings as possible.

Dust and fragments showered down around them.

"You have to watch out for the fallout. You can't just be mesmerized by it," she said to her assistant, panting with the aftermath of the exertion.

Geneva turned widened eyes on Quinn. "How did you . . . ?"

"I don't know. I just . . . I did." Quinn shook her head, getting herself back on track. Reflexes born of a mixture of her sensing the danger and calculating the likelihood of debris had kicked in. The magic she absorbed worked in the background constantly, like she was a computer with processing power. While weird, she couldn't be more grateful.

Geneva gestured toward the giant flaming golem. "That's not just a simple light for you to see by."

"No shit," Quinn said, knowing Geneva referenced one of the initial books she'd absorbed when she first arrived at the Library. She turned her attention back to the flailing golem, even as it began to disintegrate in front of her eyes. Power began to whoosh out of it, but Quinn could feel the heat and despite the very obvious melting going on around the golem, not to mention its own fracturing, Quinn didn't feel wary of the temperature at all.

It seeped through the air, ashes and debris flying all around with it, but it felt like home, like a reality she should always have known. The heat suffused her. It gave her close to a headache and a heady feeling, like she could do anything. She could make anybody talk. Anybody at all, including the person responsible for all of this pointless destruction.

More of the ceiling fell away. The entrance lay crumbled into ruins as the golem thrashed around inside the entrance hall, catching onto the only other support structures. Quinn was worried they were going to get buried alive as well. But Geneva seemed like she could almost read Quinn's mind. She held up a hand.

"Don't worry, Librarian," she said, her jaw set with determination. "I've got this. I'll reinforce it."

"What do you mean, reinforce it?" Quinn asked.

Geneva actually raised an eyebrow. "Well, you saw me. I protected us from all those spikes. I'll reinforce the area all around us and hope that . . . well, let's just hope that the golem disintegrates before it manages to cause any more structural damage. I do not want to be buried alive."

Quinn gaped at Geneva. It was the first time she'd ever heard her truly commanding when she spoke to Quinn. And she wasn't being as formal. Quinn thought that perhaps Geneva had always been on her most polite behavior with Quinn, since her words had always been deliberately chosen. After all, she was the Librarian.

Heat began to suffuse Quinn's body in an uncomfortable way. She immediately activated one of her ice skills and coated her hands and her forehead, trying to make herself cool down. She didn't understand anything about the fiery power she wielded. All she could remember was when Uncle Hal basically told her that she had a heat or fire affinity, and she hadn't believed him. She was going to have to see him sooner than later, not that that was a bad thing.

It looked like she might have another couple of contenders for his interrogation. Maybe wrapping them up in a bow would be nice.

Just as the golem began to crumble in earnest, Quinn and Nishpa realized one of the Esposians trapped in the armor was actually still alive. Quinn darted forward to pull the small being out, while Nishpa tore around trying to leverage a little bit of her meager weight against the burning golem to control its direction a little better. Apparently Nishpa didn't burn either. Quinn slotted the information away.

Geneva kept them safe from falling debris, while Aradie and Lynx darted over to help Malakai.

Finally, the golem crashed to the ground just after Quinn pulled the Esposian from the armor and managed to dash to safety. As it crashed, it exploded up into a shower of small, sharp, hot rock pieces. Geneva barely managed to get up a second shield in time, and because she was supporting the vast majority of the weight of the ceiling, the protection wasn't nearly as strong.

Quinn, Nishpa, and the poor wretch they'd managed to salvage from their otherwise fiery tomb of armor were all inundated with small, stinging, hot shards.

Quinn cried out in pain, and then it vanished.

Not that the rocks vanished from her skin, just that the heat they provided felt sort of comforting. Like it was melting into her skin. She didn't understand what that meant, but right then, everything inside her and around her needed to be hot, hotter than she'd ever felt anything before in her life. Everything suddenly seemed too cold, despite the smoldering ruin of a golem in front of her.

Quinn needed heat, sort of like she needed air.

"Quinn?"

Lynx's voice broke through to her, and yet it sounded distant, so far away. She pushed herself up from the ground and stumbled away from the Esposian she'd rescued while Nishpa tended to the wounds that they'd both suffered. Quinn yanked at the rocks, tugging them out of her skin, ignoring the fact that blood flowed freely from the wounds. With a thought, she exerted just a tiny bit of healing in the direction of the small puncture wounds in her body. They healed up, and yet the heat still remained, like it was running through her veins, as if she'd lit a fire with an ignition switch that was burning through all of her blood and turning it into molten lava.

"Lynx, I'm hot. Really, really hot." Quinn fell to the ground on her knees and her hands, like that cat pose in yoga. She didn't know where the vague thought came from, just that her insides were turning into fire.

"Breathe, Quinn."

But that wasn't Lynx's voice, that was Malakai, and even he sounded out of breath. Wait, hadn't he just been fighting?

Quinn was burning and everything else seemed to melt together.

"Ice, Quinn, ice. Form the ice." Malakai's tone soothed like a cool breeze on a hot day.

She did. She formed a thin layer of ice all over her body, and not just any old ice, hard like arctic ice, like something that had existed for millennia. It worked, just a little, at first, like somebody had put a cold compress on her head.

It helped, a lot, but not as much as she needed. She had to constantly reinforce the ice. It was melting too fast. Her body still felt like an inferno, like a volcano, but at least now she wasn't about to erupt. She shifted and sat down, putting her head between her knees, panting.

"Whoa," she said, "so hot."

"Yeah." Malakai touched her shoulder briefly and crouched down next to her. She looked at him, realizing that she still had a layer of ice all over her body.

The sensation ran under her skin and clothes, as well as on her hands, her face, her neck, and any part of her body that was visible. Malakai grinned at her. "Better?"

Quinn flashed him a grateful smile. "Thanks. For just a second there, I think I forgot breathing was possible."

"Likely," he said. He tapped her hand, still encased in ice. "Now, now I know why you smell like ice."

"What do you mean?" she cocked her head to one side, looking at him with curiosity.

"Well, you need the ice. You have a strong affinity to it because of your water affinities. You know, like a lunar dragon." He paused as he thought over his answer. "But it's also a defensive mechanism to help keep the heat that will probably engulf your body now you're awakening. You know, keep you cooler. It's like a built-in air conditioner, isn't that what you call them?"

Quinn blinked at him. "Oh, yeah, that really does make sense. Kind of, I guess. Wouldn't I just be, like, impervious to heat?"

"You'd think so." Mal smiled. "But they did mix in some other elements that might make that a little bit difficult. Still, I think you're holding it together pretty well."

"Gee," she said, her voice coming out flat. "Thank you so much."

Regaining her equilibrium, Quinn pushed herself to standing and brushed off some of the ash and debris. "How are you holding up, Geneva?"

"I'm holding up fantastically, as is the dome above us," Geneva said, the strain showing in her voice.

Malakai raised an eyebrow. "Wow, what happened? Did you bloom into a beautiful butterfly, Geneva?"

"No, I'm just short-tempered today. This whole fiasco has frayed my very last nerve!" She bit out the words like they were distasteful in her mind, and that's when Quinn realized just how right she was.

"I agree with you, Geneva." She handed her a couple of energy supplements to help her maintain the shielding above them. Quinn's mind was already on a plethora of other things, especially the traitor.

The illusions had long since dropped from the city. But even more so, everything around them began to crumble. It was all Quinn could do not to gag at the smell of seared flesh and hair now she had the raging inferno inside her back in check. The poor pool of molten golem even tugged at her heartstrings.

She turned on the now prone and bleeding Adrito. He had blood pouring from his eyes and ears and his body was emaciated. He looked like a dying fly. Latia was out cold, blood streaming from a couple of wounds that had been partially healed.

"You're a nice opponent, aren't you?" she said to Malakai, who shrugged.

"I wasn't going to leave them to bleed out. I don't need a universal diplomatic incident because I decided to kill the leaders of one of the factions." He shrugged. "Even if they deserved it."

"Yeah, probably not a good idea," Quinn said. "Still, I think it just makes you nicer."

"Careful, Quinn, I'll almost think you like me."

"I'd never go that far," Quinn said. "I'm just being nice too."

Malakai chuckled. "Good, good."

Quinn noticed Lynx standing guard over Adrito, who wasn't out cold despite the bloody appearance. He was writhing in pain, curled into a tiny ball. She walked to the top of the dais stairs and stood over him, which was quite easy to do given his diminutive stature. She looked at the prime minister. He was much paler, more transparent now than he had been when she'd initially met him. She wanted to be angry at him and yell at him.

She was pretty sure she could work herself back up to that level of anger, but right then her logic won out. He was prone. He looked small, forlorn, broken and feeble. Nothing like he'd made himself appear when they first arrived. All his power was gone. Frankly, it looked like a heavy wind would blow him away, even with his wings. Speaking of which, the ends of them were in tatters. She raised an eyebrow at Malakai and he shook his head, so he hadn't done it.

"What did you pull on so much power for?" Quinn said, unable to keep the accusatory tone from her voice. She took a breath, centering herself, thanks to all of Milaro's teachings, and tried again. " Why was it so important to finish us, to keep us from healing Eugea? Or whatever your reasoning is. You've destroyed the city. You've destroyed the lives of many of your subjects. Did you realize you've made multiple islands plummet out of the sky?

Adrito opened his eyes. They were almost colorless now. He coughed and it wracked his entire small frame. Blood gathered on his lips. Quinn felt a pang of sadness for him, that he had been slightly regal when she saw him but forty minutes ago and now, now he was a wreck, because he'd pulled on too much power, caused too much destruction. Malakai knelt down to infuse a bare minimum of healing despite the fact it wasn't as effective on Esposians as their own magic. At least it was something.

"Don't you have an answer?" Quinn asked gently.

"I don't answer to you," Adrito spat out.

Quinn rolled her eyes. "Listen," she said, taking a knee in front of him so she could be a little bit more on his level. He struggled to sit up.

"There's no need to sit up, you can just listen to what I've got to say. All of this is wrong and you know it and I know it. You've your own people. Because of your actions, people who depended on you for their safety have lost their lives. You've destroyed a magical world, for what?" Her disdain for him grew as she spoke, with each realization of how despicable he truly was.

"You wouldn't understand," Adrito spat out again.

"Of course I wouldn't, how about you tell me and try me, maybe I will." She hated the way villains vagued everything up, like, oh no, let's catastrophize it all. Maybe if he could just articulate his reasoning, she'd understand. Improbable, but possible.

Adrito laughed. It was a light sound, not pretty like she was used to from Geneva, not even like she'd heard Nishpa laugh. There was a rasping quality to it. "You don't understand. I'm not alone. We aren't alone. There are many species out there who don't agree with the filtration of chaos, who don't agree that everybody should have access to magic. The strong need the magic. We can funnel its power and make the right choices. We will usher in a new age," he coughed, spluttering, spitting out blood.

"You will usher in a new era?" Quinn asked skeptically. "You're not looking so strong right now."

"An era that allows us to make sure that only those most capable among us become the strongest." He spat out the words again, blood spittle lingering on his pale lips.

Quinn raised an eyebrow and gestured emphatically at the crumbling surroundings Geneva was barely able to keep from burying them. "You call this capable?"

Adrito actually paled, but scowled and didn't say another word.

Quinn threw her hands up in the air. "Are you happy?" she said. "What could possibly be worth all of this destruction? Destroying those who trusted you, draining them and your world for what reason? In an attempt to destroy myself and my companions? How was any of this worth it for you or anyone?"

She'd raised her voice. She was angry, her fists clenched at her side. Malakai touched her shoulder lightly, just briefly, just enough to take her away from that edge, the edge that made her want to smash Adrito in a million pieces. She calmed herself and gave the Esposian a smile full of promises he wouldn't like. "You may not want to tell us what you know. But I know somebody who can make you," she said and gestured to the two leaders and the Esposian guard they'd saved. "Gather them up."

"You okay, Quinn?" Malakai asked with concern.

She nodded. "I'm better than okay. We're taking them all back to the Library. And then . . . we're visiting Uncle Hal."

42

THIN LAYER

Returning to the Library proved easier said than done. Quinn's skin itched as if something was trying to break through from underneath, from inside. And it was hot, as if yearning to escape. The sudden heat seemed very abrupt. Yet another reason to insist on going to visit Uncle Hal.

Except, there was a spanner in the works that had to do with returning.

Instead of simply being able to retrieve Eugea and escape back to the Library, Quinn found herself stuck in a logistical nightmare.

She understood the reasons. They'd secured and healed both Adrito and Latia as best they could, given their non-Esposian heritage. Neither Nishpa nor Geneva could heal them properly. The poor Esposian they'd saved from the fiery doom of the golem's crash was still unconscious and breathing shallowly.

Thus, Nishpa ensured that Eugea was sent for, and in the process also retrieved Galetta. The one mostly Esposian healer they could trust. Or at least, Quinn hoped they could trust her. Galetta began treating Adrito and Latia with much more success. However, Quinn noticed Galetta only did the bare minimum to ensure they were out of danger before moving on to the rescued Esposian.

"Thank you for not killing them," Galetta said, her eyes fiery with an emotion Quinn didn't associate with healers. It was out of her hands now anyway. Adrito and Latia would have to pay for what they'd done to their Esposian city. Quinn didn't think they were going to appreciate their comeuppance. She also wasn't certain she would be able to deliver them to Hal . . . but that was a later problem.

Nishpa tugged on Quinn's sleeve.

She looked over at the hovering Furionas. "Sorry, what? Why did you tug? Why didn't you just call my name?"

"I did. Twice. But you didn't answer me," Nishpa said dryly. It seemed that all of her energy and ability to laugh had deserted her. Not that it was surprising.

Quinn sort of understood. The whole trip ended in a much larger mess than she'd anticipated. She sighed. "Sorry, what is it?"

"I won't be able to return to the Library with you. I have matters to take care of here." Nishpa sounded wearier than anything else, as if it took effort for her to hover.

Quinn hesitated; her curiosity piqued.

Nishpa raised an eyebrow. "I can practically hear you begging me to tell so I'll just go ahead and do so. We've had our eye on this particular Esposian city for a long time. We are . . ."

"And who's 'we'?" Quinn asked, interrupting Nishpa.

Nishpa let out a short laugh. "I forget you're not versed in intergalactic politics. The Fae Committee. It's made up of centaurs, the Furionas, Esposians who are not on this planet, and several other conglomerations of species, all stemming from the fae. I'm unsure just now how many you've already encountered. We have a council which this particular branch of the Esposians has long since forsaken, and thus we have been keeping an eye on them. I was sent to accompany Geneva while trying to heal the injured Esposians you rescued so we could figure out just what was happening here, which, as you can probably tell, is a lot worse than we initially thought."

Quinn took a moment to glance out at the ruins of the once-beautiful city. While she knew most of it had been subterfuge with magical illusions overlaying a badly maintained city, the vision of it was still burned into her mind.

The illusions had long since shattered, along with about fifty percent of the city. She couldn't see any people out there either, but she could hear the occasional sob and moan. She wondered just how many of them had been impacted, how many of them had been injured. Did they understand why Adrito had done what he had done? Did they agree with it?

She highly doubted it.

They'd been pawns.

Quinn was about to say it was fine, when Geneva floated up to her. "You'll have to go ahead without me as well, but you must take Eugea with you. While these investigators are mostly trustworthy, I don't know them as well as I know you and Nishpa. I would prefer it if you'd take Eugea somewhere she can continue to heal and not be poked and prodded because your magic snapped her out of it."

"Plus," Nishpa added, "that way it might be easier for you to figure out how you healed her in the first place. I'm betting Milaro can assist there. I have a distinct and utterly horrific feeling that there'll be more colonies out there that are affected like this."

Quinn gulped. "Fine, we'll take her with us if she's willing to go."

"I'm willing to go," Eugea said. She looked even better than when they left her a couple of hours ago. Her color was returning, well, as much as an Esposian's color returned to them at all. And yet she seemed eager. "I want to help. I think I have memories. I have recollections. Maybe, maybe that can help lead you to whatever did this to us." She glanced around as if scared someone might overhear her. "I know. I know what it did," she said, whispering the last.

Quinn raised an eyebrow at Malakai, who ushered Eugea over to the door they were about to use to enter the Library. Quinn's skin itched, that fiery sensation threatening to leak out through her pores. She took a deep, calming breath and tried to suffuse the top of her skin with a thin, thin layer of ice. It worked, for the most part. She sighed with relief, a little bit of respite, before she faced the dragon back at the Library. Milaro would have so many questions. She knew it. Everybody knew it.

"Do I need to wait to meet with these dignitaries or whatever they are?" Quinn asked.

"Oh no," Nishpa said. "In fact . . . you don't want to. Hurry up. Go. If you meet with these people, they're going to keep you here for another few hours just to talk to you about the Library, because they're all fully aware that it was gone for a while."

Quinn grimaced. "Great. I'll take that under advisement and we should leave now."

"Truer words have never been spoken," Lynx said. "Are you ready?"

"Do you have enough energy left?" Quinn asked.

"I didn't deplete myself that much," he said, shaking his head, but she could sort of tell that he was rather happy that she'd asked. She had a very good friend in Lynx. She didn't want to see him disappear and hoped that that got across to him.

"Very well, here we go." They opened the door and Quinn ushered everybody through. Aradie stuck to her shoulder, however, cooing in her ear. Malakai went first, gently guiding Eugea with him. Lynx trotted afterwards and Quinn turned to Geneva and Nishpa.

"Thank you both. Hurry back, Geneva. We miss you." Their relationship had changed, for the better. Quinn was looking forward to having her back.

"I know," Geneva said, "what I wouldn't do just to have time to sit and read a book."

Quinn chuckled as she stepped through to the Library, closing the door to the destroyed Esposian city behind her.

A sense of calm overcame Quinn as she stepped into the Library. It had truly become a home, a place she felt she belonged. Sensations swept over her, the connection with the Library clarifying and solidifying, almost like someone had retuned a guitar string. She looked around and noticed that they hadn't come through the double doors they usually did. Instead, they were standing in the door from her office into the Library.

"Interesting choice," she said to Lynx.

He shrugged. "That way we're out of the way of everybody. If you want, you can close the door and hide yourself. You don't have to talk to anybody." He gave her a wink. "Now if you'll excuse me, I'll accompany Eugea and get her settled."

The Esposian looked around the office in wonder before nodding and following Lynx who sauntered out into the main part of the Library with her in tow.

Quinn seriously debated what he'd said. She knew Eugea was in good hands now. Frankly, she'd a hundred and fifty percent prefer to just curl up with a load of books, absorb a heap of power, and ignore all of the political and intricate machinations that apparently wanted to deprive the Library of power. However, she knew that way she'd only get limited time before something else hit the fan, and she didn't really want to scoop poop.

"Fine," she said, muttering.

Calibration required.

Scanning now.

Quinn blinked. *What's happening?* she asked the Library.

There was a pause, and Quinn got a distinct sense of disbelief from it before the Library spoke. *You created a new affinity. It needs to be calibrated into the magic system, and eventually you're going to have to define how to approach it.*

Quinn was quite stumped. She remembered vaguely the strange messages popping up in front of her when she'd healed Eugea, but she hadn't thought anything more of it. *Sooooo . . .*

I need to verify the different aspects that went into creating a new affinity, then I need to catalog it and establish it. The Library sounded slightly annoyed.

Will that take long? Quinn asked, trying to figure out how long she could manage considering her to-do list wasn't getting any shorter.

The Library huffed. At least, Quinn was fairly sure it huffed. *Fine. I'll let you off the hook for creating the precursors and prerequisites required for this one. But not for too long. Just long enough to get the pressing matters taken care of.*

I'm sorry. Quinn really did feel bad, especially since this could potentially help the Esposians. *Will the delay mean others can't use it?*

No, the fact that they can't wield the number of affinities you combined to create the new one will mean they can't use it. The Library sighed. *It's okay, I just haven't had a new affinity in such a long time.*

Quinn chuckled. I *promise, as soon as I get a moment, we'll sit down and work through it.*

I'll hold you to that.

I'm counting on it. Quinn smiled.

Calibrating . . .

Mental Chaotic Fortitude Abolition added to affinity database

Restrictions in place

Quinn grinned at the last. The Library was just being the Library.

Lynx waited patiently, having already escorted Eugea to the infirmary, and was obviously aware Quinn and the Library had been talking.

"Sorry about that," she said, but didn't get any farther.

"Ah, there you are," Milaro said just as she stepped into the main part of the Library. Dottie peeked out from behind his legs.

"We were starting to get worried about you. You weren't supposed to be gone long," the bench said, talking as if she was Quinn's grandmother. She reached down and petted the bench fondly. She didn't know what she'd do without Dottie anymore.

"Well, it got a little bit more complex than we thought," Malakai drawled. "You wouldn't believe it."

"Oh, try me," his grandfather said. "I'd believe a lot of things."

Quinn chuckled and recounted the entire situation to which, at least gratifyingly, Milaro's jaw dropped. Quinn was fairly certain that Dottie's would have too, if she'd had a jaw to drop.

"So," she said, "what do you think?"

"I think . . . that's pretty screwed up," Milaro said. "I don't understand. That doesn't even make sense. I knew Adrito."

Quinn crossed her arms. "How long ago did you know Adrito?"

"Well, I mean, I didn't know know him, but we'd been to several camps together when we were children," Milaro said hesitantly.

"Seriously," Quinn said, "camps when you were children? What? Three thousand years ago?"

"Well, we take our camps seriously. There's lots of interplanetary relationships to work on, to try and maintain a peaceful element among us all. Doesn't always work. There are a lot of us in the universe. We need to get along, mostly. We have to be able to prevent war and needless loss of life." Milaro sighed. "He never struck me as somebody who'd be willing to kill hundreds of thousands of his people just to prove a point."

Quinn shrugged. "Well, just goes to show we never really know people, eh?"

She began to itch again, and as she looked down, her scales flared above her skin, like they were trying to keep in the heat too. It even made them solidify ever so slightly, and she applied cool ice to them to help keep the heat at bay. Naturally, the approximately five seconds that that took didn't escape Milaro's notice, and he raised an eyebrow in her direction that basically said, *We're going to talk about this later.*

Quinn suppressed a sigh. She knew they had to talk about it later. It didn't mean she wanted to. Quinn gave in and let them all pile back into her office with her.

"So," Milaro said, sitting himself on the couch, "this is a lot bigger than we originally anticipated?"

Quinn shrugged. "I'm not sure. I didn't really have anticipations for, you know, universal conspiracies, but from what we're seeing now that we've talked to Arnekai and sort of to Adrito, is the generalized doom and gloom rhetoric of *we will take over the world.*"

Malakai snorted. "Universe, Quinn. Universe."

She laughed, but didn't feel very mirthful.

Milaro watched her closely. "It would appear that way. Are you going to tell me why you're itching your arms or am I going to have to guess?"

"Quinn sort of," Malakai offered instead of allowing Quinn to answer, "incinerated a sandstone golem."

"What?" Milaro said. "Your affinity, your strongest affinity is—" But he paused, narrowing his eyes briefly. "Oh, wait, I see. Why in the universe didn't I think of that before . . . when are you going to visit Hal?"

Quinn shrugged. "Well, I'd like to go now, but that's not really possible, is it?"

"Nope, not possible at all," Jasper said, popping her head around the door. "You need to talk to Harish, Siliqua, Cadre, and me, because I helped."

Quinn raised an eyebrow, unable to keep the smile off her face at the exuberance her new assistant had. She'd really come to like Jasper and her company. "Okay, I'll bite. What happened and why do I have to talk to them?"

Milaro chuckled and crossed his arms as Jasper practically danced up to the desk. "They fixed it. Well, they know how to fix it. They just need you and the core to collaborate together and fix the memories. It'll take a while and it will require a partial reboot, but one that we can control."

Quinn perked up at that. "Wait, you can fix the memories and the time gaps?"

"Yep, we can fix the memories, mostly." Jasper paused contemplatively. "We can fix the retrieval process of the memories and thus likely fill most of the gaps."

"Are the memories still there?" Quinn asked.

"Yes, at least we think so. We just have to retrieve them, and that's not going to be painless, but it's doable and thus we win." Jasper grinned again.

Quinn raised an eyebrow. "Is it going to be painful for me?"

"Shouldn't be. You don't have memories to retrieve, do you?" Jasper asked.

Quinn shook her head and glanced over at Lynx.

Jasper laughed and shook her head. "Oh, it's not going to hurt Lynx. Lynx is a manifestation."

Quinn smiled. "That's true. So it's going to hurt the Library?"

"A little bit is likely. But, you know, I think it's okay with that."

Quinn felt a thrum under her feet of acquiescence and realized that, yeah, maybe the Library was okay with that. Then she remembered that Adrito had been left back on his world and she scowled. "Damn it! I wanted to take Adrito to Hal. I don't know how we're going to get a hold of him. He's conspiring against the entire universe. We need the best person to get the information out of him."

Milaro clasped his hands in front of his eyes, leaning on his hands for a moment. "Fine," he said, pushing himself upright. "I guess I'll go and start negotiating."

Quinn grinned. "And then I'll have two presents for Uncle Hal."

Milaro waved her away as he disappeared in a whirl of robes.

"He really does love to make an entrance and exit, doesn't he?" she asked no one in particular.

Malakai chuckled, Aradie cooed, and Jasper laughed outright before focusing on something probably in her HUD and gasping. "Sorry! Going to have to jet. Being called by Siliqua! They'll need you soon. Maybe tomorrow morning? You should probably get some rest," she called out over her shoulder as she left the office.

"Bit of a whirlwind, isn't she?" Quinn muttered. "Wouldn't mind some of that energy."

Mal nodded and stepped closer. "Quinn. We need to talk."

She reached up and pet Aradie, who nipped her finger, cooed angrily, and took off to see her friends in the book infirmary. Quinn sighed and turned to Mal. "I know, I just . . ." She itched at her arm again.

"How about we try and deal with this first," he said, pointedly looking at the scales only just disappearing from her arm again. "You're leaking fire."

She looked up at Malakai. Now they were alone in the room. "What do you mean I'm leaking fire?"

Mal sighed, as if he was trying to sort his thoughts. "I don't exactly know when this started, but I'm pretty sure the main trigger for your fire ability as a dragon began when you had to incinerate those infected books and accessed flames that were way above your current level."

After a couple of seconds thought, Quinn had to admit he was probably right. "That actually sounds pretty accurate. I'm a little confused. It feels like water, ice, and fire are all calling to me simultaneously. It's already noisy enough in my head without all that. There's just so much to do, so much for me to get a handle on."

He nodded, and offered a sympathetic smile. "We just need to keep you as cool as possible as you can until Hal can help you get a handle on your powers."

"You really think he can help?" Quinn said.

"He battles flames, quite literally, on a daily basis. Pretty sure no one, other than an active cosmicisodracus, can help."

He's right. Hal is our best bet, the Library chimed in unexpectedly.

Quinn was going to have words with the Library sooner rather than later. Okay, probably much later than she'd like. "Maybe I should go now, then?"

But Malakai shook his head. "You've got too much to do here first. You need another day or two's rest. Get everything sorted out. My grandfather will fetch Adrito so we can take him with us too."

Quinn could feel a mild panic start in her gut, but took a few deep breaths, calmed her mind, and tried to tell herself that there was only so much she could do. "Okay. I'll just keep up this thin layer of ice for now, I guess?"

"It's sort of helping, right?" Mal said and sighed as Quinn shrugged. "Just stick with what's working for now so we don't send the whole Library up in flames."

Quinn gulped, because he had a point. The incineration flames had triggered this result in her . . . which meant she was fully capable of burning the books should she lose control.

Damn it.

THAT'S ALL

QUINN HAD NEVER BEEN THE BIGGEST FAN OF THE HEAT.

She'd always liked summer, but most of summer involved water. Lakes. Beaches. Swimming Pools. Water took away the sting of the heat and most of the humidity, which she also wasn't a fan of because it made her hair frizzy as hell. But now, even though the Library was temperature-modified or air-conditioned or whatever it was, she felt overheated and cold on an interchangeable, constant basis.

Quinn pulled the covers on; she was too hot. She pushed them off; she was freezing cold. She walked downstairs; she felt like an icicle. When she walked into her office it felt like somebody had blasted a furnace across her skin. It was really starting to get old, but at least it was under control. She wasn't spewing flames at things, and she also wasn't constantly being interchangeably covered in scales and skin as she had when they first got back.

Although, if she was being completely honest, Quinn kind of liked the scales. They made her feel very mystical and like maybe it was possible to accomplish everything she needed to.

The next day found her extremely irritable after a very restless night's sleep. She stumbled down while the Library sun rose and found her way to the kitchen to greet Cook, who was, as always, awake.

Did golems need to sleep?

"You look unrested, Librarian," Cook said as they pushed a plate of what looked like bacon and eggs over to her.

Quinn raised an eyebrow. She'd been feeling like bacon and some fluffy eggs. "You didn't happen to whisk these eggs with salt, pepper, cheese, heavy whipping cream, into like a light fluffy batter and cook them in butter, did you?"

Cook grinned at her. "I may have."

Quinn frowned. How would they know that was how she best liked eggs? She'd learned that when she was twelve, about four weeks before the accident. She took a bite of the scrambled eggs, and a wave of nostalgia hit her, followed by a much smaller wave of melancholy.

"These are wonderful," she said.

"I am glad that you approve. Would you like me to work these into your regular rotation of different breakfast foods?" Cook asked her quite seriously.

"Go for it. I'd eat these every single day if I could. But I like the variety," she said, holding up a hand just in case Cook got the bright idea that she meant she didn't want any of the other food like cinnamon doughnuts, waffles, yogurt, and granola. She had a bit of an eclectic taste, she liked to think. Although maybe she was using that word wrong.

"Do you need to sleep?" she asked suddenly deciding there was no time like the present.

"Not in the way you think, but we do rest to . . ." Cook paused a second as if trying to figure out how to express it properly. "To recharge."

Quinn nodded.

Her mood, definitely better for having eaten one of her favorite childhood foods, managed to last with her as she walked out into the Library and looked over it. She stretched and made her way toward the check-in desk but stopped about halfway there and stood in the shadow of one of the pillars, simply watching the assistants serve the people that came to the Library. They were very deft with the books now. They knew exactly how to scan them for any potential threats and then enter them into the system. All in a fraction of the time it took them the first few days.

She observed them for maybe a quarter of an hour as they checked in about a dozen people between the two of them, and she watched and saw how Finn sort of hovered over them. Not that Finn had wings. Finn was running along a bench that was behind the check-in desk or attached to it, which Quinn had never noticed before. Yet another thing that went with the adaptability of the Library. It seemed it was much easier for Finn to keep an eye on everything when they could look over instead of up at. Made perfect sense in a magical world sort of way.

And when someone who didn't need it took over the supervisory shift, she was quite sure it would magically disappear. Very handy.

Still, Quinn felt a slight niggle in the back of her mind. Finn was fitting right in now that they'd been called to step up. Much more so than Quinn had previously noticed. They were attentive and very good at instructing those under them. Quinn frowned. It could be that their trust in Finn had simply lit a fire under the Ilgonomur. Then again, if Quinn was trying to infiltrate somewhere and spy on a group of people, she'd probably try to ingratiate herself, make herself dependable and trustworthy.

Oh, this was going to be a problem. If Quinn suspected everybody all the time, it'd get exhausting. As it stood, Finn had done nothing to alert Quinn's senses.

Yet, maybe.

Quinn frowned and moved away from her observation spot, making a note to herself to check on everybody else's views of Finn a bit later. Right now, she had traitors and potential spies up in her head like nobody's business. This constant suspicion needed to be kept under control.

Instead of heading over to the check-in desk where everything was quite obviously running smoothly, she took herself to her office. Just before she walked in, Aradie swooped down to her place on Quinn's shoulder, chattering ever so birdishly into Quinn's ear.

"You know I can't understand you when you speak that fast."

Aradie shoved a picture at her, an image of Milaro about to return, opening the door.

"Oh." As Quinn approached her office, she saw the door to the holding cell just down the way from her open. "Ah," she said, "I guess he's here with our guest."

Aradie nodded.

"You could have just said so," Quinn said.

Aradie looked away, pointedly raising her beak in the air. Quinn shook her head and decided to take the door through to the holding cells that was inside her office. It would make things smoother. She walked through the office straight into the holding cell and observed as Milaro oversaw the return of Adrito. He finished instructing the entourage with him and then turned and entered the antechamber with her.

"I thought it was better to open the door directly into the holding cell instead of disturbing all of your patrons in the Library with an entourage of guards and a pretty pitiful former ruler." Milaro offered the explanation with one of his typical smiles.

Quinn nodded. "Did you have any trouble convincing them to let us take him to Hal?"

"Surprisingly no, but I do have to admit I do think Nishpa and Geneva held more sway than me when it came to those matters." Milaro looked out over their prisoner with a sad sigh. "It's a mess."

"Yeah, pretty much destroyed the entire ruling island, right?"

"Ishiposa Island and a few of the neighboring ones," Milaro said, correcting her absent mindedly. "I must confess I don't understand his motivations. But it's not for me to understand right now; it is for me to help you figure out why, how, and who decided to do all that."

"I like the way you think." Quinn spoke gently, wishing she could alleviate the heaviness of the situation. "But I do believe you owe me food."

Milaro cringed at her comment and then smiled tightly, his eyes never leaving the prisoner in his strange trance like state. "You know, I do owe you that. How about, when we get some more of this sorted, I just make you a full-on banquet?"

Quinn narrowed her eyes. "You wouldn't be trying to get out of it, would you?"

"No, I actually genuinely enjoy cooking. It's calming and normal in a way I sometimes need." He paused and gestured beyond the glass they watched through. "However, right now I have a lot on my mind. And thus, I'm unable to give my full attention to meal preparation. How about we just have a big banquet when some of this is over? And then I will gladly cook for you once a week."

"Hmm," Quinn said. "I accept your counter-proposal, but you better keep your promise."

"I'll keep them, don't worry. I'll keep all of them," he said gravely before smiling as he changed the subject. "Anyway, we have other things to do."

Quinn sighed. "I know. Do you have any idea why he did what he did?"

Milaro shook his head. "Literally none."

Quinn watched Adrito through the glass. "What did you do to him? He looks . . . is he drooling?"

"It's a stasis. He's not aware he's asleep. It's just . . ." Milaro sounded sad.

"Why are his eyes open if he's asleep?" Quinn asked, not sure what to do with her mentor's mood.

"It's a mind stasis. He's been made comfortable. I didn't want him to have time to dream up some way to attack us from within, so I placed him in a dreamlike state." He scrunched up his face in distaste. "Basically, I'm trying to lull his mind so it's more open to our questions.

"But didn't Tenejo break out of that state and murder his supposed best friend?" Quinn asked, quite horrified.

"Yes, but I'm thinking there was a lot involved that I didn't realize at the time. The power and malice behind his . . . I think it was instigated by Kajaro, who operates at a level I didn't expect," the elven king added.

"You're not filling in a lot of blanks here, Milaro."

"I know." He winked at her, a hint of his usual self creeping out. "Anyway, Adrito's mind magic is constructs and illusions. Even though he's not the strongest when it comes to the latter. Latia appears to have been the one who maintained the illusions over the city when you arrived. His specialty is controlling objects and to a lesser extent, people, thus he controlled the golem."

Quinn frowned, "Well, I guess—"

And then Misha stomped in with three security golems that didn't look like the other eight they had. She frowned. Those were obviously from the culinary branch. Quinn hadn't expected them so soon, even though she'd left instructions to initiate their assembly. Time was getting slightly mixed up in her head. So much had happened over the last few days.

Quinn nodded in recognition as Misha inclined her head at her through the security screen. Naturally the supervisory golem knew they were watching. "I guess we have three brand new security golems watching over him while your entourage gets back to where they belong, and you and I, Mr. King of the Elves, go and see what it is that Siliqua and Harish have to show us."

"I think that's a wonderful plan," Milaro said as he took her arm with a flourish and escorted her out of the room out of the door that led to the Library.

"Where are we meeting?" Quinn asked, suddenly suspicious.

"In your office, but I thought we'd go out and make an entrance."

She raised an eyebrow at him. "So my office is kind of just the general meeting room, right?"

"Yep, I'm glad you've gathered that."

Siliqua, Harish, Cadre, and Lynx were all in Quinn's office. The Library manifestation looked positively sullen.

"Quinn, it's wonderful to see you again," Siliqua said. She seemed a lot happier and less worried than she usually was, which, in a way, was good, of course. The wood elf always seemed eager about everything she did.

"What news do you have for me?" Quinn asked, glancing at Lynx who hadn't even tried to meet her gaze.

"Ah," Harish said, "maybe we will let Cadre explain that in more detail."

Quinn raised an eyebrow. Milaro let himself fall onto the couch instead of sitting at the conference table that was set up. "Do regale me with your news," he said, a smirk on his face. Quinn wondered at the rivalry between the two of them. They seemed friendly enough.

"Well," Siliqua spoke up first. "There's actually been some, I've had some . . ." She paused as if she was trying to figure out phrasing. "I have had some progress on the Ashiron pillar."

Cadre waved her forward. "This is perhaps better addressed first."

She flashed him a small smile of appreciation before continuing. "It was a non-organic failure, not just of the filters themselves, but of the actual filtration system, which is why it cannot be flushed and cannot be reset unless we manually go down there and figure out a workaround. We'll need to figure out what's gotten into it. From everything I can tell, there might be a physical contaminant inside it. For now I believe it's safe, considering you had the foresight to seal it off, but it will require a manual inspection and reset."

Quinn frowned. "I sort of assumed that we'd have to do that."

Siliqua paused, and then hesitated before speaking again. "But there's something wrong with it on an integral level. Not like it was when you had to change the filters, though we'll likely have to do that as well. But Ashiron is at least airtight. In such a way that not even I can access it. I have no idea who set it up that way, but not even Harish, Cadre, or I can figure out how to break through the, hmm, what would you call it?"

"Code?" Milaro offered helpfully.

"No," Siliqua said, shaking her head.

"Encryption?" The elf king tried again.

Siliqua's face lit up. "That's it. Whoever sealed it away did so with such a complex encryption that I can't break it."

Quinn frowned as she considered everything else Siliqua had been able to accomplish. That had to be some next-level lock on Ashiron if even she couldn't break it. "That doesn't sound good. And with all the memory holes that we have, couldn't this be more dangerous than anything else? It's right underneath us. It's tapped into the lake of mana."

"Actually," Siliqua said, "I think whoever locked it away was on our side because whatever they did is keeping it basically out of synchronization with the rest of the mana lake and the filtration chamber. It isn't quite in contact with it. Nothing from the pillar can leak into it and contaminate the lake."

"What, they did like a dimensional shift?" Quinn asked, a part of her finding it odd that she took this in stride.

"Probably. We'd need to physically go down and check."

Quinn looked at Milaro and Lynx who wouldn't meet her eyes and back to Siliqua. "So you're telling me it's so dangerous they had to shift it out of synchronization with our current dimension that is already its own dimension? So that it wouldn't infect us?"

"Yes, precisely," Siliqua said. "I love the way you get difficult topics, Quinn."

Quinn sighed, counted to three, and decided to veer them back to the original reason they'd come together. "It's safe for now and will last until we've dealt with other stuff though, right?"

"Precisely, but I wanted you to know what we'd figured out."

Quinn didn't bother to say she had no intention of fooling around with a dimensionally shifted pillar right now, and nodded instead, "I've got it. Okay, so what about the memory retrieval?"

"Ah, the memories, the locked files," Harish said his expression just like a kid at Christmas.

Siliqua snatched the conversation away from her husband. "Don't you worry, Librarian. We've almost got everything ready to replace the corrupted and decayed sections. It's just that Lynx will require recalibration and the fix will bleed over into normal everyday Library functions. You'll need to announce that the Library is upgrading or something similar for the next ten or so days. It means physically borrowing books and extracting them from the Library won't be possible. They can still read them here. But that's all."

Quinn let the information sink in for a few seconds before counting to three under her breath again. "Oh, fantastic," she said. "That's all."

44

ANNOUNCEMENTS

Quinn pinched the bridge of her nose. Shutting the Library to borrows . . . again? All said, it could have been worse, but that still didn't mean it was good.

"Okay, fine. Can you break this down for me, on an 'I've been in a magical universe for a few months and don't understand everything yet' sort of wavelength? Why will we have technical difficulties that won't allow us to lend out books?"

"Oh," Cadre said, side-eyeing Harish and Siliqua ever so slightly before walking up and standing in front of Quinn. He was the only one who hadn't sat down yet. "You see, Librarian," he said in his very soft voice, "I have figured out that Lynx must be flushed along with the system. It means that the Library and Lynx will be mostly unavailable during such a time as they are being re-synchronized."

Quinn narrowed her eyes. "You literally just told me nothing."

Cadre shifted, his lizard-like eyes flickering briefly towards Siliqua and Harish.

"She can take it. She'll understand in a way," Siliqua amended.

"You were trying to spare my feelings and not tell me everything? Again?" Quinn said. "Because we all know how well that's gone so far."

They at least had the decency to look sheepish.

"Then a different approach," Cadre said. He cocked his head to one side like he was trying to shake the thoughts into it. "Look, the system is an organic system, unlike the more electrical and mechanical side you're used to. It permeates everything that we are. It hooks into every single person who has an affinity for magic. This is why you cannot see the system on Earth. That's why, for most of Earth's population, the system would be new. Should there be a magical signature on your home planet, they would have immediate access to a system—even if their energy level doesn't enable all of its functionalities. It is simply how the universe functions. Now the . . ."

"Wait a second, wait a second," Quinn said. "That doesn't work for me."

"What do you mean?" Cadre asked, confusion apparent on their face.

"That what you're saying doesn't track." Quinn crossed her arms. "I lived on Earth for years. I don't ever remember having a system in front of my face."

"You were a child for most of your time there, a minor. Minors are not granted full access to the system and only certain genetic aspects will cause it to take control in cases of emergency. It's a failsafe to make sure that children don't, shall we say, make mistakes when approaching magical phenomena or attempting to gain control of their magic. Your guardians would have had control until you came of age. I believe your energy levels were still replenishing when we found you, your magical energy wouldn't have had enough spare to activate the system."

"Oh," Quinn said, because it made perfect sense, in a roundabout if you believe in magic sort of way. "Wait, so children are able to access magic, but it's regulated so they don't accidentally destroy the worlds?"

"Pretty much," Siliqua said. "Wouldn't want a toddler to accidentally explode a neighborhood block because you wouldn't let it eat a drawing stick, would you?"

Quinn actually laughed and then paused. "I realize that's not funny, but just the idea of a toddler throwing a tantrum and, you know, exploding the swimming pool that they weren't allowed to swim in or something made me laugh. Sorry."

"You have an odd sense of humor," Milaro piped in.

"I know," Quinn said. "Morbid, I believe, is how some people describe it. Still, keep going, please."

"Anyway," Cadre continued on cue, "Children do not have access, or perhaps better explained, they do not have *control* of that access. Frankly, if you weren't the Librarian, I still don't think you'd have access."

"Why?" Quinn blurted out.

Cadre shrugged. "As far as years for your appearance, you might be an adult, but for your main genetic sequence? You're just a baby in terms of those years."

Quinn nodded slowly, digesting the information. Maybe it was like a Malakai thing . . . in human years, he was well into adulthood; in elven years, still a teen.

Cadre gave her a slightly concerned look before continuing. "So the system, as you know, functions within the parameters of the affinities and how magic works. Even while the Library was out of commission, all affinity users still had access to their own powers. Magic wasn't replenished as quickly and wasn't as clean. However, it didn't mean our abilities were gone. I've digressed much farther than I wanted to, but you brought up a very valid point," Cadre said. He gripped his head as if he was trying to figure out where his train of thought had led him, and Quinn watched.

She was still quite uneasy with the way they'd only sort of covered the Ashiron pillar situation. A sense of dread and urgency ate at her. It could also have come from the fact that she was having another severe hot flash that felt like it was trying to burn her up from the inside out. She really did need to get that under more control. But all this system information . . . she wished she'd have known it earlier. It was complex enough that she felt she needed more time to absorb it all.

"Systems work for everybody, but they are fueled. The magic that runs the universe, as you know, is fed through the Library. Thus, in order to make sure we're not damaging anything accidentally, we'll need to purge the affected, infected sections of the memory as we're replacing them with the good sequence." Cadre took a second and then nodded. "I guess that would be the best analogy."

"All right," Quinn said, "so while you're doing that purging of each section, you're going to require more power?"

"Not necessarily more power," Cadre corrected. "More of the Library's resources in a monitoring capacity. Thus, it'll make certain aspects of the Library itself inaccessible, or at least, not ideal to access."

"Okay," Quinn said, "I can deal with that. I understand what you're saying. It makes sense. Like if your hand is broken but not your fingers, you can't use the fingers without hurting the hand that's broken until it's whole again."

"Yes," Cadre said, his eyes shining. "Exactly! Exactly!"

"Fine. I understand, but I don't get why you weren't going to tell me."

"I apologize, Librarian," Cadre said, "I'm simply used to couching some of my research in more hidden terms."

Quinn remembered his own people weren't as open minded. "You're not quite on the same wavelength as the rest of your species, are you?"

"That is a very eloquent way to put it, Librarian." He winked one of his eyes very deliberately. "I would be somewhat less polite about it."

In that instant, he totally reminded Quinn of a gecko she'd seen on TV a lot.

"I needed to forewarn you about this so that Library patrons can be notified there will likely be intermittent outages in the Library borrowing system for the next week or even two." He blinked rapidly for a second, before nodding to reinforce his words.

"For at least a week?" Quinn said, "nobody can borrow?" She could already hear the complaints piling back up.

"But they can still use the Library services," Cadre added hurriedly. "The fact that we won't have full access to the Library borrowing system doesn't negate the fact that the golems and other assistants know the collection highly well and can recommend books within the

Library. You'll still have a lot of patrons, they just won't be able to take the books home with them for now."

Quinn smiled. He was really trying to make it less cumbersome. "We're likely to get a lot of patrons staying for longer periods of time, then?"

Cadre shrugged. "Probably, depending on what they need the books for."

"Cadre," Siliqua chimed in, sending a glare in Cadre's direction, "get to the point, unless you want me to."

"Fine, you can fill her in the rest of the way." Cadre stuck out a very long, forked tongue at the wood elf. Siliqua, point-blank, ignored him.

Quinn's tolerance was wearing thin. "Guys, I have so much work to do. Do you see my desk? It has papers on it. Papers, old-fashioned papers that Milaro tells me people on the council still like to use. Stacks of them, in fact. Since I can't simply say yes or no in the system, I need you to get this over with as quickly as possible. Tell me what we're dealing with, please."

Quinn took a breath and a drink from the water that miraculously appeared on her table. She'd have to talk to the Library about that. There still seemed to be things it could do that she still didn't know about. Bringing her water was a welcome thing.

Siliqua laughed, and there was a hint of nervousness to it. "Very well. I know you're busy."

"I've never been so busy in my life." Quinn laughed this time, but it was more of a self-deprecating laugh. She still wasn't used to this level of activity. Constant activity. Never-stopping activity. Her brain pulsed painfully for a second in protest.

And she suddenly felt overwhelmingly hot for just an instant again.

"Anyway, Cadre," Siliqua continued, "I shall proceed. Lynx requires recalibration for the sequencing to take full effect. I need you to understand that the fix, or the change, won't be instantaneous. Lynx won't immediately recall absolutely everything in the memories we make available again. There are reasons for this. We need to . . . Hmm. How do I phrase that?" She glanced at her husband for help.

"We need to figure out how best to help him and the Library access those memories, those data points, and make sure they won't re-infect the entire system," Harish said.

"Can't you do that before you reset them?" Quinn asked.

"You'd think," Cadre said, "but the way the system is set up, I won't have safe access to those pathways until we begin the process. If we access the memories through the corrupted pathways and force ourselves into it, the odds are that we completely and utterly infect the memory, thus likely destroying it, is high."

"So that data would be lost," Quinn said, having a light bulb moment.

"Yes. Right now, our, or at least my, main goal has been to retrieve the information the Library is missing so we can piece together everything it needs to know and recollect."

Quinn blinked at Cadre. He'd just said that so fast. She appreciated the candor. "Okay, so that's why it'll take several days?"

"Yes, I'd say access to those memories, those data points, are going to take at least a few to several days. Actual incorporation of them could stretch out to months. These have been sealed away for a very long time. It is my hope that one of the fail-safes of the Library kicked in in order to protect the overall system. Without the system, everything's going to crash. Without the cleansed and filtered mana and energy we all use to survive in the universe, the system is going to crash. Without the system, we don't have any measure of control over the magic that we need for day-to-day survival."

Quinn felt a shiver run down her back. "That doesn't sound good at all," she said.

"Oh no, it's actually quite horrific!" Cadre said, his tone strangely upbeat, as if he was solving the world's best puzzle, "It'd be a very bad situation if all the data points were also corrupted. Hopefully, we find good news when we dive in. But that's why it'll take so long, and require us to shut down borrowings. That is acceptable, correct?"

"I'd much prefer to maintain the magic systems in the universe than to suddenly lose them." Quinn said.

"Well, it would be catastrophic, Librarian. Rampant chaos! Nobody's magic would work. The parameters would be lost. The controls would be gone. You'd accidentally gesture and probably eliminate the person standing next to you. Not an ideal world, in any case, even if slightly fascinating," Cadre said. "Oh, and not to forget that chaos would them devour everything it could to increase its real estate.

"Okay," Quinn said, slightly put off by his enthusiasm for the end of order in the universe, "you're giving me the totally worst-case scenario. I'd love a best-case scenario option too here."

"That's easy. Best-case scenario, the whole process takes several days, and everything will be fine. We'll retrieve the information we need quickly, and you'll be able to find the people who tried to sabotage the Library and take care of all of them easily," Cadre answered promptly, a big smile on his face.

"That's a great best-case scenario." Quinn said, relieved. "How about a likely case scenario?"

"The probable case," Cadre said with a sigh, "is that it will take maybe ten days for us to calibrate Lynx. Then, Lynx, the system, and the Library. Then, it's probably going to take us at least a month or two to get all the information from those restored, because we're trying to preserve them in the process and make sure that nothing creeps in that shouldn't. We need to be cautious so it's not all for nothing, so we don't have to start from the beginning again."

Quinn nodded again, slowly this time, and Aradie nipped at her ear. "Yeah, I get it, I get it. Aradie says the night owls will help, should you need them."

"Really? Aradie, you would you lend me your magic?" Cadre asked, suddenly very serious, his focus on the owl.

The owl pulled herself up to full height, which also meant that she shed the illusion that made her slightly lighter on Quinn's shoulder. Quinn almost groaned with the exertion until she noticed the look on Cadre's face. He was half smiling, an eagerness behind the expression that Quinn hadn't quite seen the man express before. He seemed delighted to get to work with the owl.

Quinn wanted to know what was so special. "You seem so excited," she asked.

"Working with a night owl's magic is one of the things on my bucket list, if that's what you'd like to call it." His eyes shone with a thirst for knowledge.

Aradie finally nodded.

"Excellent, then I think we might have a better chance of pulling this off, Librarian. Thank you for your generous offer, Aradie." Cadre gave a little bow in the owl's direction.

Aradie cooed quick and fast. Quinn suppressed a chuckle. "She says that she'll be in charge."

Cadre laughed too. "Oh, there's no doubt in my mind that she *will* indeed be the one in charge. But this way I feel like this failsafe has an even higher chance of success."

Quinn smiled, realizing they had a lot of work ahead of them. She was nervous, getting ready to recalibrate Lynx and shut outgoings down for a couple of days. She began composing the announcement, all the while unable to shake the shivers that ran down her spine that had absolutely nothing to do with her newly onset alternating of hot and cold.

Either something was coming, or something was about to go terribly wrong.

45

A FRACTION OF THE UNIVERSE

"A higher *chance* of success doesn't exactly sound confidence inspiring," Quinn said. She couldn't shake the bad feeling about putting Lynx in stasis.

Cadre blinked and Harish nodded, leaning forward on the table. "I see your point, Librarian. There is, as always in anything, risk involved. But with Aradie's assistance as well as the Library and Lynx cooperating fully, we have a much better chance at having a successful outcome."

Quinn glanced over at Lynx, who gave her an almost imperceptible shrug. It seemed he wasn't exactly fussed either way. If she was honest, the manifestation appeared to have mostly given up. Another aspect for Quinn to worry about.

Milaro was still watching her, studying her, but he stood up suddenly and clapped his hands, startling the others in the room. "All right. I think we've got the gist of it then. We're placing Lynx in standby mode, and have the Library watching over both him and itself, while we monitor it, correct?"

Siliqua blinked in surprise. Milaro had been mostly quiet while they all talked, and the king could often be much larger than life when he chose, as he seemed to have chosen in this instant.

"Yes. That's quite correct," Siliqua said.

Quinn held a hand up. "Monitor it from where, none of you can stay in the chamber indefinitely, right?"

"That's right." Siliqua smiled, back from the slight shock Milaro's sudden interjection caused her. "We'll be able to monitor him from outside the chamber. Make sure everything is going to plan, tweak what we need to, observe the pathways. We've got it all sorted. Perfectly safe for all of us."

Quinn sighed. "I guess this plan is a go . . . Lynx, what about you? Are you okay with all of this?"

He shrugged. "I have to be. I'm not working at my usual capacity, and it's both demoralizing and frustrating. If for no other reason I want to return to being my efficient self and stop feeling as if my brain is full of holes."

She smiled at him, wishing it could just be magically fixed. Although technically she guessed it was. "That makes a lot of sense. I'm sorry you're all holey."

Lynx laughed. "Yeah, it's strange operating like I'm missing parts of what makes me myself."

Siliqua and Harish stood up, joining Cadre near the door. Milaro moved over to them as well. He smiled. "See you both in a couple of hours." The king ushered the other three out of the room before they could say another word.

Quinn watched after them, frowning. Had Milaro somehow known she wanted to talk to Lynx by himself?

She could also sense Malakai standing just beyond the doorway. Another thing she'd been perturbed about in the last couple of days. Malakai seemed to have velcroed himself to her side since the incident with the golem on Ishiposa Isle. He didn't let her out of his sight at any point during the day.

Except when she slept.

At least, she hoped when she slept. She was fairly sure he wasn't sleeping on the ground outside her room. She wasn't going to ask him. Ignorance was bliss, right?

Still, he lounged around her office door just like he was doing now when she was trying to gather her thoughts about the whole situation with Lynx and the calibration. After what happened last time they rebooted the Library, she couldn't help being worried that they might instigate a catastrophic failure in this as well.

Quinn sighed. Maybe Malakai was just taking his guard duty seriously, which was probably a good idea. Quinn seemed to be fully capable of getting herself into the most ridiculous forms of trouble ever. She sighed again.

"Will you stop sighing?" Lynx said. "It's really not all that bad."

"I know it's not a bad thing," Quinn said. "It's just that you'll be out of commission again."

Lynx laughed. "You know, I've practically been out of commission more than I've been helping you run the Library."

But the joke fell flat. Not that it was true, either. She'd been there for three months, and he'd only been in stasis for about two weeks of the time. It just felt like a very long time every time it happened.

"Don't be sad," he said. "I should be sad. I'm the one that's running the risk."

"Is it really a risk?" she asked, trying not to let the worry shine through in her words.

"I mean, they said it wasn't a big one." Lynx laughed, but the sound was forced. "But when do researchers ever fully know what they're doing, Quinn?"

She hesitated. "True. I'm worried about you. Okay? There you go. I said it. I'm worried about you. I just want to make sure you come back."

This time, there was an echo of laughter through her mind.

It was the Library. *He's going to come back, Quinn. This isn't that dire.*

"Oh, you mean the holes in your memories and data points? The inability to access them? That's not a problem or a dire situation?" Quinn snapped, quite irritated at the downplaying of the entire situation.

No, that is a problem. It's just not as dire as you're making it out, because we now have a solution. The way that Siliqua explained they're going to tackle this is the safest possible route. The paths will be replaced first, and then the infected areas. And then we should be good to connect all the memories and data points. The Library's tone held a soothing note that barely managed to calm some of Quinn's nerves.

"Okay, in theory it sounds fantastic," Quinn said. She hated theory. It rarely worked in practice.

Yes, it does, doesn't it? the Library said back to her. *Don't worry. We're good. Do you want to come down and see us go into stasis? See it for yourself? Might help put your mind at ease about the whole thing?*

Quinn perked up at that, suddenly feeling a wave of better. "Yeah? Is that okay?"

It'd be nice for us both, too, actually, because the only other person who can come down is Milaro, and we all know how stroppy he can get.

Quinn laughed although she did wonder just how it would work for the others who needed to observe Lynx. There was obviously something they hadn't told her. Perhaps they had special glasses they could use to see him with. "Okay, we'll be down there when the time comes." She said, and felt the Library fade from her immediate consciousness.

After several seconds of silence, and a few deep breaths, Quinn smiled over at Lynx.

"Do you feel better now?" he asked, raising an eyebrow.

"Much better in fact."

"Good," Lynx said and then looked at her more seriously than she'd ever seen before. "Because I need you not to get too anxious about this. It's unknown to me too, and one of us needs to stay awake and alert to make sure the Library runs smoothly. And that person should be Dottie."

Quinn blinked at him after that totally unexpected addition. "Say what now?"

"Dottie will keep an eye on them, and the Library, and everything. You know she loves to rise to a challenge. So let her just take care of the Library, along with Misha and Geneva while you're gone," Lynx concluded, looking quite pleased with himself. Sort of like a cat that got the cream.

Quinn held up a hand. "Wait, wait . . . and where am I in all of this?"

He blinked, like he didn't understand the question. "What?"

"Where am I going that I need to leave Dottie and the rest in charge of making sure you and the Library are taken care of?" Quinn racked her brains to find the information she was sure she'd just glossed over.

"You're visiting Hal," Lynx said, like it was a given.

Quinn blinked. Well, she had to go and visit Uncle Hal because of Tenejo, and now Adrito, and to be completely honest, she desperately needed some help with this whole heat trying to immolate her thing. But . . . "I don't have time to go right now. There's far too much to do."

Lynx laughed. "Do you think the Library can't run without you?"

Quinn narrowed her eyes. "I think a broken Library that can't remember its arse from its elbow probably shouldn't have prolonged Librarian absences."

He laughed again. "Okay, you've got me there. But . . . think on it. It's only portions of the system that won't be accessible. You have a great group of assistants and supervisors who can take over for the few days you'll need. It's not like you can do anything to help me anyway. And I'm pretty sure Milaro will be watching over us during the whole recalibration process."

She frowned at him. He had a very good point. "Well, I'll think about it."

Lynx raised an eyebrow. "You need to get that problem figured out, and right now, the Library has to recalibrate and sequence in order to return to its original glory. I don't think you can afford the time it'll take to wait until the Library has all of its memories intact and thus can help you." He ended the plea in a soft but serious voice.

"I think you're right," Quinn said, as she could feel the heat in her veins push to the fore again. "Okay. I'll go as soon as possible."

"Good," Lynx said and stood up, brushing himself off even though she knew he didn't need to. "Shall we proceed then?"

About twenty minutes later, Quinn found herself standing down at the core, watching as Lynx approached what looked like a small cushion perched at the base of the petrified trunk. Or at least whatever that trunk was. She'd still not asked the Library why it was presented as a tree . . . and now wasn't the time.

He looked up at her and gave her a thumbs up.

Milaro nudged her as he popped what looked like a hard candy into his mouth. "It'll all be okay. I have a good feeling about this."

She eyed the wrapper he stuck in his pocket. "Is that how you can stay down here?"

He nodded. "Yeah, only way."

"Can you stay down here indefinitely if you have enough of those?" she asked as she watched Lynx flicker ever so slightly.

"Nope. A couple of days at most." He shrugged. "If I don't leave then, it'll start killing me."

"Wow, you must really like the Library." Quinn raised an eyebrow.

Milaro watched her for a second before answering. "I like what the Library stands for, and the fact that the Library's a pretty good person, also helps. I like balance, Quinn. I would do most anything to maintain the balance that keeps our universe healthy and, you know, not imploding or devouring itself."

Quinn laughed, but it was a forced expression. Milaro was right. While she hadn't visited even a fraction of the universe, she was certain that most residents would choose to exist. Maybe.

She watched as Lynx settled down onto or into the cushion. He melted back into his lynx form, and the runes that were the stripes around him swirled lazily as he curled up onto the cushion. It sank back into the petrified core tree trunk. The Library hissed ever so softly, and then Lynx was gone.

"That's it," she said, a strange emptiness where Lynx usually was in her senses.

"That's it," the Library said, its smoky visage evident next to the trunk. "Siliqua and Harish will run the relevant sequences from above."

"Wait. There's a control room above or something?" Quinn said. She'd been trying to figure out how they were going to observe this all. A control room not only made sense, but made her feel better about perhaps leaving to get her fire under control.

The Library shimmered slightly. "I didn't think you'd be interested, considering you can always come down and see me."

Quinn smiled. She *was* a bit of an exception.

"Where do you think we've been working this entire time?" Milaro asked.

"Well, I don't know, I assumed you'd be down here . . . since you came down here when I synchronized?" Quinn laughed. "Well, how about you go show me this control room so I can at least get an idea of what's happening?"

"You could always just come down here if you wanted to visit," Milaro said softly.

"True . . ."

He was right, but Quinn was feeling very out of her depth. Lynx, while cantankerous, had been the first one to greet her, and the one who took her through her first perilous days. He'd guided her this whole time, even when he was barely present. She couldn't help the worry.

"You know this will take days, right, Quinn?" the Library asked.

"Of course," she said reluctantly.

"And you realize Lynx is right." The Library practically whispered the next in her ear. "You have to get this under control. I can't help you for days. And if, as I assume, your heritage is awakening sooner than I'd anticipated, then you really need to go and see Uncle Hal since I'm currently indisposed."

"Even you're calling him Uncle Hal," Quinn said, but she couldn't bring herself to laugh.

"It's much easier to pronounce. Let's just say that."

Quinn smiled. "Okay, okay, I'll go."

"Really? While we're out of commission?

"Sure," Quinn agreed and almost immediately wished she hadn't.

"Delegate to your supervisory staff. Milaro will be overseeing the entire transfer of sequencing anyway. If anything big comes up . . ."

"Yeah, I get it, he can take care of it." Quinn laughed. "Fine, I'll get ready to make the trip." She glanced back at where Lynx had disappeared and knew he was in the best place possible for what he was about to undergo.

"Don't forget to take Eric with you," the Library said.

"I won't," Quinn called over her shoulder as she exited the core.

"First of all," Milaro said, as he nudged her toward the exit, "we have several things to discuss. But as soon as we've done those, and as soon as Adrito and Tenejo are prepared, you're going to see Uncle Hal."

Quinn smiled. "You know, I think that sounds like an excellent plan."

"Good. Because you're going even if Eric has to shrink you and throw you in his storage."

Quinn gasped. "He can't really do that can he?"

Milaro shrugged. "I don't know. He's an imp. He can do all sorts of things."

That didn't make Quinn feel any better.

4 6

—————

LONG NIGHT AHEAD

It was vaguely lonely in Quinn's head now that the Library had receded in her mind due to its current focus. However, as they ascended the stairs, Quinn realized that this was necessary even if it made her feel oddly vulnerable.

Milaro guided her to a room behind the stairs once they were up on the main level, close to where Quinn had installed the new elevator leading to the filtration chamber. She surveyed the room. It was about twenty by twenty feet, surprisingly large for a space she'd never noticed before. To be fair, it wasn't an area she frequented.

She saw Siliqua, Harish, and Cadre hunched over readouts and screen projections. At an angle below the desks, windows overlooked the core. The view was misty, suggesting something about the atmosphere down there prevented the use of completely clear glass. It probably wasn't even glass, but some weird magically enhanced sort of thing, considering the Library created it . . .

However, the fact that they could see some of it comforted her.

"Feeling better?" Milaro asked.

"A little," Quinn replied.

"Good." He offered her a smile of commiseration. "Can we agree that he's in good hands?"

"I knew he was in—yes, we can agree," Quinn said. There was no need to argue because there was nothing to argue about. It was just her anxiety and paranoia trying to run rings around her mind.

"Now can we move on?" he asked gently.

"Fine." She gave in, knowing he was right.

"I wish I'd have been there to observe first-hand how this ability of yours is working, but I wasn't. So, Quinn, I need you to run me through exactly what happened back on Ishiposa Isle." He sighed as they approached her office. "This really shouldn't have happened to you yet. It's not within any of the calculations I ran before you were created."

"It's okay. You couldn't predict everything." She winked at him trying to soothe that blow.

"You're right," he said as they finally entered through her office doors.

She was amazed he'd admitted to it. "Okay, now, spill. What do you need from me?"

"Just give me a second." He placed a hand lightly on her forehead, murmured a few words under his breath that she couldn't quite hear, and closed his eyes. She felt a slight jolt, but she knew he wasn't doing anything dangerous. He was simply trying to get a read on her and these new skills that were developing.

He frowned and then opened his eyes, removed his hand and motioned for them to sit down on the couch. "Okay, I need details. Not what you did, because I know what you did. I saw the results of it and that was pretty impressive. I need to know how the sensations felt while you were experiencing them."

"Oh, you mean like the fire trying to eat me from the inside out?" Quinn asked. She wasn't trying to be sarcastic or snarky, but it sort of came out that way.

"Like that. But I need more detail," he said.

"What do you mean, more detail?" Quinn asked.

"Well, exactly that. I need to know exactly how it felt as you set the golem on fire."

Quinn frowned and closed her eyes, trying to bring the sensations back to her. The franticness of the situation, the smell of the crumbling stone . . . "I don't know, it was strange. It kind of suffused me and I felt warm like I was just trying to light a spark. Maybe grab some tinder and just let it burn. I was actually hoping to steam the golem out and destroy its structural integrity, but it caught on fire."

"You knew it was malleable archonite and had soaked it beforehand, right?" he asked cautiously.

Quinn nodded as she opened her eyes. "I iced and watered whatever I could. I don't even understand how it caught fire."

"That's because Adrito actually used incendiary stone as the core, which was bizarre." Milaro sounded decidedly irritated by the fact. "He's definitely changed since our childhood days." For a second, sadness passed over Milaro's expression, as if he truly missed the Adrito he'd known in his childhood, even if they hadn't been the best of friends.

Quinn supposed that finding a childhood friend had turned into a species-destroying monster probably hurt a little.

"The thing was, the fire felt welcome. It didn't seem dangerous for me in any way, like it was protecting me. It wasn't safe for the golem," she added. "Anyway, my scales—I mean, I don't know if they're scales, but they look like scales. They were darker and they hardened. They were more corporeal, like armor."

"Can you summon them now?" Milaro asked. Curiosity peaked in his voice. "Like, right now, could you just summon those scales?"

Quinn put her arm out and focused. She focused on the memory of the sensations, and willed the scales to appear so hard she almost made herself dizzy.

And they did absolutely nothing.

Her arm didn't change, and was still the same olive complexion skin she'd always had. She could almost sense the power inside her laughing at her.

"That would be a no," Quinn said.

"I'd say more of a *not yet*. That's a shame. I'd love to get to study them sooner rather than later." Milaro sounded severely disappointed.

"Maybe it's a reflexive measure," Quinn suggested. "Like, it protects me when I get in any super danger like getting smashed into the floor would probably be considered, you know, dangerous for me."

"It's likely." He leaned back and studied her for a moment. Then nodded to himself and spoke. "I'll give you a few books I think will help you over the next couple of days while we're getting everything ready for you to go and visit Halschius."

Quinn sighed. "A couple of days? Do you think it'll take longer than that for Lynx to finish the sequencing?"

Milaro laughed. "Yes, Quinn, it's going to take longer than two days. Frankly, I think the initial week-long estimate was generous, but Cadre has been known to pull out miracles before. We'll see what happens. The point is, we have to prepare Tenejo and Adrito for the trip to Halschius. They can't be knocked out of their stasis. Otherwise, we'll have hell to pay."

Quinn laughed.

"Why are you laughing?"

"Because Halschius sounds like hell, and Uncle Hal is sort of like the king of hell, and you said there'd be hell to pay." Jokes weren't nearly as funny when you had to explain them.

"Oh, I get it." Milaro laughed a little bit. More like a chuckle, really. "Anyway, before I give you those books, I want to actually take a look in your mind. Will you allow me to do that?"

"Does it have something to do with the fire?" Quinn asked.

"Your mind controls everything, Quinn. There are ways we can strengthen protections for you. There are ways we can help your mind win over matter. A lot of times, we're societally conditioned to believe certain things. Now, don't get me wrong. Fire is always going to burn, but somebody like you, who has a heritage that is largely almost immune to fire, it's not going to hurt as much, but because you were raised human, you will perceive that these flames are going to kill you, and that is a mind problem, not necessarily a fire or physique problem."

Quinn blinked at him. "You realize that only makes sense because there's magic, right?"

"Oh, Quinn, so much only makes sense because there's magic." Milaro's laugh this time was hearty.

Quinn laughed. He had a point, and she had put her foot completely and utterly in that one. "Touché, you're right. I just wish it made a little bit more sense."

"We all do, but the good thing is that it consistently makes almost no sense." He gave her a wink.

She waved his horrific logic away. "Enough, enough. What do we need to do?"

"I need you to take my hands, hold them. I need to double-check everything with your . . . with your shielding." The way he said it gave Quinn pause.

"Did something happen with your shielding, Milaro?" she asked.

"I may have been a little remiss in my own protections recently. I've been taking on a lot, you know. But I have very good friends who take extremely good care of me. And so, crisis averted, I am well. I just want to make sure your shielding is also up to snuff, shall we say." He gave her another wink, as if downplaying the danger.

Quinn nodded, but got the feeling distinctly that he wasn't telling her everything. A cold shiver suffused her body, and it had nothing to do with her current temperature regulation issues. It was almost prescient. Milaro had to be careful; he needed to take care of himself.

"You'll be careful, right?" she asked him suddenly.

He raised an eyebrow. "Of course I'll be careful. I'm fine. I fixed everything, with my friend's help."

"Is it a friend you can trust?" she asked, suddenly even more wary. Everybody around them was close to being a suspect.

"Quinn, breathe," Milaro said. "It's okay, you even know this friend. Nishpa is the friend that helped me."

"Nishpa?" Quinn digested that, and it did indeed make her feel somewhat better. She didn't know Nishpa too well, but the Furionas had seemed quite sturdy when they fought side by side. "She's a type of healer, right?"

"Yes, she's a mind medic." Milaro sounded mildly amused.

"A mind medic. I like that name," Quinn said. "Sounds pretty cool."

"It is pretty cool. Quinn, are you okay?"

"Yes, I'm fine. I just . . ." Quinn couldn't explain the sensation. It was still there, not as prevalent as it had been at the beginning, but it was still underlining everything, sort of in her bones, warning her to be cautious.

"I need you to do me a favor," she said to Milaro. "I need you to promise me that no matter what, you will tell someone where you're going, someone trustworthy, and tell someone when you arrive, so people always know where you are. Especially me. Tell me, or Lynx, or the Library."

"Quinn, I'm a very busy king, I . . ." But he paused, looking at her. "Did you get a feeling that something was going to happen to me?"

Quinn nodded. She didn't trust herself to speak. It was such a strange sensation, this sudden panic. It wasn't as bad anymore, but it was definitely still there. It wasn't due to happen now, but in the future. Now she was aware of it, it seemed to be fine with waiting in the background.

"Then I *will* take it seriously. Last time, you may have saved my life, or at least saved me a lot of pain." Milaro referred to the time she made sure he escaped Tenejo's powers. "And so I will take this seriously and do as you ask, okay? And while you go to visit Uncle Hal, I'll remain in the Library, so you definitely know where I am."

Quinn nodded. "Okay, thanks. Sorry if it seems like I blew it out of proportion, I just . . . I've never had a feeling like that before."

He chuckled. "You're going to get a lot more of those."

"Are you serious?"

"It's a good thing. It means your heritage is taking a good strong hold, and that the new magical signatures you received are mixing well together. Now let's just make sure your brain is completely and utterly safe. For you, and for everyone else."

Quinn took both of his hands in a grip, and closed her eyes, just as he'd instructed. She could sense him entering her mind. He was very gentle, very respectful. He didn't touch anything. He didn't try to move anything. All he did was inspect. He showed her where to strengthen her wards. Close to where her memories were, there was a slight crack. Something bleeding through, interfering with her protections. Stray thoughts of her own. Perhaps that had happened when she found out about the accident.

Sealing it off, she paused. No, the memory was still there. So that wasn't how she'd forgotten. Perhaps it had simply been the shock.

He guided her around, telling her to strengthen, reinforce certain walls, reinforce certain aspects of her mind. And then, he happened upon the connection she held with the Library. She could practically feel the frown on his face.

"That's odd," his voice echoed throughout her head. "This needs to be strengthened, Quinn. Can you make it less tenuous?"

She shrugged but that didn't translate into the mind world they were in, so she spoke it out loud, "I think so."

"Reinforce it. This is the one connection you cannot afford to splinter, damage, or lose. So put everything you have into making sure it's always secure. Do you understand the gravity of this situation?"

She hesitated before answering. "If it splinters, or if it were to break, would I no longer be the Librarian?"

"More than likely," he said. "But it would be more than that, Quinn. Not only would your Librarian link be hampered, if not destroyed, it would backlash the power into you, and probably break you in the process. I'm not sure even cosmicisodracus heritage could save that."

"Oh," Quinn said, not liking that bit of news in the slightest. "Let's reinforce that as much as we can."

She opened her eyes and looked at Milaro, who seemed very contemplative. She asked him the question she'd been burning to ask since she realized she could wield fire. "I thought I was supposed to be a lunar dragon. That's what the Library said. I'm supposed to have a water affinity."

But Milaro chuckled. "You do have a water affinity. You are a water dragon. But just because you're a water dragon doesn't negate your fire ability. All types of dragons have fire affinities—strong ones."

"What *is* a cosmicisodracus?" Quinn asked.

"They are the original dragons. Five of them with all the affinities, but more aptitude for particular ones. Capable of shapeshifting into any form you want. As you can, indeed see, in the case of the Library."

Quinn half smiled to herself.

Milaro continued. "There are five, six including you, even if you have smatterings of other species-specific abilities in your make up."

"There are six of us," Quinn said, and she couldn't help the little thrill that ran through her at saying that.

"Yes, there are."

"And we're all able to manipulate all of the affinities."

"Yes, but you will always, as a lunar dragon, have an extremely good relation with water and thus ice. And as a—"

"But also with fire," Quinn asked.

"Yes, always with fire. Like I said, it's the basis of any dragon. There is no fire dragon, because you all have fire abilities ingrained in your being."

Quinn nodded slowly. She got it, at least she thought she did. "Are we done in here?" she asked, wondering why they'd stopped in her mind.

"Oh, yes." Milaro's presence in her mind disappeared and Quinn's eyes fluttered open to see her office again.

She frowned. "Okay. So what are these books you think can help me?"

"Ah, yes." He mulled that over for a second. "It's my hope that absorbing these will help you keep the overheating at bay. I'm not liking the look of it from inside or out. And the information in these should amalgamate in such a way as to protect you in the short term. *Fire Control for Beginners*. We're going with that one. Straight after that, I want you to take *Honing Fire Control Without Rising from the Ashes*."

Quinn blinked. "They're not very entertaining names."

"Do you really think that we should entice people to learn how to play with fire by giving them interesting names for the books?" Milaro asked, eyebrow raised.

Quinn shook her head. "You make a very valid point! That actually sounds like a horrendous idea."

"Exactly." he said and moved onto the next one. "Okay, then I want you to get *Burning and Pyrokinesis Understood*, and then finally *Fire Misdirection and Common Malpractices.*"

"Okay," Quinn said.

"Get started on these straight away." He said, pushing for her to acknowledge his words.

Quinn sighed. "Fine. I'll start now. I guess I've got a long night ahead of me."

4 7

AFTER-EFFECTS

Quinn woke the next morning more rested than she'd anticipated, considering the books she'd devoured the night before. Frankly, she actually felt better. She wasn't having any shivers, nor was she overheated. Her body temperature seemed marginally regulated, which, after the last couple of days, was a very welcome change. It was amazing how quickly something became the norm for her.

Still, the books had helped. *Fire Control for Beginners* had been especially handy. It taught her to set temperature control from within, which was decidedly rudimentary, yet . . . also somehow instinctive once she'd understood the concept. Such a basic skill that she'd been lacking.

She paused and sat up straight. Was today the day? "Do I have that meeting, Aradie?" she asked. There was a low hoot of agreement. "Am I late? I'm not late. Fantastic. Food and then meeting, correct?"

Aradie let out a series of coos and hoots and jumped onto the bed, looking up at Quinn. "Do I want a different room for people to meet in that isn't my office?" Quinn thought about the question for a second before shaking her head. "You know, let's put that on the massive to-do list and worry about the design of it when I don't have a friend sitting in stasis hoping he can resequence the more vital parts of his system." The owl hooted again and Quinn smiled. "Excellent, I shall get ready."

Ten minutes later, Quinn was quickly showered and dressed in comfortable jeans and a shirt, and down in the lobby. She glanced around to see Finn working their little arse off as they checked in books and people, answering questions, their eyes lighting up every time they mentioned a book.

Which was all the time.

If Finn wasn't genuinely the most dedicated Librarian assistant ever, then they deserved every single acting Oscar in the universe for their role in fooling Quinn and the others into believing that they were. Quinn really hoped that Finn wouldn't prove her trust wrong. But not believing in Finn and not giving him the benefit of the doubt would simply result in her never trusting anybody again, and frankly, Quinn didn't want to be that jaded person. She wanted to believe in people, even if the reality check in the back of her mind constantly reminded her that people could, overall, be dicks.

Besides, both Aradie and Quinn's guts were telling her she was right to believe in the Ilgonomur. And thus, her mind was made up.

"Librarian?" Dottie said from her knee height. "Are you coming? We're all waiting."

Quinn blinked down at the bench. "But I'm not late. Aradie said I wasn't late."

"Oh, you aren't. We're just all early and you're the last person we're waiting for."

" I'm grabbing food I'll join you in my office shortly." Quinn wasn't giving up her breakfast.

"Excellent," Dottie said and trotted towards Quinn's office. She watched after the little bench, frowning. Dottie was definitely one of her favorite people in this new life.

Food in hand after a very brief and stop in with Cook, Quinn sat down at the head of her conference table and blinked.

Milaro was to her right. "Ah, Librarian, I'm very glad that you joined us."

There were two people in here she'd never seen before. One of them was a satyr. Like a miniature version of Uncle Hal. Maybe six feet tall, so not really miniature at all, just less massive. Even though he was sitting down, so perhaps he was taller than she estimated. His skin and fur hues had a blue undertone to the red, but somehow didn't quite make him purple, and his horns were a sleek black.

Next to them was somebody who looked surprisingly like Narilin. Quinn double-checked. No, no, definitely not Narilin. Somehow a little thicker, maybe more masculine, or perhaps they didn't go by pronouns. Quinn wasn't sure. She didn't want to offend this Salosier because they were, well, much less dainty than Narilin. Built less like a willow, and more like an aged oak.

"Are you going to introduce me?" Quinn asked, putting a smile on her face.

"Well," Milaro drawled. "That was the plan unless you'd like to introduce yourself."

Quinn rolled her eyes.

"Everyone, this is the Librarian. Quinn, you already know Siliqua." Milaro started.

But Quinn cut him off, a sudden, brief surge of panic suffusing her. "Shouldn't you be monitoring?"

"It's okay," Siliqua offered her a smile. "Harish and Cadre are taking care of everything."

"Sorry," Quinn said and took a deep breath. She forced another smile. "Carry on."

"This is Nishpa, who you already know," Milaro continued. "She's Geneva's aunt."

"Geneva is manning the front desk, or she will be shortly." Nishpa inclined her head. "I've managed to return her to you. I thought you could use her."

Quinn nodded. "She'd been missed."

Milaro cleared his throat ever so slightly before continuing. "Eric, Dottie, Malakai you already know. And these lovely two people on your left are Ikeshal. He is, well . . ."

"I'm Hal's right-hand man," Ikeshal said, cutting Milaro off. "A pleasure to meet you, Librarian." His voice was rumbly, sort of like a small earthquake happening in that very specific spot. Quinn decided she really liked Ikeshal, and she inclined her head by way of greeting, and then turned her attention to the Salosier.

"And this is Escadril." Milaro introduced the last guest. "Escadril is the first advisor to the king of the Salosiers."

"Well met, Librarian. I am here to facilitate discussions on the crisis whose approach appears imminent for all of us."

"Nice to meet you," Quinn said while thinking that Narilin's way of speaking was perhaps an entirely species-related phenomena. Salosier fascinated her. Living trees had been a part of many of Quinn's fantastical childhood imaginings. She got the distinct feeling that Escadril was the very definition of ancient.

"And you." Escadril inclined his head, rustling the leaves that made up his hair.

"Very well, what's on the agenda?" she asked, hoping she sounded professional enough, like she should be the Librarian.

"Well," Dottie spoke up. "Today we'll go over the different factions of who we believe is involved in the sabotage of the library. These include the Serpensiril, the Sedimentites, the Esposians, the Ilgono-mur, the Aracnios, and some others that we have currently have on our radar."

"Are these empty suspicions because of the actions of a few, or do we have some, you know, solid evidence to condemn an entire species?" Quinn hoped the last bit didn't come out too sarcastic.

Escadril moved slightly in his seat and the leaves in his hair crinkled, lending a soft pine scent to the air. Quinn decided she could sit there and talk to him forever. "It is, I regret to say, largely substantiated."

Quinn nodded, wondering what sort of information would come her way.

"I'll do it, shall I?" Nishpa said, fluttering up to stand on the table so she was more at eye height with everybody, or slightly above them. Quinn got the distinct impression that Geneva's Aunt Nishpa liked commanding attention in rooms full of people who were much larger than her.

Quinn grinned. "Fine, regale me with the information."

Nishpa laughed, and this time her laugh sounded musical. Quinn was happy to hear that she was in much better spirits than she had been when they were on Ishiposa Isle. "Well, I don't think we're going to like this information, but it is necessary. To start with, I'll address the Serpensiril. They're the snake in the room, I guess. There are multiple factions of Serpensiril. They rarely agree with each other, however, in this case, there are only two factions that do not support the deletion of the library."

"Wait," Quinn said, holding up a hand while she wrapped her brain around that comment. "Deletion of the Library? Like, not just shutting it down, but they actually want to kill the Library?"

"Well, yes," Nishpa said. "This isn't a fairy tale, Quinn. This isn't a story where we save our favorite character. This is reality where people disagree with what the Library stands for and what it does. They want the power for themselves, or for others not to have it. I don't think they've figured out that the power isn't picky or choosy about who it kills. I've reached out to those two factions, but am still waiting to hear from them. I'm hoping someone else can reach out to them. They might not be eager to hear from me, given my familial relations."

"I can do that," Ikeshal rumbled. "I'll endeavor to locate these factions. Do you know which ones they are? Specifically?"

"Yes, we have the Saratosh and the Dinalian."

"Wow, Dinalians? That's definitely unusual. I'd love to look into why they've turned," Ikeshal said, smiling so widely he showed all of his sharp teeth. "But as I said, I will find them if they can be found."

Nishpa nodded and gave him a grateful smile. "I did send some lesser sprites to keep an eye on a Sedimentite I would never have originally suspected. I wouldn't have thought they'd support the Serpensiril faction, but they appear to be sympathetic to them. From what I've been able to gather from our informing sprites, Sedimentite affinities are on the lower end of the power scale. It's probably being seen as a way to boost them from inferiority."

"Are you kidding me?" Ikeshal asked.

Escadril scoffed. "Their entire bodies are magical. They are comprised of magic. Do they not understand the havoc pure chaos would wreak on their forms?" The Salosier advisor seemed extremely perturbed by the information that a species would sympathize with something that could fully destroy them. Quinn couldn't help but agree. She wasn't entirely sure what she was supposed to be doing at this meeting, but right now she was learning a lot.

Escadril spoke up. "What is the conclusion about the Sedimentites?"

"I plan to keep the lesser sprites in place and have them simply observe for now." Nishpa shrugged. "Any evidence I've gathered seems far too circumstantial at this stage."

Escadril looked thoughtful before proceeding. "Are you sure the sprites can't be corrupted?"

"Of course, they can't be corrupted. They're my sprites." She paused with a slight grimace. "Sprites, by their very nature, are incorruptible. Lesser sprites even less so. They're completely devoted to their summoner. They'll disintegrate if someone manages to catch them and attempt it."

A flash of sadness passed over Nishpa's face. "Anyway. They will, however, remain invisible and keep their distance. I may miss some of the information, but this way we'll at least get a lot of information instead of relying on pure speculation."

"Very well, I agree. If there is anything I can do to assist in this way—"

"Do you think," Quinn asked, "if they're not actually in support but more sympathetic, that they would be open to discussions?"

"What would we discuss with them?" Escadril asked.

Quinn shrugged. "I don't know, but if they're not completely swayed yet, then it stands to reason that they can be leveraged back to our side."

"Hmm, food for thought, young Librarian. I like this. I will think on this and see if I can come up with a solution."

"And what of the Esposians," Milaro asked, moving the conversation along.

Quinn looked over at Malakai, standing at the door, extremely bored. She couldn't blame him. He wasn't necessarily a part of the discussion. But he did need to know all the information, which made it important that he be there.

"The Esposians." Melancholy suffused Nishpa's next words. "I . . . I don't particularly like the way things have gone for this species and our relationship to them, frankly. I was hoping I'd have better news for us. It saddens me to let you know. But since the incident a couple of days ago with Adrito and Latia and the destruction of Ishiposa Isle, most of the Esposians have gone no contact with outsiders and have performed hostile takeovers of the isles they're on. Anyone who isn't in line with their thinking . . . is probably trapped."

She let that sink in and took a breath before continuing. "They are refusing any other fae help. There are four factions not supporting the main Esposian line right now. Those who we can trust are as follows: the Ecksha, the Drayna, the Palirsh, and the Tannen. Those are the four Esposian factions we can somewhat rely on. At least not to aid their main branch. They are, however, as you are all aware, not the strongest factions. The Tannen are Eugea's faction. They are extremely grateful for us having rescued the victims. And are interested in how she was healed so that the others might be fully rescued as well. Those people you saved were on a new settlement mission when they were taken over. They are a lot angrier than I would think the rest of them are."

Quinn felt a pang of sadness for Eugea's people. "The rest of them—have you lost contact?"

"Pretty much. They've decided to separate themselves from the rest of the fae kingdom, and there is sadly nothing I can do about that." The room fell silent, and Quinn could sense the sadness in every single person.

"Is it unredeemable?" Quinn asked. "Can we not reverse it?"

Nishpa shook her head. "Right now, they're still under the influence of . . . whatever they're under the influence of. It isn't like the people on the isle we rescued and are still healing, by the way. Luckily, several of the people in the Tannen and the Drayna line have extremely strong healers and haven't given up now they've retrieved their patients. Which is why, Quinn, I really need you for the next days that you are here to work with myself and Milaro and figure out exactly what it was that you did to heal Eugea."

Quinn blinked. How could she have forgotten how important that was? Sure, she'd had that brief encounter with the Library as soon as she returned. But she'd completely forgotten to talk to Milaro about it. Maybe the fact that the fire awoke in her had simply outweighed the very real fact that she'd brought somebody back from the brink. "Of course," she said.

Milaro turned to Quinn and said, "What did you do?"

"Didn't she tell you? Did nobody tell you?" Nishpa asked, her eyes wide with shock.

"Obviously not, or I wouldn't be asking," Milaro said. Everybody else around the table blinked, including Ikeshal and Escadril.

Quinn couldn't meet her mentor's eyes. She couldn't believe she hadn't told him. "I'm so sorry. With everything else I totally forgot to mention it. "I healed Eugea of the after-effects of that book."

48

A LITTLE FRAZZLED

COMPLETE AND UTTER SILENCE FOLLOWED QUINN'S ADMISSION. MILARO stared at Quinn, who felt decidedly uncomfortable, and then he held up a hand. "Wait a second, what do you mean she healed Eugea?"

"She did!" Nishpa put her hands on her hips and gave Milaro a smug smile. "I've been trying for weeks to heal the minds of all the Esposians that were rescued, to coax them out from the torment they suffered as the aftermath of the book—*Machmüller's Theory of Dimensional Dissolution and Disintegration Through Ritual Sacrifice.*"

"I knew what you meant by the book," Milaro said with a sigh and then turned to Quinn. "But you healed it? You used mind healing?"

Quinn shrugged. "I didn't mean to, I just kind of instinctively knew how to do it."

"Why didn't you tell me?" Milaro asked.

"A lot happened on Ishiposa. I sort of forgot since it happened before the whole golem fight," Quinn said. There'd been a lot on her mind when she came back into the Library.

Milaro threw his hands up. "How would you forget something as momentous as that?"

"First," Quinn said, "to me, it wasn't exactly momentous. I don't know what I did, I don't know how I did it, and thus had absolutely no idea how amazing it was at the time. Secondly, I've kind of been engrossed with trying to prevent myself from burning to a crisp. You'll excuse me if I was a little preoccupied with not dying."

Milaro cringed. "That was pretty pompous of me, wasn't it?"

"Yes, you were only living up to the elf name," Quinn said, "You can't help it."

Milaro sighed. "I do apologize for that, but I really need to—"

"No, just wait, Milaro." Quinn held up a hand. Her mind might think quicker these days, but there was still a point where everything hit the overwhelm and she was getting close to it. They needed to finish one thing before moving onto the next. "I think we need to respect everybody's time because I know that Nishpa, Escadril, and Ikeshal all need to get back to where they're from and you should probably be running a kingdom or something. The Library has already cataloged the ability and the related affinity. I promise we'll address the healing later and I'll make sure to connect with you so you can copy the memory and figure it out or something. You know, I did it now, you'll remember, you're good like that. Let's just try and stay on track and finish this first."

Quinn turned back to the table, but even Ikeshal and Escadril were looking at her with renewed respect. She suppressed the next sigh and took a seat again, not realizing that she'd stood up to yell at Milaro. He was substantially taller than her. She had to do everything she could to make herself feel, well, less small.

Quinn clapped her hands together, startling most of them, except Malakai, who'd been watching intently from the doorway. He could have reminded her to tell everybody about the healing thing, but he hadn't. She'd probably have words with him about that. On second thoughts, that's exactly what he probably intended by his actions. Sometimes he could be such a shitstirrer.

"Right," Nishpa said, going through a few of her things on her own HUD if her eyes were anything to go by.

Dottie piped up, "We do have yet to address the state of the Ilgonomur and the Aracnio alliances or their relation to the Library."

"Ah, yes." Nishpa looked through her reports.

Escadril cleared his throat, interrupting her. "I do not mean to alarm anyone, but it is a fact that approximately five years ago, the Aracnios did break off complete and utter contact with us as trading partners." The leaves of his hair rustled as he spoke creating a lulling juxtaposition to his words.

Nishpa gasped. "Are you serious?"

"What? What's so dire about not trading anymore?" Quinn asked.

"The Aracnios have a very lucrative contract with the Salosiers. They require silk for many of their nurseries, and the Aracnio silk mines have always had a monopoly on providing it. It was a very long standing relationship." Nishpa sounded quite shocked.

"Three hundred twenty-five millennia of trade relations thrown away just like that," Escadril sighed. "But such is the fate of the worlds, I suppose."

"But not your fate," Nishpa needled him. "You'll find another supplier."

"We have already sourced an alternative, but the Aracnios have not spoken to us for many a term. That is why we were rather perturbed to hear of Narilin's report when she mentioned there were Aracnios working at the Library."

"Narilin reports to you?" Quinn asked, raising an eyebrow.

"Not in a spying way. She simply delights in telling her entire family how marvelous the Library is on the occasion that she does visit." Escadril paused and the clarified. "On the occasion that she does take a day off and come home."

"I'm glad to learn she does indeed take some days off," Quinn said. "She works so much I sometimes worry."

"Three times, Librarian," Escadril clarified further. "Three days since the Library opened."

Quinn frowned at that. "I'll encourage her to go home more often."

"I doubt you would be successful, but thank you for your concern." Escardril offered a barky smile.

"Okay," Quinn said. "So anybody else? I mean, is that definitive proof? Maybe they didn't think they were getting enough money or something."

"No," Ikeshal piped up. "No, the Aracnios have been withdrawing from trade agreements, pulling themselves from gatherings for the last few decades or so. I'm unsure why. Tell me, is anybody aware of how long the Library had left had Quinn not been found?"

Quinn shivered ever so slightly. The Library was silent and Lynx's connection was but a wisp in her mind.

When no one else spoke, Quinn did so. "As I understand it, they used up most of the last dregs of power to pull me here. From what they mentioned, the reserves were all but depleted and there would have been maybe three or four weeks remaining, I'd say. Maybe a month or two longer if they hadn't summoned me here. So basically a few months at the very most."

There was silence after Quinn answered the question.

Then Dottie spoke in a very small voice. "Do you think all those people knew?"

"Maybe, if that's the reason why they withdrew from you all," Quinn said, "then they must have had some way of tracking the levels of power in the Library."

"They couldn't get in," Milaro said, thoughtfully twining hair around a finger. "It was sealed off."

"Or maybe some far reaching calculation from when they cut the Library off?" Quinn asked. "I can't check for that right now. We need the Library for those questions."

"Surely the Library would have noticed if it was leaking information out," Nishpa said, making as if to wave that line of questioning away.

"With everything we're uncovering," Quinn said, "I don't really know."

Siliqua jumped in. "The Librarian's right. We have no idea what the Library's been able to keep track of. We're lucky it hasn't completely broken down. After the success of the current procedure they're performing, I think we'll get a lot more answers."

Quinn didn't comment, but in her mind she was thinking that maybe it was a shallow hope. How could they be so certain? "Basically, we have marginal proof that the Aracnios are against the Library or at least against the alliances the Library has?" Quinn asked.

"Yes," Nishpa stated flatly. "They've withdrawn from any and all trade agreements, any and all social engagements, and any and all political discussions, discourse between the nations, between the planets, between the solar systems. They have effectively blacklisted us all."

There were several seconds of stunned silence around the conference table. Quinn cleared her throat, before breaking it. "Wouldn't we be blacklisting them?"

Nishpa shook her head. "Well, sort of, but they've already blacklisted us from their dealings . . . I think."

They looked at each other for a few seconds in confusion before shrugging.

Quinn hesitated briefly before continuing. "I guess that leaves the Ilgonomur?" she asked, not liking that her voice wasn't nearly as strong and confident as she wanted it to be. But she was starting to get so tired of so much negativity. Not that it was anyone in the room's fault, but she just wanted a break. She already had enough drama to fill up the next several years of her life. Hopefully, they could get the Library up and operating as it should be and put all this behind them.

Wishful thinking.

"Ah, yes." Nishpa bowed toward the Librarian. "I'm sorry. I was distracted."

"By the machinations of evil," Ikeshal needled her this time.

"Yes, by that exact thing," she said. But it was clear the Furionas had recovered most of her usual disposition. Quinn heaved a slight sigh of relief.

"Anyway." Milaro clapped his hands. "There's a lot to do before Quinn makes her trip to Halschius."

Ikeshal raised an eyebrow. "I was not made aware of this."

"She has a standing invitation." Eric spoke for the first time since the meeting began, his voice grumpier than usual.

"I was made aware of that, but I did not realize she would be gracing us with her presence quite so soon," Ikeshal clarified.

"We find it necessary," Milaro said.

"We also find," Quinn butted in, "figuring out if the Ilgonomur are all against us or perhaps just a few of them necessary."

"To be honest," Escadril said, "it is in my humble opinion that the Ilgonomur have been against us and the Library for quite some time. At least as a general rule. I am quite sure there might be outliers, such as this Finn person I have glimpsed?"

Quinn nodded and Escadril continued. "Their dealings with my people, with the Salosiers, have become stagnant and practically non-existent. I did notice that they haven't attended the last four war councils."

"War councils?" Quinn asked, pinching the bridge of her nose with her fingers. She could already feel another headache coming on. "What are the war councils?"

"My apologies, Librarian. Every five years, we hold a war council to evaluate any of the less antagonistic conflicts between species. However, for the last fifteen to twenty years, they have not attended."

"Did they ever give a reason?" Quinn asked. War councils sounded like a pretty important event to her.

"No." Escadril shook his head; his leaves rustling soothingly. "And beforehand, they were always a cantankerous yet welcome addition to them."

Quinn mulled that over. "And we don't know if some of their factions have broken off and wish to distance themselves from the others?" she asked. There was hope in her still that perhaps Finn's family weren't bad people. Maybe they'd simply been overeager about . . . nope, she couldn't even lie to herself about that. Quinn sighed. "Well, I guess that rules them out, too."

"I do believe," Nishpa interjected, "that there will always be outliers, just like Cadre, who is aiding you. His species is not amenable to much of what the Library stands for. But Cadre is trusted in many of our circles because of the integrity he has shown as an individual."

"I know," Quinn said. "I'm not ruling out everybody in a species just because they have a barrel of bad apples."

"Good, I didn't think you would, but I wanted to have mentioned it." Nishpa flashed her a bright smile.

"Thank you," Quinn said. She sighed and looked out over the table, suddenly extremely tired. "Is there anything else we needed to discuss? How to move forward?"

Malakai mumbled from the doorway. "Can we track them?"

"Great point, Mal," Quinn said, suddenly just wishing she could fall asleep. Fatigue washed over her, but at least she wasn't burning to death where she sat. "Is there anything we can do to keep an eye on these species or have they all gone into hiding?"

"I do still have my agents following the Sedimentites, to be honest," Nishpa said, glancing around the room. "And I do hope this will all stay in this room." She said very pointedly, looking at Ikeshal and Escadril. They nodded their acquiescence. "Most places that we have dealings with, as the Furionas fae, have some of my agents in them at any rate."

"Have some of your agents in them," Quinn said. "Are you supposed to be telling us this?"

"No, probably not. But I do believe we are among friends," she said, glaring at each representative in turn.

It was Escadril who laughed. "You never fail to amuse, Lady Nishpa. I do know that you are aware we think along the same lines."

She smiled. "I am aware of this, but sometimes I'm not sure exactly how observant people are."

"So, basically you've got spies everywhere and should be able to gather information," Quinn said.

"Precisely." Nishpa preened a little. "It's what my spy network is for, after all."

Quinn raised an eyebrow before continuing. "Once the Library is back in full operation, we need to heighten security, but that's something I'll have to discuss with the Library and Lynx before we implement it."

"You're still sad that the Aracnio brothers aren't who you thought they were, aren't you?" Milaro asked.

"Of course I am," Quinn said. "I really thought the people who applied were excited for the Library's return."

She stopped, realizing just how upset she was. The Library had felt like a home relatively fast. And all the different people in it became a part of that feeling. Quinn realized the twisting in her gut was betrayal even though she was fully aware this wasn't personal against her at all, but a long-standing animosity.

Still, it hurt.

"Understandable," Escadril said in a grandfatherly tone not unlike how Milaro sometimes spoke. "Anyway, we have very close to proof that they have, in fact, cut all the ties. The steady distancing has added up."

"What about security when it comes to Jim and Bob's access?" Ikeshal asked.

Quinn nodded. "Lynx blocked them before he went into stasis, shortly after their no-show actually."

"Excellent," said Nishpa.

"Does anybody have anything else to add?" Quinn asked.

Everyone around the table shook their heads, and Siliqua watched Quinn closely, but the Librarian refused to make eye contact.

"I think we all have a lot of work to do," she said, and stood up immediately. Ikeshal, Escadril, and Nishpa raised an eyebrow, and everybody gathered together, including Dottie and Eric. Quinn smiled. "Thank you so much for coming. I look forward to your next visit."

It took several minutes for them all to usher themselves out after bidding each other farewells. Quinn sat in her chair, reminding herself to breathe. So much information. Such a huge scale for absolutely everything they spoke about. It was mildly suffocating.

"Well," said Milaro when everyone else but Malakai and Aradie had finally left. "That was expertly wrapped up. Well done, Quinn. Now about that heal . . ."

Quinn held up a hand to forestall him. "I . . . I can't do this right now, Milaro. I'm really happy to sit down and chat about this whole healing thing, to give you access to my own recollection. But right now, I need some downtime. I am tired. Feeling a little frazzled. No complex discussions right now even though I realize others are potentially waiting for healing. The Library scanned me through. It has a basic understanding and record of what occurred I believe."

Quinn paused, trying to push down the guilt she felt at just wanting a few hours to herself. "I'm going to go and eat. And I'm going to take a little walk around the library, I think. I don't want to listen to any political machinations. No library emergencies. No sudden visits. I'm just going to take some me time."

She paused at the door. "I'm sorry," she said softly.

With that, she turned on her heel and left her office.

49

WONDERFUL VIEW

QUINN LEFT HER OFFICE WITH PURPOSE IN HER STRIDE. IT WAS HOME, here in the Library, but for the first time in a long while, she felt utterly alone.

That's when she realized that, apart from Aradie, she was the most alone she'd been since coming to the Library.

From that first moment on, from that first landing where she'd heard the heartbeat of the Library, the sensations she'd experienced in the core room, and even Lynx's stumbling, stuttering way to guide her into the world that rubbed her the wrong way for several days, she had been connected to the Library in such an intimate way. Both Lynx and the Library were able to discern her every thought for a while until she built her defenses.

Even after that, they were always there, this solid, reassuring presence.

Right now with them barely discernable, it hit different.

Quinn paused, standing off to the side of the middle of the Library, and closed her eyes for just a second. She could still sense the people and everything about the Library, but not so much the Library itself, the personification of it. Lynx was there ever so distantly, and she had to concentrate hard to try and focus on him. It was easy to let go of the thread, and while she knew they were still there, they felt so far away that it was like her entire mind was back to being just her own.

It was a very sobering feeling, for it was strange how quickly she had grown used to their company, how quickly she had simply become a part of everything the Library was.

Quinn paused, considering the whole experience, and opened her eyes.

Nobody was looking at her, well, except Aradie, who perched nearby on the back of a chair watching her intently. Quinn patted her shoulder and the bird swooped in, but perhaps because Aradie was quite in tune with her own thoughts, the owl simply sat, offering a very soft wing brush against Quinn's cheek.

"Thanks," she whispered to the bird, who said nothing, but Quinn felt an overwhelming sense of acceptance. She was quite surprised that neither Malakai nor Milaro had followed her out of her office. After all, everybody always seemed to want a piece of her time, apart from the couple of weeks she'd spent absorbing every book in sight. Quinn hadn't really had much alone time, and even then she was fulfilling people's expectations about becoming the strong Librarian she needed to be.

It was very much a lot.

She started moving again, feeling oddly free despite the weight of the owl on her shoulder. She slipped past everybody reading books, behind them, between the seating areas and the bookshelves. They bent their heads down, discussing texts, arguing methodologies. There had to be at least a hundred people in the Library right now. She walked through the main section and worked her way through to the corridor that led to the beginner weapons area where she originally found the book short sword she'd only partially successfully used to kill the engorged bookworms.

The path to the room was no longer filled with gloom. It was easier to navigate, friendlier, and there were bookshelves spanning the floor to the ceiling the entire way through.

She frowned at the sheer amount of reading material on the way to the room.

There appeared to be a lot more than the few hundred books they required to open the combat section that had suddenly returned to the shelves. She'd have to ask the Library about that later. Had they had some locked away? Were more missing than the Library initially showed?

As she approached the small room that held all of the beginner texts for the combat branch, she marveled at the fact that it was cleaned up and presentable again. The wooden dummy that stood at the far end of the room was no longer dilapidated and partially broken. There were actually two of them and they were sturdy. They showed some signs of use and yet Quinn was quite certain they wouldn't buckle or splinter under any swings from her this time . . . her and her wooden sword.

She paused, looking around, and finally noticed next to the dummies at the end of the room was a double door.

"Do you think that's where the combat branch will open?" she asked Aradie, who cooed in her ear and didn't say anything else. It was quite marvelous how the owl just knew to let Quinn have her own time and space.

"Well, I don't care how it was done before. I think that's where the doors will open into the combat section. We should probably focus on opening some more of the Library. Gather up the right books. Expand a bit . . ." She said the words out loud and had them echo back to her. A few tables were scattered around the room too, which, if Quinn was being honest, was much larger than she remembered it being when she first came in here to learn enough skills to kill the bookworms.

Not that she was surprised. The Library changed as was necessary.

"You know what," she said, suddenly realizing, "I've never been to the upper levels. Will you show me the way, Aradie?"

The owl hooted and launched herself from Quinn's shoulder. She wasn't exactly sure how Aradie constantly flew slow enough for Quinn to keep up with. She'd never been an expert in aerodynamics, least of all magical aerodynamics, so she simply followed the owl.

Several people looked up as she entered the main part of the Library again and waved at her. Quinn waved back, feeling a warm surge of belonging. It was welcome after that brief wash of loneliness earlier. Despite how she'd got there, and all the harrying situations she'd been involved in since arriving, the Library would be gone without her. For all she knew, chaos may have even started devouring the universe again.

Purpose.

It felt good.

She smiled to herself and went about her walk with her bird. The owl led her to a series of spiral staircases. Quinn frowned at them.

They were beautiful wrought-iron spiral staircases like the sort that led up to her quarters, and down to the core.

Two led down, but the middle one led up.

"Why are there three spiral staircases in a row?" she asked. Aradie raised an owl eyebrow, which was some sort of feat of facial reconstruction for an owl perhaps, and then Aradie very slowly and deliberately shrugged.

"Oh, you're gonna be like that?"

Aradie pointed a wing up and then soared up the stairs. Quinn followed using the middle staircase. The down one probably led into some more of the specially tailored reading habitats or something. Or maybe they'd end up telling here there were Library mole people who kept the foundation of the Library intact or something.

Frankly, these days, not much surprised her anymore.

She wasn't entirely sure what she expected from the upper level. It wasn't that she never wanted to visit it, but her instructors always had Tim and Tom, or other golems fetch her books, and thus, she'd never really had a reason to venture upstairs.

After traipsing up the steps, she wasn't disappointed in the slightest.

"Wow," she said, breathing out softly. "Doesn't it look majestic from up here?"

Aradie cooed low and came to grip the railing right next to her.

Beneath her the Library sprawled out. Rows and rows of bookcases. Chairs, pillars, and books as far as she could see. The seating arrangements all made much more sense from this overhead view, too. A group of several friends walked into the dining hall and out of her view, chatting animatedly.

She watched the check in desk as well. The massive wooden structure seemed impossibly large as she watched the assistants scuttle around in it, returning books and speaking to patrons. Eric had returned to the front desk and she noticed Finn was there, as was Danio the centaur. And a couple of assistants she didn't recognize. She looked over at the different little groups scattered all throughout the large main section, heads bowed over books, books exchanging hands, excited discussions taking place.

Tim and Tom, Carty and the others, all ferrying books back and forth.

It felt like the scene was in a snow globe she'd shaken. It was something she could watch for hours if she let herself.

However, after several minutes, she turned around and took a really good look at the balconied section of the Library in which she was standing. Per Quinn's previous wish, it appeared the Library had put signs everywhere. Overhead, in beautiful filigree lettering, was "Bardic and Musical." Quinn moved around the large space. There were instruments here and there, both in and out of the bookcases. The seating arrangements up here were sort of odd and strange-looking chairs, seating areas that—

"Oh my gosh," Quinn said, "are these—are these, like, soundproof?"

Aradie nodded her head.

"So you can sit and play an instrument, or sing, or do anything musically related, and you're not disturbing anybody else."

Precisely, the words shot across Quinn's mind as Aradie snapped it out with clarity.

"This is really cool." Quinn was fascinated. Although she also understood it. Because if you were practicing magical singing in any way, wouldn't those people hearing it be affected by it? It was much safer to block out the sound.

There were obvious gaps in the shelves that Quinn could see, and yet, so many books.

"Does the Library not lend out that many books?" she asked. She'd always thought eighteen thousand books wasn't enough for a universal Library. But then again, those were the ones borrowed out at the time. She wondered if Lynx had perhaps stopped lending them out at some stage. Then again, she'd already added another almost four thousand to the list by opening the culinary branch.

Aradie shook her head from side to side, and then spoke into Quinn's mind. *It is not always the way for books to be borrowed. Most people use the books here, so eighteen thousand books being borrowed is quite a lot.*

"Makes sense, yet . . . I would think people would want to take them away and study them forever," Quinn mumbled. Although, in hindsight. Perhaps that was just her. Maybe she got her book hoarding ways from her heritage. "Anyway, let's have a look at the other sections."

So she walked through the alchemical and medicinal area. The alchemy area had different terrariums set up, along with several small alchemy stations. They looked like something only capable of assisting with beginner work.

Then came the horticulture area, which held what appeared to be a plethora of differing soil basins. Quinn wasn't even going to pretend to understand.

Across the other side, down the entire length of that terrace, was the crafting area. There were looms, and small tanning benches, and several what appeared to be anvil set ups. Quinn frowned. The way they were all set up with little cubicles could only mean this too was sound proofed. She was excited to see how these branches would eventuate.

Finally, having backtracked a bit, Quinn sighed and leaned over the railing at the very end, close to where she'd fought the bookworms.

"This really is beautiful. Sort of glad it's my home," she said out loud.

Aradie rubbed her face against Quinn's, and Quinn laughed. "Thank you. But you know what, Aradie? It's really missing something. What do you think it's missing?"

Aradie cooed, as if to ask her what.

"Stories," Quinn said. "It's missing stories."

Aradie leaned back, looking quizzically at Quinn. "It's okay, you may not understand."

But the idea wouldn't let go of Quinn, and she made a promise herself that she'd talk to the Library about it when things had calmed down a little.

Anyway, she meandered back down and toward the dining hall, intent on taking in some food, when she paused, eyeing the entrance to the Restricted Vault.

"You know what," she said to no one at all, not even her bird. "I think I would like a beautiful view with a lovely meal."

Aradie launched herself off Quinn's shoulder with a slightly reproachful hoot. "You don't have to get . . ." But the bird was already gone, and Quinn was quite sure that shortly she would have some sort of meal that her owl had gotten her.

Quinn approached the Restricted Vault, placing both hands on either side of the narrow, double filigree doors. She pushed them open. There was a hissing click as the air whooshed into the room, and Quinn was once again made breathless by the beautiful view of the starry skies beyond them.

She closed the doors, knowing that Aradie would figure out her own way in, and looked over at the seating area that was still exactly as she'd asked for it. Set up in a booth sort of dinette way so she had a table she could use while she watched the view. As she moved toward her destination, she brushed her fingers across the cages that housed all the books. She was quite certain no new ones had gone missing, which she wouldn't expect to, but she could sigh with relief at the fact that at least no insiders were still actively sabotaging them.

Maybe.

It was a relief that perhaps things wouldn't get too much worse before they got better, although she didn't want to tempt fate that way. There were too many loose threads. Stuff was going to get worse, she just hoped they could temper it.

She sighed and grabbed *DeKarlyle's Thesis of Spatial Distortion* out of its cubby. She hadn't absorbed this book. She wasn't entirely sure that she wanted to, but she did know that she could read it.

Something in the back of her mind told her that she could find answers in this. Maybe even solutions.

Perhaps it wasn't the wisest idea to go through it by herself, but she couldn't rely on everybody else all of the time. She needed to understand what they were up against, and while her mind was clear, while she wasn't being influenced in any way, shape, or form, either deliberately or inadvertently by anybody else's thoughts or wishes, Quinn decided to take control of things herself, especially of her knowledge base.

She settled herself in the corner and pulled the book up, but did not make to absorb it. She wasn't that foolish, letting that sort of information rush into her mind when she wasn't yet prepared for it. No, Quinn wanted to read it the old-fashioned way. In a cushy and comfortable place, with a wonderful view.

Aradie was suddenly there with a bag in which there was a flask of something that smelled suspiciously like spiced chai. Cook knew her all too well. She poured herself a cup from the thermos and sat it on the table. She glanced out at the starry sky above as she pulled out a meatball sub and took a vicious bite of it.

Contentment swept over her, and she realized that if she had to land anywhere in the universe, being the Librarian of a magical Library, even if it needed a little bit of rebuilding, was probably the greatest thing in the cosmos.

Well, at least it would be once she convinced the Library that it also needed a fiction wing.

5 0

CONTROL THE FIRE

QUINN WOKE LANGUIDLY THE NEXT MORNING, EARLIER THAN USUAL, without anyone needing to wake her up, and blinked slowly up at her moving ceiling.

She felt fully rested for the first time in ages. Stretching, she realized how soft her bed was and how comfortable and easy it might be to simply stay in it. But her read-through of *DeKarlyle's Thesis of Spatial Distortion* had opened her eyes to several things, the least of which was that she needed to start setting her own pace, choosing her own reading topics, and guiding her own path, just a little more forcefully.

It wasn't that Milaro, the Library, Lynx, Malakai, and every other single person she encountered weren't well-intentioned, but they were, in fact, not her.

Her owl was still asleep, her head tucked under her wings. She looked peaceful in the faint morning glow that suffused Quinn's bedchamber.

After reading *DeKarlyle's Thesis*, she found a new resolve in herself. She'd grown so used to simply absorbing all the knowledge and having it gradually make sense, even if the power was immediately available. But just reading the book gave her more understanding, and a more gradual ability to reach for the power. Less of an impetus to do so. The slow realization of what it could do was probably more terrifying than simply absorbing it might have been.

But it was also far safer for both her and others.

She understood now, with the knowledge from the book, and her experience of the ritual sacrifice, how it might be possible to end the Library and many other dimensions. The slow processing of the information felt like she was constantly unraveling and understanding truths instead of having them thrust upon her and itch to be used. She liked it that way, especially for a book that held, arguably, a lot of power.

Especially since she also needed to get over the danger these books posed and let them help her deal with the issues.

The more she read the previous evening, the more she had understood why they needed to get the three remaining sister books back as soon as possible. There was a very real prospect of the Library coming undone, being undone by saboteurs. It gave her such a heady clarity, such a different perspective.

She crawled out of bed and got herself ready for the day, only waking Aradie as she got ready to leave the room. The owl cooed in her direction, more of a question as to why she was already awake.

Quinn ruffled Aradie's feathers. "It's one of those days that needs to begin earlier, and I think from now on, I need to sleep like I did last night."

Aradie shook out her feathers and alighted to sit on Quinn's shoulder as she headed downstairs. The Librarian directed the system to summon Milaro, wherever he was, and tell him that she'd love to see him and go over all the information about the healing she'd done.

After much contemplation, Quinn wasn't entirely sure how the whole universe was in sync. Different planets went around different suns at different rates, thus giving them different years. That was how it worked, right? She'd been thinking about that a lot since the previous evening. Obviously, the Library had a standard time or something that everybody stuck to, but still, she'd like to know how they calibrated it all.

"Cook," she said by way of greeting as she walked into the kitchen. Well, the culinary wing with the equivalent of five thousand kitchens in it. Perhaps a slight exaggeration.

"Librarian, you are awake early."

Quinn shrugged. "Am I really, though, or is this more the time that normal people with a lot to do would get up?"

Cook actually laughed. "Perhaps," they said, "but you do more than enough, and sometimes, if you go to bed late, sleep is necessary."

Quinn nodded, helping herself to what looked suspiciously like bacon and eggs. "Should I ask you where you got this?"

Cook shook their head.

"Yeah, I didn't think so. Is it bacon and eggs?"

Cook shrugged. "Sort of. It is as close as I could get."

She mulled that over and chose not to pursue that line of questioning.

Belatedly, Quinn also summoned Malakai. Perhaps he could help her fill Milaro in on some of the things that happened on the Ishiposa Isle. After all, he had been there. Plus, she had to ask him where her phone went because Quinn knew she hadn't misplaced it, and she'd been fully aware he intended to modify it so that it could work on magic.

She needed to know if he'd succeeded.

She took her food and a cup of chai, and meandered back to her office in plenty of time for Milaro to arrive. When he did, she'd just finished her food and was still in an extremely good mood. A control of her own situation and circumstances mood. She liked this frame of mind better. It helped her not feel less like she was constantly scrambling.

"Why, most esteemed Librarian, you are up," Milaro said with a flourishing bow.

"I know, I know," she said, resisting the urge to roll her eyes. "Early."

"Well, I was going to say you are up and looking fine, but you are also up earlier than I'm used to." He chuckled and lounged against the doorframe.

"Were you here all night?" she asked, curious about why he was standing in the doorway.

"I've been overseeing the procedure with Siliqua while Harish got some much-needed sleep." Milaro grinned. "The lights in the core have always fascinated me."

"What about you?" Quinn asked as she made a mental note to go and spend some time observing the core through that room. "Did you get any sleep?"

Milaro shrugged. "I'm an expert at power naps."

"Is that really a thing?" Quinn asked, raising an eyebrow in disbelief.

"Technically."

"Magically enhanced?" Quinn asked.

"Sort of. Maybe more along the lines of meditatively enhanced." Milaro winked. "Okay, what do you have for me?"

"I'm just waiting. Malakai should be here—"

"Right about now," Malakai said, walking into the room.

"Close the door, please," Quinn said.

Malakai looked at her quizzically but did as she asked. "Any reason?"

"Well, it's not exactly information I want getting out. There are hundreds of people currently in the Library." She briefly closed her eyes, reaching out to sense the area. "Close to a thousand. They're in all different divisions, near all different branches. So, precautionary measures if you will. Before I get to how I healed Eugea, Malakai, where's my phone and battery pack?"

"Oh, yes." He fumbled in his storage and pulled out both of them. He placed them on the desk in front of Quinn.

She smiled as she noticed the little plug in icon. "Is that charging? Its battery is almost full. How did you manage it?"

"Okay, so what I did was I sort of Jimmy rigged some mana crystals with energy infusion. Now, you'll need to use energy tokens to replenish it, but they're easy enough to make. That way it should keep your phone charged. I'm almost done with figuring out how to integrate the mana, so it sort of . . ." He crinkled his nose like he was trying hard to figure out how to explain something. "It should, theoretically, be able to make a small gateway just for its signal so you can send and receive messages. That way you can text intermittently, so they don't worry."

Quinn's eyes opened wide in surprise. "Are you serious?"

"I saw how you sort of missed people even if you say you don't. Right now, it'll only open enough for a text message. I haven't figured out how to allow video or speech to pass through yet," He shrugged, and for once seemed sort of shy. "I thought this way, you could at least communicate with them."

"Thank you," Quinn said, suddenly feeling overwhelmed with gratitude.

For once, Malakai didn't have a snippy comeback. He just smiled.

"I'll get you to go over this with me while we're travelling," she said.

He raised an eyebrow in question.

"You're coming with me to Halschius, right?"

"Oh, yes," Malakai said, a smile back on his face. "Of course I'm coming."

"Excellent. Which is why I called you here, Milaro . . ." She paused as he held up a hand.

"When you get back, I'll need you to walk me through how you rigged that phone up, Malakai. That's fascinating." Milaro's tone was gently and full of pride.

Malakai actually blushed and cleared his throat. "Sure."

Quinn grinned. "Great. Anyway. I figured we can go over the healing I did for Eugea first. And then I need you to help me understand what's involved in preparing and moving Tenejo and Adrito for travel to Halschius and how I can help."

Milaro seemed taken aback. "Fantastic. That sounds like a great plan."

"Of course it is." Quinn smiled. She really was feeling much more prepared this morning.

"Are you feeling quite well, Quinn? You seem . . ." Milaro appeared to be reaching for words.

"Less frantically trying to figure out what we can do next that won't continue to overwhelm me?" she asked.

"Pretty much," Milaro said.

"Let's just say I read a book last night that opened my eyes to some perspective."

"What did you read?"

"I read de *DeKarlyle's Thesis.*"

Milaro gave a sharp intake of breath. "Wait, you read or you absorbed?"

"Well, I'm assuming that if I had attempted to absorb it, it would have been much like the chaos filtration not worked properly. So I didn't absorb it. I read it. And I understand things on a larger level now. I think I've gained perspective."

"Very well." Milaro's eyes narrowed. "But that's not the sort of book to test waters with. It's highly advanced. Please, next time you choose to read a restricted text, let me know. Just so I can be prepared in case something goes wrong."

Quinn nodded solemnly. She hadn't even thought about it being potentially dangerous for her. She'd been safe in her Library, after all. "I will, I promise."

"Good." Milaro seemed slightly relieve. "Now, tell me how you healed Eugea."

And so Quinn described how it happened to the best of her recollection. The very short version of her having an overwhelming feeling that she knew exactly what to do and that she simply commanded Eugea's mind to clear of the pain that was being inflicted on her. While trying to provide a gently cushion for her consciousness to land on.

"That's all you did?" he asked, leaning back in the chair in front of her desk where he'd plopped himself.

"Yeah, her mind sounded like it was sort of crying out for help. Like she wanted to get out and just didn't understand how to break through. So I reached for her and I helped her get out. It was more a matter of, I think, the victim wanting to return to whatever they had before they were placed in this mind hell hole. They had to have realized where they were wasn't their actual reality."

Milaro looked very thoughtful. Malakai simply nodded. "She's right. That's pretty much how it went. It happened inside of maybe two seconds. She went from obviously in pain and suffering to free and clear. It was quite fascinating to watch."

"Obviously, she'll still have memories," Quinn said. "That's not something I took away. I wouldn't even know how to start. And to be frank, I don't want to manipulate people's memories because that's kind of screwed up."

Milaro chuckled, but it was a dry chuckle, like he wasn't amused. "You speak the truth, Quinn. It is definitely screwed up. So there's nothing you can tell me how you did it?"

"No," Quinn said, shrugging and throwing her hands up. "That's just it. I don't understand what I did."

"Would you mind if I looked?" he asked cautiously.

"Please be my guest. Figure out what I did so we can help others."

Milaro leaned over the desk and took her hands in his as he closed his eyes. She could feel him in her mind, replaying that memory. He replayed it over and over. And then he dropped her hands.

"That's quite remarkable, Quinn. You did exactly what you said you did. You simply identified that she was desperate to get out of it. Not desperate to find other people, not desperate to be forgiven, but desperate to live. That might be the key that will help them unlock their minds from that state." He frowned thoughtfully. "It's something that Nishpa can work with them on, at least. There's an edge of desperation to survive and to continue on as they are. If she find that or can instill that in them, the odds are that she can also heal them."

"Oh good," Quinn said. "I was kind of worried. I couldn't understand exactly what I did. I just knew. A lot of this information that I've absorbed and read, it just comes to me when I need it to. Sometimes. It's like instinctive."

"Sounds like it," Milaro said. "And now I believe I owe you information."

"Why yes, you do." Quinn grinned over at him and steepled her fingers. "Explain the whole Tenejo and Adrito thing to me."

"Well, they're almost ready to go. Ikeshal, Escadril, and Nishpa brought components with them last time to help us create a force field that is that is strong enough and self-powering so it can make the jump between dimensions. If we have to jump between power sources, then the shielding would break and both of them would run free. That isn't an option. We're delivering them to Hal for the specifics of finding out what we need to know."

Quinn wanted to ask if he thought she was doing the right thing, but to be honest, she didn't really care. They'd tried. Tenejo killed his friend. He'd wanted to kill Milaro. He'd attacked them. He'd hurt Lynx. And he'd hurt Dale. So much so that the golem even needed to be repaired. So no, she wasn't about to give in anymore. After a lifetime of poor choices, Tenejo deserved whatever he got. And Adrito did too. "Okay, so they're ready to travel?"

"Yes, a few more hours and they will be."

"Excellent," Quinn said. "I propose that we leave first thing in the morning."

"Do you want Halschius's morning or our morning?"

Quinn paused. "When is Halschius's morning?"

"In about four hours. Very similar time to the peninsula you were on to visit my daughter-in-law."

Quinn nodded slowly. "Okay. Should we give Uncle Hal notice?" she asked.

"I think you should probably talk with Eric a bit. But I would assume you should just go. You have a standing invite."

Quinn nodded slowly. "There's nothing I can do to help with Tenejo and Adrito, then?"

"Nope. All been done." Milaro hesitated a second before continuing. "However, I'll instruct you on how to maintain and drop their shielding so that you can hand it off to Uncle Hal when you get there," Milaro said. "I'll remain back here to help Harish and Siliqua keep an eye on the current procedure and to help Dottie keep an eye on the Library."

"Very well," Quinn said. "Geneva's here too, yes?"

"Yes, she is."

"Okay. Then I'm going to find out what I need to be ready for my trip to see Uncle Hal." Quinn was excited to visit Halschius, not the least because she was certain he could help her control the fire within.

51

***

LAVA SPRITES

Preparing for entry to Halschius was an involved process. There were breathing techniques to go over, magically infusing her airways to compensate for the different atmospheric idiosyncrasies. Not to mention having to get their "gifts" for Hal ready for travel.

However, Quinn had to admit that when the doors opened out onto the plains of Halschius, it was more than worth the effort.

It wasn't fire and brimstone like she'd initially assumed it'd be. Instead, it opened out onto plains of igneous rock that spread out before them. Hill formations and what looked like petrified trees dotted the landscape. In the distance, she could even see what she thought were waterfalls, or, to be more precise, lava falls. It was very warm, and the air felt heavy, despite the fact that she was using an air filtration spell.

With the multicolored roaring suns in the distance lending a blood orange and purple-ish hue to the entire landscape, it was oddly scenic.

"Is this one of the three doors?" She turned and asked Eric, as the Library guards shuffled the prisoners through to the Halschius side of the opening.

"Yes," Eric said, "this is one of the three doors. The king has his own, but this is one of the three the public have access to."

"Wouldn't transporting the prisoners to Uncle Hal directly have been a better choice?" Quinn asked.

Eric shook his head. "Doesn't work that way. Uncle Hal's chambers have protections build in that wouldn't allow their stasis pods."

Quinn nodded as she took in the landscape further. A serene and peaceful feeling washed over her despite the heat.

Frankly, with the amount of work Milaro made them do the evening before, she'd been quite apprehensive about visiting in the end. He'd drilled the protective spells they'd need into them. He wanted them armed with breathing magic that would prevent them from burning their esophaguses.

The heat was so dense that without help, non-acclimated species took damage. That was part of the reason Aradie wasn't accompanying her on this trip. It took a while to get the hang of, but Quinn was fairly certain she'd be able to maintain it even in her sleep, under pain of death, or while she herself was perhaps being tortured.

On top of the breathing assistance was the body cooling system they had to apply to themselves. It was a very odd spell that constantly leached a very small amount of energy. Although in Quinn's case, she'd become used to cooling her energy ever since fire tried to devour her.

Spells it seemed, could be cast by anyone with magic and enough practice regardless of affinity. They were generally rudimentary. Abilities were directly tied only to affinities. It was a distinction she'd only learned the previous evening that left her feeling somewhat dense. Like she should have known it sooner.

Standing at the entrance to Halschius, she watched as her energy ticked up and down semi-regularly. Maintaining her body heat should be doable. From what everyone said, Halschius seemed to be one of the hottest places in the universe, or at least, one of the hottest she could visit without being charred instantly.

That was probably more accurate.

She watched as a few of the golems, security golems from the Library, ushered out the stasis blocks. She still couldn't get over the fact that they looked like they were frozen in place by some sort of frosted glass. Adrito appeared to be in mid-scream, while Tenejo's eyes were closed. The latter looked positively peaceful. What a lie . . .

"They'll be fine, Quinn," Milaro said, his tone filled with reassurance. He stepped back into the Library. "We'll maintain the door until you have been greeted and the golems can return."

Quinn nodded. "Sure. Do you think they know we're here?"

"Of course we know you're here," Ikeshal said, suddenly right there next to them.

Quinn turned around to see the . . . well, he was about eight feet tall now. Not the six feet he'd been when sitting in her conference room. She frowned. "You seem to have grown a bit."

Ikeshal laughed, and it was a deep, growly noise. "You have a sense of humor, Librarian. I am simply in my true form here. It is easier to walk through doorways in your reality when I make myself ever so slightly smaller."

Quinn nodded. "I can see that."

He eyed the blocks containing Adrito and Ikeshal up and down. "These are the prisoners?"

"Yes," Quinn said, looking around and glancing back at Milaro. He waved her attention back. "We will see you when you return, Librarian. Take care of her, Ikeshal. I'll hold you responsible."

And the doors closed, leaving the Library completely cut off. Ikeshal still had a grimace on his face when Quinn turned her attention toward him.

"Ah, I see you're not immune to Milaro's threats either." Quinn grinned at the satyr.

He laughed again, but it was more of a chuckle this time. He snapped his fingers twice and four imps, and four . . . she couldn't quite give them a name out of her own mythological knowledge, so she inspected them.

This distance from the Library, all she got was a rudimentary breakdown. But she guessed everyone lived with the system, so this was probably what everyone was used to.

Name: Tilen
Species: Citriphosa

Region: Halschius—Origin—2nd level
Status: Friendly

She watched them. They were similar to a centaur in that they had front- and hindquarters. But they had two hind legs on each side, two front legs with one on each side, and then four arms in total. Between them, the four citriphosas hefted the large blocks and began to move them toward what looked like a teleporting pad that Quinn hadn't noticed when they first stepped in. The imps gave directions and generally stayed out of the way. The portal was nestled between two of the petrified trees. She watched, curious.

"Are they taking them to hell?" she asked, knowing it wasn't the hell of the scriptures back on Earth, but unable to stop herself from making the comparison.

"In a manner of speaking." Ikeshal winked at her. "I am here to escort you. Our leader finds himself somewhat preoccupied right now and it may be better for me to accompany you to the palace farther down."

Quinn glanced around. She could see houses back away from the main path, or what at least looked like some sort of living structure. They were more like low stone huts, but larger than a hut. More like stone hip roofed houses. She glanced around. Everything was so black and grey and red. And yet the sky with its amber and purple hues really offset it. She thought it'd be extremely picturesque in a painting.

"What do you think, Librarian?"

She shrugged, still looking around curiously. "I'm not really sure. I like it here. The warmth reminds me of some places I've called home. I think I'd enjoy it here."

Ikeshal laughed again, but this time it was a booming type. "I am sure Hal will be pleased to hear that," he said. "Anyway, I will take you through the village on the way to his palace."

They'd been walking a little while now and crested a hill of igneous rock that was somehow spongy. Quinn could only hope that didn't mean it was about to break and plummet them into a river of lava.

Way to go there, overactive imagination.

But as they came up the other side of the hill, she saw the palace. The rock had somehow formed into this beautiful gothic castle. It had drippings off the spires that made it almost seem liquid. There were sheens of iridescent blacks and greens and purples and reds that wove their way through the rock.

It was quite breathtaking.

"Wow," she said. "I did *not* expect that."

"Nice view." Malakai stood next to her with a look of pure contemplation on his face as he watched over the horizon.

"Yeah." Quinn smiled.

"Now, my instructions," Ikeshal said, clearing his throat as he glanced at Eric who crossed his arms and looked off in the distance as if he was sulking, "are to guide you to the town and have Eric take you to the reception chamber."

Quinn raised an eyebrow. "Is it like an official visit-y thing?"

"Well," Ikeshal interjected, "you wanted to see his true height, and he had promised to show you. Thus, as you have come bearing gifts, I believe the only place he can truly show you his actual size under some cover is in the reception chamber."

Quinn nodded. "Shall we?"

They approached the village that lay in front of the massive gothic castle. Everything around them had a hint of the same style. It wasn't quite what Quinn would imagine from texts, drawings, and pictures of such castles, because everything was made out of igneous rock, it seemed. At least it seemed that way to her. How they'd molded it like that, she didn't know. It all had a slightly-melted-in-the-oven-after-it-was-crafted look to it, and it was positively breathtaking.

There were stalls set up along the streets, along one side all the way down. There were no vehicles to clog the streets either, but then, she guessed a lot of the residents had wings. They probably didn't require modes of transportation.

Approximately two or three dozen imps flitted about here and there. Their colors varied wildly, from deep red oranges through to the black type of red that Eric was. They were such a red-black-rainbow of different hues, and it lent to the overall relaxed aura of the area. There were no screams in the distance either, so it wasn't the counterpart to hell she'd imagined. Sadly, the joke that she constantly had running through her head about it fell a little flat.

They walked through the stalls in the streets.

"Is that candy?" Quinn asked.

"It's sort of candy," Eric said, "that'll break your teeth. Yours aren't strong enough to bite into it."

"Okay," Quinn said. "What crawled up your butt and died? You're in the worst mood today. You came home! That's not a good thing?"

"No, Quinn. No, it is not."

"Okay, tell me about it when you're ready, because it's obviously impacting your already shining personality." She grinned at him to try and take the sting out of the words.

Eric glared at her and then sighed. "I apologize, Librarian, I do not enjoy coming home."

"Why not?" She prodded gently, not wanting to sound demanding.

"Because being a Librarian assistant is apparently not a noble enough profession for somebody in my family." He sounded a bit sad.

"Well, you're going to have to tell me, at some stage, what it is your family does, so that I can tell you how wrong they are." She smiled.

Eric laughed. "I knew it. I should have told you sooner. You always make me laugh, Librarian, even if it's because you're being slightly naïve."

"Whatever tickles your fancy," Quinn said.

Malakai sighed. "Even with body and air filtration magic, it's so hot here," he said. He'd even twisted his long braid up into a sort of bun.

It made Quinn wish she had her phone and camera with her. But she'd left it back at the Library to finish charging. "Well, when you come from forests," Quinn said, "I guess it's pretty easy for you to feel really hot."

"Exactly," he said. "I'm not supposed to be here, in fire, brimstone, and lava land."

"Where are you supposed to be, then?"

"I'm supposed to be strolling around your damn Library, teaching you how to fight."

"Well, how about we just walk around here and figure out who the hell is trying to kill us?"

"Well, I mean, that does sound pretty interesting, too," he said, grinning, but sweat still beaded his brow. Malakai was trying valiantly not to let it get to him.

There were some odd things in this market that Quinn didn't quite understand the origin of, nor how they were supposed to be used. "What's this?" she asked, pointing to something that was long and looked like a horn.

"What do you think it is?" Eric asked. "What does it look like?"

"Well, it looks sort of like a horn."

"Exactly. Some of us, in these countless wars that we constantly wage on our brethren and closely or distantly related demons, we lose horns. These are prosthetics. They, once attached magically, act in a very similar way to the horns we've lost," Eric said, his voice unusually subdued for the smart-arsed little imp that he was.

"Oh," Quinn said, "that's kind of cool."

"Yes, it is." He sighed. "You know, if we didn't lose them in wars to begin with."

Eric's anger was palpable, and Quinn waited as they walked past another stall before speaking again. "Why do you wage so many wars?"

"It's literally a Halschius thing. Our entire quadrant is very closely related, all by blood, in one way or another, whether it's been magically enhanced, or created. Basically, nobody is ever happy with whoever it is who is currently running the quadrant. And thus, there are wars all the bloody time."

"Lots of death," Quinn said.

"Enough. But also not so much. It's just bloody, and drawn out, and completely and utterly unnecessary." Eric sighed. "We're damn near impossible to kill, but we can be maimed."

"Oh," Quinn said, thinking that over. "Is that what your family does?"

"Yes," Eric said. "They fight constantly. And I'm not a warrior. I'm a reader. I'm a researcher. I'm a 'let's find a way to not kill everybody and solve the problem at the same time' sort of imp."

"Well, Eric, I like your sort of imp the best," Quinn said.

He actually flashed her a genuine smile. "I'll remember that, when you're, you know, angry at me next time."

Quinn laughed. "You do that."

They approached the palace steps now, but Quinn didn't feel intimidated by them, like she had on the Isle of Ishiposa. No, these steps felt welcoming, despite the fact that they were made out rough black rock. There were several guards scattered around, but none of them paid her much attention. They only inclined their heads toward the group as they made their way up.

Finally, Ikeshal bowed and took his leave as they entered the hall.

Quinn paused on the threshold, marveling at the candelabras that hung down from the ceiling, which had to be some forty or fifty feet above them. The massive lights that she at first thought were lit by candles, but realized after closer inspection that they were a type of magical light instead. It glowed and flickered in an almost playful way.

"Lava sprites." Eric offered when he saw where she was watching.

Quinn nodded, taking the rest of it in. The long, blood red carpet that led up steps to a throne and . . .

She gulped . . .

Standing at the end, in front of a massive throne that could probably fit the entire Library staff on it, was a twenty-five-foot odd satyr.

The massive and imposing satyr looked down at them all, a wide grin on his face. Quinn had never felt so tiny in her life.

He gave a flourishing bow and a decidedly impish grin. "I apologize for not greeting you immediately, Librarian, but I *did* promise to show you my true size."

5 2

NICE AND WARM

Quinn always expected Uncle Hal to be quite a bit larger than he was when he came to visit the Library. She wasn't expecting him to be taller than a house. Imposing as he was, that smile was cheeky as ever. Eric hovered right up near Hal's face, with his hands on his hips, glaring at his uncle.

"Fine, fine," Hal intoned, his voice booming through the room. Even as he spoke, his body began to shrink, until he stood at about the eight-foot mark again, just two feet taller than Malakai. "Is that better?" he asked, his voice less encompassing, yet no less deep.

"That's much better," the imp said, having hovered back down to a normal level.

"I apologize." But Uncle Hal didn't sound contrite at all. "But it was fun, and Quinn did ask how large I actually was."

"But you can still be bigger than that," Eric called him out with a smug smile. "So you didn't do what she asked."

"No, I *can* be bigger than that. But only with effort." Hal grinned. "That was my natural size"

"Whatever," Eric grumbled, and his wings fluttered with irritation, staccato in their beat.

Malakai frowned. "That's massive," he said.

"Yes, it is rather, isn't it? Impressive, and I shall always say so myself." Hal winked at the elf.

Malakai didn't bat an eyelash. "Is that innate magic, or is it a spell?"

"Innate magic. It's a satyr thing." Hal shrugged with ease. "Power levels dictate on how large we grow naturally. But after a certain level it becomes bothersome."

"Hmm," Malakai said. "So how tall is Ikeshal actually?"

"Not as tall as me," Hal said. He looked at Quinn quizzically. "You seem a little hot. Would you like to retreat somewhere the temperature is more regulated?"

Quinn nodded, even as she looked around the charcoal dusted area. There were veins running through the walls, red, like blood, somehow illuminated through the rock.

Lava veins throughout the whole structure.

It gave the whole area this eerily wonderful sensation of being alive.

The heat seeped through her magical barriers. She wondered how Eric felt in a constantly temperature-controlled environment when he was in the Library. She'd have to try and remember to ask him that later.

"Come. Let us chat in comfort. I'll have refreshments brought to help you with the heat." Hal led them from the reception chamber through a twelve-foot door and into a small hallway. It was too small for him. He visibly pulled in on himself because his shoulders were too wide for the door. For Quinn and the others, it was easy to traverse. She and Malakai could even walk side by side.

Windows cut into the rock looked out over rocky hills, plains, and petrified trees. And she noticed people in groups performing what seemed like . . .

"Are they practicing fighting?" she asked, watching what seemed like formations of some sort.

"Yes, it's, uh, they're drills. Each regiment has a different time for drills. And you're looking at, I believe, regiment seventeen." Hal didn't seem ready for that question.

"How many regiments do you have?"

"A lot," he said, the smile gone from his eyes as he glanced back at her again. "You need to cool down."

Quinn muttered under her breath. "Isn't that why I'm here?"

If Hal heard her, he ignored it.

They walked into what seemed to be a massive living room. Quinn sank into a surprisingly plush red couch that felt like a hug. The coffee table in front of her had rivers of lava running through it in a mesmerizing way. Everything outside of those couches was formed out of the same rock as the rest of the palace. She frowned.

"Not what you were expecting?" Hal asked.

"No, not that. Is everything made out of igneous rock?" she asked.

"Technically," He gestured all around them at the malleable way things had been created even in the room. Right down to the archways that made up the windows. "We simply mold it."

"Wait, so it wasn't a massive volcanic eruption that incidentally created everything here?" Quinn glanced around. "You just mold the lava?"

"Well, despite the lava rivers we don't have that many volcanos. The heat comes from the core of the planet. Most of our worlds are powered that way in this sector. The temperature keeps the lava workable."

"What about water?" Quinn asked.

"Well, of course we've got water, but it's usually hot." Hal paused for a second, thinking. "Yes. Think hot springs, very hot springs."

"I can imagine," Quinn said. "So you have sculptors who make all of this furniture and who form the castles and the houses. Is that how it works?"

"Yes, it is." Hal offered a smile. He seemed proud. "They are sculptors, masonries, crafters. We have a very diverse architecture division in our universities. It's not for the weak of heart to take lava as it is, and form it into something useful or beautiful."

Quinn pondered that for a few moments and then thought about the army division who were fighting in the courtyard. "How do you have time to spend with us or even to come and visit the Library?

Didn't you say you frequently have wars to fight?" It was a concept Quinn couldn't quite get her head around.

"Well, we have wars, but to be honest they're more like spats where my brothers and sisters, who still disagree with decisions made millions of years ago by our forefathers, have decided to constantly irritate me by bombarding me with attacks." That steely portion of his personality was back.

Quinn wasn't sure she wanted to know more about the sibling rivalry at this point.

"What's on your mind, Quinn?" Hal asked, narrowing his eyes. "There's something you're not asking. Something you're not telling me."

"I was wondering about Tenejo and Adrito. What are you going to do to them to find out what they know?" She avoided telling him her real problem for a few more precious moments.

Hal leaned back, studying her. "Haven't we already established that, by handing them over, you've given me leeway to extract the information any way I see fit?"

"Well, yes," Quinn said, slightly reluctantly.

"That's not what you weren't telling me, though. Are you going to actually tell me why your heat levels are off the charts?"

"What do you mean my levels are off the charts?" Quinn asked.

"There's something wrong. You're"—he narrowed his eyes again, peering at her in a way that reminded Quinn of how Lynx frequently reconnected with the system and multitasked—"you are out of balance, Librarian. There is something wrong with your fire element."

Quinn sighed. "You mentioned fire, back when you were at the Library. It was the first time I realized that perhaps the hot flashes I got every now and again weren't just because I'd changed worlds and my hormones were acting up."

"Well, obviously it's something else. You're mostly a cosmicisodracus. Fire is your thing. It is a species-related affinity, and it's strong. Probably your strongest one." He waved the statement away nonchalantly.

Quinn felt completely and utterly out of her depth. She frowned.

"So, fire is my natural affinity and I shouldn't try to stop it from leaking out?"

"You definitely should be fighting its attempts to emerge," Hal said. "After all, you don't want to burn down a Library. There's a lot of books in there."

"But those books don't burn in regular fire," Eric said, laughing.

"Have you ever felt the fire of a cosmicisodracus?" Hal asked.

"Of course I haven't," Eric said. "They've been mostly absent since long before I was born. You know that."

"Precisely. So don't talk out of your arse since you have no idea what you're talking about," Hal said. "Their fire can burn magical texts. Trust me when I tell you it's hot. Even for me." He added the last almost as an afterthought.

"Oh," Quinn said, "was that the fire I gained access to when I had to destroy the contaminated books?" She asked suddenly. Malakai blinked at her, as did Hal and Eric.

"You already triggered the fire once?" Hal asked, his tone incredulous.

"Yeah, the system said it was level twenty-one or something and it said that it was way out of my power range or something like that."

Hal pinched the bridge of his nose and began to pace in the room.

"I take it that was a bad thing?" Quinn asked.

"You're extremely good at reading body language, Librarian. However, did we manage without you?" His words were clipped.

"There's no need to be snarky about it," Quinn retorted, quite irritated. She picked up one of the cups of tea on the table, marveling at how fine the material was. It didn't appear to be porcelain but almost as delicate, likely made of an igneous rock variation or something.

"Fire of that level should have been monitored. You should have been in the core to try it out the first time. You needed to be protected." Hal sighed. "Just the act of using it set off the chain reaction to alter your body on a molecular level, which you are not yet ready for because you are basically still an egg."

"I was born in an egg?" Quinn asked.

"Metaphorically speaking, you are still a baby with a lot of responsibilities thrust on you, raised in human society. This is"—he took a deep breath and appeared to count to maybe five—"absolutely none of your fault. We will fix this and get you working at the optimal level."

"Okay," Quinn said, slightly mollified and yet at the same time, rather scared. She wasn't entirely sure what she expected.

Hal seemed to take pity on her and smiled. "It's not that dangerous, or it won't be if I'm the one teaching you. We do have several reinforced chambers that can withstand the type of force that your fire creates if absolutely necessary."

"Great," Quinn said, not meaning it even for a second. What he described sounded positively terrifying. What if she couldn't withstand the force. She took a long sip of the slightly bitter tea.

Hal frowned while watching her. "I need to check a few things. May I touch your head?"

Quinn leaned back slightly.

"What do you mean, touch my head?" she asked, suddenly feeling a wave of exhaustion hit her. Had she been doing too much again?

"It's easier for me to assess the level of potential damage, the level of power you're approaching, and perhaps what techniques might best suit your very specific genetic makeup." He sounded very business-like.

"Oh, okay," Quinn said, and was surprised when he was quite gentle about it. He placed two fingers very lightly on her scalp, his thumb on the back of her head and his ring finger on the front. She tried hard not to think about the fact that Hal's hands were big enough to crush her skull in one fist.

Yep, that was something she didn't want to picture.

"Calm your thoughts. They are breaking out of your barriers." His tone was smooth and soft.

"No, they're not," she said, after checking briefly despite her increasing lethargy. Maybe it was the heat all around them, lulling her into a sense of relaxation. Like a permanent hot rock massage.

"Well, I *am* extremely perceptible to thoughts directed in my direction. Please keep them under wraps," he murmured softly.

Quinn could tell he wasn't trying to be mean, just the forthright way he spoke could sound pretty blunt. Fatigue washed over her. What she wouldn't give to sleep right then. "I apologize. That wasn't really directed at you, just in general."

"I understand," he said, and for a few moments they stayed that way. Hal looking through her mind or body for whatever it was he thought he'd find, and Quinn fighting against her growing exhaustion.

"Hmm." He said several times over the course of a couple of minutes.

Quinn didn't like the sound of his hmms. They didn't inspire confidence in her. In fact, they made her quite trepidatious. She could feel a presence at the outer edges of her barriers, testing ever so slightly and a warmth that ran through her mind, that had nothing to do with the out-of-control fire that kept threatening to take control of her and other things around her.

It had nothing to do with the sudden overwhelming freezing sensations that shot through her body. This was welcome and friendly, but in a stern teacher sort of way.

But there was that thing at the outer edges, trying to creep in, this wave of fatigue that wouldn't leave her. It only kept growing—exponentially it seemed. Gradual at first, now she could barely hold herself awake.

"Excellent," he said, as he withdrew both his hand and his probing. She frowned, feeling a strange sense of coolness suffuse her head where his fingers had rested. Granted, he was the Lord of Halschius, made out of mostly fiery stuff. It probably stood to reason he was warmer than most.

"So what is this *hmm* about?" Quinn asked, suddenly finding herself breathless now. Out of breath and tired, like she'd just run a marathon.

"This *hmm* is specifically about the fact that you have handled everything much better than I would have anticipated, given your upbringing."

"Not my heritage?" she asked.

"No, no, no. Your heritage is neither here nor there, apart from the fact that it makes you prone to use fire. You have done remarkably well, as has, I believe, Lynx in aiding you? Did Dottie not help you?"

"No." Quinn blinked rapidly, trying to keep her eyes open. "You know she has a fire affinity, right? I always thought it was weird that a wooden bench had a fire affinity."

"She's not made out of actual wood. She's made out of a type of extremely fire-resistant petrified type wood, I guess. But she's grown, you understand that, right? The superellex futora are a grown species. Anyway, you can read about them. I am disappointed that you aren't further along in your power management, but content that you haven't set the Library and other people on fire."

Hal opened his mouth to speak, but then closed it and frowned, studying her, his brow creasing with concern.

"Thanks?" Quinn asked.

"You're welcome." He paused as if he hadn't even heard her properly. His eyes narrowed again, watching her intently again before continuing. "I have some exercises I wish to run through with you. They'll be very similar to the way you built your mind protections, which are, by the way, quite exemplary, given how little time you've had to erect them. Kudos to Milaro. I'll tell him myself when I next see him."

Quinn blinked. Hal was so commanding and so simply there. Everything he said, she wanted to listen to. And she knew that everything he said held weight unlike anyone else except Milaro.

If only her head wasn't so heavy.

She reached for her cup of tea, suddenly positively parched. Her arms felt like lead . . . as if they'd been transformed into a heavy metal and then encased in concrete. Her vision swam even as she tried to make sure her breathing filtration was working.

"I think we'll begin training straight away. Now, I need you to get . . ." Hal stopped. "Quinn. What's wrong?"

He leaned in to catch her as she fell forward. "Send for Girilda right now. Quinn needs a doctor."

Hal smoothed her hair back, and she swore she could see thunderclouds behind his eyes. He muttered under his breath. "I should have looked deeper when I felt something off." Clearing his throat, he spoke to her. "It's okay. You'll be fine."

She didn't believe a word. There was simmering anger in every pore of his being.

"Fine . . ." She gulped as she lay back on the propped-up pillows. "My throat . . . drink."

Hal glanced at the teacup she was staring at. He lifted it up to his nose and sniffed, just once, before placing it back on the table, discomfort on his face. "Is this what you drank?"

Quinn nodded, barely able to keep track of the action considering her head felt like it was on a spin cycle.

Hal roared out something in a guttural language Quinn couldn't understand, perhaps it was because her head was wonky, but it might also have been because her translator didn't know how to twist the words enough to make her understand.

Either way the timbre made her shiver.

She was so very tired. All she wanted to do was close her eyes.

"Stay with me, Librarian," Hal said, his tone soothing.

She smiled. "Mm-hm. It's nice and warm here."

He frowned and muttered under his breath. She thought he said something like: "I should have done a complete scan."

"I'm sorry," she slurred ever so slightly. "I'm just suddenly so tired."

She noticed Malakai off to the side, his face ashen, and Eric was nowhere to be seen. Quinn tried to figure out why in her head.

"Stay awake. Come now. I have a wonderful beverage coming your way, much better than what you just drank." There was an overtone of concern to his voice.

Quinn nodded as the world swam in and out of view.

"Where the hell are they?" Hal growled this time, beckoning to Malakai. "Watch her. I need to find the doctor and make sure she brings the antidote."

Quinn decided she really needed to sleep . . . *antidote* didn't sound like a good thing. Maybe they could tell her all about it when she woke up.

53

FLUTTERING FRANTICALLY

THE ENTIRE ROOM CONTINUED TO SPIN, AND QUINN COULDN'T QUITE process where each and every person around her was. Her head spun like a top, and the disorientation was real. Not only did she have a sore throat, but her stomach started to swirl, inundating her senses with nausea on a level she hadn't experienced since she got food poisoning a couple of years ago.

In fact, it sort of felt like her stomach was trying to boil up out of her system and exit through her esophagus. It was not a comfortable or welcome feeling.

She frowned.

Something was wrong.

Something was wrong with her.

Ever since she drank that tea earlier . . . her eyes fluttered open, even though she swore she hadn't closed them. She could see Malakai sitting there, fanning her with something that didn't resemble the fan she thought it should even if it was giving her a nice little bit of cooler air. It just wasn't helping enough.

She checked to make sure she still had the barrier around her. Each thought took more effort than she remembered. Her magic was still in place. The spell was still holding. Something else had to be sapping her energy.

She checked her energy levels.

2,972/2,985

Nope, energy levels were absolutely fine.

"Am I sick?" she whispered.

Malakai nodded. "Yeah, we think you drank something that didn't agree with you."

"Is it like a species thing? Should I not have?" But even the words were difficult to get out. All she wanted to do was sleep, just to drift away and preferably not wake up for quite some time.

Suddenly, she could feel vibrations in the floor beneath ever so subtly as large footsteps made their way toward them. She blinked and tried to push herself up, but her strength gave out.

"Quinn, sit," Hal's tone commanded.

"Trying," she said to Hal.

He frowned. "Malakai, help her."

Malakai raised an eyebrow. He'd never been the best at taking orders, but apparently taking them from Hal, at least right then, was acceptable. Which made Quinn all the more suspicious. And yet, she couldn't quite get the thoughts into words.

She struggled, with Malakai's help, into a sitting position, leaning against the side of the couch.

"I'm so sorry," she said, her breath coming in short gasps. "I . . . I know everybody keeps telling me to sleep, but there's just been so much to do."

Hal actually laughed, but she could tell the expression didn't meet his eyes. In fact, his eyes looked positively stormy, like he was pissed off.

"What is it?" she asked.

"Let's just get this in you first," he said, holding up a cup for her.

Quinn noticed another satyr behind him. Hadn't he called for somebody? She couldn't place the name. But she was tall. Well, like most satyrs apparently, and sort of majestic. There was a sheen to her, sort of like an aura. It flashed in a soft lemon light around her.

Girilda . . . that was her name.

"I'm so sorry," Quinn said again.

"Stop it, Quinn." He reached over to Girilda and grabbed a glass from them. "Here, you need to take this."

"Will it settle my stomach?" Quinn asked. As each second passed, she felt like her strength was being sapped even more. This was one hell of a food poisoning incident.

"It will," he said. "Now, drink."

"Fine," she said, and gulped down the drink. It was even more bitter than the tea which, in hindsight, she hadn't actually liked. She'd always been a fan of tea, but this one was not their best. The liquid hit her stomach like someone dropped a ball of lead into water.

She gasped. "Oh, that hurts."

"Just give it a minute, Quinn," Hal said. "Now, just breathe. I need you to concentrate on your breathing. Don't stop."

Quinn laughed. She couldn't help it. "Why would I stop?" She took a huge intake of breath and suddenly it was difficult to breathe.

That was why he told her not to stop breathing. It hurt so bad. She almost passed out. She could see the little black dots forming in front of her vision but fought through valiantly because if it was this difficult to breathe, she wasn't sure she'd be able to involuntarily.

The agony prolonged her senses in such a way that it made time seem infinite. She really hoped hours hadn't passed and that in actuality it was simply a few minutes, and yet it just hurt so much it felt like forever. Her stomach roiled like it was boiling water and tried to exit out of her from every orifice, every pore.

The pressure inside her built and built and built until she let out one massive burp.

Quinn paused. "Oh," she said extremely embarrassed. "That . . . it's really weird. I am so sorry. I didn't mean . . . I was just trying to breathe."

Malakai snorted behind his hand. She could tell he was laughing. He'd pay later. Hal simply looked relieved.

"That was a natural release of toxins." Hal gave her a half smile. "And I promise that I've heard far worse, Librarian. You have no idea."

Quinn realized she probably didn't want to know. Girilda simply flashed her a smile, and Eric fluttered down and put a tiny hand against her forehead.

"She's still sweating." the imp informed the room.

"Of course I'm sweating," she said. "It's hot here."

"Not that type of sweat, Quinn," Eric said in a clipped voice, before turning his attention back to Hal. "Anyway, what do you make of it? Do you really think?"

The looks that passed between Eric and Hal started to grate on Quinn's nerves. As every moment passed, she felt a bit better, a little more in control of herself like she usually was, and definitely still embarrassed about the after effect of the tea she'd consumed. "Okay, enough with the looks between you two. What are you not telling me? Was that somebody else's drink? Should I not have touched it?"

"No, Librarian, and I must apologize for this. That was a hundred percent your drink, and I do *not* understand how this happened, but the reality is that someone poisoned you." Hal's skin tone darkened, and fire licked at his horns before he took a deep breath and continued. "I've already sent my guards to the kitchens to find out who procured, mixed, and made the tea. Luckily, I recognized the symptoms in time. I wish I'd have recognized them sooner. I simply thought you were fatigued from having to maintain the barriers required to keep you ventilated. I forgot, and still forget, of your heritage and the fact that maintaining a simple barrier like that isn't going to drain you."

Quinn blinked up at the satyr and held up a hand, only just making sense of his words. "Wait, somebody poisoned me?"

"Yes." He said it like it was a common occurrence. "It seems that even my domain is not immune to infiltration. I *will* get to the bottom of this."

Quinn still couldn't process it though. Somebody tried to poison her?

"Then did it almost work?" she asked.

To that, Hal simply laughed.

"Well, it *could* have poisoned you," Hal said, "but it wouldn't have killed you."

Quinn still wasn't getting it. Her head seemed to be full of cotton wool again. She understood, in theory, that someone had indeed placed poisonous substances in her drink and that she was suffering the after-effects. But for so much of her short life she'd felt meaningless and unimportant, that wrapping her head around the fact that someone had found her important enough to actually get rid of was a weird sensation. "Okay, so, they poisoned me, and I should technically have died."

"Well," Eric said, "technically, they were trying to poison the human Librarian."

"Oh," Quinn said. "So they didn't know."

"No, they didn't know."

"Does she know?" Quinn asked, nodding in Girilda's direction.

"Not precisely," Hal said, dismissing the doctor behind him. "We'll transport you to somewhere less open and have Eric fetch any other supplements we need to feed you. Perhaps it might be better to open a door to the Library and get food directly from Cook for you."

Quinn shook her head slowly, trying to clear out the fuzzy feeling. "Don't you only have three doors?"

"Technically we have four. Three public doors. The fourth door is my door. I don't share well," Hal said, then chuckled. "Anyway, this seems like as good a time as any to move you."

He reached down and easily plucked Quinn up. His skin was warm to the touch. She yelped, "What the hell, Hal?"

Hal laughed. "It'll take time for you to recuperate your physical energy. I know you've almost got more magical energy than me. So I'm just bringing you to safety."

He carried her to a room off to the side with a lock that he spoke one guttural word to and it opened. He placed her on another couch in a room that was very similarly furnished. It had high arched windows that looked out over a molten lava lake. He motioned to Eric, and they walked over to look out of the windows while they spoke.

Quinn sat quietly. She could feel her energy returning. Along with the energy came a bit of anger. She was pissed. Someone had tried to poison her with tea. Now she'd second guess every cup of tea she ever had.

"Are you doing okay?" Malakai asked.

"No," Quinn said, "not really. I'm trying not to be too angry. Trying to get over the fact that I still really want to sleep and probably shouldn't. Not to mention the fact that I'm trying to process the fact that someone tried to kill me."

"Well, to be fair," he said, "you've had Kajaro try to kill you, a demon tree try to kill you. Oh, even your new bestie Jasper tried to kill you. I mean, you should be sort of used to it by now."

Quinn laughed despite her mood. "Don't make light of it, Malakai. It's serious."

"Of course it's serious. But it's also kind of, you know, commonplace for you now. You think three attempted murders? Well, if you count Tenejo, it's probably four. And the mind bomb that Kajaro placed in you, it's probably five." He grinned at her. "If we really try, we could probably pile up a heap more of them."

"Thanks," she said to him, surprised at how much his words calmed her when it was about such a topic. "I appreciate your efforts in trying to make me feel better."

"Yeah, so you should," Malakai said. "Now, let's get rid of that dreary face and figure out what we're going to do."

"I'm slowly regaining my physical energy." She checked her magical stats again, double-checking her mana levels and checking her energy levels. "Nope, magical energy is still fine at 2,974 now of 2,985 because every now and again it ticks over and takes energy to maintain the shields and the breath masks that I've given myself. I don't know what to do, Mal."

He shrugged. "How about you drink some more of this disgustingly bitter stuff he called medicine and see if we can make you a bit healthier. Did you bring any food with you?" He asked Quinn.

"No." She shook her head. "But right now I can't stomach anything. It still feels like its own lava pit down there."

Malakai chuckled. "Well, that's polite dinner conversation."

Hal finally walked back over. There was something much more rigid in the way he held himself. "Eric went to procure you some sustenance. I'm fetching it directly from Cook. And Eric has permission currently to use my private door to do so." His words were clipped with underlying anger.

Mal raised an eyebrow. "You don't trust someone not to try and poison her again?"

"Not until I've weeded out who did this. Don't worry, I'll find them." Hal's voice held a low tremor.

The way the words resonated down Quinn's spine, she had absolutely no doubt in her mind that Hal was speaking the truth.

"In the meantime," she said, trying to lighten the mood somewhat, "What sort of poison did they use? Was it potent?"

"Oh, yes." Hal said, focusing back on her. "If you'd in fact been human, you'd have been dead in about fifteen seconds."

"Oh," Quinn said, digesting that information like it tasted bad. "But it still affected me."

"Yes, it still affected you. Because like I said, you are an egg. You are a baby who shouldn't yet be in the position she's in." He took another deep breath.

Quinn realized at that point that Uncle Hal didn't have a problem with her per se, it was more than she should have been able to grow into her powers before becoming the Librarian instead of having it all forced upon her so fast. She had to agree with him for the most part, and appreciated his concern.

"I need to let go of my irritation at how things were handled, and we need to move on from there," he continued.

Quinn, very wisely, remained silent.

"Look, your heritage, your genetics mean that you shouldn't be evolving for another several decades at least. Maybe another eighty or ninety years." Hal paused, "You are, what, twenty?"

Quinn nodded.

Hal threw up his hands. "Which is ridiculous. Your innate traits make poisoning you pretty much moot point, but your evolution has not yet come far enough, especially since you were essentially created from nothing. Anyway—we need to train your senses to scan for poisons, and anything else that might harm you. Poisons are, for most types of dragon, not necessarily even just your type of dragon, something they can simply burn off. Once we've trained you to identify harmful substances, you should, essentially, be able to incinerate them internally."

"Like I did the infection on the books?" Quinn asked.

"Yes! Quite like that in fact, except inside and all." Hal laughed. "I wish Drevicia could show you this itself, but as it is I'll give you a few exercises right now that'll take your current abilities and hone them. You'll need to focus deeply on your sensory abilities. You must learn to break down everything in an instant of observation to know whether things are safe or a danger to you. Just inanimate things. People are more complex, and Milaro is far better suited to help you with that."

"Should I recover first?" she asked, despite already feeling much better than she had.

"Quinn, you're fine. The only reason you had any trouble at all was the dose size. And soon nothing will be able to threaten you . . . at least nothing your body can purge." He flashed her a grin.

Quinn cringed. There was no time like the present. "Okay, I'm ready."

Hal began walking her through some exercises she could initiate whenever she was handed food, or beverages from people she didn't know well. It involved an almost instantaneous analysis of the air around the item, or person, as well as the item itself. And it took several tries for Quinn to understand fully what he meant. But by the end, Malakai could walk past with two cups and she could pick out the one with poison in it without having to look at the liquid or taste it.

"That's a good start," Uncle Hal said, a huge smile on his face. "You're taking to it fairly easily. Now, I have some exercises to show you that you can do on your spare time, whenever you have a moment. Make this second nature and you won't even have to think about danger identification. It'll become habit."

"I like the sound of that." She grinned at him.

"Now keep in mind, if you're in the Library, you also have the safety protocols in place there . . . so this just makes you doubly safe."

Quinn nodded.

But the exercises were going to have to wait for later, because two sunset-colored imps burst into the room, their orange-black wings fluttering frantically behind them. "We believe the prisoner is ready for you right now." they said in unison.

Hal raised an eyebrow. "What do you mean the prisoner is ready for me? I'll see the prisoners when I am ready."

"No, sire . . . you need to see this." They spoke together again. "You have to see this for yourself. It would be a good idea to come down now."

"What's happened?" he asked. "Did you push the questioning too hard?" His tone took on an iron-like quality. The imps looked at each other.

They sort of shrugged as they wrung their hands. "We didn't think we pushed it too hard, but we may have inadvertently triggered a failsafe."

Hal sighed and it reverberated through the entire room. "Very well. I guess we go visit our prisoner now."

54

HALF THE BATTLE

HAL IMMEDIATELY LEFT THE ROOM, THE REST OF THEM FOLLOWING behind him as he beckoned.

Quinn managed to have at least the presence of mind to remember she had a hover skill. She applied it with her flight skill and easily keep up with them without having to exert as much physical energy as she would have walking. She realized she'd have to be very careful with this because it was an excellent way for her to get extremely lazy. But right now, still feeling marginally like crap, she decided this was the best way to travel.

They went through halls that were much more opulent than Quinn had thought an igneous rock formation city would be.

Red drapes hung over the massive arched windows as they went along, glowing in a way that resembled the lava outside. The red carpets were bordered with gold and a strange type of cross between silver and bronze adorned the floors they traversed. She kept her eyes on Uncle Hal's back and a very subtle eye on her energy and mana levels to make sure being here wasn't causing them to run out quicker than usual.

She realized that wasn't the case, so apparently her proximity to the Library had nothing to do with her magic and energy replenishment.

It was all her.

As they went down a massive spiral staircase, she lost track of how many turns they took on the way. It opened out into a huge underground cavern that appeared almost as big as the one housing the filtration system in the Library. Granted, she knew the latter was deceptive in its size.

She looked around, taking it all in. The ceilings were impossibly high, the floor rough for the most part as it stretched out in front of them, and there were strange domes scattered all throughout.

Inside each of the domes was a weird sort of fog that was mostly transparent.

Many of them appeared to be empty.

"Climb aboard," Hal said curtly.

Quinn ripped her gaze away from watching the domes and saw that he was standing on a platform. She hurried to float onto it and turned around slowly.

The platform was about ten by twelve feet in size, maybe. It was rounded on the edges, so probably not exact. It had a wrought iron type of railing, and it hovered across the ground. It moved fast. Quinn thought the inertia should have made her stumble backwards, but somehow whatever magic it worked with allowed her to remain standing as it shot across the area between the domes. Finally, they reached a standstill only for it to rise in the air. Quinn clenched the railings until her knuckles went white and they looked down into one of the domes.

Quinn squinted her eyes. What she'd expected to see was seas of lava and people tied to walls being tortured. Images from old cartoons her foster-father used to watch in the wee hours dominated her perception of hell. But Halschius wasn't the hell from Earth mythology . . .

Halschius was nothing like that.

Tenejo stood in the middle of the dome, his eyes flickering all around him as if he was watching people she couldn't see. There were reflections in the smoke, a strange sort of mimicry, almost like they were watching a television show. She glanced up at Hal. He grunted.

"Seems he took the bait earlier than usual. This is unprecedented," he said, a big frown on his face.

"What's unprecedented?" Quinn asked.

He glanced at her and then back to watch Tenejo before speaking again. "Sometimes I forget you are not from these worlds. You don't understand the implications of what Halschius stands for. We are known for our ability to retrieve targeted information, no matter what."

"That sounds decidedly ominous." Quinn said, still watching and marveling at how it felt like her eyes were looking through binoculars. The vision below them was so clear. "What do you mean?"

"Watch."

And so, Quinn watched. Tenejo, lost in his own world, tried to break free of the bindings on his hands. He watched what looked like his jailers on the other side of his cell. He observed them carefully and closely, his eyes narrowing every now and then as he twitched his hands. Every time their backs were turned, he jiggled more at his bindings. Until finally, only several minutes later, his arms fell free. First of all, he rubbed each wrist and then he slowly moved so that he was facing the exact direction of his guards.

Except from what Quinn could tell, the guards were indeed a simple projection, an image on the smoke or the clouds or screen or whatever it was they were watching. In just a small section of the dome, Quinn frowned. "Are we seeing what he thinks?"

Hal muttered, "You're perceptive enough but you need to start trusting your own judgment. Your senses are strong enough to determine what is and isn't real. It could save all of our lives if you do." He glanced at her. "Or else you've just spent far too much time around Milaro, probably the latter, maybe a little bit of the first."

Beneath them Tenejo moved again.

Uncle Hal frowned again. "That was awfully quick. Does he already know where he thinks he is?"

The imps who'd come to fetch him earlier both shook their heads. "No, he is completely under, just like every other prisoner we take."

Quinn glanced over, still not understanding. "So what's the deal?"

Hal held up a finger to his lips and Quinn turned her attention back to the dome. Tenejo had suddenly rushed the bars of his cell and spoken a single sibilant word that Quinn couldn't quite grasp, couldn't quite hear. One guard after another slumped to the ground. Tenejo turned around and used his tail to scoop at the guards' clothing and retrieve the jacket with the keys. Quinn raised an eyebrow. Hal simply shrugged.

Malakai looked like he wanted to get some popcorn and sit down to watch the rest of this.

And Quinn noticed that Eric was simply hovering in a corner, scowling.

And the next thing they knew, Tenejo was out of his cell.

"Does he know where he is?" Quinn asked.

"Wait . . ." Hal was grinning now.

"But he's still in the dome." Quinn didn't understand the swirling of the image, and could only assume it was somehow hooked into his thought process or memory, or perhaps a dream?

"Projection imaging, is what we call it. It taps into whatever it is that our prisoner wants to happen, wants most to happen, and what they then expect as a result of that to occur." Hal didn't take his eyes off Tenejo. "Essentially, we give them an opportunity to escape to wherever it is they most desire and follow them there. You'd be surprised how much you learn when a person thinks they're beyond your reach."

"So, you essentially play on his most desperate desires?"

"Eh, not desires, more wants, goals, items they're aiming for, things they're obsessed with. In Tenejo's case, it appears to be, well, you."

Quinn was taken aback. "Me? Obsessed with me?"

"Your elimination. He appears to value that the most." Hal gave her a sly grin, but still didn't look at her. "Whatever did you get up to that made him so very angry."

"Existing?" Quinn answered, somewhat down about the whole thing.

"Ah." said Hal. "That'll do it every time. Now, shall we watch and see where he goes?"

Quinn nodded and narrowed her eyes as she observed Tenejo creep out of what looked like a portable prison and escape outside after bashing in two guards' skulls from whom he took a key and unlocked the half of the restraint still dangling off one wrist. Once out of the cuffs, he looked around to get his bearings.

Then he spoke a single word and the air around him rippled, and he vanished.

Quinn gasped, stumbling back. "What happened? Why? Where did he go?" Even after getting mostly used to magic, some stuff just still took her by surprise.

"It's okay, Quinn—" Hal started, nice and calm, but Eric interrupted.

"The barrier he's inside of is self-realizing. He can't escape from it. Instead, it'll loop him in a way that his perception fits within it no matter what. Don't worry about it," Eric snapped. He was in a fiery mood and Quinn didn't think it was only to do with what they'd discussed earlier. She'd leave that particular little quirk alone for now.

In the meantime, Hal watched the scene intently and so Quinn gave the scene below her full attention.

As if she was watching a movie, Tenejo, in what seemed like fast-forward, found himself outside a castle that rose up from the ground in a spiral that reminded her of a coiled snake. It was made of pale bricks that appeared more scalelike, especially in the areas overrun with moss.

Tenejo appeared just as he'd disappeared, in a flash and the dome shifted, its magic flawlessly compensating for his projected outcome.

The guards at the gate of snake castle let him through after double-checking something he said to them. He wandered the darkened halls. Quinn had to squint to make anything out. It appeared the moss continued inside the structure, and she could have sworn it smelled faintly of rotting vegetation.

"Careful Librarian," Hal said, his tone sharper than usual "Don't push your mental presence out too much, he'll feel you and know this is all an illusion."

"Sorry." Quinn said, sheepishly, tamping down on broadcasting. Her shields were solid, but she could see how she'd managed to push her presence beyond herself. She hadn't even realized she'd been doing that in the first place, so there was another thing she needed to work on. Pulling back her awareness a bit meant she didn't smell the nauseating stench anymore at least. So that was a win.

The halls stretched on until Tenejo finally came upon an audience chamber. After being ushered through a short hall, the room came into focus.

It was long, and narrow, with a very lean table down the center. There were several Esposians that Quinn had never seen, sitting in a cluster. There were a couple of Aracnios, neither of which were Jim and Bob, and two species Quinn could neither identify herself nor pull up the information for.

"If you're trying to figure out who or what they are," Malakai said from next to her, "it's a projected image. They're not actually there. The system can't pick up on imaginary people."

Quinn nodded. It made complete and utter sense. She turned her attention back to the dome.

There were a few more random Serpensiril, but above all, there was Kajaro. He sat at the head of the table and watched as Tenejo took each step into the room. Then he closed the open book in front of him and pushed it away so he could steeple his hands.

Everything felt so real even though she knew it was all in Tenejo's head.

"This is his goal," she said to Hal.

Hal nodded very slowly. "He has an exceptional grasp of what he wants to achieve. I'm surprised he's going for this. We made the escape a little easier than we usually would have, but I didn't believe he'd take to it so fast. He must be desperate." Hal frowned as he watched. "Kajaro does not seem pleased."

"But that's just a projection, right?" Quinn asked, peering at the book in front of the Serpensiril.

"Yes, yes it is. Unless . . ." he turned to the imps next to him. "Double-check he's not using some internal connection we managed to overlook."

Several dials on the image array in front of the two imps flared up. They shook their head and spoke in unison again. "There is nothing foreign in his mind that we can detect."

Hal frowned and everyone's attention returned to the scene below them.

"You failed to kill the Librarian, and you failed to bring us Milaro," Kajaro said, his sibilant voice full of disdain. "Just why is it you've sought an audience when we're having a meeting?"

Tenejo's voice, when he spoke, sounded raspier than Quinn remembered. He bowed low before righting himself. "I apologize but I did bring news. News that the Library is stronger than we anticipated at this point in time."

"How so?" Kajaro leaned back in his chair, the slim ridge above his eye raised.

Tenejo hesitated, as if he was trying to remember the details. "The Library was able to encase me, to prevent me from following the king's scent. And then the Librarian was able to stop me. Even after I gave in to the power you gifted me."

"You used that power already," Kajaro said, slapping a hand on the table in front of him. His tone had changed from languid to annoyed.

"Yes. I had to. They had me trapped." A note of panic entered his voice briefly, and he looked around furtively, "I almost gave away things. I almost let them know."

"You should never have let them know," a voice said that Quinn couldn't quite locate the source of. Even Hal leaned forward, confusion plain on his face.

"Is there somebody hidden in the shadows?" Quinn whispered as she peered in through the smoke.

"Yeah," Eric said as he fluttered above the railing. "Someone in a robe, I think."

"That's curious." Malakai popped a treat into his mouth, obviously thoroughly entertained. "It's definitely curious."

The robed figure continued speaking. "You should have finished the job if you accessed the power."

"Surely there's something you can do," Tenejo said, an edge of hysteria in his voice.

That's when Quinn noticed there was something wrong with his skin. Mottled and scaly he might be, but it appeared to be cracking. She could see red ridges just behind the scales, and they were widening.

"There's nothing that can save you now," Kajaro gave a cruel smile. "You should have died at the Librarian's hand. At least then you would have had a pleasant death."

"No. I have information. I can give you . . ."

"I can glean the information from your cold dead brain, Tenejo. You were warned. You knew what accessing that power would do." The voice in the shadows faded as the creature retreated into nothingness.

"But you said there was a way to reverse it." There was panic in Tenejo's voice now, and Quinn glanced at Hal, who seemed quite concerned. He motioned to the two imps that had fetched them, and they fluttered down toward the dome, taking on guises of Serpensiril guards as they attempted to cross into it. Their first effort met some resistance.

Hal grunted as the imps continued to press themselves forward.

Tenejo, panicking by now, backpedaled, appealing to every single type of person in the room. But they began to flicker in and out, and Quinn suddenly noticed why. Tenejo's face was crumbling. First the scales on the back of his head darkened, and his fingers blackened as well. The scales were rotting where they sat on his flesh and the cracks widened even more.

"You have to reverse this," he said. "Please."

"Oh, Tenejo," Kajaro said, sounding not at all contrite. "Did you honestly think that if you came to me, having failed not one but two missions, that I'd even give you the time of day? We only listened because we thought you might, on the very off chance, have something of significance to share with us."

"They moved me . . ." Tenejo's voice crackled.

"Then I guess that's where you die," Kajaro said dispassionately.

Tenejo screamed, "No, please. Please, just . . ." And then his jaw fell off. Blood and a strange black sludge dripped from his face, and he could no longer say anything. His eyes held panic, but Kajaro continued to wave him away and clean that up.

Hal's imps finally broke through the next layer in the dome, but they'd be far too late to change this.

The shadow emerged and looked right up at the observation platform for just a second. Quinn saw a flash of red eyes, and then it, along with the entire image in front of them, was gone, leaving only Tenejo decomposing and sprawled on the floor of the dome.

"Well," Hal said, "that was unexpected."

Quinn gaped at him. "Surely that wasn't all in his head."

"No . . . it wasn't. And I'm not sure how they managed to circumvent our security."

"He's dead and we didn't learn a thing," Malakai said. "Great."

"On the contrary," Hal said, grinning. "Didn't you see the book in front of Kajaro?"

Quinn sighed. She'd been hoping she was seeing what she wanted to, being an illusion and all. "Yeah . . ."

"Don't be so glum, Librarian."

She rolled her eyes. "Whyever not? It's lightyears away."

"Ah," Hal said, as the platform began to move back down to safety. "But now we know who has *Ririn's Dimensional Distortion Through Sacrificial Means*. And knowing is half the battle."

SENSE OF FOREBODING

"He seemed very aware," Quinn said, once they had settled back in the room they'd been in prior to visiting Tenejo. She was still trying to wrap her head around the fact that he'd dissolved before they could get to him.

"He did, rather," Hal said, not exactly paying attention to her.

"You seem distracted," Quinn said, not that she could blame him.

"I just had a prisoner I assumed I would have for a very long time disintegrate in front of me through some sort of subliminal magic implanted in his mind." Hal sounded perturbed. "This is unprecedented. A level of manipulation I hadn't thought anyone outside of myself and several of my siblings capable of."

"Could it have been like the mind bomb I had?" Quinn asked.

"From the reports I've read from Milaro, no. We scanned for exactly such a thing since he was sent by Kajaro in the first place. That's the problem." Hal really did seem quite disturbed by the fact. "Whatever this is, it's not something I've encountered before, and that makes me more uneasy than I like to admit."

Quinn couldn't blame him. After all, it wasn't every day you got to watch someone be vaporized by their own imagination with afterimages of people who were too close to real. "Could they have known he might end up here and have prepared just such a surprise in case?"

Hal stopped and stared at her. He blinked a couple of times. "It's possible. If you end up here, people know they'll talk. However, our methods aren't widely known. Just by certain . . ." He frowned. "There are several ways they could have found out our process. I'll look into it."

"I hope it's not widespread," Quinn said.

"You and me both, Librarian." Hal's face brightened. "But at least we know where the book is."

"Well," Malakai drawled, "we already knew approximately where the book *was*."

"Now we have a more definitive location for you. Are you happy?" Hal asked.

Malakai shrunk back just a bit. "I was just saying . . ."

"Well, don't *just say*, Malakai. Do be a little bit more like your grandfather in that instance." Uncle Hal was a hundred percent irritable.

Malakai scowled, and Quinn wisely turned away and changed the subject. "Since he seems to have been influenced by his imagination, what did you think about the shadowed figure pretty much making eye contact with us?"

"Another disturbing factor." Hal sighed. "Along with the fact that I still need to find the culprit who decided to poison your tea, this has been a trying couple of days."

As if directly on cue, another satyr walked through the door. He was shorter, kind of stocky, still taller than Quinn, at about six feet tall. And he was completely black except for blood-red eyes. He snapped his heels together and cleared his throat. "Reporting for duty."

"Ah, yes, Opier, thank you for coming. I trust you have some news for me."

Quinn didn't think that anybody facing that question was going to say no, not with Hal's current mood. He was pissed, and she swore she could see steam rising off him. Anybody in the same room, planet, nebula could probably tell Hal was currently pissed off. It radiated like an aura.

Opier cleared his throat. "We believed we'd detained the culprit, but . . ." They paused and looked decidedly uncomfortable and marginally terrified.

"Oh," Quinn said, "did they implode?"

Opier looked quite relieved at her comment. "Yes, Librarian, they imploded, but it was extremely messy. They may as well have just exploded. It would have been easier on us all."

Quinn sighed and Hal put his hand over his face. "So there's no way to question them. Is any of the brain intact, Opier?"

"There are several stems that we do believe our alchemists can extract some remaining information from."

"And you've already delivered it to Haya?" Hal's tone was still dangerous.

"Yes, Haya already has the . . ." Opier searched for some way to express what he had to say. "Shall we say, the specimens, the remnants, what we have of the corpse in its entirety?"

"Excellent." Hal sighed and began pacing the room again. "That's about all we can do right now. I want as much information as she can glean as soon as possible, preferably five minutes ago."

"Your wish is our command." Opier gave a small bow.

"What have I told you about that?" Hal barked out.

"You know, we do it just because we love you, sire." Opier grinned before dashing out of the door.

Hal's face looked like a thundercloud. Quinn scooched to the side, sitting as far as she could on the couch from where he stood closer to the door. Hal took in a deep breath and then laughed. It was a huge, guffawing sound that seemed to bounce around the entire room.

"Well," he said, "this is *not* how I pictured this day going. I have several things to investigate. Librarian, I do apologize. I had set aside two whole days for you. I want you to practice the exercises I've already given you. And Eric"—he beckoned to the perpetually sulking imp—"teach her how to access, control, and dampen the fire within her. You could have done this at the Library; it wouldn't have been hard."

"You didn't give me explicit permission. They're imp and satyr techniques." Erik pouted.

Hal raised an eyebrow. "You should know better."

Eric scowled. "Fine, I'll teach her."

"You know what?" Quinn was suddenly not in the mood to be handed around like a chattel that needed polishing. "Just give me a book. I'm great with books. If you"—she turned to Eric—"don't want to teach me, I don't want to learn from you. It makes for an extremely combative environment, and I'm not up to that right now. I just got poisoned, but look at me, I'm still alive and kicking. I'm pretty sure I can figure out how to teach myself fire control if you just give me a damn book."

Eric hovered back a few steps. "I apologize, Quinn, I'm a little angry, pissed off, upset that we're here . . ." he began like a broken record.

"Didn't want to come home, boo-hoo," Quinn said. "We don't always get to do what we want."

"Yeah." Hal laughed. "She's got you there. You are always in the worst mood when you come home. Stop it. You have a good life, nobody's making you fight wars, you're helping the Librarian. Half the time you don't even see your family. Do what you should do, what needs to be done. And stop whining about it, Eric."

Eric probably would have turned red if he hadn't already *been* shades of red. With that, Hal left the room, and Quinn sighed. "You know, you don't have to teach me if you really don't want to. I'll just get the book and read it. I'm pretty good at reading."

"No, he's right." Eric shot her an apologetic look. "I just—I don't like being here."

"Whyever not? It's lovely, it's pretty, and it's nice and warm. I didn't think it was going to be attractive. I thought it would be like blood and hell and lava and brimstone and death and . . ."

Eric gaped at her. "What in the cosmos did you think that for?"

"Well, because it's . . . never mind. It's one of those myths from

Earth that sort of coincides, but really doesn't. I just expected it to be different, that's all."

"Oh," he said, "well, I'm sorry we disappointed you. Let's get some of that fire handling know how into you. I'll teach you how to sense the fire within, and how to draw it out without hurting yourself and others around you."

"Sounds like a plan."

It would be a few hours before Hal returned. Eric hovered over to where Quinn was sitting while Malakai stood guard at the door.

"Let's get started," Eric said with a smile. "This, right here"—he focused on projecting something toward Quinn's mind—"is a fire core. You have one, but it might look subtly different given that we're not the same species. You have to look inward to find it."

Quinn nodded and closed her eyes to get a better feel of her inner self.

It took quite a while for Quinn to grasp that she had her own core, like a magical swirling vortex inside of her. It was tiny, nothing like, you know, a big world-swallowing vortex in the sky, but it was there, and there were tiny star like elements that swirled inside of it.

"So this," Quinn asked, "is a fire core?"

"Technically," came the reply.

Quinn pondered for a few moments. "Why haven't I noticed it before?"

"It's likely only recently begun to emerge from dormancy. It's always been there, but fire affinities require a catalyst to truly ignite, or an official coming-of-age ritual." Eric paused long enough to chuckle.

"Coming-of-age?" Quinn cocked her head to one side, curious.

"Ah, yes. For whenever species feel their offspring are ready to handle the species-specific powers they possess." He smiled sort of wistfully. "Anyway, you need to expel some of that energy, whether you transfer it into other abilities or whatever. You just can't let it expand and overwhelm you, or you'll, you know, accidentally set things on fire up to and including yourself."

"Why didn't the Library tell me this?" Quinn asked, curious.

"Probably at the time, it was minuscule and not a danger. The ignition required to incinerate the Library books was, but a blip compared to the power you pulled out against the golem." Eric let that sink in before continuing. "So much has happened since you ignited that golem that the Library probably didn't scan you as closely as it should have."

Quinn took in a deep breath. She could do this. She was fine. Everything was fine. It'd all stay fine.

She wasn't going to set things on fire.

"It's okay, Quinn. We'll get through this." Eric's tone was actually gentle for once.

"I know. I'm just . . ." She breathed and focused inward. The swirling mass of tiny nebula inside her definitely didn't give her a sense of calm or security. *Nebula* was probably the wrong way to describe it, but it was as close as she could get for now. She frowned. "Okay, I've got this."

Closing her eyes and casting her gaze inward, she basically massaged the little thing until it was smaller and smaller. While doing so, she siphoned the power from it as gently as possible and infused it into other things, like her mind-shielding barrier, strengthening it, helping it to organically adapt to any threats around her. She wasn't entirely sure how she understood to do that, although she'd read like eighteen different books on mind magic. But it was an instinctive thing to keep herself safe and thereby keep everybody else safe who spent time with her.

Not to mention protecting the Librarian portion. That was the first place she wanted any excess energy to go. The next place was the shielding that she always kept up on her body. She fused the powers together so that it could pull on the fire and enhance her shielding even insofar as she extended it to protect her friends.

"That's an excellent start, Quinn," Hal said.

And Quinn opened her eyes to see Uncle Hal was back.

"Oh," she said, "did you sort everything?"

"I have some news for you. But first, Eric," the satyr turned to the imp, "excellent teaching. I wasn't expecting you to fulfill my request to that extent."

Eric shot Hal a glare. "I take my duties very seriously," he said.

"I'm well aware, but I do thank you. Anyway, it appears that when you opened the Library connection to our door when you arrived in Halschius, someone was waiting to cross over with you. They were, however, not from the Library. They came from a different sector at exactly the same moment through the door. We didn't notice them because of the condensed power surrounding both Adrito and Tenejo at the time, as well as the golems who brought it over, lending their power signature to it, and Milaro standing in the doorway probably didn't help. We are upping security as we speak, and this will not happen again. I do apologize for putting you in danger, Librarian."

"How did they get into the castle?" Malakai asked.

"Still under investigation. We believe they used some sort of memory spell or device," Hal said, the words clipped.

Quinn nodded, trying to decide how she felt about this revelation. She'd really been in danger, but not for the first time. Malakai was right. She'd been almost killed a few times now, or come close to getting seriously injured. And yet, she felt oddly calm about everything.

"Are you okay, Quinn?" Malakai said, leaning on the door, watching her intently.

"I think so," she said.

"Good. You'd tell me if you weren't?" His concern leaked into his tone.

"More than likely," she said, hoping that was enough.

Hal watched them for a moment, a small frown crinkling his eyes before he spoke. "Anyway, I apologize that you did not get a chance to speak with your attacker yourself. However, I'm confident this problem will not arise again. I'm taking measures as we speak."

"Thank you," Quinn said, and felt it. She didn't doubt him for even a second. But it wasn't like she was truly safe anywhere, until her powers grew more substantial. Right now, if she concentrated, she could feel the constant energy churning at her core. It made her understand how a being like the Library could exist with all the necessary power.

She turned to Hal. "This is this something most fire users have?"

"Yes and no," Hal said. "Yours is a little different. It's not the same as what Eric and I possess. It appears to be an accretion core, but I'd have to double check with some reference materials and the Library. The similarities are enough that I can help you gain safe control over it in lieu of the Library, who will, no doubt, assist you as soon as it is able to. Now, come, there is much to do, and you need to eat."

"Oh," Quinn said, "thank you." And she realized she was actually famished.

"Come, come, I have the dining room prepared, and I have guards at every opening." Hal clapped his hands, getting everyone's attention.

As if summoned, Opier walked into the room again. "Sire, we are ready for you now. I will escort you."

"Very well," Hal said as his guard led them out of the room. Quinn decided to walk this time. She felt stronger now. It had been half a day since she was poisoned and almost died, although they'd assured her she wouldn't have died. It was still scary.

"Are you excited? I hear food here is amazing," Malakai said. "Maybe you can ask Cook to make us some when we get home."

Hal interrupted. "I actually have food under guard for you directly from Cook. They made sure to take into account the types of food you would otherwise have gotten to try here. I think you'll be pleasantly surprised."

Quinn smiled. She did appreciate them taking precautions just in case they'd all missed something. The food was amazing. And she could tell Cook's flair was in there as well. It was much homier than she thought, very similar to a shepherd's pie, but with a tang and a spice to it that she couldn't quite place. And she knew the vegetables weren't potatoes, but they tasted like she was eating a soft, buttery potato cloud. It was delicious.

Opier disappeared when they started eating and came back about twenty minutes after they'd finished when they were having several drinks. She swirled hers in her cup, enjoying the tangy and spicy taste that lingered.

"It's been a long day," Hal announced.

Quinn found herself quite exhausted and had to agree with him. "Bed sounds like bliss," she said. And she already missed Aradie.

Hal laughed. "I'll have some exercise and maintenance methods prepared for you tomorrow, so we can get you safe for the foreseeable future."

Quinn smiled. "I'd appreciate that."

Hal nodded to Opier before speaking again. "Opier will guide you to your quarters in the guest wing. And then stand guard to make sure you remain safe."

"Thanks," Quinn said, but deep down, she couldn't shake a deep sense of foreboding.

5 6

SO MUCH FUN

THE BED WAS SURPRISINGLY COMFORTABLE, AMAZINGLY SOFT. QUINN wanted to stay nestled in its depths.

It was odd to have gone to sleep without Aradie, but the owl opted to stay back at the Library once she'd delivered Quinn, due to the heat and humidity of Halschius and something about it dampening her feathers.

Quinn also didn't have any dreams, which was the oddest sensation. Unless the rapping on the door that woke her up was, in fact, a nightmare because she didn't want to get up yet. She felt like she'd only been in bed an hour or two.

"Librarian," the voice called.

Quinn frowned. She knew that voice.

"Librarian, we need your presence, please." Undoubtable tension hummed under those words.

Quinn shuffled out of bed, far more drained than she would have thought possible, until she remembered the whole poisoning incident as her brain finally woke up.

"I'll be right there." She sighed. She got out of bed, pulling on clothes fast. It sounded like an urgent matter. Given they'd woken her in what felt like the middle of the night, it probably was.

"I'm coming," she said, finally pulling the door closed behind her.

Opier stood there, a frown on his face. "Terribly sorry to have woken you this early, ma'am."

"I'm not a ma'am, please," Quinn said. "That's my grandmother. What's the problem?"

"There's no problem so much as there is . . ."

"Oh," she said, suddenly completely sure. "Has Adrito woken up?"

"Yes. We need to head there right now," he said. "We will join Hal and the others for observational purposes."

"Lead the way." Quinn dutifully followed Opier down and joined Malakai, who waited at the top of the stairs. Quinn chose to float down the spiral again because it was much easier than accidentally losing her balance and falling down the stairs to land flat on her face at the bottom, potentially breaking limbs in the process. She knew all too well how coordinated she was when she was still three-quarters asleep.

She yawned, covering her mouth. "I'm sorry, I am so tired. I didn't think I'd be this tired."

"You were poisoned yesterday. Your body's doing all sorts of healing things," Malakai said.

"But didn't I heal it?" Quinn asked, somewhat confused. "Like, didn't we actually heal it?"

"Well, yes, we healed it, as you so eloquently put it, but at the same time, your body still needs to recover. Healing uses your body's energy, Quinn. You've got to understand that."

"Well, I do, on a technical basis." She shrugged. "I just haven't been poisoned before. I didn't realize healing it would take so much out of me."

Finally, they arrived back down in what Quinn dubbed the illusion chamber. Hal was tapping his foot. "We need to hurry. I thought I told you to make sure they got here as soon as possible."

"They were asleep, sire," Opier said.

Hal sighed. "Sleep is for the weak. But I guess you *were* poisoned yesterday."

"That's what I keep telling her," Malakai said.

Eric finally fluttered down to join them. He tossed them all a withering glare.

"You're not a morning person, are you?" Quinn said.

"No, Librarian. I am not a morning person. I'm also not a still the middle of the night person. This is just typical of that Esposian to piss me off. Waking me up at this hour."

"Yes, I'm sure he did it because of you. Positively aimed for it," Hal drawled, "Now hurry up."

This time, the platform took them over to the left-hand back corner. This dome was substantially smaller, perhaps because the Esposian was smaller Quinn wasn't entirely sure, but its size made it easier to observe.

"Is that blood?" Quinn asked.

"Yes, it seems our Esposian friend is quite violent," Hal said, completely detached from the carnage in the dome.

Quinn shuddered. "Are those the imaginary remains of guards that he disemboweled?" She asked. There was nothing else it could be wrapped around the throat of one, but Quinn couldn't . . . She reached over the side and retched. Nothing came out, but the gagging wouldn't stop.

"That's just . . . you didn't know he was that violent?" Eric asked.

"No, I didn't. He took control of a stone golem, which I then somehow melted into lava. He didn't seem this, well, malevolent. I don't understand. Even when he was speaking to me at the end, I just thought he was fanatic."

"Some of them hide it better than others." Hal shrugged. "He is misguided. Although, you know, if you're in an echo chamber and everybody agrees with you, then you think you're right. Which is what's happened to him. Frankly, you could say it happened to us. We all agree with each other too, right?"

"Well, yes, but I also agree that chaos can have its uses when it's strictly monitored and carefully used," Quinn said. "I mean, we've all used it to some extent. You did to build this amazing feat of architecture."

Hal smiled. "You're a lot more observant than I give you credit for."

"I get that all the time," Quinn said. "Anyway, no, he wasn't initially this violent. He may have been trying to crush us like bugs under his feet with the massive construct he created. So I guess I should have assumed." Quinn sighed.

Malakai patted her shoulder. "There, there, Quinn. It's okay."

She shot him a withering glance.

"I knew he destroyed the city and, therefore, probably killed thousands of his citizens. I just didn't combine the two of them from where he got the materials for the golem from." Hal turned his full attention back to the dome.

"I guess he's always had violent tendencies," Quinn muttered as she watched. A tiny deeply red, slimy in appearance fae fluttered around the dome, darting here and there. "Oh, my gosh. Did he *bathe* in the blood?"

"Well, it sort of sprayed everywhere," Hal said. "He didn't hold back."

Quinn looked at the bits of viscera hanging from the Esposian's mouth. He no longer appeared civilized. He looked feral, as if something had taken control of his mind. Adrito piloted like he was an animal needing to eat to survive.

"Will he be okay?" Quinn asked.

Hal simply shot her a look and said, "You want him to be okay?"

She sighed. "I just—he looks pitiful. I feel sorry for him."

"Don't go feeling sorry for him. This is what *his* mind came up with, Quinn. This is how, if he were to get free, he would treat the guards in my castle who are literally just keeping him in a room, mostly for the safety of others."

"I guess it's against his will, though."

"Of course it's against his will. But he already killed thousands upon thousands of people. Should we just let him go?"

She knew the answer. "No. But look at him . . . how did he get so unhinged?"

That exact moment was when Adrito snarled and moved out of his imaginary jail cell. He wandered halls and suddenly came to a door. Each hall he moved through resulted in more guards being summarily ripped apart, limb from limb, body section from body section.

Shoulders and elbows at the joints, bones cracking, muscles tearing in the process. But the crack of the spine when he separated torso from hips was the worst, not to mention the viscera that came apart with it.

Quinn looked away and for several moments just couldn't look back again.

Malakai put a hand around her shoulder and gave her a quick hug. "I'll tell you when it's okay to look again."

"Thanks," she said, knowing deep within that if Adrito were to be let out again, many more hundreds of thousands maybe even millions of people would die.

The noises emanating from the dome inhabited by Adrito left little to Quinn's imagination. She couldn't quite fathom the depths of depravity he must have experienced to gnaw on bones and tear flesh apart. Suddenly, the sounds stopped.

"It's okay, Quinn. You can look again," Malakai said.

Quinn nodded and looked up. The dome's haziness had cleared slightly, leaving Adrito no longer indoors in his imagination, but instead in the dome outside his prison. It was remarkably similar to where they were, suggesting that Adrito had been aware enough during his transportation to realize he'd reached Halschius.

Or maybe it was the way the heat permeated everything even when the temperature was being controlled.

"Was he supposed to know?" Quinn asked, suddenly worried.

"Each species has their own specialties," Malakai replied. "One of the Esposians' is special awareness, because they can fly and are very sensitive to temperature changes, which you can't exactly avoid, even in stasis, when you come here."

Quinn nodded. "He knows where we brought him."

"Yes, he appears to, doesn't he? But even so, the pathways through to the jail cell weren't accurate, so his awareness isn't as heightened as it usually is. Milaro did do a good job." Hal stared at the Esposian intently.

"What exactly did he do for you?" Quinn asked.

Hal didn't take his eyes off his quarry. "Milaro set their minds at ease, so that when we got them here, it would be easier for us to instigate the process that we use to extract the information we require. We don't often have a mind mage of Milaro's caliber at our disposal, frankly. I've asked the man several hundred times to just drop everything he's doing and come and help me, but he won't do it. He said he has a kingdom to run, and now he's got the Library too."

This time, Hal laughed. "But seriously, I'm glad Milaro could prepare them to this extent. I am, however, concerned that he didn't find the trigger inside Tenejo that caused . . ."

Hal's voice petered off, and Quinn focused on the dome with him. He frowned. "That's not right," he said. This time, instead of turning to the twin imps next to him, he went to the control panel himself. "That's not—Opier, take a look." He called him over.

Quinn wisely stayed out of his way. She'd gotten the distinct impression that Hal, in a bad mood, was someone you shouldn't cross or even get in the way of. But instead, she watched as the dome fogged up, and suddenly, Adrito was standing on top of a long table in his throne room—or at least the room as it had been before he destroyed it—with several other Esposians around him, not to mention Kajaro, and two Aracnios that Quinn didn't recognize in the least.

"I made it back," he bit out.

Kajaro raised an eyebrow. "You think you made it back?"

"What do you mean by that?" Adrito's wings fluttered in irritation, still caked in blood, spattering dried bits and still wet globules all around him.

"Look around, little king. What do you see?" Kajaro's voice spoke smoothly, but not in a way Quinn would have attributed to him.

"Where's Latia?" Adrito asked, a note of panic in his voice.

Suddenly, Latia appeared beside him, but she was faded and looked injured, like she had been the last time he'd seen her. Adrito shook his head forcefully. "No, that's not right. Something's wrong."

"I told you something was wrong," Kajaro said. "When will you ever listen to me?"

"I listened to you enough," Adrito practically screeched. "You're the reason I created the golem. I destroyed my entire city because of what you told me what I should do if the Librarian arrived, and I still didn't get her."

"You're not the only one who's failed to kill the Librarian. She seems to have dumb luck on her side." Kajaro drawled the words, very different from how Quinn had ever seen him speak. She wondered if Adrito had experienced something similar to this in the real world and that he just perceived people differently in his head.

"It's not right," Hal said, practically echoing himself from earlier, not to mention Adrito. "We need to shut it down."

"If you shut it down now," Opier said, "we won't get what we want out of him. His mind will melt."

"Better that than the glitches that are appearing in the system," Hal snapped.

Quinn held up a hand. "What do you mean, glitches?" All she could think of was the Library and how vast and debilitating those glitches were proving to be. "Is it a virus?"

"No, no, it's something to do with Adrito's mind. He's not fully under. He's starting to disbelieve what he's created." Hal paused to glance over at her, must have realized how concerned it made her. "It's not a glitch in the way the Library is experiencing, but a disconnect between his brain and the projection spells in place. He's too aware. That Kajaro memory is making him too aware. The suggestion isn't taking hold like it should."

Quinn paused and looked over, whatever she'd thought to say dying on her tongue.

A hiss and a whoosh of air suddenly burst into her face, forcing her to shut her eyes. For just a second, her equilibrium shifted, close to the vertigo she'd felt when the Library first found her, and then it was all quiet.

Everyone was gone except her.

Quinn looked around slowly. It was like a rainforest, very similar to what they'd experienced when they went to retrieve the cookbook and found *Machmüller's Guide.* That's when she saw Adrito, not four feet from her, inside the dome with her.

"Oh, shit," Quinn said.

"Really?" Adrito said, happy surprise evident on his face. He sounded positively gleeful when he began to speak. "You're really here. Like really, really here. And in here I can create anything I want."

He summoned a massive pendulum, except it wasn't blunt like those on an old grandfather clock. It was sharp and apparently affixed in midair. It swung down towards Quinn, who dove out of the way, allowing her hover ability to push her farther than she'd have been able to jump without assistance. She rolled and came to a crouch on the other side.

"Oh, Librarian," Adrito said, "we are going to have so much fun."

57

A SPLIT SECOND

From where Quinn crouched on the ground, she almost thought she misheard what he'd said. Surely, he wasn't grandstanding again, not after last time. Still, that pendulum seemed quite real and very present. Testing Adrito could prove to be fatal.

Quinn couldn't afford that.

She quickly glanced around, trying to get her bearings, after all, she was quite certain that not twenty seconds prior to this she'd been standing outside of the bubble on the observation platform. She couldn't locate it through the smokey interior and realized it must have been one way viewing. Which made perfect sense.

Too much thinking was dangerous in this instance as, even condensed, she couldn't be sure what Adrito's mind was doing. She rolled out of the way of the pendulum again, only to realize it was perilously closer than last time. Her body still held definitive weakness, as she was already out of breath. Despite the healing, despite some sleep, her body hadn't fully recovered yet.

Even if the poison hadn't been capable of killing her, it had weakened her stamina.

"Why, Librarian," Adrito called out in a singsong voice as Quinn skittered behind what seemed to be a rock, even though she was fully aware it was simply an illusion. "You know I know you're there, right?"

When she didn't answer, he laughed. "You're being awfully quiet. I seem to remember you had so much to say back on Ishiposa. Do tell me what I'm doing wrong again. I'd so love to hear it."

Quinn had been in plenty of dream projections. Most of them Kajaro's fault. She could do this. There was no way she'd let him get the upper hand.

"What do *you* think you're doing wrong?" she asked and moved immediately after speaking, clouding her steps, making sure it was as difficult as possible to track her movement.

She'd hidden from Kajaro in his own mind cage; she could hide here too.

"Me?" Adrito said, his voice seemingly coming from everywhere else at once. "I'm not doing anything wrong. In fact, I'm about to do a very right thing. Something I should have done days ago, immediately once you set foot on my island, once you started messing with my people."

"I didn't mess with Eugea. I took her out of the torment you *deliberately* inflicted on her!" Quinn snapped, despite her resolution to remain calm until she'd managed to figure out a plan of escape. She moved again, as soundlessly as she could manage, tiptoeing, gently sliding, and reinforcing the illusions to hold up. She had no idea how this magic or technology worked, but it felt sort of holographic, like she could only hope it was controlled from an outside source.

"Eugea was a part of a greater whole, working toward a common goal. You don't even comprehend what you did!" His voice screeched loudly and sent shivers down Quinn's spine.

And yet . . . she wanted to know more about what he was saying. There was something in his voice. This feverish sort of reverence. She didn't understand where it came from or what it meant, but she needed to find out. There was something about it, as if her gut was trying to tell her this was all a hint. If she understood his motivations, if she realized exactly what he was saying, then she'd be just one step closer to understanding this whole entire mess.

Quinn pushed and guessed more wildly than she ever had. "Of course I comprehend what you did! You've been weaving your very own people into one big sacrificial net in order to fuel chaotic energy into overpowering the Library's filtration systems."

There, that sounded about as wild as she could manage.

For a few seconds, complete and utter silence followed, leaving only the sound of the Esposian hovering as white noise.

Adrito's wing sound changed ever so slightly. When he finally spoke, his voice was filled with suspicion. "How . . . there's no way that can be a guess. Who told you?"

Quinn blinked rapidly and kept moving so he couldn't home in on her voice. She could only distort it so much with some help from healing manuals to use vibration on her vocal cords. How could she have been even close to right? That was the most ludicrous and far-fetched thing she'd been able to muster based on the very loose information she'd gathered while healing Eugea.

Then again, the universe was magical.

As if he heard that question, Adrito continued. "Who told you about the sacrificial net? Surely you haven't captured one of us?"

His voice sounded closer, and Quinn pushed down the panic fluttering in her chest. She had to remain calm. They needed as much information as they could get. And apparently, he didn't count himself as being captured for some reason. Maybe he wasn't as aware as he thought.

Doing her best to keep her fear under control, she spoke again. "Now, why would I tell you how I know? Maybe you don't know everyone around you as well as you thought."

"Rubbish, Librarian. Now you're just making things up." His voice was way too close for comfort now. "Just who did you capture to reveal such an integral part of the plan? The rest of your guess is wildly off, but this . . ."

Not for the first time, Quinn wished she already knew how to teleport more than just to wildly escape something, but was certain it would be quite messy if she attempted to wing it. She didn't answer him this time, and concentrated instead on trying to find another place to hide, trying to get away from where she knew he hovered. All the while attempting to come up with a plausible reason for her belief other than I added two and two and got four.

"The net won't work, you know," she said, directing the sound to bounce off the sides of the dome.

They needed information. He seemed chatty as long as he thought he was playing with his prey. She infused her shielding with more power, pulling on her cosmicisodracus heritage just a tad and hoping it didn't backfire. All she had to do was outlast him and coax out everything she could.

It was a good thing she could out-stubborn most living things.

Adrito's laugh echoed throughout the area again. "And what makes you say that?" he asked, his voice dripping with slime.

"The net won't withstand the chaotic elements you want to feed through it." With everything she'd read, and how chaos ate through most things, Quinn was quite certain of that.

"Of course it won't, but it'll last long enough to guide it right to where we want it."

She could hear the malevolence in his voice, the vitriol almost dripped from his words. And suddenly clarity washed over her, and she knew exactly what they intended. With all the books they had, all the dimensionally related books . . .

"You're not going to . . ." she murmured, hardly realizing she'd just spoken out loud.

"Oh yes we are," Adrito's voice came softly from right behind her.

Quinn darted forward and sought refuge behind a series of rocks. Damn it, she'd got surprised by his agreement and dropped her guard for a second. Reinforcing her mind and body, she grimaced as the rocks around her all began to dissipate slowly.

She lashed out with a blade of wind, directly at his face, but Adrito batted it away as if it were nothing. Hers wasn't as potent as Nishpa's or Geneva's, but she'd never initiated it before.

"Really, Quinn," Adrito said, as he floated menacingly toward her.

"What did you think you were doing? Did you sincerely forget it's my imagination this entire area was created from? Everything in this dome is powered by my imagination. I can put the rock there, and I can make it vanish. Took me a while to figure it out, though."

He flexed his hand and the other rocks near her disintegrated into nothing, into pinpoints of light before vanishing.

Quinn tried desperately to figure out how to keep him villain monologuing for long enough to buy her some time. Her brain darted in and out of possibilities, dismissing them as fast as she thought of them. Even so, she made sure to watch her steps. With uneven ground, going down even once wasn't ideal.

Not only was she trying to buy time for the others to break through, but she wanted to get something from this. She was tired of operating in the dark.

Adrito, still well within her line of vision, stretched his arms over his head, joined them together, and cracked his knuckles. "I could get used to this. Controlling all of my surroundings with my mind. And I'll be able to, did you know that? Once chaos has chosen me, has realized my potential, and leant me its power. Then . . . then I'll be able to make anything a reality that I want to. Create anything I dream of."

"You could do that now," Quinn started, but Adrito screamed.

"No! I can't. No one but the Library can do everything! Don't you understand? We're all limited. Restricted *because* of the Library! It holds all that glorious magic power hostage! But chaos . . . no, it allows us to reach our full potential once we overcome the trials."

She could see his eyes and how they swirled. Fanaticism rolled off him in waves.

Trying to antagonize him as little as possible, Quinn kept her voice as steady as she could. "What trials?" She made sure her voice was small so as not to pull him out of his strange half trance.

Adrito only half looked at her, almost through her, a puzzled expression on his face. "Surely you understand the trials?"

She shook her head, wondering if he even saw her. "No." She hoped, needed, wanted him to tell her all about these trials.

Adrito spun in the air, arms outstretched. "But it is the most wonderful of chances. Once chaos is abundant, once we have eliminated the Library and thus its purpose, chaos will be free to find those of us who are not only loyal, but strong. It will choose those of us who can withstand the onslaught, and we will be baptized in fire, and reborn as the strong. The leaders. The blessed."

"That's amazing," Quinn said, and didn't elaborate that it was the most delusional load of crap she'd heard in a while, because that would get her nowhere. Instead, she wracked her brain for questions to ask, for the most important question to ask. "Who is we?"

He flew right up to her, where she stood, not having moved from where she'd been behind the now vanished boulders. His tiny face pushed close to hers, and she could smell a strange sense of rot about him. Not from his breath, but more from his entire being. There was a reason his coloring was so sickly. Something had triggered decay in his body. Perhaps his contact with chaotic magic was already too much to save him.

Not that she'd want to rescue someone like him after he'd already killed tens of thousands of his own people.

His eyes grew impossibly large for just a second before returning to normal. "We is us. All of us. Every single one of the Sölem."

Quinn didn't interject. She didn't dare interrupt the current look of contemplation on his face. She held her breath until he continued speaking. In fact, she didn't even blink.

His eyes grew wide again and something slithered in front of the iris, just for a split second, like there was a foreign body in his eyes. "We are already enlightened. We see the restrictions for what they are, a feeble attempt to control us all and to hoard the magic for yourselves. To restrict the universe instead of letting it grow freely, instead of letting it devour what it needs so that it might become greater. You? Are just the fodder so the rest of us can be whole."

He paused, blinking rapidly, a wave of confusion covering his face . . . followed by fear. His body convulsed ever so slightly, as if he was about to have a fit.

Quinn'd had a high school friend with a seizure disorder and it often began that way. She moved slightly, ignoring the pain that shot through her knees at having stood rigidly still for so long.

But Adrito shook himself out of it before she could reach him. "Do not come so close to me!" He screamed at her, sharp teeth bared as spittle flew from his lips.

Quinn could practically smell the fear. Had something been triggered by an outside source? She backed away, slowly, trying to hold out her hands in a way to show she meant no harm.

"No," he said, looking at his own hands and not at her as smoke began to rise from them. Then he turned his gaze to Quinn. "I'm supposed to be one of them. I *am* one of the chosen. They promised! All I have to do is kill you! All I have to do is sever your link to the Library and make you all pay. It's so simple!"

His wings fluttered frantically, and Quinn backed up even more, noticing now that everything around them had fallen away, and she could hear a strange scratching from far above them. She hoped it was the others and not some weird sort of wasp trying to peck its way through to her. Though she wouldn't dismiss the latter as a possibility, since her luck seemed to be going that way recently.

"Take a breath," she said, trying her best to sooth the homicidal Esposian.

But he snarled at her, even as smoke began to rise from his wings. "You're right here. I can end you and fulfill my contract. Chaos will cleanse me in his name, and you will no longer stand in our way."

"And whose name is that?" Quinn asked gently, backing up a few more steps. The smoke appeared to be hindering Adrito's wings. He was starting to lose his equilibrium.

But at her question, he looked up, confusion plain on his face. "He that is all . . . he that was there at the very beginning."

The smoke was thicker now, consuming him, eating away at his wings. The sadness and confusion on his face almost made Quinn feel sorry for him. Except for the fact that he found a momentary burst of speed and was almost upon her before she could blink.

Quinn held up her hand, reinforcing her shielding on them while she reached out with her ice-creation affinity her only thoughts to encase him and stop whatever was trying to devour him before it spread further.

At the same time, something whizzed through the air. Her ice stasis hit him at the same instant an arrow impacted his side, sending him plummeting to the ground.

He hit the ground with a thud, the arrow, blood, and fae frozen by her ice-casing as he lay at her feet unconscious.

5 8

ODDLY DISCONCERTING

QUINN LEANED DOWN, EXAMINING THE ICE-ENCASED ESPOSIAN NOW frozen in time. Not even blood flowed out from him. He was simply suspended in a clear casing. She looked at her hands, relieved that the plan she'd envisioned in her mind appeared to have worked. Ice mixed with her shielding meshed well together. She'd wanted to protect him from the damage that was obviously beginning to affect him.

She hadn't been close enough to Tenejo to help in time. But Adrito had been inches from her.

And they weren't going to get answers if everyone they captured to question kept disintegrating before they could interrogate them.

"Quinn." Malakai grabbed her arm and tugged gently, looking her over for any signs of injury. "Are you okay?"

She nodded thoughtfully, still trying to get her head around the logistics of the disintegration. "You shot the arrow, right?" she stated more than asked, not even looking at Malakai.

"Yes." He walked around her slowly, making sure she was okay. "Are you hurt anywhere? What did he do to you? We couldn't see."

The slight frantic note to his voice caused her to turn and look at him. She waved his concern away with a smile. "I'm not hurt, I'm okay. He was just . . . well, he wasn't exactly being clear, but now I know for certain there's someone behind all this crap who isn't Kajaro. And . . ."

Hal finally made it to where they were, a scowl on his face. "You should have let me disable the dome. This will take forever to repair." His commanding tone of disapproval had no effect on Malakai at all.

Instead, the elf glowered at him. "If I'd waited any longer, she could have been killed, or seriously injured at the very least."

"I wouldn't have been injured. I'm not that weak, thanks," Quinn muttered dryly. Hal seemed to ignore her statement.

"That's beside—" But Hal paused, looking at the Esposian with a frown. "What happened to him?"

The satyr commander squatted down and poked at the shielding surrounding him with one finger. A soft knock resonated from it, but nothing changed. Not the casing, not the pose Adrito was in, and not the complete and utter lack of bleeding. "How in Halschius did you manage that?" he asked, looking straight up at Quinn.

She shrugged. "I was just trying to preserve him and stop the disintegration from escalating. Just like Kajaro, his body started to break apart. In his case, it was more like when we fought the tree. How those five Esposians suddenly just fell apart."

Malakai frowned. "That was one of the worst deaths I've seen, and you halted his disintegration?"

"Well, it's what I was trying to help with when you shot him with an arrow," she said pointedly.

Malakai had the good grace to look sheepish. "In my defense, I was trying to keep you safe."

Quinn chuckled. "Goal achieved, even though I think I believe I managed quite well myself." She paused before speaking softly. "Thanks. Again."

"No problem. I'll just have to train you harder."

She nodded, most of her attention back on Adrito. "What can we do with him?" she asked Hal.

He shrugged. "Not much. I don't understand the intricacies of how you've done what you've done. What led you to even contemplate this?"

She shrugged. "I don't know. I mean, when I felt a malevolent presence near us on Ishiposa Isle, I extended my shielding around my whole party. Doing so kept them, and me, safe from whatever it was. I just did it instinctively. This was more . . . I wanted to freeze the damage so it couldn't proceed. Combining my shielding and ice together made logical sense."

Hal's eyes narrowed. "Sort of like you injured Kajaro with ice, freed the book from the possessed tree, stopped Tenejo from wreaking havoc in the Library, cured Eugea, and melted a golem?"

"Not to mention shot down a whole flock of miasma drones," Malakai inserted cheerfully.

Quinn gave him a withering glance. "Yes, just like I 'just did' those things."

"You realize that makes you unpredictable and a possible danger to yourself and everyone around you," Hal said, his stern face back on. He waved the thought away. "Hold that thought for now. Opier?"

"Yes, sire?" the shorter satyr asked.

"Carefully gather him up, check him for life signs, and let's see exactly what feat it is our Librarian has managed this time around." He glanced around at everyone, and it was only then that Quinn realized Eric was conspicuously absent.

"I've never hurt anyone," Quinn grumbled. "And most of the time my brain does the calculations so fast, I'm moving before I realize I've thought of a potential solution."

Hal let out a sigh. "I'm not angry with you. I'm irritated by the set of circumstances we find ourselves in. I am, however, not very good with communication when it's not a direct command. Follow me back and we'll see if we can't sort all of this out. It's high time I gave you an examination."

Quinn nodded, even though it felt like a bowling ball hit the bottom of her stomach. She tried to make herself feel better by convincing herself that the universe needed the Librarian and, therefore, her, but it didn't really do any good. She steeled herself against the journey back up top.

Hal might be a lot of things, but she was absolutely positive he wasn't a spy. It wasn't his fault he was named after a killer computer.

Back up in the reception room they'd used previously, Quinn sank into the couch, suddenly tired again.

"What happened in there?" Hal asked, quite gently.

Quinn gave them a run down, making sure they knew she'd managed to disguise where she was by practically throwing and modulating her voice, not to mention obfuscating her whereabouts with shielding and other methods.

"Your body acts instinctively when you're in danger," Hal muttered half to himself.

"Pretty much." Quinn suddenly felt ill. The images of her accident with her parents kept flooding her mind again. It wasn't a nice sensation. She didn't want to recall those memories.

But she also couldn't deny the specific pattern that emerged. In the case that Quinn didn't know how to save herself, it appeared her specific design stepped in and took over. Her heritage had saved her repeatedly, and a few of those times, also saved others by proxy.

"Anything else?" Hal asked, studying her face as her thoughts rampaged through her head.

"It's oddly disconcerting how much of what I've done is just a fail-safe." She didn't like this sudden realization that she had so little control over herself. Sure, she'd chosen to remain in the Library, she'd chosen to be this magical link between the Library and the rest of the universe.

But this autonomy thing? That wasn't okay. Taking it from her . . .

She looked up to find Mal standing in front of her, a frown on his face. "You know you can't be angry at an innate ability that saves your life, right?"

Quinn blinked. When he put it that way, it sounded almost childish. "But I want to make my own choices."

"What? To die because you can't react quick enough yet?"

His words were cutting, but they needed to be. It managed to slice through the momentary lapse of Quinn's steely resolve. It ripped away the self-pity she felt and replaced it with strength. "That's a good point." And if she really thought about it, the ability allowed her to see the possible paths she needed to take with her power in order to get to the solution they needed.

So technically, she guessed she *did* have a choice.

"I know we sometimes forget," Malakai continued, his expression grave and nothing like the cheeky friend she'd come to know and care for, "that you've only been here a bit over three months, right? In that time, you've had to realize that the universe is full of magic, that you have magic yourself, that you are one of the keys that feeds magic to the entire universe, and that you have a new home. Not to mention your heritage, your history revelations."

She kept nodding at each new incident he brought up. There'd been a lot going on ever since she got there. So much. And there was still so much for her to learn. So much for her to absorb. Knowledge and experience wise. "Yeah, I know."

"We sometimes forget that, Quinn. Those of us who are not you." He stepped closer and put his hands gently on her shoulders, giving them a light squeeze of encouragement. "But you should never forget that. You're not allowed to let yourself forget that. You've overcome, learned, and accomplished so much . . . don't sell yourself short."

Quinn nodded and then paused. Malakai was suppressing a laugh. She scowled. "I thought you were being serious."

He tried to fend her off, laughing full-throated now. "I am serious, it's just . . ." He paused, dancing out of her way slightly, but also to regain his breath. "I said don't sell yourself short . . . like you can help it."

And peals of laughter started again.

Quinn couldn't help but join in. The expression allowed her to let go of some of her nerves, and most of her fears. Then she grinned. "Has no one told you?"

"Told me what?" Malakai made as if to brush a tear of laughter away.

"Told you that when I fully come into my powers, I'll be able to adjust my appearance." She winked at him, feeling much better. "Thanks. I needed that."

Hal cleared his throat. "I'm glad you've got a good training partner in each other, but you also need to make sure you stay aware of the surrounding dangers. Understood?"

After they nodded emphatically, Hal clapped his hands. "Excellent. Because we have a lot to do." He clapped his hands, and first Opier appeared followed by three other satyrs slightly taller than he was, who were pushing carts. There were books placed on each of them. About ten on each.

Quinn raised an eyebrow. "Did you just borrow a heap of books?"

Hal shrugged. "Technically, no. We just removed them from the Library because you can't borrow right now. But you're the Librarian so I'm pretty sure that's a loophole."

"You stole Library books," she said flatly.

"Potayto, potahto. You're practically a piece of the Library, so technically the Library still has the books, right?"

Quinn laughed.

"Anyway, it's what I sent Eric to do once I realized you'd been sucked into that dome. I still don't know what magic trick Adrito used in order to pull you into his manifested dream-state, but it's under investigation." Hal's brow creased with a frown, and Quinn could tell he was truly upset by the invasion.

About the failure of all his security measures.

"For your protection and all of ours, we need to get you up to speed. This will do for now, but shortly, as soon as we've dealt with some of this immediate threat, you will need to absorb everything you can get your hands on."

Quinn nodded gravely. "Do I read these or absorb?" she asked.

Hal watched her closely for several seconds before breaking out in a genuine smile. "I see you've realized that only absorbing the books isn't always the correct option. However"—he held up a finger to forestall any comments—"right now, expediency is paramount, and thus, I've only taken books I consider vital to your survival."

Quinn nodded, and couldn't help but feel relief at Hal taking charge like this. She wondered why others hadn't, but then she remembered the sheer number of books the Library and Milaro had suggested to her, not to mention she also frequently sought out very specific books depending on her mood.

"I have twelve healing tomes for you. While you were fully capable of healing Eugea, you lack the awareness to do it deliberately every time. By absorbing this following pile, you should be able to execute that precise *Mental Chaotic Fortitude Abolition* that you quite literally managed to pull out of thin air, and you'll be able to create your manual for others to learn from once you do understand it to a higher degree."

"Wait, I need to write a manual?" she asked, confounded. No one had mentioned that yet.

He blinked at her. "Of course. You founded the specific principal, the initial affinity. Thus, you are responsible for sharing it and figuring out all of the adjacent and required affinities to trigger it. Don't worry, after everything is organized with the Library, you'll have plenty of time for this."

Quinn felt a wee bit overwhelmed, but she nodded her head. The books were there for her to absorb right now. She could easily do it. Her energy levels were replenishing as fast as usual.

"With me so far?" Hal asked kindly.

She nodded.

"I know it's a lot, but right now we have to strike before they learn how strong you are. I have a sneaking suspicion there's something in the heads or bodies of all of this Sölem's members that gives their leadership feedback of some sort. I'll know more after we continue the investigation." Hal paused, a thoughtful look on his face.

"Do you think they know about me?" Quinn asked.

"Perhaps, but I want you to be stronger before they can be certain, so that even if they think you're at one level, you're actually even tougher." Hal paused and rifled through the book stacks. "Excellent. This pile here is for shielding. You seem to have a proclivity for protection shielding—for yourself and those you wish to protect. We'll use that and strengthen what you can do with it. The other two piles on that last cart are for fire and ice. You must wield both with confidence."

"Sounds like a plan," she said, even though she was so tired she felt weak at the knees. "Do I start now?"

"Yes. I have you for another day before I must send you back, and I plan to get all of these absorbed. Don't worry, I've sent for the appropriate food from Cook as well."

She eyed the piles and suddenly really missed Aradie and Lynx.

"I'll stay right with you," Malakai reassured her, as if he could read her mind.

"I should hope so," she murmured under her breath. But it did make her feel slightly at ease.

"Then what are you waiting for?" Hal asked, his patience obviously on about a par with her own. "They're not going to absorb themselves."

She sat down on the couch and lifted the first healing book off the cart. "Um, I was advised not to absorb more than five a night."

Hal waved his hand, as if he was waving away the concern. "We have medical staff on hand, and a mixture of beginner and intermediate tomes. It'll be hard, and exhausting, but we'll take care of you so you can do what you must."

Quinn held his gaze for several seconds before slowly nodding. He'd take care of her like the grumpy grandad he seemed to be.

Absorbing the first one didn't hurt.

Frankly, she'd gotten so used to the pain, most of them didn't hurt anymore. The air rushed up, ruffling her hair as the information flooded her mind. "This is a lot of books," she said after *Sherman's Understanding of Multiplanar Healing Applications* was absorbed.

"It is. But it's necessary to make you stronger, faster," Hal said matter-of-factly. "We'll focus on your undeniable strengths and make you temporarily bulletproof."

"And what happens when they invent a new type of projectile?" she asked.

Hal shrugged. "By then we'll have you ready for it too."

Quinn nodded. She liked that plan.

She reached for the next book and started the absorption process all over again.

5 9

FEELING HOPEFUL

QUINN FLEXED HER HAND AND STARED AT IT FOR A FEW MOMENTS before turning to double check with Hal for the fifteenth time. "Are you sure you can handle Adrito's encasing?"

"I've been here for eons; I think I can handle a stasis-frozen fairy." Hal raised an eyebrow, but his smile softened the stern tone. "Don't forget the exercises I taught you. Make them habit, you-can-do-in-your-sleep habit. And don't forget what you've learned."

"Hard to forget what you practically punched into my head," Quinn grumbled, giving him a resentful glare. Her hands were cool, as if ice encased them, but it had much more to do with her controlling the heat than trying to combat it.

"All for your own good." Hal gave a bow with a flourish and grinned. "Once again, I thank you for my gifts."

Quinn smiled and nodded once, curtly. "See you soon."

She turned without further ado and placed her hand against the door. "Library, I need you," she muttered, and a pang of sadness in her chest told her they weren't just empty words. For days now, she'd been suppressing her worry for Lynx and the Library, and now they were finally headed back.

Quinn stepped over the threshold after Malakai and Eric had

already crossed through, bringing the books back with them. There was a fraction of a second where things around her shifted, and then she stepped in through her office doorway. It made her feel a little melancholy. She missed entering through the big double doors.

But she wasn't ready for the bustle of people and noise yet. Her head felt stuffy and full, and while she knew that'd dissipate in a couple of days, she wanted time to orient herself.

Library? she asked in her head. But there was no immediate response, meaning that most of its bandwidth was still being used. "Shouldn't they be done by now?" she asked no one in particular, feeling disgruntled.

"Quinn?" Malakai placed a gentle hand on her shoulder. "They'll be done when they're done, and I'm quite certain we'd have heard something if anything had gone wrong. Frankly, if something was wrong with the Library, you, as the Librarian, would know regardless how far away you might be."

She nodded, trying to squash her worry and not think about the whole Adrito situation. Hal would find what they needed. She hoped. "I know that deep down, but that doesn't change the fact that mental silence from the Library is eerie as hell."

He shrugged and flashed her a grin. "Nothing I can do about that, but we can—"

"Librarian!" Dottie trotted into the room, her voice light and airy. From what Quinn could tell, she was in a very, very good mood. "Welcome back!" If she'd have had eyes, they would have been shining.

Quinn couldn't help but smile in response, despite her cloudy head. "It's good to be back. I breathe so much easier here." The pressure of the heat and the atmosphere in Halschius had been almost suffocating.

"We're so happy to see you. Now, we've—" But that's as far as Dottie got.

Aradie shot into the room, pulled up right in front of Quinn with a massive blast of air, and promptly settled in her place on Quinn's shoulder. She then hooted softly as if to say, *All is well, you may carry on.* Quinn reached up to scritch her neck.

Dottie cleared her throat, or voice-box, or whatever it was that helped her speak, and continued. "We've had some very interesting returns while you were gone."

"Oh?" Quinn said, curious. "What do you mean by interesting?"

At that moment Geneva swooped into the room, positively sparkling. Her golden hair shone as if Rumpelstiltskin had woven it. "Interesting as in the number of books we need for the next two branches to open!"

"That's not fair!" Dottie wailed. "I was telling her. You promised I could tell her."

Geneva shrugged and grinned, much more confident than she'd been before the whole Ishiposa Isle incident. "You were taking too long. I wanted to get the good news to her as soon as possible. You had your chance."

"I'll remember that," Dottie grumbled.

Quinn could practically imagine the fae sticking out her tongue at the bench. But Geneva did no such thing, she simply smiled smugly and continued.

"Excellent, why don't we move into the foyer and . . ." Quinn's voice trailed off.

Milaro's voice spoke smoothly into her mind. *Welcome back. Excellent timing. Did you want to come and talk with us before we head down to wake them up?*

Be right there. You're in the observation room?

Milaro didn't answer in words, but Quinn got the distinct impression of an affirmative answer. "Sorry to interrupt this. I promise I'll come and go over possible new branches once I've taken care of the Library."

"Of course!" Dottie said, somehow giving the appearance of standing straighter than she usually did.

Geneva inclined her head. "We'll see you soon."

"Hey," Quinn said as she was about to leave the room. "Is Jasper here?"

Geneva shook her head. "Not right now. She left a bit earlier and will be back tomorrow, I believe."

Quinn nodded. "Thanks." She headed out toward the observation room. Aradie cooing at her like she was gently berating the Librarian for having been away for so long.

"Nothing I could do about it, girl," Quinn said apologetically. "You could have come with me."

Aradie shot her an image of a bedraggled owl that Quinn somehow knew was in such a state because of the heat.

"Ah, I see. You have a good point. Still, could have used you there." She really had missed the owl.

Arriving at the room, she stepped inside to find Harish, Siliqua, Cadre, and Milaro gathered around the central table in the room. They were poring over something. She stepped up softly and looked at it too but couldn't understand what might catch their attention so.

"What are we looking at?" she whispered.

Milaro chuckled as the other three were slightly taken aback.

"You didn't tell them I was coming, did you?" Quinn turned to him.

"Nope. Thought I'd wait for them to notice." Milaro smiled, and then as he looked her over, his eyes narrowed. "I was going to say welcome back, but as it stands right now, as soon as we've taken care of the Library, you're going to tell me why you're recovering from poisoning."

Quinn blinked. She'd been hoping to keep that particular fact from Milaro, especially since she knew he'd kick up a fuss. She let out a sigh. "It's a long story, but suffice it to say that Hal is taking care of it."

"He should have taken care of it before it actually happened." It was the closest to sounding angry Quinn had heard from Milaro.

"Pretty sure he feels that way too. We got it sorted, got some decent information. It's fine." She tried to reassure him with middling success.

"Still. We're going through this once we're done here. And I need to have a word with that damn satyr. He never mentioned it in any of the reports he sent back." Milaro was obviously irritated.

"Really, I'm fine. We did a good amount of training too, and I'm fairly confident in my ability not to self-combust and take the entire

Library with me." Quinn grinned. She hadn't realized Hal was sending reports back, but it made sense.

Milaro blinked. "I'd prefer it if you were completely confident, but I supposed I'll take my wins where I can, shall I?"

"So!" Quinn clapped her hands together. "What are we doing?"

Cadre bowed deeply. It was more comical than graceful given the fact that he looked like a very short human-sized insurance salesman gecko. But the gesture was sweet, nonetheless.

"Don't keep me in suspense?" she said.

"I'm transferring the information directly to you for view." Cadre's voice held such excitement that he barely gave her three seconds to check on the information that flashed up in front of her eyes before he continued. "Now, as you can no doubt see, we've been running the sequencing while recalibrating the pathways simultaneously. If you look at the graph, I'm sharing to your left, you'll notice that the synchronization in the cortex regions of the Library and Lynx are clearing up and have, in fact, been repaired."

Quinn watched the graphs and the numbers and didn't understand any of them on even one level, but Cadre seemed so excited, she didn't have the heart to tell him. Though she did understand that this meant the treatment, however it worked magically or scientifically, appeared to be successful.

"So," Cadre continued, "basically the new pathways are reestablishing the old links that were sort of deleted for want of a better phrasing."

"Do you mean the path to retrieve memories or information was obfuscated?" Quinn asked, thinking it might be similar to the way computer files were rarely ever permanently deleted by the majority of people. There were often ways to dig them up unless they were properly removed or destroyed.

"In a way. You could look at it like that." Cadre paused, frowning as he ran the idea over in his head. "But in this case, it was more the pathways to them were either rerouted or completely removed and replaced with alligator infested swamps."

Quinn blinked at the slight buzz in the translation to alligator.

Obviously, that was the closest thing they had to the word. "So it's looking pretty good?" She tried to keep the hopeful tone in her voice on the soft side, but she wasn't very successful. It'd be so nice to have a fully functioning Library and Lynx back with her.

"Yes!" Cadre exclaimed. "It's looking better than I dared hope. The only thing left for us now is to wait for the timer to tick over and for you and Milaro to go wake them. And then of course we have to wait, the retrieval will take time."

"Timer?"

Siliqua interrupted the conversation to answer that question. "The Library wanted a certain amount of time allocated so it wasn't rushed. Without worry. Although we were slightly nervous you might not make it back in time to be there when they came out of stasis."

"You mean just Lynx, right?" Quinn asked, certain that she'd been able to sense the hum of the Library in the back of her mind the whole time she'd been away. It was fainter, not as intrusive as it usually preferred to be.

Siliqua chuckled. "Yes, I mean just Lynx. However, the Library has used considerable concentration and personal resources to complete this whole process. Remember, it too has been affected by all these memory glitches."

Quinn gestured all around them. "If it doesn't repair itself, then we're all pretty much doomed anyway."

"You have such a way with words," Milaro interjected dryly. "Anyway, is it close to time yet?"

Every single one of them looked at Harish, who was frowning as he stood over the monitoring console. "Close, yes. You can probably go down and wait for my signal."

Milaro shook his head. "Reception down there to up here is always spotty at best, so let's just wait until it's . . ."

Several quick staccato beats sounded out just as Milaro spoke. All three of the others looked at one another and shrugged. "I guess that's the system telling us to get our heads out of our proverbials, then." Milaro laughed. He turned to Quinn, putting on a serious face. "Okay, are we ready to do this?"

She shook her head. "I don't even know what I'm doing."

Milaro patted her shoulder commiseratively. "That makes two of us."

"What?" Quinn stopped short. "Why would you say such a thing?"

Milaro laughed and gestured around. "None of us have ever had to deal with this before. There is only one Library. This is not a repeat measure or occurrence. For the most part, none of us had ever been near the core. I've had to guide them in the closest possible approximations. And, before you say anything, I'm not telling you this so you think I don't like to help. I'm simply saying that none of us in this room, heck, none of us in this *Library* has any clue what we're doing, given the lack of precedence."

"Well." Quinn chuckled. "When you put it that way." She danced out of the reach of Milaro's long arms.

"Take it a bit more seriously once we get down there, okay?" was all the comeback she got. Somehow Quinn was oddly disappointed not to get a rise out of Milaro.

"Okay," Harish said. "If you go down now, the veil will drop once you reach the center, or thereabouts. You'll be able to see if the core has been fully reinstated."

"How?" Quinn couldn't think of any way to figure out what he just mentioned.

"Because you'll be able to touch it, and it won't try to blast you backwards through a wall, just in case you're an intruder."

Quinn gulped and followed Milaro out of the room silently. They were going to visit Lynx, and for the first time in several days, she actually felt hopeful.

WEEDED OUT

THE CORE NEVER FAILED TO MAKE QUINN STARE IN AWE. SHE LOVED THE lights, which were slightly duller than usual, and nevertheless reminded her of frosted trees in a twilight. They lit up leaf-like centers and still reminded her of starry nights. And she was most happy to see that despite everything else, despite all their trouble, this whole procedure might actually have worked.

There were barely any red, orange, or yellow instances of lighting left.

Sure, there were several holes, but nothing that exhibited a sign of warning or infection. She let out a small sigh of relief.

"Feels like that, doesn't it?" Milaro sounded slightly strained.

Quinn glanced over at him, wresting her eyes from the beautiful sight of the lights in the cavern. He seemed a little drawn, his face slightly thinner than she remembered, even though it could probably be the lighting down here as well. "Is everything okay?" she asked, suddenly concerned.

He didn't glance down at her, but a small smile spread across his face. "I'm as well as I can be when I'm practically splitting myself in two. But thank you. It means a lot that you care."

Quinn frowned. "Of course I care." She didn't like him completely and utterly avoiding the question like that. But for now, they had bigger concerns. She'd be sure to hassle him about his wellbeing a little later.

As they approached the core, Quinn realized Lynx's presence was strong. Yet she couldn't see him anywhere.

Until they got right up close.

The trunk of the core was practically luminescent, and at the base of it was a pod filled with multicolored constantly changing iridescent light. It swirled around and moved in sync with the way the lights faded in and out all around them, almost like it was dancing.

Reinstatement in five minutes.

Quinn paused and looked up at Milaro, who'd obviously also seen the announcement. "Does that mean the process is finished?" she whispered.

He nodded and smiled. She could see so much relief in the expression.

It was easy to pass the time watching the lights. She loved the way they lit up, how they illuminated the surroundings and, at the same time, expressed such a sense of peace and wellbeing. And the swirl of lights in the pod fascinated her. Mesmerizing in the way it moved and swapped colors and light density. She didn't need to be told that was Lynx's true form.

Here he was in his natural state, without trying to be anything for anyone else. It made her wonder if he enjoyed being able to take on different forms, or if he preferred just being light.

Process completed.

Initializing reinstatement.

The pod opened, and the light spilled forth. Somehow it danced with enthusiasm, with this complete and utter joy, just for a few precious seconds. It refracted and shone, somehow, all at the same time. Surely, he had to know they were watching? Maybe he was showing off.

The light swirled into a multitude of different shapes, so fast Quinn couldn't even keep up with it. But he was there, suddenly, just like when she'd first seen him. The deep purple lynx with the gorgeous runic stripes running all around him. His eyes were bright and focused solely on Quinn as his face split into a huge grin.

"Welcome back, Lynx."

He continued to smile, even as his eyes flickered, and she knew he was checking out all manner of things that he'd missed.

"It worked," he mumbled, a look of shock coming over his feline face. "I think it actually worked."

"Well, that's good," Milaro said dryly. "Or we just wasted a whole heap of time and energy."

Lynx laughed, and it was the first free and hard laugh Quinn had ever heard from him.

"It's good to see you," she said.

"And you. How . . ." But Lynx paused, a frown on his face.

At the same time, the Library stirred within her, and the shadowy figure that was the Library when it chose to be emerged from the core.

Together, they both stared at her and spoke. "What the hell happened? Who poisoned you?"

Quinn blinked. "That was days ago now. How is it that easy to tell?"

Milaro cocked his head to the side. "It lingers in a few small places, that's all. For anyone who knows you and views you through a filtering lens, it's very apparent."

Quinn narrowed her eyes, peering at him. "Filtering lens?"

"Oh, because of your situation, I frequently make sure we took everything into account and that you're not having unforeseen interactions with generic incidents." Milaro shrugged as if it were the most natural thing in the universe.

She nodded. It tracked well enough. He had to monitor the experiment, after all. Even if she was still adjusting to having been one, it didn't make it any less true. "Enough about me for now, Lynx! How are you feeling?"

The manifestation grinned and slowly morphed into his human form. "I'm feeling . . . fine." He stretched out each arm and wiggled the fingers as if testing them. "Yep, all functional."

"But how is your head feeling?" Quinn frowned and looked around. She'd thought there was something for her to do down here.

And that's when Lynx stumbled.

She caught him, confused as to why she had to. Usually, he was able to adjust his form enough to pass through objects and the like if he fell. "What's wrong?"

Lynx laughed. "I'm fine . . . it's just this whole weird manifestation thing right now. All the information that's slowly beginning to unlock is propagating and putting me a little off kilter here."

The Library took a few steps forward, hesitating. "Lynx is still processing. We literally had to delete pathways of information and rebuild them from the ground up. A lot of new points of transfer were reopened after being addressed. It's been a lot to handle. For both of us."

Quinn grinned. "I do believe I know something about being a lot to handle."

Milaro rolled his eyes.

"Okay, so what do I need to do here?"

The elf king blinked at her. "You have to make sure your connections with the Library and Lynx haven't been affected in any way."

Quinn nodded. "Because the process could have disrupted the connections?"

"Precisely." He paused. "And I'm here to make certain nothing has gone wrong and that you don't accidentally get sucked into the system in ways we can't retrieve."

Quinn stopped and looked at him. "Excuse me?"

"It's a side effect. Although, finalization of the sequencing seems to have gone perfectly according to plan." He paused and gave her a wan smile. "You can never be too careful."

She took a deep breath, counted to three, and spoke. "If there's a next time, I'd like to be prepared for such a thing in advance. You know, just in case."

Milaro cringed. "I was being a tad insufferable, wasn't I?"

Quinn didn't even dignify that with an answer. Instead, she sat down in her usual sitting spot, where she rested against the tree trunk and beckoned for Lynx to do the same with her. Once he joined her, his busy eyes blinking rapidly, she spoke. "How do you feel connection wise?"

Lynx pondered that thoughtfully for a bit. "It's full again, but not as full as it once was. There are pathways still being forged and others that are warily renewing themselves. But I don't feel that constant sense of loss, the overwhelming sense of missing parts of me. The complete blank holes are still there, but now I can see a way to get past them, eventually anyway. Once everything has reestablished itself. Several memories have come back to me with the initial flush, nothing I believe pertinent to our current situation, but . . . I do think this worked."

"Well, that's just wonderful." Quinn was relieved. "How long do you think this whole recalibration process is going to take?"

"Weeks," he said without hesitation and then frowned. "More likely months for everything. There are convoluted paths in place now where there was once easy access. Rebuilding the roads or crafting new ones will take time, but now I have the tools to do so." He looked at Quinn with so much hope, and a smidgen of the cockiness he'd shown when she first met him. "It won't be too long in the grand scheme of things."

"That's good to hear you say." Relief swept through her. "And you?" She turned to the Library.

"I am unexpectedly well. Rejuvenated. Again, the full impact of this refresh will take a while, but . . ." Its voice sounded like it was smiling. "I do believe we can right the wrongs that were committed and get back on track."

Quinn felt a sudden calm come over her as the Library around her practically revved up. Energy flowed in a renewed, more efficient way. If she closed her eyes, she could sense everything around them with so much more clarity now. She hadn't realized it was lacking before. All the areas appeared clearer. The stacks, the kitchen, the whole culinary branch, heck, even the check-in desk gave her more information from where she was right now.

Her sense of the entire structure was more in tune with the

Library flow. She could sense the power underlying everything, from the books to the patrons, from the filtration chamber to the check-in desk; it was all in one big spiderweb of power. One she'd instinctively known was there, but never actually witnessed.

At the same time, it made her aware of just how much damage had been done to the Library. The saboteurs had done their best to mangle anything they could. But they had done so subtly. Not having anything to compare it to before, she realized now that her entire connection to the Library had been tainted.

It was like they'd been running on half-broken generator power beforehand and everything had been barely functioning. If she pushed her senses now, everything was more intricately connected to her. She could even reach as far as identifying the specific species rooms from each other.

And now, the whole entire network was lit up like a Christmas tree.

"This is wonderful," she said. "It feels brand new."

"In a way, it is," the Library said. "There were a lot more sequences that needed to be replaced than I'd thought. The suggestion was a good one. Thank you, Quinn."

Quinn waved the thanks away. "Someone would have come up with it. Was only a matter of time, really."

"Perhaps, but now we can truly rebuild. And we can begin to weed out those areas that were infected and investigate the restricted vault with so much more precision." Even the Library sounded more upbeat than Quinn remembered. More alive. More determined.

Lynx shook himself and stood up, springing into action next to Quinn.

"You've got a lot more energy," she said, standing up with a groan. She was still tired from all the training she'd done with Hal. Not back in the Library for two hours and she already felt worn out. Not to mention the amount of knowledge she was still processing had taken a bit of mental strain.

Those had been a lot of books.

"Not all of us were poisoned via etridilelum." Lynx shrugged.

"That's going to drain your energy for days regardless of how healed up you got yourself."

"Excuse me? What did you say?" No one back in Halschius had told her what the poison was.

Lynx blinked at her. "You were poisoned by etridilelum leaf. Very potent poison, although not nearly as useful on those with some reptilian blood in their ancestry. They obviously had no idea about your heritage." He finished off with a laugh.

"We've established that. But is that a poison they could have tested what I am with?" Quinn knew Hal had a growing suspicion that the poisoning incident hadn't been meant to kill her but to help determined why they'd been so unlucky in killing her thus far.

Lynx frowned for the first time since waking up. "I mean, maybe? Although that wouldn't give a definitive answer depending on how long it had been since you ingested it, your surroundings, your own magic and that of those around you. All the factors could tell them a lot, but I don't think that's what this is. For anyone that would have been a risky move to make in Halschius, and I'm quite certain they only made it because Aradie wasn't with you."

Aradie hooted angrily.

"No, it's okay. You don't have to worry about singeing your feathers by going to visit with me next time." She petted the bird on the head. "I think Hal has it sorted now. They basically hijacked our door portal in."

"They what now?" Lynx and Milaro asked, turning to stare at her.

"They hijacked our door portal into Halschius and hid behind the signature of the two containment blocks we had the prisoners in." She shrugged. "I mean, Uncle Hal seemed very put out by that, but I don't believe anyone will be able to do it again now he's aware of it."

Milaro grunted. "That's ingenious. And would have had to be perfectly timed."

"Oh no." Quinn groaned.

"Oh yes," the Library said, its tone stern. "That means we haven't weeded out all the spies yet."

61

THE MORE POWER

QUINN TOOK A DEEP BREATH AND COUNTED TO FIVE. BARELY. FRANKLY she was still ready to pop at about three, but it wasn't anyone's fault in here. More spies in the Library wasn't what Quinn wanted to hear. She liked everyone she'd had a proper chance to meet. She loved most things about the Library too.

This constant deliberate sabotage made her grit her teeth.

"Isn't there some magical sort of truth serum we could give every single person who works here to make them tell us the truth?" Quinn asked, finally. It wasn't that she wanted to yell and scream, but she was quite certain doing so would at least relieve some of the tension she felt.

Milaro cocked his head to one side. "Of course there are those sorts of potions and serums, even some tonics I believe."

"But?" Quinn butted in, knowing it was coming.

He grinned. "But those are in the advanced wing of the Library. Granted, there are people scattered all over the universe who won't need the books to create such a concoction. Why, I bet your friend Jasper would have some familial related recipes written down back at her home."

Quinn brightened slightly. "Do you think that's something we could talk people into taking?"

Milaro shrugged and Lynx spoke up instead. "We can only ask. It's not like we can force them to take it. But most people who are working here? I doubt they'd say no. And if they did, wouldn't that mean they have something to hide?"

"Exactly!" Quinn was happy to know Lynx was at least on her side, although Milaro hadn't been against it.

"The thing is," Milaro said, his brow furrowed thoughtfully, "there are many types of ingredients, and not all species can ingest or inject all of them. Some of them may cause allergic reactions in one while enhancing another. Basically you need an expert in not only the creation process, but also the application process to allow for any incidentals that might crop up."

Quinn sighed. It made her brain tangent for a second too. Didn't that mean not all mana potions, and energy potions or food would work on all species? Figuring that out sounded like some of the worst headaches a person could have.

She realized the room around her with all its sparkling glory was slowly sucking her into a lull. She wanted badly to just nap. But, at least for now, there was no time. The Library tossed her a feeling that resembled a chuckle. Like a short wave of laughter that soothed her soul. "Stop that," she muttered.

"Sorry." The Library said. "You just seemed a little stressed."

"It's not stress as such. I'm just intent on getting everything fixed." Quinn crossed her arms and looked at the shadowy form. "I'm genuinely relieved and happy that your connections are reawakening. But we still have so much to sort out and I can't afford to lose focus."

There was a momentary damper that rippled through the core chamber. But then the shadow nodded. "You make a good point. Lynx, head upstairs. You need to calibrate with all the system access points too."

"Mm-hm," the manifestation said, as if he was only partially paying attention. But then he moved away from the core and began, very slowly, heading toward the stairs.

"Take care of him for a bit. He's still got a lot to process. It'll probably come back in fragments and waves. Teleporting around like he usually does isn't the wisest for now, so I hope he refrains for a couple of days. I'll see you soon." And then the Library's shadow form was gone, and Quinn could feel the presence settling into the back of her mind like a warm and comforting blanket.

While it had never actually left her, the Library's presence had been faint at best while she was in Halschius. Quinn hadn't realized just how attached she'd become.

She activated her flight and hovered herself up the stairs, following directly after Lynx. When she arrived at the top, she turned and glanced back at Milaro. He still seemed paler than usual. "Are you sure—"

"I'm fine, Quinn," Milaro said, preempting her concern. "There are other things we need to attend to before we worry about the fact that I'm a bit tired."

"You have been doing a lot," she continued anyway.

"Astute observation." He smiled. "Let's concentrate on getting ourselves sorted first. Deal?"

"For now." Quinn narrowed her eyes at him as they continued to follow Lynx toward her office.

Dottie was trotting around the large conference table when they entered the room, while Geneva hovered in the corner, flipping through something in her interface.

"Hey," Quinn said, genuinely happy to see them, although she'd thought they'd gone back to their tasks and hadn't realized they were waiting for her.

"Librarian!" Dottie was positively beaming. The bench always gave Quinn that little rush of dopamine just by being herself.

"Dottie!" Quinn said back, trying to put as much enthusiasm into her own words as the bench. She could see Geneva not only roll her eyes, but also the small smile that tugged on the Furionas fae's mouth.

"We have all the updates for you! All prepared. Along with our recommendations." Preening. That was the right way for how the bench held herself, for the pride she took in having something for Quinn to do.

Information flashed up in front of Quinn's face, and she realized it had been a good while since she'd gone through the book retrieval statistics.

Main Branch Tome Report

4,823 are still outstanding from the initial overdue amount. 13,219 books returned. 1 book being reproduced. 417 in repair status. 18 missing restricted books.

Horticulture: 536/720

Bardic Musical: 604/897

Crafting: 493/730

Alchemical/Medicinal: 342/384

Combat: 661/837

Academy: 608/785

Culinary Arts: 282/282 - Culinary Branch Open - 3281 Books of 3795 remaining, 514 culinary specialist books returned. Would you like a categorical breakdown?

Yes or No?

Quinn shook her head absently. No, she didn't want categorical breakdowns until they'd cleared all the remaining books in the main branch. But this . . .

"We only need another forty-two books to open the Medicinal and Alchemical Branch?" she asked, somewhat incredulously.

"Exactly!" Dottie said, practically jittering in the spot with excitement.

Quinn laughed. "That's pleasant news."

Considering she really wanted to get whatever tomes memorized that would allow her to shove a truth serum down every assistant applicant's throat . . . she took a deep breath. Thinking like that was only going to have her suspecting every single person around her. Which, in a way, she sort of did.

"That's the plan?" Milaro asked as he let himself fall into the couch, very unceremoniously, and not at all king like in nature.

"Yes," Quinn said. She observed him for several moments and frowned. "Malakai?"

The elf peeled himself from the station he'd never even left by the door, and crossed his arms, staring at her. "What?"

"Take Milaro home please. Get him checked up."

"Quinn!" Milaro actually snapped out, and then sighed softly. "I am fine. There's nothing to worry about when it comes to me. A good night's sleep is all I need."

But Quinn shook her head. "I don't think it is. You're pale, and you even said your shielding had cracks. Go home, see your physician or whoever takes care of your health, and please, rest for a day or three." She tried commanding on for size so she didn't worry herself into a minor panic attack. Milaro had been a rock since she got there. Training her, giving her confidence, teaching her the ways of all the worlds around them. She didn't even want to contemplate him being sick.

"You have to take care of yourself," she continued, "You owe me a feast, remember?"

Milaro actually chuckled. There was an air of confusion from both Dottie and Geneva, but they wisely remained silent.

Malakai frowned. "I'm not sure I should leave your side."

Aradie hooted loudly and indignantly enough that Malakai cringed. "Fine, fine. She's safe if you promise to stick around."

The owl fluffed her feathers up and turned her back on the elf as if to say, *I've been around longer than you; of course she'll be fine.*

Malakai sighed. "Time to get home, you old geezer."

"Show some respect, runt." But there was a tired smile on the king's face. He paused to make direct eye contact with Quinn before allowing himself to be ushered out of the room. "Just a bit of a rest. That's all."

Quinn nodded slowly. "But you have to recuperate some of that energy. Promise?"

"Promise." Milaro nodded as Malakai practically pushed him out of the door.

He paused before following his grandfather. "I'll make sure he really does get himself checked out. Thanks, Quinn." He flashed her a smile and then dashed after Milaro.

Quinn watched them go, fighting this odd melancholic sensation she could feel rising within. It wasn't even something she could define properly. Just this absolute certainty that Milaro had to rest and do it now. She gave herself a bit of a shake as she headed to her chair and turned her attention back to Dottie. "So. Tell me all about all these reports!"

Dottie padded over and joined her behind the desk while Geneva hovered above it.

Quinn scrolled through the forty books in front of her and frowned. "So most of these are actually still with the people or families who borrowed them in the first place?"

Geneva nodded. "Yes, but they haven't responded to any of the pings to return books."

"And we're sure they're getting them?" Quinn asked. After all the Library had been on such low power for so long; maybe long-range attributes were also glitchy.

"Yes. Definitely the last few ever since the fourth filtration tower went online. With yours and the Library's levels increasing, your reach and efficiency has expanded." She smiled as if that made all the sense in the world.

"Any reason they haven't returned them yet? Are they perhaps with Serpensiril allies?" Quinn asked hesitantly.

Geneva and Dottie exchanged a glance, which was quite interesting on its own considering the bench's lack of facial features. But it was more of a sensation that flowed through the ambient surrounds.

"Spill it." Quinn said, "I know there's something you're not telling me."

"You know the locations we're currently narrowing in on to find the three restricted books we still need?" Dottie asked, like she was speaking to a child.

Quinn decided not to let it bother her for the moment, because truth be told, she still wasn't used to magic to such an extent that everything came naturally to her. "The ones that Jasper located on the map she conjured and Lynx entered into the system?" Also, Quinn couldn't remember having told Dottie or Geneva this, although the latter probably learned it from her aunt who appeared to be close with Milaro.

To be honest, Dottie had probably just kept her ears open at the right time. She could occasionally be a sneaky bench.

"Those very same ones," Dottie continued. "Anyway, a few of the books are located in close proximity to those books."

"Okay, and what's stopping us just activating the homing beacon and making the books walk back to us like some of them did last time?" Quinn really didn't understand why some things worked occasionally but not always. Then again, perhaps the artefact or book's own affinities had a huge part to play too.

"Because most of these are still attached to a living family line." Dottie said the last slowly and delicately.

"And that family line doesn't appear to want to return them?" Quinn pursed her lips in thought.

"It would seem not." She hesitated slightly before continuing. "Or they could just be certain it's a malfunction and not believe the Library is open."

That was a perfectly plausible reason too. "What about the other books?" Quinn asked.

Geneva cleared her throat and took over. "Well, those are being summoned as we speak. We've sent out a category-specific retrieval message."

Quinn raised an eyebrow. "That's a thing?"

"Of course. Wide recalls are generally frowned upon and more often than not, completely unnecessary, and as we've observed sometimes, even ignored," Geneva explained, and then caught herself. "Except in the case that we're rebooting the Library and require every single book to be returned for better power distribution."

Quinn digested that. It was a bit of a mouthful. "I get it. And I guess we'll fetch those ones that are in troublesome spaces too—especially since we already have other important things to retrieve there."

Dottie jumped from one leg to another, which was a normal thing for someone to do when they're excited, but for a superellex futora that involved hitting each foot once in a weird staccato rhythm.

"What is it?" Quinn asked.

"Does this mean we're aiming to open the alchemical and medicinal branch as soon as possible?" Dottie asked, her excitement barely contained.

Quinn watched the bench closely. She couldn't, for the life of her, figure out what was so exciting about that. Nor could she figure out a reason not to answer in the affirmative, even if Dottie was being extremely out of character in that moment. "Well, bardic and combat are getting fairly close to the books they need. But alchemical and medicinal is the one that needs the fewest books, and the sooner we open another branch, the more power we'll get flowing, right?"

"Yes. Correct," Geneva said with a sigh that sounded oddly like she'd given up.

"Okay, you two, what am I missing?" Quinn couldn't shake the sense of bewilderment she felt.

"I win!" Dottie said, her voice so high pitched it was almost a squeal.

"It was a lucky guess," Geneva said, pouting.

"No, it wasn't. I used my expert powers of deduction and I win," Dottie said smugly.

Quinn held up a hand. "What do you mean you won?"

"Oh!" Dottie had calmed down ever so slightly. "A few of us bet on which branch would be opened next! And I won!"

Quinn laughed just as Geneva groaned. Apparently, workplaces and groups of friends were the same all throughout the universe.

6 2

ENDLESS STARS

QUINN GAZED OUT OF THE WINDOW IN THE RESTRICTED VAULT, marveling at the endless stars in the vast sky.

The universe spread out before her.

It was quiet in the restricted area, with her newly adapted seating booth and all the books she could devour. However, she didn't want to devour all of these. She knew that most of them were far above her current levels. That for most things outside of mind magic, ice, and now a bit of fire, she was barely even scraping the intermediate surface. Leapfrogging ahead too far before her mind and body were ready for some of the content in here would be foolhardy.

There were still plenty of abilities and skills for her to gain in the beginner areas.

Still, she pulled *Reality Combined: Chaos Fever Dream* toward her and searched for the little mention of Ashiron pillar. It had taken her quite a while to relocate it, so long that she was starting to wonder if she'd imagined it. But just as she was about to give up, she finally located it.

Replacement Ashiron X982 faulty. Third reminder failed.

Maybe now the system was beginning to recover from its glitches she'd be able to get to the bottom of it. Pulling up her interface, she accessed the system search. Trying to simply scroll through the Library catalog and related information was only going to give her a headache if she didn't try to narrow it down.

Define: Ashiron X982 faulty.

What does Third Reminder Failed mean?

There were several moments of silence in her thoughts, before a whirring sound rushed through her mind, followed by a semi-high-pitched beep. Quinn shook her head, trying to shake the sound loose as it bounced around inside her skull. She groaned, but then sat up straight staring at the information in front of her eyes as it typed itself out.

Pillar Reminders are issued under the following circumstances:

Filtration change requires an F39B4 form, as long as it is induced by positive attrition.

Should it be faulty, filtration change requires an F39M3 form be submitted for onsite golems to be activated.

Deterioration of the inner linings and chaotic leak protection function could result in meltdown - An X7524 must be issued for an inner lining, and an X982 for the chaotic leak protection function.

Should neither of these be implemented, a shift V197G will be issued to prevent misalignment and chaotic mass breach. Reinforcing said shift requires calibration by the Librarian, Library, or the Manifestation.

Has this answered your question?

Yes or No?

Quinn blinked at all the words in front of her. And indicated *no*.

Please expand your query further.

There had been a chaotic leak that could cause a mass breach . . . and someone had sealed it? She shook her head. That wasn't enough information for her to go on, but it was a hell of a lot more than she'd initially had to go on. So at least there was that.

There were golems? Quinn frowned. Surely, they could have had them—oh, that was right. There hadn't been enough power for that back when she precariously balanced in a harness while scaling the failing pillar.

Taking a deep breath, she tried to get her head around the information. It was still too vague, but at least now she knew a potential reason Siliqua hadn't been able to initiate anything with the pillar. It had been shifted . . . a V197G shift, whatever that meant, to prevent things breaking further.

Had Lynx been the one to reinforce the shift so long ago?

She pondered a few moments and then asked another question. "Is a shift V197G in place?"

That strange whirring sound breezed through her brain again. This time the beep was softer and less prolonged.

Unable to verify.

Ashiron communications array currently inoperable.

Recommendation: Repair communications array, enable standard operating beacon.

Quinn suppressed a groan and pushed her hair out of her eyes.

Has this answered your query?

Yes or No?

"Query now, is it?" she muttered under her breath, but knew better than to tempt anything else. Clearing her throat, she spoke directly to the system. "No, it hasn't. But I'll instigate another query at a later time."

Silence filled her head again and Quinn frowned. So basically, the only answer she'd gotten was that something had gone super wrong, which she already knew. And that it had been shifted out of phase with the rest of the pocket dimension. Something she'd also known thanks to Siliqua's supposition.

It irritated her that she'd literally hit a dead end unless she went down there and tried to figure out what was wrong with it in the first place. Perhaps she'd summon the supervisory golem soon and have the golem initiate some filtration chamber helpers so they could restore the communications array . . . whatever that entailed.

Quinn put her head in her hands and just sighed.

And that was when Lynx popped into the room, directly in front of her to such an extent that he almost appeared inside the table.

Quinn started and blinked at him rapidly as his body continued to solidify. "The Library said you weren't supposed to be teleporting yet."

She'd left him on the couch in her office where he'd sequestered himself earlier while she spoke with Geneva and Dottie. After all, he'd seemed fairly engrossed in his own world then. Not that she could blame him considering all his memories were beginning to come back.

Of course he needed time for himself, and she didn't begrudge him that.

He shrugged. "I made it safely."

Despite the fact that he landed in the middle of her table, she couldn't help being relieved he was here again. Even if she was slightly wary about why he might be there. "What brings you here?" she asked when it became obvious that he wasn't going to comment first.

Lynx blinked rapidly, then focused directly on her, a massive grin spreading across his face in that way that reminded her specifically of a damned Cheshire cat. She wondered if he'd ever read the book or seen the movie.

"Lynx?"

The grin, if at all possible, got wider. "I didn't realize you'd left."

"I left like two hours ago now . . . is everything okay?" If he'd lost that much time, then she was probably right to be concerned about him. She wondered if she had to contact the Library, and tentatively began to reach out.

"No. No. There's no need to do that," he said gently nudging her feelers away. "I am perfectly okay. Perfectly me. For the first time since you met me." His grin was now a positively beaming smile.

It was difficult not to just get swept along with him when he was like this. Or at least, that's what she'd imagined. After all, it was the first time she'd experienced him in this good a mood. Not even when she arrived and saved the Library from collapsing in on the universe had he seemed so excited or happy. Granted, he'd also been in the middle of discovering that he was no longer fully functional.

"You're okay, then?" she asked, a smile tugging at her own mouth.

"As well as I can be right now, anyway," he said, a slightly more serious tone in his voice.

"Still piecing everything together?" she asked sympathetically.

"Quite, quite." His brow furrowed and his runes churned in his hair. "This'll go on for a while."

Quinn was all sorts of glad to have him back. Without him there, it simply felt like a part of the Library was missing. An extremely integral part. "Well, I'm glad you're back," she said softly.

Lynx grinned at her. "Good! Because I'll probably need your help again. Now that I'm starting to get memories and functions back. There are already a few things I didn't realize I'd lost access to that have returned."

"Really?" Quinn asked, quite curious. "Like what?"

"The ability to track any book within the Library no matter what it is or who it's with or where it's located." He frowned for a second and then brightened up just as fast. "Excellent—I should be able to access that once we boot up to the next power level. Although that's taken longer than I would have liked—what with Jasper using that locating ritual, and then having to essentially realign myself and the Library with that work around—we pulled pretty heavily on those power reserves."

Quinn held up a hand to forestall another onslaught of words. "You're telling me that we'll be able to locate the other books definitively once we move up another power level."

Lynx shrugged. "Mostly. That portion of the system wasn't activated correctly. It had been shut down, but when we were realigning ourselves with the new sequences, we managed to reset that section of the system and unlock it."

"That's very welcome news," Quinn said, suddenly feeling like there was more hope to get the books back, defeat the bad guys, and get the Library completely restored. She had a sudden thought. "Hey, who would I talk to about expanding the Library offerings?"

Lynx did a double take and stared at her. "What do you mean, expanding the Library offerings?"

"Precisely that." Quinn shrugged. "I want fiction books, stories, you know, pieces of writing made for entertainment. I'd think that way it's far easier to understand what goes on in the heads of others. Put yourself in someone else's shoes and whatnot."

Lynx sighed. "Well, perhaps I'm misunderstanding the scope, but once the academy has been unlocked, rebooted, expanded to . . . whatever you want to describe it as, there's a whole fictional section in there. Playwrights, scripts, compositions, right through to children's story books, fables, and many books. Although I don't believe there are any from Earth in there. After all . . . you can't access the Academy if you don't have magic." He paused a second and chuckled. "Or at all at the moment, it would seem."

Quinn flashed him a scowl. "No need to be facetious."

"No need. But it is fun."

"You've been hanging around Malakai too much," Quinn grumbled, despite being excited to see Lynx less grumpy. She changed the subject. "Anyway, I take it to mean that the Academy has some fiction and thus it would be very easy to expand it or implement another branch for it in the future, right?"

Lynx laughed. "Yes. That is exactly what I mean."

His eyes went distant for a second, but only that long. It didn't seem to take him a ridiculous amount of time to search or communicate now. "Wonderful," he said. "There are sections close to unlocking. Give me a few moments while I tinker with this one emerging memory."

Quinn turned her attention back to the book in front of her. Not that it was going to tell her anything more about Ashiron pillar, just that she wanted to have something else to look at other than Lynx's flickering eyes. Learning about chaos from these books had definitely helped her understanding, but she felt like there was so much more for her to comprehend.

"Damn it," Lynx said.

Quinn turned to look up at him. His coloring had changed ever so slightly and now fluctuated between a deep red and purple. From the sensations he gave off, Quinn could only imagine how angry he must be for those emotions to boil over considering he usually had such excellent control over himself. She made sure her voice was soft when she spoke. "What is it?" she asked cautiously.

"Just . . . I know there's so much more I still need to uncover. The fact that all of these holes in my mind are one person's doing. Someone I trusted explicitly and am now, even with this first memory, realizing she used to the fullest of her abilities against me." His scowl ran deep, giving him a harsh gleam to his eyes. A very unlike Lynx thing.

"But now you've got them back despite what she did, and you can put a stop to whatever machinations she had planned. You'll win this, Lynx. In the end, she only delayed the inevitable."

Lynx focused on Quinn's gaze for what seemed like an age. Then he nodded once. "You're right. I'm diving back in. I've almost got it."

Quinn didn't have to wait long this time. Lynx practically growled with rage and pulled himself out of whatever vision or memory he was in. She knew better than to ask him what was wrong. Instead, she waited for him to be ready to spill it all, to tell her.

Lynx reached out a hand to her. "Please, take it. See what I'm seeing."

Without hesitation she did so, and plunged into a deeply cold yet soothing sensation that had to be Lynx's mind. It was different from Milaro's or Eugeas, this was a sea of obsessively categorized perfect pockets of information. This was how Lynx operated on the inside.

Quinn could see boxes, stacked neatly sort of like shipping containers would be in an organized shipping yard. In each of the boxes there were images playing and replaying - except in a bunch at the far end that were all like TV from the 80s at 3 a.m. where static overtook everything.

"Those are the empty ones, the ones I've yet to reconnect to." His voice sounded hollow in here, like there was nobody attached to it. He gestured toward one box that was slowly coming into clear reception. "That one."

Quinn watched it. The beautiful, slender, cyclops-like unusceros figure of Korradine flitted across the image. It was back, close to the beginner combat section of the Library. A door opened there, revealing a person in a hood. Extremely tall, maybe close to how Hal appeared when he was in the Library but not as bulky, and he hid under a hood. Lynx . . . the one in the vision, was about to say something when he stopped and observed.

Hood guy's words were difficult to make out, but it was obvious from the relaxed way Korradine stood that she was used to dealing with him. She shook her head twice, and then her shoulders slumped slightly in defeat. "Fine," she said, "we'll do it your way this time."

The visitor's voice held a guttural rumble when he spoke, "You're being watched. Take care of it, or else I'll have to rethink my decision in molding you for this position." With a flourish of the cloak, he was gone.

Quinn could feel Lynx about to dissipate, but suddenly a hard wall slammed around him, and then Korradine was right in front of his face.

She seemed genuinely concerned, and even her tone when she spoke held the same emotion. "You should know better than to eavesdrop on me, Lynx. I can't let you keep that memory. Let's not make a habit of this."

And then there was fuzziness followed by a blank sensation.

Quinn snapped back to reality in the Restricted Vault. "Shit."

"Yeah," Lynx said, his tone melancholy. "That about sums it up."

"But now you know," Quinn said, unsure how to make him feel better.

Lynx laughed, but it was a forced sound. "Yeah. Now I know, and apparently every time I knew, she just made me forget."

Quinn didn't know what to say to him, so she stood and gave him a side-hug. At least now they had confirmation.

Korradine had been a willing plant from the start, no matter what might have happened later.

63

RESTRICTED ACCESS

The more Quinn digested the vision she'd experienced with Lynx, the more she realized how dire the ramifications were. If Korradine had wiped his memory every time he encountered anything suspicious, that potentially meant a lot more damage to his memory files—banks, whatever they were—than they'd originally expected.

So many questions popped up in Quinn's mind. Things they needed to know and sooner rather than later. A deep sense of foreboding began to form in her stomach, and she wasn't foolish enough to think this reawakened memory was a coincidence.

It had triggered something within Quinn's Library equilibrium. But the only way she knew to extract more information was to pose the questions. And she wasn't entirely certain Lynx was ready to answer any of them. Minutes were not enough to process the now irrefutable millennia of betrayal.

"After that vision, do you have any idea who she spoke to?" Quinn finally asked softly.

Lynx's eyes rippled all through the sclera, like a wave passed over the surface. He shook his head, and his shoulders sagged in defeat. "I don't know. I can't remember ever seeing him before."

Quinn hesitated to speak, unsure of how to express what she was thinking, but then the Library itself nudged her.

If you have something you think is pertinent, please don't hesitate. Despite the current power level we've achieved, Lynx and I aren't personally operating at full capacity yet.

You're still underpowered? Quinn asked incredulously.

Not like that. The power levels are fine for the moment and for us to maintain our current level of operation. However . . . It was like the Library had to figure out how to phrase what it wanted to say properly. *The holes in our memory, in our data streams, will take time to restore. During this time, we'll continue to be as vulnerable as we have been until now, and perhaps, for a time, even more so.*

And just how long will this take? Quinn asked, taking slow steady breaths to keep herself centered.

At our current rate of recovery, I would think perhaps a couple of weeks, maybe a couple of months. I do think Cadre's estimation of a month might be generous. The Library finished it off as if what it said was reassuring.

All Quinn could do was pay attention to the swell of trepidation that threatened to engulf her. She tried to parse it in her mind. For the whole next fortnight, or even longer, the Library and its manifestation would be even more vulnerable than they had been so far. Not ideal at all. *Are you capable of protecting yourself?*

The Library paused. *As in the core? Myself? Lynx? My histories vault?*

All the above . . . and perhaps the Library. Quinn could practically feel the entity that was the Library shake its head. It was just a sensation of the action mimicked in her mind. So that was a no. *Then what can you currently protect?*

My core, the essence of what I am, Lynx . . . and likely my personal vault. But right now, as it stands, there's no way my power will extend to take care of more until this restoration and sequencing is complete. As long as I can hold out until then . . .

You'll be able to make the culprits pay? Quinn asked hopefully.

That's much nicer language than I intended to use, the Library said dryly. *But essentially, yes. Just let us gain access to all of our nooks and crannies of information again, and we will be armed and dangerously ready.*

Okay. Since that's all I have to do.

The Library, perhaps very wisely, chose not to say anything else.

It wasn't as if the Library could change the past or could have foreseen what seemed to be a very long in the making, extremely complex plan. Nor could they have avoided pulling her into this crap once they found her, considering the Library would have popped out of existence if they hadn't reeled her in to help save it. Perhaps it was an oversimplification to think of it that way, but it didn't make it any less true.

Quinn mustered all the self-control she could, all the lessons she'd learned on how to process her thoughts, how to segment them to allow her to analyze things in a more efficient way . . . and took a deep breath. None of them could change the past, so they simply had to deal with the results of it now in the present.

The gut-wrenching certainty in her body told her they couldn't leave it to future Quinn and Co. no matter how much she might want to take the easy way out.

She was careful while she watched Lynx in the light of the stars shining in from outside of the restricted vault. It felt like any sudden movement would startle him, and he seemed too lost in his own deep dive that she didn't want to risk being the cause of any damage.

Cautiously, she delved into her own mind, strumming her fingers lightly on the page of the book that was still open in front of her. This time, she was determined not to segment her emotions the way she had with the whole Tenejo affair. There was a mild twinge in the back of her thoughts that she was sad about. Even if he'd been mostly evil, some part of her wanted to believe everyone was redeemable, even if it made her a tad idealistic.

Segmenting her mind to run through different exercises was, in itself, a mental stimulation technique Milaro had taught her quite early on. The ability to multitask with several thought processes at once was a true boon. The way the information filtered back into her, through to her, and allowed her brain to divide it up as relevant felt like a superpower.

As long as she didn't end up losing herself in the process as she'd so closely come to doing with Tenejo.

She set one part of her mind to work on her ice skills, honing them into sharper weapons, and to fend off overheating. To keep the pattern going on a continuous loop that would use her energy constantly and yet make sure she didn't overheat until she got the fire element completely under her control.

That set up, it was time to go through the beginner exercises that had already saved her a lot of hassle since reading the books Hal assigned. Once the loop of fire control was set, she left that segment alone as well, and set about calibrating her mental and physical shields.

Quinn was certain beyond any shadow of doubt that being able to reinforce and extend her mental and physical shields beyond her own self and to her party members, could potentially save a life. It wasn't quite prescience, but she knew it was something she must master.

Once all her multiple tasks were set up and running, she opened her eyes and watched for signs of distress from Lynx. He'd been silent ever since the Library spoke up.

Is he okay? she asked, knowing the Library would hear her.

There was a pause, but it was one where Quinn instinctively knew the Library was trying to figure out how to respond, so she waited, watching him as surreptitiously as she could.

He's trying to process. Even though we knew about Kor, he was still holding out hope that we were wrong. Plus, he's trying to reestablish his own connections and the fact that some of them weren't simply eroded maliciously but forcefully removed like this . . . he might need more time than I anticipated.

Quinn frowned, unable to help that feeling in the back of her mind that told her they didn't have time for him to need more of it. That there were things coming to a head and he had to be, that they all had to be, ready. *But what about you? Can you push past that betrayal and be available sooner than him?*

With absolutely no hesitation whatsoever, the Library answered with a clear and clipped *Yes*

Quinn nodded. *Good.*

At that moment, Lynx's eyes flickered, and he finally refocused on Quinn. "I left that note in the book."

Quinn blinked at him. "What do you mean, you left that note in the book?"

He waved his hand toward the book she was still leaning on. "There. That note. About the pillar. I have a fragment of memory that resurfaced where I witnessed a conversation that mentioned preparing a pillar for something, followed by me coming to the restricted vault to take refuge and figure out what to do. But I can't remember everything I heard. Just the name of the pillar, and something about it. I grabbed the book, jotted the information about the pillar down, and that's all I've got."

Lynx shrugged, his face contorting with the effort of trying to recall and access more of the data. Then his shoulders slumped again.

"Stop trying to force it. It's not going to do any of us any good if you blow a fuse and fizzle out." She tried to soften his frustrations with a smile.

He scowled. "Forcing won't work, but if I can use events we already know of from the owl's visions, from Carafax's recollections, then perhaps I can simply jog those memories, those data points, and bring them to the fore."

"Sound reasonable." Quinn didn't like the massive elephant in the room. But she honestly wanted him to bring it up first.

"Do you have any guesses as to who the spy is that's still in our midst?" Lynx asked finally.

Quinn shook her head. "I was really hoping you might."

Lynx laughed, but it was self-deprecating in the worst way, tinged with a side of hopelessness.

"It's not that bad. We'll get out ahead of this now," she said with much more determination than she currently felt.

He stopped and studied her for a second. "I'll hold you to that."

"Good." She grinned at him. This was more like Lynx.

"We could use the power of elimination for people we are certain it *isn't*," he offered.

"Good plan." She looked around, and then let her senses reach into different nooks and crannies, to spread out and make sure no one was possibly watching who shouldn't be there. "We're clear in here for now."

Lynx smiled tightly. "There are only a few people I'd say we can completely trust."

Quinn's interest piqued, and she let him mull over his thoughts.

"Us, of course. Milaro definitely." A pause.

Milaro was high on Quinn's list, too. The man had risked so much on a consistent basis and was even neglecting his own health. Malakai might have a lot of issues, but she really hoped Lynx would include him in the list, too.

"Malakai. He's too young to really have been a part of this anyway, and Milaro has him quite well in hand." Lynx frowned as he thought. "Eric, Dottie, and I'd extend the list to Nishpa, her niece, and Hal. I'm uncertain about every single other person, however."

Quinn blinked at him. "Including Narilin? Cook?"

Lynx shook his head. "No. The golems should be above reproach."

But there was something about his tone at the end of the sentence that made Quinn question everything.

Should be.

There were a lot of things about the Library that *should* have been some way ever since she got there and were decidedly not.

"They should be," he repeated and sighed. "You know, I don't even know anymore."

"Then what do I do, Lynx? Is there a spell, a book I can absorb, something I can concoct that'll allow me to analyze people?" Quinn was starting to feel desperate. And a little impatient.

Lynx hesitated. "We don't encourage the use of the Mind Capitulation Device."

Quinn winced. "Well, we don't even have it right now because we haven't hunted it down yet, and I doubt Milaro is going to create another one because he hates that he made the original, so that's neither here nor there."

But Aradie cut her off with a hoot.

Quinn blinked at the owl. "What?"

Aradie let out a series of hoots followed by rapid images that took Quinn several seconds to digest.

"Really?" she said, looking at the bird dubiously.

Really. With substantial preparation, I'm capable of viewing aspects of people. It would require work to translate them and won't be a hundred percent accurate. But I will teach you at the same time. And it should give us at least some measure of all the people around us past, whether or not they are lying or deceitful. The owl sighed at the end of that very long speech . . . or at least it was for her.

"Excellent." Quinn grinned. At least that was some good news. Now all she needed . . .

But Dottie spoke from the other side of the door as she knocked against it with her wooden little legs. "Librarian, we need you to come out, please. Jasper has something very important to share with you."

Quinn hadn't given Jasper restricted access yet. "Coming." Even as she called out her answer, Quinn couldn't help but hope Aradie didn't find fault with the new assistant.

As long as the disquiet making her entire skeletal structure tingle wasn't because of Jasper, Quinn would figure the rest out.

64

MOVING TOWARD

QUINN WAS ABOUT TO TELL DOTTIE TO BRING JASPER TO THE Restricted Vault, when the Library intervened in her thoughts.

If you're about to grant Jasper access, it might be better to simply meet her in your office instead.

Quinn frowned. Since she hadn't been broadcasting, the interjection made it seem that her connection to the Library was deepening. Granted, she thought she could sense subtle shifts in the Library too. *Isn't it just easier to do so here?*

I can make any room as secure as this one. However, right now, giving permission to enter this room while we're still trying to discover what tomes have gone missing and how it was done is probably not the best idea.

That did track. Quinn shrugged, deciding not to bring up that far too many people had access already. *It's not because you don't trust her at all?*

Of course it is. The Library sounded indignant. *I don't know Jasper. All I have to go on are your experiences and anything I've gleaned from her while she's been here. She's been helpful, but I can't base everything on that. If being helpful were the bar to measure by, then the Aracnio twins would have been the nicest people ever.*

True. Quinn sighed, wishing she'd at least got to ask the twins why.

She thought about it before calling out to Dottie. "Tell her I'll meet her in my office in a bit. She can wait for me in there. I'm almost done."

"Very well!" Dottie said in a singsong manner that was filled with light.

Quinn really hoped Dottie was trustworthy. She just had to be. All of this suspicion was getting way out of hand. She turned her attention back to the Library. "You can secure my office in the same way we have the vault done?"

Yes, the Library answered without hesitation. *It's not an easy task, but a necessary one in the case of the restricted area. After all, there are prerequisites to being able to come into this room. To allow people to eavesdrop would negate that purpose.*

"But they can listen to me in my office," Quinn asked, a little confused.

Of course they shouldn't be able to, and it has a level of security layered over it, but with the recent turn of events it's become obvious that's insufficient. The Library paused. *I didn't have it reinforced with the same level of restriction as in here. Granted, given the way things have been going, that's a rather large oversight on my behalf, and I am in the process of rectifying it. I guess I've been extremely naïve.*

Quinn felt a pang of sorrow for the Library. Bringing all this knowledge to everyone and assuming that others would reciprocate that love for sharing and making the universe stronger. But there were just some individuals out there who were selfish. Quinn wasn't surprised. Her world was made up of so many types, too; she knew the rest of the universe probably reflected the same.

Not everything could be a utopia.

The upgrade of your office is complete. Let me know if I missed anything. The Library interrupted her train of thought.

"Thanks." Quinn glanced back at Lynx. His eyes were flickering again, so she wasn't entirely sure he was paying any attention to her. "You ready?"

It took several seconds for Lynx to pull himself out of that mode, and he blinked at her as his eyes reverted back to their usual deep, purply black. The runes slowed in their spiral and a tight smile spread across his face. "As ready as I'm going to be for now."

Quinn paused, trying to figure out how to say what she wanted to, and then decided blurting worked perfectly well. "Any luck retrieving more of the blocked information?"

"That's not what you want to ask. I can feel it." Lynx smiled, but this time, for the first time since he recalled that memory, it wasn't filled with sadness. "And yes, I can attune to your wavelength far better than I've been able to. In the way I should always have been able to."

He frowned and his runes began to twist again. "Actually. Wow. How did you get any of the things done that we asked you to do?"

"What do you mean?" Quinn stretched and moved out toward the door, Aradie sitting tight on her shoulder. "Tell me while we walk? I can't leave her waiting forever."

Lynx blinked next to her. He didn't move like a human anymore. No, he now had access to all the power he'd been missing, to the fragments of himself that had been lost. While he might not be able to use everything yet, his lithe grace mimicked the lynx form he seemed to prefer.

"Your information centers. How we tried to transfer the information to you when you were first brought to the Library. It's all over the place, and not the correct brain chemistry configuration. I'm surprised you could access anything. That was definitely an oversight on my behalf." While he sounded regretful, there was also a businesslike air to the way he spoke. "Then again, I guess I wasn't fully informed at the time."

"You've mentioned before that my genetic makeup means the chip wasn't set up properly. What's different now?" she asked, genuinely curious.

"Now I have access to many of my abilities again, to a wider spectrum for our connection, which allows me to be more in tune with you—and you with me—when the situation calls for it or when one of us deems it necessary." Lynx kept up a smooth pace as they approached her office.

She watched him for a few seconds, unsure whether she liked the changes that had come over him or not. Perhaps they'd be end up being more useful, and he for sure had more confidence than previously. But there was a part of her who missed the Lynx who seemed to need her.

This version . . . no longer had a sense of bewilderment about him. At least when he wasn't retrieving painful memories anyway.

"You're telegraphing at me," he said without meeting her eyes. "Our connection is more stable, and your reflections reach me in a more concentrated manner than they did before." Then he stopped shortly before her office and cleared his throat.

"What?" She crossed her arms and waited.

"I need you to know that I appreciate everything you did. Every little sacrifice you've made since you got here, including fighting those damned worms. And not limited to retrieving books we needed that should never have been let out of my care. So, thank you, Quinn. For not throttling me when I couldn't help you."

She blinked at him and sincerely examined the words. "You're very welcome. Thanks for not losing your temper much with all my constant questions."

Lynx grinned at her, and there was a glimpse of the Lynx he'd been. He was still in there, just hidden beneath capability now that he had access to more of himself again.

And that's what it broke down to, really. Lynx wasn't quite repaired. Neither was the Library, but they were more whole than they'd been the entire few months she'd been the Librarian. The recovery brought with it a refreshing breeze of relief. But it was one they couldn't afford to let lull them.

"Shall we go in and not keep Jasper waiting?" Lynx winked at her.

"We shall." Quinn grinned, and they headed into the room.

Jasper crouched down, one hand resting lightly on the couch as she conversed with Dottie. "I don't see how you even eat . . . you're just fascinating."

"I'm not a scientific experiment. We eat through sustenance absorption." Dottie sounded haughty, as if she was mildly offended.

"Sorry!" Jasper held up her hands as if in defeat. "I just find you remarkable and am genuinely curious, so . . ." She trailed off and jumped to standing to twirl around and grin at Quinn. "Finally! Took you long enough."

"Like literally fifteen minutes or something," Quinn said, rolling her eyes. "Anyway, I'm sure there's something you need to tell me, and I have a to-do list that's three miles long and growing steadily every day, so spill so I can add things to the list and we can all move on."

Jasper laughed, this time a full-throated and happy sound.

Frankly, it put Quinn at ease. It had remnants of a lulling effect in it, and she wasn't sure how she could tell, except that she simply could. Had all her senses been upgraded when the Library's pathways were renewed with the sequencing? Did that mean Quinn's connection to the Library had also upgraded?

But Jasper's laughter calmed down and her eyes shifted ever so briefly in the direction of Dottie. Quinn got the hint straight away and turned to the bench. "Hey, Dottie. I think I saw them having trouble at the check-in desk as we made our way down here. Can you go help them?"

Dottie, who was no fool, gave Quinn the distinct impression she was rolling eyes she didn't have. "Fine. I know when I'm not needed."

"Silly Dottie," Quinn said. "You're always needed and welcome. I just have some stuff I have to go over right now."

Dottie didn't even say anything else as she left, which meant she was probably irritated now. Quinn would have to make it up to her later.

"Come on, Jasper." Quinn couldn't help smiling. If Jasper turned out to be a spy, she was going to be very put out. "Spill. What is it that's of such dire importance?"

A shadow came over Jasper's face and she looked down and away. "So, you're probably going to be a little angry at me for this."

Quinn took a breath and counted to three. "Just start at the beginning and we'll see," she encouraged in the most even voice she could muster, thanking Milaro in her head yet again for having taught her all of the control he had. It made dealing with situations far easier.

Lynx scowled, but Quinn sent him a mental nudge and he smoothed his expression over immediately.

Jasper paced, and it was obvious she was struggling with something, but then she stopped, planted both feet shoulder width apart as she turned to face them, and put her hands on her hips. Determination washed over her face, and she sighed before she spoke.

"You remember when I did the tracking ritual, right? The one to locate the missing books that shouldn't be missing?"

Quinn nodded. "Of course we remember. I mean, it was a bit of an ordeal with the jail being underneath us and all . . ."

"Exactly." Jasper preened slightly, but then cleared her throat. "Well, you were having difficulties, remember? With the map and the locations, not being able to pinpoint them all precisely. Then there was the transfer of the locations, and it was a whole ordeal for Lynx to shift them over to the Library's central systems."

"We do remember," Lynx said, cracking a smile as he continued. "Even I remember now, and I'm not likely to ever forget."

Quinn chuckled. "Come on, Jasper, stop drawing it out. You know you've got a captive audience as is."

"Yeah. I just . . . you see, I may have done not the wisest thing in the world." She wouldn't meet Quinn's eyes.

Quinn's gaze narrowed. "You mean less wise than lying to Savinth, stealing a Library book, trying to kill the Librarian, and then holding the tracking ritual longer than was healthy for you?"

"Yeah." She shrugged, "Perhaps even more reckless than all those things put together."

"What did you do?" Lynx's eyes shifted and his gaze let off a strange intensity. He let out a groan. "Oh no. I mean, it was a good idea in theory, but what a mess you've made. Did you even know how to execute that spell?"

Jasper scowled. "In theory. I've read up on it and practiced it a thousand times."

"But implemented it?" Lynx said, his voice flat.

Quinn looked between them, and tried to get a read on Jasper, completely lost in the conversation. She'd give them another few seconds before she demanded to know what the hell they were talking about. But even as she narrowed her eyes again, trying to take in any changes in Jasper, she thought she saw a fleeting second of guilt.

And that something triggered another flare of foreboding in her gut.

"That last book . . . the one that was so difficult to center." Jasper was beating around the bush again, and Quinn groaned because a part of her knew where this was going, or, at least, she had a very good inkling.

"*Ririn's Dimensional Distortion Through Sacrificial Means?*" Quinn provided the name.

"Yeah," Jasper said, refusing to meet Quinn's gaze. "That's the one."

"You didn't . . ." Lynx said, sounding like he already knew she'd done precisely what he anticipated.

"Yeah. I'm sorry. I tethered a tracking signal from it to me. It's weak and all, but I can tell you something." This time Jasper looked up sheepishly. "The book has now been moved from that sector."

65

WELL-DESERVED

Quinn held up a hand, stopping anything else Jasper wanted to say. "Wait, what do you mean it's moved from its location? Is it moving by itself like they do when summoned, even though we can't summon it?"

Jasper paused and genuinely seemed to think it over. "I'd assume, since you can't summon it because the Library technically hasn't restored its data of having owned the book yet, that it's moving *with* someone. I mean, it can't really know right now that it needs to come home, so to speak, right?" She closed her eyes and frowned for several seconds.

Quinn shook her head. "No. How does this tethering thing work?"

"I just imprinted their locations to my psyche and allow the thread to loosely track whether its stationery or moving."

"And how is it moving?" Lynx interjected. "Is it bee-lining for us? Or what general type of movement do you mean?"

Jasper shrugged. "It's just not where it was. The sector has changed, and you can't pinpoint its movement on the map markers you set. Those are stationary."

"So you tethered to *Ririn's Dimensional Distortion Through Sacrificial*

Means," Quinn asked, counting to a hundred in her head. All she could hope was that this hadn't placed Jasper in unnecessary danger.

"Yep!" Jasper answered promptly.

Quinn sighed. She'd known it, and yet somehow, she was still clinging to denial. "I thought so. That's the book Kajaro has." Her voice trailed off as she tried to go over the possible repercussions in her head, especially after Tenejo's gruesome death. "Wait, so you only tethered yourself to the one?"

Jasper nodded. "It was an on-the-spot decision thing."

"How do we know the other books remained where they were?" Quinn asked.

Lynx blinked, and Jasper imitated a goldfish for a second.

"Because . . ." Lynx started and then sighed. "We don't. We can't know that. We'll have to track them again to find out their precise location when we're ready retrieve them."

"Which is when?" Quinn asked, pinching the bridge of her nose and counting to three.

"Once all our memories and data have returned to being fully functional," Lynx said.

She mulled that over for a few seconds. It wasn't ideal. If this one book was moving around, what's to say the others weren't as well? Granted, she didn't believe that Kajaro had more than one of the books left in his possession. But that didn't mean he couldn't easily gain access to the two remaining ones.

"Is the book headed in the direction of the remaining two?" she asked suddenly, wondering if that'd help them narrow down intentions.

Jasper frowned and sat down on the couch in a meditative position, her eyes closed, her slender frame almost lost in the plush seat. Her eyelids twitched several times and an aura of magic rose from her. Power that tingled Quinn's every nerve, drawn to it like a moth and a flame.

It was then Quinn realized Jasper was powerful, much more so in fact that Quinn had ever realized. She wondered if she could get the system to help her analyze people's power levels since she hadn't expected Jasper to be over nine thousand.

Being able to assess people's magical extent before engaging them could only benefit her and the Library. She made a note to look into an affinity she might be able to adapt for that as soon as she had time. It had to exist.

As long as the book wasn't necessarily moving toward the Library, Quinn held out hope they could figure out their next step before Kajaro and his little band of henchmen grew wise to the fact that they could track the book. Didn't this give them some sort of advantage?

With the severing of the book's connections from the Library, however Korradine managed to do it, it gave the cahoots group, as she was now calling it because Sölem sounded like far too nice a name for their machinations, an upper hand. They had gained the ability to refine and master the techniques contained within without any danger of the Library reclaiming what belonged to it. At least until it got fixed.

Which they never expected it to.

"It's moving somewhat closer to where the second book was located," Jasper said, her voice sounding particularly tired . . . or, to be more precise, her voice sounded trancelike. "But I don't think it's headed there. I can't get more than vague imprints from it."

"This tethering you've done," Quinn started, still grasping at straws to figure out exactly what it was she was trying to say. "Just how did you attach yourself to the book?"

Jasper shook her head. "It's not like an attachment, so it's not something visual they can see or even feel. As an aside to the ritual, it lends me the sense for it, heightens and adapts my ability to sense the presence of the item I was tracking. Keep in mind, the whole tracking ritual was to locate a lost item. The books were lost, and this allows me get a minor trace read. But I can't tell specifically where it is, only vague directions starting with where we initially discovered it."

"And you're certain they can't feel you. There's no way for them to reverse track it to you?" Quinn pressed, just to make sure they weren't inviting any more danger by utilizing this specific set of lucky skills.

Lynx spoke up, however. "No, if it's the type of tracing spell I think it is, and I'm certain it is, then it's vague, one way, and barely of any use. To anyone not in our current situation, that is. Having an eye on the specific book we know Kajaro has in his possession could be very useful for us."

"As in, like, an early warning system?" Quinn asked. "Something to help us know when they head in our direction?"

"Why in the cosmos would they head to you?" But Jasper paused and shook her head. "Never mind, I see."

Lynx looked up with a frown. "Exactly. Eventually, they'll get it in their heads that the only way to make Quinn disappear is to come here and do it themselves. Which is probably, logically, a sound sort of reasoning."

Quinn scowled and Lynx hastily added. "Not that I agree with them, but you can see where that might be a conclusion they'd draw."

It was true. Quinn couldn't pretend it wasn't. But right now, it wasn't a problem. And because it hadn't got to that stage quite yet, they could all take precautions.

An idea began to form in her mind. "I'll call Misha and see if we can't beef up security just in case the inevitable happens sooner than later, and then we can discuss."

On command, Misha appeared right in front of Quinn, a disapproving frown on their face. At least, Quinn thought it was disapproving.

"What can I do for you, Librarian?" Misha asked, their tone slightly more clipped than usual.

Quinn frowned. "I needed to talk to you about security measures."

"Oh." Misha perked up a bit. "Sorry, I was in the middle of the storeroom inventory. There are several more delicate items I have had to juggle, and my attention was momentarily split. Our storage facilities have had to expand."

"Are all the supplies you ordered being delivered as they should be?" Quinn asked, trying to be polite since she'd obviously interrupted something.

"Yes. People have been more eager than anticipated." Misha turned fully to face Quinn, slightly robotic in their movements. "I am a little stiff right now, as I am running many processes. How might I help you with security?"

"How possible is it for someone to, say, lay siege to the Library?"

Misha blinked, and her silver eyes flickered briefly. "Excuse me?"

"You know, if there were a group of enemies who wanted to lay siege to the Library, is there a way they could do that with all the security we've already put in place? You know, the whole scanning process after Tenejo?" Quinn couldn't read Misha's expression and it was making her nervous.

Misha frowned, but for a split second there was an air of relief around her. "Those scans allow us to nip any trouble in the bud before it becomes a reality. Now, are you speaking theoretically, or is there a potential threat you have not yet briefed me on?"

"Theoretically for now, but it could become reality?" Quinn half said, half asked. "I just want to get ahead of things should it be necessary.

Misha sighed. "All of our current allotment of security golems are and attending to their duties around the Library. I will set the doorways to monitor our entrants on a more stringent basis. Is there something in particular I should be looking out for?"

The question caught Quinn off guard. Was there? Should they be looking out for something else? It wasn't as if their enemies were going to arrive and just attack them, right? They should have some forewarning. But in her book, it was better to be safe than sorry.

"Any large contingents that could be related to one another? And anyone suspicious or from one of the potential delegations we've flagged?" It was about as comprehensive an answer as Quinn had.

"Very well. I shall make the necessary adjustments," Misha said, and then suddenly brightened. "I do believe Carafax is on his way to see you."

"Oh, really?" Quinn asked, curious. She liked Carafax. "But how can he help us with this security thing?"

To be honest, Quinn's worry stemmed mainly from not being sure who she could trust in any given situation right now. She'd like to trust the aged slothilus and his friendly demeanor, but if she were a spy or a plant, then she'd be trying to win over everyone in precisely the most unassuming way.

Quinn kept running through all her mental exercises while she waited to hear what Misha had to say.

Misha smiled. Or it might have been a laugh, Quinn wasn't certain. "He is almost here. I believe he can help Lynx and the Library with their recovery process."

Quinn glanced at Lynx, who nodded imperceptibly, and then answered. "Sure. Why not?"

"Marvelous. I will leave you in his capable hands, as I have many things to attend to, including increased security." And Misha vanished.

"Do you ever get used to people just popping in and out?" Jasper asked incredulously, a huge grin on her face.

Quinn shrugged. "Slowly."

"Who's Carafax?" Jasper asked, moving closer, her curiosity practically glowing.

"He's a slothilus chronicler."

But whatever else Quinn had been about to say was interrupted by a slight squeal from Jasper. "Chronicler? You've met one?"

Quinn blinked, not having thought it too special a feat. "Yes. Should I not have?"

"It's just they often keep to themselves unless they're called on to testify. Sometimes you don't even know they're there." Jasper paused. "What I meant to say was they're in places you'd least expect them. As if they sometimes have an extra sense for knowing when they need to record some form of history or make a vital observation."

"That sounds like him." Except now she wanted to know if that was the reason he was in the Library to begin with.

There was a knock on the doorframe, and Quinn looked over. The lumbering slothilus with his beautifully quilled back gave her a big grin that made his upturned nose almost irresistibly boopable. She resisted the urge to do so only with great difficulty.

"Ah, Librarian." He spoke slowly, distinctly, as he shambled into the room, tomes clutched in his hands. "I wish to speak with Lynx if you would permit."

"Most definitely," Quinn said, her smile coming easily.

Lynx waved him over to sit next to him at the conference table. One of the chairs morphed immediately to accommodate the slothilus's more rotund form. It made Quinn wish everywhere in the universe was so accommodating, or at least capable of it. How much more pleasant would that make life in general for everyone?

"Tell me, Carafax, what is it you've managed to learn from our owls?" Lynx asked, leaning forward eagerly, the runes in his hair already speeding up.

Carafax spread three massive tomes on the table, a twinkle to his eye as the images in them came alive. "Well, you see . . ."

But Quinn turned away and back toward Jasper with the odd sensation that to listen in would be to eavesdrop on memories that Lynx might not want to share. Manifestation though he might be, he was also his own person and entitled to some memory privacy.

"Shouldn't we be . . ." Jasper asked, and her curiosity burned in her eyes.

Quinn shook her head and steered her friend out of the office, giving a nod to Lynx as she closed the door behind her. *Use the office as long as you need,* she thought at him.

A wave of gratefulness flowed back to her, and she smiled before turning to Jasper. "This is private time for him and the Library. Just because they do so much for everyone else doesn't mean we have the right to be privy to information that might be personal to them."

"Ah," Jasper said, her tone somber and eyes thoughtful as they headed toward the kitchen.

"Let's go get some food, and then, my friend?" Quinn said. "I'm going to get a well-deserved night's sleep."

6 6

NOT QUITE

Tumultuous clouds swirled as she looked up at them. They swam into each other, spinning into shapes that were gone just before she had a chance to identify them.

Which was when she realized this wasn't the ceiling she should be looking up at. There were no shelves or Library patrons walking around, no golems for her to watch like a fascinating video of the goings on beneath her.

No, this was a sky, and it was one that shouldn't exist, or at least one she'd never visited herself considering the lighting came from three different sources. She couldn't tell if they were moons, suns, or some other form of light she'd never heard of.

But she did know this wasn't the Library. It wasn't on Earth. And since she was mostly certain she'd just walked up to her room to finally get some sleep, Quinn also knew this was a dream.

Orienting herself accordingly, she turned around slowly, taking it all in.

Around her were trees of a type she'd never seen before. Their leaves resembled holly, with their pointed edges, but even from a distance she could tell they were sharper. The ground underfoot wasn't spongy like grass, but more coarse like sandpaper that poked at her bare feet.

Dreams were different, though. She willed shoes onto her feet and was rewarded in kind. But even then, the landscape didn't change.

Which could only mean one thing.

It was more of a dream visit to somewhere she'd never been before. She took a second to check over her mental defenses and make sure she wasn't missing something.

Her walls were still tight, her alarms set in place. There was no evidence of tampering, none of intrusion, nothing foreign at all. Convinced that she hadn't been dragged into this dream with malicious intent, she strengthened her wards and took stock of her surroundings.

The heat under her skin prickled, and a ripple of scales passed over her body. Slowly but surely, she was getting used to the sensation. She knew this was a dream and wondered, idly, if perhaps the scale sensation showed on her body back in the real world while in a dream.

"Time to figure out why I'm here," she muttered, and began moving across the coarse landscape. The ground reminded her of dried coral, but wasn't brittle. It was difficult to muffle her sound, but she deadened the air immediately around her feet so the sound wouldn't carry.

Dream or no dream, she had to be cautious. She'd already learned that whatever happened in here could have serious outside repercussions.

Quinn reached out with her senses, pushing them subtly and gently around her. There were bumps in the surroundings that, upon closer inspection, turned out to be other consciousnesses. This was a new method for locating people, and seemed to thrive in this new set of circumstances. Usually when she got pulled into dreams, they had direct correlation to the original one Kajaro tugged her into.

But this was no set of desolate halls.

Instead, this surrounding area was jagged, dangerous, and unfamiliar. Except for that one presence several hundred feet away. While the others were vaguely familiar because they resembled specific species signatures, there was only one she'd encountered before.

Kajaro was here.

But, as yet, he didn't appear aware of her.

Which was both good and bad. Had he intended to pull her here, or was there some sort of subconscious tracker where Quinn sought him out?

Milaro wasn't even in the Library right now. She'd sent him home to recuperate because he was running himself down. There was no one to pull her back from the brink if she couldn't handle this herself.

Quinn was determined to handle this.

Quinn didn't understand the technicalities of this altered consciousness she was in, but she did understand that sometimes magic just happened. Which led her to not even blink when she traversed more ground than she'd realized. Where she warped to the next place she spied.

Meanwhile, whispered snippets of conversations leaked their way to her. They brushed past her head like cobwebs in the night, threatening tidbits of information.

Librarian

Interfered

Unexpected.

She didn't need a map to draw conclusions as to what was being discussed.

Finally, she stood behind the strange trees, near the back of a jagged roofed building. Although, she was starting to suspect this landscape was simply like that. She frowned and summoned padded gear to protect her from the sharp protrusions on the trees around her as she angled herself into a good spot for eavesdropping.

It wasn't ideal. She could only see what she thought was the back of Kajaro's head, along with an Esposian, a Sedimentite, an Aracnio, a species she didn't recognize and then . . . a hooded person.

Really, wasn't that a little cliché? They appeared to be bulkier, obviously taller and of a large build. She couldn't even catch a glimpse under that hood, but she could sense a presence, even in this state.

She'd examine why this kept happening later. If she made it back.

But for now, her energy was focused on the aura emanating from the figure in the hood. Hood boy? Hooded one? Mysterious man? She needed something to call him.

Hoody would do for now.

Now positioned in an opportune way, she settled in to listen closer, ready to flee at any moment.

"She should have been dead already," Hoody hissed at Kajaro, and perhaps even the rest of the gathering. But the voice didn't sound like it came from a Serpensiril, not in Quinn's expert opinion of having come across four of them in her tenure so far.

She already knew this information—and from her recent experience in Halschius, she guessed they were quite put out about her penchant for not dying. Which made her wonder how long it would take for them to make two and two equal four.

"There were complications. We couldn't be entirely sure about the car accident." Kajaro spoke smoothly even if there was a hint of irritation in his voice, and a strange blip over the word car, letting her know there was something not quite correct about the translation.

But what she did know was they were talking about her car accident. It was all she could do not to let the anger boil up.

"We received feedback retrieved weeks later." This new voice wasn't one Quinn knew. There was a gravelly like undercurrent to it. From what she could see, she thought it might be a Sedimentite, but couldn't be sure. He continued speaking in a lumbering voice. "There were no affinity traces whatsoever, no magic we could locate. With the state of their vehicle, we assumed all had perished."

"Weeks later?" Hoody snapped. "That isn't good enough. I gave you one task, Kajaro; you have failed repeatedly."

The Serpensiril thorn in Quinn's side pushed his chair back and turned to face Hoody. With the ease of someone who didn't give two craps, Kajaro shrugged. "And what are you going to do? Kill me?" He barked out a laugh.

But it only lasted a split second before he was writhing in pain, leaning against the table and panting. Quinn could see the convulsions wracking his frame and barely resisted the inclination to shudder herself.

"I'm not going to kill you yet," Hoody said, his exasperation clear. "You still have some use."

Kajaro pushed himself up from the table. "We know where she spends her time now. All we have to do is find her and eliminate her when no one can reach her and this time." He turned to someone on the far side of him that Quinn couldn't quite see from her hiding place. "Yes, this time, don't poison her while the damned satyr is right next to her. She's not about to die on his watch."

Or on any watch, Quinn thought to herself. She wasn't about to give these beings the satisfaction.

Hoody cleared his throat, and it sounded gravelly, too. "The plan is still in place. Our extermination has all but eradicated the Librarian signature. There still aren't any other candidates that can match the Library's signature. All we have to do is get rid of one measly human."

"To be fair," Kajaro interjected, as if he hadn't just been mildly tortured, "that specific 'all we have to do' has proven quite difficult."

Quinn had to suppress a chuckle. She knew now why her mind fled to here. Perhaps Kajaro's thoughts about her triggered the link or something. It'd make sense in a weird, got pulled through into a magical dimension sort of way.

"Difficult, because we're being blocked by those protecting her. Those who don't understand what good it would do the universe to unravel the Library." Hoody pushed himself up to his full height, and Quinn had to reassess. He was definitely as tall as Uncle Hal's eight feet Library visiting size.

"But we do understand, sire." Kajaro's eyes glinted with a fervor Quinn had noticed back in the cavern where she'd first met him. This fanatical belief that he and those who thought like him were in the right.

Kajaro righted himself and began speaking quickly. So quickly, it was difficult for Quinn to understand him through the sibilant sounds. "Direct your people to find a loophole in the defenses. I don't care how they have to do it," he said to the Sedimentite, who shuffled off, finally giving her a clear view of the next person.

They were gnarled, old, similar to Narilin, but she could see the type of tree was different. This one was dark, barked and stocky, as if it could survive in the most rugged of temperatures. He rumbled forward, his thick brows accentuating his frown.

"Figure out a way to damage the pages. They can't make books if they don't have the items. And see if you can find a way in sooner rather than later." Kajaro was back to his most slimy self, and Quinn felt herself recoil. He continued on with his instructions to the others, and Quinn realized she'd lost sight of Hoody for a moment.

Suddenly painfully aware of how vulnerable her hiding spot was if she were to be discovered in it, Quinn extended her senses, and not a moment too soon. It seemed Hoody was rather too insightful for his own good. Or perhaps, more accurately, for Quinn to stay hidden comfortably.

She wasn't about to risk being caught here, regardless of the level of information she could gather. As she cast around, making sure Hoody wasn't somehow circling her to nab her, she kept an ear out for the rest of Kajaro's instructions.

In her haste to make sure she wasn't about to get pounced upon; she'd already missed several precious seconds of discussion.

A knocking sound echoed through her mind, and she shook her head. That was strange. And quite uncomfortable.

She found Kajaro again, speaking with an Esposian this time. The tiny fae creature seemed determined, its own fanatical gleam evident. "Any means necessary. She and the Library must be eliminated."

"There are ways to get in. Unconventional means give many more options." The Esposian grinned, and she could see the gleam of its teeth filed to points.

The knocking sounded in her head again, and this time she concentrated on it. Finally, she realized it came from her room back where she was projecting from. Back where her body was definitely not getting the slumber it deserved.

"Ah," drawled that voice Quinn was already coming to hate, and she turned to see Hoody close enough to have seen her hiding, even if she was still mostly obscured.

She focused on the incessant knocking, attaching visuals to it, the sensations, the slight vibrations that emanated from it.

"What do we have here?" Hoody practically growled as he began to step forward. She still couldn't see his face, but the cowl moved menacingly. She was willing to bet he was the same person in Tenejo's vision back in Halschius.

And then there was a weight on her shoulder and a peck at her ear, and Hoody disappeared with a snap.

Quinn sat up, blinking, with Aradie perched on her shoulder cooing softly. "Thanks, girl. You saved me." Quinn's breath came in gasps and she realized she needed to be more careful next time, because Hoody was far more powerful than Kajaro could even dream of. His aura was so tightly contained, it almost gave her whiplash, even from that distance.

The knocks sounded yet again, and this time she called out in aggravation. "Just come in. What is it?"

What she didn't expect was that Eric and Hal would burst into her quarters, breathless and slightly fiery.

"This doesn't bode well," she muttered to herself. Then righted herself and attempting to look in control, considering she was in an oversized nightshirt with the covers pulled up. "What brings you here?"

Eric glanced at Hal, who nodded. "We've found them."

"Found the books?" Quinn asked, suddenly more alert.

Hal laughed and pushed Eric aside. "No. Not quite. But we have found where Kajaro is, and since he has a book, why don't we just go and take it from him?"

ANY GIVEN TUESDAY

QUINN BLINKED AT THEM. "WAIT. JUST TAKE IT BACK FROM HIM? YOU act like that's so easy." She shook her head with a laugh.

"Easy." Hal shrugged. "Perhaps it won't be easy, but if we go prepared, it'll be easier."

Quinn frowned and watched as Eric hovered erratically. "I had a dream."

"Of bunnies and giliars?" Eric laughed in that cackling way he sometimes exhibited when he was extra excited.

"I don't know what a giliar is, but no." Quinn couldn't shake the shiver that ran down her spine when Hoody saw her. She was certain he recognized her, or at least that he'd be able to put two and two together and figure out who eavesdropped. Taking that further, she was also aware that Kajaro had to know they had some sort of link and would probably know more about it than she did. Hence, this whole thing could have been set up from the start. She looked up at Hal, her voice serious. "When did you find his location?"

"A few hours ago," he said, a quizzical look on his face. "As in morning in Halschius. I had several things to do to verify and figure out before I came here to deliver the news."

So that meant it was some hours ago, before Quinn was transported to eavesdrop. At least that boded for a less likely connivance. "You realize it's probably a trap, right?"

Hal shrugged easily, the fire in his eyes igniting briefly. "I've never encountered a trap I couldn't escape. Don't worry, Librarian, I'll make sure you make it out too." He said the last with a wink.

Quinn laughed, freeing up some of the anxiety she'd been feeling.

"Anyway," Hal continued, narrowing his gaze and turning serious. "Just what do you mean you had a dream?"

"Oh, since the incident to retrieve DeKarlyle's tome way back in my first few days here, where he put the mind bomb in my head, we've had this weird sort of dream link." Quinn shrugged. "Milaro and I disposed of the bomb, and cleansed my mind, erected wards and protections, and some alarms. I regularly sweep my defenses just in case, but sometimes I do wonder."

Hal held up a hand. "You had a mind bomb placed by Kajaro and now you get sucked into his dreams?"

"Not exactly," Quinn said. "Well, actually yes to the mind bomb, but no to the sucked into his dreams. It's not like that anymore. The first time it was, and I think his intent was to eliminate me. Even then he didn't have control over me like I think he thought he would. And the other times he's always been surprised to see me. As if I wasn't supposed to be there in the first place."

Hal paced and stroked his chin. He looked a bit like a huge black-and-red thundercloud. "But not dreams, so you're experiencing the place he's present in at the time he's there. Are you the topic of discussion in these instances?" he asked the last quietly, almost as if he didn't want to.

"Yeah, pretty much." She squinted at him. "Why?"

He ran his hand over his head, tugging on one horn before he spoke. "Milaro should have checked closer. That's conscious transference. Because of the connection you once had, you still possess a link to each other, which means that when Kajaro is specifically focused on you, it pulls you in."

"Does that mean he's doing it deliberately?" Quinn asked, a sickening lump forming in her stomach.

"I'm not entirely sure, but it's something you need to be careful of. How did you pull yourself out of it today?"

"I focused on the knocking, and pulled myself out by anchoring myself to Aradie when she pecked my ear." Quinn grimaced. "And I may have been seen by Hoody."

"Hoody?" Hal raised an eyebrow. "The weird, cloaked figure in the back?"

"Yeah, him. There were several people there, but I could only see about five of them, and really only enough of their features to define their species. Basically, they want to infiltrate the Library, or storm the Library and do away with me." Quinn paused as the memory hit her. She sobered and had to fight back a sudden well of emotion. "Oh. And. They were behind the people who killed my parents."

Hal sucked in a sharp breath at that. But whatever he was about to say went unsaid, because the Library interrupted, speaking out loud and not just into Quinn's head, its voice echoing throughout the bedroom.

This person in the hood, could you see anything about them that might stand out?

Quinn started at first, not expecting the Library to speak, and speak to everyone in the room. "Tall, pretty bulky. But then Uncle Hal is bulky, so that's neither here nor there, right?"

There was silence for several seconds, so much that Quinn was about to ask Hal to say what he'd been going to earlier.

But then the Library spoke again. *If you get close enough, Hal, could you tell if it's him?*

Hal sighed. "Of course, I can tell if it's him. I can smell the bastard from a thousand paces."

He's probably not hibernating at all. The Library sounded cross, quite put out in fact.

"It doesn't make sense to be him," Hal said, but Quinn could tell his stubbornness on the matter was limited. "Although . . ."

Exactly.

"If he was going to be like this, he shouldn't have agreed to it in the first place," Hal said hotly.

Quinn cleared her throat. "How about you clue me in?"

Hal blinked down at her. "Oh. Sorry. Old habits die hard."

Apologies, Quinn. I do need to run several scans to check for an inadvertent link. Otherwise it could simply be that Kajaro's mind left an imprint on yours, because of your harrowing encounter with him, and because it was one of your first magical experiences. Doubling it up like that might have established a link through causation that neither of you have complete control over.

"Sure," Quinn said. "But that doesn't actually explain any of your conversation to me at all." She waited for several seconds and glared at Hal because she knew he wasn't about to tell her unless she pressed. "Fine. I'll bite the bullet and ask. Who is Hoody?"

The Library actually tsked. As if it somehow thought she wouldn't catch onto their conversation. Quinn tapped her foot, waiting impatiently.

Finally, after what seemed like an age, it spoke up. *It could be my brother.*

Quinn raised an eyebrow, but she wasn't exactly surprised by the fact. Frankly, she'd sort of been expecting some huge dragon conspiracy what with the few mentions the Library had made of her siblings.

Wasn't that the way some of the books had been written back on Earth? It seemed like a highly logical conclusion to her. The Library had four siblings, two which were presumed to be hibernating because they were undetectable, and two who were off gallivanting around or something. "Is that supposed to shock me? We discussed your siblings if you'll remember, and you did bring him up. I'm assuming it's still that specific sibling."

Well. Yes. The Library paused, as if having the wind taken out of its sails by the revelation not being a surprise had somehow let it down. *Anyway. It could be my brother, but I can't tell much right now. It's why I'd like to look at your recollections. With permission?*

Quinn shrugged. "Don't see why not. We're pretty much joined at the hip as is. Does your brother have a name?" she asked as the

Library gained access to delve around in Quinn's immediate memories.

Yes, he does. This time, the words echoed through her mind, reverberating off the sides like one of those super bounce balls. *But names, especially our true names, have real power. Until I know that it's him, I don't wish to utter it just in case it triggers a summoning or locating portal.*

"Perfectly understandable," Quinn muttered and then directed the next to Hal. "Okay so, you're thinking of setting off toward Kajaro and his band of little helpers, even though it's very likely walking into a trap. You're determined to do this then."

Hal grinned. "Of course! That's part of the fun. They're not expecting us yet, because they think we've fallen for their trap. We can saunter in when they least expect us."

They could be expecting Quinn, the Library said, now out of Quinn's mind.

"What do you mean?" Hal sounded marginally sulky.

The landscape in Quinn's mind is extremely unique. There's only one sector they can be in, and in that sector there's only about two planets they could be inhabiting right now, as they don't appear to be wearing heavy devices. There is no way this wasn't a deliberate choice. And I'm willing to bet that Kajaro is fully aware of the connection he has to Quinn. This was orchestrated. For a second, the Library paused, and Quinn could practically feel the grin emanating around her quarters as the Library hit on something. *Of course, they don't know that we know they know.*

Quinn groaned. "Anything but this."

Hal laughed and clapped his hands. "Sounds like great minds think alike. I'm listening."

They don't realize that we know what they've done is a trap. As far as they're concerned, Quinn might bring one or two others to retrieve the book. Kajaro hasn't been shy about flashing it around everywhere. This would lead to their ambush or putting a kink in the new Librarian's trusted circle. What they won't be expecting is for Quinn to have figured this all out and bring more manpower. And if they weren't setting a trap at all, and we're overestimating their intelligence—well, then we're just over-prepared.

Quinn wasn't sure she liked this plan. It hinged a lot on playing the players against themselves. Sort of. "What about the Library's defenses?" she asked, genuinely concerned.

The Library paused before answering. *Misha has all fourteen security golems at our disposal. Plus, our regular golems have magical attributes as well and are fully capable of self-defense, not to mention taking care of their category divisions. You'd be surprised what Cook can do with a knife.*

That mental image made Quinn gulp. She could very well imagine how well Cook could filet all sorts of things with a knife if what they could do in the kitchen was anything to go by. "You make a valid point. "Still . . ."

"We won't be taking everyone from here though, Librarian." Hal said, his voice uncharacteristically tender. "You should bring Malakai, Aradie, and probably Eric over there."

"I can hear you," Eric said, sulking from where he hovered by the door.

"I know." Hal turned back to Quinn. "Anyway. I have a couple of people I am willing to bring. We'll see if Milaro has anyone he's willing to spare to go with you."

"But he needs to rest. He'll want to come with us," Quinn butted in. She was worried about the elf king. There was something off about him the last times she'd seen him, and she thought he needed more than a day or two to set it right.

Uncle Hal raised an eyebrow. "Really?" That one word held more concern for Milaro than Quinn ever thought the King of Halschius would show. There had to be so much more to that friendship rivalry. One of these days, she'd figure it out.

"Yes."

"But we have to tell him," Hal insisted. "He'll know who he can send that's trustworthy."

Quinn knew he was right, even if she didn't like the fact. "Fine. But I'll get Malakai to deliver the message. He's probably the only one who can out-stubborn his grandfather."

"Very well, then we should . . ." But Hal trailed off as he watched Quinn pull the covers up and cover her head. "What are you doing?"

She spoke from beneath the covers, her voice muffled. "You do realize I'm still in bed, right?"

"Of course I do. I'm not blind."

"I'd really like a chance to get out of bed, grab a shower, and put something other than a nightshirt on, and then we can talk about all the logistics for as long as you want." She still refused to remove the blanket. Taking a stand and shooing them out of her bedroom after like half an hour was probably a little belated, but she'd really had enough of sitting half up in the bed. It always hurt her back after a while.

Hal sighed, and Quinn could feel as he moved. No matter how much smaller he made himself, he still moved like he was massive. Only so much of his size he could shift apparently.

"Very well, Librarian. I shall meet you downstairs. Perhaps in the culinary branch. I've suddenly got quite the appetite. Fighting—or potential fighting—always seems to make me hungry."

"I'll be there shortly," Quinn called after them, still not uncovering her head. Frankly, she had a bit of a headache. It was still pounding, probably from the dream visit she'd had. Aradie hooted the all clear. "Thanks."

Her hair was filled with static electricity by the time she yanked the cover off her head, but her room was blessedly empty. Pushing herself up, she made her way to the shower, quickly washing under the hot stream of water. She knew those dreams weren't dreams, and that they were dangerous, because she'd encountered Kajaro in them more than once. He'd been reactive and present. Definitively there.

But, after encountering Hoody the potential Library brother . . . she realized just how dangerous they were.

Not only did she have to figure out how best to defend herself against being pulled in whenever the fancy struck Kajaro, but now she had to prepare for the trap they were definitely walking into.

Yanking a brush through her hair before she tossed it up in a high ponytail and wrapped it into a messy bun. Shoving two sticks in to hold it in place, she was fighting ready.

Now all they had to do was come up with a plan of attack and pull it off successfully.

Otherwise known as any given Tuesday in the Library.

68

SO INFERIOR

QQUINN'S GUT FEELINGS WOULDN'T LET UP. THEY GOT LOUDER AND stronger no matter what discussions were had, and what reassurances were given.

She tugged at the material of the protective gear hanging in front of her and frowned. Most recently, she'd absorbed a beginner shielding book that had given her more insight on how best to project her initial shielding abilities. Which, in turn, it seemed, were easily adapted by the cosmicisodracus contained within her. Because now, when she enabled it, her scales flourished.

They spread across her arm like rippling water, fast and fleeting, before disappearing back into her skin. But that's not all they did. They left behind a distinctive barrier that hardened her exterior against anything she'd tried so far.

She tried to be calm about it, but inside she was so excited that she could activate her shielding now.

Quinn wasn't entirely sure why the beginning shielding book had worked that way for her, but she was grateful. It was an extra level of self-preservation she sorely needed, especially after the poisoning incident. Her ability to trust those around her had diminished, even those people like Malakai and Milaro, Lynx and Hal. While she wasn't completely suspicious, there was still this voice in the back of her head that whispered every now and again.

What if she couldn't trust any of them?

"Quinn?" Dottie spoke, clearing her . . . voice projection box?

"Sorry." Quinn shook her head, trying to clear the negative thoughts. "Did I zone out?"

Dottie nodded. "Are you okay? You've been vaguing out every so often lately."

"I just have a lot on my mind."

"Can I help?" the bench offered, somewhat cautiously. Like she wasn't sure how the offer would be received.

It made Quinn smile. "Thank you. But not right now. I have a lot to sort out. Was there something I could help you with?"

"Oh. Yes." Dottie brightened. Quinn still found it strange that the change in aura was so apparent to her, despite Dottie having no visual cues to go off. "Branches. I realize you're in the middle of preparing to get that book back and all, but while you're gone, I'd like to direct our resources to solving some of our most pressing matters."

"Okay then." Quinn turned away from her protective gear and gave Dottie her full attention. "What is it I can do for you?"

"Did you want to pursue the bardic branch first?" Dottie suddenly sounded all business like.

Quinn blinked. "No. If I recall, those were quite a ways from having all the books returned. I think we'd settled on alchemical and medicinal. Why?"

"Checking what books we should ping, what we should pursue." Dottie paused. "There have been a few intermediate books that have made their way back since we opened the culinary branch. We have several from the combat area, but more have come in from bardic and musical."

Quinn's interest piqued. They needed the other branches open as soon as possible. More power coming in meant the Library could upgrade and better defend itself. It meant that it was less likely for anyone to break it, storm it, or hurt it. "Dottie, what do you think is the best course of action?" Quinn asked, because to be honest, the bench was probably much more attuned to what the Library needed.

Dottie paused. "Alchemical and medical is very close to finishing up, so I agree with your first choice. Forgot for a second that I won the bet. I would lean toward making bardic and musical as well as combat our next focus." She sounded a little hesitant, as if she wasn't sure she should be making these suggestions.

"True." Quinn knew combat was vitally important. She needed upgraded versions of the abilities she had, and newer, more advanced ones. Especially if she wanted to understand the added shielding, her scales appeared to be lending her in conjunction with her beginner spell. "Combat sounds vitally important in our current predicament."

Dottie laughed nervously but seemed to puff up with a bit of confidence. "Would you mind if I took it into my own hands, with Geneva's help, to pursue the missing books a bit more . . . shall we say rigorously?"

Quinn resisted the urge, with some difficulty, to quip about how Dottie was going to take anything into her hands. She wasn't trying to be mean, but it struck her as hilarious. Still, Dottie was such a devoted assistant and a good friend, Quinn got a bit irritated at herself having to exert so much self-control not to laugh. Instead, she attempted to nod gravely. "You've got it. You and Geneva do what you need to do to get what we need done."

She paused. Yeah, that sounded right.

"Really?" Dottie practically pranced in place.

"What else do you need? Do I have to adjust some permissions?"

Lynx popped into place directly in front of them in that instance, practically giving Quinn a heart attack. She gasped in shock and took a step back.

"Will you announce your arrival, please? That shortened my life-span considerably."

Lynx gave her a deadpan look. "No it didn't. Nothing can do that now. Technically. Anyway, they need permissions through the console to perform this task. Which, I encourage you to give."

Quinn pursed her lips in thought. Lynx had become a little more pompous since the memory retrieval process began. Sort of like he'd been when they'd first encountered one another after she got sucked into the core room. "You've been eavesdropping on me again."

He raised an eyebrow. "You spoke out loud. There aren't many other options than to listen."

Quinn laughed. He wasn't as bad as he'd originally been. Perhaps the experience had humbled him. "All righty, guide me through, oh wise manifestation."

Lynx rolled his eyes, which was sort of difficult to manage with the way they were colored straight through the sclera. But he'd apparently perfected the trick. "Fine. We need you to adjust their permissions to include ratified book retrieval after three non-answered notifications."

Quinn activated the system as he showed her and frowned. "This gives them the right to go out and basically knock on people's doors and demand the books back?"

Lynx nodded. "Basically. These people are probably the ones who're too lazy to open a door and drop the book at the desk. Because they also don't want to be fined."

"Fines are what makes the universe go round," Eric called out from the other end of the storage area, where he was being fitted for his protective gear.

"I thought that was magic and mana," Quinn called out to heckle him.

"Amateur!" Eric shot back.

Quinn couldn't help chuckling. "His hearing is certainly excellent when he wants it to be."

"Back to the matter at hand." Lynx turned his attention back to Dottie and observed her for several seconds. The bench skittered at first and then planted her legs somewhat defiantly.

"I guess you're up for the job?" Lynx asked. "You realize it's not just like knocking on doors?"

Dottie bobbed in place, probably the equivalent of a nod. "Of course I know that. It's why it will either be Geneva accompanied by another assistant. I will remain here to coordinate and that way the Library is never without one of us for protection."

Quinn shivered. It was what she most feared. That the Library would come under attack when she wasn't there to protect it. Even though they weren't taking Lynx, and Milaro would be nearby to assist if necessary. Geneva, Narilin, and Dottie were all remaining to oversee the Library and its assistants.

Not to mention the Library itself was doing better than it had been since Quinn had arrived. "Will Siliqua and Harish remain here?" she asked suddenly. Her extended perception of others' power levels allowed her now to realize just how strong so many of the surrounding people were. The sequencing for the Library seemed to have improved more than just Lynx and the Library's stability. It appeared to extend to Quinn's connection as well.

"Of course they'll remain. You're only taking Malakai, Eric, Hal, Ishekal, and Nishpa as far as I know." Lynx paused and glanced over at Quinn. "I mean, the people that you know, anyway. I believe Hal has a few others lined up to join you all while his generals take care of things back home, but from the Library—those are the people you'll be taking with you."

Lynx hesitated for a second and then locked gazes. "You need to come back to us. We're almost at the next power threshold, and we'll require reintegration once we reach it. Not to mention . . . we need you, okay?"

Quinn gulped and suddenly felt very self-conscious, especially of the gnawing abyss that her stomach had turned into with the portent of danger churning around in it. "Well, I plan on being back here as soon as possible."

"With the book!" Hal said, making her jump as he came around from the door behind her. "Ah, Librarian. You must work on those nerves. We can't have you breaking our cover when it's least advisable."

She shot him an exasperated scowl. Even if he was right, this was all new to her. This subterfuge and ambush strategy that she still wasn't entirely on board with.

But before she could offer a retort, Hal was moving, his great strides swallowing the distance between them and where Eric was still fiddling with his fitting while Misha glared at him. If looks could kill, the imp would have been nothing more than a stain on the wall.

"How go the fittings, Misha?" Hal boomed in that commanding voice of his. He stood with his hands on his hips, surveying the entire area with a slight frown on his face. Before Misha even got a chance to answer, he let out a laugh. "I see you are as competent as your predecessor. You are a credit to your station."

"Thanks," Misha said, which was about as dry as Quinn had ever heard them speak. "The preparations are coming along. I have had to adjust several of the resistance suits for the atmosphere. The Stachriquil in the atmosphere has to be dealt with and it's a tricky spore. These suits will emanate a frequency pulse that destroys them before they get close enough."

Misha paused, glanced at Quinn, and then continued. "They will be able to detect this frequency from close proximity. It won't be the Librarian who gives you away, but rather the suits."

Hal's eyes narrowed. "Define close proximity."

"Within two feet," Misha responded immediately.

Hal let out a guffaw that shook the room ever so slightly, and Quinn could have sworn the Library sighed in her head.

"Two feet? They'll be dead before they realize my fist hit them." He ground the words out like the threat they were.

Even though Quinn knew the words weren't directed at her, she still felt the chill down her spine. Hal might be kind to her, he might be good to the Library because he approved of it and what it did, but he was a satyr, he was powerful, and he would be formidable if he turned against them.

Not that she thought he would. She was just relieved they were on the same side.

"Very well." He cocked his head to one side for a few seconds and then sighed. "I must away to brief my men and gather those I bring with us! We leave tomorrow. Be prepared."

Just as he was about to leave the room, he paused next to Quinn and his expression grew serious. "Watch yourself. Remember. Their whole goal is to see you dead."

"Shouldn't we keep her here where she's safe, then?" Dottie piped up, her voice trembling ever so slightly.

Hal blinked and looked down at her, a smile tugging at his lips. "It would be a good choice, but also a foolish one. Just because she's here doesn't mean they can't gain access. Keeping the Librarian in plain sight where she can be protected, and learn to protect herself, is a vital point in her development."

"Valid argument," Dottie said, as if she had the power to stop the attack. "I'll allow it."

"Thank you, Miss Dottie. I do appreciate your concern." Hal's tone had softened, and he even let the smile complete itself. "I will be back tomorrow and we shall leave. Librarian . . ."

"Yes?"

"I've left instructions for you to absorb three more tomes. It's imperative that you do this before I return tomorrow. Do you understand?" His eyes practically peered into her soul.

"Sure," she said, a little intimidated.

Stop tormenting her, Hal. She'll get them done. Go and leave us in peace to finish preparations. The Library spoke up, surprising every single person in the room.

"Ah, very well. I shall. And tomorrow, we will take another step to right what's wrong." Hal winked at Quinn, opened the storage room door, and stepped into his personal study.

Quinn watched as the door shut behind him. "We really need to get the other branches open. I need more power, so I don't always feel so inferior when he's near."

That's not going to change. That's just Hal's aura, the Library provided very unhelpfully.

I really don't like the feeling of this, Quinn admitted to the Library. *Not just of us going, but there's something building even here that sends chills down my spine.*

Well, at least you're forewarned. We'll all be on the lookout.

You know about the weird premonitions I've been feeling? Quinn shouldn't have been surprised, but she still was a bit.

The Library didn't answer for a few seconds. *I can sense them. The connection is stronger, so I can't tell what you're thinking, but your emotions aren't always the best at hiding themselves.*

Yeah. Quinn sighed, unable to refute that and turned to Dottie. "We're definitely going to be needing the combat branch sooner rather than later. Make that the priority after alchemical and medical."

"Shall do!" And Dottie trotted off back out into the Library.

Quinn watched her go and silently took the three tomes that Tim appeared to hand to her. Tomorrow, they'd execute the plan that Quinn was already a hundred percent certain wouldn't work. The least she could do was be as prepared as possible.

They'd all need it.

69

EXACT REPLICA

The suit clung to Quinn's skin like it wanted to swallow her whole. She'd originally thought it a type of neoprene, but this was more like a silicone that didn't make her sweat. Or a mixture. The dark coloring belied its true nature, that was to camouflage with the surroundings. It made her head spin to look at the others before her eyes got used to the shifting colors.

At least her magic sense could tell the truth from the mirage.

The potential that they'd be moving through enemy territory made her spine tingle. She'd been here months now, but every now and again Quinn still had to pinch herself to make sure it wasn't all just a long dream. It all still seemed so surreal, like it couldn't possibly be true.

But she'd seen things, experienced things now that she couldn't refute.

Pulling her backpack around to the front, she rifled through it double-checking her rations and supplies as she ran through the books Hal had her memorize the previous evening. They'd been more difficult than she'd expected and her brain was still processing the majority of the magical information.

But they had given her a far greater understanding of how to utilize her fire, ice, and mind shielding strength. *Nordon Fires of Burning Water* was a fascinating take on how to utilize fire even in the least favorable of circumstances. As was *The Field's Guide to Ice in an Arid Habitat.* But it was the *NiChuirc's Mental Fortitude Revelations in the face of Substance Contamination* that really hit home.

All of that information was currently percolating in her mind, becoming things she'd never even considered before. Skills stewed until such a time where they clicked, and she knew precisely how to use them. Not that she minded, she preferred to have the magic meld with her mind and with her other abilities before she used them.

It gave her at least the illusion of having some control.

"Quinn!" Lynx called out, and she turned to him with a frown.

"What's up? Did you need something?"

He shook his head and then stopped, hesitating for a second. "Not really. It's more of a memory recollection thing. Carafax and I are working through the holes methodically, trying to piece events together and attempting to nudge some of the more stubborn ones loose. Well . . ." He glanced around at the large storage area, as if he didn't want their allies to hear what he had to say.

Quinn shrugged and moved with him, motioning for him to follow. Neither Milaro nor Malakai were here yet, not to mention Hal, and it wasn't like they were leaving without her trainer or the King of Halschius. She could spare some time for Lynx, especially since what he had to say seemed important.

They moved to her office, which was only a short walk away, and she closed the door behind them. "What's up? You know we don't have long, so I am *actually* trying to rush you."

Lynx laughed and looked around nervously. "I've been working on some elements that don't add up from any account, not from mine and not from the owl's Carafax retrieved them from."

Quinn nodded, and wanted to prod him to speak faster, but she waited, because she was fairly sure he was either extremely anxious about what he needed to tell her.

"Apart from all the obvious instances where Korradine was acting on her own behalf without any interest of the Library at stake whatsoever, there were several visitors she let into the Library who I would not have."

"Lynx. I want to know all of this, but I need you to get to the point faster." She tried to say the words as calmly as she could, but the point was that she really did need him to hurry up.

"Sorry. It's just . . ." He glanced nervously at the door. "I think we may have been compromised on a closer level than we originally thought."

"Explain." Quinn didn't appreciate the beating around the bush. It was flat and leafless by now, and she just wanted to pull it up by the roots. Plus, he really could have communicated telepathically.

"I'm starting to recall a conversation I had with Korradine. One that an owl overheard part of. It's helping cross reference the segments." A flash of pain crossed Lynx's face, but he pushed on. "She must have flashed my memory again in that instant, but the initial conversation was with Kajaro and someone I still can't recognize. But what's important is the snippets I remember."

He took a deep breath, before speaking again. "Korradine made sure to mention that the failsafes were being put into place and would trigger should the Library still be functioning in a millennium. This failsafe of theirs would bring down the entire Library, the filtration system, basically kill it and anyone attached to it or within it at that point in time."

Quinn balked. "I guess they really were playing the long game. Can you tell when this was?"

"That's just it. If I go on the dates, we think this occurred on, that millennia was either close then, or close now. It could even be both. It'd make sense to have more than one failsafe." Lynx frowned and his eyes took on a steely resolution. "You have to understand that this is why they're coming for you. They're set on eliminating you before this reset. Before their failsafe activates."

Quinn digested the information and wished it were more precise. Give Lynx another week or so and she was sure everything would be much clearer than the slightly watery mud they had right now. "Is this your way of trying to tell me to be careful?"

Lynx hesitated. "Sort of, but also, you need to understand that if the Library loses you, we don't have the time to hope we can create or find another Librarian. We haven't hit the energy threshold we need yet to survive yet."

"But we're close, right?" Quinn surprised herself with the question given the gravity of her own demise was on the line. But for some reason, she felt calm. The sensation of her scales shimmering under her protective gear made her feel safer. She had her own way of minimizing risk now.

"But not there yet," he insisted.

Quinn changed tactics. "You haven't found any others, have you?"

Lynx shook his head. "Nope. We've been looking, too. Can't have too many Library assistants, and it always helps to have a couple who have the affinities they need to be a Librarian too. No one is going to match your affinity level, but a backup would help, and perhaps keep you safer."

"And until you find that backup, you'd prefer it if I stayed here?" Quinn asked softly.

Lynx sighed. "Pretty much. I think it's ridiculous that you're taking this risk when you technically don't need to be there.

"Actually." Hal walked through the door that led to the interrogation room with a soft frown on his face. "She does need to be there."

"How did—" Lynx looked chagrined.

"And yes, I did just, um, *actually* you," Hal said with a grin and without skipping a beat before continuing on smoothly. "*Ririn's* book is . . ." He paused as if he was trying to search for the correct words to use.

Then he sighed, ran his hand over his scalp and spoke, his tone serious. "It is best for my kind and others like us not to touch that book. There are certain components that speak more to our primal nature in all five of those books. That is part of the reason I had them placed in the Restricted Vault here in the first place. They provide a form of power than feeds on greed, on hunger, on a want to rule and subjugate."

Quinn stayed quiet while Lynx and Hal glared at each other.

Finally, Hal spoke again. "These are, perhaps, the way my forefathers ruled, but they do not apply to my proclivities. I would prefer that my people remain where they are and do what is needed out of a loyalty to our people and where we all came from. Call me old-fashioned, but corporeal punishment, threats, and bodily torture just don't work the same way they used to."

He said the last dryly, but Quinn knew exactly what he meant. "I get it. So these books, their magic, can infect you?"

Hal nodded. "And while it can affect the species I oversee perhaps a bit faster than others, no one gets out of there unscathed. Except for you." He punctuated that last piece by pointing directly at her.

"Librarian Quinn? Or cosmicisodracus Quinn?" she asked, getting straight to the point.

"Perhaps a bit of both," Hal said, his eyes sparkling a little. She'd have described it as twinkling in anyone else, but Hal didn't twinkle.

A wave of unease crashed over Quinn. She reached out to the Library, trying to organize her thoughts. *Do we know when Ashiron broke? Do we have an approximate timeline yet?*

Yes. Approximately—But the Library stopped, and Quinn knew it was thinking exactly what she was thinking too. And none of it was a good thought.

If what we're thinking is true, which we won't know until we check, we'll need a lot of protections in place before we repair it. Correct? Quinn could feel a headache coming on.

This'll be top priority after you've retrieved the book. The Library actually sounded tired. Or perhaps that wasn't the correct term. Weary. It sounded and felt, to Quinn's extended senses, weary.

How safe do you think the seal is? Quinn asked suddenly.

Safe. None of us can gain access. We've tried. There's some sort of lock on it that we obviously placed there as a safety measure. Your sealing of it a while back helped too. I'm unsure though. The data isn't coming back to me as quickly as I wanted it to, but it has been obvious that the gaps in these recollections are strategic.

You'll have to explain that to me when we get back. Quinn sighed and noticed Hal was staring at her thoughtfully.

I'll have to explain it to you when I understand it better. The Library let out a dry chuckle that echoed through Quinn's head. *Now off with you before Hal decides to brave the core waves and come and scold me himself.*

"Are you two done?" Hal asked, and she noticed he was also outfitted in protective gear, which begged a lot more questions about the satyr species than it answered.

Quinn nodded. "Yeah. Just getting my priorities straight."

"They're pretty simple. Head to the Illukai Region, Segment 722NV. Retrieve missing ridiculously powered tome. Return and find the next book." Hal shrugged. "Sounds run of the mill, doesn't it?"

Quinn laughed. "Somewhat yes. But why doesn't the place we're headed have a name? Why does it have that designation?"

Hal cocked his head to one side, but it was Lynx who answered. "It's technically supposed to be uninhabited. The surface is dangerous to the majority of species and anyone who visits it needs to take specific safety measures, such as the suits you're wearing, and the gear you're bringing with you."

"Not to mention the ability to purify the surrounding air. Not only that you breathe but also that potentially touches your skin. It also requires regulation of your body temperature and emissions." Hal finished the list off

She grimaced at the last. "This makes airport security look like child's play."

"Airport security?" Hal asked.

Quinn shook her head. "Never mind. I'll google it for you one day and explain when we're not trying to stop this faction from destroying the Library and the universe with it."

"It's a date!"

Quinn raised an eyebrow.

Hal laughed. "Not that sort of date. Eggs aren't my thing."

"You should head out," Lynx said, looking deflated.

"I promise I'll take care of myself," Quinn started. She could see he was genuinely worried, even if she knew on some level that worry was more aimed at the Library's well-being than at herself. She understood it in the grand scheme of things.

"We'll all take care of her, Lynx.=," Hal said solemnly. "We're not about to let them get their way. It's why we need the damned book."

Lynx brightened ever so slightly and some of that cocky confidence leaked back into his demeanor. They headed back to the storage area where Misha was aiding Siliqua and Geneva with the final touches on everyone else's gear. Malakai stood in the corner, his already donned, with Milaro next to him.

Quinn was relieved to see the older elf had some color back in his face and didn't look like death warmed up anymore. Her trainer caught her eye and waved her over. She grinned as she approached. "You look like a cabbage roll."

Malakai blinked at her. "I don't know what that is, but I'm assuming it's an insult."

"Sort of." Quinn shrugged. "They do taste pretty good, though."

He raised an eyebrow, but Milaro beat him to speaking. "I'd prefer to be going with you."

"But you have a kingdom to run, and some health to recover," Quinn said. "Keep an eye on things here?"

Milaro held her gaze for a few seconds and then nodded slowly. He leaned forward and took her hand, pressing a small, smooth object into it. "Just don't do anything rash. Emergency teleporter to bring you home should you need it. Should you need us."

Quinn was touched. Not that it was a big deal. Magic made so many things easier, but the gesture was appreciated. "Got it," she said and slotted the object into her ring. "I promise. If it's too dangerous, I'll evacuate."

"Good. Good!" Hal said, appearing next to her in that stealthy way he had that no one his size rightfully should. "It's about time we get going."

Malakai pulled his pack over his shoulder, slotting it into place. The whole outfit connected to each individual item. "I'm ready."

Quinn glanced at him. There was something off about the way he held himself. He was stiffer than usual. She nudged him with her elbow as they all gathered at the storage room doors. "You okay?"

He glanced down at her and sighed. But just as she thought he was about to speak, he grimaced, shrugged and said: "I'm fine. Just concentrating. This type of spell, for the breathing, doesn't come as easily to me."

Quinn frowned. That only sort of explained his current attitude. But she'd talk to him after they retrieved the book. "Okay. But you're not getting off that easily."

His smile was tight, and he turned his attention to Hal and the rest of the gathering.

With Malakai and Quinn, there were twelve people traveling. Hal, and his right-hand satyr Ikeshal, Nishpa, and another Furionas Quinn didn't recognize. Then there was Escadril. She wasn't certain he was the right choice for a stealth mission given his size and the way the trunk and boughs that made up his figure were difficult to disguise, but as far as she'd been led to understand, he'd mostly be anchoring the doorway. Something about Segment 722NV not having a stable environment. Now that was cause for some major confidence there.

Not.

Eric fluttered irritably next to his uncle, and there were four more imps she didn't recognize. But she knew from experience how stealthy they could be.

"Very well. Let's get this done," Hal's voice commanded, and everyone fell silent. Hal reached to the storage doors, muttering under his breath, and opened them.

Quinn balked. Even though she'd known where they were going, it was still surreal to see it while awake. Just beyond the door was an exact replica of her dream, and trepidation hit her in the gut like lead.

70

SOMETHING IS COMING

Sharp.

That was the first thought Quinn had upon entering the world and taking it in. Everything around them was sharper than it had been in her dream, and even then, she'd taken measures to protect herself from it.

From the trees that looked like odd 3D renderings of particularly spiky pines, to the ground, that even through her protective clothing, she could tell was as coarse as forty-grit sandpaper.

The second thing she noticed was Hal had shrunk himself down more. He was on a par with Malakai's height instead, making him more maneuverable, which was necessary in this space.

The third thing that stood out was that they didn't enter through a doorway. The air behind the group rippled as they all moved through to stand near a couple of those spiky trees. She glanced around, trying to figure out how they got through, when she saw Milaro give her a wave from the other side of a shimmering doorway.

"I thought it could only open into another doorway," she murmured under her breath as she watched the hole close behind her.

Eric laughed, keeping his volume level low. "Anyone with a

doorway can open it. Anyone with enough magical strength can brute force a doorway anywhere."

Quinn mulled that over as everyone checked over their supplies one more time. Magic was sometimes a far too convenient excuse.

Hal checked over everyone with a quick and efficient wave of subtle magic that activated the suits they wore. Once engaged, the camouflage aspect blended them with their surroundings. He frowned as he looked at them all.

Quinn blinked. It was only because she sensed where everyone was that she could identify them properly. And even then, it took several seconds to focus. If someone concentrated on the area they occupied, then they'd see them. But, hopefully, those precious few seconds would blindside their enemies.

She took a deep breath as Hal stood next to her. He spoke once in a low voice that practically penetrated her soul. "Surface-level targeted mind communication, so we at least don't alert anyone to our presence because of the noise. I'll activate the channel and give you all access."

Suddenly, Quinn felt a gentle probe against her mind and accepted the offered tether.

Better, Hal said. *Librarian? What do you sense?*

She closed her eyes for just a second, gathering her bearings. They'd not come out where she'd been in the dream. Then again, she'd walled her mind off as tightly as she could, so she didn't get pulled back in. But she could sense, like, a whiff of something tantalizing on the air, just where they needed to go.

She missed Aradie already. But with the need for subterfuge and the camouflage, not to mention the air difference, they'd thought it better for her to stay in the Library and assist in protecting it just in case. This was the last trip she'd take without her owl, even if she had to help her with the air circulation herself.

Finally, after what felt like an age, even though she knew it'd only been a moment, Quinn opened her eyes and pointed off to the left. *Over there.* Sending magic and people had gotten easier, but it still required far too much concentration for her liking.

He nodded. *Move easily. Follow me. Make as little sound as you can. Touch nothing but the ground we walk on.*

Quinn fought the urge to roll her eyes, but the nerves about the whole situation took care of that pretty fast. She glanced to her right, watching Malakai out of the corner of her eye. He was uncharacteristically quiet. She nudged him with her elbow and he gave her a tight smile.

One that didn't reach her eyes.

Quinn wasn't sure how she felt about that. It was almost like he'd changed since coming back from making sure his grandfather rested. Or maybe he was just in a bad mood.

I'm fine.

She glanced at him. That had been on the surface of her mind only, and not through the group link. *Sure, you're fine. How about you tell me why your face looks like a cat's bum?*

Malakai's facade cracked, and a laugh leaked out momentarily. *I'll talk to you later. We should concentrate on this.*

What are you two doing? Eric was suddenly hovering in front of him. It was so disconcerting with the way the camouflage gear worked. He flickered in and out of her vision.

Sorry, Malakai said, not sounding like he meant it in the slightest.

Eric scowled, and didn't budge from their side.

Later would have to do. Quinn concentrated instead on the way the ground here, the trees, and different lighting in the sky were all precisely faithful to her dream. Having never set foot here before, she figured her mind would have filled in gaps. Which made the dream all the more suspect. At the edges of her senses, she could feel people and things.

More of the things were obviously native animals. She could sense a few bugs, beetles, and definitely some spiders. Not to mention other creepy crawly things that seemed to be native to this strange landscape. She wanted to ask what this was, the material that made up the ground.

Hal held up his hand as the tree line began to thicken. *Be careful. You can't afford to puncture the gear.*

They were getting closer now.

Escadril spoke through the bond. He'd remained behind to obfuscate their entry and stand guard for the potential exit point. *There is something amiss with the vegetation here. It is in pain.*

It's not exactly an ideal ground for anything to grow. Eric grumbled.

Quinn could practically see Escadril shaking his head as he spoke. *These are trees and shrubs from the Bishickah family. They can grow and flourish in this climate. They should not be emanating this type of pain.*

Do you have any suggestions? Hal asked, his voice echoing strangely through the link in her head.

Quinn could hear Escadril breathe and thought he wouldn't speak for a bit, but then he proved her wrong. *It could indicate that there's a torghud around. Be cautious. Their burrows are something the suits will not protect against.*

Got it, Hal said, and he sounded annoyed. *Keep an eye on where you're walking. The last thing we want to do is fall into a torghud burrow.*

A low murmur of assent whispered through their mental link. All Quinn wanted to know was what the hell a torghud was.

She could see Malakai fighting laughter next to her. Or at least, he seemed to be as far as the wispy visage their camouflage gear let them see.

Have something to say? she asked him.

Torghuds are very similar to the creatures we fought back on the Dabilian homeworld. Except their legs are powerful, more like grasshoppers. Their exoskeleton is hard as rock and the only vulnerability they have is the soft area where their joints meet.

Quinn gulped. *Sounds wonderful.* It was amazing how much easier tone was to convey through thought.

Basically, we have to dismember it if we come across one. Use anything with a cutting ability, slicing . . . that sort of thing. Malakai offered what he probably thought was a reassuring smile. But in actual fact, with the shadows and incorporeal sensations, the suits gave off, it only made her uneasy.

A thousand different thoughts flew through her mind, vying for her attention. She couldn't figure out why, if they could anchor a door anywhere, they hadn't just anchored it right to the book, grabbed it and poofed back out of existence, returning to the Library with no hint of danger.

Although, perhaps they needed space around it to pull in energy. Which would make sense as to why opening it in a group of people would be problematic.

All around them, the trees didn't move, even though Quinn could feel a light, humid breeze around her. The air still smelled strongly of stagnant algae, despite the suit's filtration, and her own magic kicking in. She'd felt none of this in her dream.

They wove their way through the Bishickah trees, all following Hal's caution and not touching them. Quinn got the distinct impression that nothing on this planet was friendly, including the people she could sense far off to the left.

Perhaps, especially them.

Walking just to the right behind Hal, she almost missed it. Just one step after Hal experienced a visible shudder, Quinn stepped over what seemed like a threshold. Only it had been dampened.

What . . .

Hal held up a hand, bringing everyone to an abrupt stop. He motioned with a finger to his lips for everyone to remain silent.

She watched as his eyes glowed briefly and felt the dampened web around them relax again. After a few seconds, with the ground calmer, he spoke. *There are security measures taken throughout the area. Most of them are underneath us, sensing vibrations and weight fluctuations, but there are also some that are airborne. Using too much magic will disturb the flow of the air and likely alert them to our presence sooner than we'd like.*

Ikeshal moved slightly to the fore. *Then what do you suggest?*

But it wasn't Hal who spoke up. Nishpa flitted up to hover next to him, a frown on her face. *I can activate my innate canceling of magic, but that might alert them more. Better to have a flux than to have a sudden absence?*

Hal shrugged like he was weighing her words. *Better leave it as is. I pushed it with my redirection just now.*

Could a shield help? Quinn asked.

What sort of shield?

Like a don't look over here sort of blanket to cover us all? Redirection—perhaps misdirection is a better term? She had several books from her arsenal that would allow her to twist the shielding in that sort of way.

Hal frowned and nodded once. *Do you know how much energy that'll cost?*

Quinn blinked. *It's not a spell. I should just be able to do it. Here, let me try it on myself and you can see. One person won't make a dent.* Quinn always wore her shielding anyway. In order for maintaining it to become second nature, constantly wearing it just made sense. Adjusting its frequency wasn't difficult. She closed her eyes, reached through the ability and changed it, pulling on one of the first books she'd ever absorbed, *Blink, and I'm Gone,* adjusting it ever so slightly. It took maybe two seconds.

She felt a sort of shimmer as the shield adjusted and then heard a mildly panicked voice.

Quinn. Malakai sounded worried, but then she felt him relax to the side of her. *That's eerie.*

But effective. Hal stroked his chin and nodded. *Do it. I didn't feel a thing.*

Quinn got to work. It took a moment, but soon all eleven remaining members of their party basically had a look-away-from-me spell cast on them. They moved out, and Quinn could already feel the resistance against them had lessened. In fact, she only realized it was there now, because she knew exactly what to look for.

They continued walking for a while, and Quinn was getting a little hungry. Probably a side effect from boredom. The landscape barely changed. There were no hills, no mountains, just nighttime in a desolate area with vegetation. Having to remain camouflaged and hidden from any potential detection meant no one gave into the temptation to touch things they shouldn't.

Are we just walking in circles? Eric asked suddenly.

But Hal shook his head. *No, we're walking toward that cluster of trees over there.* He gestured off to the left, where it was definitely closer, but still seemed so far away.

Can't I just scout? Eric asked, his impatience shining through.

Nishpa beat Hal to the answer, though. *Only if you promise to be careful.*

What she said. Hal reinforced the direction. *Take one of the others with you.*

Eric nodded, motioned to one of the other imps Quinn didn't know the name of, and took off. She reinforced the shielding as he did and it took maybe a second for her to lose sight of him in the dim light and gear he wore, but she could sense him. He lit up in her mind like a lightning bug; her shielding was always visible in her thoughts.

The rest of the group continued moving cautiously. Quinn was aware she wasn't the only one reaching out her senses to check, double, and triple check that nothing approached them. She knew full well that other people had access to camouflage gear, and she couldn't shake that damned feeling in her gut that'd been there for days now.

Her body felt like lead, heavy to move through this strange atmosphere, despite having the acclimated suit, and the breathing and air purification spells. She was tired, but not tired like she'd been when she was poisoned several days ago.

Had it really been so recently? Everything bled together in her head these days. Time was fluid and passed too fast, while sometimes too slow. Quinn had to shake her head to clear her thoughts and focus on their surroundings.

Are you okay? Malakai asked, the emphasis on you.

Quinn shrugged. She wasn't okay, but she didn't think everything was going smoothly. *I've just felt like something is coming, as if something very bad is about to happen.*

Well, Malakai said, his tone very matter-of-fact. *Can you be more specific?*

But just as Quinn was about to answer, she felt like she got punched in the gut. Stumbling, she fell to one knee, barely saving herself by putting her hand out to catch herself. The ground pressed dangerously close to puncturing her suit through her fingertips, and she unsteadily got to her feet. Nausea threatened to overwhelm her, but as it cleared, she knew one thing with certainty.

One of her shields was badly damaged, and heading directly toward them, limping along in flight.

But the other shield?

Had been obliterated.

71

OUT OF THE SHADOWS

A STRING OF PAIN SHOT THROUGH QUINN'S HEAD AS A REACTION TO HER shield evaporating. She gasped out loud.

"What's wrong, Quinn?" Hal asked.

"It's . . . it's not right. Something's wrong. One of them is coming back. I can't—" There was too much disturbance around the sensations she was experiencing, and she couldn't quite tell who it was that was returning. The feedback pounded against her head, reverberating inside her skull.

She'd have to learn to differentiate sensations better or else her ability to perceive so much at once would be utterly useless.

"Are we being ambushed?" Hal asked, but the amount of senses flooding Quinn at that point in time didn't allow her to give him an exact answer.

"Likely," she said, because one of her shields had winked out of existence. "A shield shattered . . . violently. It's gone. I think—I think," she said, but she didn't need to think anymore, because Eric fluttered into view.

Calling it fluttered was very generous. The little imp and his blood-red hair dripped actual blood this time, as he half-stumbled, half-fluttered into the group, before biting the dirt hard. Given the nature of the ground, Quinn could practically feel the fall.

"Eric," Hal said as he moved to the imp.

Quinn noted that there was a hint of concern in the word. Not that she'd ever thought Hal was heartless.

"The other . . ." Eric stuttered, not sounding like the cocksure little imp that she was used to conversing with. "He's been . . . he's gone."

Hal didn't dignify that with an *Oh, no, what do you mean, he's gone?* Instead, he took it at face value and nodded, directing the others to be on alert. Nishpa and her Furionas companion began casting protective shielding around the group's location. Malakai switched his stances, pulling out his bow and cocking it, while Ikeshal drew his weapon and began to patrol the perimeter.

Nishpa left her spot and hovered over to Eric, who was still bleeding from a tear under his arm. It looked nasty, as if something had punctured him with a sharp implement and raked it down as far as it could. It appeared he'd barely avoided being disemboweled. Not a way Quinn would choose to go. She grimaced. The smell of blood made her slightly nauseous. She looked away as Nishpa hovered down to heal the imp.

Quinn surveyed everything around her, reaching her senses out, trying to find what or who it was that had attacked them. She still couldn't sense people. They weren't any closer than they had been. Of course, it was always possible that their attackers were camouflaged, just like she and Hal had protected their group. Which was only logical.

"Stop it," she heard Nishpa say, and had to suppress a smile considering the situation.

"I'm fine," she heard Eric snap.

"You're not fine," Nishpa said. "Stop acting like a child and let me treat your wounds so that you can at least be partially useful if we're ambushed."

"It's not an ambush, it's—"He was cut off by a massive roar that sounded from underneath their feet. It made the ground tremble, shudder, like an earthquake of a four-point magnitude was hitting them.

Quinn fell to one knee. She knew it'd bruise later. Malakai switched immediately from his bow to his sword.

"Watch out," he said. "That's a torghud."

A torghud. The armored centipede-like creature that Malachi and Escadril had warned them about.

"Fantastic," she heard Hal mutter. Not meaning a word of it. "Everybody spread out. Get ready to engage. You could have told us it was a pack of torghud. I thought we were expecting people," Hal snapped at Eric.

"You didn't give me a chance," Eric said, a little more emboldened now that he'd been partially healed.

"That's going to have to do, Eric," Nishpa said, as she brushed her hands off on each other. "Your wing is fragile. Be careful. I need to conserve my energy and your physiology and mine just don't mix. We'll need to get you an actual healer for your species."

"I know," he said. "Thanks for patching it up."

"Stay in the back," Nishpa warned him. "Make sure that you don't get close to this thing."

"Wasn't gonna," he said, backing away. Hovering a little better now.

And then the torghud was upon them, bursting out of the ground in a shower of rock and debris.

Quinn blinked. She'd been expecting something more like the centipede. Kind of little mandibles up in the head and lots of little grasshopper legs. This thing was positively out of her nightmares. Instead of tiny legs, it has those big jumping grasshopper shears, and it landed right in front of her.

She dodged to the right and rolled to the side, feeling the ground prickle beneath her armor as she brought up a sheath of ice directly between one of the legs and its carapace. The creature screeched, and blood spurted everywhere.

Gross, dark brown blood that stank like rotting vegetation.

Quinn gagged and then sealed off her ability to smell because it wasn't about to do her any favors.

"Good one, Quinn," Malakai said as the leg fell to the ground, twitching. The bad thing was that the creature had about forty more of them.

"Yeah, one down, eighty-seven to go," she said. Everybody began attacking the torghud. Hal ripped at it, literally pulling limbs from its carapace, which was hard as a rock. Quinn dodged attacks as best she could. Because, by the way, the torghud could move its legs independently of one another. The serrated edges on its legs were as hard as steel.

Malakai's sword was perfect for getting between the armor plates. It became a hack and slash for him to separate limbs from the body.

"You should enhance the blade with something else," Quinn offered helpfully, as she gasped in air to keep up with the amount of running she had to do.

He sent her a glare and continued to fight.

Ikeshal dual wielded two burning blades, making quick work of several of the legs. Nishpa healed any wounds received and exacerbated from what Quinn could see the bleeding of the creature.

"Are you doing that?" she asked as blood welled and spurted out of openings when it should have been ebbing.

"It's reverse healing, not to complicate it too much." Nishpa managed a tight smile as she flitted around the battle scene, using her skills to support, heal, and attack.

Quinn had so many questions about the reverse healing, but wisely saved them for later.

The rest of the group, the two other remaining imps and the Furionas Quinn didn't know, went to work as well. Slowly, the torghud lost its limbs. They'd lopped about half of them off and Quinn actually heaved a sigh of relief.

They could do this.

Or so she thought before two more roars echoed from nearby.

Which was precisely not what Quinn wanted to hear.

Hal yelled, "Quinn, Malakai, finish that one off! Ikeshal, tank this one. Brady to Ikeshal, Garon to me. Eric, don't come near them."

The commands were crisp, direct, and helped Quinn push down the fear threatening to creep up her spine. They didn't have time to waste on fear. They had torghuds to kill.

Out of the corner of her eye, Quinn could see the others intercept the two new approaching torghuds. She checked her energy, still in the two thousands, and extended the shield ever so slightly, reinforcing it that bit more so that hopefully nobody else received a fatal injury.

The torghud Quinn and Malakai were fighting seemed emboldened by the appearance of its brethren. They fought it valiantly, but it was much more difficult now that the torghud didn't have other people to distract it from Quinn and Malakai.

Ice, sharpened and pointed, severed limbs spectacularly well, probably because it also froze the joint completely and it was therefore easy to snap off. With each freezing, the creature let out an uncomfortable yelp. It rang through Quinn's ears. And every time, just for an instant, she felt sort of sorry for it.

"Hey," Malakai said, rescuing her inadvertently from her pity, "share it around. Freeze the joints and I'll lop them off."

Quinn blinked. She didn't know why she hadn't come up with that method herself, because it sounded like the simplest solution ever. She nodded once and complied.

Methodically, they worked through the remaining limbs.

Their torghud was frantic now, flailing with multiple legs at once, with no proper direction. One of them caught Quinn with a glancing blow, and she could feel the scratches from the serrated edges of the legs bite deep into her armor.

Luckily, however, the armor absorbed most of the damage, winding around it and making the marks disappear. It still bruised her ribs, and she knew she'd be sore the next day. But she was alive, and thus promptly froze three more limbs.

Her energy was getting low, in the high thousands now, but its regeneration had always been fast. She willed an energy ball out of her inventory and popped it in her mouth, chewing away. They were a new-and-improved recipe Cook sent with her. It was enough for several freezing throws.

"Malakai, to your left!" Quinn suddenly yelled, just as one leg flailed out in that uncontrolled way. A split second after he dive rolled, the leg passed directly through where his torso would have been. He barely escaped it.

With how sharp the serrated edges were, Quinn wasn't entirely sure the armor would have protected the elf. Her gut wrenched. She didn't want him to get hurt—didn't want any of them to get hurt.

And she hated that Eric had gotten injured.

Quinn focused, bringing herself into a numbing space to allow herself to work as methodically as possible. She couldn't afford to focus on the anger at having lost someone, or the potential fear that they might lose someone else.

Quinn blocked off the fear, she blocked off any pity, and clung to her logic. She needed to be efficient and effective. The theory was there, and she knew that any theory she had, she could turn into a magical power with the skills she'd already learned.

A scream ripped through the sounds of combat off to the left. But Quinn refused to look. She couldn't afford to. *They* couldn't afford for them to lose concentration on their current target, who'd begun to slide through its own blood. Now that three-quarters of its appendages were gone, its movements became sluggish.

"It's bleeding out, Quinn. We should be fine now. Can you just freeze the joints?" Malakai spoke, his breath coming in gasps.

Quinn promptly froze the joints, then finally glanced around to see the others, to see where that scream came from while Malakai made quick work of the rest of the dozen legs that were left. When Quinn finally turned to see the rest of the fight, she realized that the battle had tipped in the torghud's favor.

Nishpa nursed what looked like a terrible gash on her arm, and was slowly healing it, while casting protections on Hal, who fought one of the torghuds single-handedly. Garon lay prone on the ground.

She couldn't tell if he was breathing and knew Nishpa would take care of him if he was.

Ikeshal and Brady were less lucky. They bled from multiple wounds, gashes, and already had darkening bruises.

Eric cast fireballs alternatively on both of the torghuds being fought, and the precious second Quinn wasted taking everything in almost cost Hal his arm. He barely avoided the leg that thrust at him, taking the serrated edge of it directly against his forearm. It cut deep, but he shook it off as if it was nothing, and the armor closed back over it. Quinn realized the King of Halschius probably had his own ridiculous self-healing properties.

And then she went to work too.

She froze the limb, adjusted her position, and heard them crack off behind her as Malakai did his work. Rinse and repeat.

Freeze.

Adjust.

She dove out of the way of flailing limbs intermittently. Taking cuts to her armor here and there, landing awkwardly against the coarse ground, she gained more than one gravel rash, even through the protective gear.

She worked methodically with Malakai through both the front half of Hal and Ikeshal's torghuds. Quinn freezing, Malakai following. Their momentum worked like a charm, and Hal was able to take a breath and heal properly.

Finally, when it felt like there was nothing left to do, Quinn looked up as Ikeshal and Hal took care of the rest of the two they'd been fighting. The massive creatures littered the area with brown and sticky blood, some of which sank into the ground.

Erik sat down, panting as he regained his strength, his bedraggled wings drooping behind him. He actually looked pale.

Brody and Ikeshal worked together as they completed their kill. But the Garon was dead, and the Esposian who'd come with Nishpa was badly wounded. Nishpa didn't look too upset. She just seemed irritated, which Quinn hoped meant that she'd be able to heal her companion.

Quinn tossed a complete regeneration snack to everyone, including to Eric who, for once, didn't respond with a snarky comment. They could only use one of those a day, but it seemed like the perfect just-in-case time.

As it was, however, the group's numbers had dwindled. Escadril remained back at the entrance, but now, instead of eleven, they were down to nine people.

Quinn had to keep her emotions at arm's length lest she mourn the people they'd lost. She might not have known them, but she'd spent the last few hours in their company, and now they were gone before she could know more about them.

The smell permeated the entirety of the area, and Quinn knew they'd move soon. Malakai reached over and squeezed her arm even as she was healing their minor wounds.

"Milaro just didn't want me to come," he said simply.

Instantly Quinn understood his earlier mood. She grimaced. "Sorry."

"Shh," Hal said. "Everybody quiet. We can't exactly camouflage with all this here." He gestured at the blood caked ground.

"My, my, my," a sibilant voice whispered out of the darkness beyond the third torghud. "I was right, after all. I *did* smell a rat."

And out of the shadows, Kajaro slithered with a very recognizable book under his arm. A few others stood behind him, including a bulky tall individual in a hooded robe. Kajaro grinned, his fangs showing. "I didn't realize there'd be so many of you."

72

BIDING HIS TIME

The shivers that ran up and down Quinn's spine had nothing to do with the atmosphere they were in. It was the voice that still haunted her in nightmares. It was a voice she apparently followed with her mind whenever he spoke of something involving her—to the extent that she could track him down and listen to his plans on a more astral presence level that she didn't understand.

And now, here he was. Kajaro, in the flesh, most definitely not dead, and not an image projected inside of her head. She slammed her shielding into place, thickening it, making it as dense around herself and her companions as she could, shoveling her own power into it.

"Oh, little Librarian," Kajaro said, his tone mocking. He moved toward her, his body swaying in that sinuous movement only snakes possess. "I see you're all grown up now."

Quinn scowled. She didn't know what to say. She hadn't imagined meeting him face to face so soon. In her mind, she'd be stronger, surer of her abilities and herself, and thrash the ever-living breath out of him. They'd been supposed to surprise the Sölem.

Hal rallied himself, only minorly surprised. He'd obviously sensed something. But he recovered quicker than Quinn could think of something to say, or not to say, or maybe to crack that emergency escape teleport that Milaro had given her. It took a lot of willpower not to do the latter.

She breathed deeply as Hal shifted his stance and plastered a cocky smile on his face. He peered toward the hooded person. "It is you under that hood. I should have taken bets on it."

Hoody didn't dignify that with a response. Instead, he withdrew into himself slightly and pulled behind Kajaro. It was comical in a morbid sort of way, given Hoody was a lot bulkier than the serpent man and wasn't hidden in any sense. Quinn was pretty sure, after listening to the Library and Hal, that she knew who it was. She just wished she was wrong.

Kajaro laughed. "It seems he doesn't want to talk to you," Kajaro said. The S was long, sibilant, so snake-like. He turned around and looked at Hoody for a second before switching his stance back to face Quinn. "What brings you to this barren world. You're not supposed to be here, Librarian."

"If you hadn't sabotaged my Library and nicked off with a bunch of my books, then I wouldn't have to be here now, would I?" Quinn surprised herself with her answer. She'd been thinking those words, but hadn't imagined she'd have the courage to say them out loud. But her fear was still locked away, and her logic had formed into bluntness fueled by the fact that she was sort of pissed off. She pointed to the book under his arm and said, "That book belongs to me and my Library, and you should bloody well give it back."

Kajaro raised the equivalent of a Serpensiril eyebrow. "What, or else you'll glare me to death? You don't even know what's in this book."

"I do know what's in that book. You've already lost two of the five set. Just give me the third one now." She put one hand on her hip and did glare at him to drive home the point.

"I practically gave you one myself," he scoffed, waving the mention of DeKarlyle's book away.

But Quinn wasn't about to be intimidated or to have the narrative changed up on her. He might have taken the chance to plant the mind bomb in her, but she was a hundred percent certain he'd never thought, not in a million years, that she and Malakai would be capable of taking him down. "We also retrieved that one from the Esposian continents."

Kajaro nodded and then yawned, his forked tongue darting out of his mouth as he glanced slyly over at Hal. "Ah, yes. Adrito. Whatever have you done with him? I can't sense him at all."

Hal grinned slowly. "Wouldn't you like to know?"

"Yes." Kajaro blinked. "I would, that's why I asked."

Hal actually laughed that full-throated laugh of his, as if he hadn't expected the response at all. "Kajaro, you and I would probably be marvelous friends if you weren't a zealous fanatic."

"Likely, but in order for that to happen, you'd have to stop being an inane oaf," Kajaro shot back.

Quinn rolled her eyes, all the while monitoring the people who surrounded the Serpensiril. She'd noticed there were two Aracnios with him. Their carapaces seemed darker than Jim and Bob's had been. All eight appendages and mandibles moved restlessly, their many eyes on everything at once as they swayed in the non-existent breeze. They looked vicious.

There were two Sedimentites directly behind Hoody and Kajaro. They looked like a living bunch of boulders, and as they shifted, the ground rumbled ever so slightly. From their demeanors, they were nothing like Larry, the jolly little Sedimentite who was one of her Library assistants. She missed the Library, and they'd only been here a few hours.

Out of the corner of her eye, she saw the one she didn't know, who looked extremely much like a Salosier, but was shorter and stockier, gnarled and almost looked like the wood he was made of was burned beyond recognition even though it obviously hadn't crumbled into charcoal. Information flashed up in front of her face and she remembered she wasn't stuck in a dream and the system had grown strong enough to reach most places.

Name: Itugo
Species: Petraligno
Library Status: Never an ally

Okay, she could deal with that. And for those few seconds, Hal and Kajaro continued to trade insults, and if Quinn wasn't mistaken, Hoody was casting a spell . . . some sort of magic swelled around him.

She shot out her right hand, having found gestures really helped her when executing something new that flashed across her mind. "Encase." She spoke the word, wrapping a shielding around Hoody's hands similar to what she'd used on Adrito, to interrupt whatever ritual or spell he was muttering under his breath.

It didn't work the same way, but it achieved her purpose of halting the spell casting.

Hoody looked up, surprise reflecting in the eyes she only saw briefly before he turned his face away and growled. The sound reverberated through the ground in a guttural noise. "You shouldn't have done that."

"What?" Quinn asked, battering her eyelashes innocently. "Am I just supposed to let you cast your spells without fighting back?"

"It'd be easier on all of us if you would." His voice held a lilting quality that sounded familiar, as if she should know the person speaking, or someone close to it.

"Obviously, it's my goal to make life as difficult as possible for you," she said. "So how about you just give me back my book and we won't have to kick your butts?"

Hoody blinked at her, and Kajaro laughed. It was a strange sound, like tree branches devoid of leaves skittering over a tin roof. The sound was brittle and yet bold as it snaked down her spine, practically rebounding off her bones within her skin. The sensation wasn't one Quinn relished. She double-checked her shielding, triple-checked her mind, and felt safe within her abilities to control. It gave her more confidence to speak to him.

But Kajaro was smirking at her as the silence grew.

"What's your deal?" she asked, her tone flat.

He laughed, full-throated, and echoed around the clearing. "Oh, Librarian, you're not even supposed to be here. You were supposed to die, what eight years ago? I don't even know how old you are. A long time ago, before you ever had the chance to come here."

Quinn scowled, but pushed away the inkling to react in anger. Instead, she shrugged. "Guess I don't like dying."

"We seem to have that in common." Kajaro actually laughed. And Hoody, well, he joined in.

Hal clapped his hands together. "Enough of this. Dravishk, it's about time you told me what you're doing here."

Dravishk stepped out from behind Kajaro and pushed his hood back, flexing the fingers on his hands that Quinn had hurt earlier. His features resembled what Quinn would think of as an upright bearded dragon. He had beautifully smooth scales accentuated by black ridges, even though they glowed a strange sort of golden-green underneath.

"Really, Halithrija? You, of all people, are telling me this is enough?" Dravishk threw his head back and laughed. His scales glistened in the strange double twilight that had settled over them in the last ten minutes. The others they'd come with moved as if of one mind. "You take all the fun out of things, and for that, I believe I owe you payback."

Quinn knew, deep down, who this Dravishk was. Who he had to be. It clicked into place because it made sense. Her own skin bristled underneath her armor. As if the scales were trying to get out, to answer whatever call Dravishk initiated. She exerted all the calm mind techniques she knew, attaining complete control over her own body and soothing the cosmicisodracus portion of her into taking a back seat for now.

Dravishk looked around, his expression confused for a second. "Where is she?" he asked, the question directed pointedly at Hal.

Hal shifted, allowing his usual resting height to emerge. His eyes followed the movement of their opponents as he did so, cracking his neck as he took everything in. "You'll have to be a bit more specific, dear cousin. After all, you know how thick I can be, right?"

Hoody looked decidedly peeved at the comment. He opened his jaw to say something but close it again as if he'd had second thoughts. "She's here. I can sense her. Do you have the manifestation hiding somewhere here? Is that it? After what he's been through, he shouldn't even be functional." He said the latter with a sneer, in such a way that

Quinn wanted to jump the distance and punch his mouth shut for him.

But she could tell this Dravishk fellow was far too powerful for her. For now, anyway. Besides, she had a sneaking suspicion that it'd be unwise to draw more attention to herself. Malakai inched closer, placing himself slightly to the side of her and a step in front of her. She appreciated the gesture, because judging from the abject terror in her gut right now despite trying to seal it away, this was what the premonitions she'd been having were all about.

"The emanations come from the fact that she outfitted us. You know that." Hal sounded convincing, but Quinn suspected she was who Dravishk sensed, and that didn't bode well for any of them. If he found out . . .

It seemed Hal was on the same page.

"Do I have to throw the first punch or are you just going to sniff us to death?" Hal asked, and didn't wait for an answer. A split second later, he hurled a massive fireball directly at the Petraligno, who'd moved closer to Nishpa, catching both him and Dravishk off guard. The latter of which caught a second fireball directly after.

The Petraligno screeched with a sound that wasn't like anything Quinn had ever heard before.

Quinn cringed. Popped a regeneration lolly and reinforced all the shielding she had.

New mission: Distract Dravishk from the truth.

Escadril! Hal yelled through their communication link. And a split second later, the massive Salosier appeared, landing in a superhero pose directly in front of the King of Halschius. He stood up, even as roots shot up through the ground, tangling themselves around the feet of every single member of their attacker's group.

"Took you a mite longer to call me than I anticipated," he mumbled to Hal.

"I was busy." Hal shrugged his answer as he raised a hand to fend off Dravishk's first attack with a shield like substance. He looked directly at Quinn. "Focus."

Hal spoke in her mind. *I'll distract him while you both pull Kajaro as far away from Dravishk as you can. Separating their complimentary fighting styles will be key to coming out on top.*

Quinn nodded. Summoning her ice balls, she sent foot-long sharpened darts aimed with deadly precision toward Kajaro's face. Preoccupying him with those allowed Malakai to herd him in the direction they wanted. It would have been great if she wasn't a hundred percent sure he was currently biding his time.

She only wished she knew for what.

73

ORIGINAL INTENTION

Quinn and Malakai had faced Kajaro before, but this time all of them were more calculating. And Kajaro's smirk hinted at ulterior motives for allowing them to pull him away.

Quinn partitioned her mind to keep an eye on anything out of the ordinary while using the main portion to devote to the fight. She penned in his movements in with ice darts.

Meanwhile, Malakai darted in and out, distracting him, breaking concentration so that Kajaro couldn't finish casting one of his vortexes. Perhaps not the best strategy, but it worked until they could figure out precisely how to defeat him.

What they wouldn't withstand well was being hit by one of those swirling masses of negative magic.

In the back of her mind, though, she knew the others might need her or Malakai's assistance. Multitasking on a battlefield wasn't on her bingo card, but she had to make it work.

Hal fought Hoody, or Dravishk, or whatever his name was. The Aracnios fought against the remaining imp, Brady, as well as Nishpa and the Furionas that Quinn just hadn't gotten around to scanning. The Sedimentites were occupied by Ikeshal with Erik as backup.

Quinn catalogued each fight separately, effectively able to be on alert for an emergency. She kept it confined and locked down from worry and fear. But even so, she couldn't help being impressed by Ikeshal's ability to reflect back the damage he took.

Kajaro's shielding this time was next level. He reinforced himself to such an extent that her ice magic barely scratched the surface. She certainly wasn't able to do actual damage to him yet. But she'd persevere.

It was the Petraligno versus Escadril fight that threatened to distract her. Their fighting style involved ripping the ground up, churning the surrounding nature. Escadril did it in such a way that enhanced the natural properties, like utilizing the roots to confine and restrict his opponent. But the Petraligno was destructive in his methodology, twisting things that were already broken or ripped apart and making something new and vulgar from them.

He used the torghud carapace in just such a way. As it screeched and scraped while being molded, Quinn cringed.

"Librarian, it's like you've never been in a fight," Kajaro drawled. Her attention hadn't been completely split from him, but she admitted even to herself that she might have been slightly fascinated by Escadril's fight. "Your opponent is me."

She raised an eyebrow as she narrowly avoided what seemed like a half-hearted electrical pulse directed her way. "It's not like you're challenging or anything. I've already killed you once. Do you have nine lives?"

Kajaro didn't laugh. He looked somewhat perplexed, and his brow pinched with worry. "How did you know I have nine lives?"

Quinn did a double take. "Well, you don't have nine anymore. You've already died at least once that I know of," she said, trying to figure out how a Serpensiril had nine lives, where the adage that she knew was about cats having nine lives.

But apparently Kajaro didn't like her comeback, because the next thing she knew, he basically manifested a damned vortex spear instantly in his hand.

"Dive to the right," Malakai yelled out at her. Quinn did so without thinking simply because of the amount of training she and Malakai had put in together. She knew that when he called out for her to move, she needed to do it. In her spot, a pool of lava opened up. She didn't feel any fear at the sign of the liquid rock, which was an odd sensation. Her gratefulness that she was mostly impervious to heat lingered in her mind.

Kajaro stood there cackling as he summoned his vortex between his hands again. The electricity swirled. It gave her flashbacks of that first fight, back when she'd literally known nothing, not understood how things worked, and basically only survived out of sheer dumb luck.

Now she wasn't that same girl anymore. She'd grown in knowledge and power now. As she reached out, sensations flooded through her, the knowledge of simply how to stop the electricity, how to siphon it off.

"*Acquiesce*," she said, and the lightning jumped from the vortex Kajaro had been creating and leapt into the lava pool, imploding it in upon itself and sealing it away into hardened rock.

Kajaro looked at her with his mouth open. "That shouldn't be possible."

Quinn put a hand on her hip and played with three large ice balls in her other hand. She twirled them and they floated as if she was juggling them with one hand. She looked at him. "Why shouldn't that be possible? Half the fun is testing out affinity relationships." At least that's how it worked for her. He didn't know she had no idea what she was doing.

Lightning passed through Kajaro's dark eyes. The black that bled to the edges of the sclera seemed to bleed even farther now, darkening his facial features. Electricity zinged around his body like an eel. This was different electricity. It belonged solely to Kajaro.

"You'll pay for that," he said. "You're not supposed to be here. You should be dead and the Library along with you. And this time, I'll see the job done properly. Because I'll do it myself."

Quinn felt shivers run down her spine, even as Malakai backed up and fired non-stop shots, trying to locate an opening in Kajaro's defenses, but the Serpensiril's new shielding was nigh impenetrable.

She couldn't figure out how to damage him. Unmaking a personal shield was a far more advanced level of magic than Quinn was ready for.

Wasn't it?

She held up her hand to get the elf to stop. "You're just wasting."

"Have unlimited arrows," Malakai grumbled, rolling his eyes, but Quinn couldn't pay him attention because she needed to find the opening in Kajaro's defenses. The jerk actually had multiple lives. While she'd been certain he was dead after their last encounter, originally she'd assumed she made a mistake. But with this revelation . . .

She could see, could sense through her extended reach, that Hal and Dravishk were sincerely evenly matched, and that worried her. How did an ancient primeval satyr not have an edge over Hoody? It only meant her hunch had to be right.

They had to win this fight, but right now, it felt shaky at best. She could already sense that Nishpa and her crew, as well as Ikeshal, Escadril, and Erik, were falling behind. None of them had expected this type of power. They'd been foolish and thought they had the upper hand.

When obviously, Kajaro's idea had been to obliterate the Librarian when she came to get the book.

They needed something to shift the fight, and she needed that bloody book back.

Calmness leached through Quinn as she reached into her thoughts and let herself breathe. In order to focus, she had to minimize distracting thoughts. *Bravo, brain,* she thought, but really, she was grateful. It allowed her to analyze the area and try to find holes in Kajaro's defenses.

While time didn't technically slow around her, she boosted her perception and thought speeds, taking in everything around her in but a split second.

Kajaro sent out electrical shocks toward her and Malakai. She dodged out of the way, using her ability to hover and blink simultaneously, and to be in spots that he wasn't expecting. That he couldn't foresee. It threw him off every time, and his eyebrows twitched in frustration.

Malakai used the same tactic and slowly but surely, they began to chip away at the Serpensiril's shielding and composure.

Quinn, knowing how to unmake her own shielding, began to leverage her ice attacks with a slight hint of what she would call an acid attack. It wasn't actually acid, but it was like a tiny spark that started a hairline, spiderweb-type fracture in his shield. Frankly, the skill was originally intended for breaking into strongholds during siege battles.

But she felt Kajaro was stronghold enough for her to use it as subtly as possible. She hoped that by the time they cracked through, he'd still be unaware of what she was doing.

Off to the right, she heard Nishpa gasp. It took all of her concentration not to run and help. It was a pained sound, but she knew Nishpa was more than capable of taking care of herself. Just like Hal's fight would end the way they needed it to, just like Ikeshal and Escadril were going to be fine.

Because they all had to be.

"Librarian, you're learning tricks," Kajaro said, his tone forever mocking her, even if she could hear a hint of strain this time. "Not too many months have passed; you shouldn't have learned this many tricks yet."

Quinn shrugged, not letting him interrupt her concentration or take away the distance she'd achieved from fear and worry. It was the best way to keep herself together, to not give in to the emotions while also not completely getting rid of them. It was a compromise for both her, the Library, Aradie, and Lynx. She didn't want to go back to that place, even if it meant she could be ruthlessly effective.

A massive roar echoed from over in the left-hand corner where Hal and Hoody were fighting. Quinn glanced briefly, her focus taking in everything at the time. Hal gripped Dravishk under the chin and turn him around as if he was going to wrestle throw him. The growl was Hoody, incensed because he was being manhandled.

Quinn took a breath, her complete focus back on Kajaro as she picked away at his shielding with her spiderweb-like cracks. It was rinse and repeat. She distracted him; she entrapped the shielding while Malakai did and then she felt it.

She knew it was about to give.

I need you to aim to the left side of his chest, just under his arm, she said to Malakai.

Malakai gave one nod and loosed the arrow.

The effect was dazzling.

It hit just under Kajaro's left arm and the shielding literally cracked like somebody had thrown a pebble through a glass window. Even the sound carried over the entire combat area. The spiderweb solidified, breaking everything forcibly, and pushed the Serpensiril to the ground as the shielding fell away.

Kajaro screamed and held his head for a second, the backlash hitting him strongly.

Maybe he thought too much of himself, maybe he thought too little of Quinn. She couldn't exactly be sure, but she'd done it; she'd broken his shielding.

Concentrating, she levied an ice attack to spear him in the chest with three more immediately to follow.

Just as they were about to hit him, he stood upright and drew himself up larger than he'd ever been. He stood taller than Malakai now, at about seven feet, and his eyes were fully red. Blood leaked down his face leaving a green trail behind.

"Enough!" he screamed.

There was power in that word.

She could tell everybody had stopped and was watching them, that the command wouldn't let her look away either to check on her comrades, so she had to use senses instead.

"I've had enough of you. You have thwarted me at every single possible turn," Kajaro said, "and I will no longer allow it."

"You don't have a choice," Quinn said, fighting through the paralysis to work her mouth. "Do and say whatever you want. But you'll give that damned book back."

"You're not getting any more books, Librarian, because I'm going to kill you. But first, you're going to watch all your little friends die." Something swirled in his eyes, it churned all around him like a vortex but a different type.

It swirled in tiny increments so fast around him that Quinn couldn't quite comprehend. A forceful thought like an ice pick allowed her to break the paralysis hold on herself and others. She reinforced her shielding and poured everything she could to protect them all.

She heard Malakai yell out a warning across the battlefield and she hunkered down, bolstering those shields repeatedly, knowing she couldn't stop what was coming.

Her stomach flip-flopped.

Nausea threatened to overwhelm her, but she held on grimly.

It was only a split second later when Kajaro released the spell. Quinn wasn't sure what she'd been expecting.

Multiple small, mini-frisbee-sized disks of electrical vortexes simply exploded out from where Kajaro stood, zooming toward every single individual, not even picky about what side they were on. She could hear them as they impacted, ripping through everybody. Even her reinforcements barely offered any resistance. She could feel it as they thunked through flesh.

The cries and the screams made it to her, and because she was shielding everyone, she could feel the damage done to every single person.

She looked up as she saw the vortexes whirling toward her, and dug down, knowing she'd get one chance to drop them like miasma drones.

But she didn't expect Malakai to dive in front of her.

Not only did he get the electrical frisbees that were meant for him, but he intercepted the ones intended for her. His scream cut off as he plummeted to the ground.

Quinn shrieked out, "Malakai!" and Kajaro cackled gleefully.

Inside her, it was like a click resounded through her entire being, teetering on the threshold of something just out of reach.

Screams echoed through to her; pain resonated in her senses.

And something inside her shattered.

Every single emotion fell away, every single one except the pure need to rectify the situation.

Quinn looked up, barely noticing that her scales had ripped portions of her armor away, and now coated some of body. It even felt like a protective helmet now encased her face.

She focused her gaze on Kajaro and held out her left hand, palm forward, before speaking. "That was a terrible choice."

74

MAKES PERFECT SENSE

Back in the Library, Milaro watched Dottie. It was amazing, in his mind, how the superellex futora operated. She helped the check in desk, organized all of the assistants, and with help from Jasper and Geneva, orchestrated the retrieval of branch opening relevant books. He was impressed and was just about to tell her so.

But a very subtle ripple of power washed over him. He glanced around, realizing that no one else had felt it and frowned. Maybe it was in his head. He'd been running himself ragged for the past few months, and a few days rest hadn't allowed him to completely recover yet.

Oh no. It was definitely there.

Milaro looked up as something shifted within the Library. Aradie perched on one of the pillars above him, and let out a low and even hoot, directed solely at him. Lynx was deep in conversation with Carafax and Siliqua somewhere else in the Library, trying to recover his memories. And so Milaro had promised to keep an eye on everything. He turned to Harish, who was fiddling with the console.

"Did you feel that?" he asked. "The slight hiccup in the Library's systems?"

"Just a bit of an adjustment I think." Harish shrugged. "I mean, they're recovering memories all the time right now, sire. It's very obvious there'll be fluctuations throughout the whole system."

"Yep, you're probably right," Milaro said, yet he was quite certain that wasn't it. He directed his conversation to the Library. *What is that?* he asked.

I don't know, the Library responded slowly, as if it too was trying to make sense of the fluctuations emanating throughout the pocket dimension. Granted, they were very subtle. It wasn't something the average layperson would notice, but for somebody like Milaro and the Library itself, who were very attuned to the different dimensional wavelengths, this was extremely obvious.

"You don't think they've gone and done something stupid, do you?" Milaro asked.

Well, the Library said and paused. *What would you define as stupid?*

Milaro chuckled. Harish raised an eyebrow, but he was used to the king speaking telepathically by now. He'd known the man for millennia.

You make a good point, Milaro said to the Library. *And yet, at the same time, I feel like we've missed something. How is the gathering of the books going?*

I mean, I know, but how do you feel it's going? the Library asked.

Dottie and Geneva are working hard to get the rest of the books for the alchemical branch. I do believe we're close. I think we're down to single figures.

Exactly. Which is marvelous. But I don't think that's the shift.

No. No, it shouldn't shift until the branch actually opens, should it? Milaro asked.

No, the Library said. *Now, this is different than that. Quinn has definitely used her power, but she hasn't . . . oh no,* the Library said, pausing suddenly.

Okay, "oh no" is a bad thing to say to somebody, and then not elaborate, Milaro said.

As if to accentuate that, there was a soft rumbling from the core of the Library. Subtle, not enough to alert anyone else. But Aradie swooped down, hooting soft and low, worry evident.

I . . . I think something may have flipped Quinn's switch, the Library muttered.

What do you mean it flipped her switch?

It seems she's tapped into some of her heritage a bit prematurely. The Library's tone was filled with worry.

Her cosmicisodracus heritage? Milaro couldn't keep the incredulity out of his tone

What other heritage would you think I meant? The Library sounded irritable. *It's strong. And I don't . . .* The Library gasped. *She's not ready for this. This isn't good.*

In what way? Milaro tried his best to stay calm, but the Library was actually getting worked up.

There was a pause before the Library spoke again. *It's not going to break the Library, but I am worried it might break Quinn. I can't tell from here.*

Should we send people to help?

Again, the Library hesitated. *I'm not sure how she's accessed this. She might not be in the right state of mind to recognize friend from foe if we send others . . .* A few precious seconds passed. *Something's happened to trigger this, something dire.*

Another slight shift echoed through the Library. No one but Aradie, Milaro, and the Library itself seemed to notice. At least that's what Milaro thought until Lynx popped into view directly in front of him at the check in desk. His eyes were fluctuating, and his body flickered. "She shouldn't be emerging this way. It's way too soon. Hal is going to be furious."

"Hal is with her," Milaro said, condensing the air around them to make sure they didn't panic any of the assistants or patrons. "He'll keep her safe."

Lynx's eyes finally settled and he studied Milaro for a long moment. "I don't think this is as simple as that."

He's right, the Library said as yet another soft ripple of power ran through.

"That does seem more controlled than the initial bursts," Milaro offered.

"More controlled and yet, she's upset . . . she's not herself." Lynx sounded so worried.

Be ready to send help, but . . . from what I'm sensing through our connection right now, sending more people will only confuse her.

"Then we have to hope she's still got enough control so Hal can help her keep her presence of mind." Milaro examined every avenue. "In the meantime, I'll figure out how we can help her."

But he couldn't help that secondary worry that gnawed at him. He had the distinct feeling Quinn wasn't the only one in danger.

Power rippled under Quinn's scales, under her skin, and she felt alive. Like she did every time her mind activated one of those new-fangled skills she didn't quite understand. Except this time, coldness crept through her, and Quinn couldn't help but revel in it. Her scales gave her an added sense of protection. Her mind was clear of everything: clear of the need to worry about anybody else, clear of the need to care about how she might damage anybody in the vicinity who wasn't her friend, and clear to objectively analyze the situation in front of her.

Her friends were covered by her shielding and thus easily identifiable.

Kajaro took a step back at the sight of her. She could feel herself grinning, even though it wasn't something she'd initiated consciously. But that didn't matter anymore. Kajaro was there, right in front of her, being more of a pest than he had been the entire time she had known about him.

And she was done.

Her arm still held out, she clenched her fist. "Crush," she said, and the ground underneath him crushed together, holding him in place.

A yelp of pain escaped him.

"What? You look surprised," she said. She didn't give him a chance to respond. Instead, as she said *surprised*, she pushed out her hand and with it, a force like a gale wind jettisoned out of her palm, straight into Kajaro's chest, pushing him over the coarse ground about twenty feet after ripping him away from the earth holding him.

She looked at her hand and frowned. "Well, that didn't go nearly as far as I meant it to," she said. Then she shrugged, not that it mattered. She could sense everybody all around her. Everybody but Hal and Hoody were injured. Hal didn't need her healing thread. They'd had enough power to protect themselves when Kajaro sent out his death disks.

She clicked her fingers, envisioning an ever-so-slight regeneration thread that she wove into the shielding she kept over everyone. All it took was a thought to create and one to direct. Simple understanding of the mechanics behind the magic allowed her to combine what she knew. She didn't have time to check and see just how much healing or energy regeneration each person needed. Her brain refused to focus on the fact that Malakai still lay motionless on the ground. All she took from that image was the anger and the fuel.

Because this time, Kajaro was going to pay.

"Did you think that would be enough?" Quinn said as she moved toward him. The fighting beyond them picked up, but there was a renewed energy in her allies. "Did you think you'd hurt my friends? The people who've been taking care of me? And that I'd suddenly cower in a corner?"

Kajaro shook his head and scrambled back up. But he was hunched over, and Quinn could smell more than she could see the blood. He must have ripped something. Out of the corner of her eye, she noticed that Hoody began to move toward them. Yet Hal intercepted him. Good. At least she could count on them to keep out of the way.

"Nishpa, I'd appreciate it if you could make sure that I don't accidentally injure anybody," Quinn said. "Heal the others up. Take care of Mal."

"Quinn?" Nishpa asked. Her voice sounded like it was concerned. "Quinn, I'm not sure he . . ."

"Heal who you can," she said, without answering the question in

Nishpa's voice. The Furionas fae also sounded like she was miles away when Quinn knew she wasn't. And that was fine.

Everything was fine.

She could sense the way the Furionas was stuck in indecision. She didn't know whether to come and help Quinn or remain and heal those she could. The healing Quinn had sent out was minuscule in comparison to what Nishpa could accomplish. But it had, luckily, stopped some of the worst gashes on every single one of them. The Librarian could sense the blood flow stopping in general in one of her many compartmentalizations.

"I don't think this is going to work out, Kajaro," she said. She thought she should be angry. Very much so. But why? Why had he wanted to make her pay by hurting her friends. That didn't even make sense. What sort of person, what sort of being did that?

She looked up and she could feel this strange light, almost see it from her eyes, coming from her eyes. She glanced down at her hands, the blue and gold scales giving her claws. She cocked her head to one side as Kajaro managed to right himself completely. He stood still about seven feet to her five odd.

"You're still tiny but you're not human?" His voice gave away his consternation. "How?"

Quinn shrugged. "I'm just being me. You, on the other hand, you need to stop being you."

And as she spoke the word, she clenched her fists again.

Suddenly, Kajaro was wracked by pain. It blitzed through his whole system like a completely different grade of electricity running through him. She made sure it worked its way out gradually. Because everybody's bodies had some element of electricity in them, didn't they? She wanted him to pay. She wanted him to hurt. And she wanted all the information in his head.

"How about this time we lock *your* mind away?" And then Quinn decided that speaking was overrated. She leveled a mind bomb at him, one she'd devised herself based upon what he'd attempted to do to her. But she'd refined it. She just wanted to dig in and pull all the information out she could, regardless of how it affected him.

He held up his hands crossed over each other in front of his face and barely managed to avoid being hit by her first strike. She shrugged and moved faster than she'd realized she could, so that she stumbled as she came to the left-hand side of him. She threw yet another mind bomb and another one aimed at his head. They were designed to simply dig into his skull and retrieve whatever she could, however she could, regardless of damage left behind.

"You hurt him," she said, some of her locked away anger leaked over and into her voice. "You hurt so many people."

But Kajaro wasn't to be outdone. He sent out shocks of his own, dangerously close to Quinn. Multiple, raging electrical shocks. At first, as she saw them coming toward her, she was mildly concerned. But calm overcame her as she assessed them, inspected them and realized that they were mundane electricity and all she had to do was swipe them to the side while channeling her earthen affinity. Grounding them and allowing them to peter out.

Doing so, she realized it looked like she blocked them from each side, sending the electricity fizzling into nothingness.

And that's when Dravishk yelled, "She can't exist. It's not possible."

But Hal actually chuckled, "You've been a little bit too busy sabotaging your sister to be able to say that."

The words clicked in Quinn's head, as definitive confirmation of who Dravishk was. Even though the voices were distant, it all made sense now.

All except Malakai being an idiot.

All except Malakai still not moving.

"And now," she said, tearing her attention back to herself, "for your next trick."

Kajaro spluttered. "This makes no sense," he ground out, the *Ses* in his words sibilant to a fault. "*You* make no sense!"

"Oh," Quinn said, suddenly very glad to be what she was. She threw out another strike of lightning combined with one of her mind bombs, and this time it hit. "I'm the only one here who makes perfect sense."

Kajaro screamed.

75

CLOSE TO DEPLETED

A PART OF QUINN BALKED AT HAVING CAUSED KAJARO PAIN. SHE LOOKED at him, blinking once as his form writhed on the floor. Her ability to detach herself and clinically analyze his predicament felt strange, yet powerful.

Compartmentalization might be dangerous, but right now, it felt potent.

She was completely preoccupied by this one individual, even though her senses extended beyond him, allowing her to understand where everybody was in relation to her and just how quickly she needed to react in case they decided to approach her. She could still sense exactly where Malakai lay.

How still he lay.

However, the other part of Quinn was cold, calculating, and felt nothing. Kajaro, writhing on the floor in agony when he'd caused so much pain to so many people, including those she cared about who were being patched up by their healer right at that moment, was just the first step.

"Tell me, Kajaro." She finally spoke out loud, her brain a whirr of thoughts trying to figure out what to do, and how to handle this, how to keep a hold over the power she could feel surging inside her. "Why do you want me dead?"

But Kajaro wasn't exactly forthcoming with answers right then, and Quinn, tired of listening to the squeals as the mind bomb she'd created worked its magic, wasn't exactly patient. What she'd cast at him was more like a mind worm, because she'd been thinking of the bookworms at the time that she created it, and it slowly wormed its way through his brain before settling somewhere.

"Oh, is that hurting you?" she asked. "Do you think that hurts as much as when you tried to kill me with yours, when I didn't know anything, and you took advantage of that?"

"Quinn?" Nishpa called out.

Quinn held up a hand, and she knew Nishpa wouldn't be able to speak, because she was keeping the sound away from her. Right now, Quinn couldn't afford to be distracted, not even by her allies. Finally, sick and tired of Kajaro's lack of coherence, she simply cut off sounds to his vocal cords.

After all. She'd absorbed the Serpensiril anatomy specifically with this meeting in mind.

"So much better," she murmured. "Maybe just direct your thoughts to me, and I'll be able to hear them. What was that? No, you're still screaming in your mind. Was I too harsh?" she asked no one in particular.

She could sense Nishpa, Ikeshal, all of them still fighting. Eric was wounded badly wounded, so she sent another healing wave out toward him, and glanced at her statistics. She frowned, with no idea why her energy had filled up. No idea why it was now over three thousand. That seemed odd. She was quite certain it had been under three thousand earlier.

3208/3622

2854/3285

Quinn paused. Something niggled at the back of her mind, like a squirrel when it had a nut in its little hands. She was forgetting something. But it obviously wasn't important, or she would have remembered it.

She stepped closer to Kajaro, who'd finally stopped spluttering as his mental screams died down. She clicked her fingers, and sound came back to him. He drew in ragged breaths and looked up at her, his eyes black, filling the entire sclera, much like a snake's eyes except those thin slits seemed absent. But this time, there was something else in them, something she'd never seen in the Serpensiril before.

"Why, Kajaro," she said, "is that fear I see?"

Quinn wasn't sure what she was doing. Her mind held focus, almost like a pristine clarity that ran through her mind. And all she wanted was to figure out how to permanently stop Kajaro and make him pay in the process.

Kajaro needed to die, but Kajaro was a conundrum in himself. He had multiple lives, and she wasn't sure how those multiple lives worked, because she did know for a fact that he had to die for them to kick back in, which begged the question: how long did she have to wait for him to come back? And where would he respawn? So, even if she killed him . . .

Well . . .

That put a kink in her plans.

The first thing they needed to do was get Kajaro out of the way.

He staggered, first to his knees, and then he put a hand down on the floor. "You," he rasped, "you will pay for this."

She cocked her head to the side. "I will pay for this," she said, as if tasting the words on her tongue.

Energy flared through her. She could sense fire creeping along her veins. She knew, without a shadow of a doubt, that her very own power would overwhelm her if she let it. It was such a vast sense of force, such a vast realization that she had to keep things balanced or it would consume her too. That was the only reason she didn't obliterate him right then. "Explain yourself. I'm getting bored."

And while he spluttered, she checked on the others. Hal fought Dravishk, not giving him any chance to interfere with Quinn and Kajaro's fight. She noticed that Brady, Escadril, Ishekal, Erik, Nishpa, all of them were fighting so that Quinn had her chance to deal with

Kajaro. And she had to, because she couldn't allow him another one of those vortex attacks.

She pushed out with her own energy, gifting an abundance to those around her, and drew in ambient energy and mana from the whole world around her. This place had it in abundance, but it was all tainted with chaos energy. Easy enough to filter out after she'd absorbed so many books on the subject.

With just a thought, just with a flick of her wrist, the energy swirled, passing through her and out to the others. For several precious seconds it gave Quinn a sense of vertigo, not unlike the one she'd had when she got pulled into the larger universe.

Kajaro finally, fully on his feet, looked worse for wear. He moved his fingers, but Quinn wasn't about to let him. "I'd stop that if I were you," she said.

"You don't have the guts to hurt me," he snarled out at her, anger replacing the wariness once again. Even still, his body was bruised and battered.

Quinn raised an eyebrow, and she pushed back at him again. This time, when he landed, she grounded him with "Gravitas," one word, bitten out in a command, so he couldn't refuse.

"I do believe I can do worse than that," she said, grinning at no one.

He tried, he fought against the pressure, trying to push himself up. "Nullify," he screamed out.

But it didn't, it couldn't, because Quinn bound his own body to the gravity, and his simplistic attempt to undo the spell didn't factor that into the equation.

Kajaro continued to thrash, and Quinn allowed the binds of gravity to keep him prone. She heard a gasp off to her side and didn't need to look to know that Ikeshal had been badly wounded. Luckily, he'd downed the last of the Sedimentites in the process. With Eric's backup, it seemed that he'd barely managed to overpower them. She could sense that their wounds weren't exactly trivial. But she didn't have in depth knowledge of all their physiologies to make sure.

Another oversight she needed to correct.

It took all her concentration to keep the shieldings up, feeding them healing and regeneration from the atmosphere she filtered. Not to mention containing Kajaro. She had to get stronger so she could protect them better.

Nishpa was low on energy despite Quinn's replenishment, but at least the Aracnios were badly wounded. While Hal and Hoody appeared to be evenly matched, she could tell that Hal was beginning to tire, perhaps because he was trying so hard to prevent Dravishk from interfering in Quinn and Kajaro's fight.

The Petraligno and Escadril worried Quinn despite how far she'd pushed her compartmentalization. It seemed some emotion was still leaking through. Escadril didn't appear to have the upper hand she thought he should have. The Petraligno's abilities were simply capable of rotting anything Escadril threw at him and she could feel that one of her allies' limbs had already been affected. She'd be able to help, she was sure of it, once Kajaro was dealt with. Ikeshal should be able to move to help the others now that the Sedimentites were out of the way.

She turned her full attention back to Kajaro just as a ripple passed through her, a power, a shuddering fiery energy.

Quinn grasped the skills Hal had taught her, everything he'd done to make her understand how to utilize her powers, but it wasn't working. Fire was a brutal element. Rarely reasonable. Often passionate.

Even with the calmness, even with the detachment, she couldn't quite grasp onto that power. It was angry. It wanted to be used and it wanted to get out of her. Not much in her readings had prepared her for such a circumstance. She wasn't entirely sure how to go about using it safely.

She tried to center herself, not let herself get carried away. Even with telling herself she could do it, the fire still bubbled just underneath the surface. A brief orange hue passed through her blue and gold scales. They still protected her.

Taking in a deep breath, Quinn reassured herself. She was part cosmicisodracus. She could do this, but just what *was* this? She hadn't been ready. They hadn't trained her fully, always acting like there was plenty of time for her to be ready. All she'd learned was rudimentary control. And right now, it was slipping.

Quinn took another deep breath, even if it was a little shakier, refusing to let it get the better of her. She could feel the heat coursing through her veins. Heat and brief pain flashed through her causing her to momentarily lose control of the gravity shield she'd placed over Kajaro. It buckled and he burst free, shattering it in all different directions. Luckily, he'd had to waste a lot of his energy to do so, and Quinn had been purifying the chaotic energy around them, turning it into mana and energy replenishment for her team.

Another thing, she had no idea how she'd done.

But at least it meant that there was less chaos energy for him to pull from.

She gasped from the string of backlash losing the shield caused, panting. Kajaro leveled one of his vortex discs directly at her. It flew true, catching Quinn in the forearm as she raised it to protect herself.

Her scales weren't as strong as a full dragon or anything. And the disc ripped into them ever so slightly because the armor wasn't yet at its peak. All her scales did right now was give her an extra layer of protection.

She screamed in pain as the scales were damaged, but not because of the vortex disc attack. The fire inside her begged to escape, pouring out like molten lava. It wanted release. It wanted to engulf Kajaro in everything it could, and she didn't know how to stop it.

Quinn held up a hand, aiming the palm toward Kajaro, and screamed in defiance as veritable lava shot out of her wound. He barely dodged out of the way. It caught his cloak, and it caught his tail, and she could smell singed cloth and flesh. She recalled some of Hal's stories about element utilization and with effort, refocused herself.

It was difficult to focus through the pain and the fire, which seemed to almost have a will of its own.

Quinn focused and pulled the fire back down into her in an attempt to calm it, to settle it. The fire, which was ripping through her veins and trying to come out the other side burned in defiance. At first she didn't realize the whimpers came from her. Even so, the good old mind concentration she'd practiced for hours with Milaro came to the rescue.

She managed to form a stream of ice over her limbs, a cooling down that hissed out of the wounds in her arms. But she didn't stop there. Aiming her right hand, the only one she could still move slightly directly at Kajaro, she leveraged an ice geyser straight into Kajaro's face.

He'd still been hoping around trying to put out his tail and cloak. His face was pale, and his entire tail had blackened, the scales already beginning to peel.

He looked up at the attack, surprise showing on his face in the split second before it smashed right into his nose. The ice spread fast, encasing his snout, head, neck, until all of him stood encased in an ice block.

The Librarian panted and fell to all fours, most of her energy gone. She only had about five hundred energy left, her mana close to depleted. She heard a massive explosion from where Hal had been, and knew, just from what her senses continued to tell her, that he had thrown Dravishk into one of the large rock formations nearby, and her draconic uncle had vanished.

It was a pity she knew he wasn't dead either.

Then Hal was there, hands on her shoulder, lending her a calm she hadn't been able to get to on her own. "Quinn, breathe, and remember to focus. Calm yourself and snap out of that damned ice prison you locked yourself in."

But Quinn didn't want to, because if she came out of that ice prison, she might find Malakai dead. She couldn't sense him properly, just his body, just that he was prone, and just that he was so badly injured she didn't think he'd recover.

Tears burned at the back of her eyes, but she didn't have time for that right now.

She turned to Hal, reaching for that cold element inside her, for that sense, that trance, that would allow her to function. "We need to finish imprisoning him."

"No, Quinn, we need to kill him," Hal said. "You have to stop this compassion you have for your damned enemies."

But Quinn laughed. "Don't be silly. It's not compassion. I want to flay him nine ways to Sunday, but he's got like nine lives, and I don't know how it works. I think he respawns elsewhere, and I'm not letting that happen. The best we can do right now is imprison him, so he can't harm anybody else, until we figure out how his nine lives work."

Hal stepped back, glancing around. She watched several emotions play over his face before he nodded. "Then do it."

Quinn stood up to finish the prison, throwing one comment over her shoulder. "This time maybe don't let him disintegrate in your custody. He needs to suffer far more than that."

Hal went to retort but Quinn's next words halted him. Her voice cracked when she spoke. "Please check on Malakai."

76

ALMOST ANYTHING

QUINN COULDN'T LET HER WORRY FOR MALAKAI INTERFERE WITH THE task before her. She tried to suppress the emotions, but without the impetus of needing to protect everyone, she couldn't seem to access that space again.

Nothing she did could erase the memory of him diving in front of her, absorbing the full force of the vortex spheres. She had to compartmentalize that image and lock it away; she couldn't afford to dwell on it.

Killing Kajaro might allow them to understand his regeneration process. It didn't matter if he was dead and encased in ice, unless it meant he would dissipate and regenerate elsewhere.

Unfortunately, she couldn't risk him regenerating elsewhere and being free of them again, no matter how much her anger wanted him to pay.

Taking a deep breath, Quinn refocused on the mind and ice magic she'd studied under Milaro and the others. She recalled the countless hours spent wrapping her head around the vast abilities and potential crossovers. The necessity to absorb books before bed so her brain could process the power.

She knew what she had to do. Kajaro needed to hibernate, to be placed into a stasis where he was still alive but essentially in a coma. It seemed like a far too humane way to handle this. Wrestling with her conscience proved more challenging than she'd anticipated.

Maybe if he hadn't hurt Malakai, she could have been more lenient, but she continued to reinforce the ice prison. This was different from what she'd done with Tenejo because she hadn't known what she was doing back then. Since that time, she'd realized how powerful ice could be when used against the Serpensiril.

Given their cold-blooded nature, this was the best way to lower their body temperature and induce a stasis without killing them. Quinn hadn't thought it through properly last time and leaving his head free had been a mistake. She'd let the Library worry about providing him sustenance. It was the least it could do.

Slowly but surely, she created the ice prison, making it tighter, not allowing him to wake up or understand where he was, nor did she allow any healing to help with the wounds he'd sustained. When they finally brought him out for his punishment, if they ever did, he should still be in pain. She took what she knew from having absorbed the Serpensiril anatomy tome, and made sure to suspend him, keeping him whole.

For now.

When she'd figured out this whole nine lives thing and knew how to stop him from coming back, she'd revisit the situation.

Her fingers hurt. Her left arm was in tatters despite the healing she'd funneled into it. In fact, her whole body ached, but Quinn kept on crafting the prison until it was done.

"Quinn." A voice startled her out of her momentary lull. She turned to see Nishpa hovering at her elbow. "Quinn, honey, I need you to come with me. You're injured."

Quinn was surprised. "No, I'm not," she started to argue, but then she looked down at her hands and realized they were caked in blood. In a sludgy red mess that was still congealing all over her body. "Oh," she said, racking her brain for when else she could have been hurt. She didn't remember.

The fire. Her own power turning on her. That wasn't a good thing.

"You have to be more careful until you can control it better," Nishpa said. "We can't lose you right now."

"Yeah, I know, I get it," Quinn snapped, taking another breath. The separation of her emotions wasn't working this time. She needed it to work.

But Nishpa didn't snap back. Instead, she patted Quinn's hand as she gently infused healing into her patient. "Quinn, he's . . . he should be okay."

"Should be?" she asked. Even though there was hope in that "should be," there was also fear. Because she'd already assumed he wasn't going to be. "What do you mean 'should be'?"

Nishpa didn't rise to the urgency in Quinn's voice, but instead kept her own measured and calm. "I mean if we can get him back to Milaro, as soon as possible, I have no doubt he'll recover. But right now, you need to get the book from Kajaro."

"Oh," Quinn said. She focused for several moments, slowly causing the ice to recede until the storage ring on Kajaro's hand became visible. "Is there a way we can just take it from him? He's not dead. Last time he was dead." Panic rose in Quinn's suddenly not-controlled center. She bit down on it and tried to look at the situation logically.

"Not really." Nishpa frowned, hovering over the finger. "But we might be able to forcefully activate it."

"Of course we can force activate it," Hal said, stomping up. His hooves made a strange sound on the scratchy ground. He tapped the now visible finger, and there was an odd screeching sound in the back of Quinn's mind. "Open."

Right in front of them all, the contents of Kajaro's ring displayed. "You'll need to take it," he said to Quinn as he gestured to the third cube, two down, on the right.

"Can everybody do this?" she asked.

"No," Hal said. "I can do it. Give yourself a couple of millennia, and you can do it too."

"Okay," she said meekly, reached in, and grabbed the book. It writhed in her hands at first until it settled, almost purring. She glanced down at it. "Well, that's unsettling," she said.

"It's an odd book. I told you we couldn't touch it. You should be beyond the reach of its corruption."

"Let me check it." She scanned it herself with the best of her ability to make sure that it wasn't going to poison her own inventory. Then she slid out a decontamination bag to rid it of any potential chaotic pollution, and then slid it into her own inventory. After which she re-extended the ice shielding around Kajaro's hand.

"I guess we're done," she said, finally stopping to look around. Her head felt dizzy, and she swayed slightly, weak all of a sudden.

"I'll open a doorway shortly," Hal said, as he reached out a hand to steady her. "I just have to tend to Ikeshal and Escadril first."

Quinn blinked and looked over at the other large satyr. He lay on the ground, wounded, hurt badly from a massive gash in his side. Quinn gasped. "I didn't . . . I didn't feel that. I could have helped."

"No, Quinn, you were fine. You did what we needed you to. It'll be okay. We'll figure this out." Hal squeezed her shoulder before moving over to his friend.

That's when Quinn took in the rest of them. Not even the landscape seemed strange anymore. They'd been here long enough and stained it with enough of their blood to make it eerily familiar.

She didn't think Brady would survive with the amount of brain matter splattered on the ground next to his still corpse. Her throat caught, and she had to remember to breathe.

Eric leaned up against one of those strange not-Christmas trees, one arm hanging limply at his side, his eyes closed. There were gashes and wounds all over him, mottling his skin with chunks of missing flesh. And one of his wings was torn.

Ikeshal lay prone, and Hal was healing him.

Escadril stood off to one side, his bark paler than she remembered and his left arm hung limp with what looked like rot. Instinctively, Quinn knew that wasn't a healable injury and she wished she'd have fought harder against coming here.

And Malakai?

Slowly, she turned to see him.

His head was propped up ever so gently. Quinn gasped in a breath and stumbled to his side.

She ignored the fact that Nishpa tsked irritably because she hadn't finished tending to Quinn's wounds. Quinn, however, exerted her own level of healing, trying to make up for it as she scrambled to Malakai. She should have a few hundred energy left. Surely that was more than Nishpa.

Healing her wounds shouldn't be a priority.

"Mal," she said. He didn't respond.

"I thought you said he was going to be okay." She glared accusingly at Nishpa.

"I said he *should* be okay. We have to get him transported and we need to do it now. So you need to help us transform the chaotic energy around us into the mana and energy we need to open the portal," Nishpa said patiently.

Quinn took the reprimand for what it was and got her head on straight. Get everyone home first. Worry about life-and-death possibilities after. She could do that. "I thought we had a portable one. I . . . wait, where did Hoody go?" she asked, even though she vaguely recalled his essence disappearing. She knelt next to Malakai and tried to recall how she'd transformed the chaotic saturation during the fight.

Hal crossed his arms. "He got away."

She could tell he was angry, but she could also sense a sort of mild relief in him. "You don't seem entirely broken up about it," she said softly.

"I'm not. I would much rather stay alive for a while longer." Hal barked out a laugh of derision.

"Aren't you like immortal?" She'd always thought he was sort of like the Library. Invincible to a certain extent.

"You should know, as well as anybody else, that immortal doesn't mean eternal. You can die. It's just hard to kill you. Case in point, over there on an ice block, because we're not sure how to really kill the bastard." He gestured back to Kajaro's prison.

Quinn didn't know how to respond to that, and paused as she caught a whiff of how she'd manipulated the chaotic energy around them. "Okay, can you explain?"

"Of course I can explain. He's exactly what you are, but he's pure-blooded, and he's been around since before the Library, who happens to be the *youngest* sibling. He's much stronger than me in a drawn-out battle when he's at full strength. So no, I didn't want to keep fighting him, and I'm glad that he's scooched off to wherever he's gone, leaving behind a multitude of corpses I'm not even sure are going to stay dead now."

Quinn paled. She was suddenly extremely tired and quite nauseous. "Nishpa. I don't feel too good."

"Did you try to heal Malakai?" Nishpa asked.

"A little. I wasn't sure exactly how. Is that bad?"

"Quinn, you're down to the dregs. Even if it still looks like a lot to you, your magic was kind of rampant back there. I need you to understand that losing control of it like that, well, did more harm to you than anybody else."

"Oh, yeah." Quinn could barely move her arms by now. They hurt like they were crusty and broken. It was all she could do to channel the chaotic energy into mana and energy rejuvenation for the rest of them.

Malakai had wounds all over his body, but at least they weren't bleeding anymore. "Mal," she said, "please wake up."

"I've done what I can. He has a mixed physiology, Quinn. I need to get him back to Milaro. Milaro is the only one I know who can fix him properly."

"Well, what are we waiting for?" Quinn demanded only she noticed her own voice was raspy and held no oomph.

"You," Nishpa said gently. "You need to filtrate more mana. We need a little more power to get back. Sorry."

Quinn suddenly felt so out of depth. She'd known what to do to help them while they were fighting. Instinctively. She hadn't even thought about it. But right now, the process was tired and sluggish and curled up in a corner of her psyche like a baby dragon that didn't want to move. She coaxed it, none too gently, into helping her increase the mana circulation for her friends.

"This should help," she said, her body aching so much she was surprised others didn't hear it.

"Thanks." Nishpa patted her hand gently.

Quinn didn't think she dozed off, but she must have, because suddenly there was a thrumming under her butt as she sat next to Malakai. She didn't even have energy to extend, to give him some added healing. Not that she knew what to do. She had no clue how to heal a freaking elf.

"Okay, little egg," Hal said. There was fondness back in his tone. "You did well. You didn't manage to kill any of us or yourself, so I think we did pretty good. You got the book back. But you've got a lot to learn. And it's high time we teach you, even if . . ."

"Even if I'm an egg," she said, giggling ever so slightly in all her exhaustion.

Hal chuckled. "Can you stand?"

"As long as I don't have to walk on my hands, I should be good," she quipped, fighting to keep her eyes open. She couldn't move her arms at all right now.

"How are your arms?" Hal asked.

"I feel like they've been through a shredder and a meat grinder and then kind of just shoved back into the skin molds."

"Oh, fantastic," Hal said. "You're doing great."

Quinn actually chuckled and coughed.

"Everyone ready?" Hal's voice boomed out.

"We're as ready as we're going to be," Eric said, stumbling, his wings not functioning.

Quinn didn't even want to look at him. She felt like this was all her fault. Her dream should have warned them. Everything was so up in the air now.

Hal finished sketching something on the ground that Quinn couldn't see, before he spoke. "Okay, opening to the Library."

Everything went so fast after that. Quinn couldn't quite control anything. She stumbled into the Library, heaving in the air, realizing how hard it had been to breathe on that planet. It rushed into her lungs, practically suffocating her for several seconds before she readapted to it and remembered to let go of the filtration spells she'd been holding onto.

There was a gasp right next to her. Quinn thought it might be Geneva, but she wasn't sure because her head and body were battling for which one was the most painful.

And Dottie, she could hear Dottie in the background. She was talking nonstop. "Oh my dear, what's happened? What did you do? Quick, over here. Let's get them to the infirmary."

She could feel everything shifting around her. Lynx was there. The Library. And suddenly, she was also in the infirmary. The Library morphed it perfectly, keeping everybody in their own little rooms, giving them all the privacy they needed.

There was a hum as people bustled in and out. It was the only word Quinn could think of at the time, half aware as she was.

Quinn reached out her senses, but it stung and backlashed, and her mind couldn't handle it. And so she pulled in on herself, trying to heal what she could, but there was no energy left. And she fell in and out of sleep.

She wasn't sure how many days had passed when she woke back up. But she looked around, and Milaro stood at a table close to her, looking over what seemed to be a projected chart of some sort. He didn't even need to see her before he spoke. "Ah, you're awake."

"I guess," Quinn said, her throat croaky.

"Tried to burn out all your magic centers, didn't you?"

"Not really," Quinn said. "I just . . . reacted."

"It's perfectly okay. You were lucky they didn't expect to fight so many people. That made them less effective."

"Pretty much," Quinn said.

Milaro turned. He looked tired. Again. She'd tried to fix that.

"I'm sorry," she said.

"Why are you sorry? You didn't ambush us. You stepped in. You took care of Kajaro. And you even, unintentionally, rejuvenated everybody's mana and energy, Quinn. You did more than enough for a completely unexpected situation. Please. Don't. Say. Sorry."

Myriad emotions hit Quinn. She knew, in her heart of hearts, that Milaro was correct. She had nothing to be sorry about. But at the same time, wasn't she supposed to be this powerful Librarian? This person who could save everyone and everything? Wasn't she supposed to be able to stand between the Library and destruction? To protect the books and the patrons who actually respected how the library worked?

"You know," Milaro said, interrupting her thoughts, "I don't know if this helps, Quinn. But you've been here like three and a half months and you've mastered a lot for a Librarian who didn't have a predecessor who passed on the position. You did this, all by yourself, with a malfunctioning Library that still isn't fixed completely, without all of the available branches, information, and tools you should have. And you did it. You knuckled down when it counted."

"But we lost people," Quinn said, her voice small. "I couldn't save them all."

"Quinn, nobody expected you to be the person to save everyone. We're all just happy you saved yourself."

"What about Malakai?" she asked, suddenly feeling very small. This was his grandfather. He had to be so upset.

Milaro sighed deeply, and she swore she could see wrinkles that weren't there before. "My grandson will recover. It'll take a bit of time. But we have time. And you know what else we have, Quinn?"

"What?" she wasn't sure what she wanted the answer to be. But she did know that she had to know what the answer was. To cling to hope.

Milaro gave her a genuine smile, even if his eyes seemed tired. "We have magic. And you know what we can do with magic?"

Quinn managed to return the smile just a little bit as she nodded ever so slightly.

"Exactly, Quinn," Milaro said. "With magic, almost anything is possible."

EPILOGUE

The Library had powered up to the next level when *Ririn's Dimensional Distortion Through Sacrificial Means* was returned.

Quinn's senses connected to the Library had deepened. She took a breath, talking to herself in a mantra. "I'm going to figure myself out, find a way to heal Mal properly, and never let anyone get hurt again."

Aradie perched nearby and hooted once in low agreement.

I'm glad to see you up and about again. You sound more like yourself. The Library spoke softly into her mind.

Quinn wasn't exactly sure how to respond. But just as she was about to speak, the Library interrupted her thoughts.

I think it's time you visited my vault.

Quinn paused. That was the last thing she'd expected. To be honest, she'd mostly forgotten the Library had ever mentioned its vault. *It's not where the restricted vault is, is it?*

It can be accessed from two locations. One of them is inside the Restricted Vault, and one is off the path that goes around the core. No one but me can enter them. They're bio locked.

What do you mean no one but you, aren't you the Library? Quinn was confused. It wasn't like the Library ever took on any other form than . . . the Library.

The Library chuckled, the sound spreading out like pure joy in Quinn's mind. *I have Lynx to move around for me, but I do have a singular corporeal form I can assume if I want to. I just haven't needed to for a very long time.*

Quinn digested that and frowned. *Okay. When should I head down then?*

Maybe now. There's information you need sooner rather than later. Information I don't currently feel safe giving you any other way. I'll conceal your presence once you're in the Restricted Vault.

I can just come down through the core.

I don't want you activating any of your power right now. Not until I've had a chance for us to analyze where you stand and what we can do to expediate your adaptation. So you can't float down the stairs, and I can't transport you yet. It's shorter for you to walk from the infirmary to the vault.

Oh. Quinn frowned. The Library had a point, but Quinn wasn't sure how it would go down if other people knew she was in there.

It's okay. I'll shield your movement as much as possible on your way there. More of a don't look at you.

Quinn sighed, and stretched. She cringed at the lingering pain. "Come on, Aradie, let's go."

Aradie cooed in Quinn's ear as Quinn made her way to the restricted section. No one looked at her as she passed, and Quinn liked being able to move around surreptitiously. *Can you do this more often?* she asked, hoping the answer was yes.

Of course, but I'll be able to teach you how to do it yourself soon enough. You've already absorbed one of the related books anyway.

Great. I'll remember that. She stopped, right in front of the restricted vault, shorter of breath than she thought she'd be. Magic can fix everything? She'd have words with Milaro next time she saw him. She swore he'd been avoiding her.

Or else . . . he was trying to take care of Mal. The latter was much more likely.

Quinn placed her hand on the beautiful twenty-foot narrow double doors of the restricted section. Their frosted glass with wrought iron filigree bars still caught her attention like they had the first day.

"Where do I go?" she murmured to the Library.

Straight through to the back seating area, but take a left and there is a small panel in between the window and the side of the bookshelf.

Quinn walked through the Restricted Vault toward the back, loving the view through the massive bay windows that looked out to the galaxy beyond. The stars lit up the interior of the vault beautifully, lending even more mystery to the books housed there.

Including Ririn's tome. It was now housed behind protective glass, with an attached alarm, given its ability to corrupt almost any magical creature that touched it.

Ripping her attention from it, she glanced around to find the panel the Library talked about. Her gaze crossed dozens of books, the shelves, and then finally landed on the panel.

She walked up to it. It was nondescript, basically just a part of where the bookcase was attached to the back wall. *This it?*

Now place your hand about a foot above your waist. There'll be a slight prick and it will take your genetic reading. And only then will you be allowed inside.

Quinn placed her hand a foot above her waist, and a panel that hadn't been visible at all suddenly popped open. There was a hand imprint device just inside it and she placed her hand palm down on it. The prick was more like a shock, it sparked through her system like a call that needed to be answered.

Genetic material recognized.

And then, the panel slid open to reveal a staircase leading into darkness.

The staircase leading down was narrow and unremarkable.

Or at least, it would have been unremarkable if Quinn discounted the fact that the stairs themselves, the walls, and the ceiling—which she was sure was far above her head—all had pinpricks that looked like stars dancing around on them.

The beauty of the universe was something she could get very used to.

Aradie cooed from up above as the door closed, shrouding Quinn in darkness. She couldn't come with her because the vault was specifically attuned to Quinn's cosmicisodracus frequency.

Or something . . .

It made Quinn feel oddly alone. Right then, there was complete and utter silence in her head. She couldn't even feel the presence of the Library around her. After months of being in constant proximity with so many mind-reading creatures, Quinn suddenly felt vulnerable.

I am here, Quinn, the Library said. The timbre of the voice had changed. It was more regal and echoed slightly through Quinn's mind. Everything around her felt the same, very echoey and not at all like Quinn had expected. The stairs appeared to go on forever and Quinn was a little confused.

"I don't understand," she said. "Aren't we directly above the filtration room?"

Not exactly, the Librarian said. *And while we're in here, you can call me by my real name. Drevicia. If you'd like to, that is.*

"Really?" Quinn said.

Well, yes, or I wouldn't have offered.

"Sorry," Quinn said, cringing slightly as she continued to pick her way down the stairs very carefully. "I just, you seemed quite irate when Uncle Hal decided to use your name and I wanted to make sure I wasn't overstepping my bounds in any way."

My name holds power, and reverberates through the universe when spoken. When Hal used it, he could have set off a chain reaction that summoned my siblings, whether I wanted them here or not. However, when you say that name in this space, you help keep that power alive and strengthen it, especially through our familial bond.

"Oh, I don't understand it at all," Quinn said. "Literally, not at all.

But it's okay, I don't need to understand it, to realize that it's a very good thing and that I'll bet it'll all make sense soon."

Drevicia, or the Library, snickered slightly.

"You seem more tangible in here."

Just you wait, we haven't even reached the proper memory vault yet.

A few more steps, gingerly taken. Quinn frowned. "Who all can get into this place?"

You and I.

"You and I as in us, or as in cosmicisodracus in general?" Quinn was curious.

Ah, yes, my siblings would be allowed to enter through the Library space. However, there are checks and balances in place, and even they can't come in without my explicit permission.

Quinn pondered that for a second before asking: "Can it be coerced?"

The permission? The Library mulled that over itself. *Technically. Or if I'm dead, I guess. But I don't think they'd get that desperate. At least . . . not all of them.*

"Did you have a falling out?" Quinn asked.

Not like you're thinking.

"I wasn't really thinking at all, I just sort of wanted to ask." Quinn took another step, and still couldn't see an end. "How much further down is it and can I teleport out of here?"

Nope, you haven't read the right texts yet.

"I'm trying to rectify that tonight," Quinn said.

Suddenly, the steps stopped and the floor flattened out in front of them. There was another door. This one, in the pale starlight, looked like one of those massive arched wooden doors with the wrought iron studs all around the outside of it.

Place your hand on it; it's another lock.

There was a slight prick against her finger again and the door shimmered and vanished. Quinn walked through and gasped. This room was big. Not cavern big, but huge.

This was simply a room. It was probably the size of a football field and in it were books that weren't books. They didn't have pages but instead there held starlight within the covers. It streamed out illuminating the entire space in a light of wonder.

These are the histories of myself, the Library and my people, Drevicia said, her tone soft and slightly melancholy.

"Are you here? Can I see you?" Quinn asked, excitably.

Oh no, Quinn. I made a sacrifice when I became the Library. I can never take my personal corporeal form again. The Library is my form now, and while I can change it and shift within it and adjust it and project a part of myself, I sadly won't ever be able to be myself again.

"Oh," Quinn said, a sudden pang in her chest making her eyes water, "that's very sad."

It is a bit, isn't it? I thought so, too. But it is what it is, you know. I made a choice. It was something that, at the time and even now, I don't regret. There were few options available to us at the time and none would enable this result—preventing the immediate destruction of all things in creation. My siblings helped me. They fused their power with mine and we created something new. My primary power is water. Hence, I am a lunar dragon. Though, as you know, we all possess fire.

Quinn took in the information. "The Library was a collaborative effort between you all?"

Yes. The Library sounded somewhat wistful as it continued to speak. *We all worked in synchronization to imbue me with the power to become the Library. The concept itself was fantastical, barely doable, but considering we sort of coaxed our oldest brother into helping. It was the space affinity he had that enabled this possibility to this extent.*

There was a swirl of lights that encompassed the room before the Library continued speaking. *This is where the majority of the history of my people is. I can't give it to anybody else. You can't share this with anyone. There are heavy magics that will prevent you from speaking about anything you witness here. But for your own safety and preservation, you need to understand exactly what went into the Library's creation. Are you willing to let me show you?*

Quinn gulped. She didn't really think she was ready for this but if the last fight had shown her anything, she knew she had to know more to become the type of powerful she needed to be. How were they supposed to fight what was coming if she didn't even understand what happened to get them here in the first place?

If she didn't even understand herself?

Will you, Quinn?

Quinn nodded. "Yeah." She didn't really think she had a choice but at the same time, she knew for a fact that if she said no, Drevicia wouldn't push her. And that mattered.

She looked around the beautiful room. There were no pillars in sight. It just felt like she was walking on a floor of stars and nobody was here to interrupt her. She could close her eyes and imagine herself floating out there through the galaxy. Quinn paused for a moment, trying to figure out how to phrase what she wanted to ask. "You said you sacrificed yourself."

Technically, I suppose. I mean, what other dragon has this wealth of knowledge? I have a horde of books, of magic, of mana, of everything. And I can partake of it without it ever having to leave, without ever having to give it up. And even better . . . I can share it with everyone!

Quinn laughed at the pure joy in the Library's voice. "You don't like it when your books go missing, do you?"

Definitely not, Drevicia said. *But it's inevitable that others will covet what you have, even if what you have is something that you share freely with everybody else.*

"So true." Quinn sighed.

When we performed this miracle, we were a hundred percent on the same page. But as time passed, my siblings may have, as you've already witnessed, changed their minds. I don't know who is in cahoots with whom, or what Dravishk is even thinking.

Quinn wanted to know what he was thinking more than anything.

These books are bound to me. They cannot be removed. But you can read them.

Quinn stood in the middle of the room and closed her eyes. She could hear a very faint thrumming, like a beat of a soft drum. She'd heard it before in the Library. The very first day when she'd been pulled through that damn door and into here, Lynx had asked her if she could feel that beat.

"Is that your heart?" Quinn asked softly.

In a way, the Library said, that wistful tone back. *It is the idea of my heart. It is my life force. And my life force is everywhere in the Library. It is me. I am it. Where it begins, I end. And where it ends, I begin.* It sighed, but it sounded like a happy sigh.

"Drevicia, why am I down here? Why did you bring me here?" Quinn asked.

I wanted you to understand where you come from, or what you come from, how vast the power that you have at your fingertips is. And in the same vein, you need to understand that you have abilities that can be triggered.

"What do you mean, abilities that can be triggered?"

All dragons possess fire. We develop our other abilities as a way to temper the fire from devouring us whole. Your power has been locked away for most of your short life. When you have no magic to feed on, the fire has nothing to combust with, and has no fuel. But the moment you stepped into the Library, your wellspring began again. Hal was right. The Library sounded oddly irritated by the fact.

"Back up," Quinn said. "Uncle Hal is right? You want me to tell him that?"

The Library chuckled. *Please don't. He's insufferable enough.* The tone turned serious. *But he is right in some things. You are still a whelp. Too young for the power you to need to wield. And yet . . . we have to do what must be done.*

Drevicia made a breeze blow through the room. *I want you to dig in deep right now, and pull out the flame that was in one of the first books you absorbed. Recall the information in* Bright Light Starters. *But I want you to concentrate on it, make it hot, make it blue, push it to white, and imagine it is protecting you.*

Quinn did what she was instructed to, and clicked her fingers. Instead of the tiny flame that popped out from her clicked fingers the first time, Quinn summoned a hot blue flame. But that wasn't all.

Even as the flame summoned it triggered her scales, and they sprang up fluidly to coat her upper body, shielding her from potential danger in a white-hot way that felt like coming home.

R ead on in Book four on Patreon!

ABOUT THE AUTHOR

Born in Australia, K.T. Hanna met her husband in a computer game, moved to the U.S.A. and went into culture shock. Bonus? Not as many creatures specifically designed to kill you.
KT creates science-fiction, fantasy, and LitRPG, with a dash of horror for fun! She is a member of the SFWA and NINC. Her hobbies include gaming, reading, and lake time!
No, she doesn't sleep. She is entirely powered by caffeine, Chipotle, and sarcasm.

Find her on her website: kthanna.com
Join her in all the places, including Discord!

ACKNOWLEDGMENTS

I have a lot of people to thank. Even those who don't contribute directly through the writing craft keep me going and help me write my best stories.

Love of my life, Trevor, and my little Bria. It's his fault I found the genre, and her fault I never give up on writing.

I wouldn't be here without the following friends (and I know I've probably forgotten to mention someone:

SSODA

Crown

Eric Ugland

Quinton Shyn

Andrea Parseneau

M Evan MacGregor

Daniel Schinhofen

Michael Chatfield

Luke Chmilenko

Tao

Jami

Geneva

Jez

Ririn

DE Sherman

Ino

Honor

J.M.

And of course my family:

Mumskin & Papilie, Tracey, Jett, & Robbie.
<u>The entire Coteh server</u>
<u>My Legion Family</u>

<u>And every one of my Patrons.</u>
Faelor
Ma & Pa
Foxies
Quinton
Matt
Warren
Kristen
Joshua
Corwin
Johann
Renn
Irene
ChaosOmega98
Erwin
Isaac
Ty
Bryan
Joe
Kagami
Onean
support!
daavko
Table Top
Kevin
Pyro4224
Doomsongs
Jorden
Silverfox#7631
Cybernetic Angel
JSC

Skye
JewBot9000
James Rutter
Emily
Colin
Oken
Naomi
Gnathrak
Persnicketykat
Ron
Ninjamode67
Monique
Bjbrewster
Naomi Bonnin
June
Brian
Samuel
Not to mention my FB Group/Page, and people in my discord.
Thank you
You all help me maintain a level of sanity.

ALSO BY K.T. HANNA

Somnia Online

System Apocalypse Australia

The Domino Project

Last Chance Trilogy

KT Hanna's Author Page

LITRPG

Do you love LitRPG?
Do you want to find more of it?

These are amazing places to do just that!
FaceBook:
LitRPG Books
LitRPG Legion
GamelitRPG Society

Reddit:
LitRPG

Adjacent genres like Progression Fantasy/Cultivation:
Reddit: Progression Fantasy
Facebook: Cultivation Novels

MORE LITRPG

Love LitRPG?

To learn more about LitRPG, talk to authors including myself, and just have an awesome time, please join the LitRPG Group!

MORE LITRPG

Love LitRPG?

To learn more about LitRPG, talk to authors including myself, and just have an awesome time, please join the LitRPG Group!

www.ingramcontent.com/pod-product-compliance
Lightning Source LLC
Chambersburg PA
CBHW061529190726
48289CB00004B/983